Monier-Williams Kalidasa

Sakuntala, a Sanskrit drama, in seven acts

The Deva-Nagari recension of the text. Second Edition

Monier-Williams Kalidasa

Sakuntala, a Sanskrit drama, in seven acts
The Deva-Nagari recension of the text. Second Edition

ISBN/EAN: 9783337131753

Printed in Europe, USA, Canada, Australia, Japan

Cover: Foto ©Andreas Hilbeck / pixelio.de

More available books at **www.hansebooks.com**

ŚAKUNTALÁ.

MONIER WILLIAMS.

London

HENRY FROWDE

OXFORD UNIVERSITY PRESS WAREHOUSE

7 PATERNOSTER ROW

श्रीकालिदासविरचितमभिज्ञानशकुन्तलं नाम नाटकम्

ŚAKUNTALĀ

A SANSKRIT DRAMA, IN SEVEN ACTS,

BY

KĀLIDĀSA.

THE DEVA-NĀGARĪ RECENSION OF THE TEXT,

EDITED WITH LITERAL ENGLISH TRANSLATIONS OF ALL THE METRICAL
PASSAGES, SCHEMES OF THE METRES, AND

NOTES, CRITICAL AND EXPLANATORY,

BY

MONIER WILLIAMS, M.A., D.C.L.,

Hon. Doctor in Law of the University of Calcutta;
Hon. Member of the Bombay Asiatic Society;
Member of the Royal Asiatic Society of Great Britain and Ireland, and of the Oriental Society of Germany;
Boden Professor of Sanskrit in the University of Oxford.

SECOND EDITION.

Oxford:

AT THE CLARENDON PRESS.

M.DCCC.LXXVI.

PREFACE.

THE following pages are the result of an endeavour to furnish
English students of Sanskrit with a correct edition of the most
celebrated drama of India's greatest dramatist. About a century
has elapsed since Sir W. Jones discovered that there existed in
India a number of Nāṭakas or Sanskrit dramas, many of them of
great antiquity; some abounding in poetry of undoubted merit,
and all of them containing valuable pictures of Hindū life and
manners. Eager to apply the means thus gained of filling what
was before an empty niche in the Temple of Sanskrit Literature,
Sir W. Jones addressed himself at once to translate into English
the Śakuntalā, which he was told was the most admired of all the
extant plays.

This work is by the illustrious Kālidāsa, who is supposed by some
native authorities (though on insufficient grounds) to have lived in
Ujjayinī, the capital of king Vikramāditya, whose reign is the
starting-point of the Hindū era called Samvat, beginning 57 years
B.C. Kālidāsa is described as one of the 'nine gems' of that
monarch's splendid court. It seems, however, more probable that
Kālidāsa flourished in the third century of the Christian era
(see p. 474 of *Indian Wisdom*, published by W. H. Allen & Co.,
13, Waterloo Place, London). The Śakuntalā is acknowledged on
all hands to be the masterpiece of the great Indian poet. Indeed, no
composition of Kālidāsa displays more the richness and fertility of
his poetical genius, the exuberance of his imagination, the warmth
and play of his fancy, his profound knowledge of the human heart,
his delicate appreciation of its most refined and tender emotions, his
familiarity with the workings and counter-workings of its con-
flicting feelings,—in short, more entitles him to rank as 'the
Shakespeare of India.' On the Continent such men as Goethe,

Schlegel, and Humboldt have all expressed their admiration of the Hindū poet's greatest work. Goethe's four well-known lines, written in 1792, are—

'Willst du die Blüthe des frühen, die Früchte des späteren Jahres,
   Willst du was reizt und entzückt, willst du was sättigt und nährt,
   Willst du den Himmel, die Erde, mit einem Namen begreifen :
   Nenn' ich Sakontalá dich, und so ist Alles gesagt[1].'

Unfortunately the Paṇḍits omitted to inform Sir W. Jones that the multiplication of manuscripts of this play, consequent upon its popularity, had led to a perplexing result,—not, however, unexampled, as has since been proved by what has happened to the Rāmāyaṇa,—namely, that the numerous manuscripts separated themselves into two classes : the one, embracing all those in Deva-nāgarī writing, which, without being uniform, had still a community of character; the other, all those in Bengālī.

These two classes of MSS. are usually distinguished by the names ' Deva-nāgarī recension ' and ' Bengālī recension,' which terms may conveniently be adopted. The Deva-nāgarī recension

---

[1] Thus translated by Mr. E. B. Eastwick :—

' Wouldst thou the young year's blossoms and the fruits of its decline,
   And all by which the soul is charmed, enraptured, feasted, fed,
   Wouldst thou the earth, and heaven itself in one sole name combine ?
   I name thee, O Śakuntalā ! and all at once is said.'

Augustus William von Schlegel, in his first Lecture on Dramatic Literature, says : ' Among the Indians, the people from whom perhaps all the cultivation of the human race has been derived, plays were known long before they could have experienced any foreign influence. It has lately been made known in Europe that they have a rich dramatic literature, which ascends back for more than two thousand years. The only specimen of their plays (Nāṭaks) hitherto known to us is the delightful Śakontalā, which, notwithstanding the colouring of a foreign climate, bears in its general structure a striking resemblance to our romantic drama.'

Alexander von Humboldt, in treating of Indian poetry, observes : ' The name of Kālidāsa has been frequently and early celebrated among the western nations. This great poet flourished at the splendid court of Vikramāditya, and was, therefore, contemporary with Virgil and Horace. The English and German translations of the Śakuntalā have excited the feeling of admiration which has been so amply bestowed upon Kālidāsa. Tenderness in the expression of feelings, and richness of creative fancy, have assigned to him his lofty place among the poets of all nations.' In another place he says : ' Kālidāsa is a masterly describer of the influence which Nature exercises upon the minds of lovers. The scene in the forest, which he introduced in the drama of Vikrama and Urvaśī, is one of the most beautiful and poetical productions which has appeared in any time.'

is thought by most scholars to be the older and purer. Many of
the readings of the Bengālī, however, have been defended by
Dr. R. Pischel and others; and this recension has been followed
by the Sāhitya-darpaṇa, one MS. of which bears the date 1504
of our era. The MSS. of the Deva-nāgarī class are chiefly found
in the Upper Provinces of India, where the great demand has
produced copyists without scholarship, who have faithfully tran-
scribed what they did not understand, and, therefore, could not
designedly alter. On the other hand, the copyists in Bengal
have been Paṇḍits whose *cacoëthes* for amplifying and interpolating
has led to much repetition and amplification. Many examples
might here be adduced; but I will only refer to the third Act
of the Bengālī recension, where the love-scene between the King
and Śakuntalā has been expanded to four or five times the length
it occupies in the MSS. of the Deva-nāgarī recension. Even the
names of the dramatis personæ have been altered: Dushyanta is
changed into Dushmanta; Anasūyā into Anusūyā; Vātāyana into
Pārvatāyana; Sānumatī into Miśrakeśī; Taralikā into Piṅgalikā;
Dhanamitra into Dhanavriddhi; Mārkaṇḍeya into San-koćana.

Unhappily it was a MS. of this recension, and not a very
good specimen of its class, that Sir W. Jones used for his trans-
lation. From him, therefore, was gained, about a century ago,
the earliest incorrect knowledge of this, the first Sanskrit play
known to Europeans. No edition of the text appeared till about
forty years afterwards, when one was produced in 1830, after
immense labour, at Paris, by M. Chézy. He deserved great credit
for the difficulties he surmounted; but his edition was also from a
MS. of the Bengālī recension. It abounded also in typographical
and other more serious errors. An edition of the Śakuntalā was
subsequently printed in Calcutta, also from Bengālī MSS. and in
Bengālī character, by Prema-ćandra, dated Śāka 1761 (A.D. 1839).
Several editions of the Bengālī recension have been printed at
Calcutta in the Deva-nāgarī character; one in 1860 by Prema-
ćandra (under the superintendence of Professor E. B. Cowell), for
European scholars; others in 1864 and 1870.

It was reserved for Dr. Boehtlingk to be the first to edit the
Deva-nāgarī recension of this play at Bonn in the year 1842. No
other edition of the text of this recension was published until my
first edition in 1853. An edition of the same recension was
published at Bombay in 1861, and one at Breslau in 1872 by

Dr. Burkhard, Professor in the University of Bonn, to which is added a glossary.

The translations which have been published since that of Sir W. Jones and the German version of his translation by Forster, in 1791, are—first, the French of M. Chézy; subsequently the German of Hirzel, Rückert, and Boehtlingk; a Danish translation by Hammerich; and more recently, another German translation in prose and verse by Meier; not to speak of Danish and Italian versions of Sir W. Jones' English; and my own English translation, the fourth edition of which was published (by W. H. Allen & Co., 13, Waterloo Place, London) in 1872.

The great Indian dramatist only wrote two other dramas. Of the Vikramorvaśī, the twin play of the Śakuntalā, two editions have appeared on the Continent; one at Bonn, by Lenz, and a more perfect one at St. Petersburg, by Bollensen: an edition of this play was also printed at the Education press in Calcutta in 1830, and one by myself in 1849, and another at Calcutta in 1869. Translations by Hoefer and Hirzel have been published in Germany, and in England by Wilson in prose and verse, and a literal translation in English prose by Professor Cowell. The third play, called Mālavikāgnimitra, was edited at Bonn, by Tullberg; and a more correct edition, with English notes, by Shankar P. Paṇḍit, was published at Bombay in 1869. This drama has been ably translated into German by Professor Weber.

I am bound to acknowledge that I made free use of Dr. Boehtlingk's edition of the text of the Śakuntalā in preparing the first edition for the press. The merit of his work can hardly be overrated; but I may, without presumption, say that I discovered many better readings, corrected a few errors, and introduced much original matter in the shape of annotations. It is no disparagement of Dr. Boehtlingk's labours to say that his edition does not adapt itself to the exigencies of an English student. The notes are in German; they are printed at the end of the volume— a practical obstacle to their utility; and they frequently contain corrections of the text. My experience has led me to prefer a system of synopsis, both in respect of the notes and metres.

In regard to the text of the present volume, if I have succeeded in producing a more correct edition of the Deva-nāgarī recension, than those of Dr. Boehtlingk and Dr. Burkhard, the merit is due to the more ample materials which have been placed at my command. In preparing the first edition I took care to avail myself of Dr. Boehtlingk's corrections of himself, and his after-thoughts at the end of his work, as well as of such critical remarks as coincided with my own views. Often working independently of him, I arrived at similar results, because I had access to all the materials whence his *Apparatus Criticus* was composed. Dr. Boehtlingk's edition was not prepared (as he has himself explained) from original MSS. Professors Brockhaus and Westergaard, having more or less carefully collated certain MSS. in the East India House Library and in the Bodleian at Oxford, and made partial extracts from three native Commentaries, handed over the results of their labours to him. All these MSS. and Commentaries were placed at my disposal, and most of them left in my possession until the completion of my work. Not a passage was printed without a careful collation of all of them, and the three Commentaries were consulted from beginning to end.

The MSS. which I principally used, were—

1. A MS. from the Colebrooke Collection, and therefore from the Eastern side of India, numbered 1718.

2. A MS. from the Mackenzie Collection, and therefore from Southern India, numbered 2696.

3. A MS. from the Taylor Collection, and therefore from Western India, numbered 1858, dated Śāka 1734.

All these belong to the India Office Library, and represent the three Indian Presidencies respectively.

4. A copy of a very good MS. at Bombay, presented to me by Mr. Shaw of the Bombay Civil Service.

5. An old Bengālī MS. belonging to the India Office Library, numbered 1060.

6. A very old Bengālī MS. from the Wilson Collection in the Bodleian.

I consulted other Bengālī MSS., but rarely admitted readings from them, unless supported by some one of the Deva-nāgarī. Thus the verses which I inserted at the beginning of the third Act are supported throughout by my own and the Taylor MS., and partially by that of the Mackenzie Collection.

The following are the three Indian Commentators—

1. Kāṭavema, whose commentary, from the Mackenzie Collection at the India Office, is the only one in the Nāgarī character. He was the son of Kāṭa Bhūpa, minister of Vasanta (himself the author

of a dramatic work called Vasanta-rājīya), king of Kumāra-giri, a place on the frontiers of the Nizām's dominions. He must have lived after the commencement of the sixteenth century, as he quotes Halāyudha, the author of the Kavi-rahasya (see Westergaard's preface to the Radices Linguæ Sanskritæ). This commentary is very corrupt, but where it is intelligible, is of great use in throwing light on the more difficult passages of this play.

2. Śaṅkara, whose commentary, from the Wilson Collection in the Bodleian Library, is on the Bengālī recension, and written in the Bengālī character. In many places it agrees with the readings of the Deva-nāgarī recension, or at least notices them.

3. Ćandra-śekhara, whose commentary, belonging to the India Office, is also on the Bengālī recension, and generally only repeats the words of Śaṅkara. If this Ćandra-śekhara is the same person as the father of Viśva-nātha,—author of the Sāhitya-darpaṇa,—he probably lived in the fifteenth century.

I never failed to consult the three commentaries before deciding on the reading of my text, and made their interpretations the basis of the literal translations of the metrical part of the play given in the notes.

In this second edition, I have constantly consulted Dr. Burkhard's text and glossary, and where better readings have been discovered, they are generally mentioned in my notes.

On comparing the present edition with the previous one, it will be observed that the red type has been dispensed with, and the Sanskrit interpretation of the Prākṛit passages has been given in small type below.

In the Hindū drama, as is well known, the women and inferior characters speak in Prākṛit—the name given to the colloquial Sanskrit, prevalent throughout a great part of India in early times. This spoken form of Sanskrit, which was really the precursor of the present vernacular tongues, must have varied greatly, and particular dialects must have belonged to particular districts and classes of men. There is, however, but one principal Prākṛit, peculiar to the plays, viz. the Mahārāshṭrī, although specimens of some varieties occasionally occur, and two of them may be found in the interlude between the fifth and sixth Acts of this play (see p. 217, note 2, and see Indian Wisdom, p. xxix, note 2).

Other improvements and alterations will be noticed. For example, the rules of Sandhi have generally been carried out, even in the Sanskrit interpretation of the Prākṛit ; the text and renderings in the notes have been carefully revised, and reference has been constantly made to Dr. Burkhard's edition ; the stage-directions and names of the speakers have been printed in small type.

Mr. E. L. Hogarth, M.A., of Brasenose College, who has acted as Deputy Professor of Sanskṛit at Oxford during my absence in India, has superintended the progress of this second edition of the Śakuntalā through the press, and has added a useful index.

My grateful acknowledgments are due to the Delegates of the Clarendon Press for the encouragement they are giving to the study of Sanskṛit and Oriental literature generally, by undertaking the publication of standard works like the Śakuntalā.

M. W.

Cairo, March 1876.

ABBREVIATIONS.

Amara-k. = Amara-kosha.
B. and R. = Boehtlingk and Roth.
Beng. = Bengālī (MSS.) or Bengālī recension.
Bhartṛi-h. = Bhartṛi-hari (Bohlen's ed.)
Bhaṭṭi-k. = Bhaṭṭi-kāvya.
C. = the commentator C'andra-śekhara.
chap. = chapter.
cl. = class of verbs.
Deva-n. = Deva-nāgarī (MSS.) or Deva-nāgarī recension.
Dict. = my Sanskṛit-English Dictionary.
Draupadī-h. = Draupadī-haraṇa in Johnson's Selections from the Mahā-bhārata.
ed. = edition.
Gīta-g. = Gīta-govinda (Lassen's ed.)
Gram. = my Sanskṛit Grammar, 4th ed.
Hari-v. = Hari-vaṇśa, the last Book of the Mahā-bhārata.
Hitop. = Hitopadeśa (Johnson's 1st ed.)
I. O. = India Office.
K. = the commentator Kāṭavema.
Kumāra-s. = Kumāra-sambhava.
l. = line.
Laghu-k. = Laghu-kaumudī.

Mahā-bh. Sel. = Johnson's Selections from the Mahā-bhārata.
Mālatī-m. = Mālatī-mādhava (the Calcutta ed. 1830).
Mālavik. = Mālavikāgnimitra (Tullberg's ed.)
Megha-d. = Megha-dūta.
Mṛiċh. or Mṛiċhak. = Mṛiċhakaṭika (Calcutta ed.)
Mudrā-r. = Mudrā-rākshasa (Calcutta ed. 1831).
Nalod. = Nalodaya.
Pāṇ. = Pāṇini (Boehtlingk's ed.)
Prāk. = Prākṛit.
Raghu-v. = Raghu-vaṇśa.
Rāmāy. = Rāmāyaṇa (Schlegel's ed.)
Ratn. = Ratnāvalī (Calcutta ed. 1832).
rt. = root.
S'. = the commentator S'an-kara.
Sāhit.-d. = Sāhitya-darpaṇa (Calcutta ed. 1828).
Sk. = Sanskṛit.
Vikram. = Vikramorvaśī.
Vishṇu-p. = Vishṇu-purāṇa (Wilson's translation, large ed.)

॥ अथ अभिज्ञानशकुन्तलम् ॥

या सृष्टिः स्रष्टुराद्या वहति विधिहुतं या हविर्या च होत्री
ये द्वे कालं विधत्तः श्रुतिविषयगुणा या स्थिता व्याप्य विश्वम् ।
यामाहुः सर्वभूतप्रकृतिरिति यया प्राणिनः प्राणवन्तः
प्रत्यक्षाभिः प्रपन्नस्तनुभिरवतु वस्ताभिरष्टाभिरीशः ॥१॥

---

[1] '(That visible form, viz. water) which (was) the first creation of the Creator; (that, viz. fire) which bears the oblation offered-according-to-rule; and (that visible form, viz. the priest) which (is) the offerer-of-the-oblation; (those) two (visible forms, viz. the Sun and Moon) which regulate time; (that, viz. ether) which perpetually pervades all space, having the quality (sound) perceptible by the ear; (that, viz. the earth) which they call the originator of all created-things; (that, viz. the air) by which living beings are furnished with breath—may Íśa [the supreme Lord], endowed with [manifested in] these eight visible forms, preserve you!' The play begins and ends with a prayer to Śiva (see the last note in this play). After every relative pronoun some case of *pratyakshā tanuḥ* must be supplied. *Srishṭir ādyā:* see Manu i. 8–10, *apa eva sasarja ādau,* '(the Creator) first created the waters.' *Vidhi-hutam = veda-vidhānena agnau kshiptam,* Ć. *Hotrī = dīkshita-mayī tanuḥ,* K., *yajamāna-rūpā tanuḥ,* Ć., 'the Brāhman who is qualified by initiation to offer the oblation.' *Kālaṃ vidhattaḥ = samayaṃ kurutaḥ,* Ć.; *= srijataḥ,* S. Hence the Sun is called *divā-kara,* 'maker of the day;' and the Moon, *niśā-kara,* 'maker of the night.' *Śruti-vi°:* the Hindūs reckon five elements, viz. water, fire, ether, earth, and air. Ether (*ākāśa*) is held to be the vehicle of sound, or of that quality which is the object of perception to the ear (see Manu i. 75). *Vyāpya sthitā,* i. e. 'keeps pervading.' Compare

---

Verse 1. The metre is SRAGDHARÁ (a variety of PRAKṚITI), in which there are twenty-one syllables to the Páda or quarter-verse, each Páda being alike.

$$- - - - \cup - - \mid \cup \cup \cup \cup \cup \cup \cup - \mid - \cup - - \cup - - \parallel$$

नान्द्यन्ते

सूत्रधार: ॥ नेपथ्याभिमुखमवलोक्य ॥

आर्ये। यदि नेपथ्यविधानमवसितम्। तर्हीतस्तावदागम्य-
ताम्।

vyāpya sthitaṃ rodasī in the opening of Vikramorvaśī. *Sthā* is joined
with an indecl. part. to express continuity of action. *Viśvam=prapañćam,*
'the whole visible universe,' K. *Sarva-bhūta-prakṛitiḥ,* so reads Kāṭa-
vema, followed by my own MS., and supported by Manu ix. 37, *Iyam
bhūmir bhūtānāṃ śāśvatī yonir ućyate,* 'this earth is called the primeval
womb [*yoniḥ = kāraṇam,* Kul.] of all created things.' The other MSS.
have *sarva-vīja-prakṛitiḥ. Prakṛitiḥ = upādāna-kāraṇam,* K.; *= utpatti-
sthānam,* Ć.; *= nidānam,* S'. *Prapannaḥ = upetaḥ,* K. The Bengālī MSS.
have *prasannaḥ.* The worshippers of S'iva, who were Pantheists in the
sense of believing that S'iva was himself all that exists as well as the
cause of all that is, held that there were eight different manifestations
of their god, called Rudras (viz. Rudra, Bhava, Sarva, Īśāna, Paśu-pati,
Bhīma, Ugra, Mahā-deva), and that these had their types or representatives
in the eight visible forms enumerated here. So the Vishṇu-purāṇa (Wilson,
p. 58, large ed.), 'Brahmā assigned to them their respective stations:
water, the sun, earth, fire, air, ether, the officiating Brāhman [*dīkshito
brāhmaṇaḥ*], and the moon; these are termed their visible forms [*tana-
vaḥ*].' In the opening of Mālavik. mention is made of S'iva upholding
the universe by means of these forms, *ashṭābhis tanubhir bibhrataḥ
kṛitsnaṃ jagad api.* See also Kumāra-s. iv. 76. S'aṅkara, with far-
fetched subtilty, points out how each of these types of S'iva is intended
by the poet to correspond with circumstances in the life of S'akuntalā.
Thus, *yā sṛishṭiḥ,* &c., is compared with the sentiment in verse 43; and
ye dve, &c., with the two female friends.

[1] 'At the end of the Nāndī, the Sūtra-dhāra (speaks).' In the Hindū
drama every piece commences with a prologue, which is preceded by the
Nāndī or opening benediction, invoking the favour of some deity. It is
called Nāndī because it rejoices the hearts of the gods; *nandanty asyāṃ
surā yasmāt tena nāndī prakīrtitā,* S'. The Sāhitya-darpaṇa (p. 135)
says, 'What is recited in praise of a deity, a Brāhman, a king, or the like,
combined with a benediction, is called Nāndī.' It is said to be employed
vighnopaśāntaye, 'for the removal of obstacles.' The Sūtra-dhāra was
the principal manager who regulated the thread or rules of the drama;

नटी ॥ प्रविश्य ॥

[a] अज्ज। इअम्हि। आणवेदु अज्जो। को णिओओ अणु-
चिट्टीअदु त्ति।

[a] आर्ये। इयमस्मि। आज्ञापयत्वार्यः। को नियोगोऽनुष्ठीयतामिति।

---

yena nartanīya-kathā-sūtram prathamam sū'yate, S. He is otherwise, especially when not a Brāhman, called the Sthāpaka, 'he who fixes or establishes the action of the play;' *kāvyārtha-sthāpanāt*, C. *Sthāpakaḥ sūtradhāra-sadṛiśa-guṇākāraḥ*, 'the Sthāpaka has qualities and an appearance like those of the Sūtra-dhāra,' Sāhit.-d. p. 137, l. 6. *Sūtra-dhāra-padena atra sthāpako 'bhimataḥ sūtradhāra-samānākāratvāt*, S. Bharata says, *Sūtradhāraḥ paṭhen nāndīm madhyamam [prathamaṃ, C.] svaram āśritaḥ*, 'the Sūtra-dhāra should recite the Nāndī, employing a tone neither high nor low.' He was generally a Brāhman, and therefore qualified to recite the Nāndī in his own person. He did so, however, as a Brāhman, and not in his character of manager, which he did not assume till he had concluded the Nāndī. *Nāndy-ante sūtradhāraḥ* is therefore equivalent to 'at the end of the Nāndī, or after reciting the Nāndī, the Sūtra-dhāra continues speaking.' So Ćandra-śekhara, *Nāndī, etad-ante sūtradhāro vadati, nāndīm paṭhitvā anyad vadati ity arthaḥ*. Hence the word *pravisya*, 'entering,' is not required; the reciter of the Nāndī remaining on the stage in the character of manager. [*Iti nayena nāndy-ante sūtradhāra-praveśo 'pāstaḥ*, C.] If the manager happened not to be a Brāhman, he seems to have had no right to the title *Sūtra-dhāra*, nor could he recite the Nāndī, but in that case some Brāhman pronounced the blessing, and the manager was called Sthāpaka. Such, at least, seems to be the meaning of Bharata's aphorism [*ranga-pūjāṃ vidhāya ādau sūtradhāre vinirgate sthāpakaḥ praviśet paśćāt sūtradhāra-guṇākṛitiḥ*], though all the extant plays make the Sūtra-dhāra first recite the benediction, and then carry on the dialogue. The Sāhit.-d., p. 137, has the following: *Idānīm pūrva-rangasya samyak-prayogābhāvād eka eva sūtradhāraḥ sarvam prayojayati iti vyavahāraḥ sa sthāpakaḥ*, 'in these days, from the want of a complete performance of the Pūrva-ranga, the custom is that the Sūtra-dhāra alone does all, and he is the Sthāpaka.' The blessing is usually followed by some mention of the author of the piece, an appeal to the favour of the audience, and a short dialogue between the manager and an attendant actor (*pāripārśvika*). In the present play, an actress sings a song for the amusement of the audience.

[2] 'Looking towards the tiring-room,' which was behind the stage,

सूत्रधारः ।

आर्ये । अभिरूपभूयिष्ठा परिषदियम् । अद्य खलु कालि-
दासग्रथितवस्तुना नवेनाभिज्ञानशकुन्तलाख्येन नाटके-
नोपस्थातव्यमस्माभिः । तत्प्रतिपात्रमाधीयतां यत्नः ।

'looking behind the scenes.' *Nepathyam = vyatiriktaṃ yavanikāntaritaṃ varṇikā-grahaṇādi-yogyaṃ naṭa-varya-sthānam,* K.; *= bhūshaṇa-sthānaṃ raṅgād vahiḥ-stham,* Ć., S'. In a Hindū theatre, a curtain [*apaṭī, paṭa, yavanikā*] suspended across the stage, answered the purposes of scenes. Behind it there was the space called *nepathya,* where the decorations were kept, and where the actors attired themselves and remained in readiness before entering the stage; whither also they withdrew on leaving it. When an actor was to come on hurriedly, the stage-direction is *paṭākshe-peṇa* or *apaṭī-kshepeṇa,* 'with a hurried toss of the curtain.' When he was to say something whilst hidden from the audience in this space behind the curtain, the direction is *nepathye,* '(a voice) in the postscenium.' As to *nepathya-vidhānam* in the next line [*= prasādhana-kriyā,* S'.], it may be translated, 'the act of decoration,' 'making the toilet,' or perhaps, 'the arrangements of the tiring-room.' *Nepathye yad vidhīyate tan nepathya-vidhānam.* Kāṭavema has *naipathya. Nepathyaṃ vidhā = nepathyaṃ raĉ* or *nepathyaṃ kri.* Compare Ratnāvalī, p. 2, l. 16.

[1] 'For the most part (composed of) learned [educated] men.' The audience consisted chiefly of good judges [*abhirūpa = vidvas, paṇḍita,* K., Ć.] So *rāshṭraṃ śūdra-bhūyishṭham,* Manu viii. 22.

[2] 'With the new drama called "Token-S'akuntalā," or "Ring-(recog-nized) S'akuntalā."' *Abhijñāna-śakuntalā* is an anomalous compound (Gram. 775); not one in which the terms are inverted, but one in which there is *uttara-pada-lopa* or *madhyama-pada-lopa,* 'elision of the second member.' On the authority of Ćandra-śekhara, the second member to be supplied is *smṛitā,* 'recognized;' and *abhijñāna* is 'the token of recog-nition—the ring.' The compound will thus be equivalent to *abhijñāna-smṛitā Śakuntalā,* 'S'akuntalā recognized by the token.' So *śāka-pārthiva,* 'the king of the era,' is equivalent to *śāka-priya-pārthiva,* 'the king beloved by the era.'

[3] 'Therefore let care be applied by each to his own part [or character],' 'let pains be taken by all in their several parts.' *Pratipātram = pātre pātre,* K. *Tat = tasmāt,* K. So *sreshu sthāneshe avahitair bhavitavyam,* Vikram., Act I.

नटी ।

[a]सुविहिदप्पओअदाए अज्जस्स ण किम्पि परिहाइस्सदि ।

सूत्रधारः ।

आर्ये । कथयामि ते भूतार्थम्[2] ।

आ परितोषाद्विदुषां न साधु मन्ये प्रयोगविज्ञानम् ।

बलवदपि शिक्षितानामात्मन्यप्रत्ययं चेतः ॥२॥

नटी ॥ सविनयम् ॥

[b]एवं णेदं । अणन्तरकरणिज्जं दाव अज्जो आणबेदु ।

<hr>

[a] सुविहितप्रयोगतया आर्यस्य न किमपि परिहास्यते ।　　　　[b] एवं न्विदम् ।
अनन्तरकरणीयं तावदार्य आज्ञापयतु ।

<hr>

[1] 'By reason of your honour's good assignment of the parts of the play (to the several actors), nothing will be wanting;' i. e. 'by reason of your skill in casting the characters, nothing is likely to go amiss in the acting;' or, 'by reason of (our) good acting, nothing will be wanting to your honour;' or, 'by reason of your honour's (skill in the) management of the play,' &c. Such are the various interpretations of Kāṭavema, Ćandra-śekhara, and S'aṅkara: the first seems preferable. So *yaḥ prayoyo bhavatīshu nibaddhaḥ*, Vikram., Act II. [*prayoyaṃ nibandh = prayoyaṃ virać*].

[2] *Bhūtārtham = satyam*, S'.; *= satyārtham*, K., 'the real truth,' 'the true state of the case.'

[3] 'I do not consider skill-in-the-representation-of-plays to be good [perfect] until (it cause) the satisfaction of the learned (audience); the mind of those even who are very well instructed has no confidence in itself.' *Balavad = sushṭhu*, Ć. *A-pratyaya*, 'distrustful of,' (with loc.)

<hr>

Verse 2. ĀRYĀ or GĀTHĀ, in which there are thirty Mātrās or measures (a short syllable containing one, and a long, two) in the first half-verse, and twenty-seven in the second. Each foot must contain four measures, except the sixth of the second half-verse, which contains one; and the half-verse must be divided by a pause at the end of the third foot.

$$- \cup \cup \mid - - \mid \cup \cup - \| \cup - \cup \mid - \mid \cup - \cup \mid - - \mid -$$
$$\cup \cup \cup \cup \mid \cup - \cup \mid - - \| - - \mid - - \mid \cup \mid - - \mid -$$

सूत्रधारः ।

किमन्यदस्याः परिषदः श्रुतिप्रसादनतः[1] ।

नटी ।

[a]अध कदमं उण उदुं अधिकरिञ गाइस्सं ।

सूत्रधारः ।

नन्विममेव तावदचिरप्रवृत्तमुपभोगक्षमं ग्रीष्मसमयमधि-
कृत्य गीयताम् । सम्प्रति हि

सुभगसलिलावगाहाः पाटलसंसर्गसुरभिवनवाताः ।
प्रच्छायसुलभनिद्रा दिवसाः परिणामरमणीयाः ॥३॥

नटी ।

[b]तह । ॥ इति गायति ॥

[a] अथ कतमं पुनश्छर्तुमधिकृत्य गास्यामि ।   [b] तथा ।

---

[1] *Śruti-prasādana-taḥ = śravaṇendriya tarpaṇāt*, K. Some MSS. insert *saṅgītāt karaṇīyam*.

[2] Lit. 'having placed over,' 'having made the prominent subject.' Hence, *adhikṛitya = kṛite*, 'about,' 'concerning,' 'with reference to,' Pāṇ. iv. 3, 87. So, in the next sentence: 'Assuredly let a song be sung concerning this very summer season, (so) suited to enjoyment [*upabhoga-kshama*], that has not long set in.' As to *nanu*, see Pāṇ. viii. 1, 43.

[3] 'For now (are) the days on-which-there-are-grateful-bathings-in-the-water (and) on-which-silvan-breezes-are-fragrant-from-contact-with-the-trumpet-flower: (now are the days) on-which-sleep-is-easily-induced-in-very-shady-spots (and) which-are-delightful-at-their-close.' *Praććhāya*° = *prakṛishṭa-ććhāyā yatra tat sthānam praććhāyam tasmin sulabhā nidrā yeshu te tathoktāḥ*, K.; see p. 37, note 1 of this book. A short vowel is the substitute for the long final of a fem. noun, when compounded with such prepositions as *pra, ati,* &c.; thus *pragrīva* from *grīvā; atimāla* from *mālā;* see Laghu-k. 1003. *Pariṇāma = virāma = sāyan-kāla,* 'the evening,' K.

Verse 3. ĀRYĀ or GĀTHĀ. See verse 2.

∪∪∪∪ | ∪ − ∪ | − − ‖ − ∪ ∪ | − − | ∪ ∪ ∪ ∪ | ∪ ∪ − | −
− − | ∪ ∪ ∪ ∪ | − − ‖ ∪ ∪ − | ∪ ∪ − | ∪ | ∪ ∪ − | −

^aईसीसिचुम्बिआइं भमरेहिं सुउमारकेसरसिहाइं।
ओदंसअन्ति दअमाणा पमदाओ सिरीसकुसुमाइं॥४॥

सूचधारः।

आर्ये। साधु गीतम्। अहो रागबद्धचित्तवृत्तिरालिखित
इव सर्वतो रङ्गः। तदिदानीं कतमत्प्रकरणमाश्रित्यैनमा-
राधयामः।

नटी।

^bएं अज्जमिस्सेहिं पढमं एव्व आक्खत्तं अहिण्णाणसउन्दलं

^a ईषदीपञ्चुम्बितानि भ्रमरैः सुकुमारकेशरशिखानि।
अवतंसयन्ति दयमानाः प्रमदाः शिरीषकुसुमानि॥

^b नन्द्वार्यमिश्रैः प्रथममेवाज्ञप्तमभिज्ञानशकुन्तलं

---

[1] 'Loving [amorous] fair-ones make ear-rings of the S'irīsha-blossoms
that-are-very-gently-kissed by bees (and) the points-of-whose-filaments-
are-very-delicate.' According to S'ankara, *kesara = kiñjalka*, and the
whole compound is a Bahuvrīhi, agreeing with *sirīsha-kusumāni*. There
is an allusion to the blossoms of the S'irīsha being thus used in Megha-
dūta 67, *čārukarṇe śirīsham;* and Raghu-v. xvi. 48, 61. Compare also
karṇa-śirīsha-rodhi, at the end of Act I. of this play; and Ritu-s. ii. 18,
kṛitāvataṉsaiḥ kusumaiḥ, &c. *Avataṉsayanti* is a nominal verb from
avataṉsa.

[2] 'On every side, the audience, having all the feelings of its soul fixed
on the melody, is as if formed into a picture,' i. e. motionless or riveted
with attention. *Ālikhita = niśćala*, K.; *ranga* applies to the audience as
well as to the stage. *Prakaraṇa*, 'a subject,' 'story,' 'poem.'

[3] 'By your reverence;' *ārya-miśraiḥ* is here an epithet of the manager,
the respectful plural being used. In Vikramorvaśī, Act I, *ārya-vidagdha-*

---

[a] णाम अपुव्वं णाडअं पञ्ओएण अधिकरीअदुत्ति ।

सूत्रधारः ।

आर्ये । सम्यगनुबोधितोऽस्मि । अस्मिन्क्षणे विस्मृतं खलु मया । कुतः ।

तवास्मि गीतरागेण हारिणा प्रसभं हृतः ।
एष राजेव दुष्यन्तः सारङ्गेणातिरंहसा ॥ ५ ॥

॥ इति निष्क्रान्तौ ॥

॥ प्रस्तावना ॥

[a] नाम अपूर्वं नाटकं प्रयोगेणाधिक्रियतामिति ।

---

miśráḥ, 'respectable and intelligent persons,' occurs as an epithet of the audience. *Miśra*, 'mixed,' in a compound of this kind has the force of 'gentleman.' *Ā-jñapta*, 'ordered,' 'arranged,' 'announced.'

[1] *Adhikriyatām* = *prakaṭī-kriyatām*, K., i. e. 'let it be made the subject of exhibition,' 'let it be brought prominently forward;' see p. 6, note 2. Some read *prayoge;* compare in Ratnāvalī, p. 2, l. 15, *nāṭikā prayogeṇa nāṭayitavyā.*

[2] The rule is, that the conclusion of the prelude should prepare the audience for the entrance of one of the dramatis personæ. Hence, the manager exclaims, 'I was forcibly carried away by the ravishing melody of thy song, like king Dushyanta here by the very fleet antelope.' *Prasabham*, a kind of adverbial indeclinable participle from an old form *sabh* (= rt. *sah*) with *pra*, and meaning 'forcibly,' 'violently;' (see Gram. 567.)

Verse 5. ŚLOKA or ANUSHṬUBH, consisting of four Pādas of eight syllables.

$$\breve{-}\ \cup\ \breve{-}\ \cup\ |\ \cup\ -\ -\ \breve{-}\ \|\ \cup\ \breve{-}\ \cup\ \breve{-}\ |\ \cup\ -\ \cup\ \cup$$
$$\cup\ \breve{-}\ \cup\ \cup\ |\ \cup\ -\ -\ \cup\ \|\ \cup\ \cup\ \cup\ \cup\ |\ \cup\ -\ \cup\ \cup$$

The first four syllables and the last syllable of each Pāda may be either long or short.

॥ अथ प्रथमोऽङ्कः ॥

॥ ततः प्रविशति मृगानुसारी सशरचापहस्तो राजा रथेन सूतश्च ॥

सूतः ॥ राजानं मृगं चावलोक्य ॥

आयुष्मन् ।

कृष्णसारे दद्चक्षुस्त्वयि चाधिज्यकार्मुके ।
मृगानुसारिणं साक्षात्पश्यामीव पिनाकिनम् ॥ ६ ॥

राजा ।

सूत दूरममुना सारङ्गेण वयमाकृष्टाः । अयं पुनरिदानीमपि
ग्रीवाभङ्गाभिरामं मुहुरनुपतति स्यन्दने बद्धदृष्टिः
पश्चार्धेन प्रविष्टः शरपतनभयाद्भूयसा पूर्वकायम् ।

---

[1] 'O long-lived one!' a respectful mode of addressing kings. Ćandra-śekhara quotes a verse of Bharata, *Vaded rājñāṃ ća ćetīṃ ća bhavatīti vidū-shakaḥ, āyushman rathinaṃ sūto vṛiddhaṃ tāteti ćetaraḥ.* Cf. Manu ii. 125.

[2] 'Casting (my) eye on the black-antelope and on thee with-thy-strung-bow I behold, as it were, S'iva visibly present chasing the deer.' *Adhi-jya*, 'having the string [*jyā*] up;' at the end of the chase the bow would be *śithila-jya*: see verse 40. *Sa-jya* is used like *adhi-jya*. *Pinākin* is S'iva, armed with his bow called *Pināka*. [So the bow of Vishṇu has a name *Śārnga*, and that of Arjuna, *Gāṇḍīva*, Megha-d. 48, 50.] In illustration, Kāṭavema refers to Raghu-v. xi. 44, *Dhanuḥ, yena vṛisha-dhvajo vāṇam asṛijad vidruta-kratu-mṛigānusāriṇam.* S'iva, not having been invited to Daksha's celebrated horse-sacrifice, was so indignant, that with his wife he suddenly presented himself, confounded the sacrifice, dispersed and mutilated the gods, and chasing Yajña, 'the lord of sacrifice,' who fled in the form of a fleet deer, overtook and decapitated him. The Vāyu-purāṇa makes S'iva create a manifestation of himself as a monstrous being named Vīra-bhadra, who pursues Yajña in the form of a deer: see Vishṇu-purāṇa, p. 65.

Verse 6. SLOKA or ANUSHTUBH. See verse.

दर्भैरर्धावलीढः श्रमविवृतमुखभ्रंशिभिः कीर्णवर्त्मा
पश्योद्ग्रन्थुतत्वाद्वियति बहुतरं स्तोकमुर्व्यां प्रयाति ॥७॥

॥ सविस्मयम् ॥

कथमनुपतत एव मे प्रयत्नप्रेक्षणीयः संवृत्तोऽयं मृगः ।

सूतः ।

आयुष्मन् । उत्खातिनी भूमिरिति मया रश्मिसंयमनाद्-
यस्य मन्दीकृतो वेगः । तेन मृग एष विप्रकृष्टान्तरः संवृत्तः ।
सम्प्रति हि समदेशवर्तिनस्ते न दुरासदो भविष्यति ।

राजा ।

तेन हि मुच्यन्तामभीशवः ।

सूतः ।

यथाज्ञापयत्यायुष्मान् । ॥ रथवेगं निरूप्य ॥ आयुष्मन् । पश्य
पश्य ।

---

[1] 'There he is now, gracefully by the bending of his neck fixing a glance ever and anon at the chariot which pursues him, by (the contraction of) the hinder half (of his body) repeatedly drawing himself into the fore-(part of his) body through fear of the descent of the arrow; strewing the road with grass half-chewed which drops from his mouth kept open from exhaustion. See! by reason of his lofty boundings he springs forward chiefly in the air, little on the ground.' For *baddha-drishti*, compare Raghu-v. i. 40, *syandanābaddha-drishtishu*. *Pravishtah pūrva-kāyam* is equivalent to *pravishta-pūrva-kāyah*, lit. 'entering the fore-part of his body,' a Bahuvrīhi compound analogous to *baddha-drishtih* and *kīrna-vartmā*. In regard to Darbha or Kuśa grass, see note to verse 15.

[2] '[With surprise.] How now! the deer has become visible with difficulty [lit. with effort] to me pursuing (him).' Dr. Burkhard reads this line thus: *Sa esha katham anupadam eva prayatna-prekshanīyah samvrittah.*

[3] 'Because the ground is full of hollows, I have slackened the speed of the chariot by drawing in the reins.' *Utkhātinī*, lit. 'full of excavations.'

[4] 'Separated by a longer interval or distance.'

[5] The expressions *nirūpya* and *nātayitvā*, which occur so frequently in

Verse 7. SRAGDHARĀ. See verse 1.

मुक्तेषु रश्मिषु निरायतपूर्वकाया
निष्कम्पचामरशिखा निभृतोर्ध्वकर्णाः।
आत्मोद्गतैरपि रजोभिरलङ्घनीया
धावन्त्यमी मृगजवाक्षममेव रथ्याः ॥८॥

the stage-directions, are synonymous, and may both be translated by 'acting,' 'gesticulating,' 'exhibiting by gesticulation.' The properties and paraphernalia of the Hindū stage were as limited as the scenery; and though seats, thrones, weapons, and cars were introduced, yet much had to be supplied by the imaginations of the spectators, assisted by the gesticulations of the actors. Thus, though the car of Dushyanta might have been represented on the stage, the horses would be left to the imagination, and the speed of the chariot would only be indicated by the gesticulations of the charioteer.

[1] 'The reins being loosed, these chariot-horses gallop along as if with impatience of the speed of the deer [i. e. impatient or emulous of its speed], having the fore-part of their bodies well stretched out, having the chowrie which forms their crest motionless, having the ears erect yet firmly fixed [or bent backwards], not to be overtaken even by the dust raised by themselves.'—The *ćámarī* or chowrie, formed of the white bushy tail of the Yak or Bos Grunniens, served for whisking off flies; and was used as an emblem of princely rank. It was placed as an ornament between the ears of horses, like the plume of the war-horse of chivalry. The velocity of the chariot caused it to lose its play and appear fixed in one direction, like a flag borne rapidly against the wind. A similar idea occurs in Act I. of the Vikramorvaśī, *ćitrārambha-viniśćalam hayaśirasi ćámaram.* There is some difficulty in *nibhritordhvakarnāh.* The commentator explains *nibhrita* by *niśćala,* 'motionless.' The most usual sense of *nibhrita* is 'secret,' 'modest,' 'depressed,' 'low' (Gīta-g. ii. 11, ii. 21; Hitop. passim). In Raghu-v. viii. 15 the sky is described as *nibhritendu,* 'having its moon nearly set' (=*astamayāsannaćandra*). Hence might flow the acceptation 'bent backwards.' The ears of a horse while running at full speed would be not only erect, but probably bent backwards so as to present the least resistance to the

<hr>

Verse 8. VASANTA-TILAKĀ (a variety of ŚAKVARĪ or ŚAKKARĪ or ŚARKARĪ), containing fourteen syllables to the Pāda or quarter-verse, each Pāda being alike.

– – ◡ – ◡ ◡ ◡ – ◡ ◡ – ◡ – – ‖

राजा ॥ सहर्षम् ॥

सत्यमतीत्य हरितो हरींश्च वर्तन्ते वाजिनः। तथा हि
यदालोके सूक्ष्मं व्रजति सहसा तद्विपुलतां
यदर्धे विच्छिन्नं भवति कृतसन्धानमिव तत्।
प्रकृत्या यद्वक्रं तदपि समरेखं नयनयो-
र्ने मे दूरे किञ्चित्क्षणमपि न पार्श्वं रथजवात् ॥९॥

___

wind. This interpretation is confirmed by the reading of the Bengālī MSS., *cyuta-karṇa-bhaṅga;* but if the sense *niścala* be insisted on, translate—'having the ears erect and immovable.'

[1] 'Truly, the horses are [or appear as if] outstripping the horses of the Sun, and the horses of Indra,' i. e. the speed of the chariot seems like that of the Sun or the Wind. *Harito* is taken by some commentators as gen. case of *harit,* 'the Sun,' and *harīn* as acc. case plural of *hari,* 'a horse.' But *ća* after *harīn* indicates that both *harito* and *harīn* are acc. cases after *atītya.* In the Ṛig-veda we find *harī* (dual) and *harayaḥ* and *haribhiḥ* (I. 16, 1; 101, 10; 16, 4; 52, 8) for 'the horses of Indra;' and *haritaḥ* for 'the seven horses of Sūrya or the Sun' (I. 50, 8; 115, 4). In Nirukta i. 15 the different vehicles of the gods are given, and among them *harī Indrasya, haritaḥ ādityasya.* Hence Indra is called *hari-haya* or *hari-vāhana* (Vikram., Act III), and in Ṛig-veda, *hari-yojana;* and the Sun is called *harid-aśva.* One name of the Sun is *saptāśva,* 'having seven horses.' The Bengālī MSS. read *katham atītya hariṇaṃ harayo,* &c., but *harito hariṇśća* is supported by all the Deva-nāgarī MSS., and by a parallel passage in Vikram., Act I, *anena ratha-vegena vainateyam api āsādayeyam.*

[2] 'That which in my sight (appeared) minute suddenly attains magnitude; that which was divided in half becomes as if united; that also which is by nature [really] crooked (appears) even-lined [straight] to my eyes. Nothing (seems) at a distance from me nor at my side even for a moment, by reason of the velocity of the chariot.' This is a method of describing great velocity of motion, which may be well appreciated by any one, in these days, who may have taken notice of the effect produced upon adjacent objects by an express railway speed of a mile a minute.

___

Verse 9. ŚIKHARIṆĪ (a variety of the ATYASHṬI), containing seventeen syllables to the Pāda or quarter-verse, each Pāda being alike.

$$\cup - - - - - \mid \cup \cup \cup \cup \cup - - \cup \cup \cup - \parallel$$

सूत । पश्यैनं व्यापाद्यमानम् । ॥ इति शरसन्धानं नाटयति ॥

नेपथ्ये ।

भो भो राजन् । आश्रममृगोऽयं न हन्तव्यो न हन्तव्यः ।

सूतः ॥ आकर्ण्यावलोक्य च ॥

आयुष्मन् । अस्य खलु ते वाणपथवर्तिनः कृष्णसारस्यान्तरे तपस्विन उपस्थिताः ।

राजा ॥ ससम्भ्रमम् ॥

तेन हि प्रगृह्यन्तां वाजिनः ।

सूतः ।

तथा । ॥ इति रथं स्थापयति ॥

॥ ततः प्रविशत्यात्मना तृतीयो वैखानसः ॥

वैखानसः ॥ हस्तमुद्यम्य ॥

राजन् । आश्रममृगोऽयं न हन्तव्यो न हन्तव्यः ।

न खलु न खलु वाणः सन्निपात्योऽयमस्मि-
न्मृदुनि मृगशरीरे पुष्पराशाविवाग्निः ।

---

[1] 'With himself as the third,' or 'with himself making the third,' i. e. himself and two others. This is a not unusual compound. Compare the expression, *Pāṇḍavā mātṛi-shashṭāḥ*, 'the Pāṇḍavas with their mother as the sixth,' i. e. five persons, or six counting their mother. Again, *chāyā-dvitīyo Nalaḥ*, 'Nala made two by his shadow,' 'umbra geminatus' (Nala v. 25). Also, *adhīte chaturo vedān ākhyāna-panchamān*, 'he reads the four Vedas with the Ākhyānas as a fifth' (Nala vi. 9). A similar idiom prevails in Greek, αὐτός being used after ordinal numbers: thus, πέμπτος αὐτός, 'himself with four others,' Thucydides I. xlvi. Similarly, τρίτον ἡμιτάλαντον, 'two talents and a half,' and ἕβδομον ἡμιτάλαντον, 'six talents and a half,' Herodotus I. 15, 50.

Verse 10. MĀLINĪ or MĀNINĪ (a variety of ATI-ŚAKVARĪ or ATI-ŚAKKARĪ), containing fifteen syllables to the Pāda or quarter-verse, each Pāda being alike.

∪ ∪ ∪ ∪ ∪ ∪ – – | – ∪ – – ∪ – – ‖

क्व वत हरिणकानां जीवितं चातिलोलं
क्व च निशितनिपाताः वज्रसाराः शरास्ते ॥१०॥
तत्साधु कृतसन्धानं प्रतिसंहर सायकम् ।
आर्तत्राणाय वः शस्त्रं न प्रहर्तुमनागसि ॥११॥

राजा ।

एष प्रतिसंहृतः । ॥ इति यथोक्तं करोति ॥

---

[1] 'Not indeed, not indeed must this arrow (of thine) be allowed to descend upon this tender body of the deer, like fire upon a heap of flowers. Where, forsooth, on the one hand (*ća*), is the very frail existence of fawns? and where, on the other (*ća*), are thy sharp-falling adamantine shafts?' i. e. Where is the suitability or congruity between the one and the other? What has the one to do with the other? How great a contrast or difference is there between the one and the other! Let not your shafts waste their strength upon an object so frail and tender, but let them be directed towards a mark more fitted to prove their adamantine qualities. This repetition of *kva* to express great contrast or unsuitability between two things is not uncommon. It is used by Kālidāsa again at the end of the Second Act of this play, *kva vayam*, &c.; also in Megha-dūta 5, thus, 'Where is a cloud which is a collection of vapour, fire, water, and wind? and where the meaning of messages to be received by intelligent mortals?' i. e. Why deliver a message intended for intelligent human beings to a cloud? What possible connection can there be between objects whose nature is so different? See also Raghu-v. i. 2, 'Where is the race sprung from the sun? and where my scanty powers of mind?' The majority of MSS. read *pushparāśau*, some *tūla-rāśau*, 'on a heap of cotton.'

[2] 'Therefore withhold your well-aimed [lit. well fitted to the bow] arrow. Your weapon is for the deliverance of the distressed, not to inflict a wound on the innocent.' *Sandhā* is properly 'to unite or fix an arrow to a bow,' hence 'to take aim' (Draupadī-h. 149); and *sandhānam*, 'the act of taking aim.' *Prahartum* is here used where *praharaṇāya* might be expected, but the infinitive is interchangeable with the dative, and frequently has the force of that case.

Verse 11. Sloka or Anushtubh. See verse 5.

वैखानसः ।

सदृशमेतत्पुरुवंशप्रदीपस्य भवंतः ।
जन्म यस्य पुरोर्वंशे युक्तरूपमिदं तव ।
पुत्रमेवङ्गुणोपेतं चक्रवर्तिनमाप्नुहि ॥१२॥

---

[1] 'This is worthy of your honour, who art the light of the race of Puru,' i. e. an illustrious descendant of Puru. Compare in Vikramorvaśī, Act I, *sadṛiśam idaṃ soma-vaṇśa-sambhavasya*. In English we have the same idiom, 'this is just like [i. e. worthy of] one born in the Lunar race.' The two great lines or dynasties of kings according to Hindū mythology were the Solar and the Lunar. The Solar begins with Ikshvāku the son of Vaivasvata, the son of Vivasvat, or the Sun, and is carried on through Kakutstha, Dilīpa, Raghu, Aja, and Daśaratha, to his son, the great Rāma-ćandra, hero of the Rāmāyaṇa. Under the Lunar come Puru, Dushyanta, Kṛishṇa, and the heroes of the Mahā-bhārata, as, 1. Soma; 2. his son, Budha; 3. his son, Purūravas; 4. his son, Āyus; 5. his son, Nahusha; 6. his son, Yayāti; 7. his sons, Puru and Yadu. From Puru were descended Taṇsu, Anila, Dushyanta, and Bharata. From his brother Yadu came Sātvata, S'ūra, Vasu-deva, and his sons Bala-rāma and Kṛishṇa. From Bharata the son of Dushyanta and descendant of Puru came, after a time, Ajamīḍha, Saṃvaraṇa, Kuru, S'āntanu, Bhīshma, and Kṛishṇa-dvaipāyana or Vyāsa. The latter was the father of Dhṛita-rāshṭra and Pāṇḍu. The quarrels of the hundred sons of Dhṛita-rāshṭra with their cousins, the five sons of Pāṇḍu (all of them being thus descended from Kuru and Puru), form the subject of the Mahā-bhārata. These two separate Solar and Lunar lines were occasionally intermixed by marriage, and a cross occurs at the very beginning, by the marriage of Ilā (Iḍā), daughter of Vaivasvata, with Budha. Paraśu-rāma, as a Brāhman, belonged to neither dynasty, but was connected with the Solar on his mother's side (see note to verse 22).

[2] 'This well becomes you, whose family belongs to the line of Puru, (therefore) be rewarded with a son gifted with all virtues, (and who shall become) a universal emperor.' A *ćakravartin* is one who reigns over a *ćakra*, or country reaching from sea to sea. According to the Vishṇu-purāṇa, a *ćakravartin* is one in whose hand the *ćakra*, or discus of Vishṇu, is delineated. There have been twelve of these emperors, commencing with Bharata, the son of Dushyanta.

Verse 12. S'LOKA or ANUSHṬUBH. See verse 5.

इतरौ ॥ बाहू उद्यम्य ॥

सर्वथा चक्रवर्तिनं पुत्रमाप्नुहि ।

राजा ॥ सप्रणामम् ॥

प्रतिगृहीतम् ।

वैखानसः ।

राजन् । समिदाहरणाय प्रस्थिता वयम् । एष खलु कण्वस्य महर्षेरुपमालिनीतीरमाश्रमो दृश्यते । न चेदन्यकार्यातिपातः । तत्प्रविश्य प्रतिगृह्यतामातिथेयः सत्कारः । अपि च रम्यास्तपोधनानां प्रतिहतविघ्नाः क्रियाः समवलोक्य । ज्ञास्यसि कियद्भुजो मे रक्षति मौर्वीकिणाङ्क इति ॥१३॥

राजा ।

अपि सन्निहितोऽत्र कुलपतिः ।

---

[1] This exclamation usually serves to ratify any auspicious prayer or prophecy uttered by a Brāhman. *Brāhmaṇa-vaćas* may be supplied, 'the word of a Brāhman is accepted.' See the same phrase in Vikram., Act II.

[2] Compare Raghu-vaṇśa xiv. 70, i. 49.

[3] *Upa-mālinī-tīram*, 'near the banks of the Mālinī;' see Gram. 760. *b*.

[4] 'If it be not (the cause of) the neglect of any other duty,' or 'if it does not interfere with the discharge of any other duty.'

[5] 'Beholding the pleasing rites of the hermits, all the hindrances to which are warded off (by you), you will think to yourself, how much this arm of mine, marked with the scar of the bow-string, defends !' *Tapodhana*, 'a devotee,' or 'one rich in devotion.' A parallel passage occurs in Raghu-v. xviii. 47, 'The earth was preserved by his arm, though without the mark of the scar formed by the bow-string' (*abaddha-maurvī-kinalāńćhanena*). The ancient Hindūs extracted from the leaves of the Mūrvā plant (Aletris) very tough, elastic threads, with which they made their bow-strings (*maurvī*), and which, for that reason, were ordained by Manu to form the girdle or zone of the military or Kshatriya class. Manu ii. 42.

Verse 13. ĀRYĀ or GĀTHĀ. See verse 2.

```
- -  | ᴗ - ᴗ | - - ‖ ᴗ ᴗ ᴗ ᴗ | - - | ᴗ - ᴗ | ᴗ ᴗ - | -
- ᴗ ᴗ | ᴗ - ᴗ | - - ‖ - ᴗ ᴗ | - - |  ᴗ  | - ᴗ ᴗ | ᴗ
```

वैखानसः ।

इदानीमेव दुहितरं शकुन्तलामतिथिसत्काराय नियुज्य
दैवमस्याः प्रतिकूलं शमयितुं सोमतीर्थं[1] गतः ।

राजा ।

भवतु । तां द्रक्ष्यामि । सा खलु विदितभक्तिर्मां महर्षेः
कथयिष्यति ।

वैखानसः ।

साधयामस्तावत् ।   ॥ इति सशिष्यो निष्क्रान्तः ॥

राजा ।

सूत । चोदयाश्वान् । पुण्याश्रमदर्शनेन तावदात्मानं[2] पुनीमहे ।

सूतः ।

यदाज्ञापयत्यायुष्मान् ।   ॥ इति भूयो रथवेगं निरूपयति ॥

राजा   ॥ समन्तादवलोक्य ॥

सूत । अकथितोऽपि ज्ञायत एव यथायमाभोगस्तपोव-[3]
नस्येति ।

---

[1] *Soma-tīrtha* is a place of pilgrimage in the West of India, on the
coast of Gujarāt, near the temple of Somanāth. It is also called Prabhāsa.
The fable is that Soma, or the Moon, was here cured of the consumption
brought upon him by the imprecation of Daksha, his father-in-law
(Mahā-bh., S'alya-p. 2011; Vishṇu-p. p. 561). A *tīrtha* is a place of
pilgrimage, generally on the bank of some sacred stream, or near some
holy spring. The word is derived from *tṝi*, 'to cross over,' implying that
the stream has to be passed through, either for the washing away of sin,
or for extrication from some difficulty or adverse destiny. Thousands of
devotees still flock to the most celebrated Tīrthas, Benares, Haridwār, &c.

[2] *Ātmānam*, 'ourselves.' The sing. is used for du. and pl., Gram. 232.

[3] *Ābhoga* = *vistāra*, 'extension,' 'amplitude;' *paripūrṇa-tā*, 'fulness.'
S'., in explaining *pariṇāha* in the sense of 'circumference,' gives *ābhoga*
as a synonym. In Megha-d. 90, *gaṇḍābhoga* is explained by *kapola-
maṇḍala*, 'the orb of the cheek;' and by *gaṇḍa-sthala*, 'the region of the
cheek;' and *stanābhoga* is said to mean 'fulness of breast.' Translate,
'Even without being told, it may be known indeed that here (we are
within) the expanse [or exuberant fulness] of the sacred grove.'

सूतः ।

कथमिव ।

राजा ।

किं न पश्यति भवान् । इह हि

नीवाराः शुकगर्भकोटरमुखभ्रष्टास्तरूणामधः
प्रस्निग्धाः क्वचिदिङ्गुदीफलभिदः सूच्यन्त एवोपलाः ।
विश्वासोपगमादभिन्नगतयः शब्दं सहन्ते मृगा-
स्तोयाधारपथाश्च वल्कलशिखानिष्यन्दरेखाङ्किताः ॥१४॥

---

[1] 'For here are the (grains of) wild-rice beneath the trees, fallen from the mouths [openings] of the hollow-trunks (*kotara*) filled with parrots; in other places the polished stones (used) for crushing the fruit of the Ingudī are plainly observed; the fawns too, with undeviating step [i. e. not starting aside] from having acquired confidence, bear the sound (of the voice); and the paths of the reservoirs are marked with lines by the drippings from the ends of the bark-clothes.' *Mukha* is used for any opening. *Garbha*, as the last member of a compound, often denotes 'filled with,' as *cūrṇa-garbhā nāḍīḥ*, 'a tube filled with powder.' The *Ingudī*, commonly called *Ingua* or *Jiyaputa*, is a tree from the fruit of which necklaces were made of a supposed prolific efficacy; whence the botanical name Nagelia Putran-jīva or Jiva-putraka. In Raghu-v. xiv. 81 there is an allusion to the fruit being used by hermits to supply oil for lamps, and in Act II. to its furnishing them with ointment. The synonym for the tree in the Amara-kosha is *tāpasa-taru*, 'the anchorite's tree.' S. calls it *muni-pādapa*. *Abhinna-gati* may perhaps be translated 'not running away.' K. explains it by *avihata-gati*, 'not stopping in their walk.' So *abhinna-svara*, 'one who does not hesitate in speaking.' The sense of the last line is determined by a passage at the end of this Act, where the dust is described as falling 'on the bark dresses, moist with water, hung up (to dry) on the branches of trees' (*vitapa-vishakta-jalārdra-valkaleshu*, verse 32). In carrying these dresses from the tank (*toyādhāra*) to the trees, a line would be formed by the drippings from the edges [*śikhā*=*añcala*, Schol.]

Verse 14. ŚĀRDŪLA-VIKRĪḌITA (a variety of ATIDHṚITI), containing nineteen syllables to the quarter-verse, each quarter-verse being alike.

‒ ‒ ‒ ∪ ∪ ‒ ∪ ‒ ∪ ∪ ∪ ‒ | ‒ ‒ ‒ ∪ ‒ ‒ ∪ ‒ ‖

अपि च ।

कुल्याम्भोभिः पवनचपलैः शाखिनो धौतमूला
भिन्नो रागः किसलयरुचामाज्यधूमोद्गमेन ।
एते चार्वागुपवनभुवि च्छिन्नदर्भाङ्कुरायां
नष्टाशङ्का हरिणशिशवो मन्दमन्दं चरन्ति ॥१५॥

सूतः ।

सर्वमुपपन्नम् ।

राजा ॥ स्तोकमन्तरं गत्वा ॥

तपोवनवासिनामुपरोधो मा भूत् । अत्रैव तावद्रथं स्था-
पय । यावदवतरामि ।

---

[1] ‘The trees have their roots washed by the waters of canals [trenches],
tremulous in the wind; the tint of (those trees which are) bright with fresh-
sprouts is diversified [partially obscured] by the rising of the smoke of the
clarified butter (burnt in oblations); and in front, these young fawns,
free from timidity, leisurely graze on the lawn of the garden, where the
stalks of Darbha grass have been mown.’ The commentators explain
bhinna by *anyathā-bhūta*, ‘altered,’ ‘made different;’ but it may also
mean ‘broken,’ ‘interrupted,’ ‘partially obscured.’ *Arvāk* = *agrataḥ*, ‘in
front,’ ‘near.’ *Darbha* is another name for *Kuśa* or sacrificial grass (Poa
Cynosuroides). This was the plant held sacred by the Hindūs, as verbena
was by the Romans. Ground prepared for a sacrifice was strewn with
the blades of this grass. The officiating Brāhmans were purified by
sitting on it, and by rubbing it between their hands. Its sanctifying
qualities were various, see Manu ii. 43, 75, 182; iii. 208, 223, 255, 256;
iv. 36; v. 115; xi. 149; and Vishṇu-p. p. 106. Its leaves are very long,
with tapering points of which the extreme acuteness is proverbial; whence
the expression *kuśāgra-buddhi* (Raghu-v. v. 4), ‘one whose intellect is as
sharp as the point of a Kuśa leaf.’ In Atharva-v. xix. 28 this grass is
addressed as a god. According to the commentators this verse and the
last afford examples of *anumānālankāra*, or figure called ‘Inference.’

Verse 15. MANDĀKRĀNTĀ (a variety of ATYASHTI), containing seventeen syllables to
the quarter-verse, each quarter-verse being alike. This is the metre of the Megha-dūta.

$$- - - - - \mid \cup \cup \cup \cup \cup \cup - \mid - \cup - - \cup - \underset{\smile}{-} \parallel$$

सूतः ।

धृताः मयहाः । अवतरत्वायुष्मान् ।

राजा ॥ अवतीर्य ॥

सूत । विनीतंवेषेण प्रवेष्टव्यानि तपोवनानि नाम । इदं तावद्गृह्यताम् ।   ॥ इति सूतस्याभरणानि धनुश्चोपनीयं ॥   सूत । यावदहमाश्रमवासिनः प्रत्यवेक्ष्योपावर्ते । तावदात्तप्रुष्ठाः क्रियन्तां वाजिनः ।

सूतः ।

तथा ।   ॥ इति निष्क्रान्तः ॥

राजा ॥ परिक्रम्यावलोक्य च ॥

इदमाश्रमद्वारम् । यावत्प्रविशामि ।   ॥ प्रविश्य निमित्तं सूचयन् ॥

शान्तमिदमाश्रमपदं स्फुरति च बाहुः कुतः फलमिहास्य ।
अथवा भवितव्यानां द्वाराणि भवन्ति सर्वच ॥१६॥

---

[1] Compare Manu viii. 2.   Dr. Burkhard has *vinīta-vesha-praveśyāni*.

[2] 'Giving over his ornaments and bow (to the care) of the charioteer.' Observe the use of the gen. after *upanīya*; see Gram. 858.

[3] Lit. 'let the horses be made wet-backed,' i. e. let them be watered and refreshed.   'Let their fatigue be removed by giving them water and by rubbing their backs,' S'.

[4] 'Acting an omen,' or 'acting as if he observed an omen,' lit. 'manifesting a sign.' *Nimitta* is any omen or sign, such as the throbbing of the arm or eyelid.   If this was felt on the right side it was a good omen in men; if on the left, a bad omen.   The reverse was true of women.

[5] 'This hermitage is tranquil [i. e. a peaceful spot, undisturbed by passion or emotion], and yet my arm throbs; whence can there be any result of this in such a place?   But yet the gates of destiny are everywhere.'   A quivering sensation in the right arm was supposed to prognosticate union with a beautiful woman.   See Raghu-v. xii. 90; Bhaṭṭi-k. i. 27; Vikram., Act II.

Verse 16.   ĀRYĀ or GĀTHĀ.   See verse 2.

$$- \cup \cup \mid \cup - \cup \mid \cup \cup - \parallel \cup \cup \cup \cup \mid - - \mid \cup - \cup \mid \cup \cup - \mid \cup$$
$$\cup \cup - \mid \cup \cup - \mid - - \parallel - - \mid \cup \cup - \mid \cup \mid - - \mid \cup$$

नेपथ्ये ।

[a]इदी इदी सहीओ ।

राजा ॥ कर्णं दत्त्वा ॥

अये । दक्षिणेन वृक्षवाटिकामालाप इव श्रूयते । यावदत्र
गच्छामि । ॥ परिक्रम्यावलोक्य च ॥ अये । एतास्तपस्विकन्याः
स्वप्रमाणानुरूपैः[2] सेचनघटैर्बालपादपेभ्यः पयो दातुमित
एवाभिवर्तन्ते । ॥ निरूप्य ॥ अहो मधुरमासां दर्शनम् ।

शुद्धान्तदुर्लभमिदं वपुराश्रमवासिनो यदि जनस्य ।
दूरीकृताः खलु गुणैरुद्यानलता वनलतांभिः[3] ॥१७॥

यावदिमां छायामाश्रित्य प्रतिपालयामि । ॥ इति विलोक-
यन्निष्यतः ॥

॥ ततः प्रविशति यथोक्तव्यापारा[4] सह सखीभ्यां शकुन्तला ॥

[a]इत इतः सख्यौ ।

---

¹ 'To the right of the grove of trees.' *Dakshiṇena* governs the acc.
case as well as the gen. See Pāṇ. ii. 3, 31; v. 3, 35.

² 'With watering-pots (of a size) proportioned to their strength,' or
'with watering-pots suited to their size,' i. e. not too large for a woman
to carry.

³ 'If this (beautiful) figure, rarely met with [or difficult to be found]
in the inner apartments of palaces [i. e. in harams], belongs to people
living in a hermitage, then indeed the shrubs of the garden are distanced
[surpassed] in excellencies by the (wild) shrubs of the forest.' Sir W. Jones
translates, 'the garden-flowers must make room for the blossoms of the
forest, which excel them in colour and fragrance.' The *śuddhānta* is the
antaḥ-pura or 'inner suite of apartments, appropriated to women;' called
also the *avarodha* or 'private quarter,' shut out from the rest of the house
and strictly guarded. *Haram* is the equivalent Arabic word.

⁴ 'Occupied in the manner described.' A noticeable Bahuvrīhi com-
pound.

Verse 17. ĀRYĀ or GĀTHĀ. See verse 2.

– –	⏑ – ⏑	⏑ ⏑ – ‖	⏑ ⏑ –	⏑ ⏑ –	⏑ – ⏑	⏑ ⏑ –	⏑			
– –	⏑ – ⏑	⏑ ⏑ – ‖	– –	⏑ ⏑ –	⏑	⏑ ⏑ –	–			

शकुन्तला ।

[a] इदो इदो सहीत्रो ।

अनसूया ।

[b] हला सउन्दले । तुवत्तोबि तादकस्सबस्स अस्समरुक्खत्रा पिश्रदेरंत्ति तक्केमि । जेण णीमालिं आकुसुमपेलवाबि तुमं एदाणं आलंवालपूरणे णिउत्ता ।

शकुन्तला ।

[c] हला अणसूए । ण केवलं तादणित्रोत्रो एव्व । अत्थि मे सोदरसिणेहोबि एदेसु । ॥ इति वृक्षसेचनं निरूपयति ॥

राज्ञा ।

कथमियं सा कखदुहिता । असाधुदर्शी खलु तच्चभवान्का- श्यपः । य इमामाश्रमधर्मे नियुंक्ते[3] ।

---

[a] इत इतः सख्यौ । [b] हला शकुन्तले । त्वत्तोऽपि तातकाश्यपस्याश्रमवृक्षाः प्रि-यतरा इति तर्कयामि । येन नयमालिकाकुसुमपेलवाबि त्वमेतेपामालवालपूरणे नियुक्ता । [c] हला अनसूये । न केवलं तातनियोग एव । अस्ति मे सोदरस्नेहोऽप्येतेषु ।

---

[1] *Mālikā* or *mallikā* is a kind of double jasmine with large flowers, sometimes called 'Arabian jasmine;' from its delicious perfume, and abundant nectar, much frequented by bees. See Raghu-v. xvi. 47.

[2] *Ālavāla*, 'the trench for water round the root of a tree.' See Raghu-v. i. 51; also Vikram., end of Act II. (*taror mūlālavālam*).

[3] 'Truly his reverence Kāśyapa is (a man) of little discrimination, inasmuch as he appoints her to the duties [manner of life] of the hermitage [i. e. imposes upon her a hermitage-life; a mode of life such as is usual in a hermitage].' The sage Kaṇva is here called 'a descendant of Kaśyapa.' As a sage and Brāhman he might especially claim this celebrated personage as his progenitor; but Kaśyapa, who was the son of Marīci [who was the son of Brahmā, and one of the seven Prajāpatis], was a progenitor on a magnificent scale, as he is considered to have been the father of the gods, demons, man, fish, reptiles, and all animals, by Aditi, and twelve other daughters of Daksha. He is supposed by some to be a personification of the race who took refuge in the central Asiatic

इदं किलाव्याजमनोहरं वपु-
स्तपःक्षमं साधयितुं य इच्छति ।
ध्रुवं स नीलोत्पलपत्त्रधारया
शमीलतां छेत्तुमृषिर्व्यवस्यति ॥१८॥

भवतु । पादपान्तरित एव विश्वस्तां तावदेनां पश्यामि ।

॥ इति तथा करोति ॥

शकुन्तला ।

[a] सहि अणसूए । अदिपिणड्डेण वक्कलेण पिअंवदाए णि-
अन्तिदम्हि । सिढिलेहि दाव णं ।

अनसूया ।

[b] तह । ॥ इति शिथिलयति ॥

[a] सखि अनसूये । अतिपिनद्धेन वल्कलेन प्रियंवदया नियन्त्रितास्मि । शिथिलय
तावदेनम् ।   [b] तथा ।

---

chain, in which traces of his name may be found, as Koh-kas (or
Caucasus), the Caspian, Kaśmīra, &c. (Wilson's Hindū Theatre, vol. ii.
p. 12.)

[1] 'The sage who expects to make this artlessly-charming form capable
of (enduring) penance, certainly attempts to cut a branch of the hard
S'amī wood with the edge of the blue lotus-leaf.' *Aryāja-manoharam*,
'that which captivates without art or ornament,' 'naturally beautiful.'
For an account of the different orders of Rishis or sages, see *rishi* in my
Sanskṛit-English Dictionary. The S'amī tree is a kind of acacia (Acacia
Suma), the wood of which is very hard, and supposed by the Hindūs to
contain fire. [*S'amī abhyantara-līna-pāvakā*, Raghu-v. iii. 9. See also
Manu viii. 247.] Sacred fire is kindled by rubbing two dried pieces
together. The legend is that Purūravas generated primeval fire by
rubbing together two branches of the S'amī and Aśvattha tree. Other
kinds of wood are also held sacred by the Hindūs, such as the Vilva (Bel),
and only Brāhmans are allowed to use them as fuel.

Verse 18. VANS'A-STHAVILA (a variety of JAGATĪ), containing twelve syllables to the
quarter-verse, each quarter-verse being alike.

◡ – ◡ – – ◡◡ – ◡ – ◡ – ‖

प्रियंवदा ॥ सहासम् ॥

"एन्थ पओहरवित्थारइत्तश्रं अत्तणो जोव्वणं उबालह । मं
किं उबालम्भेसि ।

राजा ।

सम्यगियमाह ।

इदमुपहितसूक्ष्मग्रन्थिना स्कन्धदेशे
स्तनयुगपरिणाहाच्छादिना वल्कलेन ।
वपुरभिनवमस्याः पुष्यति स्वां न शोभां
कुसुममिव पिनद्धं पाण्डुपत्त्रोदरेण ॥१९॥

अथवा काममननुरूपमस्या वपुषी वल्कलम् । न पुन-
रलङ्कारश्रियं न पुष्यति । कुतः ।

<hr>

a अत्र पयोधरविस्तारयितृक्रम् आत्मनो यौवनमुपालभस्व । मां किमुपालभसे ।

<hr>

[1] 'This blooming [or youthful] body of hers, by (reason of) the bark
dress fastened with delicate knots upon her shoulder (and) covering the
orbs of her two breasts, does not exhibit (the fulness of) its own charms,
like a flower enveloped by a calyx of pale leaves.' The first meaning of
push, like *bhri*, is 'to nourish' or 'be nourished.' Thence, like *bhri*, it
passes into the sense of 'maintain,' 'support,' 'bear;' and thence into
that of 'possess,' 'enjoy,' 'exhibit,' 'make to appear.' In these last senses
it may be used actively, though conjugated in cl. 4. (See Manu ix. 37;
Rāmāy. ii. 94, 10; Raghu-v. xvi. 58; Mahā-bh. vol. ii. p. 186, l. 2607.)
It is curious that our English word *exhibition* may have the sense of
'maintenance' (cf. Lat. *exhibeo*). Two Bombay MSS. read *svām abhi-
khyām* instead of *svām na śobhām*: the meaning would then be, 'main-
tains its own beauty' [*abhikhyā* is so used, Raghu-v. i. 46]; and this
reading would be more consistent with what follows, but by the next
word *athavā*, as the commentators observe, *svoktam ākshipati*, he corrects
his previous remark. *Pi-naddha*=*api-naddha* from *api-nah*.

[2] 'Or rather, granted that the bark dress be ill suited to her figure,
yet it really does [lit. it does not not] possess the charm of an embellish-

<hr>

Verse 19. MĀLINĪ or MĀNINĪ (a variety of ATI-ŚAKVARĪ). See verse 10.

सरसिजमनुविद्धं शैवलेनापि रम्यं
मलिनमपि हिमांशोर्लक्ष्म लक्ष्मीं तनोति ।
इयमधिकमनोज्ञा वल्कलेनापि तन्वी
किमिव हि मधुराणां मण्डनं नाकृतीनाम् ॥२०॥

ment;' or less literally, 'it really does act as an embellishment to set off the beauty of her person.' Other instances are found in Kālidāsa of two negatives employed to strengthen an affirmative. See Megha-d. 106.

[1] 'The lotus, though intertwined [or overspread] with the S'aivala, is charming; the speck, though dark, heightens [lit. extends] the beauty of the moon; this graceful one even with her bark-dress is more lovely; for what is not an embellishment of sweet forms?' i. e. everything serves as an ornament to heighten the beauty of a figure which is naturally beautiful. *Sarasi-jam*, lit. 'that which is born in a pool,' a name applicable to any aquatic plant, but especially to the different kinds of lotus (Nelumbium or Nymphæa). This beautiful plant—the varieties of which, blue, white, and red, are numerous—bears some resemblance to our water-lily. It is as favourite a subject of allusion and comparison with the Hindū poets as the rose with the Persian. It is often figuratively used to express beauty, as 'lotus-face' or 'the lotus of the face,' 'lotus-hands,' 'lotus-feet' (Gīta-g. passim). It is also used by women as an ornament (Act III. of this play), and as a cooling remedy (Ratn., Act II). The S'aivala (Vallisneria) is an aquatic plant which spreads itself over ponds, and interweaves itself with the lotus. The interlacing of its stalks is compared in the S'ringāra-tilaka (verse 1) to braided hair (*dhammilla*). See Sir W. Jones' Works, vol. iv. p. 113. The spots on the moon were thought to resemble those on an antelope, and hence one of the moon's names, *harina-kalanka*, 'deer-spotted.'

The following verse, which is found in the Beng. MSS. immediately after verse 20, and has been adopted by the Calcutta edition, is omitted in all the Deva-n. MSS., and in the commentaries of S'. and K. It is probably spurious, as it repeats the same sentiment less poetically and with some harshness of expression :—

कठिनमपि मृगाक्ष्या वल्कलं कान्तरूपं
न मनसि रुचिभङ्गं खल्वमप्पादधाति ।

Verse 20. MĀLINĪ or MĀNINĪ (a variety of ATI-S'AKVARĪ). See verse 10.

शकुन्तला ॥ अग्रतोऽवलोक्य ॥

[a] एसो वादेरिदपल्लवङ्गुलीहिं तुवरेदि विञ्र मं केसर-रुक्खत्रो । जाव एं सम्भावेमि[1] । ॥ इति परिक्रामति ॥

प्रियंवदा ।

[b] हला सउन्दले । एत्थ एव्व दाव मुहुत्तअं चिट्ठ ।

शकुन्तला ।

[c] किस्सिमि[2]न्तं ।

प्रियंवदा ।

[d] जाव तुए उवगदाए लदासँणाहो विञ्र अअं केसर-रुक्खत्रो पडिभादि ।

[a] एम वातेरितपल्लवाङ्गुलीभिस्त्वरयतीव मां केशरवृक्षकः । यावदेनं सम्भावयामि ।   [b] हला शकुन्तले । अत्रैव तावन्मुहूर्तं तिष्ठ ।   [c] किन्निमित्तम् ।   [d] यावत्त्व-योपगतया लतासनाच इवायं केशरवृक्षकः प्रतिभाति ।

विकचसरसिजाया: स्तोकनिर्मुक्तकरढं
निजमिव कमलिन्या: कर्कशं वृन्तजालम् ॥

'The bark-dress, though rough, is beautiful on this fawn-eyed one. It does not in one's mind cause the slightest impairment of her beauty [or, of my liking for her]; just as its own rough tissue of stalks on the lotus-bed whose lotuses have expanded, so as slightly to release the neck-of-the-flower,' i. e. the pedicle, or that part of the stalk immediately under the flower.

[1] 'This Keśara tree, with its fingers of young shoots set in motion by the wind, bids me hasten as it were (towards it). I will just go and pay my respects to it.' The Keśara (Mimusops Elengi) is the same as the Bakula or Vakula, frequent mention of which is made in some of the Purāṇas, and in Ratn., Act III. It bears a strong-smelling flower, which is even placed among the flowers of the Hindū paradise. The tree is very ornamental in pleasure-grounds. The caus. of *sam-bhū* often means 'to honour, or pay one's respects to another in person.' Motion towards the object seems usually, though not always, implied. Thus, *sambhāvayāmo rājarshim*, Vikram., Act I; cf. Raghu-v. v. 2, x. 56.

[2] 'What for!' Dr. Burkhard omits this.

[3] 'Possessed of a creeper.' *Sa-nātha*, lit. 'having a lord or master;'

शकुन्तला ।

[a] अदोक्खु पिअंवदासि तुमं ।

राजा ।

प्रियमपि तथ्यमाह शकुन्तलां प्रियंवदा । अस्याः खलु
अधरः किसलयरागः कोमलविटपानुकारिणौ बाहू ।
कुसुममिव लोभनीयं यौवनमङ्गेषु सन्नद्धम् ॥२१॥

[a] अतः खलु प्रियंवदासि त्वम् ।

---

it is so used towards the end of this Act, where the devotees are said
to be *sa-nāthāḥ*, 'possessed of a guardian' in Dushyanta. A compound
verb *sanāthī-kṛi*, 'to cause to be possessed of a master,' occurs in Act II.
of this play, and in Hitop. l. 797. But here *sa-nātha = sahita, dvitīya,
yukta*, 'accompanied,' 'joined,' 'furnished with.' The transition into
this meaning may be understood from Act VI. of this play, and from
Vikram., Act II, where an arbour (*maṇḍapa*) is said to be *maṇi-silā-
paṭṭa-sanātha*, 'having a slab of marble as its master,' i. e. in which the
most prominent object is a marble seat; or in plain words, 'an arbour
furnished with a marble seat.' Similarly in Act II. of this play the
surface of a stone seat (*silā-tala*) is said to be *vitāna-sanātha*, 'furnished
with a canopy' by the shade of a tree.' Cf. also *Lakshmī-sanātha*, 'pos-
sessed of Fortune,' and *kusuma-sanātha*, 'decked with flowers,' Vikram.,
Act IV. See also Mālatī-m. p. 58, l. 2; Megha-d. ver. 97; Mālavik.
p. 5, l. 9.

[1] 'Hence most truly art thou (named) Priyam-vadā' (i. e. *priyam*,
'what is agreeable,' and *vada*, 'one who speaks;' cf. μελίφθογγος).

[2] 'Though agreeable (still it is) the truth (that) Priyaṃvadā says to
Sakuntalā. Truly her lip has the colour of a young bud, her two arms
resemble flexile stalks. Attractive youth, like the blossom, pervades her
limbs.' *Adhara*, properly 'the lower lip,' as distinguished from *oshṭha*
(i. e. *ava-stha*), 'the upper lip.' *San-naddham = sarvato vyāpakam*,
Schol.

Verse 21. ĀRYĀ or GĀTHĀ. See verse 2.

$$\smile\smile- \mid \smile\smile\smile\smile \mid -- \parallel -\smile\smile \mid \smile\smile- \mid \smile-\smile \mid -- \mid -$$
$$\smile\smile\smile\smile \mid \smile-\smile \mid -- \parallel -\smile\smile \mid -- \mid \smile \mid -- \mid -$$

अनसूया ।

[a] हला सउन्दले । इअं सअंवरवहू सहआरस्स तुए किदणा-
महेआ वणजोसिणिन्ति णोमालिआ । णं विसुमरिदासि ।

शकुन्तला ।

[b] तदा अत्ताणम्मि विसुमरिस्सं । ॥ लतामुपेत्यावलोक्य च ॥ [c] हला ।
रमणीएक्खु काले इमस्स लदापाअबमिहुणस्स वइअरो

[a] हला शकुन्तले । इयं स्वयंवरवधूः सहकारस्य त्वया कृतनामधेया वनज्योत्स्नेति
नवमालिका । एनां विस्मृतासि ।   [b] तदात्मानमपि विस्मरिष्यामि ।   [c] हला ।
रमणीये खलु कालेऽस्य लतापादपमिथुनस्य व्यतिकरः

---

[1] 'Here is the young Mālikā [a kind of double jasmine, see p. 22, n. 1]
named by you the Light of the Grove, the self-elected wife of the Saha-
kāra. Have you forgotten it?' The Sahakāra is a sort of fragrant
Mango tree. Its union with other plants seems a favourite idea with
Kālidāsa; for in Raghu-v. viii. 60, allusion is made to its marriage with
the Phalinī or Priyangu. It is said to be a great favourite with bees
(Raghu-v. vi. 69). In Ratn. p. 11, l. 7, it is spoken of as *maṇḍalā-
yamāna*, 'forming a circle.' *Svayaṃvara-vadhū*, 'a wife by self-election.'
The *Svayaṃvara*, or 'selection for one's self,' was a form of marriage in
which a princess made a free public choice of a husband from a number
of assembled suitors. In very early times the princesses of India seem
to have enjoyed this singular privilege. It is not mentioned amongst the
forms of marriage in Manu iii. 21, &c.; but the provision which is made
in Manu ix. 90, proves that a similar custom prevailed at that period.
When marriageable, she is there told to wait for three years; and after
that time, if she fail to obtain a suitable husband, she is to choose for
herself; [*samāna-jāti-guṇaṃ varaṃ svayaṃ vriṇīta*, Schol.] She is then
called *Svayaṃvarā*. In the Mahā-bh. we have a beautiful account of the
Svayaṃvara of Damayantī (who chooses Nala), and of Draupadī (who
chooses Arjuna); and in Raghu-v. vi. of the *Svayaṃvara* of Indumatī,
sister of Bhoja, king of Vidarbha (who chooses Aja, the son of Raghu).
See also Nalod. i. 30. Even the goddess Lakshmī is said to have exercised
this privilege. See the allusion to the *Lakshmī-svayaṃvara* at the begin-
ning of Act III. of Vikram. *Vi-smṛita* is also used transitively between
verses 129 and 130 of this play. In Raghu-v. xix. 2, *vi-smṛita* has an
acc. after it. See Gram. 896; Pāṇ. iii. 4, 72.

[a] संवुत्तो। णवकुसुमजोव्वणा वणजोसिणी। बद्धपल्लवदाए
उब्भोअक्खमो सहआरो। ॥ इति पश्यन्ती तिष्ठति ॥

प्रियंवदा ॥ सस्मितम् ॥

[b] अणसूए। जाणासि किस्सिमित्तं सउन्दला वणजोसिणिं
अदिमेत्तं पेक्खदित्ति।

अनसूया।

[c] एक्खु विभावेमि। कहेहि।

प्रियंवदा।

[d] जह वणजोसिणी अणुरूवेण पाअवेण सङ्गदा। अवि

[a] संवृत्तः। नवकुसुमयौवना वनज्योत्स्ना। बद्धपल्लवतयोपभोगक्षमः सहकारः।
[b] अनसूये। जानासि किन्निमित्तं शकुन्तला वनज्योत्स्नामतिमात्रं प्रेक्षत इति।
[c] न खलु विभावयामि। कथय।   [d] यथा वनज्योत्स्नानुरूपेण पादपेन
सङ्गता। अपि

---

[1] 'At a charming season, indeed, has the union between this pair, the
(Mālikā or jasmine) creeper and the (Sahakāra) tree, taken place. The
Light of the Grove (has) youthfulness by (its) fresh blossoms [i. e. its
fresh blossoms give it all the bloom of a young bride], and the Sahakāra
is capable of enjoyment by reason of (its) young shoots (just) formed.'
Vyatikara is properly 'mutual action,' 'co-operation;' hence 'union,'
'blending,' 'intertwining,' 'intermingling.' See Megha-d. 15. So also
vyatikara-sukham, 'mutual enjoyment.' The prepositions *vi* and *ati* in
composition imply both reciprocity and contrariety: hence, in Hitop.
l. 2319, *vyatikara* signifies 'reverse,' 'turn in affairs.' *Baddha-pallavatayā*,
'by the state of young shoots formed on it.' This is an idiomatic use of
the instr. case of the abstract noun in *tā*, to denote 'by reason of,' 'on
account of.' *Bandh* often means 'to form,' 'produce;' thus, *badhnanti
phalam* (Raghu-v. xii. 69); *drumeshu svayam phalam baddham* (Ku-
māra-s. v. 60). *Upabhoga-kshama* occurs in connection with *grīshma-
samaya* in p. 6, n. 2, and in Vikram., Act III, with *avakāśa*. The first
meaning of *kshama* is 'patient,' 'enduring.' Here and elsewhere it =
yogya, 'capable,' 'suitable;' so *drishṭi-kshama*, 'capable of being seen,'
'visible.' So in verse 22, *kshatra-parigraha-kshamā*, 'capable of marriage
with a Kshatriya.'

[a]णामं एव्वं अहम्पि अत्तणो अणुरूबं वरं लहेअंति ।

शकुन्तला ।

[b]एसो णूणं तुह अत्तगदो मणोरही । ॥ इति कलशमावर्जयति ॥

राजा ।

अपि नाम कुलपतेरियमसवर्णाक्षेत्रसम्भवा स्यात्[2] । अथवा कृतं सन्देहेन[3] ।

असंशयं क्षत्रपरिग्रहक्षमा
यदार्यमस्यामभिलाषि मे मनः ।

[a] नाम एवमहमपि आत्मनोऽनुरूपं वरं लभेयेति ।   [b] एप नूनं तवात्मगतो मनोरथः ।

---

[1] *Api nāma*, 'would that!' In this sense it occurs also in Vikram., Act III, *api nāma Purūravā bhaveyam*, 'would that I were Purū-ravas!'

[2] 'Can this (lady) possibly be sprung from a wife dissimilar in class (to that) of the father of the family!' *Api nāma* here = 'may be,' 'can it possibly be,' 'I wonder whether,' expressive of some doubt [*evaṃ sambhā-vyate*, Schol.] *Kshetra* = *kalatra*, 'a wife;' *a-savarṇa* = *asamāna-jātīya*, 'of a different (and inferior) tribe or caste.' A Brāhman might marry a Kshatriyā, i. e. a woman of the military or kingly class next below him (Manu iii. 13), and the female offspring of such a marriage would belong to the mixed class called *mūrdhābhishikta* or *mūrdhāvasikta*, 'head-anointed' (Manu x. 6), and would be a suitable object of affection for a Kshatriya, who in his kingly character was a *mūrdhābhishikta* also. But if S'akuntalā were a pure Brāhmaṇī woman, both on the mother's and father's side, she would be ineligible as the wife of a Kshatriya (Manu iii. 13).

[3] 'But, have done with [away with] doubt.' *Athavā* is used to correct a previous thought [*pakshāntare*]. *Kṛitam* used adverbially (like *alam*) requires the instr. case.

Verse 22. VANŚA-STHAVILA (a variety of JAGATĪ). See verse 18.

सतां हि सन्देहपदेषु वस्तुषु
प्रमाणमन्तःकरणप्रवृत्तयः ॥ २२ ॥

---

[1] 'Without any doubt she is capable of marriage with a Kshatriya, since my honourable soul has a longing towards her: for in matters that are subjects of doubt, the tendencies [inclinations, promptings] of the hearts of good men are an authoritative guide (to the truth).' The meaning is, 'If this damsel be the daughter of a Brāhman by a Brāhmaṇī [or woman of the same caste], then why should I be conscious of a sudden liking for one whom I could never hope to marry? This feeling of sympathy could only arise towards a legitimate object: for in such matters, the secret prompting [inner voice] of the heart is decisive.' He therefore concludes that she must have been of mixed origin, with some Kshatriya or regal blood in her veins; and discovers afterwards that she was, in fact, the daughter of the Rājarshi Viśvāmitra (originally of the Kshatriya or regal tribe) by an Apsaras. Dushyanta, as a king, belonged of course to the Kshatriya caste. This caste came next to the Brāhmanical, and according to Manu (i. 87) sprang from the arm of Brahmā. They wore a girdle of *mūrvā* and a sacrificial cord of hemp (Manu ii. 42, 44), and were properly soldiers. They were said to have been exterminated by Paraśu-rāma, the representative of the Brāhmanical tribe, in revenge for the murder of his father, the sage Jamadagni, by the sons of Kārtavīrya. This fable is founded on the historical fact that, at some period or other, struggles, arising out of mutual jealousy of each other's encroachments, took place between the military and sacerdotal classes; and that the former did in the end succumb to the superior power and intelligence of the Brāhmans. The example of Viśvāmitra proves that it was possible for a Kshatriya, by the practice of religious austerities, to raise himself to the rank of a Brāhman. Other anomalies of caste occur. A number of men, half warriors, half priests, Kshatriyas by birth, and Brāhmans by profession, called *Āṅgirasas* or 'descendants of Aṅgiras,' were said to have sprung from Nabhāga (Vishṇu-p. p. 359; Mahā-bh. Sel. p. 23). Kings were never chosen from the Brāhmanical class, but were properly Kshatriyas (Manu vii. 2); though there was no positive law against their belonging to the two inferior classes of Vaiśyas and S'ūdras, or even to three mixed classes (*sankara*) formed by inter-marriage with the others, viz. Mūrdhābhishiktas, Māhishyas, and Karaṇas (Manu x. 6). One dynasty of kings of the line of Nanda were actually S'ūdras, and kept the Kshatriyas in subjection (Vishṇu-p. p. 467). In

तथापि तत्त्वत एवैनामुपलप्स्ये ।

शकुन्तला ॥ ससम्भ्रमम् ॥

[1] अम्मो सलिलसेअसम्भमुग्गदो णोमालिअं उज्झिअ
वत्त्रणं मे महुअरो अहिवट्टइ । ॥ इति भ्रमरबाधां नाटयति ॥

राजा ॥ ससृहं विलोक्य ॥

साधु बाधनमपि रमणीयमस्याः ।

यतो यतः षट्चरणोऽभिवर्तते

ततस्ततः प्रेरितलोललोचना ।

विवर्तितभ्रूरियमद्य शिक्षते

भयादकामापि हि दृष्टिविभ्रमम् ॥ २३ ॥

[1] अहो सलिलसेकसम्भ्रमोन्नतो नवमालिकामुज्झित्वा वदनं मे मधुकरोऽभिवर्तते ।

---

fact, the king was but a high officer appointed to train the army, instruct
in military exercises, administer justice, and execute the laws. These
onerous duties were sufficient to deter the Brāhmans from desiring a rank
inconsistent with their love of dignified repose. *Āryam=sa-maryādam,*
'correct,' 'upright' (Schol.) *Pramāṇam,* 'that by which anything is
measured;' hence, 'a criterion or standard of truth,' 'a sure guide,' 'an
authority' [*pramā-kāraṇam,* 'a cause of true knowledge,' Schol.]   In
this sense it is usually found in the singular number, neuter gender,
though in apposition to a masculine or feminine noun, or even to a plural
noun, as here. Thus also, *Vedāḥ pramāṇam,* 'the Vedas are an authority.'
See also Hitop. ll. 169, 1465. *Pravṛitti,* 'onward course;' hence, 'a
course of action,' 'tendency,' 'inclination.'

[1] 'Nevertheless [however the suggestions of my heart are to be relied
upon] I will accurately ascertain about her.' *Upalapsye=jñāsye,* 'I will
inform myself.'

[2] *Nava-mālikā,* see p. 22, n. 1.

[3] *Madhu-kara,* 'a honey-maker,' 'a bee;' cf. Lat. *mellificus, mellifer.*

[4] Literally, 'turns towards,' 'attacks,' 'assaults.'

[5] 'Good! even her repulse is charming.'

[6] 'In whichever direction the bee turns towards (her), in that direction

अपि च । ॥ साभूयमिव ॥

चलापाङ्गां दृष्टिं स्पृशसि बहुशो वेपथुमतीं
रहस्याख्यायीव स्वनसि मृदु कर्णान्तिकचरः ।
करं व्याधुन्वत्याः पिवसि रतिसर्वस्वमधरं
वयं तत्त्वान्वेषान्मधुकर हतास्त्वं खलु कृती ॥ २४ ॥

---

her rolling eye is darted; bending her brows through fear, she is already learning coquettish-movements of the eye even though (as yet) uninfluenced-by-love.' *Yatah* and *tatah* are properly 'whence' and 'thence;' *tatah=tasmāt sthānāt*, 'from that place,' S. *Shaṭ-charaṇa*, 'a six-footed insect,' 'a bee.' *Drishṭi-vibhrama*, 'coquettish play of the eye,' 'amorous or sidelong glances,' 'rolling motion of the eyes, indicative of amorous feelings' (=*drishṭi-vilāsa*, S.)

[1] 'Thou touchest repeatedly her quivering eye, whose outer-corner moves (playfully); going close to her ear, thou art softly humming as if whispering a secret (of love); thou art drinking the lip, containing all the treasures of delight, of her waving her hand; (whilst) we, O bee! through (the necessity for) inquiring into the truth (of her origin), are disappointed (of immediate fruition), thou indeed art in the full enjoyment (of thy desire).' In other words, 'Whilst I am kept in suspense by the necessity of ascertaining whether she be a Brāhmaṇī or a Kshatriyā woman, thou art in the act of enjoying her charms.' *Vyādhunvatyāḥ*, gen. case of the pres. part. fem. agreeing with *asyāḥ* understood. *Dhā* with *vi* and *ā*, 'to shake about.' Verbs of cl. 5 reject the nasal in the fem. of this participle, see Gram. 141. c, Pāṇ. vii. 1, 80. *Rati-sarvasvam = rati-nidhānam*, 'entirely made up of delight,' 'whose whole essence is delight.' So *khaḍga-sarvasvaḥ*, 'one whose whole property consists of a sword.' *Adhara*, properly 'the lower lip,' in contradistinction to *oshṭha* (i. e. *ava-stha*), 'the upper lip,' but here simply 'the lip.' *Adharam pivasi*, 'thou art drinking (the moisture of) the lip.' Cf. *adharam pātum pravṛittā* (Vikram., Act IV), and *adhara-madhu* ('the nectar of the lip') *pivanti* (Bhartṛi-h. i. 26). *Hata* here=*mano-hata*, 'disappointed,' or rather 'kept in anxious suspense.' *Kṛitī=kṛitārthaḥ* or *kṛita-kṛityaḥ*, 'one who has gained the object of his desire, and is in full enjoyment of it.'

Verse 24. ŚIKHARIṆĪ (a variety of ATYASHṬI). See verse 9.

शकुन्तला ।

ᵃ ण एसो धिट्ठो विरमदि । अण्णदो गमिस्सं । ।। पदान्तरे स्थित्वा
सदृष्टिक्षेपम् ।।   ᵇ कहं इदो वि आअच्छदि । हला परित्ताअध
परित्ताअध मं इमिणा दुव्विणीदेण दुट्ठमहुअरेण अहि-
हूअमाणं ।

उभे ।। सस्मितम् ।।

ᶜ काओ वअं परित्ताढुं । दुस्सन्दं अक्कन्द । राअ रक्खिदाइं
तवोवणाइं णाम ।

राजा ।

अवसरोऽयमात्मानं प्रकाशयितुम् । न भेतव्यम् ।   ।। इत्यर्धोक्ते
स्वगतम् ।।   राजभावस्त्वभिज्ञातो भवेत् । भवतु । एवं तावद्-
भिधास्ये ।

शकुन्तला   ।। पदान्तरे स्थित्वा ।।

ᵈ कहं इदो वि मं अणुसरदि ।

ᵃ न एष धृष्टो विरमति । अन्यतो गमिष्यामि ।   ᵇ कथमितोऽप्यागच्छति ।
हला परित्रायध्वं परित्रायध्वं मामनेन दुर्विनीतेन दुष्टमधुकरेणाभिभूयमानाम् ।   ᶜ के
आवां परित्रातुम् । दुष्यन्तमाक्रन्द । राजरक्षितानि तपोवनानि नाम ।   ᵈ कथमि-
तोऽपि मामनुसरति ।

---

¹ Literally, 'ill-trained;' hence, 'ill-behaved,' 'ill-mannered.'

² 'Who (are) we to rescue (you)?' i. e. 'who are we that we should
be able to rescue you? what power have we to rescue you?' [*āvayoḥ
ko 'dhikāraḥ*, S.] In a passage further on (*kā tvaṃ visrashṭavyasya*, &c.)
K. explains *ka* by *na prabhu, avaśa*, 'powerless.' All the Deva-n. MSS.
read *parittādum* (Sk. *paritrātum*), but the Beng. read *parittāṇe* (Sk.
paritrāṇe), and the Calcutta *kā satti amhe parittāṇe*. The infinitive
may well stand for the dative *paritrāṇāya* (see p. 14, n. 2), especially
in Prākrit, which has no dative. A precisely similar construction
occurs in the Mālavik. p. 55, l. 13, *kā vayaṃ jetum;* and again, p. 40,
l. 16, *ke āvām parigrahāya* (Prāk. *pariggahassa*, the gen. being put for
Sanskrit dative).

राजा ॥ सत्वरमुपसृत्य ॥

कः पौरवे वसुमतीं शासति शासितरि दुर्विनीतानाम् ।
अयमाचरत्यविनयं मुग्धासु तपस्विकन्यासु ॥ २५ ॥

॥ सर्वा राजानं दृष्ट्वा किञ्चिदिव सम्भ्रान्ताः ॥

अनसूया ।

[a] अज्ज । एक्खु किम्पि अच्चाहिदं । इअं णो पिअसही
महुअरेण अहिरुअमाणा कादरीभूदा । ॥ इति शकुन्तलां दर्शयति ॥

राजा ॥ शकुन्तलाभिमुखो भूत्वा ॥

अपि तपो वर्धते ।

॥ शकुन्तला साध्वसादवचना तिष्ठति ॥

[a] आर्ये । न खलु किमप्यत्याहितम् । इयं नौ प्रियसखी मधुकरेणाभिभूयमाना
कातरीभूता ।

---

[1] 'Who is this that is practising rudeness towards the gentle maidens
of the hermits, (and that too) whilst a descendant of Puru [see p. 15,
n. 1], a chastiser of the ill-behaved, is governing the earth?' *Śāsati*, loc.
of the pres. part., used here absolutely, and liable in this root and in
roots of cl. 3 to be confounded with the 3rd pers. pl. present tense.
Mugdhāsu = apraudhāsu, aprāgalbhāsu, 'gentle,' 'timid,' 'modest,' 'inno-
cent,' Schol.

[2] *Aty-āhita = mahā-bhīti*, 'great danger.' According to some, 'great
outrage,' 'great crime.' The same word occurs in the beginning of Acts
IV. and V. of Vikram. Cf. also Mālavik. 55, 19; 56, 4.

[3] 'I trust your devotion prospers,' 'does your piety thrive?' 'is all
well with your acts of devotion?' This was the regular salutation on
meeting a Brāhman. According to Manu, *kuśalam* implies an inquiry
respecting the well-being of a Brāhman's acts of penance, at all times
liable to be obstructed by evil spirits and demons. Manu ii. 127. See
also Rāmāy. i. 52, 4.

Verse 25. ĀRYĀ or GĀTHĀ. See verse 2.

$$\bar{-}\ \bar{-}\ |\ \cup\ -\ \cup\ |\ \cup\ \cup\ -\ \|\ -\ \cup\ \cup\ |\ -\ \cup\ \cup\ |\ \cup\ -\ \cup\ |\ -\ -\ |\ -\ |$$
$$\cup\ \cup\ -\ |\ \cup\ -\ \cup\ |\ \cup\ \cup\ -\ \|\ -\ -\ |\ \cup\ \cup\ -\ |\ \cup\ |\ -\ -\ |\ \cup$$

अनसूया ।

"दाणिं अदिधिविसेसलाहेण । हला सउन्दले । गच्छ
उडञ्रं । फलमिस्सं अग्घं उवहर । इदं पादोदञ्रं भविस्संदि ।

राजा ।

भवतीनां सूनृतयैव गिरा कृतमातिथ्यम् ।

" इदानीमतिथिविशेषलाभेन । हला शकुन्तले । गच्छोटजम् । फलमिश्रमर्घमुपहर ।
इदं पादोदकं भविष्यति ।

---

[1] 'Now (indeed it does prosper) by the acquisition of a distinguished
guest.' The rites of hospitality were enforced amongst the Hindūs by
very stringent regulations. The observance of them ranked as one of
the five great sacraments (*mahā-yajña*), under the title of *nṛi-yajña* or
manushya-yajña, 'the man-sacrament.' Brahmā, Prajāpati, Indra, Fire,
the Vasus, and the Sun were supposed to be present in the person of a
guest, and to partake of the food that was given to him (Vishṇu-p.
p. 306). No wonder then that reverence of him was said to be conducive
to wealth, to fame, to life, and to a heavenly reward (Manu iii. 106).
On the other hand, no punishment was thought too severe for one who
violated these rites. If a guest departed disappointed from any house,
his sins were to be transferred to the householder, and all the merits
of the householder were to be transferred to him (Vishṇu-p. p. 305;
Hitop. l. 361). Some of the things which were to be offered to a guest
by even the poorest man were food, vegetables, water for the feet, and
if more could not be given, ground on which to lie (Manu iii. 101;
Vishṇu-p. p. 308).

[2] The *argha* or *arghya* was a respectful offering to Brāhmans of rice,
Dūrvā grass, flowers, fruit, &c., with water in a small boat-shaped vessel.
Cf. Rāmāy. i. 20, 9. 10; Wilson's note, Megha-d. 5. *Upahara=ānīya
prayaččha*, 'having fetched, present.'

[3] 'This (which we have brought with us for watering our plants) will
serve as water for the feet.' Water for the feet was one of the first
things invariably presented to a guest in all Eastern countries. Should
a guest arrive, a seat is to be offered to him, and his feet are to be
washed and food is to be given him (Vishṇu-p. p. 305. Cf. also Luke
vii. 44). *Idam*, i. e. *vṛikshārtham ānītam udakam*, Schol.

[4] *Sūnṛitā gīr*, 'kind yet sincere language,' 'complimentary and friendly
words without flattery' (*priyaṃ satyaṃ ča vačanam*). This is one of

प्रियंवदा ।

[a] तेण हि इमसिं पच्छाअसीअलाए सत्तवण्णवेदिआए मुहुत्तअं उवविसिअ परिस्समविणोदं करेदु अज्जो ।

राजा ।

नूनं यूयमप्यनेन कर्मणा परिश्रान्ताः ।

[a] तेन ह्यस्यां प्रच्छायशीतलायां सप्तपर्णवेदिकायां मुहूर्तमुपविश्य परिश्रमविनोदं करोत्वार्यः ।

---

the four things with which even the poorest man was to greet a guest. 'Grass and earth to sit on, water to wash the feet, and fourthly, friendly yet sincere speech (*vāk sūnṛitā*) are never refused in the houses of the good, even though they be poor.' Manu iii. 101; Hitop. l. 301.

[1] 'On the raised-seat under the Saptaparṇa tree, cool with much shade, having sat down for a short time, let your honour cause removal of fatigue.' According to S'. *pracchāya=prakṛishṭā yā chāyā*, 'excessive shade.' The other commentators explain it by *prakṛishṭā chāyā yatra deśaḥ*, 'a place where there is excessive shade,' and by *prakṛishṭā chāyā yasyāḥ*, 'having excessive shade.' A parallel passage occurs in the Mālavik. p. 3, l. 20, *pracchāya-śītale śilāpaṭṭake nishaṇṇā*, &c. It seems clear that *pra* in this word gives intensity to the original idea. It is needless to regard it either as a Tatpurusha or Karmadhāraya compound, although it is in such compounds especially that *chāyā* becomes *chāya*. (See p. 6, n. 3, and Raghu-v. iv. 20, xii. 50; Megha-d. 103; Pāṇ. ii. 4, 22. 25.) *Sapta-parṇa*, 'a tree having seven leaves on a stalk,' called also *vishama-cchada*, 'having an odd number of leaves,' and *viśāla-tvac*, 'having a broad bark' (Raghu-v. iv. 23). *Vedikā=viśrāma-sthānam*, 'place of repose or rest.' It was probably a quadrangular raised-seat, something in the form of an altar, and covered with a roof supported by pillars, used as a kind of arbour for sitting or standing under. In this case it seems to have been erected under a Sapta-parṇa tree. *Saptaparṇa-nāmno vṛikshasya tale nirmitā yā vedikā*, S'. According to Sir W. Jones this tree, when full-grown, is very large; when young, light and elegant. *Muhūrta* is properly an Indian hour of forty-eight minutes or two Daṇḍas, but is used for any short space of time.

अनसूया ।

[a] हला सउन्दले । उइदं णो पज्जुबासणं अदिधीणं । एत्थ उबविसम्ह ।   ॥ इति सर्वे उपविशन्ति ॥

शकुन्तला   ॥ आत्मंगतम् ॥ [1]

[b] किं णुक्खु इमं जणं पेक्खिअ तवोवणविरोहिणो विआरस्स गमणीअम्हि संवुत्ता । [2]

राजा   ॥ सर्वा विलोक्य ॥

अहो समवयोरूपरमणीयं भवतीनां सौहार्देम् । [3]

प्रियंवदा   ॥ जनान्तिकम् ॥ [4]

[c] अणसूए । को णुक्खु एसो । चउरगम्भीराकिदी महुरं आ-

---

[a] हला शकुन्तले । उचितं नः पर्युपासनमतिथीनाम् । अत्रोपविशामः ।   [b] किं नु खल्विमं जनं प्रेक्ष्य तपोवनविरोधिनो विकारस्य गमनीयास्मि संवृत्ता ।   [c] जन-सूये । को नु खल्वेषः । चतुरगम्भीराकृतिर्मधुरमा-

---

[1] *Ātma-gatam* and *sva-gatam* (lit. 'gone to one's self') used in theatrical language, like 'aside,' to denote that the words which follow are spoken privately, as if to the speaker's self, and not in the hearing of any one but the audience (= *ananya-prakāśam*). *Gata*, 'gone,' is used loosely at the end of a compound to express relationship and connexion without necessary implication of motion. It may mean simply 'in connexion with,' 'in relation to ;' or, as here, 'with exclusive reference to,' 'addressed exclusively to.'

[2] 'How now! can it really be that, having looked upon this man, I am become susceptible of [lit. accessible to] an emotion inconsistent with a grove devoted to penance?' *Vikāra* is any alteration or transition from the natural and quiescent state of the soul; hence any emotion, whether of joy, grief, anger, &c. *Kim* is used *kutsāyām*, 'disdainfully,' and = *katham eva jātam*, 'how can it have happened?' The use of the gen. after *gamanīyā* is noticeable.

[3] *Sauhārda*, 'friendship,' an abstract noun from *su-hrid*. Observe that both *su* and *hrid* are vriddhied (see Gram. page 63, Prelim. Obs. *c*).

[4] *Janāntikam*, 'aside to a person standing near.' This is a theatrical direction similar to *ātma-gatam*, but the speech which follows is supposed to be audible by one other person, to whom a private signal is

[a]लबन्ती पहाववन्दो विञ्च लक्खीञदि ।

अनसूया ।

[b]सहि । ममवि अत्थि कोटूहलं । पुच्छिसं दाव णं ।

॥ प्रकाशम्[2] ॥ [c]अज्जस्स महुरालाबजणिदो विस्सासो मं मन्ताबेदि । कदमो अज्जेण राएसिवंसो अलङ्करीअदि । कदमो वा विरहपज्जुस्सुअजंणो किदो देसो । किस्सिमित्तं

[a] लपन्प्रभावचवानिव लक्ष्यते ।   [b] सखि । ममाप्यस्ति कौतूहलम् । प्रक्ष्यामि तावदेनम् ।   [c] आर्यस्य मधुरालापजनितो विश्वासो मां मन्त्रयति । कतम आर्येण राजर्षिवंशोऽलङ्क्रियते । कतमो वा विरहपर्युत्सुकजनः कृतो देशः । किन्निमित्तं

made. 'That which is spoken apart from the rest, with a signal, such as holding up three fingers of the hand (*tripatāka*), being a mutual speech (between two), is called *janāntikam*,' S'. and Sāhit.-d. p. 177.

[1] 'Who can this be (who being) lively (yet) dignified in mien, appears as if endowed with majesty (while) speaking to us sweetly.' *Ćatura*, 'lively,' 'sprightly,' 'animated,' may perhaps mean here, 'polite,' 'courteous,' in relation to *madhuram ālapan*. *Gambhīra*, 'profound,' is used metaphorically for one whose thoughts and feelings are deep or suppressed, 'reserved,' 'dignified,' 'not betraying emotion.' The oldest MS. reads *mahuram;* the others *mahuram piam;* but *piam* belongs properly to the margin.

[2] *Prakāśam*, 'aloud,' another theatrical direction denoting that the words which follow are to be made audible to all, those which precede having been spoken aside.

[3] 'Which race of royal-sages is adorned by your honour?' *Ka-tama*, 'which out of many?' A Rājarshi is a king or man of the Kshatriya and military class who has attained to the rank of a Rishi or saint by the practice of religious austerities. Such were Ikshvāku, Purūravas, Dushyanta, &c. There are six other classes of Rishis. The Rājarshi is inferior to the Brāhmarshi or 'Brāhman-saint,' but it was possible for a Rājarshi to raise himself to the rank of the latter, and therefore to the state of a Brāhman, by very severe penance, as exemplified in the story of the celebrated Viśvāmitra, son of Gādhi, and father of S'akuntalā. See p. 43, n. 1; also Rāmāy. i. 20, 20; 65, 18; Astra-śikshā, 118.

[4] 'With its people pining by separation,' i. e. by your absence.

[a]वा सुउमारदरोवि तवोवणगमणपरिस्समस्स अत्ता पदं उब्बणीदो ।

शकुन्तला   ॥ आत्मगतम् ॥

[b]हिअअ । मा उत्तम्म । एसा तुए चिन्दिदं अणसूआ मन्तेदि ।

राजा   ॥ आत्मगतम् ॥

कथमिदानीमात्मानं निवेदयामि । कथं वात्मापहारं करोमि । भवतु । एवं तावदेनां वक्ष्ये ।   ॥ प्रकाशम् ॥   भवंति । यः पौरवेण राज्ञा धर्माधिकारे नियुक्तः सोऽहमविघ्नक्रियोपलम्भाय धर्मारण्यमिदमायातः ।

---

[a] वा सुकुमारतरोऽपि तपोवनगमनपरिश्रमस्यात्मा पदमुपनीतः ।   [b] हृदय । मा उत्तम्य । एपा त्वया चिन्तितमनसूया मन्त्रयते ।

---

[1] 'Or on what account has your person, so very delicate [unaccustomed to hardships] as it (evidently) is, been brought to the point of (undergoing) the fatigue of visiting a grove of penance ?'

[2] 'O (my) heart! be not uneasy, this Anasūyā is giving utterance to all thy thoughts,' i.e. is making inquiry about all those points about which thou art anxious (such as, who this stranger is, whence he has come, &c.)

[3] 'Or how shall I make concealment of myself?' i. e. how shall I hide my real character? how shall I dissemble? *Apa-hāra* = *vañćana*, 'deception,' K., or = *ni-hnava* or *sangopana*, 'concealment,' 'dissimulation.' This is a very unusual sense of the word, but all the Deva-n. MSS. agree in reading *apahāra*. The Beng. have *parihāra*, which is also explained by *sangopana*. The oldest Beng. MS. (India Office, 1060) omits the words from *katham vā* to *karomi*.

[4] 'O lady!' voc. of *bhavatī*. A Brāhman is to be accosted with the respectful pronoun *bhavat*, and to any woman not related by blood, the address *bhavati*, 'Madam,' or *subhage bhagini*, 'amiable sister,' is to be used (Manu ii. 128, 129).

[5] 'I, that very person appointed by his majesty, the descendant of Puru, for the supervision of religion, have arrived at this sacred grove, for the purpose of ascertaining whether the (religious) rites are free from obstruction.' The sacrifices of holy men were liable to be disturbed by evil

अनसूया ।

[a] सण्णाहा दाणिं धम्मचारिणी ।

॥ शकुन्तला शृङ्गारलज्ज्ञां निरूपयति ॥

सख्यौ   ॥ उभयोराकारं विदित्वा जनान्तिकम् ॥

[b] हला सउन्दले । जइ एत्थ अज्ज तादी सन्निहिदो भवे ।

शकुन्तला   ॥ सरोषम् ॥

[c] तदो किं भवे ।

सख्यौ ।

[d] इमं जीविदसव्वस्सेण वि अदिधिविसेसं किदत्थं करिस्संदि ।

[a] सनाधा इदानीं धर्मचारिण: ।
सन्निहितो भवेत् ।   [c] तत: किं भवेत् ।
[b] हला शकुन्तले । यद्यत्राद्य तात:
[d] इमं जीवितसर्वस्वेनाप्यति-
थिविशेषं कृतार्थं करिष्यति ।

---

spirits called Rākshasas—the determined enemies of piety. No great
religious ceremony was ever carried on without these demons attempting
to impede its celebration ; and the most renowned saints were obliged on
such occasions to acknowledge their dependence on the strong arm of the
military class for protection. The idea that holy men, who had attained
the utmost spiritual power, were unable to cope with the spirits of evil,
and the superiority of physical force in this respect is remarkable. (See
Rāmāy. bk. i. chaps. 20, 21, 32 ; and end of Act III. of this play.) In
point of fact the Rākshasas were poetical representations of the wild
aborigines of the woods.

[1] *Sa-nāthāḥ*, 'possessed of a guardian ;' see p. 26, n. 3.

[2] 'Understanding the gestures of both,' i.e. of S'akuntalā and Dush-
yanta. *Ākāra*=*ćeshṭā* or *ingita*, 'a gesture,' 'sign,' or rather the state
of mind as evidenced by gestures and outward appearances, such as
change of colour, &c.

[3] 'What would then happen ?' i.e. if he were near at hand, what would
he do ? Schol.

[4] 'He would make this distinguished guest happy [possessed of the
object of his desire] with all the substance of his life,' i.e. he would do
worthy honour to his guest by offering him the best of his substance and
property. *Sarva-sva*, see p. 33, n. 1. S'. explains *sarva-svam* by *phala-
mūlādikam*, 'fruits, roots, and other necessaries of life.' Fruits and roots

शकुन्तला ।

[a] तुम्हे अवेध । किम्पि हिअए करिअ मन्तेध । ए वो वञ्चणं सुणिस्सं ।

राजा ।

वयमपि तावद्भवत्यौ सखीगतं किमपि पृच्छामः ।

सख्यौ ।

[b] अज्ज । अणुग्गहो विअ इअं अब्भत्यणा ।

राजा ।

भगवान्काश्यपः शाश्वते ब्रह्मणि वर्तते । इयं च वः सखी तदात्मजेति कथमेतत् ।

---

[a] युवामपेतम् । किमपि हृदये कृत्वा मन्त्रयेथे । न वां वचनं श्रोष्यामि ।
[b] आर्ये । अनुग्रह इवेयमभ्यर्थना ।

---

were the chief food of anchorites, and constituted their whole substance. With an offering of these they were commanded to honour every one who came to their hermitage (Rāmāy. i. 52, 16; 61, 4; Manu vi. 7). The allusion, however, evidently is to S'akuntalā, who might be regarded as the holy father's most valuable possession.

[1] 'Get off with you! having formed some (idea) in your heart, you are speaking.' *Hṛidaye* or *manasi kṛi* is not an unusual idiom for 'to turn or cogitate in the mind' (see Rāmāy. ii. 64, 8). *Apetam* is the 2nd du. impv. of *i*, 'to go,' with *apa*.

[2] *Sakhī-gatam*, 'relating to your friend.' (*Śakuntalā-vishayakam*, Schol.) This use of *gata* is noticeable, see note on *ātma-gatam*, p. 38, n. 1. Only one Deva-n. MS. reads *bhavatyau*; but this is supported by the oldest Bengālī, which also adds *kimapi*.

[3] 'His reverence Kāśyapa [see p. 22, n. 1] lives in the constant practice-of-devotion [or in perpetual celibacy].' *Brahman* is properly the Supreme Spirit from which all created things are supposed to emanate and into which they are absorbed. It may also mean the Veda, or holy knowledge. S'. explains *brahman* by *tapas*, i.e. bodily mortification and penance; K. by *brahma-charya*, 'the practice of continence.'

अनसूया ।

ᵃ सुणादु अज्जो । अत्थि कोबि कोसिओत्ति गोत्तणामहेओ
महप्पहावो राएसी ।

ᵃ शृणोत्वार्यः । अस्ति कोऽपि कौशिक इति गोत्रनामधेयो महाप्रभावो राजर्षिः ।

---

[1] 'There is a certain Rājarshi [see p. 39, n. 3] of great majesty, whose
family name is Kauśika,' i.e. the celebrated Viśvāmitra (descendant of Kuśa
or Kuśika), whose story is told in Rāmāy. bk. i. chaps. 35 and 51–65.
He is there described as the son of Gādhi (a prince of the Lunar dynasty,
king of Gādhi-pur, or the ancient Kanouj), who is the son of Kuśa-nātha,
who is the son of Kuśa or Kuśika. According to Vishṇu-p. the following
is the pedigree of Viśvāmitra. One of the sons of Purūravas, a prince
of the Lunar dynasty (see Vikramorvaśī), was Amāvasu. Thence in
direct succession came Bhīma, Kāṅćana, Jahnu, Sumantu, Ajaka, Valā-
kāśva, and Kuśa. The latter had two sons, Kuśāmba and Kuśa-nātha;
but Gādhi was son of Kuśāmba, and was said to be an incarnation of
Indra (hence sometimes called Kauśika); for Kuśāmba had engaged in
great penance, to obtain a son who should be equal to Indra; and the
latter becoming alarmed, took upon himself the character of Kuśāmba's
son. Gādhi had a daughter, Satyavatī, who married a Brāhman named
Ṛićīka, son of Bhṛigu. This Ṛićīka—with the view of securing to him-
self a son who should be an illustrious Brāhman, and to his father-in-law
a son of great prowess—made two messes of food, one for his own wife,
and the other for the wife of Gādhi; infusing into one the qualities
suited to a Brāhman, and into the other the properties of power and
heroism. The two wives exchanged messes, and so it happened that the
wife of Gādhi had a son, Viśvāmitra, who, though a Kshatriya, was born
with the inclinations of a Brāhman; and the wife of Ṛićīka had a son,
the sage Jamad-agni, who was the father of the warrior-priest Paraśu-
rāma, she having by her entreaties induced her husband to transfer the
effects of the exchange of food from her son to her grandson. There is
something like anachronism in the history of Viśvāmitra. Satyavatī, his
sister, was the grandmother of Paraśu-rāma, and it was not till the close
of the latter's career that Rāma-ćandra appeared on the field and became
the pupil of Viśvāmitra. At any rate the Ṛishi must have been very old.
Indeed, in the Rāmāyaṇa he is stated to have mortified himself for two
thousand years before he attained the rank of a Ṛishi; for many years more
before his cohabitation with Menakā, which led to the birth of Śakuntalā;

राजा ।

अस्ति । श्रूयते ।

अनसूया ।

[a] तं णो पिअसहीए पहवं अवगच्छ । उज्झिआए सरीर-
संवड्ढणादीहिं तादकस्सवो से पिदा ।

राजा ।

उज्झितशब्देन जनितं मे कौतूहलम् । आ मूलाच्छ्रोतु-
मिच्छामि ।

अनसूया ।

[b] सुणादु अज्जो । गोदमीतीरे पुरा किल तस्स राएसिणो
उग्गे तवसि वट्टमाणस्स किम्पि जादसङ्केहिं देवेहिं मेणआ
णाम अच्छरा पेसिदा णिअमविग्घकारिणी ।

<hr>

[a] तं नौ प्रियसख्याः प्रभवमवगच्छ । उज्झितायाः शरीरसंवर्धनादिभिस्तातकाश्य-
पोऽस्याः पिता ।   [b] शृणोत्वार्यः । गौतमीतीरे पुरा किल तस्य राजर्षेरुग्रे
तपसि वर्तमानस्य किमपि जातशङ्कैर्देवैर्मेनका नामाप्सराः प्रेषिता नियमविघ्नकारिणी ।

and for many thousand years more before he became a Brāhman. It
was not till after this period that he became the preceptor of Rāma-
candra. No chronological inconsistency is too monstrous for Hindū
mythology.

[1] 'Know him (to be) the father of our dear friend; but father Kaṇva
is the (reputed) father of her, through the fostering of her body, &c.,
when deserted.' *Prabhava=janma-hetu,* 'the operative cause of being,'
i.e. a father.

[2] The story of Viśvāmitra, as told in the Rāmāyaṇa, is briefly this. On
his accession to the throne in the room of his father Gādhi, in the course
of a tour through his dominions, he visited the hermitage of the sage
Vaśishṭha (one of the ten Brahmādikas or Prajāpatis, sons of Brahmā).
There the cow of plenty, which granted its owner all desires, and was
the property of Vaśishṭha, excited the king's cupidity. He offered the
Muni untold treasures in exchange for the cow, but being refused, pre-
pared to take it by force. A long war ensued between the King and
the Muni (symbolical of the struggles between the Kshatriya and Brāh-

अस्त्येतदन्यसमाधिभीरुत्वं देवानाम् ।

manical classes) which ended in the defeat of Viśvāmitra, whose vexation was such, that he devoted himself to tremendous austerities, hoping to force the gods to make him a Brāhman that he might fight with the saint Vaśishṭha on equal terms. The Rāmāyaṇa goes on to recount how, by gradually increasing the rigour of his bodily mortification through thousands of years, he successively earned the title of Rājarshi (i. 57, 5), Rishi (63, 2), Maharshi (63, 19), and finally, Brahmarshi (65, 18). Not till he had gained this last title did Vaśishṭha consent to acknowledge his equality with himself, and ratify his admission into the Brāhmanical state. It was at the time of Viśvāmitra's advancement to the rank of a Rishi, and whilst he was still a Kshatriya, that Indra and the gods, jealous of his increasing power—exhibited in his transporting king Triśanku to the region of the stars, and in saving S'unaḥśepa, the son of his own brother-in-law Rićīka, out of the hands of Indra, to whom he had been promised by king Ambarīsha as a victim in a sacrifice—sent the nymph Menakā, to seduce him from his life of continence. The Rāmāyaṇa records his surrender to this temptation, and relates that the nymph was his companion in the hermitage for ten years, but does not allude to the birth of S'akuntalā during that period. It only informs us that at the end of ten years the Rishi extricated himself from this hindrance (*niyama-vighna*), and abandoning the nymph, departed into another region. See Indian Wisdom, p. 363.

[1] 'Such is the dread which the (inferior) gods have of the devotion of others!' Indra and all the deities below Brahman are really, according to the Hindū system, finite beings, whose existence as separate deities will one day terminate, and whose sovereignty in Svarga, or 'heaven,' is by no means inalienable. They viewed with jealousy and alarm any persistency by a human being in acts of penance which might raise him to a level with themselves; and if carried beyond a certain point, might enable him to dispossess them of paradise. Indra was therefore the enemy of excessive devotion, and had in his service numerous nymphs (*apsaras*), such as Menakā, Rambhā, and Urvaśī, who were called his 'weapons' (*Indrasya praharaṇāni*, Vikram., Act I), and who were constantly sent by him to impede by their seductions the devotions of holy men.

अनसूया ।

[a] तदो वसन्तोदारसमए से उम्मादइत्तञ्चं रूवं पेक्खिंञ्च ।

॥ इत्यर्धोक्ते लज्जया विरमति ॥

राजा ।

परस्तादवगम्यत एव[2] । सर्वथाप्सरःसम्भवैषा ।

अनसूया ।

[b] अहंइं[3] ।

राजा ।

उपपद्यते ।

मानुषीषु कथं वा स्यादस्य रूपस्य सम्भवः ।
न प्रभातरलं ज्योतिरुदेति वसुधातलात् ॥२६॥

[a] ततो वसन्तावतारसमयेऽस्या उन्मादयितृकं रूपं प्रेक्ष्य ।　　　[b] अथ किम् ।

---

[1] 'Then at the season of the descent of Spring, having looked upon the intoxicating beauty [form] of that (nymph).' Some commentators consider *vasantodāra* to be a compound of *vasanta* and *udāra;* but *odāra* is a legitimate Prākṛit contraction for *avatāra*, although *avadāra* would be equally correct. Cf. *odansayanti* for *avatansayanti* (p. 7, n. 1), *hodi* for *havadi* or *bhavati*, *jedi* for *jayadi* or *jayati*, &c. *Avatāra* is from *ava-tṛī*, 'to descend,' and applies especially to the descent of a god from heaven. *Vasanta*, 'the Spring,' is often personified as a deity. See Vikram., Act II, *Pekkhadu bhavam vasantāvadārasūidam assa ahirāmattaṇam pamadavaṇassa*, 'let your honour observe the delightfulness of this pleasure-garden manifested by the descent of Spring.' *Unmādayitṛikam* is for the neut. *unmādayitṛi*, 'that which causes to go mad or be intoxicated' (=*adhairya-janakam*, 'causing unsteadiness').

[2] 'What (happened) afterwards is quite understood [or guessed by me].' The suffix *tāt*, in words like *parastāt, adhastāt*, may stand for the nominative case, as well as for abl. and loc. (Pāṇ. v. 3, 27). Hence *parastāt = para-vṛittāntaḥ*, 'the rest of the story,' 'the subsequent particulars.'

[3] 'Exactly so,' 'how can it be otherwise?' *Athakim* is a particle of assent.

[4] 'It is fitting (that she should be the daughter of an Apsaras). How

Verse 26. ŚLOKA or ANUSHTUBH. See verses 5, 6, 11.

॥ शकुन्तलाधोमुखी भूत्वा तिष्ठति ॥

राजा ॥ आत्मगतम् ॥

लब्धावकाशो मे मनोरथः[1]। किन्तु सख्याः परिहासोदा-
हृतां वरप्रार्थनां श्रुत्वा धृतद्वैधीभावकातरं मे मनः[2]।

प्रियंवदा ॥ सस्मितं शकुन्तलां विलोक्य नायकाभिमुखी भूत्वा[3] ॥

[a] पुणोबि वत्तुकामो विअ अज्जो ।

[a] पुनरपि वक्तुकाम इदार्थः ।

---

otherwise could there be the birth of this beautiful-form amongst mortal females ? the tremulously-radiant flash does not rise from the surface of the earth (but descends from the skies).' *Apsarah-sambhavatvam* is to be supplied before *upapadyate*. According to K., *prabhā-taralam* (i. e. *prabhayā čančalam*) *jyotis* = *vidyut*, 'lightning ;' but S'. applies it also to the beams of the sun and moon. The comparison of the unearthly beauty of a nymph to the radiance of lightning is common. Cf. Megha-d. 40.

[1] 'My desire has found (free) scope,' i. e. since it is certain that she is not a Brāhmaṇī woman (*asavarṇatva-niščayāt*, 'from the certainty of her not being of the same class with the holy father'), it is clear that my desire is directed towards an attainable object. *Avakāśa* means 'free course,' 'range,' 'power of expatiating.' Cf. p. 55, l. 3, *labdhāvakāśā me prārthanā;* K. there explains it by *labdhāśrayaḥ* or *sārtho me manorathaḥ.*

[2] 'Nevertheless, having heard her friend's prayer for a husband uttered in joke [see p. 30, l. 1], my heart is held in suspense and anxious,' i. e. anxious to know the truth, as to whether she is really destined for marriage, or for an ascetic life ; and fearful lest at some former time her husband may have been decided upon (*pūrvam asyā varo nirṇīto na vā,* K.) S'. interprets *vara-prārthanā* by *svāmy-abhilāsha,* 'wish for a husband.' *Dhṛita-dvaidhībhāva-kātaram* is a complex Dvandva compound. *Dvaidhī-bhāva,* 'a state of difference, distraction, doubt.'

[3] 'Looking with a smile at S'akuntalā, (and then) turning her face towards the hero-of-the-poem ;' lit. 'having become with her face turned,' &c. All the Deva-n. MSS. have this latter clause. *Nāyaka,* in dramatic poetry, is the leading character or hero of the poem, and *nāyikā,* the heroine. Romeo, in Shakespeare, would be the *nāyaka,* and Juliet the *nāyikā.* In every Hindū play there is also a *prati-nāyaka,* or 'anti-hero,' and an *upa-nāyaka,* or 'sub-hero.' See Indian Wisdom, p. 467.

॥ शकुन्तला सखीमङ्गुल्या तर्जयन्ती ॥

राजा ।

सम्यगुपलक्षितं भवत्या । अस्ति नः सच्चरित्रश्रवणलो-
भादन्यदपि प्रष्टव्यम् ।

प्रियंवदा ।

"अलं विआरिअ । अणिअन्तणाणुओग्गो तवस्सिअणो
णामं ।

राजा ।

सखीं ते ज्ञातुमिच्छामि ।

वैखानसं किमनया व्रतमा प्रदाना-
व्यापाररोधि मदनस्य निषेवितव्यम् ।

ⁿ अलं विचार्य । अनियन्त्रणानुयोगस्तपस्विजनो नाम ।

---

[1] ‘S'akuntalā threatens [reproves] her friend with her finger,’ i. e. makes a threatening or chiding gesture, as if she were angry with her friend for leading Dushyanta to pursue his interrogatories, and were ashamed at the revelation of the particulars of her history (*ātmano vrīḍā-janaka-svavrittāntodghātanam,* K.) According to S'. this is an example of the coquettish gesture called *lalita,* i. e. though she was really eager to hear all that her lover had to say, yet by her outward gestures she appeared to be the reverse (*priyajana-kathā-śuśrūshur api vahis tad-anyathā*).

[2] ‘Rightly judged by your ladyship; from an eagerness to hear (all the particulars of) the history of pious people, there is still something (that remains) to be asked by us.’

[3] ‘Enough of deliberating; ascetic people may surely be questioned unreservedly [freely].’ *Aniyantraṇānuyoga=aniyama-praśna,* ‘one to whom a question may be put without any restraint or ceremony,’ K. *Alam,* in the sense of prohibiting or forbidding, is more usually found with instr. case of a noun, but, like *khalu,* it may sometimes be used in this sense with an indeclinable participle in *tvā* and *ya,* thus *alam dattvā,* ‘enough of giving,’ or ‘having given, it is enough;’ so *khalu pītvā,* ‘having drunk, hold!’ See Gram. 918. *a.* The Beng. MSS. read *alam vicāritena.*

अत्यन्तमात्मसदृशेक्षणवल्लभाभि-
राहो निवत्स्यति समं हरिणाङ्गनाभिः ॥२७॥

प्रियंवदा ।

[a] अज्ज । धम्मचरणेवि परवसो अम्हं जणो । गुरुणो उण
से अणुरूववरप्पदाणे सङ्कप्पो ।

[a] आर्ये । धर्मचरणेऽपि परवशोऽयं जनः । गुरोः पुनरस्या अनुरूपवरप्रदाने
सङ्कल्पः ।

---

[1] 'I wish to ascertain (respecting) your friend—Is this monastic vow, (so) opposed to the ways of love, to be observed by her (merely) until her gift-in-marriage; or else (*āho*), will she dwell to the end (of her life) along with the female deer, her favourites (from) having eyes like her own?' Dr. Boehtlingk remarks that *sakhīṃ te jñātum iććhāmi kim anayā*, &c., is equivalent to *jñātum iććhāmi kiṃ sakhyā te*, &c., 'I wish to know whether this vow is to be observed by thy friend,' &c. He gives instances of a similar construction in Draupadī-h. iv. 5; Mahā-bh. iii. 269. *Vaikhānasa*, 'relating to a *vikhānasa* or hermit;' *tena kritam proktaṃ vā vrataṃ vaikhānasam, tat tu niyatāraṇya-vāsa-rūpam*, 'the vow which is performed by him or enjoined on him is called *vaikhānasa*, and that consists in always living in the woods,' S'. *Ā pradānāt=pradāna-paryantam*, or *ā vivāhāt*, 'up to the period of her marriage.' In the time of Manu every Hindū girl was given away in marriage before the season of maturity (*ritoḥ prāk pradāna-kālaḥ*), and that father incurred great disgrace who did not so give her away. It was deemed highly reprehensible if the betrothed husband did not take her to his own house, when the marriageable period of life arrived; (see Manu ix. 4, with commentary.) *Vyāpāra-rodhi madanasya=kāma-kriyā-nivārakam*, 'hindering amatory actions.' According to K. *ātma-sadṛiśekshaṇa-vallabhābhir* may be optionally resolved into *ātma-sadṛiśekshaṇa-vallabhā ābhir*. *Āho*, a particle of doubt, is used *pakshāntare* or *vikalpe*, i. e. antithetically, in stating an opposite alternative.

[2] 'Even in the practice of religious duties this person [S'akuntalā] is subject to (the will of) another [viz. Kaṇva]; nevertheless, it is the settled purpose of the Guru to give her away to a husband suited to her.' *Ayaṃ janaḥ* may possibly mean 'we.' The same expression occurs in

---

राजा ॥ आत्मगतम् ॥

न दुरवापेयं खलु प्रार्थना ।

भव हृदय साभिलाषं सम्प्रति सन्देहनिर्णयो जातः ।

आशङ्कसे यदग्निं तदिदं स्पर्शक्षमं रत्नम् ॥२८॥

Act IV. Manu (ix. 2, 3) declares that women were never to be deemed
fit for independence. Day and night they were to be held by their
protectors in subjection. But in certain matters, such as lawful recrea-
tions, and if they chose to enter upon a religious life, they were to be
left at their own disposal. It seems that even in those matters S'akuntalā
was not her own mistress. The holy father had enjoined a life of
penance upon her, but had settled that it should not be perpetual. *Api
śabdena dharmācaraṇasya sva-ćhanda-karaṇīyatvaṃ sūćitam*, 'by the
word "even" it is indicated that the duties of religion are generally to
be performed as a voluntary act,' K. Amara-siṇha explains *saṅkalpaḥ* by
mānasaṃ karma, 'a mental act or resolution.' Vararući's rule (i. 22)
by which the Sanskṛit *guru* becomes *garua* in Prākṛit only applies to the
adjective.

[1] 'This prayer is not difficult of realization,' i. e. a suitable husband,
about whom there is this wish, is not difficult to be obtained; *prārthanā-
śabdena tad-vishayo varo lakshyate*, K., i. e. *prārthanā* is the prayer
supposed to have been made by Kaṇva, that he might find a suitable
husband for his foster-child.

[2] 'O (my) heart! become hopeful [possessed of desire]; now the
certainty (of what was a matter) of doubt has come to pass. That which
thou suspectedst (to be) fire, the same (is) a gem capable of being
touched.' *Sandeha-nirṇaya*, 'arriving at positive certainty on a doubtful
point.' This was the doubt mentioned just before verse 22, see note to
verse 22. *Antaḥ-karaṇa* is there used for *hṛidaya*. *Yad [S'akuntalā-
rūpam vastu] agniṃ tarkayasi*, 'the thing [viz. S'akuntalā] which thou
imaginedst fire,' S'. The power of a Brāhman, especially if exhibited
in anger, is compared to fire (verse 41 of this play; Bhaṭṭi-k. i. 23;
Mahā-bh. i. 3010). There may be some allusion to this here, or it may

---

Verse 28. ĀRYĀ or GĀTHĀ. See verse 2.

᷉ ᷉ ᷉ ᷉ | ᷉ − ᷉ | − − ‖ − ᷉ ᷉ | − − | ᷉ − ᷉ | − − | −

− − | ᷉ − ᷉ | − − ‖ ᷉ ᷉ − | − − | ᷉ | − − | −

शकुन्तला ॥ सरोषमिव ॥

[a] अणसूए । अहं गमिस्सं ।

अनसूया ।

[b] किण्णिमित्तं ।

शकुन्तला ।

[c] इमं असम्बद्धप्पलाविणिं पिअंवदं अज्जाए गोदमीए णिवेदइस्सं ।

अनसूया ।

[d] सहि । ण जुत्तं ते अकिदसक्कारं अदिहिविसेसं विसज्जिअ सच्छन्ददो गमणं । ॥ शकुन्तला न किञ्चिदुक्त्वा प्रस्थितैव ॥

राजा ॥ ग्रहीतुमिच्छन्निगृह्यात्मानम् । आत्मगतम् ॥

अहो चेष्टाप्रतिरूपिका कामिनो मनोवृत्तिः । अहं हि

---

[a] अनसूये । अहं गमिष्यामि ।   [b] किन्निमित्तम् ।   [c] इमामसम्बद्धप्रलापिनीं प्रियंवदामार्यायै गौतम्यै निवेदयिष्यामि ।   [d] सखि । न युक्तं तेऽकृतसत्कारम-तिथिविशेषं विसृज्य स्वच्छन्दतो गमनम् ।

---

simply mean that, supposing S'akuntalā to have been a Brāhmaṇī woman, she would have been as inapproachable to a Kshatriya as a flame of fire. *Sparśa-kshama = samparka-yogya*, see p. 29, n. 1, at end.

[1] *A-sambaddha*, properly 'unconnected;' hence, 'absurd,' 'nonsensical.' *A-baddha* is used with the same acceptation.

[2] Cf. p. 36, n. 1. S'. quotes an aphorism of Bhṛigu, 'Whosoever does not reverently honour an unknown guest, weary with travelling, and hungry and thirsty, him they call (equal in guilt to) the slayer of a Brāhman.'

[3] 'Wishing [making a movement] to arrest (her departure, but) checking himself.' So read all the Deva-n. MSS. The Beng. have, *utthāya jighṛikshur iva icchām nigṛihya*, 'rising up as if desirous of holding her (and then) restraining his intention.' It appears from p. 38, l. 3, that the whole party were seated. The Bengālī reading supposes that, with the idea of arresting her departure, he started up and then checked himself.

अनुयास्यन्मुनितनयां सहसा विनयेन वारितप्रसरः ।
स्थानादनुचलन्नपि गत इव पुनः प्रतिनिवृत्तः ॥२९॥

प्रियंवदा ॥ शकुन्तलां निरुध्य ॥

हला ण दे जुत्तं गन्तुं ।[a]

शकुन्तला ॥ सभ्रूभङ्गम् ॥

किंणिमित्तं ।[b]

प्रियंवदा ।

रुक्खसेअणाइं दुवे धारेसि मे । एहि दाव । अत्ताणं[c]
मोचिञ्च तदो गमिस्ससि । ॥ इति बलादेनां निवर्तयति ॥

राजा ।

भद्रे । वृक्षसेचनादेव परिश्रान्तामभवतीं लक्षये । तथा
ह्यस्याः

---

[a] हला न ते युक्तं गन्तुम् ।   [b] किंनिमित्तम् ।   [c] वृक्षसेचने द्वे धारयसि
मे । एहि तावत् । आत्मानं मोचयित्वा ततो गमिष्यसि ।

---

[1] 'Ah! what passes in the mind [the state of mind] of a lover has
not a counterpart in his gestures: for, being about to follow the hermit's
daughter, all at once I have been restrained from advancing by decorum;
although not (really) moving from my place, as if having gone, I have
turned back again,' i. e. I feel just as if I had gone and turned back.
Vinayena=*kula-maryādayā*, S.; =*sauśīlyena*, K., 'by family honour,' 'by
honourable, gentlemanly feeling.' *Vārita-prasara*=*niruddha-gamana*.

[2] 'With a frown.' *Bhrū-bhanga*, 'bending of the brow,' was one of
the acts of feminine coquetry called *su-kumāra*, 'very delicate.' Under
this head are included all coquettish glances of the eye, S. See p. 32, n. 6;
Megha-d. 73.

[3] 'Thou owest me two waterings of trees,' or according to Sir W.
Jones, 'You owe me the labour, according to our agreement, of watering
two more shrubs.' *Me*=*mahyam*. *Dhṛi* in the causal, in the sense of
'to owe,' requires a dative of the person.

Verse 29. ĀRYĀ or GĀTHĀ. See verse 2.

⏑⏑— | —⏑⏑ | ⏑⏑— ‖ ⏑⏑— | ⏑⏑— | ⏑—⏑ | —⏑⏑ | —
—— | ⏑—⏑ | —⏑⏑ ‖ —— | ⏑⏑— | ⏑ | ⏑⏑—| —

स्रस्तांसावतिमाचलौहिततलौ बाहू घटोत्क्षेपणा-
द्द्यापि स्तनवेपथुं जनयति श्वासः प्रमाणाधिकः ।
बद्धं कर्णशिरीषरोधि वदने घर्माम्भसां जालकं
बन्धे स्रंसिनि चैकहस्तयमिताः पर्याकुला मूर्धजाः ॥३०॥
तदहमेनामनृणां करोमि ।   ॥ इत्यङ्गुलीयं दातुमिच्छति ॥
॥ उभे नाममुद्राक्षराण्यनुवाच्य परस्परमवलोकयतः ॥

---

[1] 'For her arms have the shoulders drooping, and the lower part [fore-arm] excessively red through tossing the watering-pot. Even now her unnaturally-strong breathing causes a heaving of her breast; a collection of drops of perspiration, impeding (the play of) the S'irīsha in her ears, has formed upon her face; her dishevelled locks, the fillet (that confined them) having given way [fallen], are held together with one hand.' *Bāhu* is the arm from the shoulder-joint (*aṅsa*) to the wrist, and does not include the *karabha*, or part from the wrist to the fingers. It is divided into two parts, the upper arm, *pragaṇḍa*, or that part of the arm from the elbow to the shoulder; and the lower arm, *prakoshṭha*, commonly called the fore-arm, extending from the elbow to the wrist. *Atilohita-talau* is a Bahuvrīhi comp., in agreement with *bāhū*; *talau* cannot, therefore, be translated by 'the palms of the hands.' One meaning of *tala* is 'fore-arm,' and S'. explains it by *bhujodara*. It may possibly mean the under-surface of the arms, which would be reddened by chafing against the bark-vesture in lifting the watering-pot. *Pramāṇādhikaḥ = svā-bhāvika-mānād adhikaḥ*, 'more than natural,' 'undue.' *Baddham*, 'formed' (see p. 29, n. 1). *Jālaka*, 'a net-work;' hence, 'a collection' (=*samūha*). S'. observes that her face was spotted with drops of perspiration resembling net-work. So *svedam ānana-vilagna-jālakam*, Raghu-v. ix. 68. *Karṇa-śirīsha-rodhi*, see p. 7, n. 1. The drops of perspiration would prevent the play of the pendent flower by causing it to adhere to her cheek (*sthirī-karaṇāt*, S'.; *saṃślesha-kāritvāt*, K.) A similar idea occurs in Megha-d. 28, where the lotus of the ears is described as faded by the act of removing the perspiration from the cheeks in hot weather. The lotus-flower, or one of its petals, furnished as common an ornament for the ear as the *śirīsha* (Megha-d. 69, 46). *Paryākulāḥ = vikīrṇāḥ*, 'scattered.'

[2] This is probably the ring which was afterwards given to S'akuntalā, and served as the *abhijñāna* or 'token of recognition.'

[3] 'Both, reading the letters of the seal with the name (of Dushyanta

Verse 30. S'ĀRDŪLA-VIKRĪḌITA (a variety of ATIDHṚITI). See verse 14.

राजा ।

अलमस्मानन्यथा सम्भाव्य राज्ञः प्रतिग्रहोऽयमिति रा-
जपुरुषं मामवगच्छयं ।

प्रियंवदा ।

[a]तेण हि णारुहदि एदं अङ्गुलीअग्गं अङ्गुलीविओअं ।
अज्जस्स वअणेण अणिरिणा दाणिं एसा ।। किञ्चिद्विहस्य ।।

[b]हला सउन्दले मोइदासि अणुअम्पिणा अज्जेण अहवा
महाराएण । गच्छ दाणिं ।

शकुन्तला ।। आत्मगतम् ।।

[c]जइ अत्तणो पहविस्सं ।। प्रकाशम् ।। [d]का तुमं विसज्जि-
द्व्वस्स रुन्धिदव्वस्स वा ।

[a] तेन हि नार्हत्येतदङ्गुलीयकमङ्गुलीवियोगम् । आर्यस्य वचनेनानृणेदानीमेषा ।
[b] हला शकुन्तले मोचितास्यनुकम्पिनार्येण अथवा महाराजेन । गच्छेदानीम् ।
[c] यद्यात्मनः प्रभविष्यामि । [d] का त्वं विसष्टव्यस्य रोद्धव्यस्य वा ।

___

stamped on it), look at each other;' [*asau rājā iti kritvā*, 'thinking to
themselves, This is the king,' K.] All the Deva-n. MSS. read *nāma-
mudrāksharāṇi*. *Mudrā* is here, not a 'seal-ring,' but 'the seal or
engraved stone on the ring;' *nāma-mudrā*, lit. 'name-seal,' is a seal
with a name engraved on it, a signet-seal. So in Mālavik. p. 5, l. 9, and
48, 4, *nāga-mudrā-sanātham aṅgulīyakam*, and *sarpa-mudrakam aṅgu-
līyakam*, 'a ring possessed of a snake-seal,' or 'snake-stone seal.' *Anu-
vāčya=paṭhitvā*, 'having read,' 'having deciphered.' *Vač* and *anuvač*
in the causal have generally this sense in dramatic composition.

[1] 'Enough of considering me to be different (from what I am);
(observing) that this (ring) is a present from the king, know me (to be)
the king's officer,' i. e. do not imagine me to be the king himself; I am
only the king's servant, and this is his ring, which he has given me to
serve as my credentials. *Alam anyathā sambhāvya = alam anyathā
sambhāvanayā* (see p. 48, n. 3). *Pratigraho 'yam*, i. e. *idam aṅgurī-
yakam mayi dattam*, S'. *Pratigrah*, especially 'to receive a gift,' with
gen., e. g. *na rājñaḥ* (or *nripasya*) *pratigṛihṇīyāt*, 'let him not receive
any gift from the king,' Manu iv. 84. *Pratigraha* is 'that which is
received' (*pratigṛihyate*); hence, 'any gift.'

[2] 'Who art thou (in respect) of what is to be allowed to go and what

राजा ॥ शकुन्तलां विलोक्य । आत्मगतम् ॥

किं नु खलु यथा वयमस्यामेवमियमप्यस्मान्प्रति स्यात् ।
अथवा लब्धावकाशा मे प्रार्थना । कुतः ।

वाचं न मिश्रयति यद्यपि मे वचोभिः
कर्णं ददात्यभिमुखं मयि भाषमाणे ।
कामं न तिष्ठति मदाननसम्मुखी सा
भूयिष्ठमन्यविषया न तु दृष्टिरस्याः ॥ ३१ ॥

नेपथ्ये ।

भी भोस्तपस्विनः । सन्निहितास्तपोवनसत्त्वरक्षायै भवंत ।
प्रत्यासन्नः किल मृगयाविहारी पार्थिवो दुष्यन्तः ।

तुरगखुरहतस्तथा हि रेणु-
विटपविषक्तजलार्द्रवल्कलेषु ।

---

it is to be held back?' i. e. what power have you to send me away or keep me back? *Kā=na prabhuḥ, avaśā*, K., i. e. you have no right or power (see p. 34, n. 2). This use of gen. for dat., and of the fut. pass. part. for the verbal noun, is peculiar to Prākṛit. The idiom of Sanskrit would require *visarjanāya rodhanāya vā*, 'for loosing or binding.'

¹ 'My wish has found (free) scope,' i. e. I am at liberty to indulge it. *Prārthanā=manoratha*, K.; see p. 47, n. 1.

² *Kutaḥ*, 'whence?' 'why so?' often used where a reason is about to be given in verse for some previous statement. Translateable by 'because.'

³ 'Although she mingles not her speech with my words, (nevertheless) she places her ear directly opposite to me speaking [when I speak]. Granted that she does not stand with her face towards my face, (still) her eye for the most part is not fixed on any other object.' Thus he was free to indulge his hopes, without being actually certain of their realization. *Dadāti [nikshipati, K.] karṇam*, i. e. *avahitā, tatparā asti*, 'she is very attentive,' S. *Kāmam*, 'well!' 'granted!' see p. 24, l. 10.

⁴ 'Be ye near at hand for the protection of the animals of the penance-grove.' *Sattva=jantu*, 'an animal,' S. Boehtlingk translates it by *Wesen*, 'being,' 'existence,' 'weal,' which is a legitimate acceptation of the word.

Verse 31. VASANTA-TILAKĀ (a variety of ŚAKVARĪ). See verses 8, 27.

पतति परिणतारुणप्रकाशः
शलभसमूह इवाश्रमद्रुमेषु ॥३२॥

अपि च ।

तीव्राघातप्रतिहततरुस्कन्धलग्नैकदन्तः
पादाकृष्टव्रततिवलयासङ्गसञ्जातपाशः ।
मूर्तो विघ्नस्तपस इव नो भिन्नसारङ्गयूथो
धर्मारण्यं प्रविशति गजः स्यन्दनालोकभीतः ॥३३॥

॥ सर्वाः कर्णौ दत्त्वा किञ्चिदिव सम्भ्रान्ताः ॥

[1] 'For the dust, raised by the hoofs of the horses, like a swarm of locusts shining in the fading glow of sunset, falls on the trees of the hermitage, having bark-garments, moist with water, suspended (to dry) on the branches.' For *valkaleshu*, see p. 18, n. 1. *Aruṇa* is the glow either of sunrise or sunset, more usually the former. *Pariṇatāruṇa*, as explained by K., is the evening (*sāyantana*) redness of the sun, in contradistinction to the *aruṇodaya* or ruddiness of dawn. *Śalabha-samūha* = *pataṅga-nivaha*, 'a multitude of grasshoppers.'

[2] 'An elephant, terrified at the sight of the (king's) chariot, enters the sacred grove, scaring the herd of deer, a corporeal interruption, as it were, of our penance; having a (kind of) tether, caused by the clinging of a coil of creepers dragged along by his feet; having one of his tusks fixed in the trunk of a tree, struck back with a violent blow.' Such is the reading of all the Deva-n. MSS. The Bengālī have *tīvrāghātād abhi-mukha-taru-skandha-bhagnaika-danta*, 'with a violent blow having broken one tusk against the trunk of a tree standing in his way.' For *pāda* K. reads *kroḍa*, 'the breast.' *Valaya* = *veshṭana*, 'anything that encircles.' *Pāśa* = *bandhana-rajju*, 'a binding-rope.' *Mūrta* = *mūrti-mat*, 'possessed of a body,' 'corporeal,' as opposed to the spiritual obstruction caused by evil spirits, &c. *Bhinna-sāraṅga-yūthaḥ* is a Bahuvrīhi comp. agreeing with *gajaḥ*, 'an elephant by which (*yena*) the herd of deer (*sāraṅga-yūtham*) has been scattered (*bhinnam* = *vikīrṇam*).' This was probably a wild elephant (*vanya-gaja*), from its being frightened at the sight of the chariot (*syandana*), K. Cf. a scene in Ratn. (Calcutta ed., p. 27).

Verse 32. PUSHPITĀGRĀ, containing twenty-five syllables to the half-verse; each half-verse being alike, the first and third quarter-verses ending at the twelfth syllable.

◡◡◡◡◡◡ – ◡ – ◡ – – ‖ ◡◡◡◡◡ – ◡◡ – ◡ – ◡ – ◡

Verse 33. MANDĀKRĀNTĀ (a variety of ATYASHṬI). See verse 15.

राजा ॥ आत्मगतम् ॥

अहो धिक् पौरा अस्मदन्वेषिणस्तपोवनमुपरुन्धन्ति ।
भवतु । प्रतिगमिष्यामस्तावत् ।

सख्यौ ।

[a] अज्ज । इमिणा आरण्णअवुत्तन्तेणं पज्जाउलम्ह । अणुजा-
णाहि णो उडञअगमणस्स ।

राजा ॥ ससम्भ्रमम् ॥

गच्छन्तु भवत्यः । वयमप्याश्रमपीडा यथा न भविष्यति
तथा प्रयतिष्यामहे । ॥ सर्वे उत्तिष्ठन्ति ॥

सख्यौ ।

[b] अज्ज । असम्भाविदादिहिसक्कारं भूओबि पेक्खणणिमित्तं
लज्जेमो अज्जं विण्णविदुं ।

राजा ।

मा मैवम् । दर्शनेनैव भवतीनां पुरस्कृतोऽस्मि ।

शकुन्तला ।

[c] अणसूए । अहिणवकुससूईएं परिक्खदं मे चलणं ।

[a] आर्ये । अनेनारण्यकवृत्तान्तेन पर्याकुलाः स्मः । अनुजानीहि न उटजगमनाय ।
[b] आर्ये । असम्भावितातिथिसत्कारं भूयोऽपि प्रेक्षणनिमित्तं लज्जामहे आर्यं विज्ञाप-
यितुम् ।   [c] अनसूये । अभिनवकुशसूच्या परिक्षतं मे चरणम् ।

---

[1] 'By this forest-incident.' *Vrittānta* often means 'incident,' 'event.'

[2] There is no dative case in Prākṛit, the genitive supplying its place.

[3] *Vijñāpayitum*, 'to represent respectfully' to a superior (with two
accusatives). The phrase *sambhāvitātithi-satkāro bhūyo prekshaṇa-
nimittam*, 'adequate hospitality to a guest is a cause of seeing (him)
again,' was probably a proverb. The two friends were ashamed to
represent this as an argument for a second visit from Dushyanta, as the
hospitality they had shewn him had been *a-sambhārita*, 'inadequate.'

[4] 'Nay, not so ; I have received all the honours (of a guest) by the mere
sight of your ladyships.' *Puraskṛita*=*satkṛita*, 'hospitably entertained.'

[5] 'By the point of a young Kuśa (leaf).' *Sūći*, 'a needle,' here used
for the long tapering point of the leaf of the Kuśa grass (see p. 19, n. 1).

[a]कुरवक‍साहापरिलग्गं च वक्कलं । दाव परिपालेध मं । जाव एं मोआबेमि । ॥ इति राजानमेवावलोकयन्ती सव्याजं विलम्ब्य सह सखीभ्यां निष्क्रान्ता ॥

राजा ।

मन्दौत्सुक्योऽस्मि नगरगमनं प्रति । यावदनुयाचिकान्समेत्य नातिदूरे[3] तपोवनस्य निवेशयामि । न खलु शक्नोमि शकुन्तलाव्यापारादात्मानं निवर्तयितुम् । मम हि

गच्छति पुरः शरीरं धावति पश्चादसंस्तुतं चेतः ।
चीनांशुकमिव केतोः प्रतिवातं नीयमानस्य ॥३४॥

॥ इति निष्क्रान्ताः सर्वे ॥

॥ प्रथमोऽङ्कः ॥

[a] कुरवकशाखापरिलग्नं च वल्कलम् । तावत्परिपालयतं माम् । यावदेनन्मोचयामि ।

---

[1] A kind of Barleria, with purple flowers and covered with sharp prickles.

[2] 'Pretendedly delaying,' i. e. making some pretext for lingering.

[3] 'I am become indifferent [slackened in my anxiety] about returning to the city. Meanwhile having joined my followers, I will make (them) encamp at no great distance from the penance-grove.' *Ni-viś*, 'to enter,' 'take up a station,' 'encamp' as an army (Manu vii. 188; Raghu-v. v. 42).

[4] 'From occupying myself about S'akuntalā.' *S'akuntalā-goćara-pravartanāt*, K. *S'akuntalā-vividha-ćeshṭitatvāt*, S'.

[5] '(My) body goes forward (towards my retinue); (my) heart, not being in harmony (with my body), runs back (towards S'akuntalā), like the silken flag of a banner borne against the wind.' *Puraḥ*, i. e. *agrataḥ senām prati*, 'forward towards (my) army.' *Paśćāt*, i. e. *prishṭhataḥ S'akuntalām prati*, K. *Asaṃstuta = aparićita, avaśa*, 'unacquainted,' 'unrelated,' 'not under control (of the body).' *Saṃ-stu*, properly 'to sing or praise in chorus.' Hence *asaṃstuta* probably means, 'not harmonizing,' 'not in concert.' The Beng. MSS. read *asaṃsthitam* (*=aryavastham*), 'restless,' 'unstable,' 'ill-regulated.' *Ćīnāṃśukam=ćīna-deśa-bhava-vastra-viśeshaḥ*, 'a kind of cloth produced in the land of China,' 'silk,' 'muslin.'

Verse 34. ĀRIĀ or GĀTHĀ. See verse 2.

    – ⌣ ⌣ | ⌣ – ⌣ | – – ‖ – ⌣ ⌣ | – – | ⌣ – ⌣ | – – |
    – – | ⌣ ⌣ ⌣ ⌣ | – – ‖ ⌣ ⌣ – | – – | ⌣ | – – |

॥ अथ द्वितीयोऽङ्कः ॥

॥ ततः प्रविशति विषादो विदूषकः ॥

विदूषकः ॥ निःश्वस्य ॥

[a] भो दिट्ठं । एदस्स मिस्सआसीलस्स रस्रो वअस्सभावेण
णिव्विसोम्हि । अअं मिस्सो । अअं वराहो । अअं सहूलो-

---

[a] भो दिष्टम् । एतस्य मृगयाशीलस्य राज्ञो वयस्यभावेन निर्विण्णोऽस्मि । अयं मृगः ।
अयं वराहः । अयं शार्दूल

---

[1] *Vidúshaka*, 'merry,' 'facetious,' 'good-natured,' is the title given to
the jocose companion and confidential friend of the *náyaka*, or hero of
the piece. This character is to the hero, what the female companion
and confidante is to the heroine (*náyiká*) of the play. He is his constant
attendant, and, by a curious regulation, is to be a Bráhman, that is to
say, of a caste higher than that of the king himself; yet his business
is to excite mirth by being ridiculous in person, age, and attire. S'. says
he is grey-haired (*palita*), hump-backed (*kubja*), lame (*khañja*), and with
distorted features (*vikṛitánana*); that the chief part of all that he says is
humorous and nonsensical; and that he is allowed access to the female
apartments (*antaḥpura-éara*). In fact, he is a kind of buffoon. His
attempts at wit, which are never very successful, and his allusions to
the pleasures of the table, of which he is a confessed votary, are absurdly
contrasted with the sententious solemnity of the despairing hero, crossed
in the prosecution of his love-suit. The shrewdness of the heroine's con-
fidantes never seems to fail them under the most trying circumstances;
but the clumsy interference of the Vidúshaka in the intrigues of his
friend, only serves to augment his difficulties, and occasions many au
awkward dilemma. As he is the universal butt, and is allowed in
return full liberty of speech, he fills a character very necessary for the
enlivenment of the otherwise dull monotony of a Hindú drama. He
is called by S'. the *upa-náyaka* of the piece, or the *náyakasya upa-
náyakaḥ*, a kind of assistant to the hero (see p. 47, n. 3). K. says, 'The

ᵃत्ति मज्झण्हेवि गिम्हविरलपायवच्छायासु वणराईसु आहिण्डीअदि अडवीदो अडविं। पत्तसङ्कुरकसायाणि कडुआणि गिरिणईजलाणि पीअन्ति। अणिअदवेलं सुल्लमंसभूइट्ठो आहारो अरहीअदि[2]। तुरगाणुधावण-करिडदसन्धिणो रत्तिम्मिवि णिकामं सइदव्वं णत्थि। तदो

ᵃ इति मध्याह्नेऽपि ग्रीष्मविरलपादपच्छायासु वनराजिष्वाहिण्ड्यतेऽटव्या अटवीम्। पत्रसङ्कुरकषायाणि कटूनि गिरिनदीजलानि पीयन्ते। अनियतवेलं शूल्यमांसभूयिष्ठ आहारोऽश्यते। तुरगानुधावनकर्षितसन्धे रात्रावपि निकामं शयितव्यं नास्ति। ततो

Vidūshaka is the name for a ridiculous, childish man (*māṇavaka*), who is always at the side of the hero (*nāyaka-pārśva-parivartin*). He is the companion of his sports and promoter of his amusement (*hāsya-kāri-narma-suhṛid*, or *narma-saċiva*). In effecting the three objects of human life, viz. religious merit, wealth, and pleasure, the family priests assist the king in the first; the heir-apparent (*yuva-rāja*) and the army in the second; the Vidūshaka, the parasite (*pīṭha-marda*), and the pimp (*viṭa*) in the third.' For *viṭa*, see Sanskṛit-English Dictionary.

[1] 'Oh (my evil) destiny! I am worn out by being the associate of this king, who is so addicted to the chase. "Here's a deer," "there's a boar," "yonder's a tiger;" (in the midst of) such (cries and shouts), even at mid-day, is it wandered about from forest to forest, in the paths of the woods, where the shade of the trees is scanty in the hot season.' *Vayasya* is properly 'an associate or companion of about the same age' (*vayas*). *Iti*, 'so saying,' here rather, 'so crying out.' *Vana-rāji*, 'a row of trees,' 'a long tract of forest.' *Āhiṇḍyate*, pres. pass. of rt. *hiṇḍ*, with prep. *ā*, 'to wander about' (an uncommon root); understand *asmābhiḥ*, 'by us.' The Prākṛit is answerable for the collocation of words in this sentence.

[2] 'The bad-smelling [pungent] waters of mountain-streams, astringent from the mixture of leaves, are drunk. At irregular hours a meal, consisting chiefly of meat roasted on spits, is eaten.' *Kaṭu*, 'pungent,' 'ill-scented.' *Śūlya-māṇsa*, 'roast-meat,' 'meat cooked on a spit.' *Bhūyishṭha*, see p. 4, l. 1, with note.

[3] 'Even in the night I cannot lie down comfortably (in my bed) through the dislocation of my joints by the galloping of the horse [or by my horse's pursuit of the game];' see p. 67, l. 6, and note 1. The above is the reading of all the Deva-nāgarī MSS. The Bengālī

^aमहन्ते एव्व पच्चूसे दासीएपुत्तेहिं सउणिलुड्डएहिं वणग्ग-
हणकोलाहलेण पडिबोधिदोम्हि । एत्तएण दाणिम्पि
पीडा ण णिक्कमदि । तदो गण्डस्स उवरि पिडिअ
संवुत्ता । हिओ किल अम्हेसु ओहीणेसु तब्भवदो मिआ-
णुसारेण अस्समपदं पविट्ठस्स तावसकण्ञा सउन्दला
णाम मम अधण्णदाए दंसिदा । सम्पदं णअरगमणस्स मणं

^a महत्येव प्रत्यूषे दास्याःपुत्रैः शकुनिलुब्धकैर्वनग्रहणकोलाहलेन प्रतिबोधितोऽस्मि ।
इयतेदानीमपि पीडा न निष्क्रामति । ततो गण्डस्योपरि पिटका संवृत्ता । ह्यः किला-
स्माखवहीनेषु तत्रभवतो मृगानुसारेणाश्रमपदं प्रविश्य तापसकन्यका शकुन्तला नाम
ममाधन्यतया दर्शिता । साम्प्रतं नगरगमनाय मनः

---

have *turaya-gaānam ća saddena*, 'by the noise of horses and elephants.'
Kand, 'to separate grain from the husk,' 'bruise,' 'break,' is not so
common as *khand*. *Kandita-sandheh* agrees with the gen. *mama*, 'of me,'
understood after *śayitavyam*. The instr. case is more usual after the
fut. pass. part., but not more correct.

[1] 'Then at the very earliest dawn I am awakened by the din of
taking the forest by the sons of slaves hunting the birds.' *Mahati
pratyūshe*, lit. 'at great dawn' (cf. *mahā-rātra*, 'mid-night,' and the
French 'de grand matin'). *Dāsyāh-putraih* stands for *dāsī-putraih*, and
is to be regarded as one compound. According to Pāṇ. vi. 3, 22, the
genitive in this compound is used in abusing and reviling (*ākrośe*); so
vrishalyāh-putraih for *vrishalī-putraih*. *Vana-grahaṇa*, 'surrounding and
taking possession of a wood for the purpose of hunting the animals it
contains' (*mriga-grahaṇārtham*, K.) Those who do so are called, further
on in this Act, *vana-grāhiṇah* (= *vanāvarodhakāh*, K.), 'those who inclose
a wood and obstruct the points of egress.'

[2] 'Even with all this my trouble does not come to an end; (for) after-
wards upon the (old) boil [scar], (another) small boil is produced.' *Iyatā
= etāvatā*, 'by this much,' 'by so much.' *Nishkrāmati = śāmyati*, 'ceases.'
Piṭakā = visphoṭaka, 'a pustule,' 'a small boil,' 'a pimple.' This was
probably a proverbial phrase, cf. *ayam aparo gaṇḍasya upari visphoṭah*,
Mudrā-r. p. 120, l. 14.

[3] 'For indeed yesterday, while we were left behind, a hermit's
daughter, named Śakuntalā, through my ill-luck was presented to the

[a]कहम्पि ण करेदि। अज्जवि तस्स णं एव्व चिन्तअन्तस्स अच्छीसु पभादं आसि। का गदी। जाव णं किदाचारपरि-कम्मं पेक्खामि। ॥ इति परिक्रम्यावलोक्य च ॥ [b]एसो वाणासण-हत्थाहिं जवणीहिं वणपुप्फमालाधारिणीहिं परिवुदो इदो एव्व आअच्छदि पिअवअस्सो। होदु। अङ्गभङ्गविअलो विअ भविअ चिट्ठिस्सं। जइ एव्वम्पि णाम विस्समं लहेअं।

॥ इति दण्डकाष्ठमवलम्ब्य स्थितः ॥

[a] कथमपि न करोति। अद्यापि तस्य तामेव चिन्तयतोऽक्ष्णोः प्रभातमासीत्। का गतिः। यावदेनं कृताचारपरिकर्माणं प्रेक्षे। [b] एव वाणासनहस्ताभिर्यवनी-भिर्वनपुष्पमालाधारिणीभिः परिवृत इत एवागच्छति प्रियवयस्यः। भवतु। अङ्गभङ्गवि-कल इव भूत्वा स्यास्यामि। यद्येवमपि नाम विश्रमं लभेय।

---

view of his Highness, who had entered the grounds of the hermitage in pursuit of a deer,' i.e. it was all my ill-luck that made him see her. *Asmāsu avahīneshu = paśćāt patiteshu,* 'dropped behind,' 'fallen in the rear,' S.

[1] 'Even to-day (the light of) dawn (broke) upon the eyes (of him) thinking of that very (damsel);' i.e. according to Ć. *jāgrata eva rajanī. niryatā,* 'the night passed away whilst he was still awake.' K. remarks, 'By this it may be inferred that with thinking of her he had not closed his eyes all night.' *Akshṇoh,* i.e. *dṛiśor unmīlatoh satoh,* 'on his eyes being (still) open.' *Satoh* in the commentary shews that *akshṇoh* is locative dual.

[2] 'What is to be done? Meanwhile I will (be on the look out to) see him, when he has performed (his) usual toilet. Here comes my dear friend in this very direction, attended by Yavana women, having bows in their hands, and wearing garlands of wild-flowers. Be it so; I will stand as if crippled by paralysis of my limbs.' *Kā gatiḥ,* 'what resource!' i.e. what remedy or what expedient can be devised? This is a common phrase in Prākṛit; it occurs again in Act V. *Kidāćāra-parikammam* (= Sk. *kṛitāćāra-parikarmāṇam*) is the reading of one of the oldest MSS. [India Office, 1060], and of Ć. K. reads *pratikarmāṇam;* but *parikarma* and *pratikarma* have the same sense, viz. 'decoration after purification of the body,' 'rubbing it with perfumes after bathing.' Most of the Deva-n. MSS. have *parikkamam* for *parikramam,* 'circumambula-

॥ ततः प्रविशति यथानिर्दिष्टपरिवारो राजा ॥

राजा ।

कामं प्रिया न सुलभा मनस्तु तद्भावदर्शनाश्वासि ।
अकृतार्थेऽपि मनसिजे रतिमुभयप्रार्थना कुरुते ॥ ३५ ॥

---

tion.' _Yavanī_, properly a Muhammadan woman, a native of _Yavana_ or Arabia, but applied also to a native of Greece. Wilson in the Vikramorvaśī (Act V, p. 261), where the same word occurs, remarks that Tartarian or Bactrian women may be intended. The business of these attendants was to act as the bearers of the king's bow and arrows. At the end of Act VI. a Yavanī enters again, _śārnga-hastā_, 'carrying a bow.' A commentator remarks, _Yavanī yuddha-kāle rājño 'straṃ dadāti_, 'the Yavanī in the time of war gives weapons to the king.' K. says, _Yavanī śastra-dhāriṇī_, 'the Yavanī is the weapon-bearer.' _Anga-bhanga_, properly 'palsy or paralysis of the limbs.' K. observes that the Vidūshaka here acts the _vishkambha_, which he defines as an _adhama-praveśakaḥ_, or inferior introductory scene, coming between two acts (_ankayor madhya-vartī_), and performed by inferior actors (_nīća-pātra-prayojitaḥ_). Its object is to connect or bind together the story of the drama and the subdivisions of the plot (_kathā-sanghaṭṭanārtham_), by concisely alluding to what has happened in the intervals of the acts, or what is likely to happen at the end (_bhūtānām bhāvinām api sankshepeṇa sūćanāt_). In the following stage-direction, _danda-kāshṭha_=_yashṭi_, 'a stick,' 'staff of wood.' Translate, 'he stands leaning on a staff.'

¹ 'Granted my beloved is not easy to gain, still my heart encourages (itself) by observing her gestures (of love). Even though love has not accomplished its object, the desire of both (of us) gives [causes] enjoyment.' _Kāmam_, see p. 55, n. 3. _Na sulabhā_, i. e. from her relationship to the Rishi, K. _Tad-bhāva-darśanāśrāsi_ is the reading of all the Beng. MSS. and of S'. The Deva-n. read _tad-bhāva-darśanāyāsi_, where _āyāsi_ means 'active,' 'kept in activity.' But K., though the MS. gives _āyāsi_, explains it by _santushyati_, 'is cheered,' and by _āśvāsitam_, 'consoled.'

Verse 35. ÁRYÁ or GÁTHÁ. See verse 2.

 − − | ∪ − ∪ | ∪ ∪ − ‖ ∪ − ∪ | − − | ∪ − ∪ | − − | ∪
∪ ∪ − | − ∪ ∪ | ∪ ∪ − ‖ ∪ ∪ ∪ ∪ | − − | ∪ | − ∪ ∪ | −

॥ स्मितं कृत्वा ॥ एवमात्माभिप्रायसम्भावितेऽजनचित्तंवृत्तिः
प्रार्थयिता विडम्ब्यते । तद्यथा

स्निग्धं वीक्षितमन्यतोऽपि नयने यत्प्रेरयन्त्या तया
यातं यच्च नितम्बयोर्गुरुतया मन्दं विलासादिव ।
मा गा इत्यवरुद्धया यदपि सा सासूयमुक्ता सखी
सर्वं तत्किल मत्परायणमहो कामी स्वतां पश्यति ॥३६॥

Bhāva=_śriṅgāra-ćeshṭā_, 'the expression of amorous sentiments by ges-
tures.' The gestures here referred to are described in the next verse, 36.
Darśana is either 'seeing,' 'looking at' (=_avalokana_, S'.), or 'exhibit-
ing,' 'shewing' (=_sākshāt-karaṇa_, K.) In the latter case, translate, 'by
her exhibition of amorous gestures.' _Ubhaya_ = _nāyaka-nāyikayoḥ_ or
strī-purushayoḥ. _Prārthanā_=_abhilāsha_, 'longing.'

[1] This is a long Bahuvrīhi comp., agreeing with _prārthayitā_. Translate,
'thus the suitor, who judges of the state of feeling of his beloved one by
his own desires, is deluded.' _Evam_=_vakshyamāṇa-prakāreṇa_, 'in the
following manner,' 'in the way about to be mentioned,' K. _Abhiprāya_
=_abhilāsha_. _Sambhāvita_=_kalpita_, 'imagined,' or _śaṅkita_, 'suspected.'
Ishṭa-jana=_manogata-vyakti_, 'the individual in one's thoughts.' _Prār-
thayitā_=_kāmukaḥ_ or _yāćakaḥ_. _Viḍambyate_=_apahāsyate_, 'is mocked,' 'is
made a fool of;' supply _kāmena_, 'by love.' The stage-direction _smitaṃ
kṛitvā_ implies that he is to smile at his own folly in supposing that
she was as fond of him as he was of her, merely because her gestures
were coquettish.

[2] 'Whereas by her, even though casting her eyes in another direction,
a tender glance was given [lit. it was looked tenderly]; and whereas
by the weight of (her) hips she moved [lit. it was moved by her] slowly,
as if from dalliance; and whereas by (her) detained in these (words), "Do
not go" [see p. 52, l. 4], that friend was addressed with disdain; all that
certainly had reference to me [or was directed at me]. Ah! (how) a
lover discovers (what is) his own!' _Vīkshitam_ is here the past pass. part.,
and _snigdham_ an adverb, S'. _Avaruddhayā_ or, according to some MSS.,
uparuddhayā=_krita-gamana-bādhayā_ or _krita-gati-vyāghātayā_. _Mat-
parāyaṇam_=_mad-vishayakam_, 'relating to me.' _Aho_ here denotes wonder

Verse 36. ŚĀRDŪLA-VIKRĪDITA (a variety of ATIDHRITI). See verses 14, 30.

विदूषकः ॥ तथा स्थित एव ॥[1]

ᵃ भो वयस्स । ए मे हत्था पसरन्ति । ता वाष्ठामेत्तेण जष्ठाबीष्ठसि[2] ।

राजा ।

कुतोऽयं गात्रोपघातः ।

विदूषकः ।

ᵇ कुदो किल सव्वं अच्छी आउलीकरिअ अस्सुकारणं पुच्छेसि[3] ।

ᵃ भो वयस्य । न मे हस्तौ प्रसरतः । तद्वाचामात्रेण जाप्यसे ।   ᵇ कुतः किल स्वयमक्षिणी आकुलीकृत्याश्रुकारणं पृच्छसि ।

(*āśćarye*, K.) *Svatām* = *ātmīyatām* or *svakīyatām*, i.e. *mat-kṛitaṃ sarvam idam*, 'all that was done on my account.' Although her gestures appeared to be unfavourable, yet it was easy to refer them to myself (*ātma-vishayatvāropa iti mantavyam*, K.)

[1] 'Still in the same position,' i. e. leaning on his stick, as if *anga-bhanga-vikala*, 'crippled by paralysis of his limbs.' See p. 62, l. 5.

[2] 'My hands are not capable of extension [lit. do not go forward], therefore by words merely are you wished victory [lit. you are made to be victorious],' i. e. I cannot greet you with the usual *aṅjali* or salutation made by joining the hands and applying them to the forehead; you must therefore be contented with the salutation *Jayatu!* or *Vijayī bhava!* This is the reading of two old MSS. [India Office, 1060; Bodleian, 233]. The Calcutta ed., without the support of these MSS., adds *jayatu, jayatu bhavān*, 'let your Majesty be victorious.' This is sufficiently implied in *jāpyase*, which is not derived from *jap*, 'to repeat,' 'mutter,' but rather from the causal of *ji*, 'to conquer.' If from *jap* it could only mean 'you are caused to mutter,' whereas the sense of *jāpyase*, as the 2nd pers. sing. pres. pass. of the causal of *ji*, is quite suitable, and, moreover, conforms to the interpretation of K. (*vijayī bhava*), and to that of the Calcutta ed. (*jayārho 'si*). Lassen considers Sanskrit *jāpyase* = Prākṛit *jaābīasi*, although, with Chézy, he refers it to *jap* (Instit. Ling. Prāk. p. 361). Most of the Deva-n. MSS. read *jaābaissam* for *jīvayishyāmi*, 'I will cause to live,' 'I will wish life,' i. e. I will salute you with *ćiraṃ jīva*, 'long life to you!' Cf. p. 68, l. 9.

[3] 'Why indeed, having yourself troubled (my) eyes, do you inquire the

κ

राजा ।

न खल्ववगच्छामि । भिन्नार्थमभिधीयताम् ।

विदूषकः ।

ᵃभो वअस्स । जं वेदसो खुज्जलीलं विडम्बेदि । तं किं अत्तणो पहावेण । णं णईवेअस्स ।

राजा ।

नदीवेगस्तत्र कारणम् ।

विदूषकः ।

ᵇममवि भवं ।

ᵃ भो वयस्स । यद्वेतसः कुब्जलीलां विडम्बयति । तत्किमात्मनः प्रभावेण । ननु नदी-वेगस्य ।　　ᵇ ममापि भवान् ।

---

cause of (my) tears!' Thus explained by S'. *yathā ko 'pi kasyačin netrayor aṅguly-ādikam praveśya pṛičchati bhavataś čakshushor aśru katham āyāti tathā tvam api,* 'you are like a person who, after thrusting a finger, &c., into the eyes of any one, asks, How does a tear come into your eyes?' The Vidūshaka probably here quotes some proverb, and the king observes in the next line that he does not understand its application in the present case.

[1] *Bhinnārtham = sphutārtham,* 'clearly,' 'distinctly,' Ć.

[2] 'When the reed imitates the character [gait] of the Kubja (plant), is that by its own power; (or) is it not (by the force) of the current of the river?' *Vetasa,* a large reed or cane (Calamus Rotang) growing in Indian rivers. *Kubja* or *kubjaka,* properly 'hump-backed,' but also the name for a crooked aquatic plant (Trapa Bispinosa), called also *vāri-kubja* and *jala-kubja.* S'. says it is sometimes called *kuvalaya,* but this is usually applied to a species of water-lily. He also mentions a reading *kuñja,* 'an arbour,' instead of *kubja.* Possibly this is the reading to which the *kujja* of the Deva-n. MSS. is to be referred, as (according to Vararući ii. 33) *khujja* is Prākṛit for *kubja.* There is doubtless a double meaning in the word, but the first allusion is to the Kubja plant. To appreciate the Vidūshaka's pleasantry in comparing himself to an upright reed, accidentally transformed into a crooked plant, we must bear in mind that his natural form was that of a lame, hump-backed man (see p. 59, n. 1).

राजा ।

कथमिव ।

विदूषकः ।

"एवं राअकज्जाणि उज्झित्त एआरिसे अमाणुससञ्चारे
आउलप्पदेसे वणचरवुत्तिणा तुए होदव्वं । जं सच्चं पच्चहं
साबदाणुसरणेहिं सङ्ग्लोहिअसन्धिबन्धाणं मम गत्ताणं
अणीसोम्हि संवुत्तो । ता पसादइस्सं विसज्जिदुं मं एक्का-
हम्पि दाव विस्समिदुं ।

राजा ॥ खगतम् ॥

अयं चैवमाह । ममापि काश्यपसुतामनुस्मृत्य मृगया-
विक्लवं चेतः । कुतः ।

न नमयितुमधिज्यमस्मि शक्तो
धनुरिदमाहितसायकं मृगेषु ।

ª एवं राजकार्याण्युज्झित्वैतादृशेऽमानुपसञ्चार आकुलप्रदेशे वनचरवृत्तिना त्वया
भवितव्यम् । यत्सत्यं प्रत्यहं श्वापदानुसरणैः सङ्क्षोभितसन्धिबन्धानां मम गात्राणामनी-
शोऽस्मि संवृत्तः । तत्प्रसादयिष्ये विस्रष्टुं मामेकाहमपि तावद्विश्रमितुम् ।

---

¹ 'By you, having thus relinquished the affairs of the kingdom, it is
to be lived as a forester [lit. it is to be existed by you having the manner
of life of a forester], in a wild unfrequented region like this. Since (then)
I truly am become no (longer) master of my own limbs, whose joints are
shaken about by daily chases after wild beasts, therefore I will beg you as
a favour to let me go just for one day to rest myself' (cf. p. 60, l. 5, with
note 3). *A-mānusha-sañcāre*, lit. 'untrodden by man,' Taylor MS. *Sandhi-
bandha* or *sandhi-bandhana*, properly ' the ligament or tendon which binds
the joints together.' *Pra-sad* in causal Ātm. is ' to beg a favour (*prasāda*)
from any one.'

² *Vi-klava*, according to K. = *vi-hvala*, *parāṅ-mukha*, 'distracted,'
'averse,' 'turning from,' 'disinclined.' Some read *nir-utsuka*, 'in-
different.'

सहवसतिमुपेत्य यैः प्रियायाः
कृत इव मुग्धविलोकितोपदेशः ॥ ३७ ॥[1]

विदूषकः ॥ राज्ञो मुखं विलोक्य ॥

[a]अत्तभवं किम्पि हिस्रए करिस्स मन्तेदि[2]। अरस्खे मए हदिस्रं आसिं[3]।

राजा ॥ सस्मितम् ॥

किमन्यत्। अनतिक्रमणीयं मे सुहृद्वाक्यमिति स्थितोऽस्मिं[4]।

विदूषकः ।

[b]चिरं जीव । ॥ इति गन्तुमिच्छति ॥

राजा ।

वयस्य । तिष्ठ । शृणु सावशेषं मे वचः ।

विदूषकः ।

[c]आणवेदु भवं ।

[a]अत्रभवान्किमपि हृदये कृत्वा मन्त्रयते । अरण्ये मया रुदितमासीत् ।   [b]चिरं जीव ।   [c]आज्ञापयतु भवान् ।

---

[1] 'I am not able to bend this strung bow, having-the-arrow-fixed-on-it, against the deer, by whom, possessing (the privilege of) dwelling in the society of (my) beloved, instruction in beautiful glances is as it were given (to her).' *Adhi-jya*, see p. 9, n. 2. *Ahita-sāyaka*=*arpita-sāyaka*, S'. *Upetya*, lit. 'having undergone' (=*prāpya*, S'.); hence *upeta*, 'possessed of.'

[2] Compare the same expression, p. 42, l. 2, with note.

[3] 'By me a cry has been made in the wilderness,' i. e. I have spoken in vain, no one listens (*ko 'pi na śṛṇoti*, Ć.) A kind of proverbial phrase; cf. *aham idaṃ śūnye raumi, kiṃ na śṛṇoshi me*, Mahā-bh. i. 3022; also Amaru-śataka, 76.

[4] 'What else (ought I to have in my mind)! The words of a friend ought not to be disregarded by me; so (thinking to myself) I stand here.' Understand *hridaye kartavyam* after *kim anyat;* and *hridaye kritvā* after *iti*.

Verse 37. PUSHPITĀGRĀ, in which each half-verse is alike. See verse 32.

FIRST AND THIRD QUARTER-VERSE.   SECOND AND FOURTH QUARTER-VERSE.

⏑ ⏑ ⏑ ⏑ ⏑ ‒ ⏑ ‒ ⏑ ‒ ⏑ ‒ ‒ ‖ ⏑ ⏑ ⏑ ⏑ ⏑ ‒ ⏑ ‒ ⏑ ⏑ ‒ ⏑ ‒ ⏑ ‒ ⏑ ‒ ‒

राजा ।

विश्रान्तेन भवता ममाप्येकस्मिन्ननायासे कर्मणि सहायेन
भवितव्यम् ।

विदूषकः ।

[a] किं मोदअखज्जिआए ।[1]

राजा ।

यच्च वक्ष्यामि ।

विदूषकः ।

[b] गहीदो खणो ।[2]

राजा ।

कः कोऽत्र भोः ।

दौवारिकः । ॥ प्रविश्य ॥

[c] आणवेदु भट्टा ।[3]

राजा ।

रेवतक । सेनापतिस्तावदाहूयताम् ।[4]

---

[a] किं मोदकखादिकायाम् ।   [b] गृहीतः क्षणः ।   [c] आज्ञापयतु भर्ता ।

---

[1] 'Is it in eating sweetmeats (that you require my assistance)?' The
Calcutta ed. and my own Bombay MS. read *khaṅjiâe*, which might
equally stand for the Sanskrit *khādikāyām*, but the above is the reading
of the oldest MSS. *Khādikāyām* is given on the authority of Ć. and the
Bodleian MS. (233). According to Pāṇ. iii. 3, 108, Vārt. i. *khādikā* is
an admissible form.

[2] Lit. 'the opportunity is taken,' i. e. now is a good opportunity;
now is the time; I am all attention (*avadhānaṃ kritam*, Ć.); I have
nothing else to do but to listen. *Kshaṇa* may mean *nirvyāpāra-sthiti*
or *vyāpārāntara-rahita-sthiti*, 'the state of having no other occupation,'
i. e. leisure, opportunity (see Amara-kośa). The above is the reading
of the oldest MS. and of Kāṭavema. S'. has *grihītaḥ praṇayaḥ*, and the
Deva-n. MSS. *sugrihīta ayaṃ janaḥ*.

[3] Cf. the Hindūstānī كوي هي.

[4] S'ankara quotes an aphorism of Bharata, as follows: 'A universal
monarch is to be addressed by his attendants with the title of *bhaṭṭa*
(=*bhartā*).' See Sāhit.-d. p. 178. K. remarks that only inferior attendants
ought to use this title; the others, *svāmin* or *deva*.

दौवारिक: ।

[a] **तह ।** ॥ इति निष्क्रम्य सेनापतिना सह पुनः प्रविश्य ॥ [b] एसो अक्खा-
बणुक्कण्ठो भट्टा इदो दिट्ठदिट्ठी एव्व चिट्ठदि । उबसप्पदु
अज्जो ।

सेनापतिः ॥ राजानमवलोक्य ॥

दृष्टदोषापि स्वामिनि मृगया केवलं गुण एव संवृत्ता ।
तथा हि देवः

अनवरतधनुर्ज्यास्फालनक्रूरपूर्वं
रविकिरणसहिष्णु क्लेशलेशैरभिन्नम् ।
अपचितमपि गात्रं व्यायतत्वादलक्ष्यं
गिरिचर इव नागः प्राणसारं बिभर्ति ॥३८॥

[a] तथा ।   [b] एम आणावनोत्कण्ठो भत्तेंतो दत्तदृष्टिरेव तिष्ठति । उपसर्पत्वार्यः ।

---

[1] 'There stands his Majesty eager to give (some) order, casting a look
in this direction.' *Utkaṇṭha*=*udgrīva*, 'having the neck erect with
expectation,' K. Here *utkaṇṭha*=*udyata*, 'ready,' 'on the point of.'

[2] 'Though observed to have evil effects [or regarded as a vice], the
chase has proved only an advantage [or is only a merit] in our master.'
See p. 71, n. 5 at end. One MS. reads *adrishta-doshāpi*, 'certainly hunting
shews no ill effects in our master.'

[3] 'For truly his Majesty, like a mountain-roving elephant, exhibits
[bears, possesses] a body, whose fore-part is hardened by the incessant
friction of the bow-string, patient of the rays of the sun, not affected
by the slightest fatigue [or not weakened one atom by the toils of the
chase], though losing flesh [reduced in bulk] not (in a manner) to be
observed, by reason of (increased) muscular development, (and) all life
and energy.' *Ā-sphālana*=*karshaṇa*, 'rubbing,' 'drawing;' the idea
generally implied is that of moving or flapping backwards and forwards.
Pūrva=*pūrva-bhāga*. *Kleśa-leśair*, so read S'. and the India Office MS.
1060. K. passes it over. The others read *sveda-leśair*, but *sveda* was pro-
bably accidentally written for *kheda*, the synonym for *kleśa*. *Vyāyatatvāt*
=*krita-vyāyāmatvāt* (C.) and *driḍhatvāt* (K.) It is the state produced

---

Verse 38. MĀLINĪ or MĀNINĪ (a variety of ATI-ŚAKVARĪ). See verses 10, 19, 20.

॥ उपेत्य ॥ जयतु स्वामी । गृहीतश्वापदमरण्यम् । किमिति
स्थीयते ।

राजा ।

मन्दोत्साहः कृतोऽस्मि मृगयापवादिना माठव्येन ।

सेनापतिः ॥ जनान्तिकम् ॥

सखे । स्थिरप्रतिबन्धो भव । अहं तावत्स्वामिनश्चित्तवृत्ति-
मनुवर्तिष्ये । ॥ प्रकाशम् ॥ प्रलपत्येष वैधेयः । ननु प्रभुरेव
निदर्शनम् । पश्यतु देवः ।

मेदश्छेदकृशोदरं लघु भवत्युत्थानयोग्यं वपुः
  सत्त्वानामपि लक्ष्यते विकृतिमच्चित्तं भयक्रोधयोः ।
उत्कर्षः स च धन्विनां यदिषवः सिध्यन्ति लक्ष्ये चले
  मिथ्यैव व्यसनं वदन्ति मृगयामीदृग्विनोदः कुतः ॥ ३९ ॥

---

by *ryāyāma*, 'athletic and manly exercise of the muscles of the body.'
A-lakshya = *na vibhāvya*, 'imperceptible.' Compare Act VI. ver. 138,
kshīno 'pi nālakshyate, and Act VII. ver. 174, *avatīrno 'pi na lakshyate;*
also Hitop. l. 2631, *kāyaḥ kshīyamāṇo na lakshyate. Prāṇa-sāra,* 'whose
whole essence or substance consists of life and spirit' (cf. *vajra-sāra,*
ver. 10). *Bibharti,* see p. 24, n. 1.

[1] 'The forest has its beasts of prey tracked, why then is it stayed?'
i. e. why do you delay? The first clause is the reading of the Deva-n.
MSS. ; the second is that of the oldest MS. (I. O. 1060), supported by K.
Kimiti, cf. Hitop. l. 2618; Gīta-g. ix. 7. *Grihīta* = *jñāta*, 'found out,'
'discovered.' The Beng. MSS. insert *pradāra-sūcita,* 'indicated by their
tracks,' after *grihīta.*

[2] *Māṭharya* (in the Beng. MSS. *Mādhavya*) is the Vidūshaka's name.

[3] 'Be firm in your opposition,' 'persevere in throwing obstacles in
his way.'

[4] *Pra-lap* = *yadvā tadvā bhāsh,* 'to talk nonsense,' 'to talk idly.'
Vaidheya = *mūrkha,* 'a fool,' 'blockhead.'

[5] 'The body (of the hunter) having the waist attenuated by the re-
moval of fat becomes light (and) fit for exertion; moreover the spirit of

---

Verse 39. ŚĀRDŪLA-VIKRĪḌITA (a variety of ATIDHṚITI). See verses 14, 30, 36.

विदूषकः ॥ सरोषम् ॥

[a]अवेहि रे उच्छाहहेतुअं। अत्तभवं पकिदिं आपण्णो। तुमं दाव अडवीदो अडविं आहिअडन्तो एरणासिआलोलु-बस्स जिण्णरिच्छस्स कस्सवि मुहे पडिस्संसि।

राजा।

भद्र सेनापते। आश्रमसन्निकृष्टस्थिताः स्मः। अतस्ते वचो नाभिनन्दामि। अद्य तावत्

[a] अपेहि रे उत्साहहेतुक। अत्रभवान्प्रकृतिमापन्नः। त्वं तावदटव्या अटवीमाहिअडन्-तनासिकालोलुपस्य जीर्णर्क्षस्य कस्यापि मुखे पतिष्यसि।

---

living creatures is observed (to be) affected with various emotions, through fear and anger; and that is the glory of the archers when the arrows fall true on the moving mark. Falsely indeed do they call hunting a vice; where (is) there such a recreation as this?' *Medas*, 'adeps or fat,'=*sthaulya-janaka-dhātu*, 'a secretion causing fatness,' K. It performs the same functions to the flesh that the marrow does to the bones; its proper seat is in the belly (*udara*); hence the flesh is called *medas-kṛit*, 'the maker of adeps.' *Ćheda*=*nāśa*, 'destruction,' 'removal,' 'reduction' (cf. *gharma-ććheda*, 'the cessation of the heat,' Vikram., Act IV). *Utthāna-yogyam*, the Beng. MSS. read *utsāha-yogyam*, but *utsāha* is merely a synonym for *utthāna*, which is applied to any kind of manly exertion. K. says it here refers especially to the act of mounting on horse-back. *Sattvānām*, i. e. *jantūnām siṅhādīnām*, 'of animals such as lions, &c.' *Sattva* may include both the hunters and the hunted. *Vikṛiti-mat*, 'affected with *vikṛiti* or *vikāra*,' i. e. any emotion which causes a change from the *prakṛiti*, or 'natural and quiescent state of the mind' (*parityakta-prakṛitikam*, K.); see p. 38, n. 2. *Bhaya-krodhayoḥ* (*satoḥ*)= *bhaye krodhe ća*. *Utkarsha*=*pratishṭhā*, 'fame,' 'honour,' S. *Vyasanam*, see Manu vii. 47, 50, where hunting is designated as one of the ten vices (*vyasanāni*) of kings, and is, moreover, included amongst the four most pernicious (*kashṭatama*).

[1] *Utsāha-hetuka*, 'one who encourages or incites to exertion;' opposed to *utsāha-bhanga-kara*, 'one who damps another's zeal,' Hitop. l. 1987.

[2] 'His Majesty has returned to his natural state [i. e. is no longer eager after the excitement of hunting]; but thou, wandering from forest to forest, wilt probably fall into the jaws of some old bear, greedy after a human nose.' *Prakṛiti*, 'the natural, quiescent state of the soul,' as

गाहन्तां महिषा निपानसलिलं शृङ्गैर्मुहुस्ताडितं
छायाबद्धकदम्बकं मृगकुलं रोमन्थमभ्यस्यतु ।
विश्रब्धं क्रियतां वराहततिभिर्मुस्ताक्षतिः पल्वले
विश्रामं लभतामिदं च शिथिलज्याबन्धमस्मद्धनुः ॥४०॥

opposed to *vikriti;* see above. *Āhiṇḍan,* see p. 60, l. 2 ; Daśa-kumāra-
ćarita, p. 151, l. 6, says, *bhallūkā manushyāṇāṃ nāsikāṃ gṛihṇanti,* 'bears
seize the human nose.' The Beng. read *śṛigāla-mṛiga-lolupasya,* 'eager
after a jackal or deer.' *Riććhassa* is Prākṛit for *ṛikshasya,* Vararući
iii. 30.

¹ 'Let the buffaloes agitate-by-their-plunges the water of the tanks,
repeatedly struck with their horns; let the herd of deer, forming groups
under the shade, busy themselves in rumination ; let the bruising of the
Mustā grass be made in (undisturbed) confidence by the lines [herds] of
boars in the pool ; and let this my bow, having-the-fastening-of-its-string-
loose, get repose.' *Gūhantām=lolayantu,* 'let them agitate, stir,' K.,
hence *lulāpa* is one of the names for a buffalo. *Gāh,* properly, 'to plunge
into,' 'plunge about in.' *Nipāna=ādhāra,* 'a reservoir or trough near a
well' (*upakūpa*). *Romantha=adhara-ćalana,* 'the moving of the lower
lip or lower jaw,' K., and *bhuktasya punar ākṛishya* or *udgīrya ćarvaṇam,*
'the chewing of what has been eaten after drawing or vomiting it up
again,' i. e. 'chewing the cud,' S., Ć. *Abhyasyatu=paunaḥpunyena
karotu,* 'perform again and again,' Ć. *Tatibhiḥ=yūthaiḥ,* 'by herds.'
The Beng. read *varāha-patibhir,* 'by the chiefs of the boars.' There is no
difficulty in *tatibhir;* many herds of animals form lines or tracks in
moving from one place to another, or in grazing. *Mustā,* a sort of
fragrant grass (Cyperus Rotundus) eaten by swine, which are hence
called *mustāda.* *Kshati=vidāraṇa,* 'tearing,' 'uprooting,' K. ;=*luṇṭhana,*
'rolling,' S. The grass would probably be bruised by their trampling
and rolling on it, as well as by their eating it. *Śithila-jyā-bandha =
avaropita-guṇa.* S. and Ć. observe that the above verse furnishes an
example of the figure called *Jāti* or *Svabhāvokti,* i. e. a description of
living objects by circumstances or acts suited to their character. They
also notice the change of construction from the nom. to the instr. in the
third line, and its resumption in the fourth.

Verse 40. Śārdūla-vikrīḍita (a variety of Atidhṛiti). See verses 14, 30, 36, 39.

सेनापतिः ।

यत्प्रभविष्णावे[1] रोचते ।

राजा ।

तेन हि निवर्तय पूर्वगतान्वनग्राहिणः[2] । यथा न मे सैनि-
कास्तपोवनमुपरुन्धन्ति । तथा निषेद्धव्याः । पश्य ।

शमप्रधानेषु तपोधनेषु
गूढं हि दाहात्मकमस्ति तेजः ।
स्पर्शानुकूला इव सूर्यकान्ता-
स्तदन्यतेजोऽभिभवाद्वमन्ति ॥ ४१ ॥[3]

सेनापतिः ।

यदाज्ञापयति स्वामी ।

---

[1] *Prabhavishnu*, 'the mighty one,' equivalent to our expression 'your
Majesty.'

[2] *Vana-grāhiṇaḥ = vandīvarodhakān*, see p. 61, n. 1.

[3] 'In ascetics with whom quietism [a passionless state] is predominant
(over all other qualities), there lies concealed a consuming energy [fire].
That (energy), like sun-crystals, (which are) grateful [cool] to the touch,
they put forth, from (being acted upon by) the opposing-influence of other
forces,' i. e. the inhabitants of this hermitage, however passionless they
may be, and however kind when unprovoked, contain within themselves
a latent energy, which, when roused by opposing influences, will be put
forth to the destruction of those who molest them ; as a crystal lens,
however cool to the touch in its natural state, will emit a burning heat
when acted upon by the rays of the sun. *Sama-pradhāneshu*, 'in whom
stoicism or self-control is everything ;' who regard exemption from all
passion and feeling as the *summum bonum*. *Sūrya-kānta*, lit. 'beloved
by the sun ;' also called *sūrya-maṇi*, 'the sun-gem,' and *dīptopala*, 'shining
stone,' a stone resembling crystal. Wilson calls it a fabulous stone with
fabulous properties, and mentions a fellow-stone called *Candra-kānta*,

---

Verse 41. UPAJĀTI or ĀKHYĀNAKĪ (a variety of TRISHṬUBH), each quarter-verse
being either *Upendra-vajrā* or *Indra-vajrā*, the former only differing from the latter
in the first syllable.

$$\smile - \smile - - \smile\smile - \smile - - \parallel$$

विटूपकः ।

[a]गच्छ भो दासीएंपुत्त । धंसिदो दे उच्छाहवुत्तंन्तो[2] ।

॥ निष्क्रान्तः सेनापतिः ॥

राजा ॥ परिजनं विलोक्य ॥

अपनयन्तु भवंत्यो[3] मृगयावेषम् । रेवतक । त्वमपि स्वं नियोगमशून्यं कुरु[4] ।

परिजनः ।

[b]जं देवो आणवेदि । ॥ इति निष्क्रान्तः ॥

[a] गच्छ भो दास्याःपुत्र । ध्वंसितस्त उत्साहवृत्तान्तः ।   [b] यदेव आज्ञापयति ।

'moon-beloved,' or *ćandra-maṇi*, 'moon-gem.' It may be gathered from this passage that its properties resembled those of a glass lens, which instrument may possibly have been known to the Hindūs at the time when this play was written. The following parallel sentiment is from Bhartṛi-h. ii. 30 : *Yad aćetano 'pi pādaiḥ spṛishṭaḥ prajvalati savitur atikāntaḥ, tat tejasvī purushaḥ para-kṛita-nikṛitaṃ kathaṃ sahate*, 'since even the lifeless (stone) beloved of the sun, when touched by its rays, burns ; how then can the man of spirit put up with an injury inflicted by another ?' *Abhi-bhava = tiras-kāra*, 'insult,' K. The sun's rays, disturbing the natural state of the stone, are compared to the hunter's disturbing the hermitage and provoking its inhabitants. *Vamanti*, so read all the Deva-n. MSS. and K. The Beng. have *sparśānukūlā api sūrya-kāntās, te hy anya-teja-'bhibhavād dahanti*, 'although the sun-crystals be grateful to the touch, yet, from the influence of other heat, they burn.'

[1] This is inserted on the authority of Kāṭavema and one MS. (India Office, 2696). The Beng. read *bho utsāha-hetuka nishkrama*.

[2] 'Your arguments for exertion (in the chase) have fallen (to the ground),' i.e. all that you have alleged in praise of hunting, with the view of rousing the king's ardour, has been in vain.

[3] Some read *bhavanto;* but the fem. *bhavatyo* (supported by K.) seems more correct, as the female attendants, called Yavanī, are intended. See p. 62, n. 2, in the middle.

[4] 'Fulfil your office (of door-keeper),' i. e. *dvāra-stho bhava*, 'stand at the door,' Ć.

विदूषकः ।

[a] किदं भवदा दाणिं णिम्मच्छिअं । सम्पदं इमस्सिं पा-
दवच्छाआविरइदविदाणसणाहे सिलाअले उवविसदु
भवं । जाव अहम्पि सुहासीणो होमि ।

राजा ।

गच्छायतः ।

विदूषकः ।

[b] एदु भवं । ॥ उभौ परिक्रम्योपविष्टौ ॥

राजा ।

माठव्य । अनवाप्तचक्षुःफलोऽसि । येन त्वया द्रष्टव्यानां
परं न दृष्टम् ।

विदूषकः ।

[c] णं भवं अग्गदो मे वट्टदि ।

[a] कृतं भवतेदानीं निर्मक्षिकम् । साम्प्रतमस्मिन्पादपच्छायाविरचितवितानसनाथे
शिलातल उपविशतु भवान् । यावदहमपि सुखासीनो भवामि ।   [b] एतु भवान् ।
[c] ननु भवानग्रतो मे वर्तते ।

---

[1] ' (The place) has now been made clear of flies by your Majesty,' i. e.
we are now left alone, and no one can interrupt us. *Nir-makshikam* =
nir-janam, 'free from people,' S., C. According to Pāṇ. ii. 1, 6, *nirma-
kshikam* is an Avyayībhāva compound, but it is here used adjectively.
The Prākṛit conforms to Vararuċi iii. 30. The phrase occurs again in the
beginning of Act VI. Has *makshika* here at all the sense of the French
mouchard, 'a spy,' which is derived from *mouche*, 'a fly'?

[2] 'On this stone-seat, furnished with a canopy,' &c. See p. 26, n. 3.

[3] Lit. 'thou hast not obtained the fruit [benefit] of thy eyes, since
the best of things worthy to be seen has not been seen by thee,' i. e.
until you have seen Sakuntalā, you may consider your eyes as barren,
and created in vain ; when they have fallen upon this object, they may
then be said to have yielded some fruit. So in Vikram., Act I, the king,
speaking of Urvaśī, says, *yasya netrayor abandhyayoḥ* (not barren)
pathi sthitā tvam. Cf. also Gīta-g. ix. 6, *Harim avalokaya saphalaya
nayane*, 'look upon Hari (and) make thy eyes fruitful.'

राजा ।

सर्वः कान्तमात्मीयं पश्यति । अहं तु तामेवाश्रमललामभूतां शकुन्तलामधिकृत्य ब्रवीमि ।[1]

विदूषकः ॥ खगतम् ॥

[a]होदु । से अवसरं ण दाइस्सं ।[2] ॥ प्रकाशम् ॥ [b]भो वअस्स । जइ सा तवस्सिकण्णआ अणब्भत्थणीआ । ता किं णाए दिट्ठआए ।[3]

राजा ।

सखे । न परिहार्ये वस्तुनि पौरवाणां मनः प्रवर्तते ।[4]

[a] भवतु । अस्यावसरं न दास्यामि ।   [b] भो वयस्य । यदि सा तपस्विकन्य-
कानभ्यर्थनीया । तदा किं तया दृश्या ।

---

[1] 'Every one regards his own as beautiful; but I speak in reference to that same S'akuntalā who is the ornament of the hermitage.' *Ātmīyam* is given in one Bombay MS. (India Office, 1858), and is supported by K. *Lalāma=alaṅkāra*. *Adhikṛitya*, see p. 6, n. 2. Cf. *mudrām adhikṛitya bravīmi*, Mālavik. p. 49, l. 11; also Raghu-v. xi. 62; Kumāra-s. iv. 38.

[2] 'I will not give him an opportunity (of speaking about her).' *Se = asya* or *asyāḥ;* K. here interprets it by the former. *Avasara = vāg-avasara.* 'I will not hold a conversation with him respecting S'akuntalā,' S'.

[3] 'If she be a hermit's daughter, she is not (fit) to be wooed (by you); what (good) then (is to be got) by her seen?' This reading is adopted from the Beng. MSS.

[4] 'The heart of the descendants of Puru does not engage in (the pursuit of) a forbidden object;' see p. 31, n. 1. The Beng. and two Deva-n. MSS. (India Office, 2696, and my own) insert the following curious verse before the above sentence: *Mūrkha, Nirākṛita-nimeshābhir netra-paṅktibhir unmukhaḥ Navām indu-kalām lokaḥ kena bhāvena paśyati,* 'O fool! with what feeling [or sentiment] do people look at a new digit of the moon, turning up their faces with a row of eyes free from winking?'

सुरयुवतिसम्भवं किल मुनेरपत्यं तदुज्झिताधिगतम् ।
अर्कस्योपरि शिथिलं च्युतमिव नवमल्लिकाकुसुमम् ॥४२॥

विदूषक: ॥ विहस्य ॥

[a] जह कस्सवि पिराडखज्जूरेहिं उव्वेजिदस्स तिन्तिडिआए
अहिलासो भवे । तह अन्तेउरइत्थिआरत्रणपरिभाविनो
भवदो इअं अब्भत्थणा ।

[a] यथा कस्यापि पिराडखर्जूरैरुद्वेजितस्य तिन्तिडिकायामभिलापो भवेत् । तथान्तःपुर-
स्त्रीरत्नपरिभाविनो भवत इयमभ्यर्थना ।

---

[1] '(Although the reputed) offspring of the sage, she is really sprung
from a celestial nymph, (and was) found (by him when) deserted by her;
like a severed flower of the Nava-mallikā fallen on the sun-plant.' The
Nava-mallikā (p. 22, n. 1) is a delicate and tender plant (*atikomala-
pushpa-bheda*, Ć.) which, as a creeper, depends on some other tree for
support; the *arka*, Asclepias, or Calotropis Gigantea, is a large and
vigorous one (see Sir W. Jones, vol. v. p. 102); hence the former is
compared to S'akuntalā, the latter to the sage Kaṇva. S'. explains
arkopari by *raver upari*, 'upon the sun;' but hints that some interpret
arka by *arka-pushpa*. *Sura-yuvati*, see p. 44, n. 2. According to K.,
kila is used *vārtāyām*, 'it is reported;' but S'. interprets it by *niścitam*,
'certainly.' *Śithilam = vṛintāć ćyutam*, 'fallen from the stalk,' Ć. The
correspondence of the words in the first line with those in the second
is noticeable; *sura-yuvati* with *nava-mallikā*, *muni* with *arka*, *apatya*
with *kusuma*, *ujjhita* with *śithila*, *adhigata* with *ćyuta*.

[2] 'Just as to any one [lit. of any one] having lost his relish for dates,
there may be a great desire for the tamarind; so is this desire of your
Majesty (for S'akuntalā), slighting the jewels of women in (your own)
inner apartments.' *Piṇḍa-kharjūra*, 'a kind of Kharjūra, or date tree,'
here probably used for the fruit, and therefore in the neuter. *Tintidikā*
or *tintidī*, 'the tamarind tree.' *Udvejitaḥ = vaimanasyam prāpitaḥ*,
'brought to a change of mind or feeling.' *Itthiā*, *itthikā*, and *itthī* are
Prākṛit equivalents for *strī*. See Lassen's Instit. Prāk. p. 182, note.

Verse 42. ĀRYĀ or GĀTHĀ. See verse 2.

◡◡◡◡ | ◡–◡ | –◡◡ ‖ ◡–◡ | –– | ◡–◡ | –◡◡ | –

–– | –◡◡ | ◡◡– ‖ ◡◡◡◡ | ◡◡– | ◡ | –◡◡ | –

राजा ।

न तावदेनां पश्यसि । येनैवमवादीः ।

विदूषकः ।

ᵃ तंक्खु रमणिज्जं । जं भवदोवि विम्हश्रं उप्पादेदि ।

राजा ।

वयस्य । किं, बहुना ।

चित्ते निवेश्य परिकल्पितसत्त्वयोगा
रूपोच्चयेन मनसा विधिना कृता नु ।
स्त्रीरत्नसृष्टिरपरा प्रतिभाति सा मे
धातुर्विभुत्वमनुचिन्त्य वपुश्च तंस्याः ॥ ४३ ॥

ᵃ तत्खलु रमणीयम् । यद्भवतोऽपि विस्मयमुत्पादयति ।

---

[1] 'Was she endowed with the properties of life by the Creator after
delineating her [placing her] in a picture, or was she rather formed by
the mind by a concentration [assemblage, selection] of lovely forms? She
appears to me like a matchless [the last] creation of the loveliest of women
[or like another creation of the goddess of beauty], when I recollect
[recollecting] the omnipotence of the Creator, and her (graceful) person,'
i. e. whatever was the method of her creation, whether she was formed
by the divine power of Brahmā by first painting a faultless figure and
then breathing into it the principle of life, or by the mind by collecting
into one ideal model a combination of various exquisite forms, it is clear
that she is an unequalled beauty (or, she appears to me as another creation
of the goddess Lakshmī). *Strī-ratna* is explained by S'. and C. to mean
Lakshmī; but it may be referred to the *antaḥpura-strī-ratna* mentioned
before, as *aparā*=*apūrvā*, 'matchless,' 'peerless,' 'without a fellow;' *na
vidyate parā*, K. and S. *Citre*=*ālekhye*. *Niveśya*=*vinyasya*, 'having
placed, fixed, committed.' *Parikalpita*=*sampādita* or *sampanna*, 'en-
dowed with,' 'provided with,' K. *Yoga*, at the end of a compound, is
often used in a vague manner; *sattva-yoga* may mean 'a combination of
the various properties of being and life.' K. refers to verse 146, beginning
Yat yat sādhu na citre syāt, which asserts that the figure of S'akuntalā

Verse 43. VASANTA-TILAKĀ (a variety of S'AKVARĪ). See verses 8, 27, 31.

विदूषकः ।

^aजइ एव्वं । पच्चादेसो दाणिं रूवबदीणं ।

राजा ।

इदं च मे मनसि वर्तते ।

अनाघ्रातं पुष्पं किसलयमलूनं कररुहै-
रनाविद्धं रत्नं मधु नवमनास्वादितरसम् ।
अखण्डं पुण्यानां फलमिव च तद्रूपमनघं
न जाने भोक्तारं कमिह समुपस्थास्यति विधिः ॥४४॥

^a यद्येवम् । प्रत्यादेश इदानीं रूपवतीनाम् ।

---

was faultless. *Rūpoččaya = čandrādy-upamāna-vastu-samuččaya*, i. e. collecting together such models of beauty as the moon, &c., for the purpose of forming one ideal perfect form, by a selection from each, K. *Manasā kṛi*, or *kḷṛip*, 'to form by means of the mind;' hence often simply, 'to imagine ;' and hence, *mano-kalpitam*, 'an idea.' There may be an allusion here to the mind-born sons of Brahmā. *Vidhinā = vidhātrā*. K. observes that, being dissatisfied with the thought contained in the first line, he asserts in the second that her limbs were too delicate to have been fashioned by the hand in a picture ; they must, therefore, have been formed in the mind. *Strī-ratna = strī-śreshṭha*, Č. *Jātau jātau yad utkṛishṭam taddhi ratnam praćakshate*, 'whatever is best of its kind that indeed they call *ratna* (a gem),' Č. The connection of *anučintya* with the dative case *me* is unusual, but not without precedent. The Beng. MSS. read *čitte* for *čitre*.

[1] 'The supplanter.' The verb *praty-ā-diś = nir-ā-kṛi*, 'to reject,' 're-move,' 'set aside,' and *pratyādeśa*, 'rejection,' is here used for 'the cause of rejection,' i. e. anything which, by its superiority, supplants and brings into contempt what was before highly prized. *Tayā nija-saundarya-mahimnā 'nya-rūpavatī-rūpaṃ khaṇḍitam*, S'. So also, in the beginning of Vikram., Urvaśī is called *pratyādeśo rūpa-garvitāyāḥ śrī-gauryāḥ*.

[2] 'That faultless form (is) a flower not (yet) smelt, a tender-shoot un-plucked [uncut, unhurt] by the nails, an unperforated jewel, fresh honey whose flavour (is yet) untasted, and the full [complete] reward of meri-

---

Verse 44. ŚIKHARIṆĪ (a variety of ATYASHṬI). See verses 9, 24.

विदूषकः ।

[a]तेण हि लहु परित्ताअदु णं भवं । मा कस्सबि तबस्सि-
णो इङ्गुदीतेल्लचिक्कणसीसस्स हत्थे पडिस्संदि ।

राजा ।

परवती खलु तत्रभवती । न च सन्निहितोऽत्र गुरुजनः ।

विदूषकः ।

[b]अध भवन्तं अन्तरेण कीदिसो से दिट्ठिरांओ ।

[a] तेन हि लघु परित्रायतामेनां भवान् । मा कस्यापि तपस्विन इङ्गुदीतैलचिक्कण-
शीर्षस्य हस्ते पतिष्यति । [b] अथ भवन्तमन्तरेण कीदृशोऽस्या दृष्टिरागः ।

---

torious deeds. I know not to what possessor [enjoyer] here [of this
form] Destiny will resort;' i. e. I know not whom Destiny intends to
be the enjoyer of her beauty. *A-lūna = śākhāvasthita*, 'still remaining
on the branch.' *An-āviddha = a-samutkīrṇa*, 'unperforated,' K. (cf.
Raghu-v. i. 4, *maṇau vajra-samutkīrṇe sūtrasya gatiḥ*, 'the entrance of
a thread into a gem perforated by the adamant'). The Beng. MSS. read
an-āmuktam = a-parihitam, ākarād ānīta-mātram, 'not yet put on,' 'only
just drawn from the mine,' S. *Phalam puṇyānām*, i. e. the fruit of
many virtuous acts in various former births come to its maturity (*pari-
ṇati-bhūtam*), S. *A-khaṇḍa = sam-pūrṇa*, 'unimpaired,' 'entire.' The
consequences of good deeds performed in former births are sometimes
not fully enjoyed; but sometimes they are perfected. Similarly the form
of S'akuntalā is *un-agha*, 'faultless' (= *pratyavāya-hetu-rahita*, K.) *Iha*,
i. e. *asmin rūpa-vishaye*, 'with reference to this form,' K. *Samupasthāsyati
= samprāpsyati*, 'will attain,' 'arrive at.' This verse is an example of
the figure called Rūpaka, see Indian Wisdom, p. 455.

[1] 'Therefore let your Highness quickly rescue her, lest she fall into
the hands of some wretched rustic, whose head is greasy with oil of
Inguḍī.' *Inguḍī*, see p. 18, n. 1. *Mā = yathā na*, K.

[2] 'Towards your Highness what kind of feeling (was displayed) by her
eyes?' *Atha* is used in asking a question, S. *Bhavantam antareṇa =
bhavan-nimittam*, C.; = *bhavan-madhye*, S. The same expression occurs
in Vikram., Act III, where the interpretation given is *bhavantam uddiśya*,
i. e. 'with regard to you.' *Antareṇa* (similarly used in Mālavik. p. 5, l. 3)
governs an acc. case, by Pāṇ. ii. 3, 4. *Dṛishṭi-rāga = ćakshuḥ-prīti*, 'the
love of the eyes,' K. So read the Deva-n. MSS., supported by K. and S.;
but the Beng. read *ćitta-rāga*.

राजा ।

निसर्गादेवाप्रगल्भस्तपस्विकन्याजनः । तथापि तु
अभिमुखे मयि संहृतमीक्षितं
हसितमन्यनिमित्तकृतोदयम् ।
विनयवारितवृत्तिरतस्तया
न विवृतो मदनो न च संवृतः ॥४५॥

विदूषकः ।

[a]एंक्खु दिट्ठमेत्तस्स तुह अङ्कं आरोहंदि[2] ।

राजा ।

मिथःप्रस्थाने पुनः शालीनतयापि ममाविष्कृतो भाव-
स्तत्रभवत्या[3] । तथा हि

दर्भाङ्कुरेण चरणः क्षत इत्यकाण्डे
तन्वी स्थिता कतिचिदेव पदानि गत्वा ।

[a] ननु खलु दृष्टमात्रस्य तथाङ्कमारोहति ।

---

[1] 'When I stood facing her, her glance was withdrawn, a smile was (feigned to be) raised from some other cause (than love); hence love, whose course was checked by modesty, was not (fully) displayed by her, nor (yet) concealed.' *Anya-nimitta*, i. e. some other cause than love, which was the true one (*abhilāsha-vyatirikta*, K.) 'By this her love was concealed,' K. The Beng. have *kathodayam*. *Vinaya-vārita-vrittir* is to be taken with *madano*, K. Cf. p. 52, n. 1.

[2] 'Is it really (to be expected) that she will seat herself on the lap of you, barely seen?' i.e. do you expect to gain her all at once, without some effort?

[3] 'Again, at our mutual departure, her feeling towards me was betrayed by her ladyship, although with modesty.' *Sakhībhyām* before *mithaḥ* is not supported by the commentators or best MSS.

Verse 45. DRUTA-VILAMBITA (a variety of JAGATI), containing twelve syllables to the Pāda or quarter-verse, each Pāda being alike.

∪∪∪−∪∪−∪∪−∪−∥

आसीद्विवृत्तवदना च विमोचयन्ती
शाखासु वल्कलमसक्तमपि द्रुमाणाम् ॥४६॥

विदूषकः ।

[a] तेण हि गहीदपाहेत्रो होहि । किदं तुए उववणं तवो-
वणंति पेक्खामि ।

राजा ।

सखे । तपस्विभिः कैश्चित्परिज्ञातोऽस्मि । चिन्तय तावत्
केनापदेशेन पुनराश्रमपदं गच्छामः ।

विदूषकः ।

[b] की अवरो अवदेसो । एं भवं राज्ञा ।

राजा ।

ततः किम् ।

[a] तेन हि गृहीतपाथेयो भव । कृतं त्वयोपवनं तपोवनमिति मन्ये ।   [b] कोऽप-
रोऽपदेशः । ननु भवान्राजा ।

---

[1] 'For, having proceeded only a few steps, (that) slim one stopped
without any (real) occasion, saying, "My foot is hurt by a blade of Kuśa-
grass" [p. 57, l. 16]; and remained with her face turned back (towards me),
whilst (pretending to be employed in) releasing her bark-dress, although
not (really) entangled in the branches of the shrubs.' *Darbhānkureṇa*,
see p. 57, n. 5; p. 19, n. 1. *Akāṇḍe=akasmāt*, K.; =*animittam*, S.;
=*anavasaram*, C. One sense of *kāṇḍa* is 'occasion,' 'opportunity.'
Vivṛitta-vadanā, i. e. *mad-avalokanāya*, 'for a look at me,' S. This
verse is an example of the Samādhi Alankāra, S.

[2] 'Therefore be provided with a stock of provender; I perceive that
you have made the penance-grove a pleasure-grove [pleasure-garden].'
Grihīta-pātheya, 'one who has provided himself with provender or the
necessaries for a lengthened stay from home.' According to K.=*san-
naddha*, 'equipped,' 'prepared,' i. e. for rambling in the precincts of
the hermitage. The Vidūshaka is characteristically anxious about the
provisions.

[3] 'And what of that ?'

Verse 46. VASANTA-TILAKĀ (a variety of ŚAKVARI). See verses 8, 27, 31, 43.

विदूषक: ।

[a] णीवारच्छटुंभान्नं अम्हाणं उबहरन्तुन्ति ।

राजा ।

मूर्ख । अन्यमेव भागधेयमेते तपस्विनो निर्वपन्ति । यो
रत्नराशीनपि विहायाभिनन्द्यते । पश्य ।

यदुत्तिष्ठति वर्णेभ्यो नृपाणां त्वयि तत्फलम् ।
तपःषड्भागमक्षय्यं ददत्यारण्यका हि नः ॥ ४७ ॥

नेपथ्ये ।

हन्त सिद्धार्थौ स्वः ।

राजा ॥ कर्णं दत्त्वा ॥

अये धीरप्रशान्तस्वरैस्तपस्विभिर्भवितव्यम् ।

[a] नीवारषष्ठभागमस्माकमुपहरन्तिवति ।

---

[1] A king might take a sixth part of liquids, flowers, roots, fruit, grass,
&c.; but, even though dying with want, he was not to receive any tax
from a Brāhman learned in the Vedas (Manu vii. 131–133). See Indian
Wisdom, pp. 264, 265.

[2] 'These hermits pay another (kind of) tribute, which, leaving behind
heaps of jewels, is welcomed [rejoiced in],' i. e. which is welcomed more
than heaps of jewels. This reading of the oldest Beng. MSS. seems
preferable to that of the Deva-n. *anyad bhāgadheyam eteshāṃ rakshaṇe
nipatati*, 'another tribute accrues (to me) for their protection.' *Bhāga-
dheya* in this sense is masculine, according to Amara-k. S'. and some
of the Beng. have *puṇya* for *anya*.

[3] 'That tribute which arises to kings from the (four) classes is perish-
able; but hermits [inhabitants of the woods] offer us a sixth part of (the
merit of their) penance, (which is) imperishable.' *Varṇebhyaḥ*, i. e. the four
classes of Brāhmans, Kshatriyas, Vaiśyas, and S'ūdras, according to K.,
S'., and C'. Hence it would appear that the Brāhmans were liable to
some kind of tribute as well as the other classes, though Manu exempts
them. The Beng. have *dhanam* for *phalam*. *Dadati*, third person plural
(see Gram. 331. Obs.)

[4] 'We have accomplished our object,' i. e. in gaining an audience of the
king, S'. *Hanta*, an exclamation of pleasure, S'.

[5] 'Oh! it is to be by the hermits, [it must surely be the hermits] who

Verse 47. SLOKA or ANUSHTUBH. See verses 5, 6, 11, 26.

दौवारिकः ॥ प्रविश्य ॥

[a] जेदु जेदु भट्टा । एदे दुवे इसिकुमारच्रा पडिहारभूमिं उवट्ठिदा ।

राजा ।

तेन ह्यविलम्बितं प्रवेशय तौ ।

दौवारिकः ।

[b] एसो पवेसेमिं । ॥ इति निष्क्रम्य । ऋषिकुमाराभ्यां सह प्रविश्य ॥

[c] इदो इदो भवन्ता ।

॥ उभौ राजानं विलोकयतः ॥

प्रथमः ।

अही दीप्तिमतोऽपि विश्वसनीयतास्य वपुषः । अथवा उपपन्नमेतदस्मिन्नृषिकल्पे राजनि । कुतः ।

अध्याक्रान्ता वसतिरमुनाप्याश्रमे सर्वभोग्ये
रक्षायोगादयमपि तपः प्रत्यहं सञ्चिनोति ।

[a] जयतु जयतु भर्ता । एतौ द्वावृषिकुमारकौ प्रतिहारभूमिमुपस्थितौ ।   [b] एष प्रवेशयामि ।   [c] इत इतो भवन्तौ ।

---

have deep, calm voices,' i. e. to judge by the tone of the voices which I hear, some of the hermits must have arrived.

[1] Properly 'the ground near the gate of the palace' (*rāja-dvāra-pra-deśa*, S'.), but here simply the station of the porter (*dvāra*, C̆.)

[2] The present for the future.

[3] 'Oh! the confidence (inspired by the sight) of his person, majestic though (it be)! But this is quite natural in this king very little inferior to a Rishi.' *Dîptimat*=*tejasvin*, 'splendid,' 'majestic.' *Viśvasanīyatā*, 'the state of being confided in.' *Upapanna*, 'fit,' 'proper,' 'reasonable,' 'to be expected.' Cf. Vikram., Act II, *upapannam viśeshanam asya rāyoḥ*. *Rishi-kalpa*, 'resembling a Rishi, but with a degree of inferiority;' see *kalpa* in Dict. and Gram. p. 65. LVII. Dushyanta was a Rājarshi, and therefore one degree below a Rishi, see p. 44, n. 2, in the middle; and p. 39, n. 3. The Deva-n. reading is *rishibhyo nātibhinne rājani*, but the Beng. is here preferable.

अस्यापि द्यां स्पृशति वशिनश्चारणद्वन्द्वगीतः
पुण्यः शब्दो मुनिरिति मुहुः केवलं राजंपूर्वः ॥ ४८ ॥

द्वितीयः ।

गौतम । अयं स बलभित्संखो दुषन्तः ।

---

¹ 'Although he abides in the Āśrama [order] of a royal householder where everything is to be enjoyed, yet he also day by day accumulates the-merit-of-penance through the act of protecting (his subjects). Of him also having-his-passions-in-subjection, the (same) sacred title of Muni [or Rishi], but (with this difference that it is) preceded by Rāja [i. e. Rājarshi], repeatedly ascends to heaven, being chanted by pairs of (celestial) minstrels.' *Adhyākrānta = svī-krita*, 'appropriated,' 'taken possession of,' K. *Āśrame = dharmācaraṇa-sthāne*, K.; = *gārhasthye*, 'the order of a householder,' S'. and Ć. *Rakshā-yogāt*, see p. 79, l. 7; *yogāt*, 'in consequence of,' 'by reason of,' 'through' (at the end of comps.); cf. Manu vii. 144, 'The highest virtue of a king is the protection of his subjects.' *Ćāraṇa-dvandva = gandharva-mithuna*, 'pair of Gandharvas, or celestial choristers.' These beings were the musicians or minstrels of Indra's heaven, just as the Apsarases were the dancers and actresses; and their business was to amuse the inhabitants of Svarga by singing the praises of gods, saints, and heroes. *Ćāraṇa*, 'a bard,' 'herald.' *Kevalam = eva*, 'certainly,' K. This verse is an example of Vyatireka, i. e. a description of the difference of two things compared in some respects to each other, S'.

² 'The friend of Indra.' *Bala-bhid*, 'Indra,' who crushes armies with his thunderbolt. *Sakhi* at the end of some comps. (like *rātri*, *akshi*, &c.) changes its final to *a*, and becomes a noun of the first class (see Gram. 778; Pāṇ. v. 4, 87. 91. 98. 102). Indra is the chief of the Suras or secondary gods, being inferior to the gods of the Triad; and corresponds to the Jove or Jupiter Tonans of classical mythology. In his lordship over Svarga, or paradise, he might be supplanted by any one who could perform a hundred Aśva-medhas or horse-sacrifices (see p. 45, n. 1). He and the other Suras were for ever engaged in hostilities with their half-brothers, the demons called Asuras or Daityas, the giants or Titans of Hindū mythology, who were the children of Kaśyapa by Diti, as the Suras were by Aditi (see p. 22, n. 3). On such occasions the gods seem to have depended much upon the assistance they received from the heroes of the earth, such as Dushyanta, Purūravas, &c.

Verse 48. MANDĀKRĀNTĀ (a variety of ATYASHTI). See verses 15, 33.

प्रथमः ।

अथ किम् ।

द्वितीयः ।

तेन हि

नैतच्चित्रं यदयमुदधिश्यामसीमां धरित्री-
मेकः कृत्स्नां नगरपरिघप्रांशुबाहुर्भुनक्ति ।
आशंसन्ते समितिषु सुराः सक्तवैरा हि दैत्ये-
रस्याधिज्ये धनुषि विजयं पौरुहूते च वज्रे ॥४९॥

उभौ ॥ उपगम्य ॥

विजयस्व राजन् ।

---

[1] 'This is not wonderful, that he whose arm is as long as the bar of a city (gate), should alone govern the entire earth, having the ocean as its dark [green] boundary [i. e. as far as the very ocean]. For the gods, constant in enmity, in their battles with the demons, expect victory through [in] his strung bow and the thunderbolt of Indra.' *Parigha*=*argala*, 'the bar or bolt which fastens a gate.' In a city-gate it was both massive and long (*styāna, dīrgha,* Ć.), and therefore an object of comparison highly significant of muscular strength. It should be borne in mind that length and vigour of arm were prime requisites in the ancient hero, whose fame depended on his skill and power in managing a bow. Hence the appositeness of such epithets as *mahā-bāhu* and *prānśu-bāhu,* 'long-armed.' *Bhunakti* =*pālayati,* Ć.; *bhuj* is often applied to a king in the sense of ruling and protecting the earth; cf. *kritsnām prithivīm bhunkte,* Manu vii. 148; also Raghu-v. viii. 7, iii. 4. *Āśansante*=*iććhanti,* 'wish for,' 'hope for,' 'aspire after.' *Samitishu surāḥ,* &c., this is the Beng. reading; the Deva-n. have *sura-yuratayo baddha-vairā,* &c. *Daityaiḥ,* see last note. *Adhi-jye,* see p. 9, n. 2. The loc. has sometimes the force of the instr. *Pauruhūta*=*Aindra,* 'belonging to Indra;' *Puru-hūta,* 'much-worshipped,' is one of Indra's thousand names. This verse is an example of the figure called Dīpaka or 'illustration,' S'.; its use is to throw light, as it were, upon an idea by some apposite illustration. See Indian Wisdom, p. 455.

[2] *Vi-ji,* 'to conquer,' is rightly conjugated in Ātm. (Pāṇ. i. 3, 19).

Verse 49. MANDĀKRĀNTĪ (a variety of ATYASHTI). See verses 15, 33, 48.

राजा ॥ आसनादुत्थाय ॥

अभिवादये भवन्तौ ।

उभौ ।

स्वस्ति भवते । ॥ इति फलान्युपहरतः ॥

राजा ॥ सप्रणामं परिगृह्य ॥

आज्ञामिच्छामि ।

उभौ ।

विदितो भवानाश्रमसदामिहस्थः[1] । तेन भवन्तं प्रार्थयन्ते ।

राजा ।

किमाज्ञापयन्ति ।

उभौ ।

तच्चभवतः कश्यस्य महर्षेरसान्निध्याद्रक्षांसि[2] न इष्टिविघ्न-मुत्पादयन्ति । तत्कतिपयरात्रं[3] सारथिद्वितीयेन भवता सनाथीक्रियतामाश्रम इति[4] ।

राजा ।

अनुगृहीतोऽस्मि ।

विदूषकः ॥ अपवार्य ॥

[a] एसा दाणिं अणुकूला दे अब्भत्थणा ।

राजा ॥ स्मितं कृत्वा ॥

रैवतक । मद्वचनादुच्यतां सारथिः । सवाणासनं रथमुप-स्थापयेति ।

[a] एषा इदानीमनुकूला तेऽभ्यर्थना ।

---

[1] 'Your Highness is known to the inhabitants of the hermitage (to be) staying here.' *Āśrama-sad* = *āśrama-vāsin*, 'a dweller in a hermitage,' 'a hermit;' so *nāka-sad*, 'a dweller in paradise,' 'a god;' hence *sadana*, 'a house.' *Vidita*, in construction with the gen., is noticeable; see Pāṇ. iii. 2, 188, ii. 3, 67; also Raghu-v. x. 40, *viditaṃ tapyamānaṃ tena me bhuvana-trayam*, 'the three worlds are known to me (as) being harassed by him.'

[2] *Rakshas* = *rākshasa*, see p. 40, n. 5.

[3] *Rātram*, see p. 86, n. 2. *Dvitīyena*, see p. 13, n. 1.

[4] *Sanāthī-kriyatām*, see p. 26, n. 3.

दौवारिकः ।

"जं देवी आणबेदि । ।। इति निष्क्रान्तः ।।

उभौ ।। सहर्षम् ।।

अनुकारिणि पूर्वेषां युक्तरूपमिदं त्वयि ।
आपन्नाभयसत्त्रेषु दीक्षिताः खलु पौरवाः ॥५०॥

राजा ।। सप्रणामम् ।।

गच्छतां पुरो भवन्तौ । अहमप्यनुपदमागत एव ।

उभौ ।

विजयस्व । ।। इति निष्क्रान्तौ ।।

राजा ।

माठव्य । अँप्यस्ति शकुन्तलादर्शने कुतूहलम् ।

विदूषकः ।

[b] पढमं सपरिवाहं आसि । दाणिं रक्खसवुत्तन्तेण विन्दूवि
णावसेसिदो ।

[a] यदेव आज्ञापयति ।   [b] प्रथमं सपरिवाहमासीत् । इदानीं राक्षसवृत्तान्तेन
विन्दुरपि नावशेषितः ।

---

[1] 'This is a becoming trait in you, an emulator of (your) ancestors.
Truly the descendants of Puru are ordained (to officiate) in the sacrifices
of (giving) exemption-from-fear to the distressed ;' i. e. whilst we Bráhmans
are consecrated to officiate in real sacrifices, the highest duty of kings is
the protection of their afflicted subjects (see p. 86, n. 1). So read all the
Deva-n. and some of the Beng. MSS. The Beng. (Bodleian, 234) has
satrena, and some begin the verse with *upakárini sarveshám*, 'the helper
of all.' *Yukta-rúpam*, cf. p. 15, l. 3. *Ápannábhaya-sattreshu=ápad-
gatánám bhaya-tráne*, S. *Díkshitáh=krita-pratishtháh*, 'consecrated.'

[2] *Api* may be used *prasne*, 'in asking a question' (cf. p. 35, l. 9).

[3] 'At first it was overflowing; (but) now, by the account of the
Rákshasas, not even a drop is left.' *Pariváha* is either 'an inundation,'
or 'a channel for carrying off an excess of water;' the Beng. MSS. have
aparibódham, 'unchecked.' *Vrittántena=náma-grahanena*, 'by the
mention.'

Verse 50. SLOKA or ANUSHTUBH. See verses 5, 6, 11, 12, 26, 47.

राजा ।

मा भैषीः । ननु मत्समीपे वर्तिष्यसे ।

विदूषकः ।

[a] एस तव चक्करक्खीभूदोम्हि ।

दौवारिकः ॥ प्रविश्य ॥

[b] सज्जो रधो भट्टिणो विजअप्पत्थ्थाणं अवेक्खदि । एस
उण णअरादो देवीणं आणत्तिहरओ करभओ आअंदो ।

राजा ॥ सादरम् ॥

किमम्बाभिः प्रेषितः ।

दौवारिकः ।

[c] अहं ।

राजा ।

ननु प्रवेश्यताम् ।

दौवारिकः ।

[d] तह । ॥ इति निष्क्रम्य । करभकेण सह प्रविश्य ॥ [e] एसो भट्टा । उवसप्प ।

करभकः ।

[f] जेदु जेदु भट्टा । देवी आणवेदि । आआमिणि चउत्थ-
दिअहे पुत्तपिण्डपालणो णाम उववासो भविस्सदि ।

<hr>

[a] एष तव चक्ररक्षीभूतोऽस्मि ।   [b] सज्जो रथो भर्तुर्विजयप्रस्थानमपेक्षते । एष
पुनर्नगराद्देवीनामाज्ञाहरः करभक आगतः ।   [c] अथ किम् ।   [d] तथा ।
[e] एष भर्ता । उपसर्प ।   [f] जयतु जयतु भर्ता । देव्याज्ञापयति । आगामिनि चतुर्थ-
दिवसे पुत्रपिण्डपालनो नामोपवासो भविष्यति ।

<hr>

[1] 'I will guard the wheel of your chariot.' There seems to be a
humorous double meaning in *čakra-raksha*, which may also be translated,
'the commander of the wing of your army;' the Deva-n. have *esa rakkha-
sādo rakkhidomhi*, 'I am protected from the Rákshasa.'

[2] 'The equipped chariot awaits your Majesty's advance to victory; but
here is Karabhaka just arrived from the city, bearing a message from the
queen-mother.' *Devīnām* is here in the respectful plural; so *ambābhiḥ*
two lines below.

[3] *Atha kim* (=*vāḍham*, 'yes') is used *angīkritau*, see p. 46, n. 3.

[a] तहिं दीहाउणा अवसं अम्हे सम्भावंइद्दव्वि ।

राजा ।

इतस्तपस्विकार्यम् । इतो गुरुजनाज्ञा । द्वयमप्यनतिक्रम-
णीयम् । किमत्र प्रतिविधेयम्[2] ।

चिटूपकः ।

[b] तिसङ्कू विअ अन्तरा चिट्ठ[3] ।

[a] तच्च दीर्घायुषावश्यं वयं सम्भावयितव्या इति ।   [b] त्रिशङ्कुरिवान्तरा तिष्ठ ।

---

[1] 'On the fourth day, (which is now) coming [i. e. on the fourth day after to-day], the ceremony [fast] named Putra-piṇḍa-pālana [i. e. cherishing of the body of a son] will take place; thereat [on that occasion] certainly we ought to be honoured-with-a-visit by the long-lived-one [by your Majesty, long may you live !].' Most of the Beng. MSS. read *putra-piṇḍa-pāraṇa*; but Ć. substitutes *pālana*, and interprets the phrase by *pura-deha-pushṭi-prada*. S'. gives the same interpretation, but reads *paryupāsana* for *pālana*. *Piṇḍa, deha-mātre iti Medinī*, 'according to Medinī, *piṇḍa* has the sense of body,' S'. and Ć. *Putra* refers to the king in his relation to the queen-mother. The Deva-n. reading (*pravritta-pāraṇa upavāsaḥ*, 'a fast which has come to an end') is not very satisfactory. *Upa-vāsa=vrata*, 'a religious ceremonial accompanied with fasting, but not necessarily a fast.' K. and Ć. observe that one name for this ceremonial was *putra-rāja*, and that it consisted in offering various presents to the young king of sweetmeats, clothes, &c., just as might be done in the present day on the occasion of a birth-day. *Dīrghāyus*, see p. 9, n. 1. *Vayam* is used in plural like *devīnām* above. *Sambhāvayitavyāḥ*, see p. 26, n. 1.

[2] 'In this direction the business of the hermits, in the other the command of a venerable parent (calls me). Both are not to be neglected. How, in such a case, can an arrangement be effected?' *Dvayam api*, 'both the one and the other;' *api* is often affixed to *dvi* in this sense; see Amara-k. ii. 1, 5; Mālavik. p. 16, l. 22. In Hitop., l. 2048, *dvayam* without *api* has the sense of 'both.'

[3] 'Stand between, like Triśanku.' The story of this monarch is told at length in Rāmāy. i. 57–60 (see also p. 43, n. 1). He is there described as a just and pious prince of the Solar race, who aspired to celebrate a great sacrifice, hoping thereby to ascend to heaven in his mortal body. He first requested the sage Vaśishṭha to officiate for him; but, being

राजा ।

सत्यमाकुलीभूतोऽस्मि ।

कृत्ययोर्भिन्नदेशत्वाद्द्वैधीभवति मे मनः ।
पुरः प्रतिहतं शैलैः स्रोतः स्रोतोवहो यथा ॥ ५१ ॥

॥ विचिन्त्य ॥ सखे । त्वमन्वया पुच्छ इति प्रतिगृहीतः । अतो
भवानितः प्रतिनिवृत्य मां तपस्विकार्यव्ययमानसमावेद्य

---

refused, he then applied to the sage's hundred sons, by whom he was cursed and degraded to the condition of a Ćaṇḍāla. In this pitiable state he had recourse to Viśvāmitra, who undertook to conduct the sacrifice, and invited all the gods to be present; they, however, refused to attend. Upon this the enraged Viśvāmitra, by his own power, transported Tri-śaṅku to the skies, whither he had no sooner arrived than he was hurled down again, head foremost, by Indra and the gods; but, being arrested in his downward course by Viśvāmitra, remained suspended *between heaven and earth*, forming a constellation in the southern hemisphere. The story is differently told in some of the Purāṇas (Wilson's Vishṇu-p. p. 371, note). They and the Hari-v. describe Triśaṅku as a wicked prince, guilty of three heinous sins (śaṅku). S'. adopts this view of his character, and calls him *kṛita-bahutara-malina-karmā rājā*. *Antarā = tapovana-sva-nagarayor madhye*, 'between the hermitage and the city.' The facetious allusion to Triśaṅku is quite characteristic of the Vidūshaka, and affords an example of the Vyāhāra Alaṅkāra, S'. and Ć.

¹ 'Verily I am embarrassed. From the difference of the places of the two duties [i. e. on account of the distance between the place where the two duties have to be performed] my mind is divided in two, as the stream of a river driven back [made to recoil] by rocks (lying) before it' (cf. the sentiment at verse 34). *Puraḥ = agre*, 'in front,' 'ahead.' Although *pratihataṃ śaile*, 'which has struck on a rock,' is the reading of the Beng. MS. (Bodleian, 233) and most of the Deva-n., yet the other Bengālī and S'. read *śailaiḥ*, which I prefer. The Deva-n. read *srotovaho*, gen. case of *sroto-vah*, f. 'a river.' Some MSS. have *srotovaham = nadī-sambandhi*, 'belonging to a river' (K., S'., and Ć.), an adjective agreeing with *srotaḥ*. This verse is an example of the Yathopamā Alaṅkāra, or 'comparison by the use of the conjunction *yathā*.'

Verse 51. SLOKA or ANUSHTUBH. See verses 5, 6, 11, 12, 26, 47, 50.

तच्चभवतीनां पुत्रकृत्यमनुष्ठातुमर्हन्ति ।

विदूषकः ।

[a] णंक्खु मं रक्खोभीरुञ्चं गणेसि[2] ।

राजा ॥ सस्मितम् ॥

भो महाब्राह्मण । कथमेतद्भवति सम्भाव्यते[3] ।

विदूषकः ।

[b] जह राञ्आणुएण गन्तव्वं । तह गमिस्सं ।

राजा ।

ननु तपोवनोपरोधः परिहरणीय इति सर्वानन्नुयाचि-
कांस्त्वयैव सह प्रस्थापयामि ।

विदूषकः ॥ सगर्वम् ॥

[c] तेण हि जुवराओम्हि दाणिं संवुत्तो[5] ।

राजा ॥ आत्मगतम् ॥

चपलोऽयं वटुः[6] । कदाचिदस्मत्प्रार्थनामन्तःपुरेभ्यः[7] कथ-

---

[a] ननु खलु मां रक्षोभीरुकं गणयसि ।   [b] यथा राजानुजेन गन्तव्यम् । तथा
गमिष्यामि ।   [c] तेन हि युवराजोऽस्मि इदानीं संवृत्तः ।

---

[1] 'You have been received by the queen-mother as a son; therefore let
your honour, having returned from hence and having announced that my
mind is intent on [zealous for] the business of the hermits, have the
goodness to discharge the office of a son towards her Majesty.' *Putra iti
pratigrihītah*, i. e. *tvam poshita-putro bhavasi*, 'you are an adopted
son,' S'. Some MSS. have *putratvam* for *putra-krityam*.

[2] 'Surely you do not suppose me to be afraid of the Rākshasas.'

[3] 'How is this possible in your honour?' or, 'how could such a
thing be thought of in your honour?' *Bhavati*, loc. sing. of *bhavat*.
Sambhāvyate may mean, 'is fitting,' 'is consistent.' *Mahā-brāhmaṇa*
is generally used ironically.

[4] 'I will go, as it should be gone by the younger brother of a king.'

[5] *Yuva-rāja*, 'the young prince,' who was the heir-apparent and
generally associated with the reigning monarch in the throne.

[6] *Vaṭu*, 'a youth,' 'a lad;' here it is equivalent to 'fellow,' 'chap.'

[7] *Kadāchid*, 'perchance.' *Prārthanā*=*abhilāshita*, 'desire,' 'pursuit,'

येत् । भवतु । एनमेवं वक्ष्ये । ॥ विदूषकं हस्ते गृहीत्वा । प्रकाशम् ॥

वयस्य । ऋषिगौरवादाश्रमं गच्छामि । न खलु सत्यमेव तापसकन्यकायां शकुन्तलायां ममाभिलाषः । पश्य ।

क्व वयं क्व परोक्षमन्मथो मृगशावैः सममेधितो जनः ।
परिहासविजल्पितं सखे परमार्थेन न गृह्यतां वचः ॥५२॥

विदूषकः ।

[a] अहइं ।

॥ इति निष्क्रान्ताः सर्वं ॥

॥ द्वितीयोऽङ्कः ॥

[a] अथ किम् ।

'suit;' i. e. *Śakuntalā-vishayānusandhāna-rūpa-kathā*, 'the story of my pursuit of S'akuntalā,' S'.

[1] 'From reverence for the Rishis,' lit. 'from the venerableness of the Rishis.'

[2] 'Where are we, (and) where a person brought up with fawns out of sight of love? O friend! let not a word uttered heedlessly in jest be taken in earnest.' *Kva-dvayam atyantāsambhāvanāyām*, 'two *kva*'s are expressive of excessive incompatibility,' S'. (see p. 14, n. 1). *Nāgarikāraṇya-janayoḥ sambandho nopapadyate iti bhāvaḥ*, 'the meaning is that a connection between a town-bred person and a forester is not possible,' K. *Paroksha-manmatha=apratyaksha-manmatha* or *ajñāta-manmatha* or *agoćara-kāma*, 'one who has had no perception or experience of love,' 'one who is out of the reach of its influence.' *Parihāsa-vijalpita=hāsya-bhāshita*, K.;=*kautuka-bhāshita*, S'.; cf. *parihāsa-vijalpa* in Act VI. The Beng. MSS. read *vikalpita*, 'invented.' *Paramārthena =tattvena*.

Verse 52. VAITĀLĪYA, containing twenty-one syllables to the half-verse, each half-verse being alike, the first and third quarter-verses ending at the tenth syllable.

ᵕᵕ‒ᵕᵕᵕ‒ᵕ‒ᵕ‒ ‖ ᵕᵕ‒‒ᵕᵕ‒ᵕ‒ᵕ‒

|| अथ तृतीयाङ्कादौ विष्कम्भः ||

|| ततः प्रविशति कुशानादाय यज्ञमानशिष्यः ||

शिष्यः ।

अहो महाप्रभावो राजा दुष्यन्तः । येन प्रविष्टमात्र एवा-
श्रमं तत्रभवति निरुपप्लवानि नः कर्माणि संवृत्तानि ।
का कथा वाणसन्धाने ज्याशब्देनैव दूरतः ।
हुङ्कारेणैव धनुषः स हि विघ्नानपोहति ॥५३॥

---

[1] 'A pupil of the sacrificing-(Brāhman) bearing Kuśa grass.' *Yaja-
māna*=*yajvan*, 'a sacrificer,' 'priest' (see Raghu-vaṃśa xviii. 11). In
Telugu it has acquired the sense of 'master.' Cf. *tataḥ praviśato Bharata-
śishyau*, Vikram., Act III. Some read *yajamānaḥ śishyaḥ*. The transla-
tion would then be, 'a pupil occupied about a sacrifice.' The pupil, or
religious student, certainly, did not officiate himself. *Śishya*, in fact,
denotes a Brahmacārin, or young Brāhman in that state of pupilage
through which every Brāhman had to pass, living in the house of his
preceptor, who, in return for instruction given, required his assistance
in various menial offices, in collecting materials for sacrifice, and in asking
alms. 'Let the student carry water-pots, flowers, cow-dung, fresh earth,
and Kuśa grass, as much as may be useful to his preceptor; let him bring
wood for the oblation to fire; let him go begging through the whole
district,' &c. (Manu ii. 176, &c.) *Kuśa*, see p. 19, n. 1.

[2] 'Since on his Highness having merely entered the hermitage, our rites
have become free from molestation.' So read the oldest MSS. supported
by K.; others *pravishṭa evāśramaṃ tatra-bharati*, &c.

[3] 'What mention of fitting the arrow (to the bow)? for by the mere
sound of the bow-string from afar, as if by the roar of the bow, he dispels
the obstacles.' *Kā kathā*, 'what account?' i. e. what necessity for fitting

---

Verse 53. ŚLOKA or ANUSHTUBH. See verses 5, 6, 11, 12, 26, 47, 50, 51.

यावदिमान्वेदिसंस्तरणार्थे दर्भानृत्विग्भ्य[1] उपहरामि[2] ।
॥ परिक्रम्यावलोक्य च । आकाशे[3] ॥ प्रियंवदे । कस्येदमुशीरानुलेपनं
मृणालवन्ति च नलिनीपत्त्राणि[4] नीयन्ते । ॥ श्रुतिमभिनीय ॥
किं ब्रवीषि । आतपलङ्घनादलवदस्वस्था शकुन्तला ।

---

the arrow? the expulsion of the demons who impede our rites is effected
by the mere twanging of the bow, without the use of the arrow (*śara-san-
dhānam antareṇa*, S'.), in the same manner as a threatening roar often
suffices to scare those who hear it. Cf. *pratiśabdo hi harer hinasti nāgān*,
Vikram., Act I. *Hunkāra* is the roar of any fierce animal. The use of *iva*
shews that the figure by which the sound of the bow is thus designated is
Utprekshā, see Indian Wisdom, p. 454. So Bhaṭṭi-k. (x. 44), in giving
an example of this figure, describes a mountain as stretching out, as it
were, a huge *body* between heaven and earth to protect the land from the
inroads of the sea.

[1] 'For strewing on the altar,' or 'on the ground near it,' see p. 19, n. 1.

[2] *Ṛitvij*, 'a priest,' especially 'an officiating priest,' lit. 'one who
sacrifices at the prescribed time,' from *ritu*, 'a season,' and *ij=yaj*, 'to
sacrifice.' *An-ritviy yajñam na gaććhet*, 'one ought not to go to (perform) a
sacrifice unattended by an officiating Brāhman.' See Manu iv. 57, ii. 143.

[3] 'In the air,' i. e. speaking in the air. This is an example of *ākāśa-
bhāshitam* or *ākāśa-vākyam*, which is defined by S'. to be *dūra-stha-
bhāshaṇam*, 'speech at a distance,' or *aśarīram nivedanam*, 'bodiless
statement;' and by K. as *apravishṭaiḥ saha ālāpaḥ*, 'conversation with
(characters) not on the stage.' It is, in fact, a speech addressed to some
person outside or off the stage, the actor at the same time fixing his eyes
in the air, or on some object only visible to himself. Hence in K. *ākāśe*
is followed by the words *laksham* or *lakshyam baddhvā*, 'fixing his gaze.'
Cf. *ākāśa-baddha-lakshaḥ*, Vikram., Act IV; Mudrā-r. p. 6, l. 19; p. 31,
l. 3. The answer which is supposed to be given is also *ākāśa-bhāshitam*,
and is not heard by the audience. The actor on the stage pretending to
listen (*śrutim abhinīya*) repeats the imaginary reply, always introducing
it with the words *kim bravīshi*, Sāhit.-d. p. 177.

[4] 'For whom are brought this Uśīra-ointment and lotus-leaves, with
fibres attached?' *Uśīra=vīraṇa-kanda*, 'the root of Vīraṇa,' a fragrant
grass (Andropogon Muricatum) with which a cooling ointment was made.
Mṛiṇāla=visa, 'the fibres of the stalk of the lotus.'

तस्याः शरीरनिर्वापंणायेति । प्रियंवदे यत्नादुपचर्यताम् ।
सा हि तत्रभवतः कुलपतेरुच्छ्वसितम् । अहमपि तावद्वै-
तानिकं शान्त्युदकमस्यै गौतमीहस्ते विसर्जयिष्यामि ।

॥ इति निष्क्रान्तः ॥

॥ विष्कम्भः ॥

---

[1] 'S'akuntalā is excessively indisposed, from injury inflicted by the heat [from a sun-stroke]; is it for the cooling of her body that you say (they are brought)?' *Langhanāt=āghātāt,* K. *;=abhibhavāt,* S. *;= paribhavāt,* C. Root *langh* means 'to leap over,' 'overstep,' 'transgress,' 'to inflict an injury,' 'insult.' *Nirvāpaṇa,* 'a refrigerant remedy,' from the causal of *nir-vā,* 'to refresh,' 'cool;' cf. *nirvāpayitā,* ver. 65.

[2] 'Let her be nursed with care; for she is the (very) breath of his reverence (Kaṇva), the head of (our) society. I also will just deliver into the hands of Gautamī for her the soothing water consecrated in the sacrifice.' *Upačar,* 'to attend on a patient,' 'administer remedies,' &c. *Ūčhvasitam=prāṇāḥ,* 'breath ;'=*jīvanam,* 'life,' i. e. as precious as his own life. Cf. Lam. iv. 20, 'The breath of our nostrils, the anointed of the Lord, was taken,' &c. ; also Kumāra-s. vii. 4. *Vaitānika=vitānākhya-yāya-sambandhin,* 'belonging to the sacrifice called *vitāna,*' 'sacred,' 'holy.' See Indian Wisdom, p. 197. *Vitāna* is also 'the sacrificial hearth on which the sacred fire was kept.' The *sānty-udaka* may have been a kind of holy water, like the 'eau bénite' of the Roman Catholics. *Gautamī,* the name of the sister of Kaṇva, K.

[3] The Vishkambha or Vishkambhaka, according to the Sāhitya-darpaṇa and Kātavema's commentary on the opening speech of Act II. of this play, is an introductory monologue or dialogue, so called from its concisely compressing (*vi-shkambh*) into a short space an account of those subordinate parts of the plot not enacted before the audience, a knowledge of which is essential to the comprehending of the action of the remainder of the play (*vritta-vartishyamānānāṃ kathāṃsānāṃ nidarśakaḥ, sankship-tārthas tu vishkambhaḥ,* Sāhit-d. p. 146; see also p. 62, n. 2 of this play). The Vishkambha may occur at the beginning of any of the Acts, even of the First, immediately after the Prastāvanā (*ādāv aṅkasya darśitaḥ*). It may be spoken by two out of the three sets of characters into which the dramatis personæ of an Indian play are divided, viz. the inferior (*nīča*), who speak Prākrit *anudāttoktyā,* 'in the low tone;' and the middling

O

॥ अथ तृतीयोऽङ्कः ॥

॥ ततः प्रविशति समदनावस्थो राजा ॥

राजा ॥ सचिन्तं निःश्वस्य ॥

जाने तपसो वीर्यं सा बाला परवतीति मे विदितम्।
न च निम्नादिव सलिलं निवर्तते मे ततो हृदयम् ॥५४॥

(*madhya, madhyama*), who speak Sanskrit *udāttoktyā*, 'in the high tone;' but not by the chief (*pradhāna*), such as the hero, &c. Again, it may be spoken by one character in the form of a soliloquy, or by two in the form of a dialogue; and either by characters of the middle class only, when it is called *śuddha*, 'pure;' or by those of the middle and lower combined, when it is called *miśra* or *sankīrṇa*, 'mixed' (*madhyena madhyamā-bhyāṃ vā pātrābhyāṃ samprayojitaḥ śuddhaḥ syāt tu sankīrṇo nīca-madhyama-kalpitaḥ*). Sometimes the characters are exclusively those of the inferior class, who speak Prākṛit; sometimes more than two appear on the stage at once, in which cases it is properly called Praveśaka, though these terms are regarded as identical by the MSS. and commentators (*vishkambha eva suryaktaiḥ praveśaka iti smṛitaḥ*, K.; *prave-śaka eva vishkambhakaḥ*, S'.) The Sāhit.-d. restricts the former title still further by applying it to an interlude only (*praveśako 'nudāttoktyā nīca-pātra-prayojitaḥ, anka-dvayāntar vijñeyaḥ śeshaṃ vishkambhake yathā*). In Vikram., Act V, the opening soliloquy is styled Praveśaka both in the MSS. and in the Calcutta edition. According to the Sāhit-d. the present monologue is a S'uddha-vishkambha. In the Beng. MSS. it is termed a Praveśaka.

¹ 'I know the potency of penance; it is (also) known to me that that maiden is subject to another [is in a state of tutelage]. But as water does not turn back from the valley, (neither) does my heart from that (S'akuntalā);' i.e. I know that if I attempt to carry her off by force or by stealth, the power acquired by penance is such, that the Ṛishi will effect my destruction by a curse, &c. (*śāpādinā nāśaṃ vidhāsyati*, S'.) *Nimnād*,

---

Verse 54. ĀRYĀ or GĀTHĀ. See verse 2.

$$- - \mid \smile \smile - \mid - - \mid\mid - - \mid - \smile \smile \mid \smile - \smile \mid - \smile \smile \mid -$$
$$\smile \smile - \mid - \smile \smile \mid \smile \smile - \mid\mid \smile - \smile \mid - - \mid \smile \smile \mid - \smile \smile \mid -$$

भगवन्कुसुमायुध । त्वया चन्द्रमसा च विश्वसनीयाभ्याम-
तिसन्धीयते कामिजनसार्थः । कुतः ।

तव कुसुमशरत्वं शीतरश्मित्वमिन्दो-
र्द्वयमिदमयथार्थं दृश्यते मद्विधेषु ।
विसृजति हिमगर्भैरग्निमिन्दुर्मयूखै-
स्त्वमपि कुसुमवाणान्वज्रसारीकरोषि ॥ ५५ ॥

---

scil. *desāt*, 'from low land,' see Hitop. 1. 2651. The Deva-n. MSS., un-
supported by the commentators, substitute the following for the second
line of the above verse, *Alam asmi tato hṛidayaṃ tathāpi nedaṃ nivartu-
yitum*, 'nevertheless, I am not able to turn back this heart from that
(damsel).'

[1] 'O divine flower-armed (god), by thee and by the moon, who (seem)
to be worthy of confidence, the whole company of lovers is deceived.
Why so? [because] of thee, (there is said to be) the property of having
flowers for arrows, of the moon the property of having cold beams;
both these (properties) are observed to be untrue in such as me; (for)
the moon emits fire with rays charged with cold; thou also makest (thy)
flower-arrows hard as adamant.' The Hindū Cupid or Kāma-deva, 'god
of love,' is the son of Vishṇu or Krishṇa by Lakshmī, who is then called
Māyā or Rukmiṇī. He is armed with a bow made of sugar-cane, the
string consisting of bees, and with five flower-tipped arrows (whence his
name Panća-vāṇa) which pierce the heart through the five senses. The
names of the five arrows (according to Bharata, cited by S'.) are—1.
Harshaṇa, 'Gladdener;' 2. *Prahasana*, 'Exhilarator;' 3. *Mohana*,
'Fascinator;' 4. *Mūrćhana*, 'Sense-destroyer;' 5. *Vikarshaṇa*, 'Distractor.'
According to K. the names of the five flowers which point these arrows,
and may be supposed to possess properties similar to those implied in the
names of the arrows themselves, are—1. *Aravinda*, a kind of lotus;
2. *Aśoka*; 3. *Śirīsha*; 4. *Ćūta* or *Amra*, i. e. the mango; 5. *Utpala* or
blue lotus. But according to Sir W. Jones [Hymn to Kāma-deva] they
are—1. *Ćampaka*; 2. *Ćūta* or *Āmra*; 3. *Keśara* or *Nāga-keśara*; 4.
Ketaka; 5. *Vilva* or *Bilva*. In both lists the Ćūta occurs. This is
certainly the favourite flower of the god (cf. the frequent allusions to it

---

Verse 55. MĀLINĪ or MĀNINĪ (a variety of ATI-ŚAKVARĪ). See verses 10, 19, 20, 38.

भगवन्कामदेव। न ते मय्यनुक्रोशः। ॥ मदनबाधां निरूप्य ॥ कुतस्ते
कुसुमायुधस्य सततस्तैक्ष्ण्यमेतत्। आं ज्ञातम्।

अद्यापि नूनं हरकोपवह्नि-
स्त्वयि ज्वलत्यौर्व इवाम्बुराशौ।
त्वमन्यथा मन्मथ मद्विधानां
भस्मावशेषः कथमित्थमुष्णः ॥५६॥

---

in Gīta-g. iii. 12, iv. 6, &c.); but in verse 135 the epithet *pañćābhyadhika*
is applied to this flower, and is explained by S'. to mean 'a sixth arrow,
in addition to the five' (cf. Vikram., Act II, *kimuta upavana-sahakāraiḥ*,
&c.) It is clear that some authorities do not include the mango in the list.
The Gīta-g. (x. 14) mentions five other flowers as occasionally employed
by the god, viz. the *bandhūka, madhūka, nīla-nalina* or blue lotus, *tila*, and
kuṇḍa. Another account includes the Mallikā or jasmine amongst the
five. In Hindū erotic poetry, cooling properties are attributed to the
rays of the moon, said to distil nectar; hence some of his names—*śīta-
mayūkha, hima-raśmi, hima-kara, amṛita-sū, sudhā-nidhi*, &c. On the
other hand, the heating effect of these rays on the lover is often alluded
to, e. g. *śitānśus tapanaḥ*, Gīta-g. ix. 10, iv. 7, v. 3; cf. *nandana-vana-
vātāḥ śikhina iva* (Vikram., Act II), and *pādās te śaśinaḥ sukhayanti*,
&c. (end of Act III). *Sārtha* = *samūha*, properly 'a caravan,' Hitop.
l. 2574. *Kutaḥ*, p. 55, n. 2. *A-yathārtham* = *viparīta-kriyam*, 'having
a contrary effect.' *Dvayam*, see p. 91, n. 2. *Garbhaiḥ*, see p. 18, l. 5.
Vajrasārī-karoshi, see p. 14, l. 2.

[1] 'Verily, e'en now the fire of S'iva's wrath burns in thee like the sub-
marine fire in the ocean; otherwise how couldst thou, O agitator of the
soul, with nothing left but ashes, be so scorching towards such as me?'
The story of the incineration of Kāma-deva by a beam of fire darted
from the central eye of S'iva is thus told in the Rāmāyaṇa (i. 25, 10):
'Kandarpa, whom the wise call Kāma (Cupid), had formerly a body.
He once approached S'iva, the husband of Umā (Parvatī), soon after his
marriage, that he might influence him with love for his wife. S'iva

---

Verse 56. UPAJĀTI or AKHYĀNAKĪ (a variety of TRISHṬUBH), each Pāda or
quarter-verse being either *Indra-vajrā* or *Upendra-vajrā*, the former only differing
from the latter in the length of the first syllable. See verse 41.

अथवा ।
अनिशमपि मकरकेतुर्मनसोरुजमावहन्नभिमतो मे ।
यदि मदिरायतनयनां तामधिकृत्य प्रहरंतीति ॥ ५७ ॥

---

happened then to be practising austerities, and intent on a vow of chastity.
He therefore cursed the god of love in a terrible voice, and at the same
time a flash from his terrific eye caused all the limbs of his body to
shrivel into ashes. Thus Kāma was made incorporeal [whence, as some
say, is his power over the minds of men] by the anger of the great god,
and from that time has been called "the bodiless one" (*An-anga*).' *Aurva*,
'submarine fire,' called *baḍava* or *bāḍava*, and personified as the son of the
saint Urva. The fable is told in Hari-v. (ch. xlv), and is noticed in
Troyer's Rāja-taraṅgiṇī (iii. 170). The Rishi Urva, who had gained
great power by his austerities, was pressed by the gods and others to
beget children that he might perpetuate his race. He consented, but
warned them that his offspring would consume the world. Accordingly,
he created from his thigh a devouring fire, which, when produced,
demanded nourishment, and would have destroyed the whole earth, had
not Brahmā appeared and assigned the ocean as its habitation, and the
waves as its food. The spot where it entered the sea was called *Baḍavā-
mukha*, 'the mare's mouth.' Doubtless the story was invented to suit
the phenomenon of a marine *jvālā-mukhī* or 'volcano,' which exhaled
bituminous inflammable gas, and which occasionally shewed itself above
the sea, perhaps in the form of a horse's mouth. Langlois places the
position of it on the coast north of Malabar.

¹ 'Nevertheless, the fish-bannered (god), even though incessantly bring-
ing mental anguish, (will be) acceptable to me, if employing (as the
subject about which he inflicts pain) that (maiden) with long intoxicating
eyes he so strike (me).' *Makara-ketu*, a name of Kāma-deva, is derived
from the *makara*, or marine monster, subdued by him, which was painted
on his banner (*ketu*). 'By the mention of this title, his invincibleness is
indicated,' S'. *Adhikritya*=*uddiśya*, 'with reference to,' S'. and Ć. ; see
p. 6, n. 2, and p. 77, n. 1; also Raghu-v. xi. 62, *śāntim adhikritya
anvayunkta.*

Verse 57. ĀRYĀ or GĀTHĀ. See verse 2.

भगवन्कन्दर्प । एवमुपालब्धस्य ते न मां प्रत्यनुक्रोशः ।

वृथैव सङ्कल्पशतैरजस्र-

मनङ्ग नीतोऽसि मया विवृद्धिम् ।

आकृष्य चापं श्रवणोपकण्ठे

मय्येव युक्तस्तव वाणमोक्षः ॥५८॥

।। सखेदं परिक्रम्य ।। क्व नु खलु संस्थिते कर्मणि सदस्यैरनुज्ञातः श्रमक्लान्तमात्मानं विनोदयामि । ।। निःश्वस्य ।। किं नु खलु मे प्रियादर्शनादृते शरणमन्यत् । यावदेनामन्विष्यामि । ।। सूर्यमवलोक्य ।। इमामुप्रातपां वेलां प्रायेण लतावलयवत्सु मालिनीतीरेषु ससखीजना शकुन्तला गमयति । तच्चैव

---

[1] ‘In vain, truly, O bodiless (god), hast thou perpetually been brought by me to growth by hundreds of desires. Is it becoming of you, drawing your bow to your very ear, (to) discharge (your) arrows even upon me (your votary) ?’ *Sankalpa = iććhā*, ‘wish.’ *Śravaṇopakaṇṭhe ākṛishya = karṇāntikam ānīya*, ‘drawing the string of the bow back as far as the ear.’ *Upakaṇṭha*, ‘near,’ lit. ‘near the neck ;’ cf. Raghu-v. ix. 57, *ākarṇa-kṛishṭaṃ vāṇam*. *Yukta = ućita*. The passage from *Bhagavan Kāmadeva* (p. 100) to *vāṇamokshaḥ* is given on the authority of the Taylor and my own Bombay Deva-n. MS., supported by S'. and Ć. and all the Beng. MSS. The Mackenzie MS. has part of the passage, but Colebrooke’s omits it altogether.

[2] ‘Where, indeed, at the conclusion of the rite being permitted to depart by those who were present at the sacrifice, shall I refresh myself weary with fatigue ?’ *Sadasya*, ‘any assistant or by-stander at a sacrifice.’ The Beng. have *nirasta-vighnais tapasvibhiḥ*, ‘by the hermits whose obstacles have been removed.’

[3] ‘S'akuntalā along with her female friends is passing [lit. causing to go] this intensely hot time of the day probably on the banks of the Mālinī, possessed of inclosures of creepers.’ *Valaya*, properly ‘an encircling hedge ;’ here it may mean ‘a bower.’

Verse 58. UPAJĀTI or ĀKHYĀNAKĪ (a variety of TRISHṬUBH). See verses 41, 56.

तावद्गच्छामि । ॥ परिक्रम्यावलोक्य च ॥ अनया बालपादप-
वीथ्या सुतनुरचिरं गतेति तर्कयामि । कुतः ।
सम्मीलन्ति न तावद्बन्धनकोषास्त्वयावचितपुष्पाः ।
क्षीरस्निग्धाश्चामी दृश्यन्ते किशलयंच्छेदाः ॥५९॥

॥ स्पर्शं रूपयित्वा ॥ अहो प्रवातसुभगोऽयमुद्देशः[2] ।
शक्यमरविन्दसुरभिः कणवाही मालिनीतरङ्गाणाम् ।
अङ्गैरनङ्गतप्तैरविरलमालिङ्गितुं पवनः ॥६०॥

---

[1] 'I conjecture that the very delicate one has not long since passed by
this avenue of young trees, because the cavities of the flower-stalks whose
flowers have been plucked off by her, do not yet close up, and these
fragments of tender-shoots are seen (still) unctuous with milky-juice.'
Vīthi=pankti. Sammīlanti=sankućanti, 'contract.' *Bandhana=pra-
sava-bandhana=vrinta,* 'a flower-stalk,' S'. *Bandhana-koshās=vrintā-
bhyantarāni,* S'.;*=vrinta-garbhāni,* C. *Amī,* 'these,' i. e. *puro-vartinah,*
'lying in front of us.' *Kisalaya-ććhedāh = pallava-khandāh. Kshīra-
snigdhāh=dugdha-ćikkanāh.* When a stalk has been some time broken
off, it contracts and the milk dries up. 'The duty of gathering flowers
and cutting stalks for sacrificial purposes might have been entrusted by
the hermits to S'akuntalā; hence it would be inferred that she had
passed that way. This is an example of the Anumāna Alan-kāra,' S'. and
C. Some of the Deva-n. MSS. omit the above couplet.

[2] 'Oh! how delightful is this spot by (reason of) the fresh breeze!'
Aho, an exclamation implying approbation (*prasansāyām*), S'. *Pra-
vāta = prakrishta-vāta,* K.; = *prasasta-vāta,* 'a good breeze,' S'. (see
p. 37, n. 1).

[3] 'The breeze, fragrant with the lotuses (and) wafting the spray
[particles] of the waves of the Mālini, is able to be closely embraced by

---

Verse 59. ĀRYĀ or GĀTHĀ. See verse 2.

```
⏑ ⏑ | ⏑ ⏑ ⏑ | ⏑ ⏑ ‖ ⏑ ⏑ ⏑ | ⏑ ⏑ | ⏑ ⏑ ⏑ | ⏑ ⏑ ⏑ | ⏑
⏑ ⏑ | ⏑ ⏑ | ⏑ ⏑ ‖ ⏑ ⏑ | ⏑ ⏑ ⏑ | ⏑ | ⏑ ⏑ | ⏑
```

Verse 60. ĀRYĀ or GĀTHĀ. See verse 2.

```
⏑ ⏑ ⏑ | ⏑ ⏑ ⏑ | ⏑ ⏑ ⏑ ‖ ⏑ ⏑ ⏑ | ⏑ ⏑ | ⏑ ⏑ ⏑ | ⏑ ⏑ | ⏑
⏑ ⏑ | ⏑ ⏑ ⏑ | ⏑ ⏑ ‖ ⏑ ⏑ ⏑ ⏑ | ⏑ ⏑ | ⏑ | ⏑ ⏑ ⏑ | ⏑
```

॥ परिक्रम्यावलोक्य च ॥ अस्मिन्नेतसपरिक्षिप्ते लतामण्डपे सन्नि-
हितया तया भवितव्यम् । तथा हि । ॥ अधो विलोक्य ॥

अभ्युन्नता पुरस्तादवगाढा जघनगौरवात्पश्चात् ।
द्वारेऽस्य पाण्डुसिकते पदपङ्क्तिर्दृश्यतेऽभिनवा ॥ ६१ ॥
यावद्वटपान्तरेणावलोकयामि । ॥ परिक्रम्य । तथा कृत्वा । सहर्षम् ॥
अये लब्धं नेत्रनिर्वाणम् । एषा मे मनोरथप्रियतमा

(my) limbs inflamed by the bodiless one.' *Śakya* (like *yogya* and some-
times *yukta*) gives a passive sense to the infinitive. The Beng. MSS. and
the Calcutta ed. read *śakyo* in the nom. case agreeing with *pavanaḥ*,
which would appear at first sight to be the better reading. But K.
expressly states that *śakyam* is here used adverbially, and quotes a
parallel passage from Rāmāyaṇa, *śakyam añjalibhiḥ pātum vātāḥ*, 'the
breezes are able to be drunk by the hollowed palms.' A passage may be
added from the Hitop., *vibhūtayaḥ śakyam avāptum*, 'great successes are
able to be obtained;' and another from Mālavik. verse 58, *na śakyam
upekshitum kupitā* (see also Maha-bh. i. 769). *Aravinda*, a kind of
lotus, see p. 25, n. 1. *Kaṇa-vāhin=śīkara-vāhaka*, 'wafting cool spray,'
S'. *An-aṅga*, 'the bodiless god,' see p. 100, n. 1. *A-virala*, lit. 'having
no interstices,' 'close.' The Beng. read *nirdayam=dṛiḍham*.

[1] 'At the entrance of it where-there-is-white-sand, a fresh line of foot-
steps is seen, raised in front, depressed behind through the weight of her
hips.' *Avagāḍhā=nimnā*. *Pāṇḍu-sikate* (=*dhavala-bāluke*) is a Bahu-
vrīhi comp. agreeing with *dvāre*. The weight of the hips of a beautiful
female is a favourite subject of allusion (cf. *paścād-natā guru-nitam-
batayā asyāḥ pada-panktiḥ*, Vikram., Act IV; *śroṇī-bhārād alasa-
gamanā*, Megha-d. 81). Hence one of the names of a lovely woman is
nitambinī, 'having large and handsome hips and loins.' Compare the
epithet 'Callipyge' applied to a celebrated statue of Venus.

[2] 'Through the branches.' The Calcutta ed. has *viṭapāntarito*, 'con-
cealed by the branches.'

[3] 'The highest object of my eye-sight,' 'the full bliss of my eyes' (=*netrā-*

Verse 61. ĀRYĀ or GĀTHĀ. See verse 2.

$$- - \mid \cup - \cup \mid - - \parallel \cup \cup - \mid - \cup \cup \mid \cup - \cup \mid - - \mid -$$
$$- - \mid \cup - \cup \mid \cup \cup - \parallel \cup \cup - \mid - - \mid \cup \mid - \cup \cup \mid -$$

सकुसुमास्तरणं शिलापट्टमधिशयाना सखीभ्यामन्वास्यते।
भवतु। श्रोष्याम्यासां विश्रम्भकथितानि। ॥ इति विलोकयन्निस्थितः॥

॥ ततः प्रविशति यथोक्तव्यापारा सह सखीभ्यां शकुन्तला॥

॥ सख्यावुपवीजयतः॥

सख्यौ ॥ उपवीज्य। सन्देहम्॥

ᵃ हला सउन्दले। अबि सुहाअदि दे णलिणीपत्तवादो।

शकुन्तला।

ᵇ किं वीजन्ति मं सहीओ।

॥ सख्यौ विषादं नाटयित्वा परस्परमवलोकयतः॥

राजा।

बलवदस्वस्थशरीरा शकुन्तला दृश्यते। ॥ सवितर्कम्॥ तत्कि-
मयमातपदोषः स्यात्। उत यथा मे मनसि वर्तते।
॥ साभिलाषं निर्वर्ण्य॥ अथवा कृतं सन्देहेन।

ᵃ हला शकुन्तले। अपि सुखायते ते नलिनीपत्त्रवातः।   ᵇ किं वीजयतो
मां सख्यौ।

---

nanda, K.; nayana-nirvṛiti, ćakshuḥ-sukha, S.) *Nirvāṇa* or *apavarga*
is properly 'final beatitude, consisting in emancipation from further
transmigration.'

[1] 'Yonder the best-beloved object of my wishes, reclining on a stone-
seat strewed with flowers, is attended by her two friends.' *Manoratha-
priyatamā*, 'most dear by desire,' i.e. not by actual possession or by any
other method, K. *Śilā-paṭṭa=pāshāna-khaṇḍa*, see p. 76, n. 2. *Anvās*,
'to sit near' (*anu, ās*).

[2] 'Are in the act of fanning her.' *Upa-vīj*, 'to fan;' cf. *vy-ajana*, 'a fan.'

[3] 'Is this wind from the (fan of) lotus-leaves agreeable to thee?' see p. 25,
n. 1, in the middle. *Api*, see p. 89, n. 2. Some Deva-n. MSS. read *suhaadi*
for *sukhayati*, but the above is supported by K. and the oldest MSS.

[4] 'Can this be the fault of the heat? or, as is passing in my mind (is it
owing to love)?' i.e. or is love, as I conjecture, the true cause?

[5] *Kṛitaṃ sandehena*, see p. 30, l. 6, with note.

स्तनन्यस्तोशीरं प्रशिथिलमृणालैकवलयं
प्रियायाः साबाधं तदपि कमनीयं वपुरिदम् ।
समस्तापः कामं मनसिजनिदाघप्रसरयो-
र्न तु ग्रीष्मस्यैवं सुभगमपराद्धं युवतिषु ॥६२॥

प्रियंवदा ॥ जनान्तिकम् ॥

[a] अणसूए । तस्स राएसिणो पढमदंसणादो आरहिअ
पज्जुस्सुआ विअ सउन्दला । किं णुक्खु से तण्णिमित्तो
अअं आतङ्को भवे ।

[a] अनसूये । तस्य राजर्षेः प्रथमदर्शनादारभ्य पर्युत्सुकेय शकुन्तला । किं नु खल्-
स्यास्तन्निमित्तोऽयमातङ्को भवेत् ।

---

[1] 'This form of my beloved, having the Uśīra applied to the bosom, and having only one armlet (and that formed) of lotus-fibres hanging-loose, (is certainly) disordered, but even so is lovely. Granted that the heat of the two influences of love and the hot season [or the heat induced by the prevalence either of love or of the sultry weather] be equal, still disorder is not inflicted on maidens by the hot weather in such a charming manner,' i. e. since the disorder apparent in the person of S'akuntalā only contributes to her beauty, it is clearly not caused by the hot weather, but by love. *Uśīra*, see p. 96, n. 4. Two other names for this plant are *jalāśaya*, 'growing in water,' and *avadāha*, 'allaying fever;' the slender fibres of it are now known by the name of Khaskhas, and are used in India in trellises for cooling the air. *Praśithila*=*adṛidha*, S'.;=*komala*, 'withered,' C'. 'Her body was so enfeebled that she could not bear the weight of two armlets or bracelets; she therefore had only one, and that made, not of gold, but of lotus-fibres (*mṛiṇāla-ghaṭita*) tied loosely round the arm,' S'. *Sābādha*=*sa-pīḍa*, C'.;=*sa-vyadha*, K. 'diseased,' 'deranged.' *Tadapi*, 'even so;' even in this manner or under these disadvantages; *tad* is here used adverbially. This reading is supported by the oldest MSS. and by K.; but some of the Deva-n. have *kimapi ramaṇīyam*, 'somewhat pleasing.' *Kāmam*, see p. 55, n. 3. *Prasarayoḥ*, lit. 'of the two prevalences;' *prasara*=*prasaṅga*, 'attachment,' 'connection,' S'.; but the simple meaning is 'spreading,' 'prevalence.'

[2] *Tan-nimitta*, 'resulting from it,' i. e. arising from love.

Verse 62. Śikhariṇī (a variety of Atyashṭi). See verses 9, 24, 44.

अनसूया ।

[a] सहि । ममवि ईदिसी आसङ्का हिञ्अञ्अस्स । होदु ।
पुच्छिस्सं दाव एं । ॥ प्रकाशम् ॥ [b] सहि । पुच्छिदव्वासि किम्पि ।
बलिञंक्खु दे सन्दाबो ।

शकुन्तला ॥ पूर्वार्धेन शयनादुत्थाय ॥

[c] हला । किं वत्तुकामासि ।

अनसूया ।

[d] हला सउन्दले । अणब्भन्तरा खु अम्हे मदणगदस्स
वुत्तन्तस्स । किन्दु । जादिसी इदिहासणिबन्धेसु कामञ्अमा-
णाणं अवत्था सुणीअदि । तादिसिं दे पेक्खामि । कहेहि ।
किस्सिमित्तं दे सन्दाबो । विञ्आरंक्खु परमत्थदो अजाणिञ्अ
अणारम्भो पडिञ्आरस्स ।

राजा ।

अनसूययापि मदीयस्तर्कोऽवगतः ।

<hr>

[a] सखि । ममापीदृश्याशङ्का हृदयस्य । भवतु । प्रक्ष्यामि तावदेनाम् ।   [b] सखि ।
प्रष्यसि किमपि । बलीयान्खलु ते सन्तापः ।   [c] हला । किं वत्तुकामासि ।
[d] हला शकुन्तले । अनभ्यन्तरे खल्वावां मदनगतस्य वृत्तान्तस्य । किन्तु । यादृशीति-
हासनिबन्धेषु कामयमानानामवस्था श्रूयते । तादृशीं ते प्रेक्षे । कथय । किन्निमित्तं ते
सन्तापः । विकारं खलु परमार्थतोऽज्ञात्वानारम्भः प्रतिकारस्य ।

<hr>

[1] 'We are not indeed intimately conversant with matters relating to
love; but as the condition of lovers is heard of (by us) in legendary tales,
of such a kind I perceive is thy (condition). Say, from what cause (is)
thy disorder? (for) indeed without being accurately acquainted with the
disease, (there) can be no application of the remedy.' *An-abhyantare*,
nom. du. fem. of a Bahuvrīhi or compound adjective formed from the
substantive *abhyantara*, 'interior,' 'inside,' by prefixing the privative *an*,
in the same manner as in *an-antara*, 'uninterrupted.' *An-abhyantara*,
lit. 'one not admitted to the inside.' Cf. *gaṇābhyantara*, 'one who is a
member of a religious association.' *Madana-gatasya*, see p. 38, n. 1.
Itihāsa=purā-vritta, S. *Ni-bandha*, 'a composition,' 'narrative.'

शकुन्तला ॥ आत्मगतम् ॥

[a] बलिअंखु मे अहिणिवेसो दाणिंपि । सहसा एदाएं
ण सक्कणेमि णिवेदिदुं ।

प्रियंवदा ।

[b] सहि सउन्दले । सुट्टु एसा भणादि । किं अत्तणो आतङ्कं
उबेक्खसि । अणुदिअहंक्खु परिहीअसि अङ्गेहिं । केवलं
लावण्णमई छाआ तुमं ण मुञ्चदि ।

राजा ।

अवितथमाह प्रियंवदा । तथा हि

क्षामक्षामकपोलमाननमुरः काठिन्यमुक्तस्तनं
मध्यः क्लान्ततरः प्रकामविनतावंसौ छविः पाण्डुरा ।
शोच्या च प्रियदर्शना च मदनक्लिष्टेयमालक्ष्यते
पत्त्राणामिव शोषणेन महता स्पृष्टा लता माधवी ॥६३॥

[a] बलीयान्खलु मेऽभिनिवेश इदानीमपि । सहसैतयोर्न शक्नोमि निवेदितुम् ।
[b] सखि शकुन्तले । सुष्ठ्वेषा भणति । किमात्मन आतङ्कमुपेक्षसे । अनुदिवसं खलु परि-
हीयसेऽङ्गैः । केवलं लावण्यमयी छाया त्वां न मुञ्चति ।

---

[1] 'My attachment [affection] even now is strong.' *Abhi-niveśa* implies
'firm attachment to' or 'intense pursuit of' any object (here = *abhilāsha*).

[2] 'Thy limbs are wasting away [lit. thou art abandoned by thy limbs].
Thy lovely complexion alone deserts thee not.'

[3] 'For, indeed, her face has its cheeks excessively emaciated, her bosom
has its breasts destitute of firmness, her waist is more slender, her shoulders
are quite drooping, her complexion is pale; she being tormented by love
appears both deplorable and (yet) lovely, like a Mādhavī-creeper touched
by the wind, the scorcher of (its) leaves.' *Kshāma-kshāma-kapola* =
atikriśa-gaṇḍa, S. The repetition of *kshāma* may imply 'becoming
gradually every day more and more emaciated,' as Priyaṃvadā had said
anu-divasam parihīyase aṅgaiḥ. Kāṭhinya-mukta, the Beng. have *yukta*,

Verse 63. ŚĀRDŪLA-VIKRĪDITA (a variety of ATIDHRITI). See verses 14, 30, 36,
39, 40.

शकुन्तला ।

[a]सहि । कस्स वा अखस्स कहइस्सं । किन्दु आआसइत्तिआ दाणिं वो भविस्सं ।

उभे ।

[b]अदो एव्वक्खु णिब्बन्धी । सिणिद्धजणसंविभत्तं हि दुक्खं सज्झवेदणं होदि[2] ।

राजा ।

पृष्टा जनेन समदुःखसुखेन बाला
    नेयं न वक्ष्यति मनोगतमाधिहेतुम् ।
तृष्टो विवृत्य बहुशोऽप्यनया सतृष्ण-
    मचान्तरे श्रवणकातरतां गतोऽस्मि ।।६४।।

[a] सखि । कस्य वान्यस्य कथयिष्यामि । किन्न्वायासयित्रीदानीं वां भविष्यामि ।
[b] अत एव खलु निर्बन्धः । स्निग्धजनसंविभक्तं हि दुःखं सह्यवेदनं भवति ।

---

but the loss of firmness in the breasts would rather be a sign of debility. *Prakāma*=*atyartham*, 'excessively,' S. So the commentator on Gītā-g. iv. 17, vii. 40, explains *nikāmam* by *atiśayena*. Similarly *kāmam* has the sense of *niśćitam*, 'certainly.' May the meaning not be 'stoop of their own accord,' i. e. 'languidly,' 'listlessly,' from their being allowed to fall without any effort being made to raise them? *Śoshaṇena*=*śoshakena*, i. e. by the wind that dries up the leaves and causes them to fall (*pattra-pātaka-vāyunā*), K., S. *Mādhavī*, a large and beautiful creeper bearing white fragrant flowers, constantly alluded to in the plays (see p. 112, n. 3).

[1] 'To whom else shall I relate it (if not to you, my two friends)?' *Yadi kathanīyaṃ tadā bharatībhyām*, S.

[2] 'Our importunity is on this very account. Grief shared with affectionate friends becomes supportable suffering.' *Nir-bandha*, 'urgency,' 'pressing solicitation.'

[3] 'This maiden being questioned by the persons who are the partners of her sorrows and joys, will most certainly declare the cause of her anguish (now) concealed in her breast. Although (I was) looked upon longingly by her repeatedly turning round, I (nevertheless) at the present moment

शकुन्तला ।

[a]सहि । जदो पहुदि मम दंसणपहं आअदो सो तवोवण-रक्खिदा राएसी ।   ॥ इत्यर्धोक्तेन लज्जां नाटयति ॥

उभे ।

[b]कधेदु पिअसही ।

शकुन्तला ।

[c]तदो पहुदि तग्गदेण अहिलासेण एतदवत्यम्हि संवुत्ता ।

राजा   ॥ सहर्षम् ॥

श्रुतं श्रोतव्यम् ।

स्मर एव तापहेतुर्निर्वापयिता स एव मे जात: ।
दिवस इवाभ्रश्यामस्तपात्यये जीवलोकस्य ॥ ६५ ॥

[a] सखि । यत: प्रभृति मम दर्शनपथमागत: स तपोवनरक्षिता राजर्षि: ।   [b] कधयतु प्रियसखी ।   [c] तत: प्रभृति तद्गतेनाभिलाषेणैतदवस्थास्मि संवृत्ता ।

---

experience an uneasy-anxiety for hearing (her reply).' *Jana = sakhī-jana;* though used in sing., it may have a plural signification. *Sama-duḥkha-sukha,* 'one who has the same joys and sorrows' (cf. *sama-duḥkha-sukhaḥ pīyate locanābhyām,* Vikram., Act I). *Bālā,* properly 'a girl sixteen years of age,' S'. *Na na vakshyati = vakshyati eva,* S'.; two negatives give intensity to the affirmative (*dvau nishedhau prakritam artham gamayataḥ,* S'.); see p. 24, n. 2. *Mano-gatam = hridaya-stham,* see p. 38, n. 1. *Atrāntare = asminn avasare,* K. *S'ravana-kātaratām = S'akuntalā-prativacana-śravana-bhīrutām.* According to Bharata the four ways by which a maiden encouraged the advances of her lover were *lekha-prasthāpana,* 'sending a letter;' *snigdha-vīkshita,* 'a loving glance;' *mridu-bhāshita,* 'soft speech ;' and *dūtī-sampreshana,* 'sending a messenger,' S'. Although S'akuntalā had favoured her lover with one of these tokens, yet he was fearful that, when about to reply to her friends, she might through carelessness (*pramādatas*) confess to an affection for some other person, S'.

[1] 'Met my eye,' 'crossed my sight,' lit. 'came across the path [range] of my sight.' Cf. *yasya netrayoḥ pathi sthitā tvam,* Vikram., Act I.

[2] 'Love, indeed, the cause of my fever, has himself become the cooler of

---

Verse 65. ÁRYÁ or GÁTHÁ. See verse 2.

⏑ ⏑ − | ⏑ − ⏑ | − − ‖ − − | ⏑ ⏑ − | ⏑ − ⏑ | − − | −
⏑ ⏑ ⏑ ⏑ | − − | − − ‖ ⏑ − ⏑ | − − | ⏑ − | − − | ⏑

शकुन्तला ।

[a]तं जइ वो अणुमदं । तह वट्टह । जह तस्स राएसिणो अणुकम्पणिज्जा होमि । अह्णा अवसं सिञ्चह मे तिलोदंअं ।

[a] तद्यदि वामनुमतम् । तथा वर्तेथाम् । यथा तस्य राजर्षेरनुकम्प्यनीया भवामि । अन्यथावश्यं सिञ्चतं मे तिलोदकम् ।

---

it; as, on the passing off of the heat, a day dark with clouds (which was at first hot, becomes afterwards the cooler) of living creatures.' This refers to the clouds which rise and disperse at the end of the hot season, making the air fearfully close and stifling; until at last a downpour comes and with it cool weather. *Smara*, 'the ideal one,' is one of the names of Kāma-deva, from *smṛi*, 'to recollect;' see p. 100, n. 1. *Nirvāpayitā*, 'the extinguisher,' 'refresher,' 'cooler' (see p. 97, n. 1);=*sukha-hetuḥ*, 'the cause of pleasure,' S. *Tapātyaye=grīshmānte*, 'at the end of the hot season,' K.; K. and S. quote a parallel passage from the Ratnāvali (p. 64), *tapati prā-vṛishi nitarām abhyarṇa-jalāgamo divasaḥ*, 'in the rainy season when the rain is near at hand the day is especially hot.' Some of the Deva-n. MSS. read *ardha-śyāma*, 'half-obscured,' which is not supported by any of the commentators, nor by the oldest MSS.

[1] 'Then if (it be) approved by you, so act, that I may be commiserated by the royal sage. Otherwise most certainly (it will happen that you will have to) pour out for me water with sesamum-seed;' i.e. you will have to celebrate my funeral obsequies. Oblations to the spirits of deceased relatives, called S'rāddha, generally consisted in offering a cake made of rice and milk (*piṇḍa-nirvāpaṇa*), or in pouring out water (*udaka-dāna, udaka-kriyā*), or water and sesamum seed mixed. In the latter case it was called *tilodaka-dāna, tila-tarpaṇa*, &c. The ceremony as performed by Brāhmans is described in Manu iii. 203, &c.; see especially iii. 223. *Dattvā sapavitraṃ tilodakam*, 'having poured out water with sesamum seed and Kuśa grass.' See Indian Wisdom, pp. 208, 253, &c. K. refers in illustration to a verse towards the end of Act VI. of this play, where Dushyanta says, *Nūnam prasūti-vikalena mayā prasiktaṃ dhautāśru-śesham udakam pitaraḥ pivanti*, 'in all probability my (deceased) ancestors are (now) drinking the only offering-of-water that is left to them, (consisting of) glistening tears poured forth by me destitute of posterity.' *Siñcatam=nirvapatam*, K. *Vartethām*, sometimes *vṛit* has the sense of 'to behave,' 'to act.'

राजा ।

संशयच्छेदि वचनम् ।

प्रियंवदा ॥ जनान्तिकम् ॥

[a] अणसूए । दूरगअवम्महा अक्खमा इअं कालहरणस्स । जस्सिं बद्धभावा एसा । सो ललामभूदो पोरवाणं । ता जुत्तं से अहिलासो अहिणन्दिदुं ।

अनसूया ।

[b] तह । जह भणासि ।

प्रियंवदा ॥ प्रकाशम् ॥

[c] सहि । दिट्ठिआ । अणुरूबो से अहिणिवेसो । सायरं वज्जिअ कहिं वा महाणई ओदरइ । को दाणिं सहआरं अन्तरेण अदिमुत्तलदं पल्लविदं सहेदि ।

[a] अनसूये । दूरगतमन्मथाक्षमेयं कालहरणस्य । यस्मिन्बद्धभावैषा । स ललामभूतः पौरवाणाम् । तद्युक्तमस्या अभिलाषोऽभिनन्दितुम् ।   [b] तथा । यथा भणसि ।
[c] सखि । दिष्या । अनुरूपोऽस्या अभिनिवेशः । सागरं वर्जयित्वा कुत्र वा महानद्यवतरति । क इदानीं सहकारमन्तरेणातिमुक्तलतां पल्लवितां सहते ।

---

[1] 'She is far gone in love, and unable to bear loss of time,' i. e. her love has reached that point which brooks no delay. Cf. *durārūḍho 'syāḥ praṇayaḥ*, Vikram., beginning of Act IV. *Vammaha* or *bammaha* is the proper Prākṛit equivalent for *manmatha*, according to Vararuci ii. 38, iii. 43. Lassen, Instit. Prāk. p. 245, although the MSS. give *mammaha*.

[2] 'He on whom she has fixed her affections is the ornament of the Pauravas [p. 15, n. 1], therefore her love is fit to be approved,' or 'it is proper that her love should meet with our approval.' *Yuktam* is here used like *śakyam*, see p. 103, n. 3. *Baddha-bhāvā*, cf. *yasmin baddha-bhāvā asi tvam*, Vikram., beginning of Act III.

[3] 'Where should a great river end its course excepting at the ocean? What (tree) excepting the Sahakāra [mango] can support the Atimukta [Mādhavī creeper] with (its) new sprouts?' *Ava-tṛī* (properly 'to descend' or 'alight') is here applied to the disemboguing of a river into the ocean. *Yathā mahā-nadī samudram praviśati, tathā rūpavatī tvaṃ Dushyante*

राजा ।

किमत्र चित्रम् । यदि विशाखे शशाङ्कलेखामनुवर्तेते[1] ।

अनसूया ।

[a]को उण उवाओ भवे । जेण अविलम्बिअं णिहुअं अ सहीए मणोरहं सम्पादेम्ह ।

[a] कः पुनरुपायो भवेत् । येनाविलम्बितं निभृतं च सख्या मनोरथं सम्पादयाव: ।

---

evānuraktā, S'. The Sahakāra is described p. 28, n. 1. The Atimukta is the same as the Mādhavī or vernal creeper, called also Vāsantī and Puṇḍraka (see p. 108, n. 3). 'The beauty and fragrance of the flower of this creeper give them a title to all the praises which Kālidāsa and Jayadeva bestow on them. It is a gigantic and luxuriant climber; but when it meets with nothing to grasp, it assumes the form of a sturdy tree, the highest branches of which display, however, in the air, their natural flexibility and inclination to climb,' Sir W. Jones, vol. v. p. 124.

[1] 'Why need we wonder at this, since the constellation Viśākhā courts [goes after] the young-moon?' i. e. if the constellation Viśākhā (or the sixteenth lunar asterism, which is frequently written in the dual Viśākhe, as containing two stars) is eager for a union with the Moon, why need we wonder at S'akuntalā's desire to be united with a prince of the Lunar race? *Saśāṅka-lekhā* is properly 'a digit of the moon,' or the moon in its most beautiful form when quite young. A complete revolution of the moon, with respect to the stars, being made in twenty-seven days, odd hours, the Hindūs divide the heavens into twenty-seven constellations [asterisms] or lunar stations, one of which receives the moon for one day in each of his monthly journeys. As the Moon [Ćandra] is considered to be a masculine deity, the Hindūs fable these twenty-seven constellations as his wives, and personify them as the daughters of Daksha. Of these twenty-seven wives (twelve of whom give names to the twelve months) Ćandra is supposed to shew the greatest affection for the fourth (Rohiṇī), but each of the others, and amongst them Viśākhā, is represented as jealous of this partiality, and eager to secure the Moon's favour for herself. Dushyanta probably means to compare himself to the Moon (he being of the Lunar race, p. 15, n. 1), and S'akuntalā to Viśākhā. The selection of Viśākhā, rather than Rohiṇī, may perhaps be explained by a reference to p. 6, l. 6, where we learn that the summer-season had barely set in at the period when the events of the drama were supposed to be taking place. If

प्रियंवदा ।

[a] णिहुअंति चिन्तणिज्जं भवे । सिग्घंति सुअरं ।

अनसूया ।

[b] कहं विअ ।

प्रियंवदा ।

[c] एं सो राएसी इमस्सिं सिणिद्धदिट्ठीए सूइदाहिलासो इमाइं दिअहाइं पज्जाअरकिसो लक्खीअदि ।

राजा ॥ आत्मानमवलोक्य ॥

सत्यमित्यभूत एवास्मि । तथा हि

इदमशिशिरैरन्तस्तापादिवर्णमणीकृतं
निशि निशि भुजन्यस्तापाङ्गप्रवर्तिभिरश्रुभिः ।
अनतिलुलितज्याघाताङ्कं मुहुर्मणिबन्धना-
त्कनकवलयं स्रस्तं स्रस्तं मया प्रतिसार्यते ॥ ६६ ॥

[a] निभृतमिति चिन्तनीयं भवेत् । शीघ्रमिति सुकरम् ।   [b] कथमिव ।   [c] ननु स राजर्षिरस्यां स्निग्धदृष्ट्या सूचिताभिलाष इमानि दिवसानि प्रजागरकृशो लक्ष्यते ।

therefore the season corresponded to the middle of May, the month would probably be Vaiśākha, and Viśākhā would, therefore, be appropriately chosen before Rohiṇī. This passage may also be interpreted, but not so consistently with the fable, by referring *viśākhe* to the two female friends, and *śaśāṅka-lekhā* to S'akuntalā. The meaning would then be, 'It is not to be wondered at that these two friends should follow S'akuntalā and assist in carrying out her schemes, any more than that the two stars of Viśākhā should go after the young moon.' *Anuvartete=anusarataḥ*, K. Cf. in Vikram., Act I, *Citralekhā-dvitīyām priya-sakhīm Urvaśīm grihītvā Viśākhā-sahita iva bhagavān Soma upasthitaḥ sa rājarṣiḥ.*

[1] '(Your) "unobservedly" will require thought, (your) "quickly" (is) easy.' This use of *iti* in quoting previous words is noticeable.

[2] 'For this golden bracelet, having its jewels sullied by the tears

Verse 66. HARIṆĪ (a variety of ATYASHṬI), containing seventeen syllables to the Pāda or quarter-verse, each Pāda being alike.

∪ ∪ ∪ ∪ ∪ − | − − − − | ∪ − ∪ ∪ − ∪ − ‖

प्रियंवदा ॥ विचिन्त्य ॥

[a] हला । मञ्अणलेहो से करीअदु । इमं देवदासेसावदेसेण सुमणोगोविदं करिअ से हत्यञ्चं पावइस्सं ।

[a] हला । मदनलेखोऽस्य क्रियताम् । इमं देवताशेषापदेशेन सुमनोगोपितं कृत्वास्य हस्तं प्रापयिष्यामि ।

(rendered) scorching from internal fever night after night flowing from the outer-corner-of-my-eye which rests on my arm, slipping, slipping down [i. e. as it constantly slips down] from the wrist, without pressing on [catching on, hitching on] the scars (that are caused) by the friction of the bow-string, is repeatedly pushed back by me.' *Vivarṇa-maṇī-kṛita*, lit. 'made into a colourless gem,' 'made so that its jewels are devoid of colour.' *Apān-ga=netra-prānta. Pravartibhiḥ=skhaladbhiḥ. An-atilulita=an-atisakta*, 'not closely adhering,' K.;=*nābhilupta*, S. and C. The same word occurs at the end of this Act, where allusion is made to the flowery couch of S'akuntalā, *sarira-lulita*, 'which her body had pressed.' One sense of root *lul* is certainly to 'adhere,' 'stick,' 'cleave.' The Deva-n. MSS. all have *an-abhilulita* with the same meaning, unsupported by K. and the other scholiasts, and the oldest Beng. MSS. Through emaciation and disuse of the bow (cf. p. 70, l. 8, with p. 67, l. 12) the callosities on the fore-arm, usually caused by the bow-string, were not sufficiently prominent to prevent the bracelet from slipping down from the wrist to the elbow, when the arm was raised to support the head. This is a favourite idea with Kālidāsa to express the attenuation caused by love (cf. Megha-d. 2, *kanaka-valaya-bhraṅsa-rikta-prakoshṭhaḥ*, 'having the fore-arm bare by the falling of the golden bracelet).' The Beng. have *an-atilulita-jyā-ghātānkād*, agreeing with *maṇi-bandhanāt*, which would appear at first sight to be the better reading. I have followed K. and the Deva-n. MSS. in making this compound agree with *valayam*. It may, however, as K. observes, be taken adverbially. *Maṇi-bandhana*, 'the place for binding on jewels,' 'the wrist.'

[1] 'Let a love-letter be composed for him. Having hidden it [made it hid] in a flower, I will deliver it into [cause it to reach] his hand under the pretext of [as if it were] the remains (of an offering presented) to an idol.' *Madana-lekhaḥ=ananga-lekhaḥ*, C.;=*smara-bhāva-sūćakaṃ lekham*, S. *Sumano-gopita=kusuma-saṅgupta*, S. *Devatā-seshāpade-śena*, the Beng., supported by S'., read *devatā-sevāpadeśena*, 'under pretext of honouring a divinity.' K. reads *devatā-vyapadeśena*, with the word *prasāda* inserted in the margin. *Devatā-śesha* is supported by C., and

अनसूया ।

[a] रोच्चइ मे सुउमारो पञ्ओओ । किं वा सउन्दला भणादि ।

शकुन्तला ।

[b] सहीणिओओबि विकप्पीअदि ।

प्रियंवदा ।

[c] तेण हि अत्तणो उवण्णासपुव्वं चिन्तेहि दाव किम्मि ललिअपदबन्धणं ।

शकुन्तला ।

[d] हला । चिन्तेमि अहं । अवहीरणभीरुअं पुणो वेबइ मे हिअअं ।

राजा ॥ सहर्षम् ॥

अयं स ते तिष्ठति सङ्गमोत्सुको
विशङ्कसे भीरु यतोऽवधीरणाम् ।

[a] रोचते मे सुकुमारः प्रयोगः । किं वा शकुन्तला भणति ।   [b] सखी-नियोगोऽपि विकल्प्यते ।   [c] तेन ह्यात्मन उपन्यासपूर्वं चिन्तय तावत्किमपि ललितपदबन्धनम् ।   [d] हला । चिन्तयाम्यहम् । अवधीरणभीरुकं पुनर्वेपते मे हृदयम् ।

---

explained by him as *nirmālya*, 'the remains of an offering of flowers presented to an idol.' Garlands of flowers were so offered. A love-letter was one of the four recognized modes of encouraging a lover (see p. 109, n. 3).

[1] 'This very injunction [suggestion] of my friend is weighed (in my mind),' i. e. I must consider before I can consent to it. This is the reading of the two oldest MSS. One, however, has *sahi* or *sahī*.

[2] 'Therefore just think of some pretty composition in verse, accompanied by an allusion to yourself.' *Upanyāsa-pūrva*, lit. 'preceded [headed] by an allusion.' *Lalita-pada-bandhana*, cf. *lalitārtha-bandham*, Vikram., Act II; *pada-bandhana*, lit. 'the connection or composition of quarter-verses,' cf. *padāni*, ver. 68 of this play.

लभेत वा प्रार्थयिता न वा श्रियं
श्रिया दुरापः कथमीप्सितो भवेत् ॥ ६७॥[1]

सख्यौ ।

[a] अयि अत्तगुणावमाणिणि । की दाणिं सरीरणिव्वाब-
त्तिन्नं सारदिन्नं जोसिणिं पडन्तेण वारेदि[2] ।

शकुन्तला ॥ ससितम् ॥

[b] णिओइदा दाणिंम्हि[3] । ॥ इत्युपविश्य चिन्तयति ॥

[a] अयि आत्मगुणावमानिनि । क इदानीं शरीरनिर्वापयित्रीं शारदीं ज्योत्स्नां पटान्तेन वारयति ।   [b] नियोजितेदानीमस्मि ।

---

[1] 'That very one, O timid one, from whom thou apprehendest a refusal, stands pining for a union with thee. The lover may or may not win Fortune, (but) how, being beloved (by her), should he be difficult-to-be-won by Fortune?' *Śrī=Lakshmī*, 'the goddess of beauty and fortune,' here identified with S'akuntalā or with the object of the lover's hopes and aspirations. The commentators throw no light on this passage. The meaning seems to be, 'There is always a doubt whether the suitor will gain favour with Fortune, or with the beautiful maiden who may be the object of his love, but when it is certain that he is beloved by her, how can *she* have any difficulty in gaining *him?* for there surely will be no doubt of his being willing to accept her favours, however uncertain may be her encouragement of his advances.' The verse which follows this in the Beng. MSS. is probably spurious.

[2] 'O thou undervaluer of thine own excellences, who now would ward off with the skirt of a garment the autumnal moonlight, the cooler of his body?' i.e. (according to S'.) this prince is too sensible to be averse to a union with one so beautiful as thou art. *Nirvāpayitrīm*, cf. *nirvāpayitā*, ver. 65, and see p. 97, n. 1. *Paṭāntena*, cf. in Act V. *paṭāntena mukham āvṛitya roditi.*

[3] 'I am now (acting) under (your) directions,' i.e. it is by your orders that I do this; *niyojitāsmi bhavatībhyāṃ gīti-karaṇe*, 'I am directed by you to compose verses,' S'.; 'I am only following your directions, therefore you are responsible if I meet with a repulse,' S'.

राजा ।

स्थाने खलु विस्मृतनिमेषेण चक्षुषा प्रियामवलोक-
यामि । यतः

उन्नमितैकभ्रूलतमाननमस्याः पदानि रचयन्त्याः ।
कण्टकितेन प्रथयति मय्यनुरागं कपोलेन[1] ॥ ६८ ॥

शकुन्तला ।

[a] हला । चिन्तिदा मए गीदिआ । ण क्ख सन्निहिदाणि
उण लेहणसाहणाणि ।

प्रियंवदा ।

[b] इमस्सिं सुओदरसुउमारे णलिणीपत्ते णहेहिं णिक्खित्त-
वण्णं[3] करेहि ।

---

[a] हला । चिन्तिता मया गीतिका । न खलु सन्निहितानि पुनर्लेखनसाधनानि ।
[b] अस्मिन्शुकोदरसुकुमारे नलिनीपत्रे नखैर्निश्चिप्तवर्णं कुरु ।

---

[1] 'Fitly, indeed, do I gaze on my beloved with an eye that forgets to wink, because the countenance of her composing [whilst she is in the act of composing] verses has one eyebrow raised; (and) by her thrilling cheek she discloses her affection for me.' *Vismṛita-nimeshena* is very expressive of a fixed, earnest gaze. Chézy translates, 'O spectacle enchanteur! dont je serais jaloux que le moindre clignement d'œil me privât un instant!' *Kaṇṭakita*, lit. 'having the downy hair of the cheek erect like thorns' (= *pulakāṅćita*). The erection of the hair of the body (*pulaka, roma-kaṇṭaka, romāṅćana*) indicates exquisite delight, according to the notions of the Hindūs. Cf. Vikram., Act I, *mama aṅgaṃ sa-roma-kaṇṭakam aṅkuritam.*

[2] 'But the writing-materials indeed are not at hand.' Most of the MSS. have *hu* for Sanskrit *khalu.* Lassen (Instit. Prāk. p. 192) shews that *kkhu* is the proper form after a short vowel.

[3] 'Engrave the letters [make engraving of the letters] with your nails

---

Verse 68. ÁRYÁ or GÁTHÁ. See verse 2.

$$- \cup \cup \mid - - \mid - \cup \cup \parallel - \cup \cup \mid - - \mid \cup - \cup \mid \cup \cup - \mid -$$
$$- \cup \cup \mid - - \mid \cup \cup \cup \cup \parallel - \cup \cup \mid - - \mid \quad \cup \quad \mid - - \mid \cup$$

शकुन्तला ॥ यथोक्तं रूपयित्वा ॥

[a] हला । सुणुह दाणिं सङ्गदन्यं ण वेत्ति ।

उभे ।

[b] अवहिदम्ह ।

शकुन्तला ॥ वाचयति ॥

[c] तुज्झ ण आणे हिअअं मम उण कामो दिवावि रत्तिम्पि ।
णिग्घिण तवेइ बलिअं तुइ वुत्तमणोरहाइ अङ्गाइं ॥६९॥

[a] हला । शृणुतमिदानीं सङ्गताऽर्थं न वेति ।   [b] अवहिते स्वः ।

[c] तव न जाने हृदयं मम पुनः कामो दिवापि रात्रिमपि ।
निर्घृण तपति बलीयस्त्वयि वृत्तमनोरथाया अङ्गानि ॥६९॥

---

on this lotus-leaf smooth as a parrot's breast.' *Śukodara*, 'a parrot's breast,' it also means 'a leaf of the Tālīśa tree' (=*tālīśa-pattra*); in Vikram., Act IV, the colour of a scarf is compared to the same thing (*śukodara-śyāmaṃ stanānśukam*), and in Mahā-bh. ii. 1035, the colour of horses (*śukodara-samān hayān*). The Prākṛit is answerable for *nikshipta-varṇaṃ kuru*. This is the reading of all the Deva-n. MSS.; the Beng. have *pada-ććheda-bhaktyā nakhair ālikhyatām*.

[1] 'Thy heart I know not, but day and night, O cruel one, Love vehemently inflames the limbs of me, whose desires are centred in thee.' Such is the reading of the Taylor MS. and my own. The other Deva-n. agree, but give *manorahāim* for *manorathāni*, in concord with *aṅgāni*. *Maṇorahāi* and *maṇorahae* may both stand for the Sanskṛit gen. fem. *manorathāyāḥ* (in concord with *mama*), and both are equally admissible into the metre (Lassen's Instit. Prāk. pp. 304, 305, 147). The interpretation of Ćandra-śekhara supports this reading (*nishkṛipa tapayati baliyas tvad-abhimukha-manorathāyā aṅgāni*). This verse is called by Kāṭavema the *upanyāsa* or 'allusion,' see p. 116, n. 2; see also the next note on verse 70.

Verse 69. UDGĀTHĀ or GĪTI. See verse 4.

$$- \cup \cup \; | \; -- \; | \; \cup \cup \, - \, \| \; \cup \cup \cup \cup \; | \; -- \; | \; \cup - \cup \; | \; -- \; | \; -$$
$$- \cup \cup \; | \; \cup - \cup \; | \; \cup \cup \, - \, \| \; \cup \cup \, - \; | \; \cup \cup \, - \; | \; \cup - \cup \; | \; -- \; | \; -$$

राजा ॥ सहसोपसृत्य ॥

तपति तनुगात्रि मदनस्त्वामनिशं मां पुनर्दहत्येव ।
ग्लपयति यथा शशाङ्कं न तथा हि कुमुद्वतीं दिवसः ॥७०॥

सख्यौ ॥ विलोक्य सहर्षमुत्थाय ॥

[a] साञ्चदं अविलम्बिणी मणोरहंस ।

॥ शकुन्तलाभ्युत्थातुमिच्छति ॥

राजा ।

अलमलमायासेन ।

संदष्टकुसुमशयनान्याशुक्लान्तविसभङ्गसुरभीणि ।
गुरुपरितापानि न ते गात्राण्युपचारमर्हन्ति ॥७१॥

[a] खागतमविलम्बिनो मनोरथस्य ।

---

[1] 'Thee, O slender-limbed one, Love inflames; but me he actually consumes incessantly; for the Day does not so cause the lotus to fade as it does the moon.' *Kumuda* or *kumudvatī* is a kind of lotus, which blossoms in the night and fades by day (*kumudvatī ćandra-virahena santaptā bhavati,* S'.), here compared to S'akuntalā. *Kumudvatī* is usually 'a group of lotuses.' *Śaśānka,* 'hare-marked,' i. e. the moon. Dushyanta again compares himself to the moon (cf. p. 113, n. 1). This with the preceding verse, according to S'. and Ć., is an example of the figure called Uttarottara.

[2] 'Welcome to the speedy (fulfilment of thy) desire!' or 'welcome to the object of thy desire which does not delay (its appearance).' The Beng. insert *samīhita-phalasya* or *ćintita-phalasya.*

[3] 'Thy limbs, which closely press the couch of flowers, (and are) fragrant by the crushing of the quickly-faded lotus-fibres, being grievously

---

Verse 70. ĀRYĀ or GĀTHĀ. See verse 2.

⏑⏑⏑⏑ | ⏑–⏑ | ⏑⏑– ‖ –⏑⏑ | –– | ⏑–⏑ | –– | ⏑
⏑⏑⏑⏑ | ⏑–⏑ | –– ‖ ⏑⏑– | ⏑⏑– | ⏑ | –⏑⏑ | –

Verse 71. ĀRYĀ or GĀTHĀ. See verse 2.

–– | ⏑⏑⏑⏑ | ⏑⏑– ‖ –– | –⏑⏑ | ⏑–⏑ | ⏑⏑– | ⏑
⏑⏑⏑⏑ | –– | ⏑⏑– ‖ –– | ⏑⏑– | ⏑ | –– | ⏑

अनसूया ।

[a] इदो सिलातलेक्कदेसं अणुगेण्हदु वअस्सो ।

॥ राजोपविशति । शकुन्तला सलज्जा तिष्ठति ॥

प्रियंवदा ।

[b] दुवेण्हि वी अण्णोण्णाणुराओ पच्चक्खो । सहीसिणेहो उण मं पुणरुत्तवादिणिं करेदि ।

[a] इतः शिलातलैकदेशमनुगृह्णातु वयस्यः ।   [b] द्वयोरपि युवयोरन्योन्यानुरागः प्रत्यक्षः । सखीस्नेहः पुनर्मां पुनरुक्तवादिनीं करोति ।

---

inflamed, do not deserve (to perform) obeisance;' i. e. are excused the usual salutation. In consideration of the state of your bodily frame, you are privileged to keep your recumbent posture even before me. *Upaćaram,* i. e. *mat-kṛite vinayādi-rūpam.* *San-danś,* lit. 'to press the teeth closely together;' hence *sandashṭa,* 'coming in close contact with.' Cf. Raghu-v. xvi. 65, *sandashṭa-vastreshu nitambeshu,* 'on (their) hips to which garments were closely fitted.' Our English word 'bite' has the same acceptation. *Āśu-klānta,* &c. The Beng. have *āśu-vimardita-mṛiṇāla-valayāni* or *āśu-vivarṇita* (= *mlānī-bhūta,* Ć.), &c., 'having bracelets of lotus-fibres that have quickly faded (from the heat of her limbs).' Cf. p. 106, n. 1.

¹ 'Will our friend deign to take a seat here on the stone ?' cf. p. 76, l. 3. The stone-seat served also for the couch of S'akuntalā, S'. *Anugṛihṇātu,* 'let him favour,' is the reading of K. For *anugeṇhadu* Dr. Burkhard reads *alaṇkaredu* (= Sanskrit *alaṇ-karotu*).

² 'But affection for my friend prompts me to be the speaker of something superfluous,' i. e. of what has been so often repeated as to be already sufficiently well-known. *Punar-ukta,* which properly means 'said again,' 'repeated,' has, in dramatic composition, acquired the acceptation of 'superfluous,' and sometimes simply 'additional.' Thus in the Vikram., Act III, the torches are said to be *punar-uktāś ćandrikāyām,* 'rendered superfluous in the moonlight;' and in Act V. of that play, tears dropping from the eyes on the breast are said to cause *muktāvalī-viraćanam punar-uktam,* 'the formation of an additional necklace of pearls.' Cf. also *kim punar-uktena,* Mālavik. p. 63, l. 5. *Sakhī-snehaḥ* = *sakhī-vishayaka-praṇayaḥ.*

R

राजा ।

भद्रे । नैतत्परिहार्य्यम् । विवक्षितं ह्यनुक्तमनुतापं जनयति ।

प्रियंवदा ।

[a] आवस्सस विसञ्अवासिणो जणस्स अन्तिहरेण रक्खा हो-
द्व्वन्ति एसो वो धम्मो ।

राजा ।

नास्मात्परम् [3] ।

प्रियंवदा ।

[b] तेण हि इञं णो पिअसही तुमं उद्दिसिअ इमं अवत्यन्तरं
भअवदा मञ्अणेण आरोविदा । ता अरहसि अब्भुववत्तीए
जीविदं से अवलम्बिदुं [5] ।

राजा ।

भद्रे । साधारणोऽयं प्रणयः । सर्व्वथानुगृहीतोऽस्मि ।

[a] आपन्नस्य विषयवासिनो जनस्यार्तिहरेण राज्ञा भवितव्यमित्येष वो धर्मः ।
[b] तेन हीयमावयोः प्रियसखी त्वामुद्दिश्येदमवस्थान्तरं भगवता मदनेनारोपिता ।
तदर्हस्यभ्युपपत्त्या जीवितमस्या अवलम्बितुम् ।

---

[1] 'That (which you have to say) ought not to be suppressed [omitted],
for that-which-was-intended-to-be-spoken and is not spoken produces
subsequent regret.' *Anu-tāpa*, 'after-pain,' i. e. repentance. *Vivakshita*,
from the desid. of root *vac*.

[2] 'It is to be become by the king [the king ought to be] the remover of
the suffering of one dwelling in his kingdom (who has) fallen into trouble;
such is your duty.' The Beng. have *āśrama-vāsino* for *vishaya-vāsino*.
The latter reading is supported by K.

[3] 'No other than this,' i. e. nothing short of this; this is exactly my
duty.

[4] 'Therefore (know that) this our dear friend has been reduced to this
altered condition by the divinity Love on thy account.' *Ud-diśya*, 'aiming
at,' 'regarding,' see p. 101, n. 1. *Avasthāntara*, 'another state,' i. e. an
alteration from the natural and healthy state. *Āropitā*=*prāpitā*, S.

[5] *Avalambitum*, properly 'to cling to,' 'depend upon;' here used
transitively, 'to sustain,' 'support.'

[6] Cf. Vikram., Act II, *sādhāraṇo 'yam ubhayoḥ praṇayaḥ.*

शकुन्तला ॥ प्रियंवदामवलोक्य ॥

[a] हला । किं अन्तेउरविरहपज्जुस्सुअस्स राएसिणो उबरोहेण ।

राजा ।

सुन्दरि ।

इदमनन्यपरायणमन्यथा
हृदयसन्निहिते हृदयं मम ।
यदि समर्थयसे मदिरेक्षणे
मदनवाणहतोऽस्मि हतः पुनः ॥७२॥

अनसूया ।

[b] वअस्स । बहुवल्लहा राआणो सुणीअन्ति । जह णो पिअसही बन्धुअणसोअणिज्जा ण होइ । तह णिव्वाहेहि ।

---

[a] हला । किमन्तःपुरविरहपर्युत्सुकस्य राजमेर्षिपरोधेन ।   [b] वयस्य । बहुवल्लभा राजानः श्रूयन्ते । यथा नौ प्रियसखी बन्धुजनशोचनीया न भवति । तथा निर्वाहय ।

---

[1] 'What (can you mean) by detaining the Rājarshi, who is pining (by reason of) separation from his royal-consorts?' *Antaḥ-pura*, 'the inner part of the palace,' 'the female apartments,' here put for the occupants thereof.

[2] 'O thou that art near my heart, if this heart of mine which is devoted to no other, thou judgest to be otherwise, (then) O lovely-eyed one, being (already) slain by Love's shafts, I am slain again,' i. e. I suffer a second death. Cf. Bhartṛi-h. i. 63, *hatam api nihanty eva madanaḥ*. *Hṛidaya-sannihite*=*man-mano-'vasthāyini*, 'O thou that abidest in my heart,' S.; =*chittārūḍhe*, C. *Madirā*, 'wine,' as applied to *īkshaṇa*, 'the eye,' is said by S. to be equivalent to *sundara*, 'beautiful;' or to *īshad-ghūrṇana-śīla*, 'slightly inclined to roll about.' 'Wine-eyed' may mean 'one whose eyes intoxicate like wine.'

राजा ।

भद्रे । किं बहुना ।

परिग्रहबहुत्वेऽपि द्वे प्रतिष्ठे कुलस्य मे ।
समुद्ररसना चोर्वी सखी च युवयोरियम् ॥७३॥

उभे ।

[a] णिव्वुदम्ह[2] ।

प्रियंवदा ॥ सदृष्टिक्षेपम् ॥

[b] अणसूए । जह एसो इदो दिट्ठदिट्ठी उस्सुओ मिअपो-
दओ मादरं अण्णेसदि । एहि । सज्ञोएम णं[3] । ॥ इत्युभे प्रस्थिते ॥

शकुन्तला ।

[c] हला । असरणम्हि । अण्णदरा वो आअच्छदु ।

<hr>

[a] निर्वृते खः ।   [b] अनसूये । यथैष इतो दन्तदृष्टिहृत्सुको मृगपोतको मा-
तरमन्विष्यति । एहि । संयोजयाव एनम् ।   [c] हला । अशरणास्मि । अन्यतरा
युवयोरागच्छतु ।

<hr>

[1] 'Even in the multitude of (my) wives [however numerous may be my wives] there (will be) but two chief-glories of my race, the sea-girt earth on the one hand (*ća*), and on the other (*ća*) this friend of yours,' i. e. there will be but two sources of glory to my race, viz. the sea-girt earth and S'akuntalā. *Prati-shṭhā*=*utkarsha-hetu*, 'a cause of renown,' 'a distinguished ornament,' S'.; properly 'a cause of stability,' 'a support.' *Parigraha-bahutve*=*kalatra-bāhulye*. The Deva-n. MSS. read *samudra-vasanā*, 'clothed in the ocean,' 'having the ocean for its garments' (*samudra eva vastrāṇi yasyāḥ*, S'.) The Beng. all have *samudra-rasanā*, which is literally 'sea-girt' (*rasanā*=*mekhalā*), and seems to be the better reading. Cf. Hitop. l. 2542. Confusion between *rasanā* and *vasanā* may easily have arisen. *Ća ća*, see p. 14, n. 1.

[2] In the Beng. MSS. the dialogue which follows these words has several interpolations.

[3] Lit. 'let us cause it to join (its mother),' 'let us lead it to its mother.' *Mātrā saha iti anushaṅga*, S'. Some word like *paśya*, 'See!' may be supplied before *yathā* in the sentence preceding.

<hr>

Verse 73. S'LOKA or ANUSHTUBH. See verses 5, 6, 11, 12, 26, 47, 50, 51, 53.

उभे ।

^a पुहवीए जो सरणं । सो तुह समीवे वट्टइ । ॥ इति निष्क्रान्ते ॥

शकुन्तला ।

^b कहं गदाओ एव ।

राजा ।

अलमावेगेन । नन्वयमाराधयिता जनस्तव समीपे
वर्तते ।[1]

किं शीतलैः क्लमविनोदिभिरार्द्रवाता-
न्सञ्चारयामि नलिनीदलतालवृन्तैः ।
अङ्के निधाय करभोरु यथासुखं ते
संवाहयामि चरणावुत पद्मताम्रौ ॥७४॥[2]

^a पृथिव्या यः शरणम् । स तव समीपे वर्तते ।   ^b कथं गते एव ।

---

[1] 'Does not this person, thy humble-servant [thy adorer], remain near thee?' i. e. am not I here to wait upon thee, in place of thy friends? The Beng. add *sakhī-bhūmau*. *Ārādhayitā*=*paricārakaḥ*, 'an attendant,' S'., but it is also 'the worshipper of a deity,' and therefore implies adoration as well as service. There is designedly a 'double-entendre.'

[2] 'Shall I set in motion moist breezes by (means of) cool lotus-leaf-fans which-remove langour? or placing thy feet, brown as the lotus, O round-thighed (maiden), in (my) lap shall I rub them soothingly?' *Karabhoru*, voc. case of *karabhorū*; according to Pāṇ. iv. 1, 69, *ūru*, 'a thigh or hip,' at the end of this and some other compounds becomes *ūrū*, and is declined like *vadhū*; and *karabhorūḥ* is said to be equivalent to *vrittorūḥ strī*, 'a woman with round thighs.' *Karabha* is 'the thick part of the hand,' 'the part between the wrist and the fingers;' it is also 'a young elephant.' Dr. Boehtlingk considers that the comparison is taken from the first of these senses. It may with more reason be taken from the other; for from the following gloss of Ć. it seems probable that as *kara* stands for both the human hand and the trunk of an elephant, and *karabha* for the upper

---

Verse 74. VASANTA-TILAKĀ (a variety of ŚAKVARĪ). See verses 8, 27, 31, 43, 46, 64.

शकुन्तला ।

[a] ण माणशीएसु अत्ताणं अवराहइस्सं । ॥ इत्युत्थाय गन्तुमिच्छति ॥

राजा ।

सुन्दरि । अपरिनिर्वाणो दिवसः । इयं च ते शरीरावस्था ।
उत्सृज्य कुसुमशयनं नलिनीदलकल्पितस्तनावरणम् ।
कथमातपे गमिष्यसि परिबाधापेलवैरङ्गैः ॥७५॥

॥ इति बलादेनां निवर्तयति ॥

[a] न माननीयेष्वात्मानमपराधयिष्यामि ।

---

part of the hand, so the latter word may be taken for the same part of an
elephant's trunk. *Karabhaḥ prāṇy-angam* ('is part of an animal') *tadiva
ūrur yasyāḥ śubha-lakshaṇam idaṃ tad uktam, hasti-hasta-nibhair* ('like
an elephant's trunk') *vrittair* ('round') *asthābhaiḥ karabhopamaiḥ prāpnu-
vantyūrūbhiḥ śaśvat striyaḥ sukham anangajam.* The epithet may there-
fore mean 'having thighs gracefully tapering like the trunk of an
elephant.' Cf. *karabhopamorūḥ*, Raghu-v. vi. 83, and *dvirada-nāsoruḥ*,
Bhaṭṭi-k. iv. 17. *Samvāhayāmi* = *mardayāmi; sam-vāh* (or more
correctly *sam-vah* in the causal) is applied especially to the rubbing or
shampooing of the limbs. *Padma-tāmrau*, Chézy observes that the
Hindū women extracted a rosy-coloured dye from a plant called Law-
sonia Inermis, with which they were in the habit of dyeing their nails
and fingers, as well as their feet. Cf. *strī-nakha-pāṭalaṃ kuruvakam*,
Vikram., Act II.

[1] 'I will not make myself in fault with those whom I am bound to
respect [towards those who are worthy of respect],' i. e. with my foster-
father and others.

[2] 'The day is not (yet) cool.' *A-parinirvāṇa* = *an-apagata-tīvrātapa*,
'having its great heat not yet passed off;' 'it was still noon,' S'. Some
MSS. have *a-nirvāṇa*, and others *apa-nirvāṇa* (= *a-nirvāṇa, nirvāṇa-
rahita*).

[3] 'Having left the couch of flowers (and) the covering of thy bosom

---

Verse 75. ĀRYĀ or GĀTHĀ. See verse 2.

```
— —  | ⏑ ⏑ ⏑ ⏑ | ⏑ ⏑ — ‖ ⏑ ⏑ — | ⏑ ⏑ — | ⏑ — ⏑ | — ⏑ ⏑ | —
⏑ ⏑ — | ⏑ — ⏑ | — ⏑ ⏑ ‖ ⏑ ⏑ — | — — | ⏑ | — — | —
```

शकुन्तला ।

^a पौरव । एक्ख विणअं । मञ्अणसन्तत्तावि ण हु अत्तणो
पहवामि ।

राजा ।

भीरु । अलं गुरुजनभयेन । दृष्ट्वा ते विदितधर्मा तच-
भवान्नाच दोषं ग्रहीष्यति कुलपतिः । अपि च
गान्धर्वेण विवाहेन बह्व्यो राजर्षिकन्यकाः ।
श्रूयन्ते परिणीतास्ताः पितृभिश्चाभिनन्दिताः ॥७६॥

^a पौरव । रक्ष विनयम् । मदनसन्तप्तापि न खल्वात्मनः प्रभवामि ।

---

formed of lotus leaves, how wilt thou go in the heat, with thy limbs (too)
delicate for hardships?' *Paribādhā-pelava = duḥkhāsahishṇu.* 'incapable
of bearing hardship.' The Beng. have *komala* for *pelava.*

[1] 'Even though inflamed by Love, I have not the power (of disposing)
of myself,' i.e. *yena tvam-manoratha-pūraṇaṃ kriyate*, 'so that your
wishes may be fulfilled,' S'.

[2] 'Having seen it, his reverence the head-of-your-society who knows-
the-law will not take (it as a) fault in you,' i.e. will not attribute blame
to you in this matter. *Drishṭvā te* is supported by the concurrent
authority of the Taylor, Mackenzie, and Colebrooke MSS. *Vidita-dharmā,*
see Pāṇ. v. 4, 124; *dharma* at the end of a Bahuvrīhi comp. becomes
dharman (cf. *yuvāṃ kshatriya-dharmāṇau,* Hitop. l. 2473).

[3] 'Many daughters of Rājarshis [p. 44, notes 1 and 2] are heard to have
been married by the marriage (called) Gāndharva, and (even) they have
received the approval of their fathers [been approved by their fathers].'
The Gāndharva marriage is one of the forms of marriage described in
Manu iii. 22, &c. It is a marriage proceeding entirely from love (*kāma-
sambhava*) or the mutual inclination (*anyonyecchā*) of a youth and maiden,
and concluded without any ceremonies and without consulting relatives,
see Manu iii. 32; Indian Wisdom, p. 199. *Gāndharvaḥ = paraspara-
bhāshayā krito vivāhaḥ,* K. The long scene which follows this verse in
the Beng. MSS. is omitted in all the Deva-n., and must be regarded as
an interpolation.

Verse 76. ŚLOKA or ANUSHṬUBH. See verses 5, 6, 11, 12, 26, 47, 50, 51. 53. 73.

शकुन्तला ।

[a] मुञ्च दाव मं । भूओबि सहीजणं अणुमाणइस्सं ।

राजा ।

भवतु । मोक्ष्यामि ।

शकुन्तला ।

[b] कदा ।

राजा ।

अपरिक्षतकोमलस्य ताव-
त्कुसुमस्येव नवस्य षट्पदेन ।
अधरस्य पिपासता मया ते
सदयं सुन्दरि गृह्यते रसोऽस्य ॥७७॥

॥ इति मुखमस्याः समुन्नमयितुमिच्छति । शकुन्तला परिहरति नाट्येन ॥

नेपथ्ये ।

[c] चक्कवाकवहुए । आमन्तेहि सहअरं । उवट्ठिदा रअणी ।

[a] मुञ्च तावन्माम् । भूयोऽपि सखीजनमनुमानयिष्यामि ।   [b] कदा ।
[c] चक्रवाकवधुके । आमन्त्रयस्व सहचरम् । उपस्थिता रजनी ।

---

[1] 'I will again take counsel with my female friends.' *Anu-man* in the causal may mean 'to ask the consent of,' 'to cause or to induce to assent.'

[2] '(As) by the bee (the honey) of the fresh, untouched tender blossom, (so) now by me eager-to-allay-my-thirst must the nectar of this under-lip of thine be gently stolen, O fair one, (ere I can let thee go).' *A-parikshata*, lit. 'unhurt,' 'uninjured,' applied to a virgin. *Adhara*, compare p. 33, n. 1.

[3] '[*Behind the scenes.*] O female-Ćakravāka, bid farewell to thy mate; the night is at hand [arrived].' *Ćakravāka-vadhukā* (Pāṇ. vii. 4, 13), i. e.

- - -

Verse 77. AUPAĆĆHANDASIKA, containing eleven syllables to the first Pāda or quarter-verse, and twelve to the second, each half-verse being alike.

⏑⏑−⏑⏑−⏑−⏑−− ‖ ⏑⏑−−⏑⏑−⏑−⏑−−

शकुन्तला ॥ ससम्भ्रमम् ॥

[a] पौरव । असंसञ्चं मम सरीरवुत्तन्तोवलम्भस्स अज्जा गोदमी इदो एव्व आअच्छदि । दाव विडबन्तरिदो होहि ।

राजा ।

तथा । ॥ इत्यात्मानमावृत्य तिष्ठति ॥

॥ ततः प्रविशति पात्रहस्ता गौतमी सख्यौ च ॥

सख्यौ ।

[b] इदो इदो अज्जा गोदमी ।

गौतमी ॥ शकुन्तलामुपेत्य ॥

[c] जादे । अवि लहुसन्दावाइं दे अङ्गाइं ।

[a] पौरव । असंशयं मम शरीरवृत्तान्तोपलम्भायार्या गौतमीत एवागच्छति । ताव-द्विटपान्तरितो भव ।   [b] इत इत आर्या गौतमी ।   [c] जाते । अपि लघुसन्तापानि तेऽङ्गानि ।

---

the Ćakravākī or female of the Ruddy goose, commonly called the Brāh-
manī duck (Anas Casarca).   The male and female of these birds keep
together during the day (whence one of their names, *dvandva-ćara*, 'going
in pairs') and are, like turtle-doves, patterns of constancy and connubial
affection ; but the legend is that they are doomed to pass the night apart
(whence the name *rātri-viślesha-gāmin*) in consequence of a curse pro-
nounced upon them by some saint whom they had offended.   Accordingly,
as soon as night commences, they take up their station on opposite banks
of a river, and call to each other in piteous cries.   The name *rathānga* or
ratha-pāda, 'chariot-footed,' sometimes given to them, indicates some
peculiar formation of the feet.   Constant allusion is made to their habits ;
thus in Vikram., Act IV, *sahaćarīṃ dūre matvā viraushi samutsukaḥ;*
cf. also Megha-d. 82, and Raghu-v. viii. 55.

[1] 'To ascertain the state of my bodily health.'   Prākṛit has no dative,
but gives the force of that case to the genitive.

[2] 'Concealed by the branches ;' see p. 104, n. 2.

[3] 'With a vessel in her hand.'   One MS. has *udaka-patra-hastā*, 'with
a vessel of water in her hand.'

शकुन्तला ।

[a] अज्जे । अत्थि मे विसेसो ।

गौतमी ।

[b] इमिणा दब्भोदँएण णिराबाधं एव्व दे सरीरं भविस्सदि ।

॥ शिरसि शकुन्तलामभ्युक्ष्य ॥ [c] वच्छे । परिणदो दिअहो । एहि । उडजं एव्व गच्छम्ह । ॥ इति प्रस्थिताः ॥

शकुन्तला ॥ आत्मगतम् ॥

[d] हिअअ । पढमं एव्व सुहोवणदे मणोरहे कादरभावं ण मुञ्चसि । साणुसअविहडिअस्स कहं दे सम्पदं सन्दावो ।

॥ पदान्तरे स्थित्वा । प्रकाशम् ॥ [e] लदावलअ सन्दावहारअ । आमन्तेमि तुमं भूओवि परिभोअस्स ।

॥ दुःखेन निष्क्रान्ता शकुन्तला सहेतराभिः ॥

---

[a] आर्ये । अस्ति मे विशेषः । [b] अनेन दर्भोदकेन निराबाधमेव ते शरीरं भविष्यति । [c] वत्से । परिणतो दिवसः । एहि । उटजमेव गच्छामः । [d] हृदय । प्रथममेव सुखोपनते मनोरथे कातरभावं न मुञ्चसि । सानुशयविघटितस्य कथं ते साम्प्रतं सन्तापः । [e] लतावलय सन्तापहारक । आमन्त्रये त्वां भूयोऽपि परिभोगाय ।

---

[1] 'O venerable mother! there is a change for the better in me.' *Nairujyaṃ kiñćid idānīṃ vṛittam*, 'there is now some freedom from pain,' S'. *Ajje* is the reading of the oldest MSS., supported by S'. and Ć. *Viśesha* is 'a change for the better,' in contradistinction to *vikāra*, 'a change for the worse.' The very same expression occurs in Mālavik. p. 46, l. 9.

[2] 'With this Darbha-water,' i. e. water and Kuśa grass, mixed and used for the *śānty-udaka*, mentioned at p. 97, l. 3; see also p. 19, n. 1, in the middle.

[3] 'O heart, even before, when the object-of-thy-desire readily presented itself, thou didst not abandon (thy) anxiety. How (great) now (will be) the anguish of thee regretful (and) dispirited! [*After advancing a step, standing still again, aloud*] O bower of creepers, remover of my suffering,

राजा ।। पूर्वस्यानमुपेत्य । सनिःश्वासम् ।।

अहो विघ्नवत्यः प्रार्थितार्थसिद्धयः । मया हि
मुहुरङ्गुलिसंवृताधरोष्ठं
प्रतिषेधाक्षरविक्लवाभिरामम् ।
मुखमंशविवर्ति पक्ष्मलाक्ष्याः
कथमपुन्नमितं न चुम्बितं तु ॥७८॥

I bid thee adieu, (hoping) to occupy (thee) again [to have enjoyment of thee again].' *Prathamam eva*, &c., see p. 120, l. 5. *Sukhopanate*, compare *yad upanatam duḥkham sukham tat*, Vikram., end of Act III. *Vi-ghaṭita* 'broken,' 'distracted with grief.' *Paribhoassa*, the genitive in Prākṛit used for the Sanskṛit dative, see p. 129, n. 1. *Paribhogāya*, cf. *pari-bhukta*, p. 132, l. 1.

¹ 'Alas! the fulfilment of desired objects has hindrances [there are many obstacles in the way of the accomplishment of one's wishes]; for by me the face of the lovely-eyelashed-eyed (maiden), having its upper and lower lip repeatedly protected by (her) fingers, beautiful in stammering out the syllables of denial, turning (away from me) towards the shoulder, was with some difficulty raised but not kissed.' *Anguli-saṃvṛita = angulibhyām pihita*, S. *Adharoshṭha*, see p. 33, n. 1, in the middle. *Pratishedhākshara*, i.e. *na mamādharam ćumbanīyam [unnamanīyam]*, 'my lips must not be kissed,' S'. and Ć. *Alam alam mā iti prabhṛitibhiḥ*, by such expressions as 'enough,' 'enough,' 'don't,' K. Some of the Deva-n. MSS. read *pratishedhāntara*. *Akshara* is 'a syllable,' as well as 'a letter.' *Anśa-vivarti = tiryak-kṛitam*, 'turned on one side,' Ć. It may, however, also mean 'revolving on the shoulders' (*anśayor vivarti*). S'. mentions another reading, *anga-vivarti = kroḍa-ghūrnamānam*. *Pakshmalākshī = ćāru-bahu-pakshma-yuktam*, or *praśasta-pakshma-yuktam akshi yasyāḥ*, 'who has eyes with beautiful eye-lashes,' S'. and Ć., i. e. whose eye-lashes are brown like the leaf of a lotus, Ć. The Hindū women used collyrium to darken the eye-lashes and eye-brows. *Pakshmala* is properly 'possessed of eye-lashes' (*pakshma-vat*), an adjective formed from *pakshman* as *sidhmala* from *sidhman*, Pāṇ. v. 2, 97; Gram. 80. LXXX. *Ut-pakshmala*,

Verse 78. AUPACCHANDASIKA. See verse 77.

क्व नु खलु सम्प्रति गच्छामि । अथवा । इहैव प्रियापरि-
भुक्तमुक्ते लतावलये मुहूर्तं स्थास्यामि । ॥ सर्वतोऽवलोक्य ॥

तस्याः पुष्पमयी शरीरलुलिता शय्या शिलायामियं
क्लान्तो मन्मथलेख एष नलिनीपत्ते नखैरर्पितः ।
हस्ताद्भ्रष्टमिदं विसाभरणमित्यासज्यमानेक्षणो
निर्गन्तुं सहसा न वेतसगृहाच्छक्तोऽस्मि शून्यादपि ॥७९॥

आकाशे ।

राजन् ।

सायन्तने सवनकर्मणि सम्प्रवृत्ते
वेदीं हुताशनवतीं परितः प्रकीर्णाः ।

'having upturned eye-lashes,' occurs about the middle of the Second Act
of Vikram. *Katham-api*, 'somehow or other,' 'hardly,' compare p. 128,
l. 12. *Na ćumbitaṃ tu* is the reading of the Calcutta ed. and of the
Sāhit.-d. p. 116, supported by Ć.

[1] 'Or rather, I will remain for a brief space in this bower of creepers
(once) occupied, (but now) abandoned by my beloved.' *Athavā*, see p. 30,
n. 3, and p. 24, n. 1, at the end. *Paribhukta*, compare *paribhogāya*, p. 130,
n. 3, at the end. *Muhūrtam*, see p. 37, n. 1, at the end.

[2] 'Here on the stone-seat is her flowery couch impressed by her form;
here is the faded love-letter committed to the lotus-leaf with her nails;
here is the lotus-fibre bracelet slipped from her hand—having my eyes
fixed on such (objects as these) I am not able to tear myself away [go out
hastily] from the Vetasa-arbour, even though deserted (by her).' *Śarīra-
lulitā=deha-sanghrishṭā*, 'rubbed by the body;' see *anatilulita*, p. 114,
n. 2. *Śilāyām*, see p. 105, n. 1, and p. 121, n. 1. *Klānta*, S'. and the
Beng. MSS. read *kānta*, 'charming,' 'dear.' *Visābharaṇa = mṛināla-
valaya*, see p. 106, n. 1. *Āsajyamānekshaṇa = āropyamānekshaṇa*. *Vetasa-
grihāt = latā-maṇḍapāt*, 'from the arbour of creepers,' see p. 104, l. 1.

Verse 79. ŚĀRDŪLA-VIKRĪḌITA (a variety of ATIDHṚITI). See verses 14, 30, 36, 39,
40, 63.

छायाश्चरन्ति बहुधा भयमादधानाः
सन्ध्यापयोदकपिशाः पिशिताशनानाम् ॥८०॥

राजा ।

अयमयमागच्छामि ।   ॥ इति निष्क्रान्तः ॥

॥ तृतीयोऽङ्कः ॥

---

[1] '[*In the air.*] The evening sacrificial rite being commenced, the shadows of the Rākshasas, brown as evening clouds, scattered around the altar which bears the consecrated fire, are flitting about in great numbers, producing consternation.' *Ākāśe*, see p. 96, n. 3. *Savana-karmaṇi* = *homa-karmaṇi*. *Sampravṛitte* = *vpakrānte*. *Pari-tas*, 'on all sides of,' 'around,' here governing an accusative. *Prakīrṇāḥ* is the reading of the oldest MSS.; Ś. reads *vistīrṇāḥ*; the Deva-n. *prayastāḥ*, 'striving,' 'using effort.' *Hutāśanavatīm* = *āhitāgnim*. *Bhayam ādadhānāḥ* = *trāsam utpādayantyaḥ*. *Kapiśa*, properly 'ape-coloured,' generally 'brown,' 'dark-brown.' *Piśitāśanānām* = *rākshasānām*. The Rākshasas (see p. 40, n. 5) were remarkable for their appetite for raw flesh (*piśita*).

[2] Observe the use of *ayam*, 'this one,' with the first person of the verb. Dr. Burkhard reads *ayam aham* for *ayam ayam*; cf. p. 136, l. 7, *ayam aham bhoḥ*.

Verse 80. VASANTA-TILAKĀ (a variety of ŚAKVARĪ). See verses 8, 27, 31, 43, 46, 64, 74.

॥ अथ चतुर्थाङ्कादौ विष्कम्भः ॥[1]

॥ ततः प्रविशतः कुसुमावचयमभिनयन्त्यौ सख्यौ ॥

अनसूया ।

[a] हला पिअंवदे । जइ वि गन्धव्वेण विवाहविहिणा णिव्वुत्त-
कल्लाणा सउन्दला अणुरूवभत्तुगामिणी संवुत्तेति णिव्वुदं
मे हिअअं । तह वि एत्तिअं चिन्तणिज्जं ।[2]

प्रियंवदा ।

[b] कहं विअ ।

अनसूया ।

[c] अज्ज सो राएसी इट्टिं परिसमाविअ इसीहिं विसज्जिओ
अत्तणो णअरं पविसिअ अन्तेउरसमागदो इदोगदं वुत्तन्तं
सुमरदि वा ण वेत्ति ।

---

[a] हला प्रियंवदे । यद्यपि गान्धर्वेण विवाहविधिना निर्वृत्तकल्याणा शकुन्तलानु-
रूपभर्तृगामिनी संवृत्तेति निर्वृत्तं मे हृदयम् । तथापीयच्चिन्तनीयम् ।   [b] कथमिव ।
[c] अद्य स राजर्षिरिष्टिं परिसमाप्यर्षिभिर्विसर्जित आत्मनो नगरं प्रविश्यान्तःपुरसमागत
इतोगतं वृत्तान्तं स्मरति वा न वेति ।

---

[1] See the note on the term Vishkambha, p. 97, n. 3.

[2] 'Although my heart is comforted by the thought that S'akuntalā has
become completely happy in being united to a husband worthy of her by
a Gāndharva marriage; nevertheless, there is still some cause for anxiety
[there is still something to be thought about].' *Gāndharvena*, see p. 127,
n. 3. *Anurūpa-bhartṛi-gāminī*, the Beng. have *anurūpa-bhartṛi-bhāginī*.
Iti may often be translated by 'so thinking,' see p. 140, n. 2.

प्रियंवदा ।

^aवीसद्धा होहि । ण तादिसा आकिदिविसेसा गुणवि-
रोहिणी होन्ति । किन्तु तादो दाणिं इमं वुत्तन्तं सुणिअ
ण आणे किं पडिबज्जिस्सदित्ति ।

अनसूया ।

^bजह अहं देक्खामि । तह तस्स अणुमदं भवे ।

प्रियंवदा ।

^cकहं विअ ।

अनसूया ।

^dगुणवदे कण्णआ पडिवादणिज्जेत्ति अअं दाव पढमो
सङ्कप्पो । तं जइ देव्वं एव्व सम्पादेदि । णं अप्पाआसेण
किदत्थो गुरुअणो ।

प्रियंवदा ॥ पुप्पभाजनं विलोक्य ॥

^eसहि । अवइदाइं बलिकम्मपज्जत्ताइं कुसुमाइं ।

---

^a विश्रब्धा भव । न तादृशा आकृतिविशेषा गुणविरोधिनो भवन्ति । किन्तु तात
इदानीमिमं वृत्तान्तं श्रुत्वा न जाने किं प्रतिपत्स्यत इति ।   ^b यथाहं पश्यामि ।
तथा तस्यानुमतं भवेत् ।   ^c कथमिव ।   ^d गुणवते कन्या प्रतिपादनीयेत्ययं
तावत्प्रथमः सङ्कल्पः । तं यदि दैवमेव सम्पादयति । नन्वस्यायासेन कृतार्थो गुरुजनः ।
^e सखि । अवचितानि बलिकर्मपर्याप्तानि कुसुमानि ।

---

¹ 'Such distinguished characters as these do not become opposite in
their qualities (to what they formerly were). But I know not now what
reply the father will make when he has heard this intelligence.' *Ākṛiti*,
properly 'form,' 'figure.' *Kintu* is inserted by the Mackenzie MS., supported
by K. *Pratipatsyate*=*abhidhāsyati*, S.; =*pratirakti*, K.; Westergaard
gives 'respondere' as one sense of *pratipad* (cf. *tac chrutvā tatheti pratya-
padyata*, Rāmāy. i. 10, 15). It might be translated, 'what he will think
of the matter,' 'what he will do,' 'whether he will ratify it.'

² 'The maiden is to be given to a worthy (husband), such was the first
purpose-of-his-heart.' *Sankalpa*=*mano-ratha*, S.; properly 'a resolve,'
'mental determination' (see p. 49, l. 5, with note 2 at the end).

अनसूया ।

[a] णं पिअसहीए सउन्दलाए सोहग्गदेवआ अच्-
णीआ ।[1]

प्रियंवदा ।

[b] जुज्जदि ।   ॥ इति तदेव कर्मारभेते ॥

नेपथ्ये ।

अयमहं भोः ।[2]

अनसूया   ॥ कर्णं दत्त्वा ॥

[c] सहि । अदिधिणा विअ णिवेदिदं ।[3]

प्रियंवदा ।

[d] णं उडजसण्णिहिदा सउन्दला ।   ॥ आत्मगतम् ॥   [e] अज्ज उण
हिअएण असण्णिहिदा ।[4]

---

[a] ननु प्रियसख्याः शकुन्तलायाः सौभाग्यदेवताऽर्चनीया ।   [b] युज्यते ।
[c] सखि । अतिथिरेव निवेदितम् ।   [d] ननूटजसन्निहिता शकुन्तला ।   [e] अद्य
पुनर्हृदयेनासन्निहिता ।

---

[1] 'Is not the guardian-deity of our dear friend S'akuntalā to be honoured (with an offering)?' *Saubhāgya-devatā*, 'the tutelary deity,' 'the deity who watches over the welfare of any one.' The Beng. read *devatāḥ*, 'deities,' and S'. adds *shashṭikā-gaurī-prabhṛitayaḥ*, 'such as Shashṭikā [Durgā], Gaurī, &c.'

[2] '[*Behind the scenes.*] It is I, ho there!' *Nepathye*, see p. 3, n. 2. *Ayam aham āgato 'smi iti arthaḥ*, S'. See Manu ii. 122, &c., 'After salutation, a Brāhman must address an elder, saying, "I am such a one" (*asau nāmāham*), pronouncing his own name. If any persons (through ignorance of Sanskrit) do not understand the form of salutation (in which mention is made) of the name, to them should a learned man say, "It is I" (*aham iti*), and in that manner should he address all women. In the salutation he should utter the word *bhoḥ* (*bhoḥ-śabda*), for the particle *bhoḥ* is held by sages to have the same property with names (fully expressed).'

[3] '(It seems) as if an announcement were made by a guest [as if a guest were announcing himself].' So read the Beng. MSS., the Deva-n. have *atithīnām*.

[4] 'With her heart she is not near,' i. e. her heart is absent with Dushyanta.

अनसूया ।

[a] होदु । अलं एत्तिएहिं कुसुमेहिं । ॥ इति प्रस्थिते ॥

नेपथ्ये ।

आ अतिथिपरिभाविनि ।

विचिन्तयन्ती यमनन्यमानसा
तपोधनं वेत्ति न मामुपस्थितम् ।
स्मरिष्यति त्वां न स बोधितोऽपि स-
न्कथां प्रमत्तः प्रथमं कृतामिव ॥ ८१ ॥

प्रियंवदा ।

[b] हद्दी हद्दी । अप्पिअं एव्व संवुत्तं । कस्सिंपि पूआरहे अवरद्धा सुस्सहिअम्हा सउन्दला । ॥ पुरोऽवलोक्य ॥ [c] ण हु जस्सिं कस्सिंपि । एसो दुव्वासो सुलहकोवो महेसी । तह सविस्स वेअचहुलुप्फुल्लदुव्वाराए गईए पडिणिवुत्तो ।

---

[a] भवतु । अलमियद्भिः कुसुमैः । कस्मिन्नपि पूजार्हेऽपराद्धा शून्यहृदया शकुन्तला ।   [b] हाधिक् हाधिक् । अप्रियमेव संवृत्तम् ।   [c] न खलु यस्मिन्कस्मिन्नपि । एष दुर्वासाः सुलभकोपो महर्षिः । तथा शब्दा वेगचटुलोत्फुल्लदुर्वारया गत्या प्रतिनिवृत्तः ।

---

[1] 'Woe! thou that art disrespectful to a guest! that (man) of whom (thou art) thinking to-the-exclusion-of-every-other-object-from-thy-mind, (so that) thou perceivest not me, rich in penance, to have approached, shall not recall thee to his memory, even being reminded; as a drunken-man (does not recall) the talk [speech] previously made (by himself).' *Atithi-paribhāvini*, see p. 36, n. 1; the Beng. have *katham atithim pari-bhavasi*. *Vetsi* = *vibhāvayasi*, S'. *Bodhitaḥ* = *smāritaḥ*, S'. *Kṛitām*, i. e. *ātmanaiva*, S'.; *kathāṃ kṛi* = root *kath*, 'to speak,' 'tell,' 'say;' and *kathāṃ kṛitām* = *kathitām*, 'what is spoken,' 'said.'

[2] 'A very unpleasant thing has occurred. S'akuntalā, in her absence of mind, has committed an offence against some person deserving of respect.

---

[a] की अखो हुदवहादो दहिदुं पहविस्संदि ।

अनसूया ।

[b] गच्छ । पादेसु पणमिस्स णिवत्तेहि णं । जाव अहं
अग्घोदअं उबकप्पेमि ।

[a] कोऽन्यो हुतवहाद्दग्धुं प्रभविष्यति । [b] गच्छ । पादयोः प्रणम्य निवर्तयैनम् ।
यावदहमर्ध्योदकमुपकल्पयामि ।

[*Looking on in front.*] Not, indeed, against some (mere ordinary) person ;
(for I see that) it is the great Ṛishi Durvāsas, easily-provoked to anger.
After uttering such a curse, he has turned back with a step tremulous,
bounding, and difficult to be checked through its impetuosity.' *Śūnya-
hṛidayā*, lit. 'empty-hearted,' one whose heart is engrossed with some
other object. *Veya-ćaṭula*, &c. This is the reading of the Mackenzie
MS., and seems to have been that of K. All the Deva-n. have *upphulla*
for the Sanskṛit *utphula*, from root *sphul*, 'to leap,' allied to *sphur*. As
to the Prākṛit *upphulla*, it may be observed that many consonants in
Prākṛit are too weak to sustain themselves singly, and that if elision does
not take place, the consonant is sometimes doubled. Thus *sukkha* or
suha may be written for the Sanskṛit *sukha*, and *nīhitta* or *nīhia* for
nīhita, Lassen's Instit. Prāk. p. 276, 3. The oldest Beng. MS. has *avirala-
pādoddhārayā*, and the Calcutta ed. *avirala-pāda-tvarayā gatyā*. Dur-
vāsas is a saint or Muni, represented by the Hindū poets as excessively
choleric, and inexorably severe. The Purāṇas and other poems contain
frequent accounts of the terrible effects of his imprecations on various
occasions, the slightest offence being in his eyes deserving of the most
fearful punishment. On one occasion he cursed Indra, merely because
his elephant let fall a garland which he had given to this god; and
in consequence of this imprecation all plants withered, men ceased to
sacrifice, and the gods were overcome in their wars with the demons (see
Vishṇu-p. p. 70). For Maharshi, see p. 39, n. 3, and p. 44, n. 2.

[1] 'Who beside Fire will have (such) power to consume ?' S'. alone has
tathā (*taha*) at the end of this sentence. The wrath of a Brāhman is
frequently compared to fire (see p. 74, n. 3, and p. 50, n. 2).

[2] 'Therefore, bowing down at his feet, persuade him to return, whilst
I prepare a propitiatory offering and water.' The Beng. have *patitvā*,
'having fallen,' for *praṇamya*. *Arghyodaka*, see p. 36, notes 2 and 3.

प्रियंवदा ।

a तह । ॥ इति निष्क्रान्ता ॥

अनसूया ॥ पदान्तरे स्खलितं निरूप्य ॥

b अम्मो । आवेअक्खलिदाए गईए पब्भटुं मे हत्थादो पुप्फभाअणं । ॥ इति पुष्पोच्चयं रूपयति ॥

प्रियंवदा ॥ प्रविश्य ॥

c सहि । पकिदिवक्को सो कस्स अणुणअं पडिगेरहदि । किम्पि उण साणुक्कोसो किंदो ।

अनसूया ॥ सस्मितम् ॥

d तस्सिं बहु एदम्मि । कहेहिं ।

प्रियंवदा ।

e जदा णिवत्तिदुं ण इच्छदि । तदा विण्णविदो मए । भअवं । पढमंत्ति पेक्खिञ अविण्णादतवप्पहावस्स दुहि-दुजणस्स भअवदा एक्को अवराही मरिसिदव्वोत्ति ।

---

a तथा ।　　　b अहो । आवेगस्खलितया गत्या भ्रष्टं मे हस्तात्पुष्पभाजनम् ।
c सखि । प्रकृतिवक्रः स कस्यानुनयं प्रतिगृह्णाति । किमपि पुनः सानुक्रोशः कृतः ।
d तस्मिन्वह्वेतदपि । कथय ।　　　e यदा निवर्तितुं नेच्छति । तदा विज्ञापितो मया ।
भगवन् । प्रथममिति प्रेक्ष्याविज्ञाततपःप्रभावस्य दुहितृजनस्य भगवतैकोऽपराधो मर्षयि-तव्य इति ।

---

[1] 'She acts the gathering up of the flowers.' *Uččaya* has the same sense as *samuččaya*, 'collecting together in a heap,' see p. 79, l. 8.

[2] 'Whose friendly-persuasion will this crooked-tempered (person) accept? however, he was somewhat softened [he was made a little merciful].' *Prakriti-vakra*, 'one whose disposition is crooked or harsh,' 'ill-tempered,' 'cross-grained.'

[3] 'Even this (somewhat) was much for him; say on.'

[4] 'Considering (it is) the first-time, this one offence of the daughter, who is unaware of the potency of penance, is to be pardoned by your

अनसूया ।

a तदो तदो ।

प्रियंवदा ।

b तदो मे वञणं अण्णहाभविदुं णारिहदि । किन्तु अहिण्णा-
णाभरणदंसणेण सावो णिवत्तिस्सदिति मन्तअन्तो सञ्चं
अन्तरिहिदो ।

अनसूया ।

c सक्कं दाणिं अस्ससिदुं अत्थि । तेण राएसिणा
सम्पत्थिदेण सणामहेअङ्किअं अङ्गुलीअअं सुमरणी-
अन्ति सञ्चं पिणद्धं । तस्सिं साहीणोबाआ सउन्दला
भविस्सदि ।

प्रियंवदा ।

d सहि । एहि । देवकज्जं दाव णिव्वत्तेम्ह ।

॥ इति परिक्रामतः ॥

a ततस्ततः ।   b ततो मे वचनमन्यथाभवितुं नार्हति । किन्न्वभिज्ञानाभरण-दर्शनेन शापो निवर्तिष्यत इति मन्त्रयमाणः स्वयमन्तर्हितः ।   c शक्यमिदानीमा-श्वसितुमस्ति । तेन राजर्षिणा सम्प्रस्थितेन स्वनामधेयाङ्कितमङ्गुलीयकं स्मरणीयमिति स्वयं पिनद्धम् । तस्मिन्स्वाधीनोपाया शकुन्तला भविष्यति ।   d सखि । एहि । देवकार्यं तावन्निर्वर्तयावः ।

---

reverence.' *Prathamam iti*, the Beng., supported by K., have *prathama-bhaktim avekshya*, 'in consideration of her former devotion.'

[1] '"My word must not be falsified; but at the sight of the jewel-of-recognition, the curse shall cease :" so speaking, he withdrew himself from sight [vanished].' *Abhijñānābharaṇa*, lit. 'the recognition-ornament,' 'the token-ring,' see p. 4, n. 2. *Ṇārihadi* (=Sanskrit *na arhati*) is correct, according to Lassen's Instit. Prāk. p. 193, 10. The MSS. frequently read *ṇāruhadi*, as on p. 54, l. 5. *Svayam antarhitaḥ*, lit. 'he became self-hidden.'

[2] 'A ring stamped with his name was by that Rājarshi himself, at his departure, fastened on (her finger) as a souvenir. In that [with that],

प्रियंवदा ॥ अवलोक्य ॥

[a] अणसूए । पेक्ख दाव । वामहत्थोवहिदवअणा आलि-
हिदा विअ पिअसही । भत्तुगदाए चिन्ताए अत्ताणम्पि
ण एसा विभावेदि । किं उण आअन्तुअं ।

अनसूया ।

[b] पिअंवदे । दुवेणं एव्व णो मुहे एसो वुत्तन्तो चिट्ठदु ।
रक्खणीआ खु पकिदिपेलवा पिअसही ।

प्रियंवदा ।

[c] को दाणिं उण्होदएण णोमालिअं सिञ्चेदि ।

॥ इत्युभे निष्क्रान्ते ॥

॥ विष्कम्भः ॥

[a] अनसूये । प्रेक्षस्व तावत् । वामहस्तोपहितवदनालिखितेव प्रियसखी । भर्तृगतया
चिन्तयात्मानमपि नैषा विभावयति । किं पुनरागन्तुकम् ।   [b] प्रियंवदे । द्वयोरेव
नौ मुख एष वृत्तान्तस्तिष्ठतु । रक्षणीया खलु प्रकृतिपेलवा प्रियसखी ।   [c] क इदा-
नीमुष्णोदकेन नवमालिकां सिञ्चति ।

S'akuntalā will be possessed-of-a-resource-in-her-own-power.' *Sva-nāma-dheyānkitam*, see p. 53, notes 2 and 3. *Smaraṇīyam iti*, properly 'saying, "It is a remembrance."' *Iti* often involves the sense of 'saying,' 'thinking,' &c., see p. 60, n. 1. The Beng. MSS. add *S'akuntalā-haste*, but not the Deva-n. nor K. For *tasmin*, S'. has *tasmāt*.

[1] 'Our dear friend, her face resting on her left hand, (is motionless) as if in a picture,' see p. 7, n. 2.

[2] *Bhartṛi-gata*, 'relating to her husband,' see p. 42, n. 2.

[3] 'Let this circumstance remain in the mouth of us two only. Our dear friend being of a delicate nature must be spared [preserved],' i.e. she must not be told about this imprecation, lest her feelings be so hurt, that her delicate constitution be injured. *Vṛittāntaḥ*, i.e. *sāpa-vṛittāntaḥ*, S'.

॥ अथ चतुर्थोऽङ्कः ॥

॥ ततः प्रविशति सुप्तोत्थितः[1] शिष्यः ॥

शिष्यः ।

वेलोपलक्षणार्थमादिष्टोऽस्मि तत्रभवता प्रवासादुपावृत्तेन
काश्यपेन । प्रकाशं निर्गतस्तावद्वलोकयामि कियद्वशिष्टं
रजन्या इति ।[2] ॥ परिक्रम्यावलोक्य च ॥ हन्त प्रभातम् । तथा हि

यात्येकतोऽस्तशिखरं पतिरोषधीना-
माविष्कृतारुणपुरःसर एकतोऽर्कः ।
तेजोद्वयस्य युगपद्व्यसनोदयाभ्यां
लोको नियम्यत इवात्मदशान्तरेषु ॥ ८२ ॥[3]

---

[1] 'Arisen from sleep,' = *suptānantaram utthitaḥ*, 'just arisen after sleep,' S'.

[2] 'I am commissioned by his reverence Kāśyapa, (who has just) returned from his pilgrimage [residence abroad], to observe the time of day. Having gone out into the open air, I will just see how much of the night remains.' *Pravāsāt*, i. e. *soma-tīrthāt*, see p. 17, n. 1. *Prakāśa* = *vivṛita-pradeśa*, 'an open spot,' K. ; = *ćatvara*, 'a court-yard,' S'.

[3] 'On the one side the lord of the plants [the Moon] descends to the summit of the western mountain ; on the other side (rises) the Sun, whose forerunner Aruṇa [the Dawn] has just become visible. By the contemporaneous setting and rising of the two luminaries, human beings are warned, as it were, in their different states,' i. e. by the alternations of these luminaries, the vicissitudes of human life are indicated. The Moon is called *Oshadhī-pati*, 'lord of medicinal plants,' being supposed to exercise some influence over the growth of such plants. Cf. Deut. xxxiii. 14, 'The precious fruits brought forth by the sun, and the precious things put forth by the moon.' *Oshadhī* is described as 'dying (*phala-pākāntā*, Manu i. 46) after the ripening of its fruit.' *Asta* is the name for the mountain in the West, behind which, in Hindū poetry, the sun and moon are supposed to set, as *Udaya* is the name of that over which they are supposed to rise. *Arka* is a name of Sūrya, 'the Sun.' He is represented as seated in a chariot drawn by seven green horses, or by one horse with seven heads (whence his name *Saptāśva*), and before him is a lovely youth

---

Verse 82. VASANTA-TILAKĀ. See verses 8, 27, 31, 43, 46, 64, 74, 80.

अपि च । अन्तर्हिते शशिनि सैव कुमुद्वती मे
दृष्टिं न नन्दयति संस्मरणीयशोभा ।
इष्टप्रवासजनितान्यबलाजनस्य
दुःखानि नूनमतिमात्रसुदुःसहानि ॥ ८३ ॥

---

without legs, who acts as his charioteer, and who is called Aruṇa, or Dawn
personified. Aruṇa is the son of Kaśyapa and Vinatā, and elder brother
of Garuḍa. His imperfect form may be allusive to his gradual or partial
appearance, his legs being supposed to be lost, either in the darkness of
the departing night, or in the blaze of the coming day. With this verse
cf. Mṛiććhak. p. 321, l. 4, thus translated by Wilson, 'In heaven itself the
sun and moon are not free from change (*vipattiṃ labhete*); how should we
poor weak mortals hope to escape it in this lower world? One man rises
but to fall, another falls to rise again,' &c.

[1] 'The moon having disappeared, even the lotus no longer gladdens my
sight, its beauty being now only a matter of remembrance. The sorrows
produced by the absence of a lover are beyond measure hard to be
supported by a tender-girl.' Some species of the lotus open their petals
during the night, and close them during the day, whence the Moon is
often called the Friend, Lover, or Lord of the lotuses (*kumuda-bāndhava,
kumudinī-nāyaka, kumudeśa*). For *abalā-janasya*, the Beng. have *abalā-
janena;* the genitive is equally admissible. Cf. *svabhāvas tasya durati-
kramaḥ*, Hitop. l. 1945.

The following are given after verse 83 in the Beng. MSS. and in the
Calcutta and French editions, supported by S'., but not in the Deva-n.
nor in K. :

अपि च । कर्कन्धूनामुपरि तुहिनं रञ्जयत्यग्रसन्ध्या
दार्भं मुञ्चत्युटजपटलं वीतनिद्रो मयूरः ।
वेदिप्रान्तात्खुरविलिखितादुत्थितस्थैष सद्यः
पश्चादुच्चैर्भवति हरिणः खाङ्गमायच्छमानः ॥

अपि च । पादन्यासं क्षितिधरगुरोर्मूर्ध्नि कृत्वा सुमेरोः
क्रान्तं येन द्यायततमसा मध्यमं धाम विष्णोः ।
सोऽयं चन्द्रः पतति गगणादल्पशेषैर्मयूखै-
रत्यारूढिर्भवति महतामप्यपभ्रंशनिष्ठा ॥

'Moreover, the early dawn impurples the dew-drops upon the jujubes;

Verse 83. VASANTA-TILAKĀ (a variety of ŚAKVARĪ). See verse 82.

अनसूया ॥ प्रविश्य पटाक्षेपेण ॥

^a एव्वं णाम विसअपरम्मुहस्सवि इमस्स जणस्स ण
एदं ण विदिन्नं । तेण रञ्ञा सउन्दलाए अणज्जं आ-
अरिदंत्ति² ।

^a एवं नाम विषयपराङ्मुखस्याप्यस्य जनस्य नैतन्न विदितम् । तेन राज्ञा शकुन्तला-
यामनार्यमाचरितमिति ।

---

the peacock, shaking off sleep, quits the Darbha-grass thatch of the cottage;
and yonder the antelope, rising hastily from the border of the altar im-
pressed by his hoofs, afterwards raises himself on high, stretching his
limbs. Moreover, after planting his foot on the head of Sumeru, lord of
mountains, the Moon, by whom, dispersing the darkness, the central
palace of Vishṇu has been invaded, even he, descends from the sky
with diminished beams. The highest ascent of the great terminates in
a fall.'

[1] 'With a hurried toss of the curtain.' *Paṭākshepeṇa* (so read all the
Deva-n. MSS. and K.) is from *paṭa*, with the same sense as *apaṭī*, i. e. the
curtain separating the stage from the *nepathya* (see p. 3, n. 2) and *ākshepa*,
'tossing aside.' The Beng. reading is *apaṭī-kshepeṇa*. *Paṭākshepeṇa=
yavanikāpanodanena*, K.;=*akasmāt*, 'suddenly,' S'. According to K.,
the entrance of an actor under the influence of flurry caused by joy,
sorrow, or any other emotion (*harsha-śokādi-janita-sambhrama-yuktasya*)
is made with a toss of the curtain.

[2] 'It is not unknown to this person [myself], however withdrawn (she
may be) from worldly concerns, that an indignity has been wrought
towards S'akuntalā by that king.' *Evaṃ nāma* is the reading of the
Mackenzie MS., supported by K. *Na etat na viditam* is given on the
authority of K. *Imassa* is inserted from the old MS. (India Office, 1060);
S'. has *amushya janasya*. The other Deva-n. MSS. read *yady api nāma
vishaya-parān-mukhasyāpi janasya etan na viditaṃ tathāpi tena*, &c.
The margin of the Beng. MS., as well as that of Chézy, has a note referring
vishaya-parān-mukhasya janasya to Kaṇva; but a comparison of other
passages shews that by *ayaṃ janaḥ* the person or persons speaking
are commonly intended (cf. p. 125, l. 6, and p. 156, l. 12). *An-āryam*,
lit. 'anything unworthy or dishonourable,' 'ungentlemanly conduct,' i. e.
according to S'. and C., *Śakuntalā-vismaraṇa-rūpam*, 'consisting of the
forgetting of S'akuntalā.'

शिष्य: ।

यावदुपस्थितां होमवेलां गुरवे निवेदयामि । ॥ इति निष्क्रान्त: ॥

अनसूया ।

[a]पडिबुद्धावि किं करिस्सं । ण मे उइदेसुवि णिञ्चकर-णिज्जेसु हत्थपाआ पसरन्ति । कामो दाणिं सकामो होदु । जेण असच्चसन्धे जणे सुद्धहिअआ सही पदं कारिदा[2] । अहवा दुव्वाससावो एसो विआरेदि[3] । अच्छहा कहं सो राएसी तारिसाणि मन्निअ एत्तिअस्स कालस्स लेह-मत्तम्पि ण विसज्जेदि । ता इदो अहिल्लाणं अङ्गुलीअअं से

---

[a] प्रतिबुद्धापि किं करिष्यामि । न म उचितेष्वपि निजकरणीयेषु ह स्तपादा: प्रसरन्ति । काम इदानीं सकामो भवतु । येनासत्यसन्धे जने शुद्धहृदया सखी पदं कारिता । अथवा दुर्वास:शाप एष विकारयति । अन्यथा कथं स राजर्षिस्तादृशानि मन्त्रयित्वैतावत: कालस्य लेखमात्रमपि न विसर्जयति । तस्मादितोऽभिज्ञानमङ्गुलीयकमस्य

---

[1] 'The time for (making) the burnt-offering;' see p. 148, n. 1.

[2] 'Although wide-awake, what shall I do? My hands and feet do not move-freely in their own usual occupations. Let Love now be possessed of his wish [enjoy his triumph], by whom our innocent-minded friend has been made to place confidence in that perfidious man.' *Uéiteshu karaṇī-yeshu*, such as 'gathering flowers,' &c., S. *Sa-kāmaḥ=kṛitārthī*, 'one who has attained his end,' S. (cf. *bhavatu pañca-vāṇaḥ kṛitī*, Vikram., Act II). *Asatya-sandha*, lit. 'one who is not true to his contract (*sandhā*);'=*asatya-pratijña*, S.;=*mithyā-pratijña*, C. *Suddha-hṛidayā* is the reading of two Deva-nāgarī MSS. and of the Bengālī. *Pada=sthāna*, 'a place,' S.; =*vyavasāya* or *ryavasiti*, 'industry,' 'application,' 'business,' C. and Amara-k. Hence *padaṃ kṛi* in the causal must mean 'to cause to have dealings or transactions with,' 'to cause to apply one's self,' 'to cause to take up a station;' whence may easily flow the interpretation, 'made to trust.' Cf. a similar phrase in Kumāra-s. vi. 14, where also the commentators explain *pada* by *vyavasāya*.

[3] 'Or rather, it is the curse of Durvāsas that has caused the change.' *Athavā*, see p. 24, l. 10; p. 30, n. 3. *Vikārayati*, see p. 130, n. 1.

[a] विसज्जेम । दुक्खसीले तवस्सिजणे को अब्भत्थी-अदु । एं सहीगामी दोसोत्ति ववसिदावि ण पारेमि पवासपडिणिउत्तस्स तादकस्सवस्स दुस्सन्दपरिणीदं आबस्सत्तं सउन्दलं णिवेदिदुं । इत्थंगए अम्हेहिं किं करणिज्जं ।

प्रियंवदा ॥ प्रविश्य । सहर्षम् ॥

[b] सहि । तुवर तुवर सउन्दलाए पत्थाणकौदुअं णिव्वत्तिदुं ।

अनसूया ।

[c] सहि । कहं एदं ।

---

[a] विसर्जयावः । दुःखशीले तपस्विजने कोऽभ्यर्थ्यताम् । ननु सखीगामी दोष इति व्यवसितापि न पारयामि प्रवासप्रतिनिवृत्तस्य तातकाश्यपस्य दुष्यन्तपरिणीतामापन्न-सत्त्वां शकुन्तलां निवेदयितुम् । इत्थंगतेऽस्माभिः किं करणीयम् ।   [b] सखि ।
त्वरय त्वरय शकुन्तलायाः प्रस्थानकौतुकं निर्वर्तयितुम् ।   [c] सखि ।
कथमेतत् ।

---

[1] 'Among ascetics inured-to-hardships, who is to be solicited (to carry the ring to the king)? Assuredly, even though I were convinced that blame was attributable to S'akuntalā, I should not have the power to make known to father Kāśyapa, (just) returned from his pilgrimage, that S'akuntalā is married to Dushyanta, and is pregnant. Such being the case, what is to be done by us?' *Duḥkha-śīle*, so read all the Deva-n.; the oldest Bengālī, supported by *C.*, has *nirduḥkha-śītale*. *Sakhī-gāmin*, see p. 42, n. 2. *Vyavasitā*, past pass. part. of *vy-ava-so*, 'to determine,' 'resolve,' 'strive;' also 'to be persuaded,' 'convinced,' as in Rāmāy. ii. 12, 61, *satīṃ tvāṃ vyavasyāmi*. *Pārayāmi* is either the causal form of *pṛi*, meaning 'to conduct across,' 'bring over,' 'accomplish,' 'fulfil,' and thence 'to be able,' or is a nominal from *pāra*, 'the opposite bank (of a river),' 'the other side,' 'the end.' *Ittham-gate*, i. e. *evam-prāpte karmaṇi*.

[2] 'Hasten to celebrate [complete] the festivities at the departure of S'akuntalā.' *Prasthāna-kautuka*=*prayāṇa-maṅgala*, 'festive solemnities which take place at the departure of a member of the family.'

प्रियंवदा ।

[a]सुणाहि दाणिं । सुहसइदं पुच्छिदुं सउन्दलासआसं
गदम्हि ।

अनसूया ।

[b]तदो तदो ।

प्रियंवदा ।

[c]दाव एणं लज्जावणदमुहिं परिस्सजिअ सञ्जं तादकस्स-
बेण एव्व अहिणन्दिदं । दिट्ठिआ । धूमाउलिददिट्ठिणोबि
जञ्जमाणस्स पावअ एव्व आहुदी पडिदा । वच्छे ।
सुसिस्सपरिदिण्णा विअ विज्जा असोअणिज्जा संवुत्ता ।
अज्ज एव्व इसिपडिरक्खिदं तुमं भत्तुणो सआसं विसज्जे-
मित्ति ।

<hr>

[a] शृणुखिदानीम् । सुखशयितं प्रष्टुं शकुन्तलासकाशं गतास्मि ।   [b] ततस्ततः ।
[c] तावदेनां लज्जावनतमुखीं परिष्वज्य स्वयं तातकाश्यपेनैवमभिनन्दितम् । दिष्ट्या ।
धूमाकुलितदृष्टेरपि यजमानस्य पावक एवाहुतिः पतिता । वत्से । सुशिष्यपरिदत्तेव
विद्याशोचनीया संवृत्ता । अद्यैव ऋषिप्रतिरक्षितां त्वां भर्तुः सकाशं विसर्जयामीति ।

<hr>

[1] 'To inquire (whether she had had) a comfortable sleep.' *Pucchidum*
for *prashtum*, so reads my own Bombay MS., supported by a parallel
passage in Mālavik. 44, 7, *suham pucchidum āgatā*. The other Deva-n.
have *suha-saida-pucchiā* for *sukha-sayita-pracchikā*, which is given as
another reading in Mālavik. Dr. Boehtlingk remarks that the agent may
be used with the sense of a fut. part. active, and refers to Pāṇ. iii. 3, 10.

[2] 'By father Kaṇva [see p. 22, n. 3] having of his own accord em-
braced her whilst her face was bowed down with shame, she was thus
congratulated [congratulation was made], "Hail (to thee)! the oblation of
the sacrificing priest, although his sight was obscured by the smoke, fell
directly into the fire;"' see n. 3 below. *Dhūmākulita*, cf. p. 65, l. 7.
Yajamāna, see p. 95, n. 1.

[3] 'My child, as knowledge delivered over to a good student (is not to
be deplored, so has it) come to pass that thou art not to be sorrowed for.
This very day I dismiss thee protected by [under the escort of some]

U 2

अनसूया ।

[a] अह केण सूइदो तादकस्सबस्स वुत्तन्तो ।

प्रियंवदा ।

[b] अग्गिसरणं पविट्ठस्स सरीरं विणा छन्दोमईए वाआए ।

[a] अथ केन सूचितस्तातकाश्यपस्य वृत्तान्तः ।   [b] अग्निशरणं प्रविष्टस्य शरीरं विना छन्दोमय्या वाचया ।

Ṛishis to the presence of (thy) husband.' Compare Manu ii. 114, 'Learning having approached a Brāhman said to him, "I am thy divine treasure, deliver me not to a scorner, but communicate me to that student who will be a careful guardian of the treasure."' The Beng. and K. insert *me* before *aśočanīyā*, and read *parigrihītām* for *pratirakshitām*.

[1] 'By an incorporeal [without body, without visible speaker] metrical speech (addressed to him from heaven), when he had entered the fire-sanctuary.' *Śarīraṃ vinā*, i. e. *ākāśe Sarasvatyā niveditaḥ*, 'he was informed by Sarasvatī (by a voice) in the sky,' S'.; see p. 96, n. 3. *Agni-śaraṇa=agny-āgāra*, 'the place where the sacred fire was kept;'=*yajña-śālā*, 'hall of sacrifice.' Fire is an important object of veneration with the Hindūs, almost as much so as with the ancient Persians. Perhaps the chief worship recommended in the Vedas is that of Fire and the Sun. According to Manu, Brāhmans when they married and became house-holders, were to kindle with two pieces of the hard S'amī, Araṇi, or Khadira wood, or with a piece of the S'amī and Aśvattha wood (see p. 23, n. 1), a sacred fire (*homāgni, grihyāgni, hutāgni*), which they were to deposit in a cavity or hearth called *agni-kuṇḍa* or *vitāna* (Indian Wisdom, p. 197), in some hallowed part of the house (or, like the Persians, in some sacred building proper for the purpose) called *agny-āgāra* (Manu iv. 58), *homa-śālā, agni-griha*, and which they were to keep lighted throughout their lives, using it first for their nuptial ceremony (Manu ii. 231, iii. 171); and for the regular morning and evening oblations to Agni (*homa, hotra*), performed by dropping clarified butter &c. into the flame, with prayers and invocations (Manu xi. 41, iii. 81, 84, 85; see also p. 133, n. 1 of this play); for the performance of solemn sacrifices (Manu ii. 143); for the S'rāddha or obsequies to departed parents and ancestors (Manu iii. 212 sqq.; see also p. 111, n. 1 of this play); and, finally, for the funeral pile. The perpetual maintenance of this sacred fire was called *agni-hotra, agny-ādhāna, agni-rakshaṇa*; and the consecration of it, *agny-ādheya*

अनसूया ॥ सविस्मयम् ॥

^a कहेहि ।

प्रियंवदा ॥ संस्कृतमाश्रित्य ॥

दुष्यन्तेनाहितं तेजो दधानां भूतये भुवः ।
अवेहि तनयां ब्रह्मन्नग्निगर्भां शमीमिव ॥ ८४ ॥

^a कथय ।

(Manu ii. 143); and the Brāhman or householder who maintained it, *agni-hotrin, āhitāgni, agny-āhita, sāgnika*. At Benares even to this day many Agni-hotras are kept burning. Sometimes the householder did not him-self attend to the sacred fire, but engaged an officiating priest (*ritvij, yajamāna, agnīdhra,* see p. 95, n. 1; p. 96, n. 2). The Brāhman who did not maintain a fire was called *an-āhitāgni* (Manu xi. 38). According to Manu iii. 212 (with commentary) there were three periods when he was necessarily without it, viz. just before his investiture, before his marriage after the completion of his studentship, and at the death of his wife; but the usual daily oblation was then to be placed in the hand of a holy Brāhman, who is said to be one form of fire (see p. 74, n. 3; p. 50, n. 2). Sacred fire is sometimes considered to be of three kinds (*tretā,* 'the triad of fires'): 1. *Gārhapatya,* 'nuptial or household;' 2. *Āhavanīya,* 'sacrificial,' taken from the preceding; 3. *Dakshina,* 'that placed towards the south,' taken from either of the former; see Manu ii. 231. The man who maintained all these three was called *tretāgni.* See Indian Wisdom, p. 198, n. 1.

¹ '[*Having recourse to Sanskrit.*] Know that (thy adopted) daughter, O Brāhman, has conceived a glorious-germ [seed] implanted [lodged, deposited] by Dushyanta for the welfare of the earth, as the S'amī-tree is pregnant with fire.' *S'amī,* 'a kind of thorny acacia' (see the last note, and p. 23, n. 1). The legend is that the goddess Pārvatī, being one day under the influence of strong passion, reposed on a trunk of this tree, whereby an intense heat was generated in the pith or interior of the wood, which ever after broke into a sacred flame on the slightest attrition. *Āhita=arpita. Tejah=śukra,* C. (cf. Raghu-v. ii. 75; Megha-d. 45.) 'By this it was indicated that S'akuntalā would have a son in glory equal to Agni,' S'.

Verse 84. S'LOKA or ANUSHTUBH. See verses 5, 6, 11, 12, 26, 47, 50, 51, 53, 73, 76.

अनसूया ॥ प्रियंवदामाश्लिष्य ॥

[a] सहि । पिअं मे । पिअं मे । किन्दु अज्ज एव्व सउन्दला
णीअदित्ति उक्कण्ठासाहारणं परितोसं अणुहोमि ।

प्रियंवदा ।

[b] सहि । वअं दाव उक्कण्ठं विणोदइस्सामो । सा तवस्सिणी
णिव्वुदा होदु ।

अनसूया ।

[c] तेण हि एदस्सिं चूदसाहावलम्बिदे णारिएरसमुग्गए
एदणिमित्तं एव्व कालन्तरक्खमा णिक्खित्ता मए केसर-
मालिआ । ता इमं हत्थसण्णिहिदं करेहिं । जाव अहम्पि से

<hr>

[a] सखि । प्रियं मे । प्रियं मे । किन्त्वद्यैव शकुन्तला नीयत इत्युत्कण्ठासाधारणं
परितोषमनुभवामि ।   [b] सखि । आवां तावदुत्कण्ठां विनोदयिष्यावः । सा
तपस्विनी निर्वृता भवतु ।   [c] तेन हि एतस्मिंश्चूतशाखावलम्बिते नारिकेरसमुद्गक
एतन्निमित्तमेव कालान्तरक्षमा निक्षिप्ता मया केशरमालिका । तदिमां हस्तसन्निहितां
कुरु । यावदहमप्यस्या

<hr>

[1] 'O friend, how pleased I am ! but when I think that this very day
S'akuntalā is being conveyed away (to her husband's house), I feel a satis-
faction mingled with regret.' *Iti*, 'so thinking,' see p. 140, n. 2. *Utkaṇṭhā-
sādhāraṇa*, lit. 'in common with regret or sorrow.' 'I am partly glad,
partly sorry,' S.

[2] '(Only) let this (our) poor-sister be made happy.' *Tapasvin*, 'a
devotee,' also denotes 'a person in a pitiable state,' 'a poor wretch.' *Nir-
vṛitā* = *susthita-ćitta*, S.

[3] 'Therefore in this cocoa-nut box, suspended on a bough of the mango,
a Keśara-garland, capable of (keeping fresh for) the intervening period,
was with this very object deposited by me. Therefore make it rest on
(my) hand [take it down and give it to me].' *Nārikera* or *nārikela*, 'the
cocoa-nut,' 'the fruit of the cocoa-nut tree.' *Ćūta* or *āmra*, 'the mango
tree.' *Kālāntara-kshamā* = *virala-kāla-sthāyinī*, S. *Keśara-mālikā*, 'a
wreath made of the flowers of the Bakula,' see p. 26, n. 1. This was

ᵃमिस्सलोश्रं तित्थमित्तिश्रं दुव्वाकिसलश्राणिं मङ्ग-
लसमालम्भणाणि विरएमि¹ ।

प्रियंवदा ।

ᵇतह करीश्रदु ।

॥ अनसूया निष्क्रान्ता । प्रियंवदा नाट्येन सुमनसो गृह्णाति ॥

नेपथ्ये ।

गौतमि । आदिश्यन्तां शाङ्गैरवमिश्राः² शकुन्तलानयनाय ।

ᵃ मृगरोचनां तीर्थमृत्तिकां दूर्वाकिसलयानीति मङ्गलसमालम्भनानि विरचयामि ।
ᵇ तथा क्रियताम् ।

---

probably a *mangala-pushpa-mayī srak*, or 'garland made of auspicious
flowers,' to be suspended round the neck of S'akuntalā, such as that
described in Raghu-v. vi. 84. S'. and the Beng. read *keśara-guṇḍāḥ* or
keśara-čūrṇāḥ, and S'. observes that the fragrant dust of this plant is
much used by women in making unguents (*udvartanāni*).

¹ 'Whilst I also will compound auspicious unguents composed of
Mṛiga-roćanā, holy earth, (and) Dūrbā sprouts.' *Mṛiga-roćanā* is said to
be either the concrete bile of a deer or an exudation from his head, used
as a medicine, a yellow dye or a perfume (see *go-roćanā* in Dict.) The
latter word is the reading of the Beng. MSS. *Tīrtha-mṛittikā* is earth
brought from Tīrthas or holy bathing-places (see p. 17, n. 1). *Dūrbā* or
dūrvā, 'bent-grass,' a kind of sacred grass, not quite so sacred as *darbha*,
but possessing many virtues, and used for the *argha* (see p. 36, n. 2). Sir
W. Jones says of it, 'Its flowers, in their perfect state, are among the
loveliest objects in the vegetable world, and appear, through a lens, like
minute rubies and emeralds. It is the sweetest and most nutritious
pasture for cattle, and its usefulness, added to its beauty, induced the
Hindūs to believe that it was the mansion of a benevolent nymph.' *Samā-
lambhana* is the act of smearing the body with coloured perfumes, such
as saffron, sandal, &c.; the plural is here used for the unguents them-
selves, which are said to be *mangala*, 'conducive to good fortune.' The
Beng. have *samālambhanam*.

² 'S'ārn-garava and the (other) good-people;' see p. 7, n. 3. The Beng.
have *Śārngarava-śāradvata-miśrāḥ*. According to S'. and Ć. these were
the names of two *śishyāḥ*, 'religious students,' pupils of Kaṇva.

प्रियंवदा ॥ कर्णे दत्त्वा ॥

[a] अणसूए । तुवर तुवर । एदे खु हत्थिणाउरगामिणो इसीओ सद्दावीअन्ति ।

अनसूया ॥ प्रविश्य समालम्भनहस्ता ॥

[b] सहि । एहि । गच्छम्ह । ॥ इति परिक्रामतः ॥

प्रियंवदा ॥ विलोक्य ॥

[c] एसा सुज्जोदए एव्व सिहामज्जिदा पडिच्छिदणीवार-हत्थाहिं सोत्तियवाअणकाहिं तावसीहिं अहिणन्दीअमाणा सउन्दला चिट्टुइ । उवसप्पम्ह णं । ॥ इत्युपसर्पतः ॥

a अनसूये । त्वरय त्वरय । एते खलु हस्तिनापुरगामिन ऋषयः शब्दाय्यन्ते ।
b सखि । एहि । गच्छावः ।   c एषा सूर्योदय एव शिखामार्जिता प्रतिष्ठितनी-वारहस्ताभिः स्वस्तिवाचनिकाभिस्तापसीभिरभिनन्द्यमाना शकुन्तला तिष्ठति । उपसर्पाव एनाम् ।

---

[1] 'Truly these Ṛishis who are to go to Hastināpur are being called.' *Śabdāyyante = āhūyante*, S'. and Ć. It is the passive form of the nominal *śabdāyate;* S'. has *śabdāyante*, which would properly mean 'they sound,' 'make a noise,' Pāṇ. iii. 1, 17. *Hastināpura*, 'city of elephants,' was the ancient Delhi, situated on the Ganges, and the residence of Dushyanta.

[2] 'There stands S'akuntalā at earliest sunrise, with her locks combed-and-washed, in the act of being congratulated by the holy-women, (having) consecrated wild-rice in their hands, (and) invoking-blessings-with-their-offerings.' *Śikhā-mārjitā*, lit. 'having her top-knot combed and cleansed,' a compound similar to *śiraḥ-snāta*, 'having the head bathed.' The Beng. MSS. have *kṛita-majjanā*. *Svasti-vāćanikābhiḥ* is here an epithet of the women who make the *svasti-vāćana*, i. e. according to K. 'a gift of flowers, sweetmeats (*prahelaka*), fruit, or any eatables presented with good wishes and prayers for the blessing of some deity.' It is especially the blessing which is coupled with the gift. In the present case the hallowed rice which they held in their hands, might have constituted the offering which accompanied the *svasti-vāćana*. In Vikram. the Vidūshaka is propitiated by a *svasti-vāćana* (or *-naka*), consisting of a *modaka-śarāva*, 'dish of sweetmeats.' Birthday-gifts, wedding-presents, Christmas-boxes,

॥ ततः प्रविशति यथोद्दिश्यव्यापारासनस्था शकुन्तला ॥

तापसीनामन्यतमा ॥ शकुन्तलां प्रति ॥

[a] जादे । भत्तुणो बहुमाणसूअअं महादेईसद्दं लहेहि ।

द्वितीया ।

[b] वच्छे । वीरप्पसविणी होहि ।

तृतीया ।

[c] वच्छे । भत्तुणो बहुमदा होहि ।

॥ इत्याशिषो दत्त्वा गौतमीवर्जं निष्क्रान्ताः ॥

सख्यौ ॥ उपसृत्य ॥

[d] सहि । सुहमज्जणं दे होदु ।

शकुन्तला ।

[e] साअदं मे सहीणं । इदो णिसीदह ।

उभे ॥ मङ्गलपात्राण्यादाय । उपविश्य ॥

[f] हला । सज्जा होहि । जाव मङ्गलसमालम्भणं विरएम ।

[a] जाते । भर्तुर्बहुमानसूचकं महादेवीशब्दं लभस्व ।   [b] वत्से । वीरप्रसविनी भव ।
[c] वत्से । भर्तुर्बहुमता भव ।   [d] सखि । सुखमार्जनं ते भवतु ।   [e] स्वागतं मे
सखीभ्याम् । इतो निषीदतम् ।   [f] हला । सज्जा भव । यावन्मङ्गलसमालम्भनं
विरचयावः ।

&c., with their accompanying compliments, are the *svasti-vácanaka* of our
day. The words *váyana* and *váyanaka* seem to have a similar significa-
tion, though without any necessary implication of *good-wishes*. *Nívára*,
'wild-rice,' Manu vi. 16.

[1] 'My child, take the title of "Great Queen," indicative of the high
esteem of (thy) husband.' *Játá*, 'a child,' is used affectionately in
addressing any young female. *Mahá-deví*, 'chief queen;' cf. p. 124, n. 1.

[2] 'May it be to thee an auspicious ablution!' i. e. may it bring thee
good fortune! May it be an omen of happiness to thee!

[3] 'Taking up the propitiatory-vessels,' i. e. the vessels containing the
flowers, unguents, &c., intended to propitiate Fortune in favour of
S'akuntalá. So read all the Deva-n. MSS., excepting one (Colebrooke's),
which has *patráni*.

शकुन्तला ।

a एदम्पि बहुमन्तव्वं । दुल्लहं दाणिं मे सहीमराडणं भविस्सदि । ॥ इति वाष्यं विसृजति ॥

उभे ।

b सहि । उइदं ण दे मङ्गलकाले रोइदुं । ॥ इत्यश्रूणि प्रमृज्य नाट्येन प्रसाधयतः ।

प्रियंवदा ।

c आहरणोइदं रूवं अस्समसुलहेहिं पसाहणेहिं विप्प-आरीअदि ।

॥ प्रविश्योपायनहस्तावृषिकुमारकौ ॥

उभौ ।

इदमलङ्करणम् । अलङ्क्रियतामत्रभवती ।

॥ सर्वा विलोक्य विस्मिताः ॥

गौतमी ।

d वच्छ णारअ । कुदो एदं ।

प्रथमः ।

तातकाश्यपप्रभावात् ।

a एतदपि बहुमन्तव्यम् । दुर्लभमिदानीं मे सखीमराइनं भविष्यति ।　　b सखि । उचितं न ते मङ्गलकाले रोदितुम् ।　　c आभरणोचितं रूपमाश्रमसुलभैः प्रसाधनैर्विप्रकार्यते ।　　d वत्स नारद । कुत एतत् ।

---

[1] 'This (friendly service of yours) too ought to be highly valued (by me). The being attired by (you) my friends, will now be a rare occurrence. [*So she sheds tears.*]' *Visṛjati* is the reading of my own Deva-n. MS.; the others have *viharati*.

[2] '(Thy) person worthy of (the costliest) ornaments is slighted [or disfigured] by decorations easily procured in a hermitage,' i. e. thy beauty, which deserves to be set off by golden ornaments, &c., is impaired by such decorations as sprouts of Dūrvā grass, &c., S'. *Viprakāryate*, K. has *vikāryate*, the Beng. *vipralabhyate* and *vipratāryate*.

गौतमी ।

[a] किं माणसी सिद्धी ।

द्वितीयः ।

न खलु । श्रूयताम् । तत्रभवता वयमाज्ञप्ताः । शकुन्तला-
हेतोर्वनस्पतिभ्यः कुसुमान्याहरतेति । तत इदानीं
क्षौमं केनचिदिन्दुपाण्डु तरुणा माङ्गल्यमाविष्कृतं
निष्ठ्यूतश्चरणोपभोगसुलभो लाक्षारसः केनचित् ।
अन्येभ्यो वनदेवताकरतलैरापर्वभागोत्थितै-
र्दत्तान्याभरणानि तत्किसलयोद्भेदप्रतिद्वन्द्विभिः ॥८५॥

[a] किं मानसी सिद्धिः ।

---

[1] ' Was it a mental creation ?' i. e. were these ornaments created by the power of his mind ? K. has *srishṭiḥ* for *siddhiḥ*.   Cf. p. 79, n. 1.

[2] ' Bring hither flowers for S'akuntalā from the trees of the forest.'

[3] ' By a certain tree a fine-linen-robe white-as-the-moon indicative-of-good-fortune was made to appear [produced]; by another, juice-of-lac, ready for the use of [the dyeing of] the feet was distilled [exuded]; from others, ornaments were presented by the hands [palms] of wood-nymphs stretched out (so as to be visible) as far as the wrist, emulating the first sprouting of the young-shoots of those (trees).' *Kshauma=vālkala-vastra-bheda*, Ć. *Kshaumam māngalyam=dukūlam maṅgalārham*, S'. *Māngalya* may mean 'with words of good omen,' 'with blessings and prayers for good fortune (*kalyāṇa-vākyaiḥ*), such as, "May she be the beloved wife of her lord,"' &c., S'. *Indu-pāṇḍu=ćandra-dhavala*. *Āvish-kṛitam=ud-bhāvitam*, K.; *=dānāya prakāśitam*, S'. *Nishṭhyūtaḥ= udgīrṇaḥ*. *Ćaraṇopabhoga-sulabho*, some Beng. MSS. have *ćaraṇoparāga-subhayo*; the oldest have *upabhoga*. Here *sulabha=kshama* or *yogya*, 'adapted' (cf. Kumāra-s. v. 69). *Lākshā=alakta* or *alaktaka*, 'lac,' 'a red dye,' prepared from an insect, analogous to the cochineal insect. This minute red insect is found in great numbers in the Palāśa, Indian fig tree, and some other trees. It punctures the bark, whence exudes a resinous

---

Verse 85. S'ĀRDŪLA-VIKRĪḌITA (a variety of ATIDHṚITI). See verses 14, 30, 36, 39, 40, 63, 79.

X 2

प्रियंवदा ॥ शकुन्तलां विलोक्य ॥

[a]हला । इमाए अब्भुवबत्तीए सूइदा दे भत्तुणो गेहे अणुहोदव्वा राअलच्छित्ति ।

॥ शकुन्तला व्रीडां रूपयति ॥

प्रथमः ।

गौतम । एह्येहि । अभिषेकोत्तीर्णायं[2] काश्यपाय वनस्पतिसेवां निवेदयावः ।

द्वितीयः ।

तथा ।

॥ इति निष्क्रान्तौ ॥

सख्यौ ।

[b]अए । अणुबहुत्तभूसणो अञं जणो । चित्तकम्मपरिञएण अङ्गेसु दे आहरणविणिओअं[3] करेम्ह ।

[a] हला । अनयाभ्युपपत्त्या सूचिता ते भर्तुर्गृहेऽनुभवितव्या राजलक्ष्मीः ।   [b] अये । अनुपभुक्तभूषणोऽयं जनः । चित्रकर्मपरिचयेनाङ्गेषु त आभरणविनियोगं कुर्वः ।

---

milky juice, with which it surrounds itself in a kind of nest, and which when dry may be broken off, and used for various purposes. This hardened and reddened substance is variously called gum-lac, shell-lac, stick-lac, &c. *Á-parva*, &c.=*parva-bhága-paryantam udgataih*. *Parva-bhága*=*maṇi-bandha*, 'the wrist,' K. *Á*, 'as far as,' generally requires the abl. of a word not in composition; thus, *á-maṇi-bandhát páṇih*, 'the hand as far as [from] the wrist.' *Tat-kisalaya*, &c., the Beng. and S'. read *naḥ*, 'to us,' for *tat*, and *kisalaya-cchháya-parispardhibhih*, 'rivalling the hue of young shoots.' According to Kavikaṇṭha-hára, quoted by S'., ornaments are divided into four kinds: 1. *Ávedhya*, as ear-rings, &c.; 2. *Bandhaníya*, as flowers, &c.; 3. *Kshepya* or *prakshepya*, as anklets, foot-ornaments, &c.; 4. *Áropya*, as necklaces, garlands, &c.

[1] 'By this favour, royal fortune is indicated as (ever) to be enjoyed by thee in the house of thy husband.' *Abhyupapattyá*=*vṛikshánugraheṇa*, 'by the favour of the sylvan deities.'

[2] 'Returned [come up] from bathing.' *Ut-tṛí* is 'to come out of the water,' 'to come to land.' So *jalád uttírya*, Mahá-bh. iii. 211.

[3] 'We [these persons] are unused to ornaments. By our acquaintance

शकुन्तला ।

^aजाणे वी णेउणं । ॥ उभे नाट्येनालङ्कुरुतः ॥

॥ ततः प्रविशति स्थानोन्नीर्णः काश्यपः ॥

काश्यपः ।

यास्यत्यद्य शकुन्तलेति हृदयं संस्पृष्टमुत्कण्ठया
कण्ठः स्तम्भितवाष्पवृत्तिकलुषश्चिन्ताजडं दर्शनम् ।
वैक्लव्यं मम तावदीदृशमपि स्नेहादरण्यौकसः
पीड्यन्ते गृहिणः कथं नु तनयाविश्लेषदुःखैर्नवैः ॥८६॥

॥ इति परिक्रामति ॥

^a जाने वां नैपुणम् ।

---

with the art of painting we will make the arrangement of the ornaments on thy limbs.' *Anubahutta* for *anupabhukta* is the reading of my own MS. and the Mackenzie, supported by K. *Ćitra-karma*, &c., 'by our knowledge of painting,' i. e. we will decorate thee in the manner we have seen in paintings (*ćitra-likhane yathābharaṇa-prayogo dṛishṭo 'sti tenaiva prakāreṇa, S'.*)

[1] ' "This very day will S'akuntalā depart," at such (a thought), my heart is smitten with melancholy [grief for her loss] ; my voice [throat] is agitated by suppressing the flow of tears ; my sight is paralysed by anxious thought. So great indeed through affection (is) the mental-agitation even of me a hermit. How (much more) then, are householders afflicted by new pangs at separation from their daughters !' *Iti*, see p. 140, n. 2. *Saṃsprṛishṭam*, &c., one MS. (India Office, 1060) reads *sprṛishṭam samutkanṭhayā*. *Kanṭhaḥ*, &c., the Beng. have *antar-vāshpa-bhāro-parodhi gaditam*, 'my voice is obstructed by the weight (*ādhikyena, S'.*) of suppressed tears.' *Vāshpa*, i. e. *aśruṇaḥ pūrvāvasthā*, 'the first stage or state of a tear,' 'the hot moisture that overspreads the eye, before the tear-drop is formed,' K. *Darśana=nayana*, 'eye-sight.' *Jaḍa=vishayā-grāhaka*, 'having no perception of external objects ;' or =*kartavyāpari-ćchedaka*, but in this case *darśana=jñāna, S'.* The effect of deep thought

---

Verse 86. SĀRDŪLA-VIKRĪDITA (a variety of ATIDHṚITI). See verses 14, 30, 36, 39, 40, 63, 79, 85.

सख्यौ ।

[a]हला सउन्दले । अवसिदमण्डणासि । परिधेहि सम्पदं खोमजुअलं[1] ।

॥ शकुन्तलोत्याय परिधत्ते ॥

गौतमी ।

[b]जादे । एसो दे आणन्दपरिवाहिणा चक्खुणा परिस्सजन्तो विअ गुरू उवट्ठिदो । आआरं दाव पडिवंज्जस्स[2] ।

शकुन्तला ॥ सव्रीडम् ॥

[c]ताद । वन्दामि ।

[a] हला शकुन्तले । अवसितमण्डनासि । परिधत्स्व साम्प्रतं क्षौमयुगलम् ।
[b] जाते । एष त आनन्दपरिवाहिणा चक्षुषा परिष्वजमान इव गुरुरुपस्थितः । आचारं तावत्प्रतिपद्यस्व । [c] तात । वन्दे ।

---

and abstraction of mind might be to paralyse for the moment the organs of vision. S'. quotes an aphorism of Bharata, *Nidrā-nāśaś ća ćintā ća bhrāntiś ćotsuka-ćetasām.* *Nu* is used *praśne*, 'in asking a question,' S'. *Araṇyaukas*=*vānaprastha* or *araṇya-vāsin,* 'one whose dwelling (*okas*) is in the woods,' 'a hermit,' see *vanaukas.* *Grihin*=*grihastha,* 'a householder,' 'the father of a family.' The Brāhman was required to divide his life into four orders (*āśrama*). In the first he was a *Brahmaćārin,* or 'student of religion;' in the second, a *Grihastha,* or 'householder;' in the third, a *Vānaprastha* (*Vaikhānasa*), or 'anchorite;' in the fourth, a *Bhikshu,* or 'religious mendicant;' see Indian Wisdom, p. 245.

[1] 'Thy decoration [toilet] is completed. Now do thou put on the pair of linen vestments.' A Hindū woman's dress generally consisted of two pieces; one covered the breast and shoulders, the other was a long robe enveloping the person. *Avasita-maṇḍanā*=*nishpanna-prasādhanā.*

[2] 'Here close-at-hand-stands thy spiritual-father as if (already) embracing thee [about to embrace thee], with an eye overflowing with joy. Perform now the customary-salutation.' *Ānanda-parivāhiṇā,* the Beng. have *ānanda-vāshpa-parivāhiṇā,* cf. p. 89, l. 13. *Āćāra,* 'good manners,' 'the usual complimentary greeting.' *Paḍibajjassa* for *pratipadyasva* is the reading of my own MS. and the Mackenzie, cf. p. 135, l. 4. The same expression occurs in Vikram., Act II.

काश्यपः ।

वत्से ।

ययातेरिव शर्मिष्ठा भर्तुर्बहुमता भव ।
सुतं त्वमपि सम्राजं सेव पुरुमवाप्नुहिं ॥ ८७ ॥

गौतमी ।

[a] भत्रवं । वरोक्खु एसो । ए आसिंसा[2] ।

काश्यपः ।

वत्से । इतः सद्यो हुताग्नीन्प्रदक्षिणीकुरुष्व[3] ।

॥ सर्वे परिक्रामन्ति ॥

[a] भगवन् । वरः खल्वेष: । नाशी: ।

---

[1] 'Daughter, be thou highly honoured of thy husband, as was S'ar-mishṭhā of Yayāti. Do thou also obtain a son, a sovereign monarch, as she (obtained) Puru.' S'armishṭhā, according to K., was the daughter of Vṛisha-parvan, king of the Asuras or demons, and wife of Yayāti, son of Nahusha, one of the princes of the Lunar race, and ancestor of Dush-yanta, see p. 15, n. 1. The Sāhitya-darpaṇa (p. 190) cites this verse as an example of *āśir-vāda*, 'benediction,' but reads (as also do the Beng.) *patyur* for *bhartur*, and *putram* for *sutam*. *Samrāj* is a sovereign prince, who has performed a *Rājasūya* sacrifice, and exercises despotic sway over others.

[2] 'This is actually a boon (conferred), not a (mere) benediction.' *San-tushṭa-devādīnām avaśyam-bhāvi vacanaṃ varaḥ, āśis tu kadācit phala-dāyinī vāk*, 'a *vara* is the promise of a propitiated deity, &c., which must necessarily come to pass; an *āśis* is a benediction which occasionally bears fruit [comes true],' Ĉ. and S'.

[3] 'My child, this way! do thou at once circumambulate the sacrificial fires,' see p. 148, n. 1. *Sadyo-hutāgnīm=tatkshaṇa-kṛita-homāgnīm*, S'. The Taylor and my own MS. have *sadyohutān*. *Sadyo* may, however, be separated from the next word, and translated 'at once,' 'immediately.' The rite of circumambulation is performed by slowly walking round any object, keeping the right side towards it.

Verse 87. SLOKA or ANUSHTUBH. See verses 5, 6, 11, 12, 26, 47, 50, 51, 53, 73, 76, 84.

कश्यपः ॥ ऋक्छन्दसाशास्ते ॥

अमी वेदिं परितः क्लृप्तधिष्ण्याः
समिद्वन्तः प्रान्तसंस्तीर्णदर्भाः ।
अपघ्नन्तो दुरितं हव्यगन्धै-
र्वैतानास्त्वां वह्नयः पावयन्तु ॥८८॥

प्रतिष्ठस्वेदानीम् । ॥ सदृष्टिक्षेपम् ॥ क्व ते शाङ्गरवमिश्राः ।

---

[1] '[*Pronounces a blessing in the metre of the Ṛić*, i. e. according to the usual metre of the Ṛig-veda.] Let these fires, taken-from-the-sacred-hearth [*vaitānas*] whose places are fixed round the altar, fed with (consecrated) wood, having Darbha [Kuśa] grass strewed around the margin, destroying sin by the perfume of the oblations, purify thee.' Each stanza of the Sūktas or hymns of the Ṛig-veda is called a *ṛić*. *Asya vṛittasya vedoktāśīrvāda-sadṛiśatvam agni-prayuktatvādi boddhavyam*, 'it is to be understood that there is a similarity between the metre of this verse and that of the benedictions uttered in the Vedas addressed to fire,' &c., K. The verse itself does not occur in the Ṛig-veda, but the metre is Vedic. Doubtless Kālidāsa intended it as an imitation of Vedic poetry. That it is addressed to Agni constitutes in itself a point of resemblance. *Vaitāna*, see Indian Wisdom, p. 197. *Klṛipta-dhishnyāḥ = raćitādhishṭhānāḥ*. *Prānta-saṃstīrṇa-darbhāḥ*, i. e. *pārśveshu ćatasṛishu dikshu sankīrṇā darbhā yeshām*. At a sacrifice, the fires, severally termed *Āhavanīya*, *Mārjālīya*, *Gārhapatya*, and *Āgnīdhrīya*, were lighted at the four cardinal points, east, west, north, and south, and Kuśa grass (see p. 19, n. 1) was scattered round each fire. See Indian Wisdom, p. 205; see also Sāyaṇa's commentary on Ṛig-v. i. 1, 4, and cf. Ṛig-v. i. 31, 13, 'thou, four-eyed

---

Verse 88. TRISHṬUP ĆATUSH-PADĀ, a form of Vedic metre, consisting of four times eleven syllables, the first and third Pādas resembling the VĀTORMĪ, and the second and fourth, the ŚĀLINĪ variety of TRISHṬUBH. In the second, however, the first syllable is short.

$$\cup - - - \cup \cup \cup - - \cup - - \; \| \; \cup - - - - \cup - - \cup - -$$
$$\cup - - - \cup \cup - - \cup - - \; \| \; - - - - - \cup - - \cup - -$$

In Ṛig-veda i. 59, 5, the first Pāda is exactly like the first in the above scheme, but the other Pādas are arranged differently, as far at least as the seventh syllable. Kālidāsa, accustomed to the strictness of the later Sanskrit metres, seems here to have endeavoured to imitate the Vedic rhythm, in which greater liberty was allowed. Thus he produced a verse too irregular to come under any of the later metres, but rather too regular for a Vedic hymn.

शिष्यः ॥ प्रविश्य ॥

भगवन् । इमे स्मः ।

काश्यपः ।

भगिन्यास्ते मार्गमादेश्यय[2] ।

शार्ङ्गरवः ।

इत इतो भवती । ॥ सर्वे परिक्रामन्ति ॥

काश्यपः ।

भो भोः सन्निहितास्तपोवनतरवः ।

पातुं न प्रथमं व्यवस्यति जलं युष्मास्वपीतेषु या
नादत्ते प्रियमण्डनापि भवतां स्नेहेन या पल्लवम् ।
आद्ये वः कुसुमप्रसूतिसमये यस्या भवत्युत्सवः
सेयं याति शकुन्तला पतिगृहं सर्वैरनुज्ञायताम्[3] ॥८९॥

Agni, blazest as the protector of the worshippers,' &c. *Pālayantu*
(=*rakshantu*) is the reading of all the Beng. MSS., supported by K.,
S'., and C., but all the Deva-n. MSS. have *pārayantu*.

[1] S'. quotes a verse of Bharata, *Devāś ća, munayaś ćaiva, linginaḥ,
sādhanāś ća* [*sādhakāś ća*, C.] *ye, bhagavann iti te vāćyāḥ sarvaiḥ strī-
pun-napunsakaiḥ*, 'both gods and also Munis, Lingins and Sādhanas
(? *sādhavas*, "saints," see Vishṇu-p. p. 300) are to be addressed as "Bha-
gavan," by all women, men, and eunuchs.'

[2] Cf. Vikram., Act II, *bhavān pramada-vana-mārgam ādeśayatu.*

[3] 'Listen! listen! ye neighbouring trees of the penance-grove. She
who never attempts to drink water first, when you have not drunk, and
who, although fond of ornaments, never plucks a blossom, out of affection
for you, whose greatest-holiday [highest-joy] is at the season of the first
appearance of your bloom, even that same S'akuntalā now departs to the
house of her husband. Let her be affectionately-dismissed by (you) all.'
Bhoḥ is a vocative particle, often joined with *śrūyatām*, 'listen!' *Vyava-
syati*, 'makes effort,' may also mean 'resolves upon,' 'makes up her mind;'
(with *na*), 'it never enters into her head.' *A-pīteshu*, the Beng. have *a-sik-
teshu*, i. e. 'as long as you remain unwatered.' The Deva-n. reading is
supported by K., who includes *pīta* among the passive participles, like

---

Verse 89. S'ĀRDŪLA-VIKRĪḌITA (a variety of ATIDHṚITI). See verses 14, 30, 36,
39, 50, 63, 79, 85, 86.

Y

॥ कोकिलरवं सूचयित्वा ॥

अनुमतगमना शकुन्तला
तरुभिरियं वनवासबन्धुभिः ।
परभृतविरुतं कलं यथा
प्रतिवचनीकृतमेभिरीदृशम् ॥ ९० ॥

आकाशे ।

रम्यान्तरः कमलिनीहरितैः सरोभि-
श्छायाद्रुमैर्नियमिताकमयूखतापः ।

---

gata, sthita, ārūḍha, &c. (Pāṇ. iii. 4, 72), which may have an active signification. *Vismṛita* may be included in the same list, see p. 28, l. 3. *Priya,* in the sense 'fond of,' may stand at the beginning of a compound, cf. φιλοσοφία, φιλόξενος (*priyātithi*), &c.; sometimes at the end, e. g. *jala-priya,* 'fond of water.'

[1] 'Acting as if he heard the note of a cuckoo,' lit. 'shewing the note of a cuckoo.' Compare *nimittaṃ sūćayitvā,* Vikram., Act II.

[2] 'This S'akuntalā is permitted to depart by the trees, the foresters'-kinsfolk; since a song to this effect, warbled by the cuckoo, was employed as an answer by them.' *Vana-vāsa-bandhubhiḥ* = *araṇya-vāsa-snigdhaiḥ,* 'beloved by foresters.' It may be translated 'her sylvan relatives.' *Para-bhṛita* (= *pika*), lit. 'nourished by a stranger.' The Indian Koïl or cuckoo is supposed to leave her eggs in the nest of the crow to be hatched, but has little resemblance to the bird known as the cuckoo in Europe. One of its names is *vasanta-dūta,* 'messenger of spring.' Its song is said to be sweet (*madhura,* Ritu-s.), but cannot be compared to that of the nightingale. 'The beauty of cuckoos is their song,' Hitop. l. 839. 'On a journey (*yātrāyām*) the note of a cuckoo is indicative of good-fortune (*śubha-sūćakaḥ*). The answer of the trees was effected by the song of the cuckoo (*pika-ravenaiva sampannam*). Next the answer of the sylvan deities is given (by a voice in the air),' S'. *Kala* as an adj. means 'soft,' 'sweet,' and *parabhṛita-virutaṃ kalam* may be 'the sweet notes of the cuckoo' (cf. Raghu-v. viii. 58).

Verse 90. APARA-VAKTRĀ, containing eleven syllables to the first Pāda or quarter-verse, and twelve to the second, each half-verse being alike.

◡ ◡ ◡ ◡ ◡ ◡ – ◡ – ◡ – ‖ ◡ ◡ ◡ ◡ ◡ – ◡ ◡ – ◡ – ◡ –

भूयात्कुशेशयरजोमृदुरेणुरस्याः
शान्तानुकूलपवनश्च शिवश्च पन्थाः ॥९१॥

॥ सर्वे सविस्मयमाकर्णयन्ति ॥

गौतमी ।

[a] जादे । णादिजणसिणिद्धाहिं[2] अणुण्णादगमणासि तवो-
वणदेवदाहिं । पणम[3] भअवंदीणं ।

[a] जाते । ज्ञातिजनस्निग्धाभिरनुज्ञातगमनासि तपोवनदेवताभिः । प्रणम भगवतीभ्यः ।

---

[1] 'May her path be pleasantly-diversified [pleasant at intervals] by lakes (that are) verdant with-lotus-beds, (may it have) the heat of the sun's rays moderated by shady trees, (may) its dust be soft with the [as the] pollen from the lotuses, and (may it be cheered by) gentle favourable breezes and (be altogether) prosperous.' *Ramyāntaraḥ=manohara-madhyaḥ*, S.; = *manojña-madhyaḥ*, C., 'having its middle space delightful,' 'pleasant throughout the intervening distance,' an epithet of *panthāḥ*. *Chāyā-drumaiḥ = chāyā-pradhānair-vṛikshaiḥ*, 'trees chiefly abounding in shade,' K.; = *chāyā-lakshita-drumaiḥ*, 'trees characterized by shade,' C. It is a compound similar to *śāka-pārthiva* and *abhijñāna-śakuntalā*, see p. 4, n. 2. 'That is called a *chāyā-taru*, 'shade-tree,' whose under-part (*talam*) excessively cool shade (*atyanta-śītala-chāyā*) does not quit either in the forenoon or afternoon,' S. and C. *Niyamita= apanīta. Kuśe-śaya*, lit. 'lying in water;'= *śata-pattra*, 'a lotus.' *Śānta = śānta-vega, manda*, K.; = *pāṭachcharādi-śunya*, 'free from robbers,' &c., S. and C. The compound may therefore be translated 'free from molestation and having favourable breezes.' *Śivaś cha bhūyāt panthāḥ*, this seems to have been a phrase commonly used as a parting benediction, like 'A pleasant journey to you!' Cf. *panthānas te santu śivāḥ*, Hitop. l. 1442, Sāhit.-d. p. 344, Mudrā-r. p. 30, l. 17, and p. 179, l. 4 of this play.

[2] 'Dear to thee as (thy own) kinsfolk.' Cf. *vana-vāsa-bandhubhiḥ* in verse 90. My own Bombay MS. has *ṇṇādi* (supported by the Calcutta edition), the others all *ṇādi* for *jñāti*. There is no doubt about the doubling of the *ṇ* when not initial, as Vararuchi, iii. 44, gives *viṇṇāṇa* for *vijñāna*.

[3] *Bhaavadīṇam*, a Prākṛit gen. for Sanskṛit dat., see p. 129, n. 1.

Verse 91. VASANTA-TILAKĀ (a variety of ŚAKVARĪ). See verses 8, 27, 31, 43, 46, 64, 74, 80, 82, 83.

शकुन्तला ॥ सर्वासां परिक्रम्य । जनान्तिकम् ॥

[a] हला पिअंवदे । यां अज्जउत्तदंसणुस्सुआएवि अम्हं परिच्चअन्तीए दुक्खेण मे चलणा पुरदो पवट्टन्ति ।

प्रियंवदा ।

[b] ण केवलं तवोवणविरहकादरा सही एव्व । तुए उव्वट्टिदविस्सोस्सस तवोवणस्सवि दाव समवत्था दीसइ [2] ।

उग्गलिअदब्भकवला मिआ परिच्चत्तणच्चणा मोरा ।
ओसरिअपराउपत्ता मुअन्ति अंसू विअ लदाओ ॥९२॥

[a] हला प्रियंवदे । नन्वार्यपुत्रदर्शनोत्सुकायाः अप्याश्रमं परित्यजन्त्या दुःखेन मे चरणौ पुरतः प्रवर्तेते । [b] न केवलं तपोवनविरहकातरा सख्येव । त्वयोपस्यि-
तवियोगस्य तपोवनस्यापि तावत्समवस्था दृश्यते ।

उद्गलितदर्भकवला मृगाः परित्यक्तनर्तना मयूराः ।
अपसृतपाण्डुपत्रा मुञ्चन्त्यश्रूणीव लताः ॥९२॥

---

[1] My own MS., supported by K., has *duḥkhena*, the others *duḥkha-duḥkhena*.

[2] 'One may observe the same (troubled) condition [the same condition is observed] of the penance-grove, as the (time of) separation from thee approaches.' *Samavasthā*=*samāvasthā*, as in Raghu-v. viii. 41. The Taylor MS. reads *samāvatthā*.

[3] 'The deer let fall the mouthfuls of Darbha-grass, the peacocks cease (their) dancing, the creepers, as they cast [in casting] their pale leaves, appear to shed tears [as it were shed tears].' *Udgalita*, from *ud-gal*, lit. 'to trickle out,' 'drop from.' The Beng. MSS. read *ugginṇa* (=*udgīrṇa*), 'ejected from the throat or mouth.' *Mṛigāḥ*, all the Deva-n. read *miïo* for *mrigyaḥ*, and in the next line *assūṇi* for *aśrūṇi*, apparently in violation of the metre. Dr. Boehtlingk has suggested *miā* and *aṇsū*, the latter is a legitimate acc. pl. from *aṇsu*, the masc. Prākrit equivalent of the neuter *aśru; see* Vararući iv. 15. *Parityakta-nartanā*, the dancing of

---

Verse 92. ĀRYĀ or GĀTHĀ. See verse 2.

⏑⏑⏑|⏑–⏑|⏑⏑–‖⏑–⏑|––|⏑–⏑|––|–
–⏑⏑|⏑–⏑|––‖⏑–⏑|––|⏑|⏑⏑–|–

शकुन्तला ॥ स्मृत्वा ॥

[a]ताद। लदाबहिणिश्रं वणजोसिणिं दाव आमन्तइस्सं।[1]

काश्यपः।

अवैमि ते तस्यां सोदर्यस्नेहम्। इयं तावद्दक्षिणेन।[2]

शकुन्तला ॥ लतामुपेत्य ॥

[b]वणजोसिणि। चूदसङ्गदादि मं पच्चालिङ्ग इदोगदाहिं
साहाबाहाहिं। अज्जप्पहुदि दूरपरिवत्तिणी दे खु भविस्सं।[3]

काश्यपः।

सङ्कल्पितं प्रथममेव मया तवार्थे
भर्तारमात्मसदृशं सुकृतैर्गता त्वम्।

[a] तात। लताभगिनीं वनज्योत्स्नां तावदामन्त्रयिष्ये।   [b] वनज्योत्स्ने। चूतसङ्ग-
तापि मां प्रत्यालिङ्गेत्तोगताभिः शाखावाहाभिः। अद्यप्रभृति दूरपरिवर्तिनी ते खलु
भविष्यामि।

---

the Indian peacock, especially at the approach of rain, in which it is
said to take especial delight, is frequently alluded to in Hindū poetry.
Cf. Megha-d. 46, 78; Ritu-s. ii. 6; Bhartṛi-h. i. 43. *Osaria* for *apasṛita*,
see Lassen's Instit. Prāk. p. 363. Raghu-v. xiv. 69 contains a sentiment
precisely parallel to the above, *Nṛityam mayūrāḥ, kusumāni vṛikshā,
darbhān upāttān vijahur hariṇyaḥ,* &c.

[1] 'Father, I will just bid farewell to (my) tendril-sister, the Light of
the Grove,' i.e. the Nava-mālikā, or young jasmine-creeper, mentioned at
p. 28, l. 3.

[2] 'I know thy sisterly affection for it. Here it is now to the right.'
Sodarya, 'of whole blood,' 'born from the same womb' (*udara*); compare
p. 22, l. 9.

[3] 'O Light of the Grove, though united with the mango-tree, embrace
me with (thy) arms-of-branches turned in this direction.' *Ćūta-sangatā,*
see p. 28, n. 1. *Ito-gatābhiḥ,* &c., is the reading of all the Deva-n. MSS.
(supported by K.) excepting one, which has *idogadehim sāhā-bāhūhim* for
ito-gataiḥ śākhā-bāhubhiḥ. The feminine noun *bāhā* is more appropriately
joined with *śākhā,* but *bāhu* is admissible, compare p. 26, l. 2. The Beng.
have *śākhāmayair bāhubhiḥ,* 'with arms consisting of branches.'

चूतेन संश्रितवती नवमालिकेय-
	मस्यामहं त्वयि च सम्प्रति वीतचिन्तः ॥ ९३ ॥

इतः पन्थानं प्रतिपद्यस्व ।

शकुन्तला ॥ सख्यौ प्रति ॥

ᵃ हला । एसा दुवेणं वो हत्थे णिक्खेबो ।

सख्यौ ।

ᵇ अब्अं जणो कस्स हत्थे समप्पिंदो । ॥ इति वाष्पं विहरतः ॥

काश्यपः ।

अनसूये । अलं रुदित्वा । ननु भवतीभ्यामेव स्थिरीकर्तव्या शकुन्तला ।

॥ सर्वे परिक्रामन्ति ॥

ᵃ हला । एषा द्वयोर्वां हस्ते निक्षेपः ।   ᵇ अयं जनः कस्य हस्ते समर्पितः ।

---

[1] 'Thou by (thy) merits hast obtained [hast gone to] a husband suited-to-thyself, just as originally determined upon by me on thy account : this young Mālikā (creeper) has united itself with the mango-tree ; now (therefore) I am free from solicitude about it and about thee.' *Saṅkalpitam*, &c., see p. 49, l. 5 ; and p. 135, l. 10 with note 2. *Tavārthe*=*tava kṛite*, K. *Ātma-sadṛiśam* = *tvat-samam*, K. ; *rūpa-kulādinā sva-sadṛiśam*, 're-sembling thyself in beauty, family,' &c., S'. ; see p. 31, n. 1. *Gatā* = *prāptā*, K. ; see p. 161, n. 3 at the end. *Saṁśṛitavatī*=*saṅgatavatī*, K. My own MS. has *saṅskṛitavatī*, and the Colebrooke *sammitavatī*. *Vīta-cinta* = *tyakta-varānusandhāna*, 'ceased from searching after a hus-band,' S'.

[2] 'Set out on thy journey hence.' *Pratipadyasva*, see p. 135, n. 1.

[3] 'This (creeper) is (entrusted) as a pledge into the hand of you two.' *Nikshepa*=*sthāpya*, S'. *Yathā sthāpyo rakshyate tatheyam*.

[4] 'Into whose hands are we committed (by thee)?' *Ayaṁ janaḥ*, i.e. *asmad-rūpaḥ*, S'. and C'.

[5] *Vi-hṛi* seems here used in the sense of 'to wipe away.'

[6] 'Enough of weeping ! Surely S'akuntalā should be cheered [rendered

---

Verse 93. VASANTA-TILAKĀ (a variety of S'AKVARĪ). See verses 8, 27, 31, 43, 46, 64, 74, 80, 82, 83, 91.

शकुन्तला ।

[a] ताद् । एसा उडजपज्जन्तचारिणी गब्भमन्थरा मित्तबहु
जदा अणघप्पसवा होइ । तदा मे कम्पि पिअणिवेदइत्तअं
विसज्जइस्सह ।

काश्यपः ।

नेदं विस्मरिष्यामः ।

शकुन्तला ॥ गतिभङ्गं रूपयित्वा ॥

[b] की गुक्खु एसो णिवसणे मे सज्जइ । ॥ इति परावर्त्तते ॥

काश्यपः ।

वत्से ।

यस्य त्वया व्रणविरोपणमिङ्गुदीनां

तैलं न्यषिच्यत मुखे कुशसूचिविद्धे ।

श्यामाकमुष्टिपरिवर्धितको जहाति

सोऽयं न पुत्रकृतकः पदवीं मृगस्ते ॥ ९४ ॥

[a] तात । एपोटजपर्यन्तचारिणी गर्भमन्थरा मृगवधूर्यदानघप्रसवा भवति । तदा मे कमपि प्रियानिवेदयितारं विसर्जयिष्यप ।　　[b] को नु खल्वेप निवसने मे सज्जति ।

---

firm, supported] by you indeed ?' i. e. you are the very persons who should rather support and comfort your friend. *Alaṃ ruditvā*, see p. 48, n. 3. *Sthirī-kartavyā=tapovana-viraha-kheda-rahitā vidheyā*, S.

[1] 'When this doe [female deer] grazing in the neighbourhood of the hut, slow by (the weight of) her young, has happily brought forth ; then you will send some one to announce [as an announcer of] the agreeable news to me.' *Anagha-prasavā=vyasana-rahita-prasūtiḥ*, 'bringing forth without any mishap,' K. *Priya*, i. e. *priya-vārtā*, S.

[2] 'That same fawn, thy adopted child, tenderly reared with handfuls of S'yāmāka-grains, on whose mouth, when pricked by the sharp-points of the Kuśa-grass, sore-healing oil of In-gudī-plants was sprinkled by thee,

---

Verse 94. VASANTA-TILAKĀ (a variety of Śakvarī). See verses 8, 27, 31, 43, 46, 64, 74, 80, 82, 83, 91, 93.

शकुन्तला ।

[a] वच्छ । किं सहवासपरिच्चाइणिं मं अणुसरसि । अचिरप्पसूदाए जणणीए विणा विवड्ढिदो एव्व । दाणिम्मि मए विरहिदं तुमं तादो चिन्तइस्सदि । णिवत्तेहि दाव । ॥ इति रुदती प्रस्थिता ॥

काश्यपः ।

उत्पक्ष्मणोर्नयनयोरुपरुद्धवृत्तिं
वाष्पं कुरु स्थिरतया विरतानुबन्धम् ।

[a] वत्स । किं सहवासपरित्यागिनीं मामनुसरसि । अचिरप्रसूतया जनन्या विना विवर्धित एव । इदानीमपि मया विरहितं त्वां तातश्चिन्तयिष्यति । निवर्तस्व तावत् ।

---

will not forsake thy footsteps [path].' *Vrana-viropana*=*kshata-praro-haka*, S'., lit. 'that which causes a scar to cicatrize.' See *ropana* in Dict. *Ingudīnām*, see p. 18, n. 1. *Kusa-sūći*, see p. 57, n. 5. *Parivardhitaka*= *anukampayā vardhitaḥ*, 'compassionately reared,' K.;=*atiśayena poshitaḥ*, 'excessively nourished,' S'. and Ć. The suffix *ka* sometimes gives the sense of compassionating (*anukampāyām*). So *putrakaḥ*=*anukampitaḥ putraḥ* according to Pāṇ. v. 3, 76. The preposition *pari* may give the sense of *atiśayena* noticed by the other commentators. *Syāmāka*=*vrīhi-viśesha*, 'a kind of rice,' S'. It is rather the grain of a kind of Panic grass, eaten by the Hindūs. *Mushti*, 'a handful,' is the first measure of capacity, equivalent to $\frac{1}{4}$th of a *kuñji*, $\frac{1}{16}$th of a *kudava*, $\frac{1}{48}$th of a *prastha*. *Putra-kritaka*=*kritrima-putra*, 'a factitious or adopted son,' S'. and Ć. K. explains this compound by referring to Pāṇ. ii. 1, 59, so that *putra-krita*, 'made into a son' (i. e. *a-putra*, 'not really a son'), is like *śreni-krita*, 'made into a line,' and *pūga-krita*, 'made into a heap.'

[1] 'Why dost thou follow me, an abandoner of (my) companions? Thou indeed wast reared (by me) without (thy) mother [when deprived of thy mother] shortly after she had brought thee forth.' *Saha-vāsa*, lit. 'one who lives with another.' The Beng. have *aćira-prasūtoparatayā*=*pra-savāvyavahita-kāla-mritayā*, 'that died directly after bringing thee forth.'

असिन्नलक्षितनतोन्नतभूमिभागे
मार्गे पदानि खलु ते विषमीभवन्ति ॥ ९५ ॥

शाङ्ग्ररवः ।

भगवन् । ओदकान्तात्स्निग्धो जनोऽनुगन्तव्य इति श्रूयते ।
तदिदं सरस्तीरम् । अच सन्दिश्य प्रतिगन्तुमर्हसि ।

---

[1] 'By-a-vigorous-effort [by firmness] make the tears cease to hang [cling] in (thy) upturned-eyelashed eyes, obstructing (their) free-action [impeding our business]. In this path in which the undulations of ground [the depressed and elevated portions of ground] are not discernible, thy footsteps must certainly be uneven.' *Utpakshmaṇoḥ*, see p. 131, n. 1 in the middle. *Uparuddha-vrittim = pratiruddha-vyāpāram*, 'impeding the functions or proper action of the organs of vision,' Ć. *Uparuddhā antaritā vrittir vyāpāro yena*, K. In p. 157, l. 6, *vritti* is applied to the course of a tear; but if so translated here, the other epithet, *viratānubandham*, would be superfluous. It is not necessary, however, to connect it with *nayanayoḥ*, as the passage might be rendered 'make the tears that impede our business cease to cling in (thy) upturned-eyelashed-eyes.' *Vāshpa* is 'the hot moisture that precedes the formation of tears,' see p. 157, n. 1. It is used in the singular. Cf. *muñćato vāshpam ushṇam*, Megha-d. 12. *Viratānubandha*, my own MS. has *vihatānubandha*; *anubandha*, lit. 'binding after,' 'following after;' hence 'cleaving,' 'adhering.' The Beng. MSS. have *sithilānubandham = sāntārambham* (sic?), S. *Vishami-bhavanti = skhalitāni syuḥ*, 'are liable to trip or stumble,' S. and C. Cf. p. 139, l. 3.

[2] '"A friend is [or friends are] to be escorted as far as the water's brink"—such is the sacred precept. This, then, is the margin of a lake. Here having given (us) directions, be pleased to return.' *Odakāntāt*, i.e. *ā + udakāntāt = ā jalāntāt* (see p. 155, n. 3 near the end). *Odakāntāt* is found in all the Deva-n. MSS.; my own has *odakāntam*. *Snigdho janaḥ* may be either 'a friend' or 'friends,' cf. *sakhī-jana*, p. 128, l. 2, with note 1. *Srūyate*, lit. 'it is heard,' i.e. it is enjoined in *sruti*, 'scripture,' 'holy writ.'

Verse 95. VASANTA-TILAKĀ (a variety of ŚAKVARĪ). See verses 8, 27, 31, 43, 46, 64, 74, 80, 82, 83, 91, 93, 94.

काश्यपः ।

तेन ह्रीमां क्षीरवृक्ष[1]च्छायामाश्रयामः ।

॥ सर्वे परिक्रम्य स्थिताः ॥

काश्यपः ॥ आत्मगतम् ॥

किं नु खलु तत्रभवतो दुष्यन्तस्य युक्तरूपमस्माभिः
सन्देष्टव्यम्[2] । ॥ इति चिन्तयति ॥

शकुन्तला ॥ जनान्तिकम् ॥

[a] हला । पेक्ख । णलिणीपत्तन्तरिदं पिअसहअरं
अदेक्खन्ती आदुरा चक्कवाई आरडदि । दुक्करं अहं
करेमिन्ति[3] ।

[a] हला । प्रेक्षस्व । नलिनीपत्रान्तरितं प्रियसहचरमपश्यन्त्यातुरा चक्रवाक्यारटति ।
दुष्करमहं करोमीति ।

---

[1] *Kshīra-vṛiksha*, lit. 'milk-tree,' a kind of fig tree, not the Vaṭa or
Banyan tree (Ficus Indica), nor the Pippala (Ficus Religiosa), but the
glomerous fig tree (Ficus Glomerata), which yields a resinous milky juice
from its bark (see p. 155, n. 3 in the middle) and is large enough to afford
abundant shade.

[2] 'What message is to be sent by us (that will be) most appropriate for
his majesty Dushyanta?' *Yukta-rūpa*, cf. p. 89, n. 1; and p. 15, l. 3.

[3] 'Friend, see! the poor female-Cakravāka, not perceiving her dear
mate hidden by the lotus-leaves, calls to (him) thus, "Hard (is the lot) I
suffer;"' see p. 128, n. 3, and cf. in Vikram., Act IV, *Sarasi nalinī-
pattreṇāpi tvam āvṛita-vigrahām nanu sahaćarīm dūre matvā viraushi
samutsukaḥ*, 'thou indeed (i. e. the male Cakravāka) art sorrowfully crying
to thy mate thinking her to be far away, although her body is only concealed
from thee by a lotus-leaf in the lake.' A few lines before this passage, the
cry is compared to the sound *ka ka*. Possibly this may account for the
somewhat peculiar phrase *dukkaram karemi*, here employed as the cry of
the bird. K. has *dushkaram khalu ahaṃ tarkayāmi*. It is true that *kṛi*
sometimes has the sense of *tark*, 'think,' 'imagine' (cf. p. 42, n. 1), but
dushkaram kṛi is not more harsh than *śokam kṛi*, 'to make or suffer
sorrow.' S. has *dushkaram ayaṃ ćakravākaḥ karoti*. Instead of *pia*

अनसूया ।

[a] सहि । मा एव्वं मन्तेहि ।

एसा वि पिएण विणा गमेइ रञणिं विसाद्अदीहत्तरं ।

गरुअम्मि विरहदुक्खं आसाबन्धो सहावेदि ॥ ९६ ॥

काश्यपः ।

शार्ङ्गरव । त्वया मद्वचनात्स राजा शकुन्तलां पुरस्कृत्य [2]

वक्तव्यः ।

शार्ङ्गरवः ।

आज्ञापयतु भवान् ।

[a] सखि । मैवं मन्त्रयस्व ।

एषापि प्रियेण विना गमयति रजनीं विपाद्दीर्घतराम् ।

गुर्वपि विरहदुःखमाशाबन्धः साहयति ॥ ९६ ॥

---

three of the MSS. have *hi* for *api*. 'This verse indicates that S'akuntalā
foresees she is about to experience similar sorrow, in having to endure
separation from Dushyanta in consequence of the curse' (*śāpa-tirohita-
Dushyantam a-lapsyamānā*), K.

[1] 'Speak not so. Even she [the female Cakravāka], without her
beloved, passes away the night made too long by sorrow. Expectation (of
meeting again) makes the pain of separation, however severe, supportable.'
Gamayati, lit. 'causes to go,' i. e. brings to an end. The Prākṛit *visāa*
=*vishāda*, 'melancholy.' S. explains the phrase by *visūraṇā-dīrghām*,
kheda-dīrghām, *duḥkha-dustarām*. *Āśā-bandha*, 'hope,' i. e. *prātar mām
sangamayishyati*, 'in the morning he will be united to me.' S. makes
this verse an example of the Āśvāsa Alankāra. K. refers to a parallel
passage in the Megha-d. 10, *Āśā-bandhaḥ kusuma-sadriśaḥ* [sic] *prāyaśo
hy anganānām sadyaḥ-pāti praṇayi hṛidayam viprayoge ruṇaddhi.*

[2] 'Having placed in front,' i. e. 'having introduced,' 'having pre-
sented.'

Verse 96. ĀRYĀ or GĀTHĀ. See verse 2.

   – – | ◡ ◡ – | ◡ ◡ – || ◡ – ◡ | ◡ ◡ – | ◡ – ◡ | – ◡ ◡ | –
   ◡ ◡ – | ◡ ◡ ◡ ◡ | – – || – – | – – | ◡ | – – | ◡

काश्यपः ।

अस्मान्साधु विचिन्त्य संयमधनानुच्चैःकुलं चात्मन-
स्त्वय्यस्याः कथमप्यबान्धवकृतां स्नेहप्रवृत्तिं च ताम् ।
सामान्यप्रतिपत्तिपूर्वकमियं दारेषु दृश्या त्वया
भाग्यायत्तमतःपरं न खलु तद्वाच्यं वधूबन्धुभिः ॥९७॥

शार्ङ्गरवः ।

गृहीतः सन्देशः ।

---

¹ 'Having well considered us as rich in devotion, and the exalted family of thyself, and that (free) flow of affection of this (maiden) towards thee [or the spontaneous flow of affection springing up in you for her] not in any manner brought about by relatives; she is to be regarded by thee, as (one) amongst (thy) wives, after raising her to an equality of rank [or with equal respect]. Beyond this is dependent on destiny, nor indeed ought that to be called in question by a wife's relations.' *Saṃyama-dhanān*, 'this implies that they were worthy of respect,' K. *Uććaiḥ-kulam*, &c., 'this implies that he would act with justice,' K.; see p. 15, n. 1. *Kathamapi*=*dur-grahena*, S'. and C'. Cf. p. 131, l. 6. *A-bāndhava-kritām*, see p. 127, n. 3. *Sneha-pravrittim*=*prema-ćeshṭām*, C'. *Sāmā-nya-pratipatti-pūrvakam*=*sādhāraṇa-gaurava-puraḥsaram*, 'preceded by equal respect;' *yādriśena gauraveṇa aparā vadhūr ālokyate tādriśena iyam*, &c., S'. *Pratipatti* is either 'the act of preferring to rank,' or 'the respect paid to rank.' *Pūrva* or *pūrvaka* at the end of a compound often simply denotes the manner in which anything is done, translateable by 'with' or 'after' (cf. *sa bhavantam anāmaya-praśna-pūrvakam idam āha*, p. 198, l. 2; also p. 116, n. 2). *Dāreshu*, S'. explains thus, *dāra-śabdaḥ puṃ-liṅgaḥ kalatra-vāćako nitya-bahuvaćanāntaḥ*, 'the word *dāra*, meaning a wife, is of the masculine gender, and always has a plural termination.' *Dārāḥ* therefore may be either wives or wife. *Ataḥ-param*, &c., 'here he tells the reason why he does not demand higher rank or greater honour for S'akuntalā,' S'. In the first line, my own MS. reads *asmān sādhu samīkshya saṃyama-parān*. All marriages in the East are arranged by the relatives of the parties.

Verse 97. S'ĀRDŪLA-VIKRĪDITA (a variety of ATIDHRITI). See verses 14, 30, 36, 39, 40, 63, 79, 85, 86, 89.

काश्यपः ।

वत्से । त्वमिदानीमनुशासनीयासि । वनौकसोऽपि सन्तो लौकिकज्ञा वयम् ।[1]

शार्ङ्गरवः ।

न खलु धीमतां कश्चिदविषयो नाम[2] ।

काश्यपः ।

सा त्वमितः पतिकुलं प्राप्य

शुश्रूषस्व गुरून्कुरु प्रियसखीवृत्तिं सपत्नीजने
भर्तुर्विप्रकृतापि रोषणतया मा स्म प्रतीपं गमः ।
भूयिष्ठं भव दक्षिणा परिजने भाग्येष्वनुत्सेकिनी
यान्त्येवं गृहिणीपदं युवतयो वामाः कुलस्याधयः ॥९८॥

कथं वा गौतमी मन्यते ।

---

[1] 'We (are) acquainted with worldly affairs,' 'we know the ways of the world' (=*loka-vyavahāra-jñāḥ*, S'.)

[2] 'There is no subject out of the reach [*agocaraḥ*, S'.] of the intelligent,' i.e. wise men are conversant with all subjects.

[3] 'Pay respectful attention to (thy) superiors. Act the part of a dear friend towards (thy) fellow-wives [rival wives]. Even though wronged [treated harshly] by thy husband, do not out of anger shew [go to] a refractory-spirit. Be ever courteous towards (thy) attendants; not puffed up [arrogant] in prosperity—in this manner young-women attain the station [title] of housewife [matron]. Those of an opposite character are house-banes [banes of the family].' The Sāhit.-d. p. 185 adduces this as an example of the figure Upadishṭa, which is defined as *manohāri vākyaṃ śāstrānusārataḥ*. S'. quotes the following aphorism, *Parisaṅgṛihya śāstrārthaṃ yad vākyam abhidhīyate vidvan manoharaṃ jñeyam upadishṭaṃ tad eva tu*. *Gurūn*=*svaśurādīn*, 'father-in-law,' &c., C. A Guru is not only a father or a father-in-law, but also a preceptor, and in fact any male relation entitled to *gaurava*, 'respect.' *Śuśrūshasva*=*ārādhaya*. *Vrittim*, some of the Beng. and the Sāhit.-d., supported by S'., read *vrittam*

Verse 98. ŚĀRDŪLA-VIKRĪDITA (a variety of ATIDHṚITI). See verses 14, 30, 36, 39, 40, 63, 79, 85, 86, 89, 97.

गौतमी ।

"एत्तिओ वहूजणस्स उवदेसो । जादे । एदंक्खु सव्वं
ओधारेहि ।

काश्यपः ।

वत्से । परिष्वजस्व मां सखीजनं च ।

शकुन्तला ।

"ताद । इदो एव्व किं पिअंवदामिस्साओ सहीओ
णिवत्तिस्सन्ति ।

काश्यपः ।

वत्से । इमे अपि मे देये । न युक्तमनयोस्तच गन्तुम् ।
त्वया सह गौतमी यास्यति ।

शकुन्तला ।। पितरमाश्लिष्य ।।

"कहं दाणिं तादस्स अङ्कादो परिब्भट्ठा मलअतरुम्मूलिआ

<hr>

ª एतावान्वधूजनस्योपदेशः । जाते । एतत्खलु सर्वमवधारय ।   ᵇ तात ।
इत एव किं प्रियंवदामिश्राः सख्यो निवर्तिष्यन्ते ।   ᶜ कथमिदानीं तातस्याङ्कात्प-
रिभ्रष्टा मलयतटोन्मूलिता

=*charitram*, 'action,' 'deed,' 'behaviour,' 'demeanour.' *Viprakritā*=
pīḍitā, C.;=*krita-vipriyā*, 'offended,' S'. *Pratīpam*=*pratikūlyam*. *Bhū-
yishṭham*=*atiśayena*. *Dakshiṇā*=*sa-snehā*. *Bhāgyeshu*, the Beng. and
S'. have *bhogeshu*=*sukheshu*, 'in enjoyments,' 'in pleasures,' in which case
anutsekinī will mean 'not given to excess.' The latter word is literally
'spouting up' like a fountain. Compare *anutseko lakshmyām*, Bhartṛi-h.
ii. 54. *Padam*=*śabdam*, 'a title,' S'.;=*vyavasāyam* or *pratishṭhām*, C.
Vāmāḥ=*tad-viparīta-kāriṇyaḥ*, S'.;=*tad-viruddhāḥ*, C.

[1] 'Lay to heart,' 'treasure up in thy heart,' 'ponder well.'

[2] 'Priyaṃvadā and my other dear friends;' cf. *Śārṅgarava-miśrāḥ*,
p. 151, l. 7, with note. My own MS. and two others insert *kim*.

[3] 'Are to be given away in marriage.' Cf. p. 48, l. 10, with note
thereon. *Ime api*; the dual terminations ī, ū, e do not coalesce with
following vowels, see Gram. 38; Pāṇ. i. 1, 11.

[a] चन्दणलदा विञ्च देसन्तरे जीविञं धारइस्सं ।

काश्यपः ।

वत्से । किमेवं कातरासि ।

अभिजनवतो भर्तुः श्लाघ्ये स्थिता गृहिणीपदे
विभवगुरुभिः कृत्यैस्तस्य प्रतिक्षणमाकुला ।
तनयमचिरात्प्राचीवार्कं प्रसूय च पावनं
मम विरहजां न त्वं वत्से शुचं गणयिष्यसि[2] ॥ ९९ ॥

॥ शकुन्तला पितुः पादयोः पतति ॥

[a] चन्दनलतेव देशान्तरे जीवितं धारयिष्यामि ।

---

[1] 'How now, removed from my foster-father's side, like a tendril of the
sandal-tree uprooted from the slopes of Malaya, shall I support life in a
strange place?' The Candana or sandal tree (σάνταλον), Sirium Myrti-
folium, is 'a large kind of myrtle with pointed leaves,' the wood of which
affords many highly esteemed perfumes, unguents, &c., and is celebrated
for its delicious scent. It is found chiefly on the slopes [*taṭa, upatyakā*,
Raghu-v. iv. 46, 48] of the Malaya mountains, which are thence called
candanācala, the tree being sometimes called *Malaya-ja*, 'Malaya-born.'
Frequent allusion is made to this tree being infested by snakes (see
Raghu-v. iv. 48; Hitop. l. 1582). *Tara*, of which the Sanskrit equivalent
is probably *taṭa*, is the reading of all the Deva-n. MSS. It is synonymous
with *utsanga*, 'the slope of a hill,' so that *Malayasya utsangāt* exactly
answers to *tāṭasya-ankāt* [*anka=utsanga*, Amara-k. iv. 1, 4]. *Ḍ* and *r*
are certainly interchangeable in Sanskrit and Prākrit, and the substitution
of *ḍ* for *ṭ* is usual. *L*, however, is the more common substitute, and it
might be supposed that *Malaya-tara* was for *Malaya-tala=Malayasya
upatyakā*, Raghu-v. iv. 46.

[2] 'Stationed in the honourable post of wife to a nobly-born husband;
(and) incessantly [every moment] distracted with his affairs important
from his dignity; having very shortly given birth to a pure son, like as
the Eastern-quarter (gives birth to) the Sun, thou wilt not take account,
O daughter, of the sorrow produced by separation from me.' *Abhijana-*

Verse 99. HARIṆĪ (a variety of ATYAṢṬI). See verse 66.

काश्यपः ।

यदिच्छामि ते तदस्तु ।

शकुन्तला ॥ सख्यावुपेत्य ॥

[a] हला । दुवेवि मं समं एव्व परिस्सजह ।

सख्यौ ॥ तथा कृत्वा ॥

[b] सहि । जइ णाम सो राञा पच्चहिस्साणमन्थरो भवे । तदो से इमं अत्तणोमहेअङ्किअं अङ्गुलीअअं दंसेहि ।

शकुन्तला ।

[c] इमिणा सन्देहेण वो आकम्पिदम्हि ।

सख्यौ ।

[d] मा भाआहि । अदिसिणेहो[2] पाअसङ्की ।

शार्ङ्गरवः ।

युगान्तरमारूढः[3] सविता । त्वरतामत्रभवती ।

---

[a] हला । द्वे अपि मां सममेव परिष्वजेयाम् ।   [b] सखि । यदि नाम स राञा प्रत्यभिज्ञानमन्थरो भवेत् । ततोऽस्मायिदमात्मनामधेयाङ्कितमङ्गुलीयकं[1] दर्शय । [c] अनेन सन्देहेन वामाकम्पितास्मि ।   [d] मा बिभीहि । अतिस्नेहः पापशङ्की ।

---

vato=kulinasya, see p. 15, n. 1. *Ākulā=vyagrā*, 'perplexed,' 'intently occupied,' S.; =*sasambhramā*, 'bewildered,' K. *Adirāt=gamanāryarahita-samaye*, 'immediately on thy arrival.' *Prāći iva*, &c.=*yathā pūrva-dik pavitra-janakaṃ sūryam*, S.

[1] *Ātmanāmadheyānkita*, see p. 53, notes 2 and 3, and p. 140, l. 9, with note 2.

[2] 'Excessive affection is apt to suspect evil.' *Ati-snehaḥ*, so reads the Taylor MS. as well as my own, supported by K. S'. observes, *tathā ćoktaṃ kirāte, prema paśyati bhayāni apade 'pi*, 'and so it is said in the Kirā-tārjunīya, "Affection sees causes of alarm [or dangers], even without foun-dation."' (See Kirāt. ix. 70.)

[3] 'The sun has ascended to another division (of the sky).' The Mackenzie MS. has *yugāntam adhirūḍhaḥ*; the Calcutta edition, *dūram adhirūḍhaḥ*; Chézy, *gaganāntaram adhirūḍhaḥ*. According to C., *yuga*

शकुन्तला ॥ आश्रमाभिमुखी स्थित्वा ॥

[a]ताद । कदा णु भूओ तवोवणं पेक्खिस्सं ।

काश्यपः ।

श्रूयताम् ।

भूत्वा चिराय चतुरन्तमहीसपत्नी
दौष्यन्तिमप्रतिरथं तनयं निवेश्य ।
भर्त्रा तदर्पितकुटुम्बभरेण साधं
शान्ते करिष्यसि पदं पुनराश्रमेऽस्मिन् ॥१००॥

[a] तात । कदा नु भूयस्तपोवनं प्रेक्षिष्ये ।

---

is by some considered equivalent to *prahara*, 'a division of the day, comprising one-eighth of the sun's diurnal revolution, or three hours;' by others, to *hasta-ćatushṭaya*, 'a space of four cubits.' Dr. Boehtlingk translates, 'The sun has already entered the afternoon-quarter of the heavens.'

[1] 'Having become for a long time the fellow-wife of the Earth bounded by the four cardinal-points, having settled-in-marriage thy matchless-warrior son Daushyanti, in-company-with thy husband (Dushyanta), who shall have (first) transferred the cares of government [the burthen of family-cares] to him, thou shalt again set foot in this tranquil hermitage.' *Ćatur-anta-mahī* seems to be equivalent to *ćatur-dig-anta-mahī*, i. e. 'the earth as far as the four quarters,' 'the entire earth.' The Beng. have a parallel phrase *sa-dig-anta-mahī.* K. explains it by *ćatvāraḥ antāḥ yasyāḥ sā.* Cf. p. 124, l. 4. *Daushyanti* is a regular patronymic, from Dushyanta, as Dākshi, 'a descendant of Daksha,' from Daksha; Aindri from Indra, &c. (see Gram. 81. X). *A-pratiratham = asat-paripanthinam,* 'having no antagonist,' = *a-pratirathikam,* K.; *ratha* being put for *rathika* or *rathin,* 'a warrior who fights from a chariot.' *Niveśya = vivāhya,* 'having caused to marry,' K.; *niviś* has this sense in Mahā-bh. i. 7138. *Tad* refers to *Daushyanti.* *Arpita,* &c., cf. *aham api sūnau vinyasya rājyam,* Vikram., Act V; also

---

Verse 100. VASANTA-TILAKĀ (a variety of ŚAKVARĪ). See verses 8, 27, 31, 43, 46, 64, 74, 80, 82, 83, 91, 93, 94, 95.

गौतमी ।

[a] जादे । परिहीञ्चदि गमणवेला । णिवत्तेहि पिदरं । अहवा चिरेणवि पुणो पुणो एसा एव्वं मन्तइस्सदि । णिवत्तदु भवं ।

काश्यपः ।

वत्से । उपरुध्यते तपोऽनुष्ठानम् ।[2]

शकुन्तला ॥ भूयः पितरमालिङ्ग्य ॥

[b] तवच्चरणपीडिदं तादसरीरं । ता मा अदिमेत्तं मम किदे उक्कण्ठ ।[3]

---

[a] जाते । परिहीयते गमनवेला । निवर्तय पितरम् । अथवा चिरेणापि पुनः पुनरेवैवं मन्त्रयिष्यते । निवर्त्तां भवान् ।   [b] तपश्चरणपीडितं तातशरीरम् । तन्मातिमात्रं मम कृते उत्कण्ठस्व ।

Manu vi. 2, 3, 'When the father of a family perceives his own wrinkles and grey hair, committing the care of his wife to his sons, or accompanied by her, let him repair to the woods,' i. e. let him enter upon the third quarter of his life, that of a hermit (see p. 157, n. 1 at the end). *Sānte*, cf. p. 20, l. 12. *Karishyasi padam*, cf. p. 145, n. 2 at the end.

[1] 'Allow the father to return; or rather, (since) even for a long time she will go on talking again and again in this manner, let your reverence return,' i. e. return at once yourself, without asking her permission. To depart without asking leave, is contrary to all Hindū ideas of politeness. *Athavā*, see p. 30, n. 3.

[2] 'The prosecution of (my) devotions is interrupted (by this detention).' Compare in Vikram., Act V, *uparudhyate me āśrama-vāsa-dharmaḥ.*

[3] 'Therefore do not beyond measure sorrow on my account.' *Ukkaṇṭha* for Sanskrit *utkaṇṭha* or *utkaṇṭhasva* is the reading of my own MS. *Mā ukkaṇṭhidum* seems questionable. K. has *Bhūyo 'pi tapaś-caraṇa-pīḍitaṃ tātasya śarīram atimātram mama kṛite utkaṇṭhitam bhavishyati.*

काश्यपः ॥ सनिःश्वासम् ॥

शममेष्यति मम शोकः कथं नु वत्से त्वया चरितपूर्वम् ।
उटजद्वारविरूढं नीवारबलिं विलोकयतः ॥१०१॥
गच्छ । शिवास्ते पन्थानः सन्तु ।

॥ निष्क्रान्ता शकुन्तला सहयायिनश्च ॥

---

¹ 'How, my child, will the grief of me, looking at the oblation of rice-grains formerly offered by thee, germinating at the door of the cottage, ever be assuaged [ever go to assuagement]?' *Ćarita*, so reads the Colebrooke MS.; the others have *raćita-pūrvam*=*purā-vihitam*, S'. *Ćarita* is supported by *ćaru*, 'an oblation of rice.' The *bali*, or *gṛiha-bali*, is a particular kind of offering, identical with the *bhūta-yajña*, i. e. a sacrifice for all creatures, but especially in honour of those demigods and spiritual beings called *gṛiha-devatāḥ*, 'household deities,' which are supposed to hover round and protect households (Manu iii. 80), or to whom some particular part of the house is sacred. This offering was made by throwing up into the air (Manu iii. 90), in some part of the house, generally at the door (Manu iii. 88), the remains of the morning and evening meal of rice or grain; uttering at the same time a *mantra* or prayer to some of the inferior deities, according to the place in which it was made (Manu iii. 87, &c.), whether to Indra with his followers the Maruts, or to Kuvera with his followers the Guhyakas, Kinnaras, Yakshas, &c., or to the spirits of trees, waters, &c. (Manu iii. 88, 89). According to Colebrooke it might be presented with the following Paurāṇik prayer, 'May gods, men, cattle, birds, demigods, benevolent genii, serpents, demons, departed spirits, blood-thirsty savages, trees, and all who desire food given by me—may reptiles, insects, flies, and all hungry beings or spirits concerned in this rite, obtain contentment from this food left them by me!' It was sometimes offered by the women of the house, who might assist in any sacrifice, provided they abstained from repeating the Mantras (Manu iii. 121), and as the offering was intended for all creatures, even the animals were supposed to have their share in it (Manu iii. 92). In point of fact the crows, dogs, insects, &c. in the neighbourhood of the house were the real consumers of it (whence *bali-pushṭa, bali-bhuj, gṛiha-bali-bhuj*, as names

---

Verse 101. ĀRYĀ or GĀTHĀ. See verse 2.

```
∪ ∪ − | ∪ ∪ ∪ ∪ | − − ‖ ∪ − ∪ | − − | ∪ − ∪ | ∪ ∪ − | −
∪ ∪ − | − ∪ ∪ | − − ‖ − − | ∪ ∪ − | ∪ | − ∪ ∪ | −
```

सख्यौ ॥ शकुन्तलां विलोक्य ॥

[a] हड्डी हड्डी । अन्तलिहिदा सउन्दला वणराईए ।

काश्यप: ॥ सनिःश्वासम् ॥

अनसूये । गतवती वां सहधर्मचारिणी । निगृह्य
श्योकमनुगच्छतं मां प्रस्थितम् ।

उभे ।

[b] ताद । सउन्दलाविरहिदं सुखं विश्र तवोवणं कहं
पविसामो ।

काश्यप: ।

स्नेहप्रवृत्तिरेवंदर्शिनी[2] । ॥ सविमर्शं परिक्रम्य ॥ हन्त[3] भीः । शकुन्त-

[a] हा धिक् हा धिक् । अन्तर्हिता शकुन्तला वनराज्या ।   [b] तात ।
शकुन्तलाविरहितं शून्यमिव तपोवनं कथं प्रविशाव: ।

---

of a crow, crane, sparrow, &c., compare Hitop. l. 1076), and such of the
grains as escaped being devoured by them would be likely to germinate
about the threshold. This *bali* formed one of the five great religious rites,
sometimes called sacraments, which the householder who maintained a
perpetual fire (see p. 148, n. 1) had daily to perform (Manu iii. 67, iv. 21).
See Indian Wisdom, pp. 203, 251. It was in honour of all creatures of
every description, but particularly of those not provided for by the other
four sacrifices. It might have reference, however, to the deities and beings
honoured in the other sacraments. That it had especial reference to the
Griha-devatāḥ is indicated in Manu iii. 117, with commentary; and in the
Mṛicchakaṭikā, where Cārudatta, after fulfilling the Deva-kārya, or second
of the five rites (cf. p. 140, l. 17), is described as offering the *bali* to the
houschold gods around the threshold. His speech, as he offers it, corre-
sponds remarkably with that of Kāśyapa, *Yāsām baliḥ sapadi mad-
griha-dehalīnām, haṃsaiś ca sārasa-ganaiś ca vilupta-pūrvaḥ, tāsv eva sam-
prati virūdha-tṛiṇāṅkurāsu, vījāñjaliḥ patati kīṭa-mukhāvalīḍhaḥ*. See
Mṛicch., Act I, verse 1. For *śivās te panthānaḥ santu*, in the next line,
see p. 163, n. 1 at the end.

¹ So read all the Deva-n. for *antarihidā*, cf. p. 140, l. 6.

² 'The course of affection views it thus.' The Beng. MSS. have *sneha-
vrittir*, and one (I. O. 1050) *evaṃ śaṃsinī* for *evaṃ darśinī*. *Yasmin
vishaye sneho bhavati tad-asānnidhyād etādṛiśa eva kramo bhavati*, S.

³ *Hanta*, here an exclamation of joy (*harshe*, S.)

लां पतिकुलं विसृज्य लब्धमिदानीं स्वास्थ्यम् ।[1] कुतः ।

अर्थो हि कन्या परकीय एव
तामद्य सम्प्रेष्य परिग्रहीतुः ।
जातो ममायं विशदः प्रकामं
प्रत्यर्पितन्यास इवान्तरात्मा ॥[2]१०२॥

॥ इति निष्क्रान्ताः सर्वे ॥

॥ चतुर्थोऽङ्कः ॥

---

[1] 'My natural serenity of mind,' 'my natural good spirits.' A load of anxiety is taken off my mind.

[2] 'Verily a girl is another's property. Having to-day sent her to her husband, this my conscience has become quite clear, as if (after) restoring a deposit.' *Kanyā-rūpo 'rthaḥ*, &c., 'the property consisting of a girl belongs to another,' S'. and C'. *Parigrahītuḥ=pariṇetuḥ.* Hence *parigraha*, 'a wife,' see p. 124, l. 3. The ceremonies of marriage are described by Colebrooke in the Asiatic Researches, vol. vii. pp. 288–311, thus:—The bridegroom goes in procession to the house of the bride's father. The bride is given to him by her father, and their hands, on which turmeric has been previously rubbed, are bound together with Kuśa grass. The bridegroom next makes oblations to the sacred household fire, and the bridegroom drops rice into it. The bridegroom solemnly takes her hand in marriage (whence he is called *pāṇi-grahītṛi*, and marriage *pāṇi-grahaṇa*), and leads her round the sacred fire (whence he is called *pariṇetṛi*). The bride steps seven times, and the marriage is then irrevocable. *Viśadaḥ=prasannaḥ*, 'serene,' 'tranquil,' K.; *=susthaḥ*, S'. Cf. *manasaḥ prasādaḥ*, Vikram., Act V. *Prakāmam=atyartham*, see p. 108, n. 3. The Beng. reading is *jāto 'smi samyag viśadāntarātmā, ćirasya nikshepam ivārpayitvā.*

Verse 102. INDRA-VAJRĀ (a variety of TRISHṬUBH), containing eleven syllables to the Pāda or quarter-verse, each Pāda being alike.

– – ◡ – – ◡ ◡ – ◡ – – ‖

॥ अथ पञ्चमोऽङ्कः ॥

॥ ततः प्रविशत्यासनस्थो राजा विदूषकश्च ॥

विदूषकः ॥ कर्णं दत्त्वा ॥

"भो भो वयस्स । सङ्गीदसालन्तरे अवधाणं देहि ।
कलविसुद्धाए गीदीए सरसञ्जोओ सुणीअदि । जाणे ।
तत्तहोदी हंसवदिआ वण्णपरिअअं करेदि त्ति ।

राजा ।

तूष्णीं भव । यावदाकर्णयामि ।

a भो भो वयस्य । सङ्गीतशालान्तरेऽवधानं देहि । कलविशुद्धायां गीत्यां स्वरसंयोगः
श्रूयते । जाने । तत्रभवती हंसपदिका वर्णपरिचयं करोतीति ।

---

[1] In the Beng. MSS. the speech of the Chamberlain at p. 186 commences the Act.

[2] 'Turn (thy) attention to the interior of the music-hall. In a soft and clear song harmonious sounds are heard [the union of notes is heard].' *Íśvarāṇāṃ yatra nṛityādikam bhavati sā saṅgīta-śālā*, 'a music-saloon is a place where dancing &c. is performed before princes,' S'. *Avadhānam*, K. has *avadhāraṇam*. *Gītyām=dhruvāyām*, K. Prākṛit *gīdīe* may stand for instr., gen., or loc. cases. *Svara-saṃyoga*, K. has *svara-yoga*. Both expressions occur in Mṛićh. (p. 33, l. 2; p. 94, l. 1; p. 222, l. 5; p. 339, l. 9), and in the Mālavik. (p. 67, l. 6, with note).

[3] 'Is practising singing,' lit. 'is making acquaintance with the Varṇas.' *Parićaya=abhyāsa*, C. *Varṇa*, 'the order or arrangement of a song.' It may also mean 'a musical mode.' These modes are numerous, personified either as male (Rāga) or female (Rāgiṇī). According to S'. and C., the Varṇas intended here are of four kinds, the first two corresponding with the division of the Bhāvas, or 'affections.' *Gītishu ćatvāra varṇā bhavanti yad āha Bharataḥ, Sthāyī tathaiva Sanćārī tathā Rohāva-rohiṇau. Varṇāś ćatvāra evaite kathitāḥ sarva-gītishu.*

|| आकाशे गीयते ||

^aअहिणवमहुलोलुबो तुमं
तह परिचुम्बिअ चूअमञ्झरिं ।
कमलवसइमेत्तणिब्बुदो
महुअर विम्हरिदोसि एं कंहं ॥१०३॥

राजा ।

अहो रागपरिवाहिणी गीतिः ।

^a अभिनवमधुलोलुपस्त्वं तथा परिचुम्ब्य चूतमञ्जरीम् ।
कमलवसतिमात्रनिर्वृतो मधुकर विस्मृतोऽस्येनां कथम् ॥

---

[1] 'O Bee, how (can it be) that thou, eagerly-longing for fresh honey, after having so kissed the mango-blossom, shouldst (now) be forgetful of it, being altogether satisfied with (thy) dwelling in the lotus!' *Cūta-mañjarī=āmra-kalikā*, S'. Cf. in Vikram., Act II, *Ishad-baddha-rajaḥ-kaṇāgra-kapiśā cūte navā mañjarī*. *Kamala-vasati=kamalāvasthiti*, C. The fondness of the bee (which in Sanskrit is masculine) for the lotus is so great that he will remain for a long time in the interior of the flower. Cf. *na pankajaṃ tad yad alīna-shaṭpadam*, 'that is not a lotus which has no bee clinging to it,' Bhaṭṭi-k. ii. 19; also *guñjad-dvirepho 'yam ambuja-sthaḥ*, 'the murmuring bee remaining in the lotus,' Ṛitu-s. vi. 15; and *idaṃ ruṇaddhi mām padmam antaḥ-kvaṇita-shaṭpadam*, Vikram., Act IV. *Madhu-kara*, see p. 33, n. 1. *Vismṛita*, see p. 161, n. 3. In Prākṛit, two forms *mar* and *sumar* are used for *smṛi;* the first becomes *mhar* after a preposition (as in *vimhao* for *vismayaḥ*, Vararuéi iii. 32); but *vimariḍo* would be equally correct according to Vararuéi iii. 56. K. observes that, under the figure of a bee, Haṃsapadikā covertly reproves the king for having forgotten her. S'. and C'. call this verse a *Praééhādaka*, and the following from Kavi-kaṇṭhahāra is quoted, *anyāsaktam patim matvā prema-viééheda-manyunā vīṇā-puraḥsaraṃ gānam striyāḥ praééhādako mataḥ.*

[2] 'Oh, what an impassioned strain!' lit. a song overflowing with affection or passion. *Rāga-parivāhinī=anurāga-nishyandinī*, S'.;=*kāma-sampūrṇā*, K. Cf. p. 89, n. 3.

Verse 103. APARA-VAKTRA. See verse 90.

विदूषकः ।

[a] किं दाव गीदीए अवगदो अक्खरत्थो ।

राजा ॥ स्मितं कृत्वा ॥

सकृत्कृतप्रणयोऽयं जनः । तदस्या देवीं वसुमतीमन्तरेण महदुपालम्भनं गतोऽस्मि । सखे माठव्य । मद्वचनादुच्यतां हंसपदिका । निपुणमुपालब्धोऽस्मीति ।

विदूषकः ।

[b] जं भवं आणबेदि । ॥ उत्थाय ॥ [c] भो वअस्स । गहीदस्स ताए परकीएहिं हत्थेहिं सिहरडए ताडीअमाणस्स अच्छराए वीदराअस्स विअ णत्थि दाणिं मे मोक्खो ।

[a] किं तावद्गीत्या अवगतोऽक्षरार्थः ।   [b] यद्भवानाज्ञापयति ।   [c] भो वयस्य । गृहीतस्य तया परकीयैर्हस्तैः शिखरडके ताड्यमानस्याप्सरसा वीतरागस्येव नास्तीदानीं मे मोक्षः ।

---

[1] 'The meaning of the words,' lit. 'of the letters or syllables.'

[2] 'This person [i. e. I] once made love (to her); therefore I am incurring her severe censure on account of the queen Vasumatī.' *Krita-praṇayaḥ = krita-premā. Ayaṃ janaḥ*, i. e. *mad-rūpaḥ*, 'consisting of me,' S. Cf. p. 144, n. 2. *Vasumatī* is a name for the earth, cf. p. 124, n. 1. *Antareṇa*, with accusative, see p. 81, n. 2. After *krita-praṇayo 'yaṃ janaḥ*, the Calcutta edition adds *ity aksharārthaḥ*, 'such is the meaning of the words.'

[3] 'There is not now any liberation for me (suffered to be) seized by her with the hands of others by-the-hair-on-the-crown-of-my-head (and) beaten, any more than for a sage-with-suppressed-passions (if taken unawares) by a lovely-nymph.' *Śikhaṇḍaka* is 'the lock of hair left on the crown of the head at tonsure.' This was the only portion of hair suffered to remain on the head of a Brāhman; but in the case of the military class, three or five locks, called *kāka-pakshāḥ*, were left on each side. The two ceremonies of tonsure are included by Manu among the twelve Saṃskāras or rites which every Brāhman had to undergo. The first, or *ćūḍā-karaṇa*, took place from one to three years old, generally after teething (Manu ii. 35); the second, or final tonsure *keśānta*, in the sixteenth year from conception (ii. 65). *Moksha* has here a double sense, 'liberation of the body

राजा ।

गच्छ । नागरिकवृत्त्या सञ्ज्ञापयैनाम् ।

विदूषकः ।

[a] का गंई । ॥ इति निष्क्रान्तः ॥

राजा ॥ आत्मगतम् ॥

किं नु खलु गीतार्थमाकर्ण्यैष्टजनविरहाट्टनेऽपि बल-
वदुत्कण्ठितोऽस्मि । अथवा ।

रम्याणि वीक्ष्य मधुरांश्च निशम्य शब्दा-
न्पर्युत्सुकीभवति यत्सुखितोऽपि जन्तुः ।
तच्चेतसा स्मरति नूनमबोधपूर्वं
भावस्थिराणि जननान्तरसौहृदानि ॥ १०४ ॥

॥ इति पर्याकुलस्तिष्ठति ॥

[a] का गतिः ।

---

from danger,' and 'liberation of the soul from further transmigration;'
see n. 3 below. The last was the great object of sages and devotees in
their bodily mortifications, but was often obstructed by the seductive
artifices of Indra's nymphs (see p. 45, n. 1).

[1] 'In the courtly [fashionable] style.' *Pravīṇasya ṛityā*, K. *Nāgarika*
here means more than 'polite.' It implies 'insincerity,' as when a man
shews exaggerated attention to his first mistress, while he is courting some
one else.

[2] *Kā gatiḥ*, see p. 62, l. 2, with note 2.

[3] 'When a being (in other respects) happy becomes conscious-of-an
ardent-longing on seeing charming objects and hearing sweet sounds, then
in all probability, without being aware of it, he remembers with his mind
the friendships of former births, firmly-rooted in his heart.' *Ramyāṇi*, i. e.
vastūni, S. For *ramyāṇi* K. has *rūpāṇi* and *sthitāni* for *sthirāṇi*. *A-bodha-
pūrvam*, 'without any previous intimation or suggestion,' 'unconsciously.'
Compare the similar expressions, *a-mati-pūrvam, a-buddhi-pūrvam*, 'without
any previous idea.' The doctrine of transmigration is an essential dogma

---

Verse 104. VASANTA-TILAKĀ (a variety of ŚAKVARĪ). See verses 8, 27, 31, 43, 46,
64, 74, 80, 82, 83, 91, 93, 94, 95, 100.

॥ ततः प्रविशति कञ्चुकी ॥

कञ्चुकी ।

अहो नु खल्वीदृशीमवस्थां प्रतिपन्नोऽस्मि ।
आचार इत्यवहितेन मया गृहीता
या वेत्रयष्टिरवरोधगृहेषु राज्ञः ।
काले गते बहुतिथे मम सैव जाता
प्रस्थानविक्लवगतेरवलम्बनार्थम् ॥ १०५ ॥

---

of the Hindū religion; see Indian Wisdom, p. 67. Dim recollections of occurrences in a former life are supposed occasionally to cross the mind, and the present condition of every person is supposed to derive its character of happiness or misery, elevation or degradation, from the virtues or vices of a previous state of being. The consequences of actions in a former birth are called *vipāka*.

¹ The Kañćukin or Chamberlain was the attendant on the women's apartments. S'. and C'. quote the following from Bharata : *Antahpura-ćaro vriddho vipro guṇa-gaṇānvitaḥ sarva-kāryārtha-kuśalaḥ kañćukīti abhidhīyate. Jarā-vaiklavya-yuktena viśed gātreṇa kañćukī*, 'the character styled Kañćukin is an attendant in the inner apartments, an old man, a Brāhman, endowed with numerous good qualities, and a clever man of business. The Kañćukin should enter with a body decrepit and tottering from age.' Compare this scene, and the speeches of the Chamberlain, with the opening scene of Act III. of Vikram.

² 'The wand [staff of office] which was assumed by me, having to watch over the royal female apartments, thinking, "It is a matter of form," much time having elapsed since then, that same (wand) has become (indispensable, or a useful crutch) for the support of me whose step falters in walking.' *Vetra-yashṭi*, properly 'a cane-stick,' used as a badge of office, like the gold stick or black rod in European courts. *Avahitena*, lit. 'attentive,' 'careful,' 'watchful,' i. e. appointed to a careful superintendence or watch. So read all the Deva-n.; the Beng., with S'., have *adhikṛitena*, i. e. 'by me set over,' &c. *Avarodha-griheshu*, see p. 21, n. 3. *Bahutithe* = *bahu-sankhye*, Chézy. K. observes that *bahu* is here treated as a numeral, *titha* being a kind of ordinal suffix (Gram. p. 66. LXIII).

Verse 105. VASANTA-TILAKĀ (a variety of ŚAKVARĪ). See verses 8, 27, 31, 43, 46, 64, 74, 80, 82, 83, 91, 93, 94, 95, 100, 104.

भोः । कामं धर्मकार्यमनतिपात्यं देवस्य । तथापीदानीमेव
धर्मासनादुत्थितस्य पुनरुपरोधकारि कथशिष्यागमन-
मस्मै नोत्सहे निवेदयितुम् । अथवा । अविश्रामोऽयं
लोकतन्त्राधिकारः । कुतः ।

भानुः सकृद्युक्ततुरङ्ग एव
राचिन्दिवं गन्धवहः प्रयाति ।
शेषः सदैवाहितभूमिभारः
षष्ठांशवृत्तेरपि धर्म एषः ॥१०६॥

यावन्नियोगमनुतिष्ठामि । ॥ परिक्रम्यावलोक्य च ॥ एष देवः ।

प्रजाः प्रजाः स्वा इव तन्त्रयित्वा
निषेवते श्रान्तमना विविक्तम् ।

---

[1] 'But (why should I hesitate?) this office of supporting the world does not (admit of) repose.' *Athavā*, see p. 30, n. 3. *Loka-tantra*, one meaning of *tantra* is 'supporting a family.'

[2] 'Because the Sun having but once (and once) only yoked his steeds travels onwards; night and day the wind (also travels); S'esha has the burden of the earth always resting (on his head). This also is the duty of him whose subsistence is on the sixth part (of the produce of the soil).' *Kutah*, see p. 55, n. 2. *Bhānu*, 'the Sun;' see p. 142, n. 3. 'In other chariots the horses are yoked again after an interval of rest, but the horses of the Sun are allowed no repose,' S'. *Sūrya evambhūtaḥ san prayāti*, S'. *Gandha-vaha*, lit. 'the scent-bearer,'=*vāyu*, S'. *S'esha*=*Ananta*, a mythological serpent, the personification of eternity (*ananta-tā*) and king of the Nāgas or snakes who inhabit the lowermost of the seven Pātālas or infernal regions. His body formed the couch of Vishṇu, reposing on the waters of Chaos, whilst his thousand heads were the god's canopy. He is also said to uphold the world on one of his heads. He has become incarnate at various times, especially in the god Bala-rāma, the elder brother of Krishṇa. *Āhita*, see p. 149, n. 1. *Shashṭhānśa-vṛitter*, see p. 84, n. 1.

Verse 106. INDRA-VAJRĀ (a variety of TRISHṬUBH), containing eleven syllables to the Pāda or quarter-verse, each Pāda being alike.

— — ◡ — — ◡ ◡ — ◡ — — ‖

यूथानि सञ्चार्य रविप्रतप्तः
शीतं दिवा स्थानमिव द्विपेन्द्रः ॥१०७॥

।। उपगम्य ।। जयतु जयतु देवः । एते खलु हिमवतो
गिरेरुपत्यकारण्यवासिनः काश्यपसन्देशमादाय सस्त्रीका-
स्तपस्विनः सम्प्राप्ताः । श्रुत्वा देवः प्रमाणम् ।

राजा ।। सादरम् ।।

किं काश्यपसन्देशहारिणः ।

कञ्चुकी ।

अथ किम् ।

राजा ।

तेन हि मद्वचनाद्विज्ञाप्यतामुपाध्यायः सोमरातः ।
अमूनाश्रमवासिनः श्रौतेन विधिना सत्कृत्य स्वयमेव
प्रवेशयितुमर्हतीति । अहमप्यत्र तपस्विदर्शनोचिते प्रदेशे
स्थितः प्रतिपालयामि ।

---

[1] 'Having supported his subjects as his own children, wearied in mind he seeks seclusion, as the chief of the elephants scorched by the sun, after conducting the herds to their pastures, in the (heat of the) day (seeks) a cool spot.' *Tantrayitvā*, from a nominal verb *tantraya* (see p. 187, n. 1), is the reading of all the Beng. MSS., supported by K.; two of the Deva-n., *śāntrayitvā*; the Mackenzie, *harshayitvā*. *Śrānta-manāḥ* is the reading of the Mackenzie, supported by K.; the other Deva-n., *śānta-manāḥ*, 'composed in mind.' *Sañćārya*, lit. 'having caused to move about or graze,' = *bhramayitvā*, S. *Vivikta* = *vijana-pradeśa*. *Divā* = *madhyāhne*, 'in the middle of the day.' *Dvipendraḥ* = *hasti-rājaḥ* = *yūtha-nāthaḥ*, 'a large elephant, the leader of a wild herd.'

[2] 'Having heard, your Majesty must decide (what is to be done).' K. supplies *yat kartavyam*. *Pramāṇam*, see p. 31, n. 1 at the end.

[3] *Atha kim* is used *svīkāre*, S. (see p. 46, n. 3).

[4] 'In the form enjoined by the scriptures' (= *śruti-bodhitena prakāreṇa*, S.)

Verse 107. UPAJĀTI or ĀKHYĀNAKĪ (a variety of TRISHṬUBH). See verse 41.

कञ्चुकी ।

यदाज्ञापयति देवः ।   ॥ इति निष्क्रान्तः ॥

राजा   ॥ उत्थाय ॥

वेचवति । अग्निशरणमार्गमादेशय[1] ।

प्रतीहारी ।

[a]इदो इदो देवी ।

राजा   ॥ परिक्रामति । अधिकारखेदं निरूप्य ॥

सर्वः प्रार्थितमर्थमधिगम्य सुखी सम्पद्यते जन्तुः । राज्ञां
तु चरितार्थता दुःखोत्तरैव[2] ।

औत्सुक्यमात्रमवसादयति प्रतिष्ठा
क्लिश्नाति लब्धपरिपालनवृत्तिरेव ।
नातिश्रमापनयनाय न च श्रमाय
राज्यं स्वहस्तधृतदण्डमिवातपत्रम् ॥१०८॥

[a] इत इतो देवः ।

---

[1] *Agni-śaraṇa*, see p. 148, n. 1.   *Mārya*, see p. 161, l. 4, with note.

[2] 'The attainment of the object (of their ambition) is followed by pain.' *Caritārthatā* = *rājya-prāptiḥ*, 'the attainment of the throne,' S'. *Duḥkhottarā* = *kheda-saṃvalitā*, 'encompassed with trouble,' S'.

[3] 'The-attainment-of-the-object-of-ambition satisfies anxious longing merely; the very business of guarding what has been obtained, harasses. Royalty [the office of king], like a parasol, the handle of which is held in the hand, is not for the removal of great fatigue without leading to fatigue.' *Autsukyam* = *utkaṇṭhā*, 'longing,' 'eager desire;' such as *kadā rājā bhavishyāmītyādi*, 'when shall I become king, &c.?' *tam eva duḥkha-dāyinī pratishṭhā avasādayati*, 'that (desire) certainly the harassing attainment-of-the-highest-rank allays,' C. S'. reads *pratishṭhām*, and places it in opposition to *autsukya-mātram*, making *rājyam* nom. to *avasādayati*. The Beng. MS. [I. O. 1060] gives *pratishṭhām* in the margin, and this reading is certainly supported by a parallel passage (*sādayanti pratishṭhām*, &c.) in the beginning of Act III. of Vikram. C. also notices

---

Verse 108. VASANTA-TILAKĀ (a variety of ŚAKVARĪ). See verses 8, 27, 31, 43, 46, 64, 74, 80, 82, 83, 91, 93, 94, 95, 100, 104, 105.

॥ नेपथ्ये ॥

वैतालिकौ ।

विजयतां देवः ।

प्रथमः ।

स्वसुखनिरभिलाषः खिद्यसे लोकहेतोः
प्रतिदिनमथवा ते वृत्तिरेवंविधैव ।

---

this reading, but adopts the one in the text and censures the interpretation of S. *Pratishṭhā* may have the sense I have given, which agrees with the *prārthitārthādhigamaḥ* and *ćaritārthatā* of the preceding lines. *Ati-śrama* may either refer to the trouble which the king has undergone in arriving at the object of his ambition, or to the troubles of his subjects which it is his office to remove. In the latter case *na ća śramāya* will mean 'without leading to personal trouble or weariness.' The Indian *ćhattra*, or parasol, from the shelter it affords has been chosen as one of the insignia of royalty. It is very heavy, and being fixed on a long pole greatly fatigues the person holding it. It is always borne by a servant; but here the king is figuratively made to bear it himself, so that he cannot give shelter to himself and others, without undergoing great personal fatigue. *Na ća śramāya* is found in all the Deva-n. MSS.; the Beng. have *yathā śramāya*, i.e. 'royalty does not so much lead to the removal of fatigue as to fatigue.' According to K., who repeats the first negative before *na ća śramāya*, the two negatives are here employed affirmatively, i. e. to affirm that royalty does lead to personal fatigue. 'It is not for the removal of great fatigue and not not for fatigue.' Cf. a similar use of two negatives on p. 24; l. 10, with note.

[1] *Vaitālika=vandin*, 'a herald,' Ć.;=*stuti-pāṭhaka*, 'a panegyrist,' S. He was a kind of herald or crier, whose duty was to announce, in measured verse, the fixed periods into which the king's day was divided. The strain which he poured forth usually contained allusions to incidental circumstances. In Vikram. and Ratn., only one Vaitālika appears, but here and in the Mālavik. there are two. In Vikram., Act II, he announces the sixth hour or watch of the day, about two or three o'clock, at which period alone the king is allowed to amuse himself. From the Daśakumāra it appears that a king's day and night were supposed to be divided into eight portions of one hour and a half, reckoned from sunrise, for distributing which strict directions are given, thus: Day—1. The king being dressed, is to audit accounts; 2. He is to pronounce judgment in appeals; 3. He is to breakfast; 4. He is to receive and make presents;

अनुभवति हि मूर्धा पादपस्तीव्रमुष्णं
शमयति परितापं छायया संश्रितानाम् ॥१०९॥

द्वितीय: ।

नियमयसि विमार्गप्रस्थितानात्तदण्डः
प्रशमयसि विवादं कल्पसे रक्षणाय ।
अतनुषु विभवेषु ज्ञातयः सन्तु नाम
त्वयि तु परिसमाप्तं बन्धुकृत्यं प्रजानाम् ॥११०॥

---

5. He is to discuss political questions with his ministers; 6. He is to amuse himself; 7. He is to review his troops; 8. He is to hold a military council. Night—1. He is to receive the reports of his spies and envoys; 2. He is to sup or dine; 3. He is to retire to rest, after the perusal of some sacred work; 4 and 5. He is to sleep; 6. He is to rise and purify himself; 7. He is to hold a private consultation with his ministers, and instruct his officers; 8. He is to attend upon the *Purohita*, or family priest, for the performance of religious ceremonies. See Wilson's Hindū Theatre, vol. i. p. 209.

[1] 'Indifferent to thine own ease, thou endurest toil every day for the sake of (thy) people. But thy regular-business is of this very kind. For the tree suffers intense heat with its head (while) it allays by (its) shade the heat of those seeking (its) shelter.' *Athavā*, see p. 30, n. 3. *Vrittir*, some of the Beng., supported by K. and S'., have *srishtir*.

[2] 'Having assumed the mace [sceptre] thou restrainest those who advance on the wrong road [set out on bad courses]; thou composest differences; thou art adequate to the protection (of thy people). Let kinsmen make their appearance forsooth in affluent circumstances [when there is abundant property], but in thee the whole duty of a kinsman is comprehended towards thy subjects.' *Ātta-danḍa = grihīta-danḍa; danḍa*, 'a magistrate's staff,' taken as a symbol of punishment and justice; it is sometimes 'the sceptre of a king;' hence *danḍa-dhara, danḍin*, 'staff-bearer,' &c., are names for Yama, the god of justice and lord of punishment. *Vimārga*, some have *kumārga*, 'bad ways.' *Kalpase = sampadyase*, K. Manu furnishes several examples of *klṛip* in the sense of 'to be sufficient,' 'to be fit' (see ii. 151, ii. 266, vi. 20; also Raghu-v. viii. 40).

Verses 109 and 110. MĀLINĪ or MĀNINĪ (a variety of ATI-S'AKVARĪ). See verses 10, 19, 20, 38, 55.

राजा ।

ऐते क्लान्तमनसः पुनर्नवीकृताः स्मः । ॥ इति परिक्रामति ॥

प्रतीहारी ।

[a]अहिणवसम्मज्जणससिरीओ सन्निहिदहोमधेणू अग्गि-सरणालिंदी । आरुहदु देवी ।

राजा ॥ आरुह्य परिजनांसावलम्बी तिष्ठति ॥

वेचवति । किमुद्दिश्य भगवता काश्यपेन मत्सकाशमृषयः प्रेरिताः स्युः ।

किं तावद्व्रतिनामुपोढतपसां विघ्नैस्तपो दूषितं
धर्मारण्यचरेषु केनचिदुत प्राणिष्वसच्चेष्टितम् ।
आहो स्वित्पसवो ममापचरितैर्विष्टम्भितो वीरुधा-
मित्याऋूढबहुप्रतर्कैमपरिच्छेदाकुलं मे मनः ॥१११॥

<hr>

[a] अभिनवसम्मार्जनसथ्रीकः सन्निहितहोमधेनुरग्निशरणालिन्दः । आरोहतु देवः ।

<hr>

Atanushu vibhaveshu = *utsaveshu*, 'at times of festivity.' *Kukshim-bhari-bhis taih kim prayojanam*, 'what is the use of these parasitical gluttons as relations?' K. The Calcutta ed. and S′. have *samvibhaktāh* for *santu nāma*. The meaning may certainly be, 'let kinsmen make their appearance (i. e. start up they will on all sides) when there is plenty of property to divide.' K. refers to verse 155, towards the end of Act VI. of this play, *yena yena viyujyante prajāh*, &c., 'let it be publicly announced that of whatever dear kinsman his subjects are deprived, Dushyanta will be (in the place of) that (kinsman) to them, the wicked excepted.'

[1] The use of *ete* with 1st pers. pl. of the verb is noticeable, see p. 133, n. 2.

[2] 'The terrace of the fire-sanctuary, with the cow (that yields the ghee) for the oblations close by, is beautiful after its recent purification.' *Sa-śrīka*, lit. 'possessed of the goddess of beauty;' a bold metaphor, used elsewhere by Kālidāsa. *Homa-dhenu*, *agni-śaraṇa*, see p. 148, n. 1.

[3] 'Has the devotion [penance] of the ascetics, who have collected a store of penitential merit, been frustrated by impediments? or else has any harm been inflicted by any one on the animals grazing in the sacred

<hr>

Verse 111. ŚĀRDŪLA-VIKRĪḌITA (a variety of ATIDHṚITI). See verses 14, 30, 36, 39, 50, 63, 79, 85, 86, 89, 97, 98.

प्रतीहारी ।

[a]सुअरिदणन्दिणो इसीओ देवं सभाजंइदुं आअदेन्ति तक्केमि ।

॥ ततः प्रविशन्ति गौतमीसहिताः शकुन्तलां पुरस्कृत्य मुनयः । पुरस्वैषां कञ्चुकी पुरोहितश्च ॥

कञ्चुकी ।

इत इतो भवन्तः ।

शार्ङ्गरवः ।

शारद्वत ।

महाभागः कामं नरपतिरभिन्नस्थितिरसौ
न कश्चिद्वर्णानामपथमपकृष्टोऽपि भजते ।
तथापीदं शश्वत्परिचितविविक्तेन मनसा
जनाकीर्णं मन्ये हुतवहपरीतं गृहमिव ॥११२॥

[a] सुचरितनन्दिन ऋषयो देवं सभाजयितुमागता इति तर्कयामि ।

---

grove? Or is it that the flowering of the creeping plants has been checked [stopped, stunted] through my misdeeds? Thus my mind, in which so many doubtful-conjectures have arisen, is perplexed with an inability to decide.' *Upoḍha=samprāpta*, K. *Vighnais*, see p. 40, n. 5. *Dharmā-raṇya-chareshu prāṇishu*, cf. p. 13, l. 3. *Aho svit*, used as particles of doubt, see Gram. 717. *h. Prasaraḥ*, i. e. *pushpa-phalādi*, 'the flower, fruit, &c.,' K. *Apa-charitaiḥ=dur-āchāraiḥ*.

[1] 'To pay homage to.' *Sabhāj* is one of the few dissyllabic roots.

[2] 'Granted that this king eminent-in-virtues [of high parts] swerves not from rectitude; (and that) not one of the classes, (not) even the lowest, addicts itself to evil courses; nevertheless with my mind perpetually familiarized to seclusion I regard this thronged (palace) as a house enveloped in flames.' *Kāmam* occurs frequently in this sense (cf. p. 24, l. 10; p. 55, n. 3). *Abhinna-sthitiḥ=avihata-maryādaḥ*, K.; =*sa-mar-yādaḥ*, S. *Asau*, so read the Beng. and the Mackenzie MSS.; the others have *aho*. *Varṇānām*, i. e. *brāhmaṇādīnām*. *Apakrishṭo 'pi*, 'even the lowest (class).' The castes were originally four in number: 1. Brāhmans or priests; 2. Kshatriyas or soldiers; 3. Vaiśyas or merchants and husband-men; 4. Śūdras or slaves; see p. 84, n. 3. *A-patha*, 'a wrong road,' 'a bad

Verse 112. ŚIKHARIṆĪ (a variety of ATYASHṬI). See verses 9, 24, 44, 62.

शारद्वतः ।

स्थाने भवान्पुरप्रवेशादित्यम्भूतः संवृत्तः । अहमपि
अभ्यक्तमिव स्नातः शुचिरशुचिमिव प्रबुद्ध इव सुप्तम् ।
बद्धमिव स्वैरगतिर्जनमिह सुखसङ्गिनमवैमि ॥ ११३ ॥

शकुन्तला ॥ निमित्तं सूचयित्वा ॥

[a] अम्महे । किं मे वामेदरं[3] एच्छणं विप्फुरदि ।

गौतमी ।

[b] जादे । पडिहदं अमङ्गलं । सुहाइं दे भत्तुकुलदेवदाओ
वितरन्तु । ॥ इति परिक्रामति ॥

पुरोहितः ॥ राजानं निर्दिश्य ॥

भो भोस्तपस्विनः । असावत्रभवान्वर्णाश्रमाणां रक्षिता
प्रागेव मुक्तासनो वः प्रतिपालयति । पश्यतैनम् ।

[a] अहो । किं मे वामेतरं नयनं विस्फुरति ।   [b] जाते । प्रतिहतममङ्गलम् ।
शुभानि ते भर्तृकुलदेवता वितरन्तु ।

---

road ;' a common metaphor, like *a-mārga, un-mārga, vi-mārga*, to express
wicked courses. *Idam janākīrṇam*, i. e. *idam puro-varti nṛipāṅyaṇam*,
'this royal court before my eyes,' S'. ; *janākīrṇam* may perhaps be used,
as in Vikram., Act II, l. 2, for a substantive, meaning 'a crowded thorough-
fare.' *Hutavahā-parīta = lagnāgni*, S'.

[1] 'I also regard (these) people here devoted to pleasure, as one-who-
has-performed-his-ablutions (regards) one-smeared (with dirt), as the pure
the impure, as the waking the sleeping, as he-whose-motion-is-free the
bound.'

[2] See p. 20, n. 4.   One MS. has *durnimittam*, 'a bad omen.'

[3] *Vāmetara*, 'other than left,' 'right.'

[4] 'The protector of the (four) classes and (four) orders;' see p. 193,
n. 2, and p. 157, n. 1 at the end.

[5] 'Having but just quitted the seat (of justice);' see p. 190, n. 1.

Verse 113. ĀRYĀ or GĀTHĀ. See verse 2.

```
-- | ᴗᴗ- | -- ||ᴗᴗᴗᴗ| ᴗᴗ-| ᴗ-ᴗ|ᴗᴗ-|-
-ᴗᴗ| -- |ᴗᴗ-||ᴗᴗᴗᴗ| ᴗᴗ-| ᴗ |ᴗᴗ-|-
```

शाङ्गैरवः ।

भो महाब्राह्मण । काममेतदभिनन्दनीयम् । तथापि
वयमत्र मध्यस्थाः । कुतः ।

भवन्ति नम्रास्तरवः फलागमै-
र्नवाम्बुभिर्भूरिविलम्बिनो घनाः ।
अनुद्धताः सत्पुरुषाः समृद्धिभिः
स्वभाव एवैष परोपकारिणाम् ॥११४॥

प्रतीहारी ।

[a] देव । पसण्णमुहवण्णा दीसन्ति । जाणामि । विस्सद्धकज्जा
इसीओ ।

[a] देव । प्रसन्नमुखवर्णा दृश्यन्ते । जानामि । विश्रब्धकार्या ऋषयः ।

---

[1] 'This is certainly a subject of rejoicing [to be rejoiced at]; nevertheless we here are indifferent parties [have nothing to do with it],' i. e. our merits and interests have nothing to do with his conduct. This favour and protection is only what might be expected from his benevolent nature. It is possible that by *vayam madhyasthāḥ* may be meant, 'we are indifferent persons,' 'we have no suit to urge nor petition to present.'

[2] 'Because trees become bent down by the growing-weight of fruit; clouds hang down the more (when charged) with fresh rain; good men are not made arrogant by abundant riches; this is the very nature of the benefactors of others.' *Kutaḥ*, see p. 55, n. 2. *Bhūri*, generally found in composition, but not always; see Mahā-bh. xii. 1410. Most of the Beng. MSS. have *dūra*. This verse occurs in Bhartṛi-h. (ii. 62, ed. Bohlen), where *udgamaiḥ* is adopted for *āyamaiḥ*, and another reading *bhūmi* for *bhūri* is noticed. Oriental poets are fond of adducing trees and clouds as examples of disinterested liberality. 'The tree does not remove its shade from him who cuts it down,' Hitop. I. 353.

[3] 'The Ṛishis appear to have serene complexions. (Hence) I conclude they have some business that inspires confidence,' or 'some quiet and easy business.' *Prasanna-mukha-varṇāḥ*, so read two of the Deva-n. MSS., supported by a similar compound in Mālavik. p. 55, l. 20. The Cole-brooke MS. has *maṇḍana*, and my own *pankaū* for *vaṇṇā*.

Verse 114. VAṆŚA-STHAVILA (a variety of JAGATĪ). See verses 18, 22, 23, 67, 81.

राजा ॥ शकुन्तलां दृष्ट्वा ॥

अथाच्चभवती ।

का स्विदवगुण्ठनवती नातिपरिस्फुटशरीरलावण्या ।
मध्ये तपोधनानां किसलयमिव पाण्डुपत्त्राणाम् ॥ ११५ ॥

प्रतीहारी ।

[a] देव । कुतूहलगब्भो पडिहिदो ण मे तक्को पसरँदि । एं
दंसणीआ उण से आकिदी लक्खीअदि ।

राजा ।

भवतु । अनिर्वर्णनीयं परकलत्त्रम् ।

शकुन्तला ॥ हस्तमुरसि कृत्वा । आत्मगतम् ॥

[b] हिअअ । किं एव्वं वेवसि । अज्जउत्तस्स भावं ओधारिअ
धीरं दाव होहि ।

पुरोहितः ॥ पुरो गत्वा ॥

एते विधिवदर्चितास्तपस्विनः । कश्चिदेषामुपाध्यायसन्देशः ।

[a] देव । कुतूहलगर्भः प्रतिहितो न मे तर्कः प्रसरति । ननु दर्शनीया पुनरस्या
आकृतिर्लक्ष्यते ।   [b] हृदय । किमेवं वेपसे । आर्यपुत्रस्य भावमवधार्य धीरं तावद्भव ।

---

[1] 'Who is this veiled-one, the loveliness of whose person is not
fully displayed?' *Svid* is a particle of question and doubt. *Avaguṇṭhana*
=*mastakācchādana-vastra*, C. The second half of this verse is clear.

[2] 'My conjecture full of curiosity being hindered (by the veil) does not
succeed.' The Mackenzie MS., supported by K., has *paḍihāḍi* for *prati-
bhāti* (in place of *pasaradi* for *prasarati*, the reading of the other Deva-n.)
and *paḍihaḍo* for *pahido*, the reading of the others.

[3] 'Ought not to be gazed at.' *A-nirvarṇanīya*=*a-darśanīya*.

[4] 'Having reflected on [called to mind] the affection of thy lord, be
firm.' *Bhāva*=*sneha* (cf. p. 112, n. 2). The Beng. have *smṛitvā* for *ava-
dhārya*. *Ārya-putra*, 'son of a venerable parent,' is the regular dramatic
mode of addressing a husband.

[5] 'They have some message from the preceptor.'

Verse 115. ĀRYĀ or GĀTHĀ. See verse 2.

$$- \cup \cup \; | \; \cup - \cup \; | \; \cup \cup - \; || \; - \cup \cup \; | \; - \cup \cup \; | \; \cup - \cup \; | \; - - \; | \; -$$
$$- - \; | \; \cup - \cup \; | \; - - \; || \; \cup \cup \cup \cup \; | \; \cup \cup - \; | \; \cup \; | \; - - \; | \; -$$

तं देवः श्रोतुमर्हति ।

राजा ।

अवहितोऽस्मि ।

ऋषयः ॥ हस्तानुद्यम्य ॥

विजयस्व राजन् ।

राजा ।

सर्वानभिवादये ।

ऋषयः ।

इष्टेन युज्यस्व ।

राजा ।

अपि निर्विघ्नतंपसी[1] मुनयः ।

ऋषयः ।

कुतो धर्मक्रियाविघ्नः सतां रक्षितरि त्वयि ।
तमस्तपति घर्मांशौ कथमाविर्भविष्यति ॥११६॥[2]

राजा ।

अर्थवान्खलु मे राजशब्दः[3] । अथ भगवाँल्लोकानुग्रहाय
कुशली काश्यपः[4] ।

---

[1] *Nirvighna-tapasah*, cf. p. 35, n. 3. *Api*, see p. 89, n. 2.

[2] 'Whence (can there be) obstruction to the religious rites of the good, thou being (their) defender? How should darkness appear, the Sun emitting light [when the Sun shines]?' *Tapati*, loc. of the pres. part., here used absolutely. *Gharmānśau=sūrye*, S.

[3] 'My title of Rāja has indeed significancy.' The Rishis had, in the preceding verse, compared the king to the Sun, and *rājan* is derived from *rāj*, 'to shine.' It is, however, probable that the play is on the words *rājan* and *rakshitri*. Cf. Manu vii. 3, *rakshārtham asya sarvasya rājānam asrijat prabhuḥ*, 'the Supreme Being created a king for the protection of this universe.' Dr. Boehtlingk remarks that in these cases it little signifies whether the derivation be true or false. In Mahā-bh. xii. 1032, *rājan* is derived from *ranj*, 'to conciliate.'

[4] 'Is his reverence Kāśyapa prosperous for the welfare of the world?'

Verse 116. ŚLOKA or ANUSHTUBH. See verses 5, 6, 11, 12, 26, 47, 50, 51, 53, 73, 76, 84, 87.

ऋषयः ।

स्वाधीनकुशलाः सिद्धिमन्तः । स भवन्तमनामयप्रश्न-
पूर्वकमिदमाह ।

राजा ।

किमाज्ञापयति भगवान् ।

शाङ्गैरवः ।

यन्मिथःसमयादिमां मदीयां दुहितरं भवानुपायंस्त[2] ।
तन्मया प्रीतिमता युवयोरनुज्ञातम् । कुतः ।

त्वमर्हतां प्रायसरः स्मृतोऽसि नः
  शकुन्तला मूर्तिमती च सत्क्रिया ।
समानयंस्तुल्यगुणं वधूवरं
  चिरस्य वाच्यं न गतः प्रजापतिः[3] ॥११७॥

Kuśalin, see p. 35, n. 3. *Bhagavāl,* &c., when the letter *l* is preceded by
t, d, or *n* dental, it requires the assimilation of the letters to itself, and in
the case of dental *n,* the mark called C'andra-vindu is written over, to shew
that the *l* substituted for it has a nasal sound, Laghu-k. No. 79, see Gram. 56.

[1] 'Saints have prosperity in their power. He with inquiries about
your safety says this to your Highness.' It will be readily remarked that
the character of these Rishis is evidently that of plain, honest, independent
men. *Siddhimantaḥ,* lit. 'men endowed with or capable of perfection,'
'saints,' Vishṇu-p. p. 45. *Anāmaya,* see Manu ii. 127, 'Let a man ask a
Brāhman, on meeting him, as to his *kuśala;* a Kshatriya, as to his *anā-
maya;* a Vaiśya, as to his *kshema;* and a Sūdra, as to his *ārogya.'* The
king was of course a Kshatriya, see p. 31, n. 1.

[2] The third sing. aor. Ātm. of *upa-yam,* 'to marry,' is either *upāyata* or
upāyaṇsta, Pāṇ. i. 2, 16. The Beng. have *upayeme,* perf.

[3] 'Thou art esteemed by us the chief of the worthy, and Sakuntalā, in-
carnate virtue. Brahmā [Fate], bringing together a bride and bridegroom
of equal merit, has after a long time (now first) incurred no censure.'
Naḥ, the Colebrooke MS. reads *yat. Vadhū-varam,* a Dvandva comp.
in the neuter gender. *Vācyam na gataḥ,* probably this refers to the blame
popularly laid on Fate for preventing the smooth course of true love.

Verse 117. VAṆŚA-STHAVILA (a variety of JAGATĪ). See verses 18, 22, 23, 67, 81, 114.

तदिदानीमापन्नसत्त्वा प्रतिगृह्यतां सहधर्मचरणायेति[1] ।

गौतमी ।

[a] अज्ज । किम्पि वत्तुकामम्हि । ण मे वञ्अणावसरो
अत्थि । कहंति ।

णावेक्खिदो गुरुअणो इमिणा ण तुएवि पुच्छिदो बन्धू ।
एक्कं एव्व चरिए किं भणदु एक्क एक्कस्स[2] ॥११८॥

शकुन्तला ॥ आत्मगतम् ॥

[b] किं णुक्खु अज्जउत्तो भणादि ।

[a] आर्ये । किमपि वक्तुकामास्मि । न मे वचनावसरोऽस्ति । कथमिति ।
नापेक्षितो गुरुजनोऽनया न त्वयापि पृष्टो बन्धुः ।
एकैकमेवं चरिते किं भणन्त्येक एकस्य ॥११८॥

[b] किं नु खल्वार्यपुत्रो भणति ।

---

[1] 'Therefore now let her, being quick with child, be received, for the joint discharge of religious-rites,' i. e. those Saṇskāras or rites, which were performed for the child before and after birth, probably by the parents conjointly (saha); see Manu ii. 27, &c.

[2] 'Her elder-relatives were not referred to by her; nor by you was any kinsman asked; (the affair) having been transacted quite privately [lit. one with the other], what has each one to say to the other?' Guru-jana, see p. 173, n. 3 in the middle. The Deva-n. MSS. have imāe for iminā. The latter, which is the reading of the oldest Beng., I have retained on account of the metre. There is no reason why in Prākrit iminā should not be used for the fem. instr., since imassim is admissible for the fem. loc.; see p. 37, l. 2. Ekaikam = anyonyam, 'mutually,' S. and C. Bhaṇnadu is the reading of some of the Beng. MSS. followed by the Calcutta edition; I have written bhaṇnadu for bhaṇādu, on account of the metre, and on the authority of Lassen's Instit. Prāk. p. 277. The Deva-n. have kim bhaṇāmi, which reading violates the metre and makes the construction of the sentence very obscure. They also read ekkam ekkassa. Eka may be for eka-janaḥ, applicable to either gender. The commentary of C. is in favour of the above interpretation.

Verse 118. ĀRYĀ or GĀTHĀ. See verse 2.

```
– – | ⏑ – ⏑ | ⏑ ⏑ – ‖ ⏑ ⏑ – | ⏑ ⏑ – | ⏑ – ⏑ | – – | –
– – | ⏑ – ⏑ | ⏑ ⏑ – ‖ – – | ⏑ ⏑ – | ⏑ | – – | ⏑
```

राजा ।

किमिदमुपन्यस्तम् ।

शकुन्तला ॥ आत्मगतम् ॥

[a] पावओक्खु एसो वअणोबंखासो ।[1]

शार्ङ्गरवः ।

कथमिदं नाम । भवन्त एव सुतरां लोकवृत्तान्तनिष्णाताः ।[2]
सतीमपि ज्ञातिकुलैकसंश्रयां
जनोऽन्यथा भर्तृमतीं विशङ्कते ।
अतः समीपे परिणेतुरिष्यते
तदप्रियापि प्रमदा स्वबन्धुभिः ॥११९॥[3]

राजा ।

किं चाचभवती मया परिणीतपूर्वा ।

शकुन्तला ॥ सविषादम् । आत्मगतम् ॥

[b] हिअअ । सम्पदं दे आसङ्का ।

<hr>

[a] पावकः खल्वेष वचनोपन्यासः ।   [b] हृदय । साम्प्रतं त आशङ्का ।

<hr>

[1] 'Truly, the import of this speech [that which is proposed by this speech] is (like) fire.' The Mackenzie MS. inserts *eso* after *kkhu*.

[2] 'Such-persons-as-your-Majesty are certainly full well acquainted with the ways of the world.' *Loka-vrittānta-nishnātāḥ* = *loka-vyavahāra-jñātāḥ*, S. *Ni-shnāta* (=*abhijña*, C.), lit. 'bathed in;' hence 'conversant with.' The Sāhit-d. (p. 193) reads *bhavān loka-vrittānte nishnātaḥ*.

[3] 'People suspect a married woman [woman who has a husband] residing wholly in her kinsmen's family, although chaste, (to be) the reverse. Hence a young woman is preferred by her own relatives (to be) near her husband, even though she be disliked by him.' *Jñāti-ku°*=*nija-griha-rāsinīm*, S. *Anyathā*, i. e. *vyabhićāriṇīm*, 'unchaste,' S. *Ishyate*=*ākānkshyate*, S. *Tad-apriyāpi*, the Beng., my own MS., and the Sāhit.-d. read *priyāpriyā vā*, 'liked or disliked;' but K. supports the other reading.

<hr>

Verse 119. VANŚA-STHAVILA (a variety of JAGATĪ). See verses 18, 22, 23, 67, 81, 114, 117.

शार्ङ्गरवः ।

किं कृतकार्यद्वेषाद्धर्मं प्रति विमुखतोचिता राज्ञः ।[1]

राजा ।

कुतोऽयमसत्कल्पनाप्रश्नः ।[2]

शार्ङ्गरवः ।

मूर्छन्त्यमी विकाराः प्रायेणैश्वर्यमत्तेषु ।[3]

राजा ।

विशेषेणाधिक्षिप्तोऽस्मि ।[4]

गौतमी ।

[a] जादे । मुहुत्तअं मा लज्ज । अवणइस्सं दाव दे अोउरठणं । तदो तुमं भट्टा अहिजाणिस्सदि ।   ॥ इति यथोक्तं करोति ॥

राजा   ॥ शकुन्तलां निर्वर्ण्य । आत्मगतम् ॥

इदमुपनतमेवं रूपमक्लिष्टकान्ति
प्रथमपरिगृहीतं स्यान्न वेत्यव्यवस्यन् ।

[a] जाते । मुहूर्तं मा लज्जस्व । अपनेष्यामि तावन्नेऽवगुण्ठनम् । ततस्त्वां भर्तीभिज्ञास्यति ।

---

[1] 'On account of dislike to a deed done, is opposition to justice becoming in a king?' This is the reading of the oldest Bengālī, and I have adopted it as preferable to that of the Deva-n., *kiṃ kṛita-kārya-dvesho dharmam prati vimukhatā kṛitāvajñā*. Dr. Boehtlingk suggests that *kṛitāvajñā* is probably an interpolation from the margin.

[2] 'Whence is this inquiry (accompanied) by the fabrication of a falsehood?' *Avidyamānārthasya kalpanayā kṛitaḥ praśnaḥ*, K. According to Dr. Burkhard, 'inquiry about a crime which has not been committed.'

[3] 'These changes-of-purpose [fickleness of disposition] mostly take effect [wax strong] in those who are intoxicated with sovereign-power.' *Mūrchanti=vardhante*, S. ; =*vyāpnuvanti*, K. (cf. Raghu-v. xii. 57, vi. 9, x. 80). Root *mūrch* has generally the opposite sense, 'to lose strength,' 'faint away.' It is applied to the thickening of darkness, in Vikram., Act III, *tamasāṃ niśi mūrchatām*.

[4] 'I am especially aimed-at-by-this censure,' i. e. I am the especial object of this censorious remark about 'persons intoxicated with power.'

D d

भ्रमर इव विभाते कुन्दमन्तस्तुषारं
न खलु च परिभोक्तुं नैव शक्नोमि हातुम् ॥१२०॥[1]
॥ इति विचारयन्निस्यतः ॥

प्रतीहारी ।

[a] अहो धम्मावेक्खिदा भट्टिणी । ईदिसं णाम सुहोबणदं रूबं देक्खिञ्च को अण्णो विआरेदि ।

शाङ्गैरवः ।

भो राजन् । किमिति जोषमास्यंते[2] ।

राजा ।

भोस्तपोधनाः । चिन्तयन्नपि न खलु स्वीकरणमत्रभवत्याः स्मरामि । तत्कथमिमामभिव्यक्तसत्त्वलक्षणां प्रत्यात्मानं क्षेत्रिणमाशङ्कमानः प्रतिपंत्स्ये ।[3]

[a] अहो धर्मावेक्षिता भर्तुः । ईदृशं नाम सुखोपनतं रूपं दृष्ट्वा कोऽन्यो विचारयति ।

---

[1] 'Not settling-in-my-mind [not deciding or determining] whether this form of unblemished beauty thus presented (to me) [brought near to me] may or may not have been formerly married [by me]; verily I am neither able to enjoy nor to abandon (it), like a bee at the break of day, the jasmine-blossom filled with dew.' *Aklishṭa-kānti* = *anavadya-saundaryam*, K. *Parigṛhītam*, see p. 181, n. 2. *A-vyavasyan* (= *a-niścinvan*), so reads K.; I have ventured to follow him, although nearly all the Deva-n. MSS. have *vyavasyan* (cf. p. 146, l. 2, n. 1; and p. 161, l. 9). If *vyavasyan* is retained, it must be translated 'deliberating,' 'striving to discover.' *Antas-tushāra*, lit. 'having dew in the interior.'

[2] 'Why do you sit [is it sat] so silent?' *Kimartham maunam kritam asti*, S'. Cf. *kiṃ tūshṇīm evāste*, Vikram., Act IV.

[3] *Svīkaraṇam* (= *vivāham*, S'.), 'making one's own,' i.e. 'taking in marriage.'

[4] 'How, then, shall I act towards her, bearing evident signs of pregnancy, doubting myself to be her husband.' *Katham pratipatsye* may mean 'how shall I make any reply?' referring to *kiṃ josham āsyate* in the previous speech; or, 'how shall I receive her?' see p. 135, n. 1.

Verse 120. MĀLINĪ or MĀNINĪ (a variety of ATI-ŚAKVARĪ). See verses 10, 19, 20, 38, 55, 109, 110.

शकुन्तला ॥ अपवार्य ॥

^aअज्जस्स परिणए एव्व सन्देहो । कुदो दाणिं मे दूराहिरोहिणी आसा ।

शाङ्गरवः ।

मा तावत्

कृताभिमर्शामनुमन्यमानः
सुतां त्वया नाम मुनिर्विमान्यः ।
मुष्टं प्रतिग्राहयता स्वमर्थं
पात्रीकृतो दस्युरिवासि येन ॥१२१॥

शारद्वतः ।

शाङ्गरव । विरम त्वमिदानीम् । शकुन्तले । वक्तव्यमुक्त-
मस्माभिः । सोऽयमभवानेवमाह । दीयतामस्मै प्रत्यय-
प्रतिवचनम् ।

^a आर्यस्य परिणय एव सन्देहः । कुत इदानीं मे दूराधिरोहिण्याशा ।

---

¹ 'Is the sage after-consenting to his daughter, who had been seduced [carnally-embraced] by thee, to be (thus) insulted forsooth? (he) by whom allowing his stolen property [i. e. S'akuntalā] to be kept [taken], thou hast been made as it were a justified ravisher [robber].' *Kritābhimarśām = krita-saṃsparśām = krita-saṅgrahaṇām*, K. The first sense of *abhi-mriś* is 'to touch,' 'to handle.' Here, as in *parā-mriś* (Bhaṭṭi-k. xvii. 38), there is an implication of carnal connexion. *Mushṭam*, the Taylor MS. has *ishṭam*, and the Beng. *dushṭam*. It must be borne in mind that S'akuntalā was married to Dushyanta, according to the Gāndharva form (p. 127, n. 3), during the absence of her foster-father (see pp. 134, 135, with notes). *Pratigrāhayatā*, the causal may sometimes give the sense of 'allowing' or 'permitting,' as in *nāśayati*, 'he suffers to perish.' *Pātrī-krita*, is a C'vi compound, formed from *pātra*, neut. 'a receptacle,' applied to express any deserving or worthy person (see Manu iv. 227).

Verse 121. Upajāti or Ākhyānakī (a variety of Trishṭubh). See verses 41, 107.

शकुन्तला ॥ अपवार्य ॥

[a] इमं अवत्थन्तरं गदे तारिसे अणुराए किं वा सुमराविदेण । अत्ता दाणिं मे सोअणीओत्ति ववसिदं ।

॥ प्रकाशम् ॥ [b] अज्जउत्त । ॥ इत्यर्धोक्ते ॥ [c] संसइदे दाणिं परिणए ण एसो समुदाआरो । पोरव । ण जुत्तं णाम दे तह पुरा अस्समपदे सहावुत्ताणहिअअं इमं जणं समअपुव्वं पतारिअ ईदिसेहिं अक्खरेहिं पच्चाचक्खिदुं ।

राजा ॥ कर्णौ पिधाय ॥

शान्तम् । पापंम् ।

[a] इदमवस्थान्तरं गते तादृशेऽनुरागे किं वा स्मारितेन । आत्मेदानीं मे शोचनीय इति व्यवसितम् । [b] आर्यपुत्र । [c] संशयित इदानीं परिणये नैष समुदाचारः । पौरव । न युक्तं नाम ते तथा पुराश्रमपदे स्वभावोत्तानहृदयमिमं जनं समयपूर्वं प्रतार्य-दृशैरक्षरैः प्रत्याचष्टुम् ।

---

[1] K., S., and the old Beng. MS. interpret *soanīo* by *śocanīya*, 'to be sorrowed for;' but C. has *śodhanīya*, and is followed by Chézy and the Calcutta edition. The meaning will then be, 'I myself am now to be cleared [justified] by myself.' All the MSS., except one, insert *me*.

[2] 'Now that my marriage is called-in-question, this is not the (proper) form-of-address;' see p. 196, n. 4. All the MSS. agree in reading *samu-dāāro* for *samudáćáro*; otherwise it might be suspected that *samudāhāro* was the correct word, to which *samudáćáro* must be here equivalent.

[3] 'It is not becoming in thee, having awhile since in the hermitage so seduced, after-a-formal-agreement, this person [myself] naturally open-hearted, to repudiate her with such words.' *Uttāna*, 'shallow,' 'unre-served,' is the opposite of *gambhīra*, 'deep,' 'reserved;' see p. 39, n. 1. *Samaya-pūrvam*, cf. p. 198, l. 3; and p. 172, l. 4, with note.

[4] 'Peace! a sin!' i. e. Silence! let me not listen to such sinful words; or, if no stop is placed after *śāntam*, 'May the sin be palliated!' This seems to be the usual formula in the plays for averting the ill effects of blasphe-mous, malevolent, or lying words. Sometimes the stage-direction *karṇau pidhāya* is omitted, compare Acts vii. 57; Mṛiććhak. p. 36, l. 5; p. 230, l. 6; p. 306, l. 9; p. 329, l. 1; Mālavik. p. 69, l. 10; Mudrā-r. p. 24, l. 5.

व्यपदेशमाविलयितुं किमीहसे जनमिमं च पातयितुम् ।
कूलङ्कषेव सिन्धुः प्रसन्नमम्भस्तटतरुं च ॥१२२॥

शकुन्तला ।

^a होदु । जइ परमत्थदो परपरिग्गहसङ्किणा तुए एव्वं पउत्तं ।
ता अहिट्ठाणेण इमिणा तुह आसङ्कं अवणइस्सं ।

राजा ।

उदारः कल्पः ।

शकुन्तला ॥ मुद्रास्थानं परामृश्य ॥

^b हद्धी । हद्धी । अङ्गुलीअ असुद्धा मे अङ्गुली ।

॥ इति सविषादं गौतमीमवेक्षते ॥

गौतमी ।

^c णूणं दे सक्कावदाराब्भन्तरे सचीतित्थसलिलं वन्दमाणाए
पब्भट्टं अङ्गुलीअं ।

---

^a भवतु । यदि परमार्थतः परपरिग्रहशङ्किना त्वयैवं प्रवृत्तम् । तदभिज्ञानेनानेन
तवाशङ्कामपनेष्यामि ।   ^b हाधिक् । हाधिक् । अङ्गुलीयकशून्या मेऽङ्गुलिः ।
^c नूनं ते शक्रावताराभ्यन्तरे शचीतीर्थसलिलं वन्दमानायाः प्रभ्रष्टमङ्गुलीयकम् ।

---

[1] 'Why seekest thou to sully the royal-title [race, family] and to ruin
this person [myself]; as a stream that-carries-away-its-own-banks (disturbs)
the clear water (and overturns) the tree on its margin?' *Vyapadeśam*, i. e.
kulaṃ nāma vā, 'either family or name,' C.; *vyapadiśyate anena iti vya-
padeśaḥ kulam*, S. *Āvilayitum*, infin. of a nom. verb from *āvila*, 'turbid.'
Sindhuḥ, 'a river,' in classical Sanskṛit is generally fem., in the older
language generally masc.; when *Sindhu* means 'the district Scinde' it is
usually masc.

[2] 'In all probability the ring slipped from (the finger of) thee as thou
wert offering homage to the water at Saćī's holy-pool, within Śakrāvatāra.'
Sakra is a name of Indra, and Śakrāvatāra some sacred place of pilgrimage
where he descended upon earth. Saćī is his wife, to whom there was pro-
bably a Tīrtha, or holy bathing-place (see p. 17, n. 1), consecrated at this
place, where Śakuntalā had performed her ablutions.

Verse 122. ĀRYĀ or GĀTHĀ. See verse 2.

राजा ॥ सस्मितम् ॥

इदं तत्प्रत्युत्पन्नमति स्त्रैणमिति यदुच्यते ।[1]

शकुन्तला ।

[a] एत्थ दाव विहिणा दंसिदं पहुत्तणं । अवरं दे कहिस्सं ।

राजा ।

श्रोतव्यमिदानीं संवृत्तम् ।[3]

शकुन्तला ।

[b] णं एक्कदिअहे णोमालिआमरण्डबे णलिणीपत्तभा-
अणगअं उअअं तुह हत्थे सण्णिहिदं आसि ।

राजा ।

शृणुमस्तावत् ।

शकुन्तला ।

[c] तक्खणं सो मे पुत्तकिदओ दीहावंग्गो णाम मिअपोदओ

---

[a] अत्र तावद्विधिना दर्शितं प्रभुत्वम् । अपरं ते कथयिष्यामि ।　　[b] नन्वेकदिवसे नवमालिकामण्डपे नलिनीपत्रभाजनगतमुदकं तव हस्ते सन्निहितमासीत् ।　　[c] तत्क्षणं स मे पुत्रकृतको दीर्घापाङ्गो नाम मृगपोतक

[1] 'This is that which is said [thus is proved the truth of the proverb], "Woman-kind is ready-witted."' $Strainam = str\bar{\imath}$-$j\bar{a}ti\dot{h}$, 'the female sex,' K. The Beng. have *idaṃ tat pratyutpanna-matitvaṃ strīṇām;* cf. Hitop. l. 2320, where *pratyutpanna-matiḥ* is the name given to the ready-witted fish. See also Hitop. l. 2338, 'The food of women is said to be two-fold, their wit four-fold, their cunning six-fold, and their passion eight-fold.'

[2] 'Here, however, sovereignty has been shewn by destiny.' A similar sentiment occurs further on in this play, and at the beginning of Act IV. of Vikram., *bhavitavya-tā atra balavatī,* 'here destiny has shewn its power.'

[3] Dr. Boehtlingk considers that *śrotavyam* is here taken as a substantive, and construes, 'The moment-for-hearing (what else you have to say) has now arrived' (cf. p. 110, l. 9). As the pass. part. is often used substantively the translation may be, 'what took place is now to be heard.'

[4] 'Lying in a lotus-leaf-cup.' As to *gatam,* see p. 38, n. 1.

[5] *Sannihitam,* see p. 150, l. 10, with note 3.

[6] 'Having eyes with long outer corners.' This was the fawn mentioned in verse 94.

[a]उवट्टिदो । तुए अच्चं दाव पढमं पिअउत्ति अणुअम्पिआण
उवच्छन्दिदो उअएण । ण उण दे अपरिचआदो हत्थब्भासं
उवगदो । पच्छा तस्सिं एव्व मए गहिदे सलिले एण
किदो पणओ । तदा तुमं इत्थं पहसिदोसि । सव्वो सगन्धेसु
विस्ससदि । दुवेबि एत्थ आरण्णाणि ।

राजा ।

एवमादिभिरात्मकार्यनिवर्तिनीनामनृतमयवाङ्मधुभिरा-
कृष्यन्ते विषयिणः ।

गौतमी ।

[b]महाभाअ । ण अरुहसि एव्वं मन्तिदुं । तवोवणसंवड्ढिदो
अणभिण्णो अच्चं जणो कइदवस्स ।

[a] उपस्थितः । त्वयायं तावत्प्रथमं पिवन्त्वित्यनुकम्पिनोपच्छन्दित उदकेन । न
पुनस्तेऽपरिचयाद् हस्ताभ्यासमुपगतः । पश्चात्तस्मिन्नेव मया गृहीते सलिलेऽनेन कृतः
प्रणयः । तदा त्वमित्थं प्रहसितोऽसि । सर्वैः सगन्धेषु विश्वसिति । द्वावप्यत्रारण्यका-
विति । [b] महाभाग । नार्हस्येवं मन्तयितुम् । तपोवनसंवर्धितोऽनभिज्ञोऽयं जनः
कैतवस्य ।

---

[1] *Upaćchanditaḥ* = *jala-pānāya preritaḥ*, 'was coaxed to drink the water,'
S.; = *pralobhitaḥ*, 'enticed,' 'coaxed,' Chézy. According to Pāṇ. i. 3, 47,
upa-ćhand means 'to conciliate privately by flattering or coaxing language.'
Cf. Raghu-v. v. 58, where Stenzler translates it by *obsecro*, 'supplicate,' 'beg.'

[2] *Hastābhyāsa*, lit. 'use of the hand,' i. e. 'stroking with the hand,'
'caressing;' with *upa-gam*, 'to approach for fondling,' 'to allow to be
caressed,' 'to entrust one's self into any one's hands' (cf. p. 209, l. 10).

[3] *Praṇayaḥ* here, 'trust,' 'confidence' (= *viśvāsaḥ*, S.) *Sagandheshu*, 'in
relatives.' *Sagandha* = *sadṛiśa* = *sannihita*. *Gandha* = *sambandha*, S.

[4] So reads my own MS. K. has *āraṇṇaa* (Lassen's Instit. Prāk. p. 187),
and interprets it by *āraṇyakau*. Some read *āraṇṇao*, which seems to be
an error for *araṇṇaāo* nom. pl. fem. The feminine is admissible on the
principle of the superiority of the human species over animals.

[5] 'Voluptuaries are allured by such false honied words as these of
women turning (them) away from their own duty.' The Taylor and my
own MS. have *nirvartinīnām*, which has been adopted in B. and R.'s
dictionary and by Dr. Burkhard; if this reading be preferred, translate

राजा ।

तापसवृद्धे ।

स्त्रीणामशिक्षितपटुत्वममानुषीषु
सन्दृश्यते किमुत याः प्रतिबोधवत्यः ।
प्रागन्तरिक्षगमनात्स्वमपत्यजात-
मन्यैर्द्विजैः परभृताः खलु पोषयन्ति ॥१२३॥

शकुन्तला ।। सरोषम् ।।

[a] अणज्ज । अत्तणो हि अआणुमाणेण पेक्खसि । को
दाणिं अस्सो धम्मकञ्चुअप्पवेसिणो तिणच्छण्णकूवोवमस्स
तव अणुकिदं पडिबज्जिस्सदि ।

राजा ।। आत्मगतम् ।।

सन्दिग्धबुद्धिं मां कुर्वन्नकैतव इवास्याः कोपो लक्ष्यते ।
तथा ह्यनया

[a] अनार्य । आत्मनो हृदयानुमानेन प्रेक्षसे । क इदानीमन्यो धर्मकञ्चुकप्रवेशिनस्तृ-
णच्छन्नकूपोपमस्य तवानुकृतं प्रतिपत्स्यते ।

'of women seeking to accomplish their own ends.' The Mackenzie has
yoshitām madhura-gīrbhiḥ for *anṛitamaya-vān-madhubhiḥ*.

[1] According to Pāṇ. ii. 2, 38, *tāpasa-vṛiddhā* is a legitimate compound,
although *vṛiddha-tāpasī* would be more usual.

[2] 'The untaught cunning is observed of females (even) in-those-that-are-
not-of-the-human-race [i. e. even in animals]; how much more (of those)
who are endowed with reason [i. e. of women]! The female cuckoos, as-
is-well-known [*khalu*] allow their own offspring to be reared by other birds,
before soaring in the sky.' *A-mānushīshu*, i. e. *mānusha-jāti-ryatiriktāsu
tiryay-jātishu*, K. *Pratibodhavatyaḥ* = *jñāninyaḥ* = *ćaitanya-bhājaḥ*, S.;
the most obvious sense, if the context would allow it, would be, 'those
women who have received instruction.' *Para-bhṛitāḥ*, see p. 162, n. 2.

[3] 'What other (person) now would act like [in imitation of] thee, that
putting on the garb of virtue resemblest a grass-concealed well?' *Prati-
patsyate*, see p. 135, l. 4, with note 1.

Verse 123. VASANTA-TILAKĀ (a variety of ŚAKVARĪ). See next verse.

मय्येव विस्मरणदारुणचित्तवृत्तौ
वृत्तं रहःप्रणयममप्रतिपद्यमाने ।
भेदाद्भुवोः कुटिलयोरतिलोहिताक्ष्या
भग्नं शरासनमिवातिरुषा स्मरस्य ॥ १२४ ॥

॥ प्रकाशम् ॥ भद्रे । प्रथितं दुष्यन्तस्य चरितम् । तथापीदं न
लक्ष्ये ।

शकुन्तला ।

[a] सुट्ठु दाव अत्त सच्छन्दचारिणी किदम्हि । जा अहं
इमस्स पुरुवंसप्पच्चएण मुहमहुणो हिअट्ठिअविसस्स
हत्थब्भासं उवगदा । ॥ इति पटान्तेन मुखमावृत्य रोदिति ॥

शाङ्गरवः ।

इत्यमात्मकृतमप्रतिहतं चापलं दहति ।

[a] सुष्ठु तावदत्र स्वच्छन्दचारिणी कृतास्मि । याहमस्य पुरुवंशप्रत्ययेन मुखमधोहृदय-
स्थितविषस्य हस्ताभ्यासमुपगता ।

<hr>

[1] 'For (when) I, whose state of feeling was dreadfully-severe from the
absence of (all) recollection, (persisted in) not admitting that affection had
privately existed (between us); it (seemed) as if (the god) Smara's bow
was snapped asunder by that very-red-eyed one with excessive anger, on
the parting of her curved eyebrows.' The double-entendre in the word
Smara, which means 'recollection' as well as 'the god of Love,' is notice-
able (see the notes on Kāma-deva, p. 99, n. 1, and p. 100, n. 1). The figure
by which the eyebrows of a beautiful woman are compared to Cupid's bow
is common, and the glances from the eye are by a similar metaphor often
likened to arrows discharged from it. Śakuntalā is said to break the bow
by the parting of her eyebrows, which were contracted in anger. Possibly
one effect of anger might be to wrinkle the brow, which would appear to
separate the eyebrows.

[2] Lit. 'a wilful, self-willed woman,' 'one who acts on the impulse of
the moment.' It may have this sense here, but S. interprets it by *ganikā*,
'a wanton, unchaste woman.'

[3] 'Thus a self-committed hasty action, when not counteracted, leads-to-

<hr>

Verse 124. VASANTA-TILAKĀ (a variety of ŚAKVARĪ). See verses 8, 27, 31, 43, 46,
64, 74, 80, 82, 83, 91, 93, 94, 95, 100, 104, 105, 108, 123.

अतः परीक्ष्य कर्तव्यं विशेषात्सङ्गतं रहः ।
अज्ञातहृदयेष्वेवं वैरीभवति सौहृदम् ॥१२५॥

राजा ।

अयि भोः । किमञ्चभवतीप्रत्ययादेवास्मान्सम्भृतदोषैरधि-
क्षिपथ ।

शाङ्गरवः ॥ सासूयम् ॥

श्रुतं भवद्भिरधरोत्तरम् ।

---

keen-remorse [burns].' Most of the Deva-n. MSS. have *parihatam* for
apratihatam; the Mackenzie has *pratihatam;* the oldest Beng. *apratihatam.*
Cāpalam is 'any action proceeding from thoughtlessness or over-precipita-
tion.' *Dahati,* the Hindūs connect a burning or smarting sensation with the
idea of remorse of conscience (cf. *manas-tāpa, paścāt-tāpa, anu-tāpa,* &c.)

[1] 'Therefore a union, especially (when) in private, ought to be formed
with-great-circumspection [after having made proper inquiry or ex-
periment, i. e. after investigating each other's character and circum-
stances]. Thus (is it that) between those who know not (each other's)
hearts, friendship becomes enmity.' *Parīkshya,* the Beng. have *samīk-
shya. Samyatam rahah = rahasi sangamah,* K.

[2] 'Do you reproach us with accumulated accusations [faults]?' Most of
the Deva-n. MSS. have *samyuta-doshāksharena kshinutha.* The above is
the reading of the oldest Beng., supported by K., who has *sambhrita-dosha-
karshanena.*

[3] *Sāsūyam,* 'scornfully,' 'sarcastically;' lit. 'with detraction.'

[4] *Adharottaram* = *nikrishta-prādhānyam,* 'ascendancy of the low,'
'placing that at the top which ought to be at the bottom,' C. In Manu
viii. 53, the word occurs in the sense of 'confused and contradictory state-
ment;' and again in vii. 21, it is applied to express the confusion of ranks
[*adharam = śūdrādi; uttaram = pradhānam*] which would ensue, if justice
were not duly administered by the king. It may be translated here ' con-
fusion of principles,' 'inversion of the proper order of things,' and pro-
bably refers to the ironical statement in the succeeding verse. Hence the
meaning may be, 'You have been taught upside down or backwards.' In
other words, 'The usual definition of the fourth Pramāna (*śabda*) is *āpta-
vākya,* you would make it *anāpta-vākya,* the words of an improper
person.' See Indian Wisdom, pp. 72, 92. *Adharottara* may mean ' reply
to a statement' or 'question and answer.'

Verse 125. Sloka or Anushtubh. See verses 5, 6, 11, 12, 26, 47, 50, &c., 87.

आ जन्मनः शाठ्यमशिक्षितो य-
स्तस्याप्रमाणं वचनं जनस्य ।
परातिसन्धानमधीयते यै-
र्विद्येति ते सन्तु किलाप्तवाचः ॥१२६॥

राजा ।

भोः सत्यवादिन् । अभ्युपगतं तावदस्माभिरेवम् । किं
पुनरिमामतिसन्धाय लभ्यते ।

शार्ङ्गरवः ।

विनिपातः ।

राजा ।

विनिपातः पौरवैः प्रार्थ्यत इति न श्रद्धेयमेतत् ।

शारद्वतः ।

शार्ङ्गरव । किमुत्तरेण । अनुष्ठितो गुरोः सन्देशः ।
प्रतिनिवर्तामहे वयम् । ॥ राजानं प्रति ॥

तदेषा भवतः कान्ता त्यज वैनां गृहाण वा ।
उपपन्ना हि दारेषु प्रभुता सर्वतोमुखी ॥१२७॥

---

[1] 'The declaration of that person who from birth is untrained to guile
(is) without authority. Let those persons, forsooth, by whom the de-
ceiving of others is studied, calling it a science, be (alone considered)
worthy of belief.' *Ā janmanah*, see p. 155, n. 3 at the end. *A-pramāṇam*
= *a-yathārtham*, S. *Ati-sandhānam*, cf. p. 99, l. 2. *Āpta-vācaḥ* = *ya-
thārtha-vacanāḥ*, S. ;=*pramāṇa-vācaḥ*, K.

[2] *Vinipāta*, 'ruin,' 'destruction,' = *pratyavāya*, K.; = *naraka-ga-
mana*, S.

[3] 'She is, then, your wife; either abandon her or take her; for the
authority over wives is admitted to be unlimited [reaching everywhere,
unbounded].' *Kāntā*, the Beng. MSS. have *patnī*. *Sarvato-mukhī*, lit.
'looking or facing in every direction ;'=*sarva-karaṇa-samarthā*, 'omni-
potent,' 'able to do everything,' C.;=*sarva-prakāreṇa*, 'of every kind,' S.

Verse 126. Upajāti or Ākhyānaki (a variety of Trishṭubh). See verses 41, 107, 121.
Verse 127. Sloka or Anushṭubh. See verses 5, 6, 11, 12, 26, 47, 50, 51, &c., 125.

गौतमी ।

गच्छायतः । ॥ इति प्रस्थिताः ॥

शकुन्तला ।

[a] कहं इमिणा किदवेण विप्पलद्धम्हि । तुम्हेवि मं
परिदेविविणिं परिच्चअह । ॥ इत्यनुमतिष्ठते ॥

गौतमी ॥ स्थित्वा ॥

[b] वच्छ सङ्गरव । अणुगच्छदि इअंखु णो करुणपरि-
देविणी सउन्दला । पच्चादेसपरुसे भत्तुणि किं वा मे
पुत्तिआ करिस्सदि ।

शाङ्गरवः ॥ सरोषं निवृत्य ॥

किं पुरोभागिनि स्वातन्त्र्यमवलम्बसे । ॥ शकुन्तला भीता वेपते ॥

शाङ्गरवः ।

शकुन्तले ।

यदि यथा वदति क्षितिपस्तथा
त्वमसि किं पितुरुत्कुलया त्वया ।
अथ तु वेत्सि शुचि व्रतमात्मनः
पतिकुले तव दास्यमपि क्षमम् ॥१२८॥

[a] कथमनेन कितवेन विप्रलब्धास्मि । यूयमपि मां परिदेविनीं परित्यजत ।   [b] वत्स
शाङ्गरव । अनुगच्छतीयं खलु नः करुणपरिदेविनी शकुन्तला । प्रत्यादेशपरुषे भर्तरि
किं वा मे पुत्री करिष्यति ।

---

[1] 'O naughty one, dost thou affect independence [art thou determined
to have thy own way]?' *Puro-bhāgini = dushṭe*, K.; = *doshaikadarśini,
doshaika-dṛik*, S. and C. *Puro-bhāgin* first means 'one who takes the first
share or more than his proper share,' i. e. 'a grasping character' (cf. Vikram.,
end of Act III, *mā mām puro-bhāginī iti samarthayasi*); then, 'malevo-
lent,' 'censorious;' lastly, as here, 'a wilful, perverse person.' Most of the
Deva-n., unsupported by the commentators, have *purobhāge*. *Svātantrya*,
cf. Manu ix. 3, *na strī svātantryam arhati*; and see p. 49, n. 1.

[2] 'If thou art so, as the king asserts, what (connexion will remain) to

---

Verse 128. DRUTA-VILAMBITA (a variety of JAGATI). See verses 45, 72.

तिष्ठ । साधयामो वयम् ।

राजा ।

भोस्तपस्विन् । किमत्रभवतीं विमलभसे । कुतः ।

कुमुदान्येव शशाङ्कः सविता बोधयति पङ्कजान्येव ।

वशिनां हि परपरिग्रहसंश्लेषपराङ्मुखी वृत्तिः ॥१२९॥

शाङ्गैरवः ।

यदा तु पूर्ववृत्तमन्यसङ्गाद्विस्मृतो भवान् । तदा कथम-
धर्मभीरुः ।

राजा ।

भवन्तमेवात्र गुरुलाघवं पृच्छामि ।

---

the father with thee fallen from thy family [an outcast from thy family] ?
but if thou art conscious that thy own marriage-vow [conduct] is free-from-
taint [pure], even slavery will be supportable in thy husband's household.'
Kim pitur, some Beng. MSS. have *kim punar utkulayā*, i. e. *kula-vyava-
hārātikramena vidyamānayā*, S. *Vrata*=*ćaritra*, K.;=*pati-vrata*, S.

[1] 'We must set off on our return,' lit. 'we must finish our business.'

[2] 'The moon awakes [expands] the night-lotuses only, the sun the day-
lotuses only; for the character [feelings] of those who control their
passions recoils [turns away with abhorrence] from embracing the wife
of another.' *Kumuda* is a kind of lotus, which blossoms in the night
(see p. 120, n. 1); the *panka-ja*, or mud-born lotus, opens its petals only
in the day. *Bodhayati*=*prakāśayati*. *Parigraha*, see p. 181, n. 4.

[3] *Anya-sangāt*, i. e. *anyasyāh kāntāyāh sangāt*, 'on account of union
with another wife.' *Vismrita*, see p. 161, n. 3 at the end; Gram. 896.

[4] *Guru-lāghava* is properly a kind of abstract noun formed from the
Dvandva *guru-laghu*, the Vriddhi taking place in the second member of
the compound instead of the first. The sense will then be, 'I ask your
reverence as to the greater and the less [i. e. the heavier and the lighter]
sin.' This is addressed to the Brāhman who acts as the Purohita, whose
duty it would be to advise the king as to which was the more or less sinful
course. This sense of *guru-lāghava* is supported by several other passages
(Mahā-bh. xii. 1273, iii. 10572; Manu ix. 299). The more obvious sense
would be, 'the alleviation [solution] of a grave matter.'

Verse 129. ÁRYÁ or GÁTHÁ. See verse 2.

⏑ ⏑ – | – ⏑ ⏑ | – – ‖ ⏑ ⏑ – | – ⏑ ⏑ | ⏑ – ⏑ | – – | ⏑

⏑ ⏑ – | ⏑ ⏑ ⏑ ⏑ | – ⏑ ⏑ ‖ – – | ⏑ ⏑ – | ⏑ ⏑ | – – | –

मूढः स्यामहमेषा वा वदेन्मिथ्येति संशये ।
दारत्यागी भवाम्याहो परस्त्रीस्पर्शपांशुलः ॥१३०॥[1]

पुरोहितः ॥ विचार्य ॥

यदि तावदेवं क्रियताम् ।

राजा ।

अनुशास्तु मां भवान् ।

पुरोहितः ।

अत्रभवती तावदा प्रसवादस्मद्गृहे तिष्ठतु । कुत इदमुच्यत इति चेत् । त्वं साधुभिरुद्दिष्टः । प्रथममेव चक्रवर्तिनं पुंचं[2] जनयिष्यसीति । स चेन्मुनिदौहित्रस्तल्लक्षणोपपन्नो भवि-ष्यति । अभिनन्द्य शुद्धान्तमेनां प्रवेशयिष्यसि[3] । विपर्यये तु पितुरस्याः समीपनयनमवस्थितमेव ।

राजा ।

यथा गुरुभ्यो रोचते ।

पुरोहितः ।

वत्से । अनुगच्छ माम् ।

शकुन्तला ।

[a] भअवदि वसुहे । देहि मे विवरं[4] ।

[a] भगवति वसुधे । देहि मे विवरम् ।

---

[1] 'In a doubt as to whether I may be infatuated or she may speak falsely, shall I become a repudiator of my wife, or defiled by contact with another's wife?' *Āho*, see p. 49, n. 1 at the end.

[2] 'A son who has the mark of the Cakra [or discus] in his hand.' When the lines of the right hand formed themselves into a circle, this was the mark of a future hero and emperor. *Cakra-vartin*, 'one whose empire extends to the horizon (*cakra*) or from sea to sea' (see p. 15, n. 2).

[3] 'If the Muni's daughter's-son shall be endowed with this mark, having congratulated her thou shalt introduce her to the female-apartments.' *Dauhitra*, from *duhitṛi*, is like *pautra*, from *putra*. *Suddhānta*, see p. 21, n. 3.

[4] 'Grant me admission or entrance,' 'open to receive me,' i. e. let me

---

॥ इति रुदन्ती प्रस्थिता । निष्क्रान्ता सह पुरोधसा सह तपस्विभिश्च । राजा
शापपर्यवहितस्मृतिः शकुन्तलागतमेव चिन्तयति ॥

नेपथ्ये ।

आश्चर्यम् ।

राजा ॥ आकर्ण्य ॥

किं नु खलु स्यात् ।

पुरोहितः ॥ प्रविश्य । सविस्मयम् ॥

देव । अद्भुतं खलु संवृत्तम् ।

राजा ।

किमेवम् ।

पुरोहितः ।

देव । परावृत्तेषु कणविशिष्येषु
सा निन्दन्ती स्वानि भाग्यानि बाला
बाहूत्क्षेपं क्रन्दितुं च प्रवृत्ता ।

राजा ।

किं च ।

पुरोहितः ।

स्त्रीसंस्थानं चाप्सरस्तीर्थमारा-
दुत्क्षिप्यैनां ज्योतिरेकं जगाम ॥१३१॥

॥ सर्वे विस्मयं रूपयन्ति ॥

---

remain no longer in the land of the living. *Mama praveśāya dvidhā bhava,* S. The Beng. MSS. have *antaram = avakāśam* instead of *vivaram.*

[1] 'That young-creature upbraiding her own fortunes, throwing up her arms, and beginning to weep,' or 'and beginning to weep with repeated uplifting of her arms.' *Bāhūtkshepam* (so read all the MSS.) = *bāhū utkshipya;* this is an instance of an adverbial indecl. part. of repetition compounded with a noun (*bhujoččālanaṃ yathā bhavati evaṃ kranditum pravṛittā,* S.) Examples of this participle are numerous in Bhaṭṭi-k., as in ii. 11, *Latānupātaṃ kusumāni agṛihṇāt,* &c.; see Gram. 567.

[2] 'A single flash-of-light in female shape having snatched her up near

Verse 131. ŚĀLINĪ (a variety of TRISHṬUBH), consisting of eleven syllables to the Pāda or quarter-verse, each Pāda being alike.

– – – – | – ◡ – – ◡ – – ||

राजा ।

भगवन् । प्रागपि सोऽस्माभिरर्थः प्रत्यादिष्ट एव । किं
वृथा तर्केणान्विष्यते । विश्राम्यतु भवान् ।

पुरोहितः ॥ विलोक्य ॥

विजयस्व । ॥ इति निष्क्रान्तः ॥

राजा ।

वेत्रवति । पर्याकुलीऽस्मि । शयनभूमिमार्गमादेशय ।

प्रतीहारी ।

"इदो इदो देवो । ॥ इति प्रस्थिता ॥

राजा ।

कामं प्रत्यादिष्टां स्मरामि न परिग्रहं मुनेस्तनयाम् ।
बलवत्तु दूयमानं प्रत्याययतीव मां हृदयम् ॥१३२॥

॥ इति निष्क्रान्ताः सर्वे ॥

॥ पञ्चमोऽङ्कः ॥

" इत इतो देवः ॥

Apsaras-tírtha went off (with her).' *Strī-saṃsthānam*, i. e. *striyā iva
ākṛitir yasya*, S. *Ārāt*=*antike, nikaṭe*, K. and S. *Jyotiḥ*=*tejaḥ. Jayāma*,
the Beng. and the Mackenzie MSS. have *tiro-'bhūt*, 'disappeared.'

[1] 'Granted, I remember not the repudiated Muni's daughter (to be my)
wife; nevertheless (my) heart being powerfully agitated forces me as it
were to believe (her).' *Kāmam*=*atyartham*, K. *Kāmaṃ kāmānumatau*,
S. (cf. p. 24, l. 10; p. 55, n. 3). *Pratyāyayati*, i. e. *tatparigrahe*, S.

Verse 132. ĀRYĀ or GĀTHĀ. See verse 2.

।। अथ पञ्चमषष्ठाङ्कमध्ये प्रवेशकः ।।

।। ततः प्रविशति नागरिकः श्यालः पश्चाद्बद्धपुरुषमादाय रक्षिणौ च ।।

रक्षिणौ ।। ताडयित्वा ।।

[a] अले कुम्भिलँआ । कहेहि । कहिं तुए एशे मणिबन्ध-गुक्किषणामहेए लाञ्चकीए अङ्गुलीञ्अए शमाशादिए ।

[a] अरे कुम्भिलक । कथय । कुत्र त्वयैतन्मणिबन्धनोत्कीर्णनामधेयं राजकीयमङ्गु-लीयकं समासादितम् ।

---

[1] *Pravesaka*, see p. 97, n. 3.

[2] 'Then enters the king's-brother-in-law (as) superintendent of the city-police, and two policemen [guards] bringing a man (with his hands) bound behind.' *Nāgarikaḥ = nagarādhikārī*, 'superintendent of the city,' S.; *= nagare niyuktaḥ*, 'one set over the city,' K.; here 'the chief of the police.' *Syāla* (also written *syāla*) = *rāshṭriya* or *rāshṭrīya* (Amara-k.) The king's brother-in-law, who here acts as superintendent of police, is a character not unfrequently introduced in the plays (cf. Mṛicchak. p. 224, l. 4; p. 227, l. 12; p. 230, l. 1, in which passages he is called *rāja-śyālaḥ* and *rāshṭriya-śyālaḥ*). K. observes that the policemen and the fishermen in this scene speak the Māgadhī form of Prākṛit (see Lassen's Instit. Prāk. p. 391), but S. affirms that the fisherman speaks the Śakāra dialect (*ćaura-pātras tu śakāra-nāmadheyaḥ śakāra-prāya-bhāshaṇāt*), see Lassen's Instit. Prāk. p. 422. Both S. and K. have omitted to make mention of the dialect spoken by the Śyāla or Nāgarika. According to Viśvanātha (Sāhit.-d. p. 180, l. 12) he ought to speak the Dākshiṇātyā form of Prākṛit. In the Beng. MSS., and some of the Deva-n., he is certainly made to speak a dialect distinct from the other characters of this scene, but in the best MSS. pure Prākṛit forms are found in the speeches attributed to him. Indeed, as brother-in-law of the king, he must have been a Kshatriya, or one of the military caste.

[3] 'O thief!' *Kumbhila* or *kumbhilaka* seems to be identical with *kum-bhīla, kumbhīlaka, kumbhīra, kumbhīraka*, &c. Compare in the beginning of Act V. of Vikram., *maṇi-kumbhīraka*, 'gem-stealer' (applied to the bird who swallowed the crest-jewel); and at the end of Act II, *loptreṇa sūćitasya kumbhīrakasya;* and in Mālavik., *aho kumbhīlakaiḥ parihara-ṇīyā ćandrikā.*

[4] 'The setting of which is engraven with his name.' *Maṇi-bandhana*, which usually signifies 'the wrist,' is here the place of the setting

मुहुंयः ॥ भीतिनाटितकेन ॥

[a] पसीदन्तो भावमिस्से । अहके ण ईदिशकम्मकाली ।

प्रथमः ।

[b] किं खु शोहणे बम्हणोत्ति कलिञ्च लक्खा पडिग्गहे दिंस्ते ।

मुहुयः ।

[c] शुणुह दाणिं । अहके शक्कावदालब्भन्तलवाशी धीवले ।

द्वितीयः ।

[d] पाडच्चला । किं अम्हेहिं जादी पुच्छिदा ।

श्यालः ।

[e] सूञ्च । कहेदु सव्वं अणुक्कमेण । मा एं अन्तरा पडिबन्धह ।

[a] प्रसीदन्तु भावमिश्राः । अहं नेदृशकर्मकारी ।   [b] किं खलु शोभनो ब्राह्मण इति कृत्वा राज्ञा प्रतिग्रहो दत्तः ।   [c] शृणुतेदानीम् । अहं शक्रावतारभ्यन्तरवासी धीवरः ।   [d] पाटच्चर । किमस्माभिर्जातिं पृष्टः ।   [e] सूचक । कथयतु सर्वमनुक्रमेण । मैनमन्तरा प्रतिबध्नीतम् ।

[technically, the collet, نگين داں *niyīn dān*] of the jewel which formed the *mudrā* or seal of the ring, mentioned p. 53, n. 3. *Maṇiḥ khaćyate yasminn iti maṇi-bandhanaḥ*, K. The name might have been engraven on the stone itself, or on the gold in which it was set. *Utkṛī* is used in the sense of 'excavating,' in Mahā-bh. i. 5813; and *samutkīrṇa* with the meaning 'perforated,' in Raghu-v. i. 4.

[1] 'With a gesticulation of fear.' The *ka* added to *nāṭita* may possibly signify a poor, sorry, or ludicrous gesture. It is often pleonastic, but in the plays it will sometimes be found affixed to the past passive participle, to which it gives the sense of a verbal noun. Thus *udbhrāntaka* and *apavāritaka* (Mṛićchak. p. 171) for *udbhrānti* and *apavāraṇa*.

[2] 'Your honour.' *Bhāva = mānya*, S., 'venerable,' 'respectable,' to which *miśra* may be added (see p. 7, n. 3).

[3] 'Was it forsooth a present given by the king (to thee), imagining (thee to be) an illustrious Brāhman?' *Pratigraha* (see p. 54, l. 2, with note) is especially 'a donation to a Brāhman at suitable periods.' *Kṛitvā*, 'thinking,' see p. 170, n. 3 in the middle; and cf. Mālavik. p. 23, l. 9, *parakāryam iti kṛitvā;* also Mṛićchak. p. 147, l. 5.

[4] Verbs of 'asking' in Sanskrit govern a double accusative case, one of which is retained after the past passive participle.

[5] *Sūćaka*, 'informer,' is the name of one of the *rakshiṇaḥ*, or 'policemen.'

उभौ ।

[a] जं आबुत्ते आणवेदि । कहेहि ।

पुरुषः ।

[b] अहके जालुग्गालादीहिं मच्छबन्धणोबाएहिं कुडुम्बभ-लणं कलेमि ।

श्यालः ॥ विहस्य ॥

[c] विसुड्डो दाणिं आजीवो ।

पुरुषः ।

[d] भट्टा । मा एव्वं भण ।

शहजे किल जे विणिन्दिए णा हु दे कम्म विवज्जणीअए ।
पशुमालणकम्मदालुणे अणुकम्पामिदु एव्व शोत्तिए ॥१३३॥

[a] यदावुत्त आज्ञापयति । कथय ।   [b] अहं जालोद्धारादिभिर्मत्स्यवन्धनोपायैः
कुडुम्बभरणं करोमि ।   [c] विशुद्ध इदानीमाजीवः ।   [d] भर्तः । मैवं भण ।
सहजं किल यद्विनिन्दितं न खलु तत्कर्म विवर्जनीयम् ।
पशुमारणकर्मदारुणोऽनुकम्पामृदुरेव श्रोत्रियः ॥

---

[1] *Ábutta*, 'a sister's husband,' or 'brother-in-law,' according to Amara-k. vii. 12. In Mṛicchak. p. 339, l. 12, this word is applied as a title of respect by a son to his father; but Dr. Boehtlingk conjectures that this may be an error for *ávuka*, the regular theatrical term for 'father.' According to Dr. Burkhard, *ábutta* = Sanskrit *bháva*, 'an honourable sir,' 'gentleman.'

[2] 'I make the support of my family by nets, hooks, and the other contrivances for catching fish.' *Udgála* or *udgára* = *valiśa* or *vaḍiśa*, 'a fish-hook,' K. *Jála-valiśa-ppahudihim* = *jála-vaḍiśa-prabhṛitibhiḥ* is the reading of the Bengálí Recension. *Jálodgára* may mean 'the casting of nets.'

[3] This is spoken ironically, as, according to Manu (x. 46–48), the *nisháda*, or fisherman caste, was one of the lowest. 'Those who are considered as low-born shall subsist only by such employments as the twice-born despise. Nishádas (must subsist) by catching fish,' &c. Any occupation which involved the sin of slaughtering animals (excepting in the case of sacrificing to the god S'iva) was considered despicable. Butchers and leather-sellers were as great, or even greater, objects of scorn.

[4] 'That occupation in which one was born, as-the-saying-is (*kila*),

श्यालः ।

a तदौ तदौ ।

पुरुषः ।

b एक्कस्सिं दिअसे खरडशो लोहिअमच्छे[1] मए कप्पिदे जाव ।

a ततस्ततः ।   b एकस्मिन्दिवसे खरडशो रौहितमत्स्यो मया कल्पितो यावत् ।

---

though in-bad-repute, verily must not be abandoned. The same Brāhman,
who is savage in the act of slaughtering animals, may be (of a disposition)
tender with compassion.' *Saha-ja = kula-kramānugata*, 'inherited from
one's forefathers.' See Indian Wisdom, p. 140 and note. Manu is very
peremptory in restricting special occupations to the different castes,
especially to the mixed and lowest castes, formed by intermarriage with
the others. 'A man of the lowest class, who, through covetousness, lives
by the acts of the highest, let the king strip of all his wealth and banish.
His own office, though badly performed, is preferable to that of another,
though well performed; for he who lives by the duties of another class,
immediately falls from his own' (Manu x. 96, 97). Hence we find the
employments of fishing, slaughtering animals for food, leather-selling,
basket-making, burning the dead, &c. &c., assigned to men born in certain
impure castes, and confined perpetually to their descendants. To the
higher and purer castes a greater variety of employment was allowed.
S. observes that the Brāhman is called *Shaṭ-karman*, from the precept of
Manu (i. 88), which enjoins upon him six occupations, viz. reading,
teaching, sacrificing, assisting others to sacrifice, giving, and receiving.
See Indian Wisdom, p. 244. Under certain circumstances he was allowed
by Manu to engage even in trade, and other employments. The sacrifice
of animals was enjoined only on the priests of the god S'iva. The
Brāhman, in the worship of this god, might have to kill animals; but
this was as much a necessary part of his business, as killing fish, of the
fisherman, and was no proof of any natural cruelty of disposition. S'.
defines a S'rotriya Brāhman thus: *Janmanā Brāhmaṇo jñeyaḥ, sanskā-
rair dvija ućyate, vidyayā yāti vipratvam, tribhiḥ śrotriya ućyate*, 'birth
constitutes the title Brāhman; sacramental rites (especially that of in-
vestiture with the sacred thread), the title Dvija, or twice-born; know-
ledge, the title Vipra; and all three S'rotriya.' The usual definition of
this word is, a Brāhman conversant with *śruti*, or scripture.

[1] The *Rohita* or *Rohi* fish (Cyprinus Rohita), lit. 'red-fish,' is a kind of
carp, found in lakes and ponds in the neighbourhood of the Ganges. It
grows to the length of three feet, is very voracious, and its flesh, though

^aतश्श उदलब्भन्तले एदं लदणभाशुलं अङ्गुलीअञ्अं देक्खिअं। पच्छा अहके शे विक्कआअ दंशअन्ते गहिदे भाव-मिश्शेहिं। मालेह वा। मुञ्चेह वा। अअं शे आअमवुत्तन्ते।

श्यालः।

^bजाणुअ। विस्सगन्धी गोहादी मच्छबन्धो एव्व णिस्संसअं। अङ्गुलीअञ्अदंसणं से विमरिसिदव्वं। राउलं एव्व गच्छामो।

रक्खिणौ।

^cतह। गच्छ अरे गण्ठिभेदअ। ॥ सर्वे परिक्रामन्ति ॥

श्यालः।

^dसूअअ। इमं पुरदुवारे अप्पमत्ता पडिबालह। जाव इमं

---

^a तस्योदराभ्यन्तर एतद्रत्नभासुरमङ्गुलीयकं दृष्टम्। पश्चादहमस्य विक्रयाय दर्शयन्गृ-हीतो भावमिश्रैः। मारयत वा। मुञ्चत वा। अयमस्यागमवृत्तान्तः। ^b जानुक। विस्रगन्धिर्गोघाती मत्स्यबन्ध एव निःसंशयम्। अङ्गुलीयकदर्शनमस्य विमर्ष्टव्यम्। राजकुलमेव गच्छामः। ^c तथा। गच्छ अरे ग्रन्थिभेदक। ^d सूचक। इमं पुरद्वारेऽप्रमत्तौ प्रतिपालयतम्। यावदिदम्

---

coarse, is eaten. Its back is olive-coloured, its belly of a beautiful golden hue, its fins and eyes red.

[1] 'O Jānuka, the villain stinking (as he does) of raw flesh (is) doubtless a fisherman.' Jānuka is the name of the other policeman, who is supposed to have detected the thief (*jānuka iti ćora-jñātur apara-padāter nāma*, S.) Some Beng. MSS. have *jālua* (=*jāluka*). *Visra-gandhi*=*āmisha-gandhi*, C. *Go-ghātī*, the killing of a cow (*go-hatyā*), is reckoned by the Hindūs a most heinous crime (cf. Hitop. 1. 162). Hence *go-ghātin*, 'cow-killer,' is applied as a reproachful epithet to any rogue or low person. Thus in the Mṛićchak. p. 299, l. 4; p. 317, l. 2, the Ćāṇḍāla is called *go-ha* or *go-ghna*.

[2] '(But) the finding [seeing, shewing] of the ring by him must be (more closely) inquired into.' *Vimarshṭavyam*=*jijñāsitavyam*, S. Root *mṛiś* with *vi* has usually the sense of 'to consider,' 'investigate ;' but if the root be *mṛij*, the sense would be 'must be pardoned,' 'overlooked.' K. has *vimārshṭavyam*, from *mṛij*.

[3] *Granthi-bhedaka*, 'cut-purse,' lit. 'knot-breaker' or 'knot-cutter.' The Hindūs generally carry their money tied up in a knot in one end of a cloth, which is bound round the waist.

a अङ्गुलीअं जहागमणं भट्टिणो णिवेदिअ तदो सासणं पडिच्छिअ णिक्कमामि ।

उभौ ।

b पविशदु आउत्ते शामिपशादश्श ।

॥ निष्क्रान्तः श्यालः ॥

प्रथमः ।

c जाणुअ । चिलाअदि खु आउत्ते ।

द्वितीयः ।

d अं अवशलोवशप्पणीआ लाआणो ।

प्रथमः ।

e जाणुअ । फुलन्ति मे हत्था इमश्श वज्झश्श शुमणो पिणंदुं । ॥ इति पुरहं निर्दिशति ॥

पुरहः ।

f ण अलुहदि भावे अकालणमालणो भविदुं ।

द्वितीयः ॥ विलोक्य ॥

g एशे अम्हाणं शामी पन्नहत्ये लाअशाशणं पडिच्छिअ इदोमुहे देक्खीअदि । गिड्डवली भविश्शशि शुणो मुहं

a अङ्गुलीयकं यथागमनं भर्तुर्निवेद्य ततः शासनं प्रतीष्य निष्क्रमामि ।   b प्रवि-शत्वावुत्तः स्वामिप्रसादाय ।   c जानुक । चिरायति खल्वावुत्तः ।   d नन्वव-सरोपसर्पणीया राजानः ।   e जानुक । स्फुरतो मे हस्तावस्य वध्यस्य सुमनः पिनद्धुम् ।   f नार्हति भावोऽकारणमारणो भवितुम् ।   g एष नौ स्वामी पन्नहस्तो राजशासनं प्रतीष्येतोमुखो दृश्यते । गृध्रबलिर्भविष्यसि शुनो मुखं

---

1 'My hands tingle [my fingers itch] to bind a flower (about the head) of this victim [criminal about to be executed].' All the Deva-n. MSS. have *sumanaḥ pinaddhum*, excepting the Mackenzie, which has *sumaha-ṇam* for *śumaṇo*. The Beng. have got rid of the difficulty by substituting *vyāpādayitum*, 'to kill.' It is clear from what follows that the two policemen expected that their master would return with the king's order for putting the fisherman to death. From the Mālati-m. and other plays, it is evident that a person about to be offered as a victim to Śiva or Durgā had a wreath of flowers bound round the head. This was also the case with common criminals, previous to their execution.

[a]वा देक्खिस्सश्शि ।

श्यालः ॥ प्रविश्य ॥

[b]सूञ्अ । मुञ्चेदु एसो जालोअजीवी । उववस्त्रो किल अस्सं अङ्गुलीअञ्अस्स आञ्अमो ।

सूचकः ।

[c]जह आबुत्ते भणादि ।

द्वितीयः ।

[d]एस्से जमसदॅणं पविशिअ पडिणिवुत्ते ।

॥ इति पुरुषं परिमुक्तबन्धनं करोति ॥

पुरुषः ॥ श्यालं प्रणम्य ॥

[e]भट्टा । अह कीलिशे मे आजीवे ।

श्यालः ।

[f]एस भट्टिणा अङ्गुलीअञ्अमुल्लसम्मिदो पसादोवि दाविदो ।

॥ इति पुरुषायार्धं प्रयच्छति ॥

[a] वा द्रक्ष्यसि । [b] सूचक । मुच्यतामेष जालोपजीवी । उपपन्नः किलायमङ्गुलीय-कस्यागमः । [c] यथाबुत्तो भणति । [d] एष यमसदनं प्रविश्य प्रतिनिवृत्तः । [e] भर्तः । अथ कीदृशो म आजीवः । [f] एष भर्त्राङ्गुलीयकमूल्यसम्मितः प्रसादोऽपि दापितः ।

---

[1] 'Thou wilt be food for [an offering to] the vultures, or wilt see the face of a dog.' *Gṛidhra-bali,* see p. 179, n. 1. *Śuno mukham,* so read all the Deva-n. MSS., excepting the Mackenzie, which omits the clause entirely. Dr. Boehtlingk has adopted as an emendation, *śiśuno muham,* i. e. *śiśor* [not *śiśuno*] *mukham,* and translated 'or thou wilt see the face of (thy) child (once more).' He has supported this interpretation by a reference to two other passages, one in Act VII. of this play (*putra-mukha-darśanena*), another in Mṛicchak. p. 303, l. 4. Doubtless *putra-mukham dṛiś* is a common phrase, but the whole point of this passage seems to me to lie in the ludicrous substitution of *śunaḥ* for *putrasya.*

[2] *Yama-sadana,* 'the abode of Yama,' i. e. the infernal city, Yama-pur, whither the Hindūs believe a departed soul immediately repairs, and receives a just sentence from Yama, the Hindū Pluto or Minos. The name Yama, i. e. Restrainer or Punisher (from *yam,* 'to restrain'), is given to him as judge of departed spirits and god of punishment.

[3] This is said ironically, in reference to p. 219, l. 7, n. 3.

[4] *Prasāda,* properly 'a favour,' here 'a present,' 'a gift.'

मुहप: ॥ समयामं प्रतिगृह्ण ॥

[a] भट्टकेण अणुग्गहिदम्हि ।

सूचक: ।

[b] एशे णाम अणुग्गहिदे जे शूलादो अवदालिञ हत्थिक्खन्धे पडिट्ठाबिदे ।

जानुक: ।

[c] आबुत्त । पालिदोशिअं कहेदि तेण अङ्गुलीअएण भट्टिणो शम्मदेण होदंव्वं ।

श्याल: ।

[d] ण तस्सं महाग्हं रदणं भट्टिणो बहुमदंति तक्केमि । तस्स दंसणेण भट्टिणो अभिमदो जणो सुमरिदो । मुहुत्तञं पकिदिगम्भीरोबि पज्जुस्सुअमणो आसिं ।

सूचक: ।

[e] शेविदं णाम आबुत्तेण ।

---

[a] भर्त्रानुगृहीतोऽस्मि ।   [b] एष नामानुगृहीतो यः शूलादवतार्य हस्तिस्कन्धे प्रतिष्ठापितः ।   [c] आवुत्त । पारितोषिकं कथयति तेनाङ्गुलीयकेन भर्तुः सम्मतेन भवितव्यम् ।   [d] न तस्मिन्महार्हं रत्नं भर्तुर्बहुमतमिति तर्कयामि । तस्य दर्शनेन भर्तुरभिमतो जनः स्मृतः । मुहूर्तं प्रकृतिगम्भीरोऽपि पर्युत्सुकमना आसीत् ।   [e] सेवितं नामावुत्तेन ।

---

[1] 'This (fellow) forsooth (may well say he) has been favoured, who, after being made to descend from the stake, has been mounted on the withers of an elephant.' *Śūla*, 'a stake for impaling criminals.' The act of impaling was called *śūlāropaṇa*, and one who deserved it *śūlya*. 'Mounting on an elephant' denotes elevation to high dignity, elephants being used in triumphal processions.

[2] This is the reading of K. Most of the Deva-n. have *palidośam ka-hehi* (=*paritoshaṃ kathaya*). Translate : 'The present proves [betokens, bespeaks] that this ring must be highly prized by the king.'

[3] 'Though naturally reserved [unruffled, deep, profound] he became for a moment agitated in mind.' *Gambhīra*, see p. 39, n. 1, and p. 204, n. 3. K. reads *pajjassu-ṇaṇo* (=*paryaśru-nayanaḥ*). All Asiatics are skilful in concealing emotion.

जानुक: ।

[a] खं भणाहि । इमश्श कए मच्छिआभत्तुणोत्ति ।

॥ इति पुरुषमसूयया पश्यति ॥

पुरुष: ।

[b] भट्टालके । इदो अड्ढं तुम्हाणं शुमणोमुल्लं होदु ।

जानुक: ।

[c] एत्तके जुज्जइ ।

श्याल: ।

[d] धीवर । महत्तरी तुमं पिअवअस्सको दाणिं मे संवुत्तो ।
कादम्बरीसक्खिअं अम्हाणं पढमसोहिदं इच्छीअदि । ता
सोणिआपणं एव्व गच्छामो ।

सर्वे ।

[e] तह ।

॥ इति निष्क्रान्ताः सर्वे ॥

॥ प्रवेशक: ॥

[a] ननु भण । अस्य कृते मत्स्यिकाभर्तुरिति ।   [b] भट्टारका: । इतोऽर्धं युष्माकं सुमनोमूल्यं भवतु ।   [c] एतावद्युज्यते ।   [d] धीवर । महत्तरस्त्वं प्रियवयस्यक इदानीं मे संवृत्त: । कादम्बरीसाक्षिकमस्माकं प्रथमसौहृदमिष्यते । तच्छौणिडकापणमेव गच्छाम: ।   [e] तथा ।

---

[1] So read most of the Deva-n. MSS. *Matsyikā* is not given in the Dictionary. Dr. Boehtlingk translates it by *Fisch-brut*, 'the fry of fish,' and observes that it is also the name for a kind of fish called in German *Schaar*. Had the word been *matsyika* or *mātsyika*, 'a fisherman,' there would have been no difficulty. May it not mean 'a fish-woman,' and *matsyikā-bhartri*, 'this husband of a fish-woman?' K. and the Bengālī have *matsya-śatroḥ*, 'enemy of fishes.' Burkhard follows this, and reads *maććha-śattaṇotti*, but in the Vocabulary prefers *maśchiā = matsyikā*, 'a fish' (?).

[2] 'Let the half of this be the price of your flower (for binding about my head).' The fisherman is again ironical. The allusion of course is to the flower mentioned at p. 222, l. 11. There is probably a double-entendre in *sumanaḥ*, which may signify 'good-will,' as well as 'flower.'

[3] 'Our first friendship requires to be attested over (some) wine,' i.e. we must pledge ourselves over our cups or in drinking each other's health. *Kādambarī*, 'an intoxicating liquor distilled from the Kadamba flower.' *Sākshikam*, compare Mālavik. p. 53, l. 7; Raghu-v. xi. 48; Hitop. l. 842.

॥ अथ षष्ठोऽङ्कः ॥

॥ ततः प्रविशत्याकाशयानेन सानुमती नामाप्सराः ॥

सानुमती ।

[a] णिव्वत्तिदं मए पज्जाअणिव्वत्तणिज्जं अच्छरातित्थ-
सण्णिज्झं । जाव साहुजणस्स अभिसेअकालोत्ति सम्पदं
इमस्स राएसिणो उदन्तं पच्चक्खीकरिस्सं । एं मेणआ-
सम्बन्धेण सरीरभूदा दाणिं मे सउन्दला । ताएस्स

[a] निर्वर्तितं मया पर्यायनिर्वर्तनीयमप्सरस्तीर्थसान्निध्यम् । यावत्साधुजनस्याभिषेक-
काल इति साम्प्रतमस्य राजर्षेरुदन्तं प्रत्यक्षीकरिष्यामि । ननु मेनकासम्बन्धेन शरीर-
भूतेदानीं मे शकुन्तला । तया च

---

[1] 'Attendance at Apsaras-tîrtha (which is wont) to be performed (by us) in regular-rotation has been performed by me. Now, whilst (it is) the bathing-time of the good people [i. e. of Śakuntalā and the nymphs], I will with my own eyes ascertain the circumstances [news] of this Râjarshi.' *Sânnidhyam* (from *san-nidha*), lit. 'proximity;' here it denotes 'close attendance or waiting,' as in Hitop. l. 1112, *anujîvinâ sânnidhyam avaśyaṃ karaṇîyam.* In the interlude before Act IV. of Vikram., *upasthâna* occurs with the same sense in a parallel passage : *Apsaro-vyâpâra-paryâyeṇa sûryasya upasthâne vartamânayâ priya-sakhyâ vinâ vasanta-samaya âgata iti balavad utkaṇṭhitâsmi,* 'I am mightily troubled that the spring season has arrived during the absence of my dear friend, who is in attendance upon Sûrya, according to the regular cycle of nymph's duty.' *Ud-anta* (lit. 'reaching to the end'), 'telling to the end,' 'full tidings,' 'news.'

[2] 'Verily by (my) connexion with Menakâ, Śakuntalâ has now become part of myself,' lit. 'my own body,' i. e. 'part of my own flesh and blood,' 'identified with myself.' As to the nymph Menakâ, the mother of Śakuntalâ, see p. 44, l. 11 with n. 2, and p. 45, n. 1. *Sarîra-bhûtâ*, this is the same sort of compound as *pûja-kṛita* or *pûja-bhûta;* see Pâṇ. ii. 1, 59, and p. 167, n. 2 at the end. Cf. *śarîram asi me,* 'thou art my body,' Mâlavik. p. 33, l. 12.

[a] दुहिदुणिमित्तं आदिट्ठपुव्वम्हि । ॥ समन्तादवलोक्य ॥ [b] किं
सुक्खु उदुस्सवे[1] वि णिहस्सवारम्भं विश्र एदं राश्रउलं
दीसइ । अत्थि मे विहवो पणिधाणेण[2] सव्वं परिश्रादुं ।
किन्दु सहीए आदरो मए माणइदव्वो । होदु । इमाणं एव्व
उज्जाणपालिआणं तिरक्खरिणीपरिच्छन्ना[3] पस्सपरि-
वत्तिणी भविश्र उवलम्भिस्सं । ॥ इति नाट्येनावतीर्य स्थिता ॥

[a] दुहितृनिमित्तमादिष्टपूर्वासि । [b] किं नु खलु ऋतूत्सवेऽपि निहत्सवारम्भि-
चैत्राज्ञकुलं दृश्यते । अस्ति मे विभवः प्रणिधानेन सर्वं परिज्ञातुम् । किन्नु सख्या
आदरो मया मानयितव्यः । भवतु । अनयोरेवोद्यानपालिकयोस्तिरस्करिणीपरिच्छन्ना
पार्श्वपरिवर्तिनी भूत्वोपलप्स्ये ।

---

[1] *Ritūtsava*, lit. 'the festival of the season,' i.e. the *Vasantotsava*, or 'great vernal festival,' in celebration of the return of spring, and said to be in honour of the god Krishna. Originally his son Kāma-deva, the god of love, must have been the object of worship in this festival. It is identified with the Holi or Dolā-yātra, the Saturnalia, or rather, Carnival of the Hindūs, when people of all conditions take liberties with each other, especially by scattering red powder and coloured water on the clothes of persons passing in the street, as described in Ratnāvali, pp. 5, 6, 7, where syringes and waterpipes are used by the crowd. Flowers, and especially the opening blossoms of the mango, would naturally be much used for decoration at this festival, and as offerings to the god of love. It was formerly held on the full moon of the month Caitra, or about the beginning of April, but now on the full moon of Phālguna, or about the beginning of March. The other great Hindū festival, held in the autumn, about October, is called *Durgotsava* or *Durgā-pūjā*, being in honour of the goddess Durgā.

[2] *Pranidhāna*, 'profound meditation,' or that mental faculty by which divine beings were supposed to be able to ascertain future events. The verb *pra-ni-dhā* (sometimes with *manas*) is primarily 'to fix in;' hence 'to fix the mind on,' 'be intent on.' Compare *mayā pranidhāna-sthitayā atyāhitam upalabdham*, Vikram. (interlude before Act IV).

[3] *Tiras-karinī*, a kind of magical veil, rendering the wearer invisible.

॥ ततः प्रविशति चूताङ्कुरमवलोकयन्ती चेटी । अपरा च पृष्ठतस्याः ॥

प्रथमा ।

[a] आअम्बहरिअपण्डुर वसन्तमासस जीअसव्वस्स ।
दिट्ठोसि चूदकोरअ उदुमङ्गलं तुमं पसाएमि[1] ॥१३४॥

द्वितीया ।

[b] परहुदिए । किं एआइणी मन्तेसि ।

प्रथमा ।

[c] महुअरिए । चूदकलिअं देक्खिअ उम्मत्तिआ[2] परहुदिआ होदि ।

[a] आताम्रहरितपाण्डुर वसन्तमासस्य जीवसर्वस्व ।
दृष्टोऽसि चूतकोरक ऋतुमङ्गलं त्वां प्रसादयामि ॥१३४॥

[b] परभृतिके । किमेकाकिनी मन्त्रयसे ।   [c] मधुकरिके । चूतकलिकां दृष्ट्वोन्मत्ता परभृतिका भवति ।

---

[1] 'O reddish pale-green mango-blossom, the very essence of the life of the vernal month, thou art seen (by me, and) I bid thee hail, auspicious-harbinger of the season.' *Ā-tāmra-harita-pāṇḍura*, this kind of Dvandva Bahuvrīhi compound, expressing varieties of colour, is noticed by Pāṇ. ii.1, 69 (cf. *krishṇa-śukla, lohita-śavala*, &c.) *Ā* prefixed, implies diminution, and is equivalent to *ishat*. So *ā-pāṇḍu*, 'yellowish,' or 'slightly yellow,' Vikram., Act II. *Jīva-sarvasva*, lit. 'whose whole substance is constituted of life,' see p. 33, n. 1 in the middle. Some MSS. have *jīva-sarvasvam*, agreeing with *tvām*. *Mangalam*, 'anything auspicious,' 'any symbol or sign of happiness;' in this latter sense it seems to be used here. The goddess Durgā is called in the same way *sarva-mangalā*, 'presiding over the happiness of the whole world.' *Ṛitu* is evidently here the season *par excellence*, the season of all others. *Prasādayāmi*, lit. 'I ask thee to be favourable,' 'I entreat thee to be propitious.'

[2] *Para-bhṛitikā*, 'the female of the Indian cuckoo,' see p. 162, n. 2.

Verse 134. ĀRYĀ or GĀTHĀ. See verse 2.

$$- - \mid \cup \cup \cup \cup \mid - \cup \cup \parallel \cup - \cup \mid - - \mid \cup - \cup \mid - - \mid \cup$$
$$- - \mid \cup - \cup \mid - \cup \cup \cup \parallel \cup \cup - \mid \cup - \cup \mid \cup \mid \cup - \cup \mid -$$

In the last Pāda the syllables *mam* and *c* are considered short by a license peculiar to Prākṛit prosody.

द्वितीया ॥ सहर्षं त्वरयोपगम्य ॥

[a] कहं उवट्टिदो महुमासो ।

प्रथमा ।

[b] महुअरिए । णव दाणिं कालो एसो मद्दविब्भमगीदाणं ।

द्वितीया ।

[c] सहि । अवलम्ब मं । जाव अग्गपादट्ठिआ भविअ चूदकलिअं गेण्हिअ कामदेवच्चणं करेमि ।

प्रथमा ।

[d] जइ ममबिक्खु अङ्घं अच्चणफलस्स ।

द्वितीया ।

[e] अकहिदेबि एदं सम्पज्जइ । जदो एक्कं एव्व णो जीविदं । दुधाठिदं सरीरं । ॥ सखीमवलम्ब्य स्थिता चूताङ्कुरं गृह्णाति ॥ [f] अए । अप्पडिबुड्डोबि चूदप्पसवो एत्थ बन्धण[1]भङ्गसुरभी होदि[2] ।

॥ कपोतहस्तकं कृत्वा ॥

<hr>

[a] कथमुपस्थितो मधुमासः । [b] मधुकरिके । नवेदानीं काल एष मदविभ्र-मगीतानाम् । [c] सखि । अवलम्बस्व माम् । यावदग्रपादस्थिता भूत्वा चूतकलिकां गृहीत्वा कामदेवार्चनं करोमि । [d] यदि ममापि खल्वर्थमर्चनफलस्य । [e] अक-थितेऽपि एतत्सम्पद्यते । यत एकमेव नौ जीवितम् । द्विधास्थितं शरीरम् । [f] अये । अप्रतिबुद्धोऽपि चूतप्रसवोऽत्र बन्धनभङ्गसुरभिर्भवति ।

<hr>

[1] *Bandhana*, i. e. *prasava-bandhana*, 'the foot-stalk of the flower,' see p. 103, l. 3, n. 1.

[2] 'Having joined the hands together,' or 'having placed them one over another.' *Kapota* is properly 'a dove or pigeon;' but K. informs us that it is also the name for a mode of joining the hands. Probably the hands and fingers were brought into a position bearing some fancied resemblance to a pigeon. S. and C. quote the following verse, which seems to intimate that this position was significant of humble entreaty, respectful representation, or fear: *Sarva-pārśva-samāśleshāt kapotaḥ sarva-śīrshakaḥ [sarpa-śīrshakaḥ, S.], bhūtau vijñāpane ćaiva vinaye ća prayujjyate.*

[a] तुंसि मए चूदङ्कुर दिण्णो कामस्स गहिदधणुअस्स ।
पहिअजणजुवइलक्खो पञ्चब्भहिओ सरो होहि ॥१३५॥

॥ इति चूताङ्कुरं क्षिपति ॥

कञ्चुकी ॥ प्रविश्य पटाक्षेपेण कुपितः ॥

मा तावदनात्मज्ञे । देवेन प्रतिषिद्धे वसन्तोत्सवे त्वमाम्र-
कलिकाभङ्गं किमारभसे ।

उभे ॥ भीते ॥

[b] पसीददु अज्जो । अग्गहीदत्थाओ वअं ।

कञ्चुकी ।

न किल श्रुतं युवाभ्याम् । यद्वासन्निकैस्तरुभिरपि देवस्य
शासनं प्रमाणीकृतं तदाश्रयिभिः पक्षिभिश्च । तथा हि

[a] त्वमसि मया चूताङ्कुर दत्तः कामस्य गृहीतधनोः ।
पथिकजनयुवतिलक्ष्यः पञ्चाभ्यधिकः शरो भव ॥१३५॥

[b] प्रसीदन्त्वार्यैः । अगृहीतार्थे वयम् ।

---

[1] 'O mango-sprout, thou art offered by me to Kāma-deva (now in the act of) taking-up-his-bow. Become the most excellent arrow of the five, having-for-thy-mark maidens whose lovers are journeying (to some distant land).' As to Kāma and the epithet *pañćābhyadhika* (=*śreshṭha*, K.; = *shashṭha*, S.), see p. 99, n. 1. *Pathika-jana-yuvati*, cf. Megha-d. ver. 8, *pathika-vanitāḥ*. With reference to the offering of flowers to Kāma-deva, cf. Ratn. pp. 14, 17.

[2] 'With a hurried toss of the curtain,' see p. 144, n. 1.

[3] 'Do not so, thou thoughtless woman!' *An-ātmajña* (=*ātma-parićaya-rahita*), lit. 'one who does not know his own nature.' It denotes here, 'one who is thoughtless about orders.' As to the Kañćukin or Chamberlain, see p. 186, n. 1.

[4] 'When even by the vernal shrubs, and by the feathered tribes [birds] their inhabitants, the commands of the king are made the rule [obeyed].' *Pramāṇa* is 'a rule or standard of action,' and *pramāṇī-kri*, 'to receive as a rule,' 'to admit as authority' (cf. p. 188, l. 5).

Verse 135. ĀRYĀ or GĀTHĀ. See verse 2.

‿ ∪ ∪ | – – | – ∪ ∪ ‖ – – | – – | ∪ ∪ ∪ ∪ | ∪ ∪ – |
∪ ∪ ∪ ∪ | ∪ ∪ ∪ ∪ | – – ‖ – – | ∪ ∪ – | ∪ | – – | ∪ |

चूतानां चिरनिर्गतापि कलिका बध्नाति न स्वं रजः
सन्नद्धं यदपि स्थितं कुरुवकं तत्कोरकावस्थया ।
कण्ठेषु स्खलितं गतेऽपि शिशिरे पुंस्कोकिलानां हतं
शङ्के संहरति स्मरोऽपि चकितस्तूणार्धकृष्टं शरम् ॥१३६॥[1]

उभे ।

[a] णत्थि सन्देहो । महप्पहावो राएसी ।

प्रथमा ।

[b] अज्ज । कदि दिअहाइं अम्हाणं मित्तावसुणा रट्ठिएण
भट्टिणो पाअमूलं पेसिदाणं[2] । इत्थं च णो पमदवणस्स

[a] नास्ति सन्देहः । महाप्रभावो राजर्षिः ।   [b] आर्ये । कति दिवसान्यावयोर्मित्रा-
वसुना राष्ट्रियेण भर्तुः पादमूलं प्रेषितयोः । इत्थं च नौ प्रमदवनस्य

---

[1] 'The bud of the mangoes, though long since protruded, does not form [gather] its own pollen [dust]. The Kuruvaka flower, though all ready to blossom, remains in its budding state. The note falters in the throats of the male-cuckoos, though the cold-dews are passed. I suspect even Smara, being daunted, arrests [replaces] the shaft half-drawn from (his) quiver.' *Badhnāti*, see p. 29, n. 1 in the middle; and compare *ishad-baddha-rajaḥ-kaṇāgra-kapiśā ćūte navā mañjarī*, Vikram., Act II. *Sannaddham* = *pushpitam udyatam*, S.; = *vikāsonmukham*, K. (cf. p. 27, l. 6, n. 2). *Sthitam*, cf. p. 1, l. 2. *Kuruvaka* is either the crimson amaranth, or a purple species of Barleria. *Tat-korakāvasthayā* = *kalikā-daśayā*, S.; i. e. *na vikāsitam*, C. *Skhalitam* = *gadgaditam*, K. *Śiśira*, properly 'the dewy season,' or 'season of hoar-frost.' The Hindūs divide the year into six seasons of two months each, viz. 1. Spring, *Vasanta*, beginning about the middle of March, or according to some, February; 2. Summer, *Grīshma*; 3. Rains, *Varshā*; 4. Autumn, *Śarad*; 5. Winter, *Hemanta*; 6. Dews, *Śiśira*. *Puns-kokilānāṃ rutam*, cf. *parabhrita-virutam*, p. 162, l. 4, with note. *Saṃharati*, cf. p. 14, l. 3. It is clear that *sam-hri* and *prati-sam-hri* may have the sense of 'replace,' in reference to a quiver, as in Mahā-bh. iii. 772; we have *saṃharasva punar vāṇam*. See also Raghu-v. iii. 64. *Smara*, see p. 209, n. 1.

[2] '(But) few days (have elapsed) to us sent to the feet of his Majesty

---

Verse 136. ŚĀRDŪLA-VIKRĪDITA (a variety of ATIDHRITI). See verses 14, 30, 36, 39, 40, 63, 79, 85, 86, 89, 97, 98, 111.

[a]पालणकम्म समप्पिदं । ता आअन्तुअंदाए अस्सुदपुव्वो अम्हेहिं एसो वुत्तन्तो ।

कञ्चुकी ।

भवतु । न पुनरेवं प्रवर्तितव्यम् ।

उभे ।

[b]अज्ज । कोदूहलं णो । जइ इमिणा जणेण सोदव्वं । कहेदु भअवं । किस्सिमित्तं भट्टिणा वसन्तूसवो पडिसिद्धो ।

सानुमती ।

[c]उस्सवप्पिआ खु मणुस्सा । गरुणा कारणेण होदव्वं ।

कञ्चुकी ।

बहुलीभूतंमेतत्किं न कथ्यते । किमत्रभवत्योः कर्णपथं नायातं शकुन्तलाप्रत्यादेशकौलीनम् ।

---

[a] पालनकर्म समर्पितम् । तदागन्तुकतयाश्रुतपूर्वं आवाभ्यामेष वृत्तान्तः ।　[b] आर्य । कौतूहलं नौ । यद्यनेन जनेन श्रोतव्यम् । कथयतु भवान् । किन्निमित्तं भर्त्रा वसन्तोत्सवः प्रतिषिद्धः ।　[c] उत्सवप्रियाः खलु मनुष्याः । गुरुणा कारणेन भवितव्यम् ।

---

by Mitrā-vasu, the king's brother-in-law.' *Kati*, like *kiyat*, may be either interrogative or indefinite. So *kati padāni gatvā*, Ratn. p. 14, l. 6. After *divasāni*, K. supplies *gatāni*, 'have passed.' This construction of the genitive after *gata*, expressing the lapse of time, is not uncommon. Cf. *ashṭa-pañćāśatam rātryaḥ śayānasya adya me gatāḥ*, Mahā-bh. xiii. 7732; *adya daśamo māsas tātasya uparatasya*, Mudrā-r. p. 80, l. 11. *Māso jātasya*, Pāṇ. ii. 2, 5. *Pāda-mūlam*, lit. 'the root of the feet,' 'the heel.' The phrase *pāda-mūlam preshitaḥ*, expressive of the most humble servitude, occurs elsewhere; see Mudrā-r. p. 16, l. 8; and p. 64, l. 16. *Rāshṭriyeṇa*, see p. 217, n. 2; the king's brother-in-law probably acted as a kind of viceroy.

[1] *Āyantukatayā*, 'since we are but just arrived,' or 'by reason of our being strangers;' see note on *baddha-pallavatayā*, p. 29, l. 1.

[2] 'By us;' see note to *ayaṃ janaḥ*, p. 144, l. 2, and cf. p. 109, l. 8.

[3] *Utsava-priyāḥ*, 'fond of festivals,' see p. 161, n. 3 at the end.

[4] *Bahulī-bhūtam = sakala-viditam*, 'generally known,' 'notorious,' S.

[5] 'Has not the scandal about the repudiation of Śakuntalā reached your ladyships' ears?' *Karṇa-patha*, lit. 'the path or range of the ears,' cf.

उभे ।

[a]सुदं रट्टिणी मुहादो जाव अङ्गुलीअअदंसणं ।

कञ्चुकी ।

तेन ह्यल्पं कथयितव्यम् । यदेव खलु स्वाङ्गुलीयकदर्श-
नादनुस्मृतं देवेन सत्यमूढपूर्वा मया तत्रभवती रहसि
शकुन्तला मोहात्मत्यादिष्टेति । तदा प्रभृत्येव पश्चात्तापमु-
पगतो देवः । तथा हि

रम्यं द्वेष्टि यथा पुरा प्रकृतिभिर्नं प्रत्यहं सेव्यते
    शय्याप्रान्तविवर्तनैर्विगमयत्युन्निद्र एव क्षपाः ।
दाक्षिण्येन ददाति वाचमुचितामन्तःपुरेभ्यो यदा
    गोत्रेषु स्खलितस्तदा भवति च व्रीडाविलक्ष[2]श्चिरम् ॥१३७॥

[a] श्रुतं राष्ट्रियस्य मुखाद्यावदङ्गुलीयकदर्शनम् ।

---

darśana-patha, p. 110, l. 2; and *locana-patham yāntyā,* Ratn. l. 2.
Kaulīna = *loka-vāda,* 'report,' K.; = *parīvāda* or *apavāda,* 'evil report,' C.
It is derived from *kula,* 'a family,' and may signify 'report relating to
family or private matters,' 'family scandal.' It is so used in Vikram.,
Act II, *etat kaulīnaṃ vijṛimbhate.*

[1] This supposes a Sanskrit stem *rāshṭṛi* or *rāshṭṛin* instead of the
more usual *rāshṭriya.*

[2] 'He abhors (everything) pleasurable. He is not, as formerly, respect-
fully-waited-on every day by (his) courtiers [counsellors, ministers]. He
spends his nights, without even closing his eyes, in tossing [rolling] about
on the edge of his couch. When, out of politeness, he addresses the usual-
civil speeches to the women of the palace, then he blunders in (their)
names and becomes for a long while disconcerted [abashed] with shame.'
Ramyam, i.e. *srak-čandana-vanitādi,* 'garlands, sandal, women, &c.,' K.;
in fact, 'the pleasures of sense.' *Prakṛitibhiḥ* = *sačivaiḥ,* C.; = *śishṭaiḥ,* S.
Učitām = *arhām* = *tatkāla-yogyām,* K.; see p. 145, l. 5. *Antaḥpurebhyo,*
see p. 123, n. 1. *Gotreshu* = *nāmasu,* S. and C.; = *nāmadheyeshu,* K.
Skhalitaḥ = *viparyastaḥ,* K., i.e. 'by mistake he utters the name of
Śakuntalā,' K. and S. To indicate a lover's absence of mind or rather

---

Verse 137. SĀRDŪLA-VIKRĪḌITA (a variety of ATIDHṚITI). See verse 136.

H h

सानुमती ।

[a] पिश्रं मे ।

कञ्चुकी ।

अस्मात्प्रभवतो वैमनस्यादुत्सवः प्रत्याख्यातः ।

उभे ।

[b] जुज्जइ ।

नेपथ्ये ।

[c] एदु एदु भवं ।

कञ्चुकी ॥ कर्णं दत्त्वा ॥

अये । इत एवाभिवर्त्तते देवः । खकर्मानुष्ठीयताम् ।

उभे ।

[d] तह । ॥ इति निष्क्रान्ते ॥

॥ ततः प्रविशति पश्चात्तापसदृशवेशो राजा विदूषकः प्रतीहारी च ॥

कञ्चुकी ॥ राजानमवलोक्य ॥

अहो सर्वास्ववस्यासु रमणीयत्वमाकृतिविशेषाणाम् ।
एवमुत्सुकोऽपि प्रियदर्शनो देवः । तथा हि

[a] प्रियं मे ।   [b] युज्यते ।   [c] एतु एतु भवान् ।   [d] तथा ।

---

the one engrossing object of his thoughts, Hindū poets are fond of making him fall into the trap of calling others by the name of his mistress (cf. Kumāra-s. iv. 8; also Raghu-v. xix. 24, *nāma vallabha-janasya te mayā prāpya bhāgyam api tasya kānkshyate iti taṃ gotra-viskhalitam ūćur angaṇāḥ,* 'the women thus addressed him, making mistakes in their names [calling them by the name of his beloved], since I have received the name of thy beloved I desire also her lot;' also Praveśaka to Act II. of Vikram., *yan-nimittam bhartā utkaṇṭhitas tasyāḥ striyā nāmnā bhartrā devī ālapitā;* and another passage in the Vishkambha at the opening of the next Act, *tayā purushottama iti vaktavye purūravasīti niryatā vāṇī).*

[1] 'In consequence of this mental derangement of his Majesty.' *Vaimanasya,* abstract noun from *vi-manas,* 'disordered or changed in mind,' 'absent in mind' (Gram. p. 67, LXXVII). *Prabhavato* (= *rājñaḥ,* Chézy; = *prabhoḥ,* K.), gen. of *prabhavat,* 'ruling,' 'one who rules;' it seems to be used like *prabhu* and *prabhavishṇu* in addressing or speaking of kings (cf. *nāsti prabhavato 'parādhaḥ,* Vikram., Act II. at the end).

प्रत्यादिष्टविशेषमण्डनविधिर्वाममप्रकोष्ठार्पितं
बिभ्रत्काञ्चनमेकमेव वलयं श्वासापरक्ताधरः ।
चिन्ताजागरणप्रताम्रनयनस्तेजोगुणादात्मनः
संस्कारोल्लिखितो महामणिरिव क्षीणोऽपि नालक्ष्यते ॥१३८॥

सानुमती ॥ राजानं दृष्ट्वा ॥

a ठाणेक्खु पच्चादेसविमाणिदाबि इमस्स किदे सउन्दला
किलम्मदि ।

राजा ॥ ध्यानमन्दं परिक्रम्य ॥

प्रथमं सारङ्गाक्ष्या प्रियया प्रतिबोध्यमानमपि सुप्तम् ।
अनुशयदुःखायेदं हतहृदयं सम्प्रति विबुद्धम् ॥१३९॥

a स्याने खलु प्रत्यादेशविमानिताप्यस्य कृते शकुन्तला क्राम्यति ।

---

[1] 'Scorning distinguished [superior] forms of decoration; wearing but a single golden bracelet fastened [placed] on the left fore-arm; with lips bloodless from sighing; with eyes very red from sleeplessness (caused) by thought (upon S'akuntalā); through the excellence of his own (inherent) lustre, though he be attenuated he is not observed (to be so), like a magnificent gem (whose surface is) ground away by the polishing-stone.' *Pratyādishṭa-viśesha-maṇḍana-vidhiḥ = nirākṛita-viśishṭālankāra-vidhānaḥ*, S'. (cf. Megha-d. ver. 92, and *prasādhana-vidheḥ prasādhana-viśeshaḥ*, Vikram., Act II). *Prakoshṭha* (see p. 53, n. 1)=*kūrpara-maṇi-bandhana-madhyabhāga*, K. (cf. p. 114, n. 2). *Bibhrat=dadhat;* in the pres. part. Par. of verbs of cl. 3, the nom. is identical with the stem (Gram. 141.*a*). *Apa-rakta=nī-rakta, rakta-hīna*, 'bloodless,' 'pale.' The effect of long and deep sighs would be to draw the blood away from the lips (cf. Megha-d. verses 83, 89). *Cintā-jāgaraṇa*, i. e. *S'akuntalā-vishayiṇyā cintayā*, S'. *Guṇāt=utkarshāt*, K. *Sanskāra=śāṇa*, K.;=*prastara-viśesha;* (*sanskāra* has the sense 'polishing;' cf. Hitop. l. 15); *śāṇollikhitaḥ=śāṇodghṛishṭaḥ*, K. *Nālakshyate* (i. e. *na āl*c), see p. 70, n. 3 at the end.

[2] 'Previously this paralysed [blighted] heart slumbered even whilst-it-was-being-roused-from-sleep by my fawn-eyed beloved. Now it is broad-

---

Verse 138. S'ĀRDŪLA-VIKRĪḌITA (a variety of ATIDHṚITI). See verses 14, &c., 137.
Verse 139. ĀRYĀ or GĀTHĀ. See verse 2.

$$\cup \cup - \mid - - \mid - - \parallel \cup \cup - \mid \cup \cup - \mid \cup - \cup \mid \cup \cup - \mid -$$
$$\cup \cup \cup \cup \mid - - \mid - - \parallel \cup \cup \cup \cup \mid - - \mid \cup \mid \cup \cup - \mid -$$

सानुमती ।

[a] एं ईदिसाणि तवस्सिणीए भाग्गहेआणि ।

विदूषक: ॥ अपवार्ये ॥

[b] लच्छिदो एसो भूओवि सउन्दलावाहिणा । ण आणे ।
कहं चिकिच्छिदव्वो भविस्सदित्ति ।

कञ्चुकी ॥ उपगम्य ॥

जयतु जयतु देव: । महाराज । प्रत्यवेक्षिता: प्रमदवन-
भूमय: । यथाकाममध्यास्तां विनोदस्थानानि महाराज: ।

राजा ।

वेत्रवति । मद्वचनादमात्यमार्यपिशुनं ब्रूहि । चिरप्रबोधान्न
सम्भावितमस्माभिरद्य धर्मासनमध्यासितुम् । यत्प्रत्यवेक्षितं
पौरकार्यमार्येण । तत्पत्त्रमारोप्य दीयतामिति ।

प्रतीहारी ।

[c] जं देवो आणवेदि । ॥ इति निष्क्रान्ता ॥

राजा ।

वातायन । त्वमपि स्वं नियोगमशून्यं कुरु ।

कञ्चुकी ।

यदाज्ञापयति देव: । ॥ इति निष्क्रान्त: ॥

[a] नन्वीदृशानि तपस्विन्या भागधेयानि ।   [b] लङ्घित एप भूयोऽपि शकुन्तला-
व्याधिना । न जाने । कथं चिकित्सितव्यो भविष्यतीति ।   [c] यदेव आज्ञापयति ।

---

awake to the anguish of remorse.' *Anuśaya-duḥkhāya*=*paścāttāpa-khe-dāya.* *Samprati,* i. e. *tad-virahe,* S. *Vibuddham*=*jāgritam,* S.

[1] 'He is again attacked [seized, afflicted] by a S'akuntalā-fever,' i. e. he is again love-sick for S'akuntalā. *Langhita,* see p. 97, n. 1.

[2] 'Having committed that to writing [to a letter], let it be sent to me;' or, 'having written that in a letter, let it be given (to some messenger).' *Dīyatām*=*prahīyatām,* S.

[3] *Sva-niyogam antaḥpurāvekṣā-rūpam,* 'thy stated business consisting of superintendence of the female apartments,' S. *Vātāyana,* this is the name of the Kañćukin, see p. 186, n. 1.

विदूषकः ।

"किदं भवदा णिम्मच्छिअं । सम्पदं सिसिरातवच्छेत्र-
रमणीए इमस्सिं पमदवणुद्देसे अत्ताणं रमइस्ससि ।

राजा ।

वयस्य । रन्ध्रोपनिपातिनोऽनर्था इति यदुच्यते । तद्व्य-
भिचारि वचः । कुतः ।

मुनिसुतामयणयस्मृतिरोधिना
मम च मुक्तमिदं तमसा मनः ।
मनसिजेन सखे प्रहरिष्यता
धनुषि चूतशरश्च निवेशितः ॥ १४० ॥

^a कृतं भवता निर्मक्षिकम् । साम्प्रतं शिशिरातपच्छेदरमणीयेऽस्मिन्प्रमदवनोद्देश
आत्मानं रमयिष्यसि ।

---

[1] *Nirmakshikam*, see p. 76, l. 2, n. 1. *Makshikāyā apy abhāvān nirja-
nam*, S'.

[2] 'Misfortunes rush in through the (first) hole (they can find),' i. e. mis-
fortunes are continually on the watch for an opening or vulnerable point
by which to assail us; they seize the first opportunity that offers for
attacking us; they quickly succeed each other before we have time to
stand on our guard. This must have been a common proverb, something
like our 'Misfortunes never come alone.' The king observes that 'this
which is a saying commonly current among men is quite consistent and
true [*a-vyabhićāri*] in his own case,' and he then proceeds to explain why
[*kutas*, see p. 55, n. 2] in the subsequent verse. *Randhra=ćhidra*, K.
Upanipātino = samāpatanti, K. *Anarthāḥ = āpadaḥ*, K. *Yad ućyate*,
i. e. *lokena*, K.; *avyabhićāri=aviparyāsi* (i. e. *nānyathā bhavati*), K.;
=avaśyam-bhāvi or *yathārtham*, S'. Dr. Boehtlingk translates, 'The un-
fortunate fall into a hole [grave],' which seems supportable by a reading
randhroparipātino 'narthā, noticed by K., although not adopted by him.
Cf. Bhartṛi-h. ii. 86, *prāyo gaćchati yatra bhāgya-rahitas tatraiva yānty
āpadaḥ*.

[3] 'No sooner is this my soul freed from the darkness that obstructed
the remembrance of my love for the sage's daughter, than a mango-
blossom-shaft, O my friend, is fixed on (his) bow by the heart-born (god)

विदूषकः ।

a चिट्ठ दाव । जाव इमिणा दण्डकट्ठेण कन्दप्पवाणं णासइस्सामि । ॥ इति दण्डकाष्ठमुद्यम्य चूताङ्कुरं पातयितुमिच्छति ॥

राजा ॥ सस्मितम् ॥

भवतु । दृष्टं ब्रह्मवर्चसम् । सखे । क्रोपविष्टः प्रियायाः किञ्चिदनुकारिणीषु लतासु दृष्टिं विलोभयामि ।

विदूषकः ।

b एं आसण्णपरिआरिआ चदुरिआ भवदा सन्दिट्ठा । माहवीमण्डवे इमं वेलं अदिवाहिस्सं । तहिं मे चित्तफलअगदं सहत्थलिहिदं तत्तहोदीए सउन्दलाए पडिकिदिं आणेहित्ति ।

a तिष्ठ तावत् । यावदनेन दण्डकाष्ठेन कन्दर्पबाणं नाशयिष्यामि ।　　b नन्वासन्नपरिचारिका चतुरिका भवता सन्दिष्टा । माधवीमण्डप इमां वेलामतिवाहयिष्यामि । तस्मिन्मे चित्रफलकगतां स्वहस्तलिखितां तत्रभवत्याः शकुन्तलायाः प्रतिकृतिमानयेति ।

---

now-about-to-shoot-at-me.' The occurrence of *ća* in each clause denotes immediate connexion or succession, expressed in English by 'no sooner— than,' 'so soon as,' 'scarcely—when,' &c. (cf. verse 131 and Kumāra-s. iii. 58). *Manasi-ja,* 'born in the mind or heart,' a name of Kāma-deva (see p. 100, n. 1). *Praharishyat,* 'about to strike,' participle of the 2nd future. *Ćūta-sara,* see p. 99, n. 1 in the middle. The verse which follows this in the Beng. and Mackenzie MSS. is probably spurious.

[1] I have adopted *vāṇam* from the oldest Beng. MSS. S'. and C'. have *vāṇān.* The Deva-n. *vvāhim* (=*vyādhim*). K. reads *vvāham* (=*vyādham*), 'a hunter,' 'shooter.' May not *vyādhi,* like *vyādha,* signify 'hunting,' 'shooting,' 'sport?' in which case the Deva-n. reading might be retained.

[2] 'The mighty power of a Brāhman is seen (by me).' This is said ironically in reference to the Vidūshaka's ridiculous attempt to destroy the arrows of Kāma-deva.

[3] Lit. 'a near attendant,' i. e. an attendant about one's person.

[4] *Ati-vah,* in causal, has the sense 'to pass time.' Cf. Raghu-v. xix. 47, ix. 70.

[5] *Ćitra-phalaka,* 'a picture-tablet,' 'a tablet for painting.' The same expression occurs in Ratn. p. 21, l. 8, and p. 22, l. 1, and Vikram., Act II. As to *gatam,* here meaning 'committed to,' see p. 206, n. 4.

राजा ।

ईदृशं हृदयविनोदस्थानम् । तत्तमेव मार्गमादेशय ।

विदूषकः ।

[a] इदो इदो भवं ।   ॥ उभौ परिक्रामतः । सानुमत्यनुगच्छति ॥

विदूषकः ।

[b] एसो मणिसिलापट्टृअसणाहो माहवीमण्डवो उवहार-
रमणिज्जदाए णिस्संसअं साअदेण विअ णो पडिच्छदि ।
ता पविसिअ णिसीददु भवं ।

॥ उभौ प्रवेशं कृत्वोपविष्टौ ॥

सानुमती ।

[c] लदासंस्सिदा देक्खिस्सं दाव सहीए पडिकिदिं । तदो से
भत्तुणो बहुमुहं अणुराअं णिवेदइस्सं ।   ॥ इति तथा कृत्वा स्थिता ॥

राजा ।

सखे । सर्वमिदानीं स्मरामि शकुन्तलायाः प्रथमवृत्तान्तम् ।
कथितवानसि भवते । सं भवान्प्रत्यादेशवेलायां मत्समी-
पमुपगतो नासीत् । पूर्वमपि न तया कदाचित्सङ्कीर्तितं
तच्चभवत्या नाम । कच्चिदहमिव विस्मृतवानसि त्वम् ।

[a] इत इतो भवान् ।   [b] एष मणिशिलापट्टकसनाथो माधवीमण्डप उपहाररमणीय-
तया निःसंशयं स्वागतेनेव नौ प्रतीच्छति । तत्प्रविश्य निषीदतु भवान् ।   [c] लतासंश्रिता
द्रक्ष्यामि तावत्सख्याः प्रतिकृतिम् । ततोऽस्या भर्तुर्बहुमुखमनुरागं निवेदयिष्यामि ।

---

[1] *Maṇi-śilūpaṭṭaka-sanātha*, 'furnished with a marble seat,' see p. 26,
n. 3.

[2] 'With the agreeableness of its flowery offerings,' 'with its charming
flowery gifts.' *Upahāra*, or according to the commentators *upaćāra* =
kusumādi-vistāra, S.   Flowers were used as complimentary presents or
offerings, especially to the god of love.

[3] *Bahu-mukha* (lit. 'having many faces'), 'manifold,' 'excessive.' *Bahu-
madam* (=*bahu-matam*) is another reading.

[4] So read all the MSS. except my own, which omits *sa*.   *Sa* may be used
to emphasize other pronouns, and *sa bhaćān* therefore = *ille tu*, i. e. 'your
honour, that same person to whom alone I mentioned the circumstances.'

विदूषकः ।

^a ण विस्सुमरामि । किन्तु सव्वं कहिश्र अवसाणे उण तुए परिहासविश्रप्पो एसो ण भूदत्थोत्ति आचक्खिदं । मए वि मिप्पिरंडवुज्जिणा तह एव्व गहीदं । अहवा भविदव्वदा बलवदी ।

सानुमती ।

^b एवं ण्वेदं ।

राजा ॥ ध्यात्वा ॥

सखे । न्यायस्व माम् ।

विदूषकः ।

^c भो । किं एदं । अणुबबखंखु ईदिसं तुइ । कदाचि सप्पुरिसा सोश्रपत्तप्पाणो ण होन्ति । एं पव्वादे वि णिक्कम्पा गिरीश्रो ।

राजा ।

वयस्य । निराकरणविक्लवायाः प्रियायाः समवंस्थाम-नुस्मृत्य बलवदशरणोऽस्मि । सा हि

---

^a न विस्मरामि । किन्तु सर्वं कथयित्वावसाने पुनस्त्वया परिहासविजल्प एष न भूतार्थ इत्याचक्षितम् । मयापि मृत्पिरंडबुद्धिना तथैव गृहीतम् । अथवा भवितव्यता बलवती ।   ^b एवं न्वेतत् ।   ^c भोः । किमेतत् । अनुपपन्नं खल्वीदृशं त्वयि । कदाचित्सादृशा शोकपात्रात्मानो न भवन्ति । ननु प्रवातेऽपि निष्कम्पा गिरयः ।

---

¹ *Parihāsa-vijalpa*, see p. 94, l. 5.   As to *bhūtārtha*, see p. 5, n. 2.

² 'Whose brains [intellect] are like a lump of clay,' 'whose understanding is dense as a clod of earth.'   (Cf. the expressions 'clod-pated,' 'clod-poll,' 'blockhead,' &c.)   Some MSS. have *manda-buddhinā*.   As to *bhavitavya-tā balavatī*, see p. 206, n. 2.

³ 'Have not hearts that give place to sorrow,' 'do not give themselves up to uncontrolled grief.'   *Pātra*, 'a receptacle,' see p. 203, n. 1 at the end.   I have followed Kāṭavema's reading.   That of the other Deva-n. MSS., *sva-vattaevā*, is hardly intelligible.

⁴ *Sam-avasthā*, with the sense of *avasthā*, 'state,' 'condition,' occurs not unfrequently in the plays.   Cf. Mālavik. p. 66, l. 1; p. 68, l. 15.   See also p. 164, l. 6 of this play, where it has the sense of *samāvasthā*.

इतः प्रत्यादेशात्स्वजनमनुगन्तुं व्यवसिता
मुहुस्तिष्ठेत्युच्चैर्वदति गुरुशिष्ये गुरुसमे ।
पुनर्दृष्टिं वाष्पप्रकरकलुषामर्पितवती
मयि क्रूरे यत्तत्सविषमिव शल्यं दहति माम् ॥१४१॥

सानुमती ।

[a] अम्हहे । ईदिसी सकज्जपरदा । इमस्स सन्दावेण अहं रमामि ।

विटूपकः ।

[b] भो । अत्थि मे तक्को । केणवि तब्भहोदी आआसचारिणा णीदेत्ति ।

राजा ।

कः पतिदेवतामन्यः परिमार्ष्टुमुत्सहेत । मेनका किल

---

[a] अहो । ईदृशी स्वकार्यपरता । अस्य सन्तापेनाहं रमे ।　　[b] भोः । अस्ति मे तर्कः । केनापि तत्रभवत्याकाशचारिणा नीतेति ।

---

[1] '(The thought) that after her repudiation from hence, (when) she attempted to follow her attendants, the Guru's pupil, (who claimed obedience) like-the-Guru-himself, repeatedly saying to her in a loud voice, "Stay," she cast on me inexorable [cruel, hard-hearted] a second look bedimmed with gushing tears; that (it is which) torments me like an envenomed shaft.' *Itaḥ,* i.e. *mattaḥ,* 'by me,' S. *Vyavasitā=yatnaṃ kritavatī,* S. *Muhus tishṭha,* &c., see p. 213, l. 1. *Guru-same,* i.e. *alaṅghyādeśatayā.*

[2] 'Alas! such is the force of absorption in one's own object that I am actually pleased by his distress (instead of compassionating it).' *Paratā* means here 'the being addicted to.' Some Beng. MSS. have *a-kajja-paradā.* *Sva-kārya,* i.e. 'relating to Śakuntalā,' S. Cf. p. 207, l. 7.

[3] 'Who else could presume [would have the power] to-lay-a-finger-on [touch, bear off] the idol of (her) husband?' *Kaḥ anya,* cf. p. 208, ll. 8, 9. *Pati-devatā,* 'the goddess of her husband,' or as we should say, 'a wife idolized by her husband.' This is probably the sense of this expression, which is found in all the Deva-n. MSS. The Beng. have *pati-vratām,* 'a wife devoted to her husband.' *Pari-mārshṭum* (so read all the Deva-n.) must come from *pari-mṛij,* 'to wipe off,' 'remove.' It may be used like

---

Verse 141. ŚIKHARIṆĪ (a variety of ATYASHṬI). See verses 9, 24, 44, 62, 112.

सख्यास्ते जन्मप्रतिष्ठेति श्रुतवानस्मि । तत्सहचारिणीभिः
सखी ते हतेति मे हृदयमाशङ्कते ।

अनुमती ।

[a] सम्मोहो क्खु विम्हअणिज्जो ण पडिबोहो ।

विदूषकः ।

[b] जइ एव्वं । अत्थिक्खु समाश्रमो कालेण तब्भोदीए ।

राजा ।

कथमिव ।

विदूषकः ।

[c] णक्खु मादापिदरा भत्तुविओअदुक्खिदं दुहिदरं देक्खिदुं
पारेन्ति ।

राजा ।

वयस्य ।

स्वप्नो नु माया नु मतिभ्रमो नु
क्लिष्टं नु तावत्फलमेव पुण्यम् ।

<hr>

[a] सम्मोहः खलु विस्मयनीयो न प्रतिबोधः ।   [b] यद्येवम् । अस्ति खलु समागमः
कालेन तत्रभवत्या ।   [c] न खलु मातापितरौ भर्तृविियोगदुःखितां दुहितरं द्रष्टुं पारयतः ।

pari-mṛiś, 'to lay hold of;' cf. p. 203, n. 1.   One MS. (I. O. 1060) has
parā-marshṭum (from parā-mṛiś), 'to seize,' 'lay violent hands on,' and this
reading is adopted by the St. Petersburg dictionary and by Dr. Burkhard.

[1] Janma-pratishṭhā = janma-sthānam, 'place of birth;' = mātā,
'mother,' Chézy. Janma-pratishṭhā=jananī, S'. Dushyanta speaks of
S'akuntalā to the Vidūshaka as, 'thy friend.' So the Yaksha speaks of
his wife to the Cloud, in Megha-d. 87, 93.

[2] 'Truly the state-of-mental-delusion [delirium, hallucination] is to be
wondered at, not the recovery-from-it [the awakening from it].' S'. ex-
plains sammoha by 'forgetfulness,' and pratibodha by 'recollection.'

[3] Pārayataḥ, 'are able,' from the causal of root pṛi, meaning properly
'to carry over,' 'conduct,' 'achieve,' &c.; cf. p. 146, l. 2.   In Prākṛit
and more modern Sanskrit (as also in Bengālī) it has, as here, the sense
'to be able.'   It may come from a nominal verb from pāra, 'the other
side.' (Cf. πέρα, πέρας, περάω, περαίνω.)

असन्निवृत्त्यै तदतीतमेव
मनोरथानामततटप्रपातः ॥१४२॥

विदूषकः ।

[1]मा एव्वं । यं अङ्गुलीअअं एव्व णिदंसणं । अवस्सम्भा-
विणो अचिन्तणिज्जो समाअमो होदि त्ति[2] ।

राजा ॥ अङ्गुलीयकं विलोक्य ॥

अये । इदं तावदसुलभस्थानभ्रंशि शोचनीयम् ।

[a] नैवम् । नन्वङ्गुलीयकमेव निदर्शनम् । अवश्यम्भाविनोऽचिन्तनीयः समागमो भवतीति ।

---

[1] 'Was it a dream? or an illusion-of-magic? or a mental-delusion? or (the result of my) good-works so far indeed rewarded (and then) marred? It has certainly passed away, never to return; (and so has become) the steep precipice of my heart's-fondest-hopes.' Such is the reading of all the Deva-n. MSS., and doubtless the true one. In the third and fourth Pādas I have adopted *eva* and *prapātaḥ* (in place of *ete* and *prapātāḥ*) from the Mackenzie, the former supported by K. *Māyā*, i.e. *indra-jālādi-kriyā*, S. *Bhrama*, one so affected imagines that to be present which does not really exist (*asad api sākshāt-karoti*, S. and C.) *Puṇyam*, i.e. *svakīyaṃ sukṛitam*, K. *Tāvat-phalam eva*, i.e. *darśana-phalam eva*, K.; *darśana-mātra-phalam*, C., 'fruitful so far only as the sight of S'akuntalā,' K. *Klishṭam* (cf. p. 201, l. 13); the best explanation of this idea will be found in p. 80, l. 7, with n. 2, and in n. 2 below. *Asannivrittyai*, cf. Raghu-v. viii. 48, *para-lokam asannivrittaye gatāsi*, 'thou art gone to the other world never to return.' S'. thus explains the second half of the verse, 'As a man after ascending the peak of a mountain falls headlong, so my hopes after ascending to the sight of S'akuntalā are precipitated.' As to *taṭa*, see p. 175, n. 1. Amara-k. (ii. 3, 4) gives *ataṭa* as a synonym of *prapāta* and *bhṛigu*, each of these words signifying 'a precipice,' but there is no reason why *ataṭa* should not be used as an epithet of *prapāta*, to denote a very precipitous declivity. The Beng. MSS. read *klṛiptam nu tāvat phalam eva puṇyaiḥ, asannivrittau tad [asannivrittyai tad] atīva manye manorathānām ataṭa-prapātam*.

[2] 'Is not the very ring a proof that there may be an unexpected meeting with that which must necessarily come?' *Nanu* often = Latin *nonne*.

Verse 142. UPAJĀTI or ĀKHYĀNAKĪ (a variety of TRISHṬUBH). See verses 41, 107, 121, 126.

तव सुचरितमङ्गुलीय नूनं
प्रतनु ममेव विभाव्यते फलेन ।
अरुणनखमनोरमासु तस्या-
स्च्युतमसि लब्धपदं यदङ्गुलीषु ॥ १४३ ॥

सानुमती ।

[a] जइ अस्सहत्थगदं भवे । सच्चं एव्व सोअणिज्जं भवे ।

विदूषकः ।

[b] भो । इअं णाम मुद्दा केण उद्देसेण तब्भोदीए हत्थसंसग्गं पाविदा ।

सानुमती ।

[c] ममवि कोदूहलेण आआरिदो एसो ।

राजा ।

श्रूयताम् । तदा स्वनगराय प्रस्थितं मां प्रिया सवाष्पमाह । कियच्चिरेणार्यपुत्रः प्रतिपत्तिं दास्यतीति ।

विदूषकः ।

[d] तदो तदो ।

[a] यद्यन्यहस्तगतं भवेत् । सत्यमेव शोचनीयं भवेत् ।   [b] भोः । इयं नाम मुद्रा केनोद्देशेन तत्रभवत्या हस्तसंसर्गं प्रापिता ।   [c] ममापि कौतूहलेनाकारित एषः ।   [d] ततस्ततः ।

---

[1] 'Verily, O ring, the-merit-of-thy-good-works like mine is judged [proved] to be insignificant [slender] by the reward [result]; since after-gaining-a-station on the charming-rosy-nailed fingers of that-lady thou hast fallen (from it).' The doctrine of laying up a store of merit by good deeds performed in the present and former births is an essential part of the Hindū creed (see last verse, and cf. p. 185, n. 3). *Aruṇa-nakha*, see p. 125, n. 2 at the end. *Aruṇa* may imply 'ruddy as the dawn,' see p. 142, n. 3.

[2] 'By my curiosity also he (would be) incited (to tell the reason).' *Kautūhala* = *śravaṇotkaṇṭhā*, 'desire of hearing,' S'. *Ākārita* = *āhata*, *prerita*, K. Cf. *taṃ vara-dānāya ākārayāmāsa*, Rāmāy. ii. 13, 2. S'. reads *vādita*, 'made to speak,' for *ākārita*. The Beng. MSS. have *vyāpārita*.

[3] *Pratipatti*, cf. p. 172, l. 4, with note thereon.

Verse 143. PUSHPITĀGRĀ. See verses 32, 37.

राजा ।

पश्चादिमां मुद्रां तदङ्गुलौ निवेशयता मया प्रत्यभिहिता ।
एकैकमच्च दिवसे दिवसे मदीयं
नामाक्षरं गणय गच्छसि यावदन्तम् ।
तावन्मिये मद्वरोधगृहप्रवेशं
नेता जनस्तव समीपमुपैष्यतीति ॥ १४४ ॥

तच्च दारुणात्मना मया मोहान्नानुष्ठितम् ।

सानुमती ।

[a] रमणीओक्खु अवही विहिणा विसंवादिंदो ।

विदूपकः ।

[b] कहं धीवलकप्पिअस्स लोहिअमच्छस्स उदलब्भन्तले
आसि ।

---

[a] रमणीयः खल्ववधिर्विधिना विसंवादितः ।   [b] कथं धीवरकल्पितस्य रोहित-
मत्स्योदराभ्यन्तर आसीत् ।

---

[1] 'Count [spell] hereon [i. e. on this ring] one by one each day the
letters of my name until thou reachest the end. So soon, O loved one,
(as thou hast spelt the whole name) a messenger will come into thy
presence who-will-conduct thee to the entrance of my private-apartments.'
Nāmāksharam, cf. p. 53, l. 6. *Gacchasi*, so reads the Taylor MS. as well
as my own, supported by the Calcutta ed. ; the others, *gacchati*. *Netā*,
the noun of agency has sometimes the sense of a future participle, and
may govern the case of the verb. So *vaktā vākyam*, 'one who is about
to speak a speech,' Draupadī-h. 32. Indeed the nom. masc. of this form
of noun is identical with the 3rd pers. of the 1st future.

[2] 'Verily (this) charming period (of expectation) was by Destiny made
(to pass away) without-the-appointment-being-kept,' or 'Destiny caused
that the delightful appointment-of-a-period (for the reunion of these lovers)
should fail of being kept.' *Vi-sam-vad* is 'to fail in keeping a promise
or agreement.' Cf. *phale visamvadati*, Vikram., Act II.

[3] The Vidūshaka designedly uses the dialect of the fisherman; see
p. 220, l. 4 sq.; p. 217, n. 2.

Verse 114. VASANTA-TILAKĀ (a variety of ŚAKVARĪ). See verses 8, 27, 31, 43, 46,
64, 74, 80, 82, 83, 91, 93, 94, 95, 100, 104, 105, 108, 123, 124.

राजा ।

शचीतीर्थे वन्दमानायाः सख्यास्ते हस्तात्रङ्घास्त्रोतसि
परिभ्रष्टम् ।

विदूषकः ।

[a] जुज्जइ ।

सानुमती ।

[b] अदो एव्व तवस्सिणीए सउन्दलाए अधम्मभीरुणो
इमस्स राएसिणो परिणए सन्देहो आसि । अहवा ।
ईदिसो अणुराओ अहिणाणं अवेक्खदि । कहं विअ एदं ।

राजा ।

उपालभ्ये तावदिदमङ्गुलीयकम् ।

विदूषकः ॥ आत्मगतम् ॥

[c] गहीदो येण पन्था उम्मत्तआणं ।

राजा ।

कथं नु तं बन्धुरकोमलाङ्गुलिं
करं विहायासि निमग्नमम्भसि ।
अथवा । अचेतनं नाम गुणं न लक्ष्ये-
न्मयैव कस्मादवधीरिता प्रिया ॥१४५॥

[a] युज्यते ।   [b] अत एव तपस्विन्याः शकुन्तलाया अधर्मभीरोरस्य राजर्षेः परिणये
सन्देह आसीत् । अथवा । ईदृशोऽनुरागोऽभिज्ञानमपेक्षते । कथमिवैतत् ।   [c] गृही-
तोऽनेन पन्था उन्मत्तानाम् ।

---

[1] Compare p. 205, ll. 12, 13, n. 2.

[2] 'How (couldest) thou (allow thyself) to be immersed in the water,
having abandoned that hand with (its) slender delicate fingers? But
(where is the wonder? for) an inanimate-object may well not distinguish
excellence. How (was it that) even by me (my) beloved was rejected?'
Bandhura=*unnatānata*, 'undulating;'=*ramya*, 'beautiful,' C. *Athavā*,
see p. 30, n. 3.

Verse 145. VANŚA-STHAVILA (a variety of JAGATI). See verses 18, 22, 23, 67, 81,
114, 117, 119.

विदूषकः ॥ आत्मगतम् ॥

[a] कहं बुभुक्खाए खादिदव्वोम्हिं[1] ।

राजा ।

अकारणपरित्यक्ते । अनुशयतप्रहृदयस्तावदनुकम्प्यतामयं
जनः पुनर्दर्शनेन ।

॥ प्रविश्य पटाक्षेपेण चित्रफलकहस्ता ॥

चतुरिका ।

[b] इअं चित्तगदा भट्टिणी । ॥ इति चित्रफलकं दर्शयति ॥

विदूषकः ।

[c] साहु वअस्स । महुरावत्थाणदंसणिज्जो भावाणुप्पवेसो ।
खलदि विअ मे दिट्ठी णिसुस्सअप्पंदेसेसु ।

सानुमती ।

[d] अम्मो एसा राएसिणो णिउणदा । जाणे । सही अग्गदो
मे वट्टदित्ति ।

राजा ।

यद्यत्साधु न चिचे स्यात्क्रियते तत्तदन्यथा ।
तथापि तस्या लावएयं रेखया किञ्चिदन्वितं ॥१४६॥

[a] कथं बुभुक्षया खादितव्योऽस्मि ।   [b] इयं चित्रगता भर्त्री ।   [c] साधु वयस्य ।
मधुरावस्थानदर्शनीयो भावानुप्रवेशः । खलतीव मे दृष्टिर्निम्नोन्नतप्रदेशेषु ।   [d] अहो
एषा राज्ञेर्निपुणता । जाने । सख्यग्रतो मे वर्तैत इति ।

---

[1] 'Why am I to be devoured by hunger (while he is apostrophizing his
ring)?' A very characteristic remark, see p. 59, n. 1 in the middle.

[2] 'The presence of the prevailing sentiment (love, *rati*) is delightful by
its sweet abiding in every part. My sight stumbles as it were amidst
the depressions and prominences;' i. e. the relief or appearance of pro-
jection and depression in the picture is so well managed that my eye is
deceived, and seems to follow the inequalities of surface. For *anu-praveśa*,
cf. Raghu-v. iii. 22; and for *avasthāna*, Sāhit.-d. p. 75, l. 2. It may
mean 'by the sweet position of the figures,' but *bhāva* means here *rati*.

[3] 'Whatever is not well (executed) in the picture [whatever falls short

Verse 146. ŚLOKA or ANUSHTUBH. See verses 5, 6, 11, 12, 26, 47, 50, 51, 53, 73,
76, 84, 87, 125, 127, 130.

सानुमती ।

[a] सरिसं एव्वं पच्छादावगरुणो सिणेहस्स अणवलेबस्स अ ।

विदूषकः ।

[b] भो । दाणिं तिण्णि तत्तहोदीओ दीसन्ति । सव्वाओ च्च दंसणीआओ । कदमा एत्थ तत्तहोदी सउन्दला ।

सानुमती ।

[c] अणभिण्णो क्खु ईदिसस्स रूवस्स मोहदिट्ठी अअं जणो ।

राजा ।

त्वं तावत्कतमां तर्कयसि ।

विदूषकः ।

[d] तक्केमि । जा एसा सिढिलकेसबन्धणुब्बन्तकुसुमेण केसन्तेण उब्भिन्नसेअविन्दुणा वअणेण विसेसदो ओसरिआहिं बाहाहिं अवसेअसिणिद्धतरुणपल्लवस्स चूअपाअवस्स पासे इसिपरिस्सन्ता विअ आलिहिदा । एसा सउन्दला । इदराओ सहीओत्ति ।

[a] सदृशमेवं पश्चात्तापगुरोः स्नेहस्यानवलेपस्य च ।   [b] भोः । इदानीं तिस्रस्तत्रभवत्यो दृश्यन्ते । सर्वाश्च दर्शनीयाः । कतमात्र तत्रभवती शकुन्तला ।   [c] अनभिज्ञः खल्वीदृशस्य रूपस्य मोघदृष्टिरियं जनः ।   [d] तर्कयामि । यैषा शिथिलकेशबन्धनोद्भ्रान्तकुसुमेन केशान्तेनोद्भिन्नस्वेदविन्दुना वदनेन विशेषतोऽपसृताभ्यां बाहुभ्यामवसेकस्निग्धतरुणपल्लवस्य चूतपादपस्य पार्श्वे ईषत्परिश्रान्तेवालिखिता । एषा शकुन्तला । इतरे सख्याविति ।

of perfect beauty], all that is wrongly (portrayed). Nevertheless her loveliness is in some measure possessed by the drawing;' i.e. the artist has to some extent made a likeness, though very inferior to the original. *Rekhā=lekhana*, 'a sketch,' 'delineation,' K. The Beng. have *lekhayā*.

[1] *Mogha-drishṭi*, cf. p. 76, l. 10, n. 3; Bhaṭṭi-k. v. 19.

[2] 'I imagine that she who is delineated as if a little fatigued at the side of the mango-tree, the tender shoots of which are glistening after her watering (of them), with arms extended in a peculiar manner, with a face having drops of perspiration breaking out (upon it), with locks of hair the flowers of which have escaped through the slackened hair-band—this (I imagine) is Śakuntalā, the other two (are her) female friends.' *Uttama,*

राजा ।

निपुणो भवान् । अस्त्यत्र मे भावचिह्नम् ।
स्विन्नाङ्गुलिविनिवेशो रेखाप्रान्तेषु दृश्यते मलिनः ।
अश्रु च कपोलपतितं दृश्यमिदं वर्णिकोच्छ्वासात् ॥१४७॥
चतुरिके । अर्धलिखितमेतद्विनोदस्थानम् । तस्मादागच्छ ।
वर्तिकां तावदानय ।

चतुरिका ।

[a] अज्जमाठव्व । अवलम्ब चित्तफलञ्झं । जाव आअच्छामि ।

राजा ।

अहमेवैतदवलम्बे । ॥ इति यथोक्तं करोति ॥

॥ निष्क्रान्ता चेटी ॥

[a] आर्यमाठव्य । अवलम्बस्व चित्रफलकम् । यावदागच्छामि ।

---

lit. 'vomited up,' here 'dropped off,' 'fallen down.' *Udbhinna-sveda-vindunā*, cf. p. 70, n. 3; hence in line 9 of that page, *sveda-lesair abhinnam* is a better reading than *klesa-lesair*. *Viseshato 'pasritābhyām*, it appears from a subsequent passage that she is represented in the act of warding off the bee mentioned at p. 32, l. 4. *Itare*, nom. dual feminine.

[1] 'Here is a sign of my passion; the soiled impression of (my) perspiring fingers is observed on the edges of the picture, and a tear here [this tear] fallen from (my) cheek is perceptible from the coming out of the colour.' However offensive to our notions of good taste, it is certain that in Hindū erotic poetry, perspiration is considered to be one of the signs of passionate love. So in the Vikram., *anguli-svedena me lupyante aksharāni;* cf. also Raghu-v. vii. 19, *svinnāngulih samvavrite kumārī,* &c. *Varṇikā* (=*varṇa*) is the reading of K., supported by most of the Beng. MSS., which have *varṇakā*. The other Deva-n. have *vartikā*, which may, like *varti*, mean 'collyrium,' 'pigment.' *Varṇikocchvāsāt* means 'from the brightness (i. e. coming out) of the pigment;' Prema-éandra explains it by *rangasya utphullatvāt*. *Kapola-patita*, 'fallen from my cheek,' or perhaps 'fallen on the cheek' (of the portrait).

[a] Lit. 'pleasure-ground,' i. e. landscape; *lieu de la scène*, Chézy.

Verse 147. ĀRYĀ or GĀTHĀ. See verse 2.

$$- - \ | \ \cup \cup \cup \cup \ | \ - \underline{-} - \ \| \ - - \ | \ - - | \ \cup - \cup \ | \ - \cup \cup \ | \ -$$
$$- \cup \cup \ | \ \cup - \cup \ | \ \cup \cup - \ \| \ - \cup \cup \ | \ - - \ | \ \cup \ | \ - - \ | \ -$$

K k

राजा ।

अहं हि

साक्षात्प्रियामुपगतामपहाय पूर्वं
चिच्चार्पितां मुहुरिमां बहुमन्यमानः ।
स्रोतोवहां पथि निकामजलामतीत्य
जातः सखे प्रणयवान्मृगतृष्णिकायाम् ॥ १४८ ॥[1]

विदूषकः ॥ आत्मगतम् ॥

[a] एसो अत्तभवं एदिं अदिक्कमिअ मिअतिण्हिआए सङ्कन्तो । ॥ प्रकाशम् ॥ [b] भो । अवरं किं एत्थ लिहिदव्वं ।

सानुमती ।

[c] जो जो पदेसो सहीए मे अहिरूबो । तं तं आलिहि-
दुकामो भवे ।

राजा ।

श्रूयताम् ।

कार्या सैकतलीनहंसमिथुना स्रोतोवहा मालिनी
पादास्तामभितो निषण्णहरिणा गौरीगुरोः पावनाः ।

[a] एषोऽत्रभवान्नदीमतिक्रम्य मृगतृष्णाया सङ्क्रान्तः ।   [b] भोः । अपरं किमत्र
लिखितव्यम् ।   [c] यो यः प्रदेशः सख्या मेऽभिरूपः । तं तमालिखितुकामो भवत् ।

---

[1] '(While) again and again making much of her (image) committed to
a picture, having previously repudiated my beloved when she came into
my presence, I have become, O friend, (as it were) possessed of a longing
for the waters-of-the-mirage, after passing by a river in-my-road having-
plenty-of-water;' i. e. I am like one who prefers the shadow to the sub-
stance, the semblance to the reality. *Citrārpitām*=*citra-gatām*, see p. 238,
n. 5. *Sroto-vahā*, beautiful women are often compared by Hindū poets
to rivers, which in Sanskṛit are generally feminine. *Nikāma-jalām*,
'yielding abundance of water, as much as can be desired;' as to *nikāma*
in this sense, see p. 108, n. 3 in the middle. *Mṛiga-trishṇikā*, lit. 'thirst
of deer,' 'a vapour floating over waste places, which appears at a distance
like water, and deceives men and animals.'

Verse 148. VASANTA-TILAKĀ (a variety of ŚAKVARĪ). See verses 8, 27, 31, &c., 144.

शाखालम्बितवल्कलस्य च तरोर्निर्मातुमिच्छाम्यधः
शृङ्गे कृष्णमृगस्य वामनयनं कण्डूयमानां मृगीम्॥१४९॥

विदूषकः ॥ आत्मगतम् ॥

[a] जह अहं देक्खामि । पूरिदव्वं णेण चित्तफलअं
लम्बकुच्चाणं तावसाणं कदम्बेहिं ।

राजा ।

वयस्य । अन्यच्च शकुन्तलायाः प्रसाधनमभिप्रेतमत्र
विस्मृतमस्माभिः ।

विदूषकः ।

[b] किं विअ ।

[a] यथाहं पश्यामि । पूरयितव्यमनेन चित्रफलकं लम्बकूर्चानां तापसानां कदम्बैः ।
[b] किमिव ।

---

[1] 'The river Mālinī ought to be drawn [made] with a pair of swans [flamingoes] resting on a sandbank; (and) on both sides of it the sacred hills-contiguous to Himālaya [Gaurī's father], with-some-deer-reclining (on them); and I wish under a tree, on-whose-boughs-some-bark-garments-are-suspended, to form a doe rubbing (her) left eye on the horn of a black antelope.' *Haṇsa*, a kind of wild-goose of a white colour, with golden wings; something between a swan and a flamingo. It serves the god Brahmā as a vehicle, and hence the *haṇsa-nāda* or 'cry' of this bird has a sacred character, just as the cry of the swan, with the Greeks; the voice of a beautiful woman is even compared to it (Bhaṭṭi-k. v. 18). *Mālinī*, cf. p. 103, l. 6; p. 16, l. 7. *Pādāḥ=pratyanta-parvatāḥ*, S.;=*paryanta-parvatāḥ*, K. *Gaurī-guroh=Himālayasya*, S'.; Himālaya, the god of the great snowy range, was the father of Gaurī, the wife of S'iva, whence she is called Pārvatī, Himavat-sutā, Hima-jā, &c. *Sākhā-lambita-valkala*, cf. *viṭapa-vishakta-jalārdra-valkaleshu*, verse 32, and p. 18, n. 1 at the end.

[2] 'With multitudes of long-bearded monks.' *Lamba*, lit. 'hanging down;' *kūrća=śmaśru*, S'. The Mackenzie reads *lamba-kuććhāṇaṃ paḍi-kamma kuevāṇeṇa tāhasaṇiṃ ṇiareṇa*.

[3] The meaning may be, 'there is another of S'akuntalā's ornaments intended (to be drawn) on this picture (but) forgotten by me.'

Verse 149. ŚĀRDŪLA-VIKRĪDITA (a variety of ATIDHRITI). See verses 14, 30, 36, 39, 40, 63, 79, 85, 86, 89, 97, 98, 111, 137, 138.

सानुमती ।

^aवणवासस्स सोउमारस्सञ्च जं सरिसं भविस्सदि ।

राजा ।

कृतं न कर्णार्पितबन्धनं सखे
शिरीषमागण्डविलम्बिकेशरम् ।
न वा शरच्चन्द्रमरीचिकोमलं
मृणालसूचं रचितं स्तनान्तरे ॥ १५० ॥

विदूषकः ।

^bभो । किं णु तत्तहोदी रत्तकुवलअपल्लवसोहिणा
अग्गहत्थेण मुहं आवारिअ चइदचइदा विअ ठिदा ।

॥ सावधानं निरूप्य । दृष्ट्वा ॥ ^cआ । एसो दासीएपुत्तो कुसुमरस-
पाअञ्चरी तत्तहोदीए वअणं अहिलङ्घदि महुअरो ।

राजा ।

ननु वार्यतामेष धृष्टः ।

विदूषकः ।

^dभवं एव्व अविणीदाणं सासिदा इमस्स वारणे पहविस्सदि ।

^a वनवासस्य सौकुमार्स्य च यत्तदृशं भविष्यति ।   ^b भोः । किं नु तत्रभवती
रक्तकुवलयपल्लवशोभिनाग्रहस्तेन मुखमावार्य चकितचकितेव स्थिता ।   ^c आः ।
एष दास्याःपुत्रः कुसुमरसपाठचरस्तत्रभवत्या वदनमभिलङ्घति मधुकरः ।   ^d भवानेवा-
विनीतानां शासितास्य वारणे प्रभविष्यति ।

---

[1] 'A S'irīsha-blossom, with its stalk fastened in her ear, (and) its-fila-ments-hanging-down-to-her-cheek, has not been drawn [made], O friend. Nor has a necklace-of-lotus-fibres, soft-as-the-rays-of-the-autumnal-moon, been formed in the midst of her bosom.' *Bandhana*=*prasava-bandhana* =*vṛinta*, S'. and C'. (cf. p. 103, n. 1, and p. 229, n. 1). *S'irīsha*, see p. 7, n. 1, and p. 53, n. 1. The blossom of a plant is neuter in Sanskrit.

[2] With regard to this passage and what follows, compare pp. 32, 33, 34. As to *rakta-kuvalaya*, &c., see p. 25, n. 1. As to *dāsyāḥ-putra*, see p. 61, n. 1.

Verse 150. VAṂS'A-STHAVILA (a variety of JAGATĪ). See verses 18, 22, 23, 67, 81. 114, 117, 119, 145.

राजा ।

युज्यते । अयि भोः कुसुमलताप्रियातिथे । किमत्र परि-
पतनखेदमनुभवसि ।

एषा कुसुमनिषण्णा तृषितापि सती भवन्तमनुरक्ता ।
प्रतिपालयति मधुकरी न खलु मधु विना त्वया पिवति ॥१५१॥

सानुमती ।

[a] अज्ज अभिजादंक्खु एसो वारिदो ।

विदूषकः ।

[b] पडिसिद्धाबि वामा एसा जादी ।

राजा ।

एवं भो न मे शासने तिष्ठसि । श्रूयतां तर्हि सम्प्रति ।

अक्लिष्टबालतरुपल्लवलोभनीयं
पीतं मया सदयमेव रतोत्सवेषु ।
बिम्बाधरं स्पृशसि चेद्भ्रमर प्रियाया-
स्त्वां कारयामि कमलोदरबन्धनस्थम् ॥१५२॥

[a] श्रद्धाभिजातं खल्वेष वारितः ।   [b] प्रतिषिद्धापि वामैषा जातिः ।

---

[1] 'Wherefore dost thou undergo the fatigue of hovering round about ? There [*eshā*] resting-on-a-flower the-devotedly-attached female-bee, although being thirsty, waits for thee; nor indeed without thee will she sip (its) nectar.' *Paripatana*, 'flying round about,' the first sense of *pat* is 'to fly.'

[2] 'For-once-now this (bee) is warned-off [kept off] quite in a courteous manner.' The meaning is somewhat obscure, but there seems to be a satirical allusion to the king's polite address to the bee, followed as it is by a threat.

[3] 'This race (of animals), however (it may be) driven off, is perverse.' The Beng. MSS. and K. have *pratishiddha-vāmā*. *Vāma*, properly 'left,' 'not right;' hence 'turned from the right,' 'reverse,' 'perverse,' 'refractory.'

[4] 'If, O bee, thou touchest the Bimba-lip of (my) beloved, charming as

Verse 151. ĀRYĀ or GĀTHĀ. See verse 2.

$$- - \;|\; \cup \cup \cup \;|\; \cup \;|\; - - \;\|\; \cup \cup - \;|\; \cup \cup - \;|\; \cup - \cup \;|\; \cup \cup - \;|\; -$$
$$- \cup \cup \;|\; \cup - \cup \;|\; \cup \cup - \;\|\; \cup \cup \cup \;|\; \cup \cup - \;|\; \cup \;|\; - \cup \cup \;|\; -$$

Verse 152. VASANTA-TILAKĀ (a variety of ŚAKVARĪ). See verses 8, 27, 31, &c., 148.

विदूषकः ।

ᵃ एव्वंतिअएहदअडस्स किं ण भाइस्संदि । ॥ सहस्य । आत्मगतम् ॥

ᵇ एसो दाव उम्मत्तो । अहम्मि एदस्स सङ्गेण ईदिसवञ्चणो विञ्च संवुत्तो । ॥ प्रकाशम् ॥ ᶜ भो । चित्तंक्खु एदं ।

राजा ।

कथं चित्रम् ।

सानुमती ।

ᵈ अहम्मि दाणिं अणवगदत्था । किं उण जहलिहिदाणुभावी एंसो ।

राजा ।

वयस्य । किमिदमनुष्ठितं पौरोभाग्यम् ।

ᵃ एवंतीक्ष्णदण्डस्य किं न भेष्यति ।   ᵇ एष तावदुन्मत्तः । अहमप्येतस्य सङ्गेनेदृश्यचन इव संवृत्तः ।   ᶜ भोः । चित्रं खल्वेतत् ।   ᵈ अहमपीदानीमनवगतार्था । किं पुनर्यथालिखितानुभाव्येष: ।

---

the uninjured blossom of a young tree, that very (lip which has been) tenderly drunk by me in love's banquets, (then) I will make thee imprisoned in the hollow of a lotus' (cf. verse 77, with note). *Bimbādhara*, 'lip like the Bimba,' i. e. of a bright red colour, like the gourd of the Bimba (Momordica Monadelpha), a cucurbitaceous plant. So *bimbādharā-laktakaḥ*, Mālavik. p. 30, l. 1; Raghu-v. xiii. 16. Compare our expression, 'cherry-lip.' *Kamalodara-ba°*, see p. 183, n. 1. *Bandhana* seems here to mean 'the place of imprisonment.'

[1] 'How should he not stand in awe of one who has (threatened him with) so severe a punishment?' *Tīkshṇa-daṇḍa*, 'severe in punishing,' 'a strict disciplinarian.' The Prākṛit equivalent of *tīkshṇa* is *tiṇha*, according to Vararući iii. 33, although most of the MSS. have *tikkhaṇa*. Root *bhī* in Sanskrit is usually joined with an abl., but the gen. is admissible (Gram. 855, 859); K., however, observes that this construction is peculiar to Prākṛit (cf. *dākshiṇya-paścāttāpasya bibhemi*, Vikram., end of Act II).

[2] 'Even I now did not understand the thing; how much less should he perceive that it was painted?' *An-avagatārthā*, so reads the Mackenzie MS., supported by K.; the others, *avagatārthā*.

[3] 'Why has this ill-natured-act been perpetrated (by you)?' *Pauro-bhāgya*, see p. 212, n. 1. K. observes, *purobhāgī = doshaika-darśī = dush-ṭaḥ, tasya karma paurobhāgyam*, and refers to Pāṇ. v. 1, 124.

दर्शनसुखमनुभवतः साक्षादिव तन्मयेन हृदयेन ।
स्मृतिकारिणा त्वया मे पुनरपि चिच्चीकृता कान्ता ॥१५३॥
॥ इति बाष्पं विहरति ॥
सानुमती ।
" पुव्वावरविरोही अपुव्वो एसो विरहमग्गो ।
राजा ।
वयस्य । कथमेवमविश्रान्तदुःखमनुभवामि ।
प्रजागरात्खिलीभूतत्तस्याः स्वप्ने समागमः ।
वाष्पस्तु न ददात्येनां द्रष्टुं चिच्चगतामपि ॥१५४॥
ᵃ पूर्वापरविरोध्यपूर्व एष विरहमार्गः ।

---

[1] 'My beloved is once more transformed into a picture by thee reviving the recollection of me enjoying the bliss of beholding her just-as-if (she were) present before my eyes, having my (whole) soul wrapped-up-in-her.' *Tan-mayena=Śakuntalā-mayena*, S'., lit. 'with a heart made of S'akuntalā,' i.e. wholly absorbed by her.

[2] *Viharati*, 'wipes away,' or 'sheds;' see p. 166, n. 5, and p. 154, n. 1.

[3] 'This demeanour of (one in a state of) separation, opposing first one thing and then another, is singular [unexampled, without a precedent].' *Pūrvāpara-virodhī* may mean 'setting itself against everything from first to last,' or 'from first to last untoward.' Lovers, when separated from each other, were supposed to find comfort and amusement in various trifling employments expressive of their passion (see Megha-d. 86); but here was the case of one whom nothing could divert.

[4] '(The hope of) meeting her in sleep is rendered vain through (my) wakefulness. Moreover the (blinding) tears (that fill my eyes) will not permit me to behold her even represented-in-a-picture.' *Vāshpa*, see p. 157, n. 1 in the middle. *Khilī-bhūta=dur-labha*, S'. In Hindū poetry dreams and pictures are the regular standing artifices of lovers for tricking themselves into fictitious unions with their mistresses; just as sleeplessness and tears are the regular standing impediments to such devices. Cf.

Verse 153. ĀRYĀ or GĀTHĀ. See verse 2.

```
— ◡ ◡ | ◡ ◡ ◡ ◡ | ◡ ◡ — ‖  — —  | ◡ ◡ — | ◡ — ◡ | ◡ ◡ — | ◡
◡ ◡ — | ◡ — ◡ | — — ‖ ◡ ◡ ◡ ◡ | — — | ◡ | — — | —
```

Verse 154. ŚLOKA or ANUSHṬUBH. See verses 5, 6, 11, 12, 26, 47, 50, 51, 53, 73, 76, 84, 87, 125, 127, 146.

सानुमती ।

[a] सव्वहा पमंज्जिदं तुए पच्चादेसदुक्खं सउन्दलाए ।

चतुरिका ॥ प्रविश्य ॥

[b] जेदु जेदु भट्टा । वट्टिआकरण्डअं[2] गेण्हिअ इदोमुहं पत्थिदम्हि ।

राजा ।

किं च ।

चतुरिका ।

[c] सो मे हत्थादो अन्तरा[3] तरलिआदुद्दिआए देवीए वसुम-दीए अहं एव्व अज्जउत्तस्स उबणइस्संति सबलक्कारं गहिदो ।

विदूषकः ।

[d] दिट्ठिआ तुमं मुक्का ।

चतुरिका ।

[e] जाव देवीए विडवलग्गं उत्तरीअं तरलिआ मोचेदि । ताव मए णिव्वाहिदो[4] अत्ता ।

---

[a] सर्वथा प्रमार्जितं त्वया प्रत्यादेशदुःखं शकुन्तलायाः ।   [b] जयतु जयतु भर्ता । वर्तिकाकरण्डकं गृहीत्वेतोमुखं प्रस्थितास्मि ।   [c] स मे हस्तादन्तरा तरलिकाद्वि-तीयया देव्या वसुमत्या अहमेवार्यपुत्रस्योपनेष्यामीति सबलात्कारं गृहीतः ।   [d] दिष्ट्या त्वं मुक्का ।   [e] यावद्देव्या विटपलग्नमुत्तरीयं तरलिका मोचयति । तावन्मया निर्वाहित आत्मा ।

Megha-d. 104, *Tvām ālikhya aśrais tāvan muhur upaćitair dṛishṭir ālupyate me krūras tasminn api na sahate saṅgamaṃ nau kṛitāntaḥ.* See also Megha-d. 89, and Vikram., Act II, *Katham upālabhe nidrāṃ svapne samāgama-kāriṇīm; na ća suvadanām ālekhye 'pi priyāṃ sama-vāpya tām mama nayanayor udvāshpatvaṃ sakhe na bhavishyati.*

[1] *Pramārjita*, 'atoned for,' lit. 'wiped clean,' 'wiped out.'

[2] *Vartikā-karaṇḍaka*, 'box of colours,' see p. 249, n. 1.

[3] *Antarā*, 'on the way,' 'midway.' The same expression occurs in p. 257, l. 14. See also Mālavik. p. 8, l. 18. As to Vasumatī, see p. 184, n. 2.

[4] 'I took myself off,' 'I made my escape,' lit. 'by me my own person was carried off.' The Prākṛit is responsible for this idiom and con-struction. *Nirvāhita* is the reading of most of the Deva-n. MSS., and

राजा ।

वयस्य । उपस्थिता देवी बहुमानगर्विता च । भवानिमां प्रतिकृतिं रक्षतु ।

विदूषकः ।

[a] अत्ताणंत्ति भणाहि । ॥ चित्रफलकमादायोत्थाय च ॥ [b] जइ भवं अन्तेउरकालकूडादो मुञ्बीअदि । तदो मं मेहप्पडिच्छन्दे पासादे सद्दावेहि । ॥ इति दूतपदं निष्क्रान्तः ॥

सानुमती ।

[c] अण्णसङ्कन्तहिअओबि पढमसम्भावणं अवेक्खदि । अदिसिढिलसोहदो दाणिं एसो ।

प्रतीहारी ॥ प्रविश्य पत्रहस्ता ॥

[d] जेदु जेदु देवो ।

राजा ।

वेत्रवति । न खल्वन्तरा दृष्टा त्वया देवी ।

<hr>

[a] आत्मानमिति भण । मेघप्रतिच्छन्दे प्रासादे शब्दय । अतिशिथिलसौहृद इदानीमेषः ।

[b] यदि भवानन्तःपुरकालकूटादुच्यते । ततो मां

[c] अन्यसङ्क्रान्तहृदयोऽपि प्रथमसम्भावनामपेक्षते ।

[d] जयतु जयतु देवः ।

<hr>

there seems no reason why it should not stand with the sense 'carried away,' 'borne off.' K. has *nirvāsita*, 'expelled.' Some of the Bengālī, *nihnavida* for *nihnuta*, 'concealed.' S'. has *niryata*.

[1] 'Rendered insolent by my great attention to her.'

[2] 'From the bane of the inner apartments.' *Kāla-kūṭa*, at the churning of the ocean, after the deluge, by the gods and demons, for the recovery or production of fourteen sacred things, a deadly poison called Kāla-kūṭa or Halāhala was generated, so virulent that it would have destroyed the world, had not the god S'iva swallowed it. Its only effect was to leave a black mark on his throat, whence his name Nīla-kaṇṭha. K. has *kala-hādo* (= *kalahāt*), 'from the strife,' and S'. *kūṭāt*, 'from the snare.'

[3] 'Call me in the palace (named) Megha-pratiććhanda.' *Sabda* may form either a nominal or a verb of the 10th class; cf. p. 152, n. 1.

[4] 'Although his heart [affection] is transferred to another.' Cf. in Vikram., Act III, *Anya-sankrānta-premāṇo nāgarā adhikaṁ dakshiṇā bhavanti*.

I. l

प्रतीहारी ।

[a] अहइं । पत्तहत्यं मं देक्खिस्र पडिणिउत्ता ।

राजा ।

कार्यज्ञा कार्योपरोधं मे परिहरति ।

प्रतीहारी ।

[b] देव । अमच्चो विण्णवेदि । अत्थजादस्स गणणाबहुलदाए एक्कं एव्व पोरकज्जं अवेक्खिदं । तं देवो पत्तारूढं पच्चक्खीकरेदुन्ति ।

राजा ।

इतः पत्त्रिकां दर्शय । ॥ प्रतीहार्युपनयति ॥

राजा ॥ अनुवाच्य ॥

कथम् । समुद्रव्यवहारी सार्थवाहो धनमित्रो नाम नौव्यसने विपन्नः । अनपत्यश्च किल तरस्वी । राजगामी तस्यार्थ-सञ्चय इत्येतदमात्येन लिखितम् । कष्टं खल्वनपत्यता । बहुधनत्वाद्बहुपत्नीकेन तत्रभवता भवितव्यम् । विचार्य-ताम् । यदि काचिदापन्नसत्त्वा तस्य भार्यासु स्यात् ।

प्रतीहारी ।

[c] देव । दाणिं एव्व साकेदस्स सेट्टिणो दुहिआ णिव्वुत्त-पुंसवणा जाआ से सुणीअदि[2] ।

<hr>

[a] अथ किं । पत्त्रहस्तां मां दृष्ट्वा प्रतिनिवृत्ता । [b] देव । अमात्यो विज्ञापयति । अर्थजातस्य गणनाबहुलतयैकमेव पौरकार्यमपेक्षितम् । तद्देवः पत्त्रारूढं प्रत्यक्षीकरोत्विति । [c] देव । इदानीमेव साकेतकस्य श्रेष्ठिनो दुहिता निर्वृत्तपुंसवना जायास्य श्रूयते ।

<hr>

[1] 'By reason of the length of the calculation of the various-items-of-revenue, only one case among the citizens has been brought under consideration.' *Artha-jātasya*, &c., some of the Beng. have *rāja-kāryasya bahulatayā*. *Bahulatayā*, cf. *pallavatayā*, p. 29, n. 1.

[2] 'It is reported that his wife, the daughter of the foreman of a guild belonging to Ayodhyā, has even now just completed the ceremony (performed) at the quickening (of the unborn child).' *Sāketakasya*, Sāketa is a name of Ayodhyā, 'the invincible city,' the ancient capital of Rāma-

राजा ।

ननु गर्भः पित्र्यं रिक्थमर्हति । गच्छ । एवममात्यं ब्रूहि ।

प्रतीहारी ।

[a] जं देवो आणवेदि । ॥ इति प्रस्थिता ॥

राजा ।

एहि तावत् ।

प्रतीहारी ।

[b] इअम्हि ।

राजा ।

किमनेन सन्ततिरस्ति नास्तीति ।

येन येन वियुज्यन्ते प्रजाः स्निग्धेन बन्धुना ।
स स पापादृते तासां दुष्यन्त इति घुष्यताम् ॥१५५॥

प्रतीहारी ।

[c] एवं ण्णाम घोसइदव्वं । ॥ निष्क्रम्य । पुनः प्रविश्य ॥ [d] काले
पवुट्टं विअ अहिणन्दिदं देवस्स सासणं ।

राजा   ॥ दीर्घमुष्णं च निःश्वस्य ॥

एवं भोः सन्ततिच्छेदनिरवलम्बानां कुलानां मूलपुरुषा-

[a] यदेव आज्ञापयति ।   [b] इयमस्मि ।   [c] एवं नाम घोषयितव्यम् ।
[d] काले प्रवृष्टमिवाभिनन्दितं देवस्य शासनम् ।

candra and founded by Ikshvāku, the first of the monarchs of the Solar
dynasty (see p. 15, n. 1).   It was situated on the river Sarayu in the
North of India, and is now called Oude.   *Sreshthin*, 'the head of a guild
or corporation practising the same trade.'   *Puṃ-savana*, 'the rite per-
formed on the quickening of the fœtus,' is the second of the twelve purifi-
catory ceremonies enjoined by Manu on the three superior classes (ii. 27,
&c.)   It comes next in order to the *garbhādhāna* or 'ceremony on con-
ception;' cf. p. 199, l. 1, with note; see Indian Wisdom, p. 246.

[1] *Garbhaḥ=garbha-sthaḥ putraḥ*, 'the child in the womb,' K.

[2] See the translation of this verse, p. 191, n. 2 at the end.

[3] 'Like grateful-rain at the right season.' *Pravṛishṭam=prahṛishṭa-
varshaṇam.* Some of the Beng. have *pariṭṭham* (=*pravishṭam*).

Verse 155. SLOKA or ANUSHTUBH. See verses 5, 6, &c., 154.

वसाने सम्पदः परमुपतिष्ठन्ति । ममाप्यन्ते पुरुवंशश्रीर-
काल इवोप्तवीजा भूरेवंवृत्ता ।

प्रतीहारी ।

[a] पडिहदं अमङ्गलं ।

राजा ।

धिग्ग्रामुपस्थितश्रेयोऽवमानिनम् ।

सानुमती ।

[b] असंसअं सहिं एव्व हिअए करिञ्ज णिन्दिदो एण अप्पा ।

राजा ।

संरोपितेऽप्यात्मनि धर्मपत्नी
त्यक्ता मया नाम कुलप्रतिष्ठा ।
कल्पिष्यमाणा महते फलाय
वसुन्धरा काल इवोप्तवीजा ॥१५६॥

सानुमती ।

[c] अपरिच्छिस्सा दाणिं दे सन्ददी भविस्सदि ।

[a] प्रतिहतममङ्गलम् ।   [b] असंशयं सखीमेव हृदये कृत्वा निन्दितोऽनेनात्मा ।
[c] अपरिच्छिन्नेदानीं ते सन्ततिर्भविष्यति ।

---

[1] 'The goods of families who are bereft of support through the failure of lineal descendants, pass over to a stranger at the decease of the representative-of-the-original-stock.' *Mūla-purusha*, 'the man who represents the original progenitor, from whom, in a direct line, the family is descended,' 'the eldest surviving son,' lit. 'the stock-man.'

[2] 'The misfortune be averted!' compare p. 194, l. 8.

[3] 'Although myself was implanted (in her womb), verily (my) lawful wife, the glory of (my) family, was repudiated by me, like the earth sown with seed at the right-season, about to become adequate to the production of mighty fruit.' *Saṃropite ātmani* = *svasmin upte sati*, K., lit. 'myself being sown,' 'she being sown with myself,' i. e. 'she bearing my second self in her womb.' According to the Hindū notion, a child is a reproduction of one's self. *Ātmaiva patnyā jāyate*, K. *Kula-pratishṭhā*, see p. 124, n. 1. *Kalpishyamāṇā*, see p. 191, n. 2 in the middle. *Vasundharā*, cf. p. 184, n. 2.

Verse 156. UPAJĀTI or ĀKHYĀNAKĪ (a variety of TRISHṬUBH). See verses 41, &c., 142.

चतुरिका ॥ जनान्तिकम् ॥

[a] अए । इमिणा सत्थवाहवुत्तन्तेण विउणुव्वेओ भट्टा । यं अस्सासिदुं मेहप्पडिच्छन्दादो अज्जं माठव्वं गेण्हिअ आणच्छेहि ।

प्रतीहारी ।

[b] सुट्ठु भणासि । ॥ इति निष्क्रान्ता ॥

राजा ।

अहो दुष्यन्तस्य संशयमारूढाः पिण्डभाजः । कुतः ।

अस्मात्परं वत यथाश्रुति सम्भृतानि
को नः कुले निवपनानि नियच्छतीति ।
नूनं प्रसूतिविकलेन मया प्रसिक्तं
धौताश्रुशेषमुदकं पितरः पिवन्ति ॥१५७॥

॥ इति मोहमुपागतः ॥

[a] अये । अनेन सार्थवाहवृत्तान्तेन विगुणोद्वेगो भर्ता । एनमाश्वासयितुं मेघप्रति-च्छन्दादायै माठव्यं गृहीत्वागच्छ ।   [b] सुष्ठु भणसि ।

---

[1] 'Woe is me! the ancestors of Dushyanta are brought to a critical situation; because—Thinking to themselves, Who, alas! after this (man), in our family, will offer (us) the oblations prepared according to scriptural-precept? in all probability,' &c.; see p. 111, n. 1. *Pinda-bhājaḥ=pitaraḥ*, S'., lit. 'partakers of oblations to the dead,' i.e. the Manes of deceased ancestors for whom the S'rāddha was performed. *Kutaḥ*, see p. 55, n. 2. *Asmāt*, i.e. *Dushyantāt*, S'. *Dhautāśru-śesha*, compare the analogous compounds *tvag-asthi-śesha*, 'having nothing left but skin and bone;' *nāma-śesha*, 'having nothing surviving but a name.' The Beng. MSS. read *dhautāśru-sekam*. The duty of performing the S'rāddha devolved on the eldest son or on the nearest surviving relative. If no one survived to celebrate this rite, the Manes of deceased progenitors sank from their celestial abode to the lower regions. Cf. Raghu-v. i. 66, 67; see Indian Wisdom, p. 253 sqq.

Verse 157. VASANTA-TILAKĀ (a variety of S'AKVARĪ). See verses 8, 27, 31, 43, 46, 64, 74, 80, 82, 83, 91, 93, 94, 95, 100, 104, 105, 108, 123, 124, 144, 148, 152.

चतुरिका ॥ ससम्भ्रममवलोक्य ॥

[a] समस्ससदु समस्ससदु भट्टा ।

सानुमती ।

[b] हड्डी हड्डी । सदिक्खु दीबे ववधाणदोसेण एसो अन्धआ-रदोसं अणुहोदि । अहं दाणिं एव्व णिव्वुदं करेमि । अहवा सुदं मए सउन्दलं समस्सासअन्तीए महेन्दजणणीए मुहादो । जण्णभाओसुआ देवा एव्व तह अणुचिट्ठिस्सन्ति जह अइरेण धम्मपदिणिं भट्टा अहिणन्दिस्सदित्ति । ता जुत्तं एदं कालं पडिपालिदुं । जाव इमिणा वुत्तन्तेण

[a] समाश्वसितु समाश्वसितु भर्ता । [b] हा धिक् हा धिक् । सति खलु दीपे व्यवधानदोषेणैषोऽन्धकारदोषमनुभवति । अहमिदानीमेव निर्वृतं करोमि । अथवा श्रुतं मया शकुन्तलां समाश्वासयन्त्या महेन्द्रजनन्या मुखात् । यज्ञभागोत्सुका देवा एव तथा-नुशासन्ति यथाचिरेण धर्मपत्नीं भर्ताभिनन्दिष्यतीति । तस्माद्युक्तमेतं कालं प्रतिपा-लयितुम् । यावदनेन वृत्तान्तेन

---

[1] 'A light being really (near at hand) this-man by reason [fault] of the screen (which covers it) experiences (all the) ill-effects of darkness.' Dr. Boehtlingk proposes to interpret *andhaāra-dosam* by *andhakāra-doshām*, 'dark night,' or 'the darkness of night,' but this seems hardly a legitimate compound, nor does the sense require it.

[2] 'Longing for their portions of the sacrifice.' *Janna* is the Prākṛit equivalent for *yajña* (Vararuči iii. 44). Great sacrifices were performed by kings in celebration of auspicious events, especially after marriage, in the hope of securing issue, and Indra as well as the inferior gods were invited to partake of portions set apart for them. These sacrifices were accompanied by largesses to the Brāhmans, and festivities, in which the gods were supposed to be eager to participate. Cf. Rāmāy. i. 13, 6. 8. The mother of Indra was Aditi, who was the wife of Kaśyapa (see p. 22, n. 3). It appears from Act VII. of this play that Śakuntalā was at this time enjoying an asylum with the illustrious pair Kaśyapa and Aditi in some sacred retreat, where they were engaged in acts of mortification and penance.

[3] 'Therefore it is proper to wait for this period.' This is the reading of K. Some of the Deva-n. have *tā na juttam kālam*, &c. (=*tasmān na yuktam kālam*, &c.)

[a] पिञ्असहिं समस्सासेमि ।   ॥ इत्युद्भ्रान्तकेन निष्क्रान्ता ॥

नेपथ्ये ।

[b] अब्म्हसं अब्म्हसं[2] ।

राजा   ॥ प्रत्यागतप्राणः[3] । कर्णं दत्त्वा ॥

अये । माठव्यस्येवार्तस्वरः । कः कोऽत्र भोः ।

प्रतीहारी   ॥ प्रविश्य ॥

[c] परित्ताअदु देवी संसञ्अगदं[4] वअस्सं ।

राजा ।

केनात्तगन्धी[5] माणवकः ।

प्रतीहारी ।

[d] अदिट्ठरूवेण केणवि सत्तेण अदिक्कमि अ मेहप्पडिच्छन्दस पासादस्स अग्गभूमिं आरोविंदो ।

[a] प्रियसखीं समाश्वासयामि ।   [b] अब्रह्मण्यम् अब्रह्मण्यम् ।   [c] परित्रायतां देवः संशयगतं वयस्यम् ।   [d] अदृष्टरूपेण केनापि सत्त्वेनातिक्रम्य मेघप्रतिच्छन्दस्य प्रासादस्याग्रभूमिमारोपितः ।

---

[1] See p. 218, n. 1, i. e. *udbhramaṇena ākāśam pratyudgamena*, K.

[2] *Abrahmaṇyam* ('Help! to the rescue!'), according to Amara-k. i. 7, 14, is *abadhyoktau*, i. e. implies an assertion that the thing in question is not to be killed. *Abadhyo 'ham ity arthaḥ*, S., 'the meaning is that, as a Brāhman, my person is sacred and inviolable.' Cf. in the Uttara-Rāma-ćaritra, p. 30, 'Then by a Brāhman, having placed his dead son at the royal gate, a cry of "Abrahmaṇya" was set up, accompanied by a smiting on the breast.' *A-brahmaṇya*, lit. '(anything) unworthy of a Brāhman.'

[3] So reads my own MS. One Deva-n. has *pratyāgataḥ*, the others simply *karṇaṃ dattvā*. The Beng. *pratyāyata-ćetanaḥ*.

[4] 'Fallen into danger,' 'placed in jeopardy.' As to *gata*, see p. 38, n. 1.

[5] *Ātta-gandha* = *ātta-garva*, 'humbled,' 'having the pride taken down,' 'insulted.' Compare in the Mahā-bh. *rājyam ātta-lakshmi*, 'a kingdom stripped of its wealth.' According to some, *ātta-gandha* = *ārta-kaṇṭha*, 'throttled,' 'strangled.'

[6] 'By some demon of invisible form, having seized [overpowered] him, he has been mounted on a pinnacle of the palace (called) Megha-prati-ćchanda.' *Sattva* = *bhūta*, 'a goblin,' 'evil spirit.'

राजा ॥ उत्थाय ॥

मा तावत् । ममापि सद्भैरभिभूयन्ते गृहाः[1] । अथवा ।

अहन्यहन्यात्मन एव ताव-

ज्ज्ञातुं प्रमादस्खलितं न शक्यम् ।

प्रजासु कः केन पथा प्रयाती-

त्यशेषतो वेदितुमस्ति शक्तिः ॥१५८॥[2]

नेपथ्ये ।

[a]भो वयस्स । अविहा[3] अविहा ।

राजा ॥ गतिभेदेन[4] परिक्रामन् ॥

सखे । न भेतव्यं न भेतव्यम् ।

[a] भो वयस्स । अविधा अविधा ।

---

[1] *Griha*, 'a house,' or 'a wife,' is masc. in the plural (Amara-k. ii. 5). The Sāhit.-d. (p. 190) inserts *nāma*, 'forsooth,' after *mamāpi*.

[2] 'Even one's own false-steps (proceeding from) heedlessness (occurring) day by day cannot be altogether ascertained. Is there (then) the power to know in every case by what road each of my subjects is walking?' lit. 'by what road who among my subjects,' &c. *Tāvat=sākalyena*, K. *Pramāda-skhalitam*, 'tripping from carelessness,' 'stumbling,' 'blundering.' *A-śeshataḥ=sākalyena*, K. According to K., this last clause presents an example of *kāku*, which is defined as 'a change in the tone of the voice,' 'giving emphasis.' Thus, 'Is there the power?' becomes equivalent to 'there certainly is not the power' (see Sāhit.-d. p. 24). *Kāku* is constantly used by Paṇḍits of a sentence spoken interrogatively, and so with a change of voice.

[3] *Avidhā ity ākrośe.* The interjection *avidhā* is used in calling for assistance, K. Translate, 'Help! help!' Two of the MSS. have *aviha* for *avidhā*; the Mackenzie, *aviddho;* my own, *avidū.* *Aviha* and *avihā* seem to be interchangeable. *Avihā* occurs in Mālavik. p. 12, l. 22; p. 24, l. 7; p. 56, l. 8. Dr. Boehtlingk suggests that *avida* in Mṛicchak. p. 213, l. 6; p. 312, l. 9, may be for *aviha* or *avihā*.

[4] *Gati-bhedena*, 'with hurried broken steps;' *tvarita-gamanena ity arthaḥ*, K.

Verse 158. UPAJĀTI or ĀKHYĀNAKĪ (a variety of TRISHṬUBH). See verse 41, 107, 121, 126, 142, 156.

नेपथ्ये ॥ पुनस्तदेव पठित्वा ॥

^a कहं ण भाइस्सं । एस मं कोवि पच्चावणदसिरोहरं इक्खुं विञ्ज तिण्हभङ्गं करेदि ।

राजा ॥ सदृष्टिक्षेपम् ॥

धनुस्तावत् ।

यवनी ॥ प्रविश्य शार्ङ्गहस्ता ॥

^b भट्टा । एदं हत्थावावसहिदं सरासणं ।

॥ राजा सशरं धनुरादत्ते ॥

नेपथ्ये ।

एष त्वामभिनवकण्ठशोणिताथीं

शार्दूलः पशुमिव हन्मि चेष्टमानम् ।

आर्तानां भयमपनेतुमात्तधन्वा

दुष्यन्तस्तव शरणं भवत्विदानीम् ॥१५९॥

राजा ॥ सरोषम् ॥

कथं मामेवोद्दिशति । तिष्ठ कुणपाशन । त्वमिदानीं न भविष्यसि । ॥ शार्ङ्गमारोप्य ॥ वेत्रवति । सोपानमार्गमादेशय ।

^a कथं न भेष्यामि । एष मां कोऽपि पश्चादवनतशिरोधरमिषुमिव तीक्ष्णभङ्गं करोति ।
^b भर्तः । एतद्धस्तावापसहितं शरासनम् ।

---

¹ *Paścād-avanata-śirodharam*, a Bahuvrīhi compound agreeing with *mām*. Some MSS. have *praty-avanata*.

² As to *Yavanī* and *śārnga-hastā*, see p. 62, n. 2.

³ *Hastāvāpa*=*jyāghāta-vāraṇa*, K.;=*anguli-trāṇa*, 'a guard to protect the hand or fore-arm from the bow-string,' 'an arm-guard,' 'a finger-guard;' from *hasta*, 'a hand,' or 'the lower arm,' and *āvāpa*, 'a band' or 'bracelet;' cf. p. 114, n. 2. The Beng. have *hastāvāra*.

⁴ 'Here, thirsting for (thy) fresh throat-blood, will I slay thee struggling, as a tiger (slays) a beast. Let Dushyanta now, who grasps his bow to remove the fear of the oppressed, be thy refuge [protector].' *Ārtānām*, &c., cf. p. 14, l. 4. *Atta-dhanvā*, cf. p. 230, l. 1.

Verse 159. PRAHARSHIṆĪ (a variety of ATIJAGATĪ), containing thirteen syllables to the Pāda or quarter-verse, each Pāda being alike.

$$- - - \mid \cup \cup \cup \cup - \cup - \cup - - \parallel$$

प्रतीहारी ।

ᵃ इदो इदो देवो ।

॥ सर्वे सत्वरमुपसर्पन्ति ॥
राजा ॥ समन्ताद्विलोक्य ॥

शून्यं खल्विदम् ।

नेपथ्ये ।

ᵇ अविहा अविहा । अहं अत्तभवन्तं पेक्खामि । तुमं मं
ण पेक्खसि । विडालग्गहिदो मूसओ विअ णिरासोम्हि
जीविदे संवुत्तो ।

राजा ।

भोस्तिरस्करिणीगर्विंत । मदीयमस्त्रं त्वां द्रक्ष्यति । एष
तमिषुं सन्धत्ते ।

यो हनिष्यति बध्यं त्वां रक्ष्यं रक्षति च द्विजम् ।
हंसो हि क्षीरमादत्ते तन्मिश्रा वर्जयत्यपः ॥१६०॥

॥ इत्यस्त्रं सन्धत्ते ॥

ᵃ इत इतो देवः ।   ᵇ अविधा अविधा । अहमत्रभवन्तं प्रेक्षे । त्वं मां न प्रेक्षसे ।
विडालगृहीतो मूषक इव निराशोऽस्मि जीविते संवृत्तः ।

---

[1] *Avidhā*, see p. 264, n. 3. My own MS. has *avihā* in this place.

[2] 'Priding thyself on the power of rendering thyself invisible.' *Tiras-karinī* is properly a veil to cover the head, used by celestial beings to render themselves invisible (cf. p. 227, l. 5). It is here the science or art, peculiar to such beings, of so concealing themselves. This interpretation is supported by the gloss of Ranganātha on *tiraskariṇī-praćchannā* in Act II. of Vikram.; *tiraskariṇī = antardhāna-vidyā*. It answers to the *śikhā-bandhanī vidyā*, 'art of tying [covering] the top-knot,' called *a-parājitā* in a preceding page.

[3] 'He it is fits the arrow (to the bow) who will slay thee worthy-of-death, and save a Brāhman worthy-of-preservation. For the flamingo extracts [takes] the milk (and) leaves behind the water that is mixed with it.' The Hindūs imagine that the Haṃsa or flamingo (see p. 251, n. 1) has the power of separating milk from water. Compare Mahā-bh.,

---

Verse 160. ŚLOKA or ANUSHṬUBH. See verses 5, 6, 11, 12, 26, 47, 50, 51, 53, 73, 76, 84, 87, 125, 127, 130, 146, 154, 155.

॥ ततः प्रविशति विदूषकमुत्सृज्य मातलिः ॥

मातलिः[1] ।

कृताः शरव्यं हरिणा तवासुराः
शरासनं तेषु विकृष्यतामिदम् ।
प्रसादसौम्यानि सतां सुहृज्जने
पतन्ति चक्षूंषि न दारुणाः शराः[2] ॥१६१॥

राजा ॥ अस्त्रमुपसंहरन् ॥

अये मातलिः । स्वागतं महेन्द्रसारथे ।

विदूषकः ॥ प्रविश्य ॥

[a] अहं जेण इट्टिपसुमारं मारिदो । सो इमिणा सान्त्रदेण अहिणन्दीअदि ।

[a] अहं येनेष्टिपशुमारं मारितः । सोऽनेन स्वागतेनाभिनन्द्यते ।

S'akuntalopākhyāna, vii. 88, *Prājñas tu jalpatām puṇsāṃ śrutvā vāćaḥ śubhāśubhāḥ, guṇavad vākyam ādatte, haṇsaḥ kshīram ivāmbhasaḥ* (i. 3078). Bhartṛi-h. (ii. 15) has the following sentiment : 'Brahmā [whose vehicle is the flamingo] when very angry with this bird, can destroy his nest among the lotuses, but cannot deprive him of that celebrated and inestimable faculty which he possesses, of separating milk from water.' The reference is probably to the milky juice of the water-lily, which would be its natural food, and to which allusion is often made by the Hindū poets. As to *rakshati*, see p. 85, n. 2.

[1] *Mātali* is the charioteer of Indra. In the pictures which represent this god mounted on his other vehicle, an elephant (called Airāvata), Mātali is seen seated before him on the withers of the animal, acting as its driver. In the drama, however (see p. 12, n. 1), Indra is generally borne in a chariot drawn by two horses (called Harī or Harayaḥ), which were guided by Mātali.

[2] 'The demons are made by Indra thy mark ; let this bow (of thine) be drawn against them. Not on a friendly-person are dreadful arrows directed [fall] by the good, [but rather] eyes soft-with-(looks of)-favour.' *Asurāḥ*, &c., see p. 86, n. 2 ; p. 87, n. 1.

[3] 'He by whom I was being slaughtered like a sacrificial victim, is

Verse 161. VAṆŚA-STHAVILA (a variety of JAGATĪ). See verses 18, 22, 23, 67, 81, 114, 117, 119, 145, 150.

मातलिः ॥ सस्मितम् ॥

आयुष्मन् । श्रूयताम् । यदर्थमस्मि हरिणा भवत्सकाशं
प्रेषितः ।

राजा ।

अवहितोऽस्मि ।

मातलिः ।

अस्ति कालनेमिप्रसूतिर्दुर्जयो नाम दानवगणः ।

राजा ।

अस्ति श्रुतपूर्वं मया नारदात् ।

मातलिः ।

सख्युस्ते स किल शतक्रतोरजय्य-
स्तस्य त्वं रणशिरसि स्मृतो निहन्ता ।
उच्छेतुं प्रभवति यन्न सप्तसप्ति-
स्तन्नैशं तिमिरमपाकरोति चंद्रः ॥१६२॥

---

greeted with a welcome by this man!' *Ishṭi-paśu-māram māritaḥ=ishṭi-
paśur iva māritaḥ*, K. This kind of adverbial compound is noticed in
Pāṇ. iii. 4, 45. 46. So *aja-nāśam nashṭaḥ* is equivalent to *aja iva nash-
ṭaḥ*, and *ghṛita-nidhāyam nihitaḥ* to *ghṛita iva nihitaḥ*.

[1] The Mackenzie MS. has *yadartham*, supported by some of the Bengālī.

[2] *Kālanemi*, son of the demon Hiraṇya-kaśipu, was a Daitya or Asura
(see p. 86, n. 2) with a hundred arms and as many heads. These Daityas
were sometimes called Dānavas, from their mother Danu, who as well as
Diti was one of the wives of Kaśyapa and daughters of Daksha. The
Rākshasas, or cannibal demons who, for the sake of human flesh, waged
perpetual war with men, as the Daityas did with the gods, were related to
the Daityas.

[3] *Nārada* is a celebrated divine sage or Rishi, usually reckoned among
the ten Prajāpatis or Brahmādikas first created by Brahmā, and called his
sons. He acts as a kind of messenger of the gods (see the end of Act V.
of the Vikramorvaśī).

[4] 'Verily that (troop of demons) is not to be subdued by thy friend
Indra; thou, at the head of the fight, art appointed [termed, called] its
destroyer. That nocturnal darkness which the sun has no power to

---

Verse 162. PRAHARSHIṆĪ (a variety of ATIJAGATĪ). See verse 159.

स भवानात्तशस्त्र एवमिदानीं तमैन्द्ररथमारुह्य विजयाय
प्रतिष्ठताम् ।

राजा ।

अनुगृहीतोऽहमनया मघवतः सम्भावनया । अथ माठव्यं
प्रति भवता किमेवं प्रयुक्तम् ।

मातलिः ।

तदपि कथ्यते । किञ्चिन्निमित्तादपि मनःसन्तापाद-
युष्मान्मया विक्लवो दृष्टः । पश्चात्कोपयितुमायुष्मन्तं तथा
कृतवानस्मि । कुतः ।

ज्वलति चलितेन्धनोऽग्निर्विप्रकृतः पन्नगः फणं कुरुते ।
प्रायः स्वं महिमानं क्षोभात्प्रतिपद्यते हि जनः ॥१६३॥

राजा ॥ जनान्तिकम् ॥

वयस्य । अनतिक्रमणीया दिवस्पतेराज्ञा । तदत्र परिगतार्थं

---

remove, the moon dispels.' *Sata-kratu*, 'lord of a hundred sacrifices;'
another of Indra's thousand names. He is so called because the rank
which he occupies is unattainable excepting through a hundred Aśva-
medhas, or 'horse-sacrifices' (see p. 86, n. 2). *Sapta-saptiḥ*, 'drawn by
seven steeds;' see p. 12, n. 1. *Candraḥ*, the appositeness of this com-
parison depends on the fact that Dushyanta's pedigree was traceable to
the moon (see p. 15, n. 2; p. 113, n. 1).

¹ *Ātta-śastra*, cf. *ātta-daṇḍaḥ*, p. 191, l. 4, and *ātta-dhanvā*, p. 265, l. 12.

² 'Fire blazes up when the fuel is stirred; the snake when irritated
expands its hood; verily a man generally regains his own high-spirited-
ness [greatness, courage] through being roused-to-action [shaken, excited].'
Phaṇaṃ kurute, lit. 'makes a hood;' *phaṇa*, 'the expanded hood of the
cobra.' *Kshobhāt*, K. has *kopāt*. My own MS. and the Mackenzie have
jantuḥ for *hi janaḥ*. Most of the Bengālī MSS. read *tejasvī saṅkshobhāt
prāyaḥ pratipadyate tejaḥ*.

³ Indra, as the Hindū Jove, is lord of the atmosphere and winds (see
p. 86, n. 2).

Verse 163. ĀRYĀ or GĀTHĀ. See verse 2.

```
⏑⏑⏑⏑ | ⏑‒⏑ | ‒‒ ‖ ‒⏑⏑ | ‒‒ | ⏑‒⏑ | ‒⏑⏑ | ‒
‒‒ | ‒⏑⏑ | ‒‒ ‖ ‒‒ | ⏑⏑⏑̇ | ⏑ | ‒⏑⏑ | ‒
```

कृत्वा मद्वचनादमात्यपिशुनं ब्रूहि ।

तन्मतिः केवला तावत्परिपालयितुं प्रजाः ।

अधिज्यमिदमन्यस्मिन्कर्मणि व्यापृतं धनुः ॥१६४॥

इति ।

विदूषकः ।

जं भवं आणवेदि ।   ॥ इति निष्क्रान्तः ॥

मातलिः ।

आयुष्मानयमारोहतु ।

॥ राज्ञा रथारोहणं नाटयति ॥

॥ इति निष्क्रान्ताः सर्वे ॥

॥ षष्ठोऽङ्कः ॥

a यद्ब्रवानाज्ञापयति ।

---

[1] 'Having made acquainted with the circumstance;' Piśuna, 'informer,' is the name of the minister (cf. p. 236, l. 10).

[2] 'Let the-powers-of-thy mind be wholly and solely (exerted) to protect-by-good-government (my) subjects. This (my) braced [strung] bow is (for a time) occupied in a different employment.' *Tāvat*, cf. p. 264, l. 3. The root *pāl*, 'to protect,' in reference to a king or his officers, implies protection by a just administration of the laws. *Samyak pāl* occurs frequently in the sense of 'to govern justly.' *Adhi-jyam*, see p. 9, n. 2; and cf. p. 67, l. 12; p. 87, l. 8.

Verse 164. ŚLOKA or ANUSHTUBH. See verses 5, 6, 11, 12, 26, 47, 50, 51, 53, 73, 76, 84, 87, 125, 127, 146, 154, 155, 160.

॥ अथ सप्तमोऽङ्कः ॥

॥ ततः प्रविशत्याकाशयानेन रथाधिरूढो राजा मातलिश्च ॥

राजा ।

मातले । अनुष्ठितनिदेशोऽपि मघवतः सत्क्रियाविशे-
षादनुपयुक्तमिवात्मानं समर्थये ।

मातलिः ॥ सस्मितम् ॥

आयुष्मन् । उभयमप्यपरितोषं समर्थये ।

प्रथमोपकृतं मरुत्वतः प्रतिपत्त्या लघु मन्यते भवान् ।
गणयत्यवदानतोषितो भवतः सोऽपि न सत्क्रियागुणान् ॥१६५॥

राजा ।

मातले । मा मैवम् । स खलु मनोरथानामप्यभूमिर्विसर्जना-
वसरसत्कारः । मम हि दिवौकसां समक्षमर्धासनोपवेशितस्य

---

[1] 'Although I have executed (his) commission, after-such-a-distinguished
reception (on the part) of Indra, I consider myself as unworthy (of so
much honour).' *Satkriyā-viśeshāt,* cf. p. 41, l. 9; p. 134, l. 18. The
ablative may imply 'in consequence of,' 'after.' *An-upayuktam,* i.e. *tādṛik-
satkriyāyā ayogyam,* Chézy. *Samarthaye = avagaććhāmi.*

[2] *Āyushman,* cf. p. 9, n. 1.

[3] 'Your Highness makes light of the prior benefit (conferred by you)
on Indra, (compared) with the (subsequent) mark-of-distinction (conferred
by him on you). He too (Indra) takes no account of the distinguished
honours (bestowed) on your Highness, being-filled-with-admiration at your
heroic-achievement.' *Prathamopakritam,* i.e. *rākshasa-jaya-rūpam pūrvo-
pakāram,* K. *Pratipattyā = sambhāvanayā. Avadāna = paurusha,* 'a deed
of heroism,' K. The Colebrooke MS. has *toshito* for *vismito. Satkriyā-
guṇān = sambhāvanā-viśeshān,* K. *Guṇa* is used at the end of a com-
pound with the sense of *viśesha* (cf. *sambhāvanā-guṇa,* verse 168). The
Beng. reading is, *Upakritya hares tathā bhavān laghu satkāram avekshya
manyate, gaṇayaty avadāna-sammitām bhavataḥ so 'pi na satkriyām
imām.*

[4] 'That honorary-distinction on the occasion of (his) dismissing (me)

Verse 165. VAITĀLĪYA. See verses 52, 133.

अन्तर्गतप्रार्थनमन्तिकस्थं
जयन्तमुद्वीक्ष्य कृतस्मितेन ।
आमृष्टवक्षोहरिचन्दनाङ्का
मन्दारमाला हरिणा पिनद्धा ॥ १६६ ॥

मातलिः ।

किमिव नामायुष्मानमरेश्वरान्ब्राह्येति । पश्य ।

सुरसखस्य हरेरुभयैः कृतं
चिदिवमुद्धृतदानवकण्टकम् ।
तव शरैरधुना नतपर्वभिः
पुरुषकेशरिणश्च पुरा नखैः ॥ १६७ ॥

---

was certainly beyond the compass [reach, place] of my hopes,' i. e. exceeded
all my expectation. *A-bhūmi*=*a-sthāna*, 'want of place;'=*a-vishaya*,
'beyond the reach,' K. Cf. p. 285, l. 7, and Mālavik. p. 35, l. 4, *abhūmir
iyam mālavikāyāḥ.*

[1] 'For a garland of Mandāra (flowers), marked with yellow-sandal from
(its) rubbing on (his) breast, was fastened (round the neck) of me, made
to sit on half his throne, before the eyes of the gods, by Indra, smiling
and looking up at (his son) Jayanta, (who was) standing by and inwardly
longing (for the same honours).' *Āmṛishṭa*, the breast of Indra was dyed
yellow with a fragrant sandal-wood called Hari-ćandana (cf. Kumāra-s.
v. 69), and the garland, from coming in contact with it, became tinged
with the same colour. Wreaths and garlands of flowers were much used
by the Hindūs as marks of honorary distinction, as well as for ornaments
on festive occasions, and to adorn sacrificial victims (cf. p. 222, l. 11, n. 1).
They were suspended round the neck (see p. 150, n. 3), or placed on the
head. Mandāra is one of the five ever-blooming trees of Svarga, or Indra's
heaven. Another of these trees is said to be the Hari-ćandana mentioned
above, and another the Santāna; but the two most celebrated are the
Pārijāta and the Kalpa-druma, or tree granting all desires. Jayanta is
the son of Indra by his favourite wife Paulomī or S'aćī.

[2] 'The heaven of Indra, friend of the gods, has been made free from
the plague of the Dānavas by two (means); now by thy flat-jointed arrows,

---

Verse 166. UPAJĀTI or ĀKHYĀNAKĪ (a variety of TRISHṬUBH). See verses 41, &c., 158.
Verse 167. DRUTA-VILAMBITA (a variety of JAGATĪ). See verses 45, 72, 128, 140.

राजा ।

अच खलु शतक्रतोरेव महिमा स्तुत्यः ।
सिध्यन्ति कर्मसु महत्स्वपि यन्नियोज्याः
सम्भावनागुणमवेहि तमीश्वराणाम् ।
किं वाभविष्यदरुणस्तमसां विभेत्ता
तं चेत्सहस्रकिरणो धुरि नाकरिष्यत् ॥१६८॥

and formerly by the claws of the man-lion.' *Sura-sakha*, see p. 86, n. 2. *Tri-diva=svarga*, each of the superior Hindū gods has a heaven or paradise of his own. That of Brahmā is called Brahma-loka, situated on the summit of Mount Meru; that of Vishṇu, Vaikuṇṭha, on the Himālayas; that of S'iva and Kuvera, Kailāsa, also on the Himālayas; that of Indra, Svarga or Nandana. The latter, though properly on one of the points of Mount Meru, below Brahmā's paradise, is sometimes identified with the sphere of the sky or heaven in general. *Uddhṛita-dā°*, lit. 'having the thorns of Dānavas extracted.' *Kaṇṭaka*, 'a thorn,' is often used for a noxious person or thing. *Dānava*, see p. 268, n. 2. *Nata-parvabhiḥ = nimna-parvabhiḥ* (*natāni anunnatāni parvāṇi yesham*, K.) Cf. *nata-nāsika*, 'flat-nosed;' also Rāmāy. i. 1, 64, *śareṇānata-parvaṇā* [*bibheda sapta-tālān*], which should be resolved into *śareṇa ānata-parvaṇā*, not *anata*, &c. *Purusha-keśarin=nara-siṅha*, 'the man-lion,' i. e. Vishṇu; for in this monstrous shape of a creature half-man, half-lion, which was his fourth Avatāra or incarnation, Vishṇu delivered the three worlds, or earth, Pātāla, and heaven, from the tyranny of an insolent demon called Hiraṇya-kaśipu, who had usurped the sovereignty of Indra (see Vishṇu-p. p. 126; Indian Wisdom, p. 331).

[1] 'Verily, when servants [delegates] succeed in mighty enterprises, understand thou that (there has been) peculiar condescension [distinguished capacity] on-the-part-of (their) masters. How indeed could Aruṇa be the disperser of the-shades-of-night, if the thousand-rayed-one did not place him in front (of his car)?' *Niyojyāḥ=sevakāḥ*, S'. *Sambhāvanā-guṇam =satkāra-viśesham*, K. (see p. 271, n. 1). *Sambhāvanā* may mean 'fitness,' 'capability,' as well as 'honour.' The condescension consisted in placing Dushyanta in front of the battle, just as the Sun places the Dawn in front of his chariot. *Sahasra-kiraṇa* is one of the innumerable names for the Sun. As to Aruṇa, 'the Dawn,' see p. 142, n. 3. *Dhuri=rathāgre*, S'.; *=agre, puro-bhāge*, K.

Verse 168. VASANTA-TILAKĀ (a variety of S'AKVARĪ). See verses 8, 27, 31, &c., 157.

मातलिः ।

सदृशमेवैतत् । ॥ स्तोकमन्तरमतीत्य ॥ आयुष्मन् । इतः । पश्य

नाकपृष्ठगतस्य सौभाग्यमात्मयशसः ।
विच्छित्तिशेषैः सुरसुन्दरीणां
वर्णैरमी कल्पलतांशुकेषु ।
सञ्चिन्त्य गीतिक्षममर्थबन्धं
दिवौकसस्त्वच्चरितं लिखन्ति ॥१६९॥

राजा ।

मातले । असुरसम्ग्रहारोत्सुकेन पूर्वेद्युर्दिवमधिरोहता न

---

[1] 'Behold the sublimity [beauty, auspiciousness] of (thy) own fame that has reached to the vault of heaven. With the tints remaining from the colours (used in the toilet) of the heavenly fair-ones, these inhabitants of the sky are painting [tracing] thy exploits on vestments [tapestry, leaves] of the Kalpa-tree, thinking of verses suitable for singing.' *Vićchitti* = *ranga, rāga*, S'. and C'. *Vićchitti-śeshaih* = *viśishṭair varṇaiḥ*, K., i. e. *kusuma-kasturikā-ćandanādibhiḥ*, 'with flowers, musk, sandal, and other cosmetics.' The first sense of the word is 'excision,' 'cutting off;' it rarely has the sense required here, of 'rouge,' 'paint.' Compare *bhakti-ćcheda*, 'the coloured streak (marking Vaishṇava) devotion,' Megha-d. verse 20. *Sura-sundarīṇām* = *divya-strīṇām*. *Kalpa-latānśukeshu* = *kalpa-latā-vastreshu*, S'. and C'. The first sense of *anśuka* is 'cloth,' 'tapestry;' it is said to bear the meaning 'leaf,' and may be so used here; in which case the idea may be that the gods are writing Dushyanta's memoirs on the leaves of the Kalpa tree. K.'s comment is not quite clear, *kalpa-latāsu anśukābharaṇādi* [*na*] *vidyante iti prasiddha;* but it seems likely, especially if reference is made to p. 155, n. 3 of this play, that he intends to imply that the Kalpa tree, which was a tree yielding everything (see p. 272, n. 1), produced the vestments or tapestry on which they might be supposed to design the adventures of Dushyanta. *Gīti-kshamam* = *gāna-yogyam* is the reading of K. and the Bengāli; most of the Deva-n. MSS. have *gīta-kshamam* (cf. p. 29, n. 1 at the end). *Artha-bandham* = *padam*, 'a verse,' 'word;' *artho badhyate anena iti artha-bandhaḥ padam*, K.; cf. *tulyānu-rāga-piśunam lalitārtha-bandham pattre niveśitam udāharaṇam priyāyāḥ*, &c., Vikram., Act II.

Verse 169. UPAJĀTI or ĀKHYĀNAKĪ. See verses 41, 107, 121, 126, 142, 156, 158, 166.

लक्षितः स्वर्गमार्गः । कतरस्मिन्मरुतां पथि वर्तामहे ।
मातलिः ।
चित्स्रोतसं वहति यो गगनप्रतिष्ठां
ज्योतींषि वर्तयति च प्रविभक्तरश्मिः ।
तस्य द्वितीयहरिविक्रमनिस्तमस्कं
वायोरिमं परिवहस्य वदन्ति मार्गम् ॥१७०॥

---

[1] 'In which course [path, orbit] of the (seven) winds are we now moving?' The Hindūs divide the heavens into seven Mārgas or Pathas, i. e. paths, courses, orbits (like the stories of the Mussalmān creed), assigning a particular *vāyu* or wind to each. Cf. Vishṇu-p. p. 212. The first of these seven, *vāyu-mārgāḥ* or *vāyu-pathas*, is identical with the *bhuvar-loka*, or atmospheric region, extending from the *bhūr-loka*, or terrestrial region [comprising the earth, and the *adho-loka*, called Pātāla], upwards to the sun. The wind assigned to this Mārga is called *āvaha*, and its office is to bear along the atmosphere, clouds, meteors, lightning, &c. The other six make up the *svar-loka* or heavenly region with which Svarga is often identified (cf. p. 272, n. 2) in the following order :—The 2nd Mārga is that of the sun, and its wind, called *pravaha* or *pravāha*, causes the sun to revolve ; 3rd, that of the moon, its wind *saṃvaha* or *saṃvāha* impels the moon ; 4th, that of the *nakshatra*, or lunar constellations, its wind *udvaha* causes the revolution of these asterisms ; 5th, that of the *graha*, or planets, its wind *vivāha* bears along the seven planets ; 6th, that of the *saptarshi*, or seven stars of the Great Bear, its wind *parivaha* bears along these luminaries, as well as the *svar-gaṅgā*, or heavenly Ganges [*saptarshi-čakraṃ svar-gaṅgāṃ shashṭhaḥ parivahas tathā*]; it appears from the next verse that this was the Mārga in which Indra's car was at the moment moving ; 7th, that of *dhruva*, or the polar-star, the pivot or axis of the whole planetary system, to which, according to the Vishṇu-p. (pp. 230, 240), 'all the celestial luminaries are bound by aerial cords, and are made to travel in their proper orbits, being kept in their places by their respective bands of air.' According to the Brah-māṇḍa-p., from which, as quoted by K., the above account is taken, the wind of the seventh Mārga, causing the revolution of the polar-star, is *parāvāha* [? *parāvaha*]. All the Deva-n. MSS. read *katarasmin* for *katamasmin;* sometimes *katara* is used for *katama*.

[2] 'They call this road, freed-from-all-impurities-by-the-second-stride-of-

---

राजा ।

मातले । अतः खलु सबाह्यान्तःकरणो ममान्तरात्मा

Vishṇu, (the road) of that wind Parivaha, which bears along the triple-flowing-river [Ganges] located in heaven, and causes the stars [of the Great Bear] to revolve, duly-distributing-their-rays.' See the last note. *Tri-srotas=svar-gangā=mandākinī*, K. The Ganges was supposed to take its rise in the toe of Vishṇu [whence one of its names, *Vishṇu-padī*]; thence it flowed through the heavenly sphere, being borne along by the wind Parivaha and identified with the Mandākinī, or Milky way: its second course is through the earth; but the weight of its descent was borne by S'iva's head, whence after wandering among the tresses of his hair, it descended through a chasm in the Himālayas: its third course is through Pātāla, or the lower regions, the residence of the Daityas and Nāgas, and not to be confounded with Naraka, 'hell,' 'the place of punishment.' *Gagana-pratishṭhām=ākāśa-sthām*, S'. and C'.; were it not for this interpretation I should translate 'the glory of the skies;' cf. p. 260, l. 11. There is doubtless a double-entendre. *Jyotīnshi*, &c., i. e. *saptarshīnāṃ dhishnyāni*, K. *Pravibhakta-raśmiḥ*, i. e. *asankīrṇa-raś-mayas tejānsi yasmin karmaṇi tat tathoktam*, K. *Vartayati=sañcārayati*, K. *Dvitīya-hari°*, i. e. *dvitīyena harer vishṇor vikrameṇa pāda-nyāsena nirdosham*, K. *Tasya vāyor*, &c., i. e. *tasya parīvāhākhyasya vāyor mārgam panthānam imam gṛihṇanti āmananti*. *Parivāho* [sic] *nāma svar-gangāṃ saptarshi-maṇḍalam pravartayati shashṭho vāyu-skandho yathoktam Brahmāṇḍa-purāṇe*, K. The story of Vishṇu's second stride was this—An Asura or Daitya (see p. 86, n. 2) named Bali or Mahābali, a descendant of Hiraṇya-kaśipu had, by his devotions, gained the dominion of Heaven, Earth, and Pātāla. Vishṇu undertook to trick him out of his power, and assuming the form of a Vāmana, or dwarf (his fifth Avatāra), he appeared before the giant, and begged, as a boon, as much land as he could pace in three steps. This was granted, and the god immediately expanded himself till he filled the world, deprived Bali at the first step, of earth; at the second, of heaven; but, in consideration of some merit, left Pātāla still under his rule. Another account makes him comprehend earth in his first step, the region of the air in his second, and heaven in his third. Hence *tri-vikrama*, *tri-pāda*, as names of Vishṇu. See Indian Wisdom, p. 331, n. 1. The Beng. MSS. have, in place of *tasya dvitīya* &c., *tasya vyapeta-rajasaḥ pravahasya vāyor mārgo dvitīya-hari-vikrama-pūta eshaḥ.*

[1] 'Hence, indeed, do-I-feel-a-delightful-repose in all my senses [organs] external and internal,' lit. 'hence my inner soul along with my external

प्रसीदति । || रथाङ्गमवलोक्य || मेघपदवीमवतीर्णौ स्वः ।

मातलिः ।

कथमवगम्यते ।

राजा ।

अयमरविवरेभ्यश्चातकैर्निष्पतद्भि-
र्हरिभिरचिर्भासां तेजसा चानुलिप्तैः ।
गतमुपरि घनानां वारिगर्भोदराणां
पिशुनयति रथस्ते शीकरक्लिन्ननेमिः ॥१७१॥

organs feels (a pleasurable) repose.' Cf. in Vikram. end of Act IV, *tvad-darśanena prasanno me savāhyāntarātmā*, i. e. 'body and soul,' 'my external and internal being,' 'my outer and inner man.' And again, *Urvaśī-gātra-sparśād iva nirvritam me sa-hridayaṃ śarīram*. The organs of sense (*indriya*) according to the Sānkhya system are divided into two classes, external, *vāhyendriya;* and internal, *antar-indriya*. The external are of two kinds : the five 'organs of perception,' *jñānendriya*, viz. the ear, eye, skin, tongue, and nose; and the five 'organs of action,' *karmendriya*, viz. the throat, hand, foot, organ of excretion, and that of generation. The internal organs are three, viz. *manas*, 'the mind,' or organ of thought; *buddhi*, 'the reason,' or organ of apprehension ; *ahankāra*, 'individuality,' or 'self-consciousness.' *Ćitta*, 'the heart,' or organ of feeling, is sometimes added. The Amara-k. (i. 4, 17) divides the Indriyas into two grand classes : 1. *karmendriyāṇi;* and 2. *buddhīndriyāṇi* or *dhīndriyāṇi*, 'intellectual organs ;' the latter comprises the *jñānendriyāṇi* with *manas;* this seems to be the popular division. Cf. Vikram., Act III, *bhavitavya-tānuvidhayīni buddhīndriyāṇi*.

[1] 'We have descended to the path of the clouds,' i. e. to the atmospheric region between the sun and the earth, the Mārga of the clouds and of the Āvaha wind (see p. 275, n. 1). The chariot must, therefore, have traversed with the speed of lightning, the four intervening Mārgas of the planets, lunar constellations, moon, and sun. If the Beng. reading, *pravahasya*, be adopted in the last verse, the transition would merely be from one Mārga to the next.

[2] 'Here [*ayam*] by the Ćātakas flying forth through the interstices of the spokes, and by the horses glistening with the flash of the lightnings, thy chariot, the rings [circumferences] of whose wheels are bedewed with

<hr>

Verse 171. MĀLINĪ or MĀNINĪ. See verses 10, 19, 20, 38, 55, 109, 110, 120.

मातलिः ।

स्थणादायुष्मान्स्वाधिकारभूमौ वर्तिष्यते ।

राजा ॥ अधोऽवलोकम ॥

वेगावतरणादाश्चर्यदर्शनः संलक्ष्यते मनुष्यलोकः । तथा हि
शैलानामवरोहतीव शिखरादुन्मज्जतां मेदिनी
पर्णाभ्यन्तरलीनतां विजहति स्कन्धोदयात्पादपाः ।
सन्तानान्त्रनुभावनष्टसलिला व्यक्तिं भजन्त्यापगाः
केनाप्युत्क्षिपतेव पश्य भुवनं मत्पार्श्वमानीयते ॥१७२॥

---

mist, betrays (our) progress over clouds whose bellies are pregnant with
rain.' *Ara=nemy-avashṭambha;* the Beng. MSS. and the Mackenzie
read *aga,* 'a mountain.' *Ara-vivarebhyaś ćakrāvayavānāṃ vivarebhyo
antarāla-pradeśebhyaḥ,* K. *Nishpatadbhiḥ=nirgaćchadbhiḥ,* K. (see p. 253,
n. 1 at the end). The Cātaka is a kind of cuckoo. The Hindūs suppose
that it drinks only the water of the clouds, and their poets usually intro-
duce allusions to this bird in connexion with cloudy or rainy weather
(see Megha-d. verses 9, 23, 113; Raghu-v. xvii. 60). So *trishūkulaiś
ćātaka-pakshiṇāṃ kulaiḥ prayāćitā valāhakāḥ,* Ritu-s. ii. 3. *Haribhir=
aśvaiḥ,* especially Indra's horses (see p. 12, n. 1, and cf. Raghu-v. iii. 43).
Aćira-bhāsām = vidyutām, S. *Gatam,* &c., *teshām meghānām upari
ūrdhva-bhāge gatam gamanam,* K. *Piśunayati=sūćayati,* K.

¹ 'The earth descends as it were from the summit of the upward-rising
[emergent] mountains. The trees, from the elevation [coming-into-view,
rising, appearing] of (their) trunks, lose their state of being enveloped
[concealed, wrapped] in their foliage. The rivers whose-waters-were-lost-
in-narrowness, become visible [acquire manifestation] from the expansion
(of their waters). Behold! the earth is being brought up to my side
[near me], as if by some one flinging it upwards.' In the same way to a
voyager in a balloon at a very great height, the surface of the earth would
seem flat, the trees would be compressed within their foliage like mush-
rooms, and the rivers shrivel into threads or tiny rivulets; but, on
descending, the mountains would appear to stand out, and the earth to
recede from them, the trees would exhibit their elevation, and the rivers
their breadth of water. *Unmajjatām=udgaćchatām,* K. *Avarohati=adho-
gaćchati,* K. *Parṇābhyantara°.* The Colebrooke MS. and my own have

---

Verse 172. ŚĀRDŪLA-VIKRĪḌITA. See verses 14, 30, 36, 39, 40, 63, 79, 85, &c., 149.

मातलिः ।

साधु दृष्टम् । ॥ सबहुमानं विलोक्य ॥ अहो उदाररमणीया पृथिवी ।

राजा ।

मातले । कतमोऽयं पूर्वापरसमुद्रावगाढः कनकरसनि-
स्यन्दी सान्ध्य इव मेघपरिघः सानुमानालोक्यते[1] ।

मातलिः ।

आयुष्मन् । एष खलु हेमकूटो[2] नाम किम्पुरुषपर्वतस्तपसां
सिद्धिक्षेत्रम् । पश्य ।

स्वायम्भुवान्मरीचेर्यः प्रबभूव प्रजापतिः ।
सुरासुरगुरुः सोऽत्र सपत्नीकस्तपस्यति[3] ॥१७३॥

---

parṇa-svāntara; the Taylor, *parṇeshvantara;* the Mackenzie, *parṇa-pra-stara;* K., *parṇāntara-vilīnam. Skandhodayāt=kroḍāvirbhāvāt,* K. *San-tānat=jala-vistārāt,* K.; the other Deva-n. have *santānais. Tanubhāra°, tanubhāvena sūkshmatvena adrishṭaṃ salilaṃ yāsāṃ,* K. *Vyaktim bha-janti,* i. e. *vyaktā bhavanti,* K.

[1] 'What mountain yonder is seen, bathing itself in the eastern and western ocean, pouring down a golden stream like a bar [bank, gate] of evening clouds?' *Parigha* occurs in p. 87, l. 6, meaning 'the bar of a gate,' but it may also denote the gate itself. *Sānu-mat,* lit. 'possessed of table-land,' 'a mountain having extensive level ground on its summit.'

[2] *Hema-kūṭa,* 'golden-peaked,' a sacred range of mountains lying among the Himālaya chain, and apparently identical with, or immediately ad-jacent to Kailāsa, the paradise of Kuvera, the god of wealth, as it is here described as the mountain of the Kimpurushas, or servants of Kuvera. They are a dwarfish kind of monster, with the body of a man and the head of a horse, and are otherwise called Kinnara (*aśva-mukha, turanga-mukha*). This mountain is also here described as 'the scene [place, field] of the perfect fulfilment of penance.' The Mackenzie MS. has *tapasvinām* for *tapasām.*

[3] 'That Prajāpati [Kaśyapa], who sprang from Marīci, the Self-existent's-son [i. e. from Marīci, son of Brahmā], (and who is) the father of the gods and demons, practices penance here along with his wife (Aditi).' An account of Kaśyapa, who, as son of Marīci, is called Mārīca, is given

Verse 173. ŚLOKA or ANUSHṬUBH. See verses 5, 6, 11, 12, 26, 47, 50, 51, &c., 164.

राजा ।

तेन ह्यनतिक्रमणीयानि श्रेयांसि । प्रदक्षिणीकृत्य[2] भगवन्तं
गन्तुमिच्छामि ।

मातलिः ।

प्रथमः कल्पः[3] ।

॥ नाभ्येनावतीर्णौ ॥

राजा ॥ सविस्मयम् ॥

उपोढशब्दा न रथाङ्गनेमयः
प्रवर्तमानं न च दृश्यते रजः ।
अभूतलस्पर्शतया निरुन्धत-
स्तवावतीर्णोऽपि रथो न लक्ष्यते ॥१७४॥

---

in p. 22, n. 3, and p. 86, n. 2. He is here said to be one of the Prajāpatis,
or fathers of all created things, who were Brahmā's sons, created by him
to supply the universe with inhabitants, and who, after fulfiling their
mission, retired from the world to practise penance and prepare for death.
The Vāyu-purāṇa certainly reckons Kaśyapa, with his father-in-law Daksha
and other sages, among the Prajāpatis, but he does not belong to the seven
original Prajāpatis of whom his father Marīci is one, nor to the ten enume-
rated by Manu (i. 35). Of the thirteen daughters of Daksha married to
Kaśyapa, the eldest, and his favourite wife, was the Aditi introduced here,
from whom were born the gods and particularly the twelve Ādityas, the
several representatives of the sun in the twelve months of the year. From
Diti, Danu, and others of the remaining twelve, came the Asuras or demons ;
and, from Vinatā, Aruṇa, 'the Dawn' (see p. 142, n. 3), and Garuḍa, 'the
vehicle of Vishṇu and king of birds.' *Svāyambhuvāt=Brahma-sunoḥ*, K.
Surāsura-guruḥ, as to *guru*, see p. 173, n. 3, and p. 91, l. 3. *Sa-patnīkas*,
i. e. *patnyā Aditya saha* (cf. *sa-strīka, sa-śrīka*, &c.)

[1] *Anatikramaṇīya*, cf. p. 68, l. 7 ; p. 91, l. 3. *Sreyāṇsi = śubhāni*,
kaśyapa-darśana-namaskārādīni, 'lucky occasions,' 'opportunities for
obtaining blessings, such as visiting and paying homage to Kaśyapa.'

[2] *Pradakshiṇī-kritya*, see p. 159, l. 8.

[3] 'A noble resolve,' 'a prime idea,' = *mukhyaḥ pakshaḥ*, K. ; cf.
p. 205, l. 7.

[4] 'The circumferences of the chariot-wheels cause no sound, and no

Verse 174. VAṆŚA-STHAVILA (a variety of JAGATĪ). See verses 18, 22, 23, &c., 161.

मातलिः ।

एतावानेव शतक्रतोरायुष्मतश्च विशेषः ।

राजा ।

मातले । कतमस्मिन्प्रदेशे मारीचाश्रमः ।

मातलिः ॥ हस्तेन दर्शयन् ॥

वल्मीकार्धनिमग्नमूर्तिरुरसा सन्दष्टसर्पत्वचा
कण्ठे जीर्णलतामतानवलयेनात्यर्थसम्पीडितः ।
अंसव्यापि शकुन्तनीडनिचितं बिभ्रज्जटामण्डलं
यत्र स्थाणुरिवाचलो मुनिरसावभ्यर्कबिम्बं स्थितः॥१७५॥

---

dust is seen rising-in-advance (of us); the chariot of thee reining-in (thy
steeds), although it has descended (to the earth), is not observed (to have
done so) by-reason-of-its-not-touching the surface of the ground.' *Upodha-
śabdāḥ=prāpta-dhvanayaḥ*, K. (cf. *upodha-rāya*, Vikram., Act II). *Pra-
vartamāna* may mean 'rising in front of us' (cf. p. 11, l. 3). *Nirundha-
taḥ=niyrihnatah*, K. *Na lakshyate*, see p. 70, n. 3 at the end. In Vikram.,
Aet I, when the car of Purūravas touches the ground, the direction is
rathāvatāra-kshobham nāṭayantī, 'acting the concussion (caused) by the
descent of the chariot.' Such, Mātali remarks, is the difference between
the car of Indra and that of mortal heroes.

[1] 'Where stands yon sage, towards [facing] the sun's orb, immovable
as the trunk-of-a-tree, (his) body half-buried in an ant-hill, with (his)
breast closely-encircled by a snake's-skin, round the throat excessively
pinched by a necklace (formed) of the tendril of a withered creeper, wear-
ing a circular-mass-of-matted-hair enveloping (his) shoulders (and) filled
with bird's-nests.' *Valmīkārdha*, &c., so read K. and the Mackenzie MS.;
the other Deva-n., *valmīkāgra*. *Valmīka* (=*kṛimi-kṛita-mṛittikāćaya*) is
the mound of earth thrown up by the large ants of India. These hillocks
sometimes rise, in Bengal, to the height of eight or ten feet, and are held
sacred; (see Manu iv. 46. 238.) Such was the immovable impassiveness
of this ascetic, that the ants had thrown up their mound as high as his
waist, without being disturbed, and the birds had built their nests in his
hair. *Sandashṭa-s°=āślishṭa-nirmokena*, cf. p. 120, n. 3. The serpent's
skin was used by the ascetic in place of the regular Brahmanical cord,
called *yajñopavīta;* see Indian Wisdom, p. 201. *Latā-pratāna=latā-san-*

Verse 175. ŚĀRDŪLA-VIKRĪḌITA (a variety of ATIDHṚITI). See verses 14, &c., 172.

राजा ।

नमस्ते कष्टतंपसे[1] ।

मातलिः ॥ संयतप्रग्रहं रथं कृत्वा ॥

महाराज । एतावदितिपरिवर्धितमन्दारवृक्षं[2] प्रजापतेराश्रमं प्रविष्टौ स्वः ।

राजा ।

स्वर्गादधिकतरं निर्वृत्तिस्थानम् । अमृतंह्रदमिवावगा-[3] ढोऽस्मि ।

मातलिः ॥ रथं स्थापयित्वा ॥

अवतरत्वायुष्मान् ।

राजा ॥ अवतीर्य[4] ॥

मातले । भवान्कथमिदानीम् ।

मातलिः ।

संयन्त्रितो मया रथः । वयमप्यवतरामः । ॥ तथा कृत्वा ॥ इत आयुष्मन् । ॥ परिक्रम्य ॥ दृश्यन्तामत्रभवतामृषीणां तपो- वनभूमयः ।

---

tāna, 'the spreading part of a creeper.' *Jaṭā-maṇḍala* is the circle or bundle of matted entangled hair which ascetics allowed to grow on the crown of their heads, and which fell in long clotted tresses over the back and shoulders. *Jaṭā* is, especially, S'iva's hair so plaited and arranged, through which the Ganges meandered before its descent upon the earth. *Nicitam = pūritam*, K. *Sthāṇuḥ = śākhā-hīnas taru-skandhaḥ*. *Abhyarkavimbam = sūrya-maṇḍalābhimukham*, K. The Mackenzie MS. has *adhyarka°*.

[1] *Kashṭaṃ kṛićchram tapo yasya sa tathoktaḥ*, K.

[2] 'Possessed of the Mandāra-tree reared by Aditi.' This was one of the five trees of Svarga (see p. 272, n. 1), and is probably the tree intended here, as, in verse 176, the Kalpa tree also is said to have graced Kaśyapa's retreat, which the commentator thence infers to have been located in part of Svarga. *Mandāra*, 'the coral tree,' may also mean 'swallow-wort.'

[3] *Amṛita*, 'the beverage of immortality,' 'the nectar' of the Hindū gods, supposed to be a liquid substance distilled by the moon, who is thence called *amṛita-sū*, 'nectar-producer;' *amṛitādhāra*, 'nectar-repository.'

[4] *Avatarishyati iti śeshaḥ*, S'.; i. e. supply *avatarishyati*.

राजा ।

ननु विस्मयादवलोकयामि ।

प्राणानामनिलेन वृत्तिरचिता सत्कल्पवृक्षे वने
तोये काञ्चनपद्मरेणुकपिशे धर्माभिषेकक्रिया ।
ध्यानं रत्नशिलातलेषु विबुधस्त्रीसन्निधौ संयमो
यत्काङ्क्षन्ति तपोभिरन्यमुनयस्तस्मिंस्तपस्यन्त्यमी ॥१७६॥

मातलिः ।

उत्सर्पिणी खलु महतां प्रार्थना । ॥ परिक्रम्य । आकाशे ॥ अये
वृद्धशाकल्य । किमनुतिष्ठति भगवान्मारीचः । किं ब्रवीषि ।
दाक्षायण्या पतिव्रताधर्ममधिकृत्य पृष्टस्तस्यै महर्षि-
पत्नीसहितायै कथयंतीति ।

---

[1] '(The place) to which other sages aspire by (their) penances, (where there is) habitual [suitable, adequate] support of life by air in a grove in-which-the-Kalpa-tree-is-found; (where there is) the performance of religious ablutions in water, brown with the dust of the golden lotus; (where there is) meditation (while seated) on jewelled slabs of marble, (and) restraint (of the passions) in the presence of celestial nymphs; in (such a place as) this these (sages) are performing penance.' *Praṇānāṃ vrittiḥ = jīvanam*, K. The Hindūs imagine that supporting life upon air is a proof of the highest degree of spirituality to which a man can attain. *Sat-kalpa-vrikshe = vidyamāna-kalpa-drume*, K.; *= vidyamāna-kalpa-tarau*, S. and C. The Colebrooke MS. has *sankalpa-vrikshe*; this use of *sat* is noticeable. *Śilā-tala*, 'the surface of a stone slab or seat;' cf. p. 76, l. 3. *Vibudha-strī = divyāṅganā*, K. *Saṃyama = niyatendriyatva*, K. *Ebhiḥ sat-kalpa-vrikshatvādikair viśeshair ayam pradeśaḥ svarga iti pratīyate*, 'by these attributes of the Kalpa tree, &c., it is inferred that this place was part of Svarga,' K. As to the Kalpa tree, see p. 272, n. 1. *Yat*, &c., i.e. *yat sthānam anye kānkshanti tasmin svarga-pradeśe amī munayas tāni phalāni parihritya tapasyanti iti anena teshām mokshārthitvaṃ gamyate*, K.

[2] 'Verily the aspirations [desire] of the great soar upwards [are ever mounting upwards].' *Utsarpiṇī = udyamana-śīlā = atiśayinī*, K.

[3] As to *ākāśe* and *kim bravishi*, see p. 96, n. 3.

[4] 'Being questioned by Dākshāyaṇī [i. e. his wife Aditi] respecting the

Verse 176. ŚĀRDŪLA-VIKRĪḌITA. See verses 14, 30, 36, 39, 40, 63, 79, 85, &c., 175.

राजा ॥ कर्णं दत्त्वा ॥

अये । प्रतिपाल्यावसराः खलु मुनयः ।

मातलिः ॥ राजानमवलोक्य ॥

अस्मिन्नशोकवृक्षमूले तावदास्तामायुष्मान् । यावत्त्वा-
मिन्द्रगुरवे निवेदयितुमन्तरान्वेषी भवामि ।

राजा ।

यथा भवान्मन्यते । ॥ इति स्थितः ॥

मातलिः ।

आयुष्मन् । साधयाम्यहम् । ॥ इति निष्क्रान्तः ॥

---

duties [duty] of a wife devoted to her husband, he is recounting them [it] to her, in company with the wives of the Maharshis.' *Dākshāyaṇī* is a patronymic applicable to any of the daughters of Daksha (see p. 279, n. 3). *Pati-vratā*, cf. p. 241, n. 3. *Adhikṛitya*, see p. 6, n. 2. *Maharshi*, 'a great saint;' the Maharshi was one step in advance of the Ṛishi or simple 'saint.' The classification of Ṛishis varies, but the following seems to be the usual gradation : 1. Ṛishi; 2. Maharshi; 3. Paramarshi; 4. Devarshi; 5. Brahmarshi. Amara mentions two other orders, Kāṇḍarshis and S'rutarshis. The Rājarshi was a mixed order (see p. 39, n. 3).

[1] 'We must await the leisure of saints.' So reads the Mackenzie MS., supported, apparently, by K. *Munayaḥ* is of course the nominative, but such is the terseness of compounds like *pratipālyāvasarāḥ* that a literal English translation is impossible. The other Deva-n. have *pratipālyāvasaraḥ khalu prastāvaḥ*.

[2] The Aśoka (Jonesia Asoka) is one of the most beautiful of Indian trees. Sir W. Jones observes that 'the vegetable world scarce exhibits a richer sight than an Aśoka tree in full bloom. It is about as high as an ordinary cherry tree.' The flowers are very large, and 'beautifully diversified with tints of orange-scarlet, of pale yellow, and of bright orange, which form a variety of shades according to the age of the blossom.'

[3] 'Opportune time' is one of the meanings of *antara*. As to *gurave*, cf. p. 173, n. 3 in the middle. Kaśyapa was the reputed father of Indra.

[4] 'I go-to-do (what I proposed),' 'I will-do (as I said);' cf. p. 213, l. 1, and p. 17, l. 8.

राजा ॥ निमित्तं सूचयित्वा ॥[1]

मनोरथाय नाशंसे किं बाहो स्पन्दसे वृथा ।
पूर्वावधीरितं श्रेयो दुःखं हि परिवर्त्तते ॥१७७॥[2]

नेपथ्ये ।

[a] मा खु चावलं करेहि । कहं गदो एव्व अत्तणो पर्किदिं ।

राजा ॥ कर्णौ दत्त्वा ॥

अभूमिरियमविनयस्य । को नु खल्वेष निषिध्यते ।[3][4]

॥ शब्दानुसारेणावलोक्य । सस्मितम् ॥ अये । को नु खल्वयमनुबध्य-
मानस्तपस्विनीभ्यामबालसत्त्वो बालः ।[5]

अर्धपीतस्तनं मातुरामर्देक्लिष्टकेशरम् ।
प्रक्रीडितुं सिंहशिशुं बलात्कारेण कर्षति ॥१७८॥[6]

[a] मा खलु चापलं कुरु । कथं गत एवात्मनः प्रकृतिम् ।

---

[1] *Nimittaṃ sūcayitvā* (=*śakunaṃ nirūpya*, K.), see p. 20, n. 4.

[2] 'I expect not to (obtain my) desire; why, O arm, throbbest thou (thus) vainly? For happiness formerly scorned turns to misery.' K. observes that *manorathāya* here=*manoratham prāptum*, and refers to Pāṇ. ii. 3, 14; so *phalebhyo yāti*=*phalāny āhartum yāti*. As to the throbbing of the arm, see p. 20, n. 5. *S'reyaḥ*=*śubham*, i. e. *S'akuntalā-rūpam*, 'consisting of S'akuntalā,' K. *Hi parivartate*, K. has *vipari-vartate* and *sat parivartate*.

[3] 'Act not so wildly [do not commit such a wild, wilful act]. What! has he gone already to his own nature?' Cf. Raghu-v. iii. 42. *Prakṛiti*, 'one's natural character;' cf. p. 72, n. 2. *Gata*, see p. 161, n. 3 at the end.

[4] 'This is no place for petulance [insolence];' cf. p. 271, l. 11.

[5] 'Who is this child with unchild-like disposition [nature], closely attended by two female ascetics?' *Anubadhyamāna*, the Mackenzie MS. has *anugamyamāna*. *Anubandha*, lit. 'tying after,' 'following at the heels,' 'sticking closely to,' very forcibly expresses the close attendance of a nurse upon a child.

[6] 'He forcibly drags to play (with him) a lion's cub that-has-but-half-sucked-its mother's dug, (and) whose-mane-is-disordered-by-rough-hand-ling,' or 'he forcibly drags from its mother,' &c.

Verses 177 and 178. S'LOKA or ANUSHṬUBH. See verses 5, 6, 11, 12, 26, 47, 50, 51, 53, 73, 76, 84, 87, 125, 127, 146, 154, 155, 160, 164.

॥ ततः प्रविशति यथानिर्दिष्टकर्मा तपस्विनीभ्यां बालः ॥

वालः ।

[a] जिम्भ सिङ्घ । दन्ताइं दे गणइस्सं ।

प्रथमा ।

[b] अविणीद । किं णो अपच्चणिविसेसाणि सत्ताणि विप्प-
अरेसि । हन्त वड्ढइ दे संरम्भो । ठाणे क्खु इसिजणेण
सव्वदमणोत्ति किदणामहेओसि ।

राजा ।

किं नु खलु बालेऽस्मिन्नौरस इव पुत्रे स्निह्यति मे मनः ।
नूनमनपत्यता मां वत्सलयति ।

द्वितीया ।

[c] एसा खु केसरिणी तुमं लंघेदि । जइ से पुत्तअं ण मुञ्चेसि ।

वालः ॥ सस्मितम् ॥

[d] अम्हहे । बलिअं क्खु भीदोम्हि । ॥ इत्यधरं दर्शयति ॥

[a] जृम्भस्व सिंह । दन्तांस्ते गणयिष्यामि ।   [b] अविनीत । किं नोऽपत्यनिर्वि-
शेषाणि सत्त्वानि विप्रकरोषि । हन्त वर्धते ते संरम्भः । स्याने खलु ऋषिजनेन सर्वदमन
इति कृतनामधेयोऽसि ।   [c] एषा खलु केशरिणी त्वां लङ्घयति । यद्यस्याः पुत्रकं
न मुञ्चसि ।   [d] अहो । बलीयः खलु भीतोऽस्मि ।

---

[1] 'Why dost thou teaze the animals (cherished by us as if) not-differing-
from-our-offspring?' *Sattvāni*, cf. p. 55, n. 4. *Nir-viśeshāni*, cf. *suta-
nirviśeshaḥ nakulaḥ*, 'the ichneumon dear to him as a son,' Hitop. l. 2721,
and *mūshika-nirviśesha*, Hitop. l. 2395.

[2] 'It must certainly be my childlessness that causes me to yearn
(towards this child).' *Vatsala* or *vātsalya* is, properly, the yearning
affection of a cow for its calf, or a parent for its offspring.

[3] *Langhayati* = *ākramati*, K.   Cf. p. 97, n. 1.

[4] K. quotes a passage from the Vasanta-rājīya to shew that different
movements of the lips, such as biting the lip, pouting the under-lip, &c.,
were significant of various emotions.   The text is corrupt, but it appears
that *adhara-darśana* = *adhara-prasāraṇa* is [*an-ādare*] a gesture of con-
tempt.   Cf. Psalm xxii. 7, 'All they that see me laugh me to scorn; they
shoot out the lip.'

राजा ।

महत्तेजसो बीजं बालोऽयं प्रतिभाति मे ।
स्फुलिङ्गावस्थया वह्निरेधापेक्ष इव स्थितः ॥१७९॥

प्रथमा ।

[a] वच्छ । एदं बालमिन्दत्रं मुञ्च । अवरं दे कीलणत्रं दाइस्सं ।

बालः ।

[b] कहिं । देहि णं ।   ॥ इति हस्तं प्रसारयति ॥

राजा ।

कथं चक्रवर्तिलक्षणमप्यनेन धार्यते । तथा ह्यस्य
प्रलोभ्यवस्तुप्रणयप्रसारितो
विभाति जालग्रथिताङ्गुलिः करः ।
अलक्ष्यपत्त्रान्तरमिद्रागया
नवोषसा भिन्नमिवैकपङ्कजम् ॥१८०॥

[a] वत्स । एतं बालमृगेन्द्रकं मुञ्च । अपरं ते क्रीडनकं दास्यामि ।   [b] कुत्र ।
देहेनम् ।

---

[1] 'This child appears to me (to possess) the germ [rudiment] of mighty energy [spirit, courage]. He stands like fire in a state of scintillation [in a smouldering state], waiting (only) for fuel (that it may blaze up).' *Edhāpekshah=indhanāni kāṅkshiṇī,* K. The Bengālī MSS. have *edhaḥkshayaḥ.*

[2] 'The mark of a universal emperor;' see p. 15, n. 2, and p. 214, n. 2.

[3] 'His hand stretched forth to beg for a coveted object, having the fingers connected by a web, appears like [shines like] a single lotus-blossom, the spaces between whose petals is imperceptible, expanded by the early dawn, whose-glow-is-just-kindled.' *Praṇaya = prārthana,* S. *Jāla,* &c.; *jāleshu antareshu grathitāḥ saṃhatā aṅgulayo yasya,* K. For *grathitāṅgulih,* S. has *saṃhatāṅgulih = saṃślishṭāṅgulih,* and remarks

---

Verse 179. ŚLOKA or ANUSHTUBH. See verses 5, 6, 11, 12, 26, 47, 50, 51, &c., 178.
Verse 180. VANŚA-STHAVILA (a variety of JAGATĪ). See verses 18, 22, 23, &c., 174.

द्वितीया ।

[a] सुव्वदे । ण सक्को एसो वाश्रामेत्तेण विरमाबिदुं । गच्छ । मम किँरए उडए मङ्करडेअस्स इसिकुमारअस्स वष्षचित्तिदो मित्तिश्रामोरत्रो चिट्टदि । तं से उबहर ।

प्रथमा ।

[b] तह । ॥ इति निष्क्रान्ता ॥

[a] सुव्रते । न शक्य एप वाचामात्रेण विरमयितुम् । गच्छ । मदीय उटजे मार्किरडेयस्य ऋषिकुमारस्य चर्यैर्चिचितो मृत्तिकामयूरकस्तिष्ठति । तमस्योपहर ।   [b] तथा ।

---

that a hand whose fingers were thus united was indicative of great valour (*mahā-purushatva*). He adds *jāla-pāda-bhujāviti nara-nārāyaṇa-viśesha-ṇam uktam*, 'webbed-feet and webbed-hands are said to be character-istics of Nara and Nārāyaṇa.' Hindū poets reckon thirty-two marks of greatness, and he who possessed them all was said to be *dvātriṅśal-laksha-ṇopetaḥ*. The child's fingers, being drawn together by this membrane or web, would bear some resemblance to an expanding lotus-flower, the fingers answering to the long petals, which would be only separated towards the top. This seems to be the sense: my first inclination was to translate, 'having the fingers regularly marked with reticulated lines,' or 'having the fingers drawn together into (the form of) a bud.' *Alakshya* (=*adriśya*, K.), so read all the Deva-n. MSS. excepting my own, which has *ālakshya*, with the Beng.; S′., however, has *alakshya*. *Pattrāntaram* =*dala-vivaram*, K. and S′. *Iddha-rāgayā navoshasā*, &c.; *ushas*, 'the dawn,' is usually neuter in classical Sanskrit. In the Vedas, as here, it is feminine. Thus in Ṛig-v. i. 46, 1, *Esho ushā apūrvyā vyućdhati priyā divaḥ;* see also Ṛig-v. i. 48, 3. 5. 7. 8. 13; i. 62, 8; i. 92, 4; and i. 113, 4, &c. It is possible that the feminine noun *ushā* may form its vowel cases from *ushas*, as *jarā* from *jaras;* nom. *jarā, jarasau, jarasaḥ;* instr. *jarasā, jarābhyām, jarābhiḥ*, &c. (see Gram. 171). The following is the corrupt gloss of S′.: *ushaḥ-pratyushasi klīvam pihaprasvāntu yoshatīti koshaḥ.* K. explains *navoshasā* as a Bahuvrīhi, 'by the early-dawned one,' *navam usho yasyāḥ sā navoshā prātaḥsandhyā tayā bhinnaṃ vikasitam.* As to *pankaja*, see p. 213, n. 2.

[1] This pleonastic word, according to Lassen (Instit. Prāk. p. 118), is derived from the Sanskrit *kṛite*, and is equivalent to *pertinens ad*, 'in the cottage belonging to me,' &c. Some MSS. omit the word.

बालः ।

[a] इमिणा एव्व दाव कीलिस्सं । ॥ इति तापसीं विलोक्य हसति ॥

राजा ।

स्पृहयामि खलु दुर्ललितायास्मै[1] ।

आलक्ष्यदन्तमुकुलाननिमित्तहासै-
र्व्यक्तवर्णैरमणीयवचःप्रवृत्तीन् ।
अङ्काश्रयप्रणयिनस्तनयान्वहन्तो
धन्यास्तदङ्गरजसा मलिनीभवन्ति ॥१८१॥[2]

[a] एनेनैव तावत्क्रीडिष्यामि ।

---

[1] 'I have a great fancy for this unmanageable (child).' *Durlalita*, i. e. *durlabham īpsitaṃ yasya* (S'.), 'difficult to be coaxed or pleased,' 'wayward,' 'naughty.' K. reads *durlasitāya* and interprets by *dhūrtāya*, 'roguish,' 'mischievous.' The causal sense of the root *lal* is 'to coax,' though *dur-lālita* might then be expected. The primitive idea is certainly that of 'sporting,' 'toying,' 'taking pleasure,' as in the root *las*. So in Vikram., Act II, the king complains that his eye-sight has become *durlalitam*, i. e. 'difficult to be pleased,' 'fastidious,' by looking on Urvaśī, and that the beauties of Nature have no longer any charms for him; *upavana-latāsu ćakshur na badhnāti dhṛitiṃ tad-anganāloka-durlalitam*. The commentator there explains the word by *dur-āgrastam*. In Sāhit.-d. p. 193, l. 1, the following is cited from the Mahā-bh.: *Dhik dhik sūta kiṃ kṛitavān asi vatsasya me prakṛiti-durlalitasya*, where *durlalita* is explained by *durvilasita*.

[2] 'Happy (those parents who), carrying (their) little-sons fondly-soliciting-a-refuge-in-their-lap, having-buds-of-teeth-just- [scarcely, slightly] visible by their innocent [causeless, without reason] smiles, while-attempting-charming-prattle-in-indistinct-accents, are soiled by the dust of their (infantine) limbs !' *Ā-lakshya, ā* is here the prefix of diminution (see p. 228, n. 1). *Praṇayinaḥ=prārthakāḥ*, S. and C. *Malinī*, the Beng. have *parushī*. This is the verse with which Chézy is enraptured : '. . . strophe incomparable, que tout père, on plutôt toute mère, ne pourra lire sans sentir battre son cœur, tant le poète a su y rendre, avec les nuances les plus délicates, l'expression vivante de l'amour maternel.'

Verse 181. VASANTA-TILAKĀ (a variety of ŚAKVARĪ). See verses 8, 27, 31, &c., 170.

तापसी ।

[a] हीदु । एा मं अञ्चं गर्यैदि । ॥ पार्श्वमवलोकयति ॥ [b] को एत्य इसिकुमाराएं । ॥ राजानमवलोक्य ॥ [c] भद्रमुह । एहि दाव । मोएहि इमिणा दुम्मोअहत्थग्गाहेण डिम्भलीलाए बा-हीअमाणं बालमिइन्द्अं ।

राजा ॥ उपगम्य । सस्मितम् ॥

अयि भो महर्षिपुत्र ।

एवमाश्रमविरुद्धवृत्तिना
संयमः किमिति जन्मनस्त्वया ।
सत्त्वसंश्रयसुखोऽपि दूष्यते
कृष्णासर्पशिशुनेव चन्दनम् ॥१८२॥

[a] भवतु । न मामयं गणयति । [b] कोऽत्र ऋषिकुमाराणाम् । [c] भद्रमुख । एहि तावत् । मोचयानेन दुर्मोचहस्तग्राहेण डिम्भलीलया बाध्यमानं बालमृगेन्द्रकम् ।

---

[1] 'O gentle sir,' lit. 'O thou with auspicious countenance.' According to the Sāhit.-d. (p. 179, l. 16) *bhadra-mukha* and *saumya* are the titles used by the inferior characters in addressing the king's son : *saumya bhadra-mukhety evam adhamais tu kumārakaḥ.* They do not seem to be so restricted, as in Act V. the Beng. MSS. make Gautamī address the king himself as *bhadra-mukha;* and K. extends the application of both terms to any *mānya,* honourable person : *Bhadra-mukheti mānyasyāmantraṇe yathoktaṃ saumya bhadra-mukhety evam mānyo rājñaḥ suto vā.*

[2] 'Release the young lion being tormented in childish play by this (boy) the-grasp-of-whose-hand-is-difficult to unloose.' Some MSS. have *maindam* or *maindaam* for *mṛigendram;* the Mackenzie, *miindam.*

[3] 'How is it that by thee, whose behaviour is opposed to (the peaceful character of) a hermitage, (thy) father's humanity [forbearance], that-delights-in-the-protection-of-the-animals, is thus outraged; like the sandal-tree by the young of the black serpent ?' *Aśrama-viruddha,* cf. p. 38, l. 5. *Saṃyama=śama,* K., 'a vow to forbear hurting animals.' *Kim iti=kim-*

Verse 182. RATHODDHATĀ (a variety of TRISHTUBH), containing eleven syllables to the Pāda or quarter-verse, each Pāda being alike.

– ◡ – ◡ ◡ ◡ – ◡ – ◡ – ॥

तापसी ।

[a]भहमुह । एा हु अत्रं इसिकुमारत्रो ।

राजा ।

आकारसदृशं चेष्टितमेवास्य कथयति । स्थानप्रत्ययात्तु
वयमेवंतर्किणः ।

॥ यथाभ्यर्थितमनुतिष्ठन्वालस्पर्शमुपलभ्य । आत्मगतम् ॥

अनेन कस्यापि कुलाङ्कुरेण
स्पृष्टस्य गाचेषु सुखं ममैवम् ।
कां निर्वृतिं चेतसि तस्य कुर्या-
द्यस्यायमङ्गात्कृतिनः प्ररूढः ॥१८३॥

[a] भद्रमुख । न खल्वयमृषिकुमारः ।

---

artham, K. ; *iti* is frequently thus joined with *kim* (compare p. 71, l. 1).
Janmanas = janmano hetoh, K. So *prabhara = janma-hetu*, p. 44, l. 4,
n. 1 ; otherwise I should translate 'from thy birth.' The Beng. MSS. have
janmadas and *sanyami* agreeing with it. *Sukho*, the Mackenzie and K.
have *guṇo* (= *dharmaḥ*, K.) *Candanam*, as to the sandal, see p. 175, n. 1.
This celebrated tree seems to have paid dearly for the fragrance of its
wood : 'The root is infested by serpents ; the blossoms by bees ; the
branches by monkeys ; the summits by bears. In short, there is not a
part of the sandal-tree which is not occupied by the vilest impurities'
(Hitop., Book II, verse 163).

[1] 'His behaviour, (which is) conformable to his mien, says as much
[bespeaks it, betokens it].' *Kathayati*, compare p. 224, l. 7.

[2] 'Such (being) the-thrill-of-delight in the limbs of me touched by this
scion of the family of some one (unknown to me) ; what bliss must he
cause in the heart of that happy-man from whose body [loins] he sprang !'
Hindū poets are fond of alluding to the thrilling effect of the touch of a
child on the limbs of its parent, and *vice versâ*. Compare the parallel
passages in the Vikram., Act V, and the following from the Mahā-bh.,
Putra-sparśāt sukhataraḥ sparśo loke na vidyate. Aṅgāt, some MSS.,
including my own, have *aṅkāt*, 'from whose loins.' *Kritinaḥ = bhā-
gyaratah*, 'fortunate.' *Kritin* is properly 'one who has accomplished the
desire of his heart.'

Verse 183. UPAJĀTI or ĀKHYĀNAKĪ (a variety of TRISHṬUBH). See verses 41, &c., 169.

तापसी ॥ उभौ निर्वर्ण्य ॥

[a] अच्छरिअं अच्छरिअं ।

राजा ।

आर्ये । किमिव ।

तापसी ।

[b] इमस्स बालअहूवस्स देवि संवादिणी आकिदिन्ति विम्हा-
विदम्हि । अपरिइदस्सवि दे अप्पडिलोमो संवुत्तोत्ति ।

राजा ॥ बालमुपलालयन् ॥

न चेन्मुनिकुमारोऽयं । अथ कोऽस्य व्यपदेशः ।

तापसी ।

[c] पुरुवंसो ।

राजा ॥ आत्मगतम् ॥

कथमेकान्वयो मम । अतः खलु मदनुकारिणमेनमचभवती
मन्यते । अस्त्येतत्पौरवाणामन्यं कुलव्रतम् ।

भवनेषु रसाधिकेषु पूर्वं
    क्षितिरक्षार्थमुशन्ति ये निवासम् ।
नियतैकयतिव्रतानि पश्चा-
    त्तरुमूलानि गृहीभवन्ति तेषाम् ॥१८४॥

॥ प्रकाशम् ॥

[a] आश्चर्यम् आश्चर्यम् । [b] अस्य बालकरूपस्य तेऽपि संवादिन्याकृतिरिति
विस्मापितास्मि । अपरिचितस्यापि तेऽप्रतिलोमः संवृत्त इति । [c] पुरुवंशः ।

---

[1] 'The speaking-resemblance of form;' 'la ressemblance parlante,'
Chézy.

[2] *Upalālayan*, 'fondling;' see p. 289, n. 2.

[3] *Vyapadeśaḥ*, 'family;' see p. 205, n. 1.

[4] 'This (custom of retiring to a hermitage) is the last family-observance
of the descendants of Puru. (They) who first of all for the sake of pro-
tecting the earth choose a residence in palaces abounding-in-all-the-

Verse 184. AUPACCHANDASIKA. See verses 77, 78.

न पुनरात्मगत्या मानुषाणामेष विषयः ।

तापसी ।

[a] जह भट्टमुहो भणादि । अच्छरासंबन्धेण इमस्स जणणी
एत्थ देवगुरुणो तवोवणे पसूदा ।

राजा || अपवार्यं ||

हन्त द्वितीयमिदमाशाजननम् । || प्रकाशम् || अथ सा
तत्रभवती किमाख्यस्य राजर्षेः पत्नी ।

तापसी ।

[b] को तस्स धम्मदारपरिच्चाइणो णाम सङ्कीतिदुं चिन्ति-
स्सदि ।

राजा || सगतम् ||

इयं खलु कथा मामेव लक्ष्मीकरोति । यदि तावदस्य

[a] यथा भट्टमुखो भणति । अप्सरःसम्बन्धेनास्य जनन्यत्र देवगुरोस्तपोवने प्रसूता ।
[b] कस्तस्य धर्मदारपरित्यागिनो नाम सङ्कीर्तितुं चिन्तयिष्यति ।

---

pleasures-of-sense, to them [of them] the roots of trees, where the one reli-
gious vow of ascetics [i. e. control of the passions, mortification] is *rigidly*
maintained, become a dwelling-place.' *Rasādhikeshu*, the Bengāli MSS.
have *sudhāsiteshu*, 'white with stucco or chunam.' *Uśanti* (3rd pl. pres.
of *vaś*, Gram. 324, 656)=*ićchanti*, S'.;=*vāṅćhanti*, K. *Taru-mūlāni*, so
Manu enjoins that the hermit is to be *vijitendriyo dharāśayo vriksha-mūla-
niketanah*, 'his passions kept in subjection, sleeping on the bare ground,
dwelling at the roots of trees,' vi. 26. It seems to have been a practice
in ancient India for kings when they had reigned sufficiently long, to
retire from the charge of government and betake themselves to penitential
exercises. They first associated the Yuva-rāja or heir-apparent with
themselves, and then left him in quiet possession of the throne.

[1] 'But this (sacred) place is not (accessible) to mortals by their own
means [condition].' *Vishayaḥ=pradeśaḥ*, Chézy. The Mackenzie MS.
has *katham* for *na*.

[2] 'In consequence of her relationship to a nymph.' *Deva-guros*=*Kaś-
yapasya*.

शिशोर्मातरं नामतः पृच्छेयम् । ॥ विचिन्त्य ॥ अथवा । अन्यायः परदारपृच्छाव्यापारः[1] ।

तापसी ॥ प्रविश्य मृन्मयूरहस्ता ॥

[a] सव्वदमण[2] । सउन्दलावण्यं पेक्ख ।

बालः ॥ सदृष्टिच्छेपम् ॥

[b] कहिं वा मे अम्बा[3] ।

उभे ।

[c] णामसारिस्सेण वञ्चिदो माउवच्छलो ।

द्वितीया ।

[d] वच्छ । इमस्स मित्तिआमोरअस्स रम्मत्तणं देक्खन्ति भणिदोसि ।

राजा ॥ आत्मगतम् ॥

किं वा शकुन्तलेत्यस्य मातुराख्या । सन्ति पुनर्नामधेय-सादृश्यानि । अपि नाम मृगतृष्णिकेव नाममात्रप्रस्तावो मे विषादाय कल्पते[4] ।

[a] सर्वदमन । शकुन्तलालावण्यं प्रेक्षस्व ।   [b] क्व वा मे अम्बा ।   [c] नामसादृश्येन वञ्चितो मातृवत्सलः ।   [d] वत्स । अस्य मृत्तिकामयूरकस्य रम्यत्वं पश्येति भणितोऽसि ।

---

[1] So reads the Mackenzie MS. The others *tarhy anāryaḥ para-dāra-vyavahāraḥ.*

[2] *Sakunta=pakshin,* 'a bird.' By joining it with *lāvanyam,* the hermitess unconsciously pronounces S'akuntalā. *Sakuntasya pakshino lāvanyam. Sakunta-lāvanyam śleshena Sakuntalā-śabdaḥ uktaḥ,* Chézy.

[3] For *ambā* (the reading of the Mackenzie MS., supported by K.) some have *ajjū* for Sanskrit *ajjukā,* and again, subsequently, *ajjuā* for *ajjukā,* where K. has *ajjaā* for *āryakā* or *āryā.* I have everywhere followed K. in rejecting *ajjukā,* as, according to Amara-k. (i. 1, 7, 11) and Sāhit.-d. (p. 179 at the end), this word, in theatrical language, is applied only to a *veśyā* or harlot.

[4] 'Perhaps the mention of a mere name, like the mirage-of-the-desert, is destined to (cause) me bitter-disappointment.' *Mriga-trishṇikā,* see

बालः ।

[a] अज्जए । रोअदि मे एसो भद्रमोरओ । ॥ इति क्रीडनकमादत्ते ॥

प्रथमा ॥ विलोक्य । सोद्वेगम् ॥

[b] अम्महे । रक्खाकरण्डअं से मणिबन्धे ण दीसदि ।

राजा ।

अलमलमावेगेन । नन्विदमस्य सिंहशावविमर्दात्परि-
भ्रष्टम् । ॥ इत्यादातुमिच्छति ॥

उभे ।

[c] मा खु मा खु । एदं अविलम्बिअ कहं गहिदं णेण ।

॥ इति विस्मयादुरोनिहितहस्ते परस्परमवलोकयतः ॥

राजा ।

किमर्थं प्रतिषिद्धाः स्मः ।

प्रथमा ।

[d] सुणादु महाराओ । एसा अवराजिदा णाम ओसही इमस्स

[a] आर्यिके । रोचते म एष भद्रमयूरकः ।   [b] अहो । रक्षाकरण्डकमस्य मणिबन्धे
न दृश्यते ।   [c] मा खलु मा खलु । एतदचिलम्ब्य कथं गृहीतमनेन ।   [d] शृणोतु
महाराजः । एषापराजिता नामौषधिरस्य

---

p. 250, n. 1 at the end. *Nāma-mātra-prastāvo* may mean 'the occasion
of a mere name,' but the verb *pra-stu* has the sense of 'mentioning,'
'declaring.' *Kalpate*, 'is sufficient,' or simply 'becomes a cause of;' cf.
p. 191, l. 5; p. 260, l. 12.

[1] A peacock, whether living or in the form of a toy, seems to have been
a favourite plaything. So the boy in the fifth Act of the Vikramorvaśī,
yaḥ suptavān madanke tam me jāta-kalāpam preshaya śikhinam. For
āryake the Beng. have *antike*. *Antikā = bhaginī jyeshṭhā = dhātrī*, S'.

[2] 'The amulet,' 'the talisman,' lit. 'the guardian casket,' 'the magical
casket.' One sense, however, of *karaṇḍaka* is 'a kind of plant' or 'herb'
(cf. next note). It was probably a kind of locket, containing some herb
with talismanic properties, worn round the waist, to serve as an amulet.
Karaṇḍaka certainly usually signifies 'a little box,' but it may possibly be
the name for the herb itself. K. explains it by *rakshā-ghuṭikā* [? *guṭikā*],
'a magical ball.' Some of the Beng. have *rakshā-kāṇḍo;* S'. and C.,
rakshā-gaṇḍo and *rakshā-gaṇḍako.*

[3] 'This herb, called Aparājitā [unconquered, invincible], was given

जादकम्मसमए भश्रवदा मारीएण दिष्णा । एदं किल मादापिदरो अप्पाणं च वज्जिश्र अवरो भूमिपडिदं ण गेएहादि ।

राजा ।

अथं गृह्णाति ।

प्रथमा ।

^bतदो तं सप्पो भविश्र दंसइ ।

राजा ।

भवतीभ्यां कदाचिदस्याः प्रत्यक्षीकृता विक्रिया ।

उभे ।

^cअणेञ्रसो ।

राजा ॥ सहर्षम् । आत्मगतम् ॥

कथमिव सम्पूर्णमपि मे मनोरथं नाभिनन्दामि ।

॥ इति बालं परिष्वजते ॥

द्वितीया ।

^dसुब्बदे । एहि । इमं वुत्तन्तं णिश्रमव्वाबुडाए सउन्दलाए निवेदेम्ह । ॥ इति निष्क्रान्ते ॥

बालः ।

^eमुञ्च मं । जाव अव्वाए सश्रासं गमिसं ।

---

^a जातकर्मसमये भगवता मारीचेन दत्ता । एतां किल मातापितरावात्मानं च वर्ज-यित्वापरो भूमिपतितां न गृह्णाति ।　^b ततस्तं सर्पो भूत्वा दशति ।　^c अनेकशः ।　^d सुव्रते । एहि । इमं वृत्तान्तं नियमव्यापृतायै शकुन्तलायै निवेदयावः ।　^e मुञ्च माम् । यावदम्बायाः सकाशं गमिष्यामि ।

---

by his reverence Kaśyapa to this child, on the occasion of the natal (ceremony).' As to the name *aparājitā*, compare p. 266, n. 2. The *jāta-karman* is the fourth of the twelve Saṇskāras or purificatory rites, described in Manu (ii. 27, &c.), and the first after the child's birth (cf. p. 258, n. 2; p. 199, n. 1). It was performed by giving the child honey and clarified butter out of a golden spoon, before separating the navel-string.

¹ *Atha* here = *yadi tu*, 'supposing now,' 'but if' (cf. *atha tu*, verse 128).

राजा ।

पुत्रक । मया सहैव मातरमभिनन्दिष्यसि ।

बालः ।

[a] ममक्खु तादो दुस्सन्दो । ण तुमं ।

राजा ॥ सस्मितम् ॥

एष विवाद एव प्रत्याययति[1] ।

॥ ततः प्रविशत्येकवेणीधरा[2] शकुन्तला ॥

शकुन्तला ।

[b] विआरकालेवि[3] पकिदिन्यं सव्वदमणस्स ओसहिं सुणिञ्च
ण मे आसा आसि[4] अत्तणो भाअहेएसु । अहवा जह
साणुमदीए आचंक्खिदं । तह सम्भावीअदि एदं ।

राजा ॥ शकुन्तलां विलोक्य ॥

अये । सेयमत्रभवती शकुन्तला । यैषा

वसने परिधूसरे वसाना
नियमक्षाममुखी धृतैकवेणिः[5] ।

<hr>

[a] मम खलु तातो दुष्यन्तः । न त्वम् ।   [b] विकारकालेऽपि प्रकृतिस्यां सर्वदम-
नस्यौषधिं श्रुत्वा न म आशासीदात्मनो भागधेयेषु । अथवा यथा सानुमत्याचष्टितम् ।
तथा सम्भाव्यत एतत् ।

<hr>

[1] 'Even this contradiction convinces me.' *Pratyāyayati*, 'causes me to
believe,' 'me inducit ad credendum' (cf. p. 216, l. 12).

[2] *Eka-veṇi-dharā*, cf. Megha-d. verse 90, *sārayantī eka-veṇīm kareṇa;*
and verse 98, *abalā-veṇi-mokshotsukāni.* The Hindū women collect their
hair into a single long braid, as a sign of mourning, when their husbands
are dead, or absent for a long period.

[3] 'Even at the time of metamorphose,' i. e. even on an occasion when it
ought to have changed its form. As to *prakṛiti*, 'the natural form or
state,' as opposed to *vikāra*, cf. p. 71, l. 10. *Oshadhi*, see p. 295, n. 3.

[4] 'I had no hope in my own destiny,' 'I had no trust in my fortunes.'

[5] Compare p. 262, lines 7 and 8.

अतिनिष्करुणस्य शुद्धशीला
मम दीर्घं विरहव्रतं बिभर्ति ॥१८५॥

शकुन्तला ॥ पश्चात्तापविवर्णं राजानं दृष्ट्वा ॥

[a] एक्खु अज्जउत्तो विअ । तदो की एसो दाणिं किद-
रक्खामङ्गलं दारअं मे गत्तसंसग्गेण दूसेदि ।

बालः ॥ मातरमुपेत्य ॥

[b] अम्ब । की एसो पुरिसो मं पुत्तेत्ति आलिङ्गदि ।

[a] न खल्वार्यपुत्र इव । ततः क एष इदानीं कृतरक्षामङ्गलं दारकं मे गात्रसंसर्गेण
दूषयति ।   [b] अम्ब । क एष पुरुषो मां पुत्रेत्यालिङ्गति ।

---

[1] 'She who, wearing a pair of dark-grey vestments, having a countenance emaciated by penitential-exercises, bearing (on her head) a single braid of hair, chaste [pure] in her behaviour, undergoes a long vow of separation from me, excessively unmerciful.' *Vasane*, acc. du. neut.; see p. 158, n. 1, and cf. *vāsasī* in Mṛicchak., Act IV. It seems that men's clothes, as well as women's, consisted of two pieces (cf. Bhaṭṭi-k. iii. 20, *manorame vastre*, which in one commentary is rendered by *manoramaṃ vastra-dvayam* and in the other by *ćeto-hāriṇī vastre*). *Pari-dhūsare*, as the preposition *ā* is employed diminutively, so the prepositions *pari* and *sam* give force and intensity, much as περί and σύν in Greek, and *per* and *con* in Latin. *Pari* is even more intensive than *sam:* thus, *sam-āpti*, 'completion,' *pari-samāpti*, 'entire completion;' *sam-pūrṇa*, 'very full,' *pari-pūrṇa*, 'completely filled;' *sam-śushka*, 'dried up,' *pari-śushka*, 'quite dried up;' *ā-pāṇḍu*, 'palish,' *pari-pāṇḍu*, 'very pale;' *pari-śrānta*, 'completely wearied,' &c. &c. *Dhṛitaika-veṇi*, see p. 297, n. 2. S. and C. quote the following from Bharata: *amalāsv avadhāraṇam* [? *amalā avadhāraṇam*, S.] *alakānāṃ ća kalpanam anulepana-saṇskāraṃ na kuryāt pathikāṅganā* ('a woman whose husband is absent on a journey,' cf. p. 230, n. 1); *pāṇḍu-ćchāyā kṛiśa-tanur veṇī-yuta-śiroruhā lambālakā dīna-veśā vibhūshaṇa-vivarjitā*.

[2] *Ārya-putra*, see p. 196, n. 4.

[3] 'Furnished with a lucky talisman,' 'protected by an auspicious amulet.'

[4] The feminine *ambā* makes its vocative *amba*, see Gram. 108. *d.*

Verse 185. AUPAĆCHANDASIKA. See verses 77, 78, 184.

राजा ।

प्रिये । क्रौर्य्यमपि मे त्वयि प्रयुक्तमनुकूलपरिणामं संवृत्तम् ।
यदहमिदानीं त्वया प्रत्यभिज्ञातमात्मानं पश्यामि ।

शकुन्तला ॥ आत्मगतम् ॥

[a] हिअत्र । समस्सस समस्सस । परिच्चत्तमच्छरेण अणु-
अम्पिदम्हि देव्वेण । अज्जउत्तोक्खु एसो ।

राजा ।

प्रिये ।

स्मृतिभिन्नमोहतमसो दिच्छ्या प्रमुखे स्यितासि मे सुमुखि ।
उपरागान्ते शशिनः समुपगता रोहिणी योगम् ॥१८६॥

शकुन्तला ।

[b] जेदु जेदु अज्जउत्तो । ॥ इत्यर्धोक्ते वाष्पकंरठी विरमति ।

[a] हृदय । समाश्वसिहि समाश्वसिहि । परित्यक्तमत्सरेणानुकम्पितासि देवेन ।
आर्य्यपुत्रः खल्वेषः । [b] जयतु जयत्वार्य्यपुत्रः ।

---

[1] 'By-the-kindness-of-fortune, O lovely-faced-one, thou standest (once
again) before me, the darkness of whose delusion is dispelled by recollec-
tion. At the end of the eclipse, Rohiṇī has been (again) brought to a
union with the moon.' *Dishṭyā* is generally an exclamation equivalent
to 'Hail!' 'good luck!' corresponding to Shakespeare's 'Now fair befall
thee!' I have preferred to regard it here as an adverbial instr. case, 'by
the kindness of destiny,' 'fortunately,' 'happily.' *Uparāga*, the following
is the Hindū notion of eclipses:—A certain demon, which had the tail of
a dragon, was decapitated by Vishṇu at the churning of the ocean; but,
as he had previously tasted of the Amṛita or nectar reproduced at that
time, he was thereby rendered immortal, and his head and tail, retaining
their separate existence, were transferred to the stellar sphere. The head
was called Rāhu, and became the cause of eclipses, by endeavouring, at
various times, to swallow the sun and moon. *Rohiṇī*, as to the love of
the Moon for Rohiṇī, the fourth lunar constellation, see p. 113. n. 1.

[2] Lit. 'having tears in her throat,' i.e. 'having her voice choked with

---

Verse 186. ĀRYĀ or GĀTHĀ. See verse 2.

$$\smile\smile-|\overset{'}{\smile}\smile-\smile|\smile\smile-\|\;--\;|\smile\smile-|\smile-\smile|-\smile\smile|\smile$$
$$\smile\smile-|\;--\;|\smile\smile-\|\smile\smile\smile\smile|\;--\;|\smile\;|\;--\;|-$$

राजा ।

सुन्दरि ।

वाष्पेण प्रतिषिद्धेऽपि जयशब्दे जितं मया ।
यत्ते दृष्टमसंस्कारं पाटलोष्ठपुटं मुखम् ॥१८७॥

बालः ।

[a] अम्ब । की एसो ।

शकुन्तला ।

[b] वच्छ । दे भाग्गहेआइं पुच्छेहि ।

राजा ॥ शकुन्तलायाः पादयोः प्रणिपत्य ॥

सुतनु हृदयात्प्रत्यादेशव्यलीकमपैतु ते
किमपि मनसः सम्मोहो मे तदा बलवानभूत् ।

[a] अम्ब । क एषः ।   [b] वत्स । ते भागधेयानि पृच्छ ।

---

tears.' *Vāshpa*, not the tear itself, but the lachrymal moisture (see p. 169, n. 2) which may find its way into the throat and impede the utterance.

[1] 'Though the (utterance-of) the word "victory" be obstructed by (thy) weeping, victory-has-been-gained by me, since thy unadorned countenance, having-the-surface- [skin] -of-its-lips-pale-red, has been seen (by me).' *Jaya-śabda*, the word 'Victory!' i.e. *jayatu* or *vijayī bhava* was the regular form of saluting kings (cf. p. 65, n. 2). *Asaṇskāram*, so reads the Taylor MS.; the others have *asaṇskāra-p*°, which violates the usual cæsura. If the latter be retained, translate 'the skin of whose lips is pale red from the absence of colouring or paint.' There is no doubt that unpainted lips were a sign of mourning, but this is sufficiently implied in *pāṭaloshtha*, and it is a question whether *saṇskāra* can ever mean 'paint.' Some of the Beng., and amongst them the old MS. (Bodleian, 233), supported by S'. and C'., read *a-saṇskārāl lolālakam idam mukham*, 'this countenance, having its curls hanging loosely from want of dressing.' *Oshtha-puṭa*, 'the covering of the lip;' so *akshi-puṭa*, 'the skin covering the eye,' 'the eye-lid.' The student is reminded that in a compound, *oshtha* optionally causes the elision of a preceding *a* (Gram. 38. *k*). The Mackenzie MS. has *pāṭaloshtham mukham priye*.

[2] S'ankara quotes the following from Bharata: *Kākubhiḥ praṇipātaiś ća bhāgya-nindādibhis tathā, evam kṛite ća narīṇām purusho 'ti-priyo bhavet*.

Verse 187. SLOKA or ANUSHTUBH. See verses 5, 6, 11, 12, 26, 47, 50, 51, &c., 179.

प्रबलतमसामेवम्प्रायाः शुभेषु हि वृत्तयः
सजमपि शिरस्यन्धः क्षिप्तां धुनोत्यहिशङ्कया ॥१८८॥

शकुन्तला ।

[a] उट्ठेदु अज्जउत्तो । णूणं मे सुञ्चरिञ्प्पडिबन्धञं पुराकिदं
तेसु दिअहेसु परिणाममुहं आसि । जेण साणुक्कोसोवि
अज्जउत्तो मइ विरसो संवुत्तो । ॥ राजोन्निश्रति ॥ [b] अह कहं
अज्जउत्तेण सुमरिदो दुक्खभाई अञ्ं जणो ।

[a] उत्तिष्ठत्वार्यपुत्रः । नूनं मे सुचरितप्रतिबन्धकं पुराकृतं तेषु दिवसेषु परिणाममुख-
मासीत् । येन सानुक्रोशोऽप्यार्यपुत्रो मयि विरसः संवृत्तः ।   [b] अथ कथमार्यपुत्रेण
स्मृतो दुःखभाग्ययं जनः ।

---

[1] 'O fair one! let the unpleasant-feeling [unpleasantness] of (my) repudiation (of thee) depart from thy heart. Somehow-or-other at that time
the infatuation of my mind was strong. For such, for the most part,
is the behaviour of those over-whom-(the quality of)-darkness-has-the-
mastery, on happy-(auspicious)-occasions. A blind man shakes off even
the garland thrown on his head, suspecting it to be [with the suspicion of
its being] a snake.' *Vyalīkam=apriyam*, K.;=*vipriyam*, C. *Apaitu*,
some of the Beng. MSS. have *upaitu*, which is unintelligible. *Kimapi*,
i. e. *anirvaćanīya-rūpam yathā syāt*, 'in a manner not to be explained,' S.
Tadā=pratyādeśa-kāle, 'at the time of repudiation.' *Prabala-tamasām*,
i. e. *prabalam ajñānam yesham te tathoktāḥ*, K. According to the Hindū
philosophy there were three qualities or properties incident to the state of
humanity, viz. 1. *Sattva*, 'excellence' or 'goodness' [quiescence], whence
proceed truth, knowledge, purity, &c. 2. *Rajas*, 'passion' or 'foulness'
[activity], which produces lust, pride, falsehood, &c., and is the cause of
pain. 3. *Tamas*, 'darkness' [inertia], whence proceed ignorance, infatuation, delusion, mental blindness, &c. *Śubheshu=sat-karmasu*, 'in
auspicious matters,' S. *Vrittayah=vyavahārāḥ*, S. *Dhunoti=nirasyati*,
K. *Srajam*, see p. 272, n. 1.

[2] 'Assuredly my (evil deeds), committed in a former (birth), opposed
to virtuous conduct, were in those days drawing towards (their appointed
evil) issue, (seeing) that my husband, although of-a-compassionate-nature,
became unfeeling towards me.' *Purā-kritam*, i. e. *janmāntara-karma*, S.

Verse 188. HARINĪ (a variety of ATYASHTI). See verses 66, 99.

राजा ।

उद्धृतविषादंशल्यः कथयिष्यामि ।
मोहान्मया सुतनु पूर्वमुपेक्षितस्ते
यो वाष्पविन्दुरधरं परिबाधमानः ।
तं तावदाकुटिलपक्ष्मविलग्नमद्य
वाष्पं प्रमृज्य विगतानुशयो भवेयंम् ॥१८९॥
॥ इति यथोक्तमनुतिष्ठति ॥

शकुन्तला   ॥ नाममुद्रां दृष्ट्वा ॥

[a] अज्जउत्त । एदं तं अङ्गुलीअअं ।

राजा ।

अस्मादङ्गुलीयोपलम्भात्खलु स्मृतिरुपलब्धा ।

[a] आर्यपुत्र । एतत्तदङ्गुलीयकम् ।

(see p. 185, n. 3 at the end). *Pariṇāma-mukham* [*pariṇatābhimukham*, K.], 'about to issue in their appointed fruit, in their matured result,' 'ripe for an evil result.' *Pariṇāma* is 'the last stage of anything,' 'the stage of maturity,' 'the final result :' *mukha*, like *unmukha* (lit. 'looking towards'), has here the sense of 'tending towards,' 'being about,' 'being on the point.'

[1] Cf. p. 272, l. 8; and *uddharen no hridaya-śalyam*, Vikram., Act I.

[2] 'O graceful lady ! I should in a manner be freed from (my) remorse by wiping off that moisture now clinging to thy slightly curved eye-lashes, which formerly, (in the form of) a tear-drop corroding thy lip, was un-noticed [overlooked] by me through mental-delusion.' *Pūrvam*, i. e. *pratyādeśa-velāyām*. *Paribādhamānaḥ*=*pīḍayan*, S. *Ā-kuṭila*, cf. *ā-tāmra*, p. 228, l. 3, and p. 298, n. 1. *Vigatānuśayo*=*apagata-paścāttāpaḥ*. For *vāshpam* some of the Beng. have *kānte*, unsupported by any of the Deva-n. MSS. The repetition of *vāshpa* seems at first unnecessary, but not if it be borne in mind that *vāshpa* is properly 'the moisture in the eye,' and *vāshpa-vindu*, 'the tear-drop when it has left the eye' (see p. 169, n. 1 in the middle).

Verse 189. VASANTA-TILAKĀ (a variety of ŚAKVARĪ). See verses 8, 27, 31, 43, 46, 64, 74, 80, 82, 83, 91, 93, 94, 95, 100, 104, 105, 108, 123, 124, 144, 148, 152, 157, 168, 170, 181.

शकुन्तला ।

"विसमं किदं एेण । जं तदा अज्जउत्तस्स पच्चाश्रयणकाले
दुल्लहं आसि ।

राजा ।

तेन ह्यृतुसमवायचिह्नं प्रतिपद्यतां लता कुसुमँम् ।

शकुन्तला ।

ᵇण से विस्ससामि । अज्जउत्तो एव्व णं धारेदु ।

॥ ततः प्रविशति मातलिः ॥

मातलिः ।

दिष्ट्या । धर्मपत्नीसमागमेन पुत्रमुखदर्शनेन चायु-
ष्मान्वर्धते ।

राजा ।

अभूत्सम्पादितस्वादुफली मे मनोरथः । मातले । न खलु
विदितोऽयमाखण्डलेन वृत्तान्तः स्यात् ।

मातलिः ॥ सस्मितम् ॥

किमीश्वराणां परोक्षम् । एतवायुष्मान् । भगवान्मारीचस्ते

<hr>

ᵃ विषमं कृतमनेन । यन्नदार्यपुत्रस्य प्रत्यायनकाले दुर्लभमासीत् ।   ᵇ नास्मै
विश्वसामि । आर्यपुत्र एवैनद्धारयतु ।

<hr>

[1] A noun formed from the causal verb explained at p. 297, n. 1.

[2] 'Therefore let the creeper receive again (its) flower', as a pledge [mark,
token] of its inseparable-union with the (spring) season,' i. e. receive thou
back this ring, as the beautiful twining plant receives again its blossom,
in token of its reunion with the spring. *Tena hi*, with the sense of
'therefore,' occurs very frequently in dramatic composition (cf. p. 81, l. 2,
p. 83, l. 4, and p. 85, l. 5). *Ritu*, see p. 228, n. 1 at the end. *Samavâya*,
'inseparable or intimate connexion.' The Bengâlî MSS. have *ritu-
samâgamâśansi* (the Bengâlî recension, *ritu-samâgama-éihnam*), and S´.
ritu-saṅgama-sûéakam.

[3] *Dishtyâ*, see p. 299, n. 1. As to *putra-mukha*, &c., see p. 223, n. 1.

[4] *Âkhaṇḍala* is one of a class of epithets (such as *puran-dara, bala-bhid,
giri-bhid*, &c.) applied to Indra, as breaking cities, mountains, &c., into
fragments with his thunderbolt (see p. 86, n. 2).

दर्शनं वितरति ।

राजा ।

शकुन्तले । अवलम्ब्यतां पुत्रः । त्वां पुरस्कृत्य भगवन्तं
द्रष्टुमिच्छामि ।

शकुन्तला ।

*हिरिआमि अज्जउत्तेण सह गुरुसमीबं गन्तुं ।

राजा ।

अपाचरितव्यमभ्युदयकालेषु । एह्येहि ।

॥ सर्वे परिक्रामन्ति ॥

॥ ततः प्रविशत्यदित्या सार्धमासनस्थो मारीषः ॥

मारीचः ॥ राजानमवलोक्य ॥

दाक्षायणि ।

पुत्रस्य ते रणशिरस्ययमग्रयायी
दुष्यन्त इत्यभिहितो भुवनस्य भर्ता ।
चापेन यस्य विनिवर्तितकर्म जातं
तत्कोटिमत्कुलिशमाभरणं मघोनः ॥१९०॥

ᵃ जिह्रेम्यार्यपुत्रेण सह गुरुसमीपं गन्तुम् ।

---

[1] 'Allows thee a sight (of him),' i.e. 'graciously permits thee to be pre-
sented to him,' 'vouchsafes thee an audience.'

[2] 'But on joyful [festive] occasions the (usual) practice must be ob-
served.' The Mackenzie MS. has *gantavyam* for *āćaritavyam*.

[3] 'O Dākshāyinī [i.e. Aditi, see p. 284, n. 3], this is he that marches
foremost at the head of thy son's [Indra's] battles, the so-called Dush-
yanta, the lord [protector] of the earth, through whose bow that edged
thunder-bolt of Indra, having rested from its work, has become (a mere)
ornament.' *Raṇa-śirasi*, cf. p. 268, l. 12, and p. 87, n. 1. *Koṭimat=*
sāgram=tīkshṇam. Kuliśam=vajram. Maghonaḥ, gen. of *Maghavan*,
a name of Indra, see declension in Gram. 155. *c.*

Verse 190. VASANTA-TILAKĀ (a variety of ŚAKVARĪ). See verses 8, 27, 31, 43, 46, 64,
74, 80, 82, 83, 91, 93, 94, 95, 100, 104, 105, 108, 123, 124, 144, 148, 152, 157, 168, 170, 181, 189.

अदितिः ।

ᵃसम्भावणीयाणुभावा मे आकृती ।

मातलिः ।

आयुष्मन् । एतौ पुत्रप्रीतिपिशुनेन चक्षुषा दिवौकसां
पितरावायुष्मन्तमवलोकयतः । तावुपसर्प ।

राजा ।

मातले । एतौ

प्राहुर्द्वादशधास्थितस्य मुनयो यत्तेजसः कारणं
भर्तारं भुवनत्रयस्य सुषुवे यद्यज्ञभागेश्वरम् ।
यस्मिन्नात्मभुवः परोऽपि पुरुषश्चक्रे भवायास्पदं
द्वन्द्वं दक्षमरीचिसम्भवमिदं तत्स्रष्टुरेकान्तरम् ॥१९१॥

ᵃ सम्भावनीयानुभावास्याकृतिः ।

---

[1] 'His dignity may be inferred from his form,' lit. 'his form has its dignity inferrible.'

[2] 'With an eye that betrays [betokens] affection for (thee as for) a son.' *Piśuna*, cf. p. 277, l. 8.

[3] 'This is that pair [Aditi and Kaśyapa], the offspring of Daksha and Marīci, one remove from the Creator [Brahmā], which (said pair) sages call the cause [origin, author, maker] of the solar-light subsisting in twelve forms [having a twelve-fold subsistence], which (pair) begot the ruler of the three worlds, the lord of the (gods who are the) sharers of (every) sacrifice, (and) in which (pair) Nārāyaṇa (or Vishṇu), he (who was) even superior to the Self-existent [Brahmā], chose [made] the site for (his) birth.' *Dvādaśa-dhā*, there are twelve Ādityas or forms of the Sun, which represent him in the several months, or, as some say, attend upon his car (see p. 279, n. 3). They are the children of Aditi and Kaśyapa, and the gods Vishṇu and Indra are reckoned among them. The other ten, according to the Vishṇu-p. (p. 234), are Dhātṛi, Aryaman, Mitra, Varuṇa, Vivasvat, Pūshan, Parjanya, Aṇśa, Bhaga, and Tvashṭṛi; but the names of the Ādityas vary in the other Purāṇas. *Tejasaḥ*, i. e. *sūryātmakasya*, 'consisting of the sun,' K.;=*sūryasya*, S.;=*ādityasya*, Chézy. *Bhuvana-trayasya*, i. e. *svarga-martya-pātālasya*, S. (see p. 314, n. 2). *Yajña-bhāgeśvaram* may simply mean 'the lord of a share of (every) sacrifice;'

Verse 191. ŚĀRDŪLA-VIKRĪDITA. See verses 14, 30, 36, 39, 40, 63, 79, 85, &c., 176.

R r

मातलिः ।

अथ किम् ।

राजा ॥ प्रणिपत्य ॥

उभाभ्यामपि वासवानुयोज्यो दुष्यन्तः प्रणमति ।

मारीचः ।

वत्स । चिरं जीव । पृथिवीं पालय ।

अदितिः ।

[a] वच्छ । अप्पडिरंहो होहि ।

[a] वत्स । अप्रतिरथो भव ।

---

it seems, however, likely that *yajña-bhāga* is here synonymous with *kratu-bhuj*, 'a god,' though *yajña-bhāj* would be the more usual form. *Ātma-bhuvaḥ* [abl. from *ātma-bhū*] = *svayambhuvaḥ* = *brahmaṇaḥ*, K. and C. *Paraḥ* = *śreshṭhaḥ*. *Purusha* = *Vishṇu*, K.; = *Nārāyaṇa*, S. and C. *Bhavāya* = *janmane*, K.; = *avatārāya*, S. *Āspadam* = *pratishṭhām* = *sthitim*, K. and S. *Upendrāvatārasya kāraṇam uktam bhavati*, K. *Dvandvam* = *mithunam* = *strī-puṃsayor yugalam*. *Srashṭur* = *Brahmaṇah*, K. and S. *Ekāntaram* = *ekāntaritam*, S.; *ekaḥ purusho antaram vyavadhānaṃ yasya tat tathoktam*. *Brahmaṇo Marīćiḥ, Marīćeḥ Kaśyapaḥ, Brahmaṇo Dakshaḥ, Dakshād Aditir iti ekāntaram*, K. *Ekaḥ purusho antaram antardhānaṃ yasya tad dvandvam*, Chézy. As Kaśyapa and Aditi were the grandchildren of Brahmā, they were only removed from him by Marīći and Daksha, their parents and his children (see p. 279, n. 3). Vishṇu, as Nārāyaṇa, or the Supreme Spirit (*purusha*), moved over the waters before the creation of the world, and from his navel came the lotus from which Brahmā sprang. As Vishṇu, or the Preserver, he became incarnate in various forms, and chose Kaśyapa and Aditi, from whom all human beings were descended, as his medium of incarnation or place of birth, especially in the Avatāra in which he was called 'Upendra' (or *Indrānuja, Indrāvaraja*), 'Indra's younger brother' (according to some identified with Krishṇa), and in his Vāmana or Dwarf-Avatāra (see p. 275, n. 2). *Purusha* is properly 'that which sleeps or abides in the body' [*puri śete*]. The worshippers of Vishṇu identify him with Nārāyaṇa and with Brahma, and name him Mahā-purusha, Purushottama, i. e. 'the Supreme Spirit,' thus exalting him above Brahmā, the Creator. Kālidāsa seems by this verse to include himself among the Vaishṇavas.

[1] *Ubhābhyām* [dat. dual], i.e. *Aditi-Mārīćābhyām*, S. *Vāsavānuyojyaḥ* = *Indrājñākārī*, 'Indra's servant,' S. The Bengālī MSS. have *vāsava-niyojyo* (cf. p. 273, l. 3).

[2] *A-pratiratha*, 'an invincible hero;' see p. 177, l. 6, n. 1 in the middle.

शकुन्तला ।

[a]दारकसहिदा वो पादवन्दणं करेमि ।

मारीचः ।

वत्से ।

आखण्डलसमो भर्ता जयन्तप्रतिमः सुतः ।
आशीरन्या न ते योग्या पौलोम्या सदृशी भव ॥१९२॥

अदितिः ।

[b]जादे । भत्तुणो बहुमदा होहि । अवस्सं दीहाऊ वच्छो
उहअकुलणन्दणो होदु । उवविसह ।

॥ सर्वे प्रजापतिमभित उपविशन्ति ॥

मारीचः ॥ एकैकं निर्दिशन् ॥

दिष्ट्या शकुन्तला साध्वी सदपत्यमिदं भवान् ।
श्रद्धा वित्तं विधिश्चेति त्रितयं तत्समागतम् ॥१९३॥

<hr>

[a] दारकसहिता वां पादवन्दनं करोमि ।   [b] जाते । भर्तुर्बहुमता भव । अवश्यं
दीर्घायुर्वत्स उभयकुलनन्दनो भवतु । उपविशत ।

<hr>

[1] '(Thy) husband (being) like Indra, thy son resembling Jayanta [Indra's son], no other blessing (would be) suitable to thee; mayst thou be like Paulomī!' (see p. 272, n. 1 at the end.) As to *Ākhaṇḍala*, see p. 303, n. 4.

[2] As to the title Prajāpati, see p. 279, n. 3.

[3] 'All hail! the virtuous S'akuntalā, (her) noble offspring, your Highness (Dushyanta)! Piety [faith], Fortune [wealth], Action; this trio is here combined.' *Sad*, i. e. *ubhaya-kula-guṇa-sampannam*. *S'raddhā*, being feminine, of course represents S'akuntalā; *vittam*, being neuter, her offspring (*apatyam*), viz. Sarva-damana or Bharata; and *vidhi*, being masculine, Dushyanta. *Vidhi*, according to C., is *veda-bodhitāćaraṇa*, 'putting in practice the precepts of the Vedas;' it may, perhaps, imply power as exhibited in action. Cf. Raghu-v. ii. 16, *babhau sā tena satām matena s'raddheva sākshād vidhinopapannā*, 'she (accompanied) by him, who was honoured by all good men, appeared [shone forth] like Faith visibly manifested, accompanied by action [works].'

<hr>

Verses 192, 193. S'LOKA or ANUSHTUBH. See verses 5, 6, 11, 12, 26, 47, 50, &c., 187.

राजा ।

भगवन् । प्रागभिमतसिद्धिः । पश्चाद्दर्शनम् । अतोऽपूर्वः
खलु वोऽनुग्रहः[1] । कुतः ।

उदेति पूर्वं कुसुमं ततः फलं
घनोदयः प्राक्तदनन्तरं पयः ।
निमित्तनैमित्तिकयोरयं क्रम-
स्तव प्रसादस्य पुरस्तु सम्पदः ॥१९४॥[2]

मातलिः ।

एवं विधातारः प्रसीदन्ति[3] ।

राजा ।

भगवन् । इमामाज्ञाकरीं वो गान्धर्वेण विवाहविधिनोप-

---

[1] 'First (came) the accomplishment of my desires; afterwards, the sight (of thee). Hence thy favour (towards me) has indeed been un-precedented.' S'. explains thus—*Sakuntalā-prāpakam bhavad-darśanam bhavishyati iti evam mamābhipretam āsīt, tāval prabhāvād darśana-pūr-vam nirvyūḍham. Tathā ća naimittikānantaram nimittotpattir iti anu-grahasyāpūrvatvam iti bhāvaḥ,* 'my desire was that the sight of thee might lead to my recovery of S'akuntalā. But (my meeting her) was arranged through (thy) divine power, before my presentation to thee. Thus after the effect was the appearance of the cause. The meaning is, that the favour (of my seeing thee and receiving thy blessing) did not precede (the attainment of my desire), and hence that the favour was unprecedented, as the accomplishment of my wishes ought naturally to have resulted from thy blessing.' There seems to be a double meaning in *apūrvaḥ.*

[2] 'First appears the blossom, then the fruit; first the rising of clouds, afterwards the rain. This (is) the regular-course of cause and effect; but the success-of-my-wishes (came) before thy favour.' *Naimittika,* 'what is connected with the *nimitta* or is dependant on it,' 'the effect.' *Puras= prathamatas,* S'. *Sampadah* (nom. pl.)=*abhīshṭa-siddhiḥ,* S'.; it is clearly meant to be synonymous with *abhipreta-siddhiḥ* just above.

[3] 'Thus (it is that) the creators of-all-beings perform favours.' *Vidhātṛi* must here be equivalent to Prajāpati (see p. 279, n. 3).

Verse 194. VAṆŚA-STHAVILA (a variety of JAGATĪ). See verses 18, 22, 23, &c., 180.

यस्य कस्यचित्कालस्य बन्धुभिरानीतां स्मृतिशैथिल्यात्प्र-
त्यादिशन्नपराद्धोऽस्मि तत्रभवती युष्मत्सगोत्रस्य कण्वस्य ।
पश्चादङ्गुलीयकदर्शनादूढपूर्वां तद्दुहितरमवगतोऽहं । तच्चि-
त्रमिव मे प्रतिभाति ।

यथा गजो नेति समक्षरूपे
तस्मिन्नतिक्रामति संशयः स्यात् ।
पदानि दृष्ट्वा तु भवेत्प्रतीति-
स्तथाविधो मे मनसो विकारः ॥१९५॥

मारीचः ।

वत्स । अलमात्मापराधशङ्कया । सम्मोहोऽपि त्वय्यनुप-
पन्नः । श्रूयताम् ।

राजा ।

अवहितोऽस्मि ।

मारीचः ।

यदैवापसरस्तीर्थावतरणात्प्रत्यक्षवैक्लव्यां शकुन्तलामादाय

<hr>

¹ *Kasyaćit kālasya*, i. e. *kasminśćit kāle*, *C.*

² Called Kāśyapa as being of the race of Kaśyapa (see p. 22, n. 3).

³ 'As if one were to say, "(that) is not an elephant," its form being before one's eyes, and doubt were to arise (in one's mind) on its walking past, but conviction were to take place after seeing its footsteps; of such a kind has been the change of my mind,' i. e. my mind has passed through similar transitions. Thus, as K. observes, when Dushyanta first saw S'akuntalā, he repudiated her (see p. 200, l. 2, and p. 201, l. 4); when she passed out of his presence, he began to relent and doubt (see verse 131); and when he saw the ring, he was convinced she was his wife. *Neti*, see p. 140, n. 2. *Samaksha-rūpe*, i. e. *samaksha-vidyamāna-rūpe*, *C.* *Padāni* =*pada-ćihnāni*, *C.* *Vikāra*=*svarūpānyathā-bhāva*, *S.* May not *sam-śayaḥ* apply to both lines? thus: 'As if there were a doubt that that is not an elephant, while he is marching along, his form obvious to the eye.'

⁴ The Mackenzie MS. and my own have *aparādha;* the others, *apaćāra.*

⁵ 'After [in consequence of] her descent to Apsaras-tīrtha,' see p. 271,

<hr>

Verse 195. Upajāti or Ākhyānakī. See verses 41, 107, 121, 126, 142, 156, &c., 183.

मेनका दाक्षायणीमुपगता । तदैव ध्यानादवगतोऽस्मि ।
दुर्वाससः शापादियं तपस्विनी सहधर्मचारिणी त्वया
प्रत्यादिष्टा नान्यथेति । स चायमङ्गुलीयकदर्शनावसानः[1] ।

राजा ॥ सोच्छ्वासम् ॥

एष वचनीयान्मुक्तोऽस्मि[2] ।

शकुन्तला ॥ स्वगतम् ॥

[a]दिट्ठिआ । अकारणपच्चादेसी ण अज्जउत्तो । ण हु सत्तं[3]
अत्ताणं सुमरेमि । अहवा पत्तो मए स हि सावो विरह-
सुहहिअआए ण विदिदो । जदो सहीहिं सन्दिट्ठुम्हि ।
भत्तुणो अङ्गुलीअअं दंसइदव्वंति ।

मारीचः ।

वत्से । चरितार्थासि[5] । सहधर्मचारिणीं प्रति न त्वया मन्युः
कार्यः । पश्य ।

शापादसि प्रतिहता स्मृतिरोधरूक्षे
भर्तर्यपेततमसि प्रभुता तवैव ।

[a] दिष्ट्या । अकारणप्रत्यादेशी न आर्यपुत्रः । न खलु शप्तमात्मानं स्मरामि । अथवा
प्राप्तो मया स हि शापो विरहशून्यहृदयया न विदितः । यतः सखीभ्यां सन्दिष्टास्मि ।
भर्तुरङ्गुलीयकं दर्शयितव्यमिति ।

---

n. 1, and p. 215, l. 18. According to S'., *Apsaras-tīrtha = sací-tīrtha* (see
p. 205, l. 12). Menakā was S'akuntalā's mother (see p. 44, l. 11).

[1] 'That this thy poor faithful [lawful] wife was repudiated in consequence
of the curse of Durvāsas, and on no other account, and this same (curse) has
terminated on the sight of the ring.' *Durvāsas*, see p. 137, n. 2. *Tapasvinī*
= anukampyā, S'. (cf. p. 246, l. 7). *Saha-dharma-cārinī = pati-vratā*, S'.

[2] *Vacanīyāt*, i. e. *sādhvī-nirākaraṇa-rūpāpavādāt*. *Vacanīyam = vā-*
cyam, p. 198, l. 12.

[3] The Colebrooke and Mackenzie MSS. and my own have *sattam* or
satam (*= śaptam*), supported by S'. The Taylor has *saccam* (*= satyam*),
supported by K. and the Bengālī.

[4] *Śūnya-hridayayā*, cf. p. 137, l. 11, with n. 2.

[5] 'Thou hast gained thy object.' *Caritārthā = labdhārthā = kritārthā*.
The Mackenzie has *viditārthā*.

छाया न मूर्छति मलोपहतप्रसादे
शुद्धे तु दर्पणतले सुलभावकाशा ॥१९६॥

राजा ।

भगवन् । अर्चं खलु मे वंशप्रतिष्ठा । ॥ इति बालं हस्तेन गृह्णाति ॥

मारीचः ।

तथाभाविनमेनं चक्रवर्तिनमवगच्छतु भवान् । पश्य ।

रथेनानुत्खातस्तिमितगतिना तीर्णजलधिः
पुरा सप्तद्वीपां जयति वसुधामप्रतिरथः ।
इहायं सत्त्वानां प्रसभदमनात्सर्वदमनः
पुनर्यास्यत्याख्यां भरत इति लोकस्य भरणात् ॥१९७॥

---

[1] 'Thou wast repulsed in consequence of the curse, (thy) husband being harsh [cruel] through the obstruction of (his) memory; (but now) indeed, on (the heart of) him freed from darkness, thy influence-is-supreme. (Even as) an image has no effect on the surface of a mirror whose brightness is tarnished with dirt, but on a clean-one easily makes impression [gains admission].' *Smṛiti-rodha*, the Mackenzie has *smṛiti-dosha*. *Apeta-tamasi*, cf. p. 301, n. 1. *Prabhutā*, K. refers to verse 73, p. 124. *Ćhāyā* =*prativimbam*. *Mūrćhati*=*vyāpnoti*, K.;=*sphurati*, S'. (see p. 201, n. 3). *Malopahata-prasāde* = *malāpagata-prasannatve*, S'.; = *mālinyena nashṭā prasannatā*, K. *Sulabhāvakāśā*=*sukhena labhyaḥ praveśo yasyāḥ*=*prāptāvasthitiḥ*, S'. (cf. p. 47, l. 3). S'. observes that *darpaṇa-tale* answers to *bhartari*; *malopahata* to *smṛiti-rodha*; *ćhāyā* to *prabhutā*; and, we may add, *śuddhe* to *apeta-tamasi*.

[2] *Atra*, &c., i.e. *asyāṃ Śakuntalāyām, kuloddhāraka-putrotpādakatvena*, 'in this S'akuntalā, because she has given birth to a son, the upholder of my family?' K.; cf. p. 260, l. 11, and p. 124, l. 3.

[3] *Tena prakāreṇa kuloddhārakatvena bhavishyantam*, K. *Ćakravartinam*=*sārvabhaumam*, 'a monarch of the whole earth,' K. (see verse 12).

[4] 'Previously (as) an-invincible-warrior, having crossed the ocean in a chariot whose motion is not (made) unsteady by uneven-ground, he will

---

Verse 196. VASANTA-TILAKĀ (a variety of S'AKVARĪ). See verses 8, 27, 31, 43, 46, 64, 74, 80, 82, 83, 91, 93, 94, 95, 100, 104, 105, 108, 123, 124, 144, 148, 152, 157, 168, 170, 181, 189.
Verse 197. S'IKHARIṆĪ (a variety of ATYASHṬI). See verses 9, 24, 44, 62, 112, 141.

राजा ।

भगवता कृतसंस्कारे सर्वमस्मिन्वयमाशास्महे ।

अदितिः ।

^aभअवं । इमाए दुहिदुमणोरहसम्पत्तीए कखोवि दाव

^a भगवन् । अस्या दुहितृमनोरथसम्पत्तेः कखोऽपि तावत्

---

subjugate the earth, consisting of seven islands. Here, from his forcible taming of the animals, he (is called) Sarva-damana; but (then) he will acquire the appellation Bharata, from his support of the world.' *Rathena*, see p. 9, l. 2. *An-utkhāta*° (*nimnonnata-pradeśasyābhāvād anutkhātam*, K.), so reads the Mackenzie MS., supported by K.; the others, *an-udghāta*; cf. p. 10, l. 6, with n. 1. *Stimita*=*anishkampa*, K.;=*apratibandhārtha-durgamanena*, S'. 'By this epithet it is indicated that the chariot would have the power of going in the air' (*tena viśeshaṇena rathasya ākāśagāmitvaṃ sūćitam*), K. *Sapta-dvīpām*, according to the mythical geography of the Hindūs, the earth consisted of seven islands, or rather insular continents, surrounded by seven seas. That inhabited by men was called Jambu-dvīpa, and was in the centre, having in the middle of it the sacred mountain Meru or Sumeru, inhabited by the gods. About Jambu flowed the sea of salt-water (*lavaṇa*), which extends to the second Dvīpa, called Plaksha, which is in its turn surrounded by a sea of sugar-cane juice (*ikshu*). And so with the five other Dvīpas, viz. S'ālmali, Kuśa, Krauńća, S'āka, and Pushkara, which are severally surrounded by the seas of wine (*surā*), clarified butter (*sarpis*), curds (*dadhi*), milk (*dugdha*), and fresh-water (*jala*), Vishṇu-p. p. 166; see Indian Wisdom, p. 419. *A-pratiratha*=*a-tulyaratha*=*mahāratha*, S'. (see p. 177, n. 1 in the middle). *Iha* = *asmin āśrame*, K. *Sattvānām* = *prāṇinām siṅhādīnām*, S'.; = *śarabha-siṅhādīnām*, K. *Prasabha-damanāt* = *balātkāreṇa mardanāt*. The name Bharata is derived from root *bhṛi*, 'to bear,' 'support.' Many Indian princes were so named, but the most celebrated was this son of Dushyanta and S'akuntalā, who so extended his empire that from him the whole of India was called Bhārata or Bharata-varsha; and whose descendants, the sons of Dhṛita-rāshṭra and Pāṇḍu, by their quarrels, formed the subject of the Mahā-bhārata (see p. 15, n. 1).

¹ 'We invoke all blessings on him for whom the prescribed-rites were performed by your Holiness,' or 'we have high hopes and expectations of him,' &c. As to *kṛita-saṇskāre*, see p. 258, n. 2, and p. 199, n. 1.

सुदत्तित्थारो करीअदु । दुहिदुवच्छला मेणआ इह एव्व
मं परिचरन्ती चिट्ठुइ ।

शकुन्तला ॥ आत्मगतम् ॥

मणोरहो क्खु मे भणिदो भअवदीए ।

मारीचः ।

तपःप्रभावात्प्रत्यक्षं सर्वमेव तच्चभवतः ।

राज्ञा ।

अतः खलु ममानतिक्रुड्डो मुनिः ।

मारीचः ।

तथाप्यसौ प्रियमस्माभिः प्रष्टव्यः । कः कोऽत्र भोः ।

शिष्यः ॥ प्रविश्य ॥

भगवन् । अयमस्मि ।

मारीचः ।

गालव । इदानीमेव विहायसा गत्वा मम वचनात्तच्च-
भवते कण्वाय प्रियमावेद्य । यथा पुत्रवती शकुन्तला
तच्छापनिवृत्तौ स्मृतिमता दुष्यन्तेन प्रतिगृहीतेति ।

शिष्यः ।

यदाज्ञापयति भगवान् । ॥ इति निष्क्रान्तः ॥

a श्रुतविस्तारः क्रियताम् । दुहितृवत्सला मेनकेहैव मां परिचरन्ती तिष्ठति ।
b मनोरथः खलु मे भणितो भगवत्या ।

---

1 'Let Kaṇva also be made acquainted with all the circumstances.' S. has *jñāta-vistaraḥ;* the Beng. MSS., *vijñātārthaḥ.*

2 Here, and in the insertion of *me* in the next line, I have followed the Mackenzie MS. and my own, as I have often done, if supported by K.

3 'Notwithstanding, he must be questioned by us about (this) joyous-event. Ho! there!' *Sishyānām madhye ko atra tishṭhati iti arthaḥ,* 'which among my pupils is in waiting here? such is the meaning of *kaḥ,* &c.,' S. Compare p. 69, l. 11; p. 263, l. 5.

मारीचः ।

वत्स । त्वमपि स्वापत्यदारसहितः सख्युराखण्डलस्य
रथमारुह्य ते राजधानीं प्रतिष्ठस्व ।

राजा ।

यदाज्ञापयति भगवान् ।

मारीचः ।

अपि च ।

तव भवतु विडौजाः प्राज्यवृष्टिः प्रजासु
त्वमपि विततयज्ञः स्वर्गिणः प्रीणयालम् ।
युगशतपरिवर्तानेवमन्योन्यकृत्यै-
र्नयतमुभयलोकानुग्रहश्लाघनीयैः ॥ १९८ ॥

राजा ।

भगवन् । यथाशक्ति श्रेयसे यतिष्ये ।

मारीचः ।

वत्स । किं ते भूयः प्रियमुपहरामि ।

---

¹ Here I have followed the Colebrooke MS. The others have *sāpatya-dāra-sahitaḥ;* the Bengālī, *sāpatya-dāraḥ.*

² 'May Indra be bountiful of (his) rain towards thy subjects! Do thou also, abundantly-dispensing [diffusing] sacrifices, gratify [satisfy] the gods [inhabitants of heaven] to the full. Thus pass (both of you) periods [revolutions] of hundreds of ages with reciprocal friendly acts, laudable on account of the favours (thus conferred) on both worlds;' i. e. you by sacrificing, and Indra by showers, confer benefits on the inhabitants of Svarga and the earth respectively. The two worlds are of course Heaven and Earth, not including the third world Pātāla (see p. 275, n. 2). *Viḍaujas* or *Viḍojas* is one of Indra's names, see p. 303, n. 4. *Prājya-vṛishṭi=pracura-varshaṇa. Vitata-yajña=vistṛita-yāga,* K. *Svargiṇaḥ=devān,* K. *Prīṇaya alam=alam bhāvaya,* K.; =*atyarthena santoshaya,* S. *Yuga-śata-parivartān=yugānāṃ śatāni tesham parivartanāni.*

³ K. has *śreyasi* and interprets it by *dharme.* S. has the same and explains it by *praśasta-kṛitye.*

Verse 198. MĀLINĪ or MĀNINĪ (a variety of ATI-ŚAKVARĪ). See verses 10, &c., 171.

राजा ।

अतः परमपि प्रियमस्ति । यदिह भगवान्प्रियं कर्तुमिच्छति ।
तर्हीदमस्तु भरतवाक्यम् ।

प्रवर्तंतां प्रकृतिहिताय पार्थिवः
सरस्वती श्रुतिमहतां महीयंताम् ।

---

[1] 'Is there any favour still greater than this? As (however) on this occasion his Holiness desires to confer a favour, then let this saying of Bharata be (fulfilled).' *Ataḥ param*, i. e. *adhikam*. *Atra praśnārthe kākur anusandheyā*, see p. 264, n. 2. The Bharata here intended must not be confounded with the young prince. He was a holy sage, the director or manager of the gods' dramas, and inventor of theatrical representations in general. He wrote a work containing precepts and rules relating to every branch of dramatic writing, which appears to have been lost, but is constantly quoted by the commentators. He seems to have superintended the exhibition of the drama called Lakshmī-svayaṃvara (composed by Sarasvatī, see p. 28, n. 1) in Indra's heaven. See Vikram., Act III, and middle of Act II, *Muninā Bharatena yaḥ prayoyo bharatīshu ashṭa-rasāśrayo nibaddhaḥ*, &c. It was not unusual to close the plays by quoting one of Bharata's verses; compare the conclusion of the Ratnāvalī. The commentator supposes that there is here an intentional ambiguity as to whether this verse is spoken in the name of the young prince or of the sage.

[2] 'Let the king exert himself for the welfare of his subjects. Let Sarasvatī be honoured among (those who are) mighty in the scriptures [lovers of literature]. Moreover, may the purple-god [S'iva], who-is-self-existent, (and) whose-Energy-is-everywhere-diffused, put an end to my future birth [deliver my soul from passing into another state of being].' *Pravartatām = prayatatām*. *Sarasvatī (= Bhāratī*, K.) is the wife of the god Brahmā. She is the goddess of speech and eloquence, patroness of the arts and sciences, and inventress of the Sanskrit language. *Sarasvatī* signifies 'flowing,' and is also applied to a river. *S'ruti-mahatām*, &c., some MSS. have *śruti-mahatī mahīyasām*; K. *śruta-mahatām*. According to the latter, *śruta = śāstra*, *mahatām = śreshṭhānām*. I see no reason why *mahatām* should not be the gen. pl. of the pres. part. regularly formed from *mah*, 'to honour.' *S'ruti-mahatām* might then mean 'lovers of literature.' *Mahīyatām = pūjyatām*, K. *Nīla-lohitāḥ*, 'blue and red;' i. e. according to K., *vāma-bhāge nīlaḥ, dakshiṇa-bhāge lohitaḥ*, 'on the

ममापि च क्षपयतु नीललोहितः
पुनर्भवं परिगतशक्तिरात्मभूः ॥१९९॥

॥ इति निष्क्रान्ताः सर्वे ॥

॥ सप्तमोऽङ्कः ॥

॥ समाप्तमिदमभिज्ञानशकुन्तलं नाम नाटकम् ॥

॥ शुभं भूयात् ॥

---

left side blue, on the right side red.' S'iva is usually represented as borne on a bull, his colour, as well as that of the animal he rides, being white, to denote the purity of Justice over which he presides. In his destroying capacity, he is characterized by the quality *tamas* (see p. 301, n. 1) and named Rudra, Kāla, &c., when his colour is said to be purple or black. 'In the beginning of the Kalpa, as Brahmā purposed to create a son, a youth of purple complexion [blue and red, *nīla lohita*] appeared, crying and running about [*ru, dru,* whence Rudra],' Vishnu-p. p. 58. Some refer this name to the colour of his throat (see p. 257, n. 2). *Parigata-śaktiḥ; prāptā śaktiḥ Pārvatī yena sa tathoktaḥ.* Hence, *Śakti = Pārvatī,* S'iva's wife. The wives of the deities were supposed to personify their energy or active power. *Ātma-bhū,* although properly a name of Brahmā, is applied equally to Vishnu and S'iva by those who give the preference to these deities. Exemption from further transmigration and absorption into the divine Soul is the *summum bonum* of Hindū philosophy (cf. p. 184, n. 3 at the end). Kālidāsa indulges the religious predilections of his fellow-townsmen by beginning and ending the play with a prayer to S'iva, who had a large temple in Ujjayinī, the city of king Vikramāditya, and abode of the poet. Both actors and spectators would probably repeat the prayer after the speaker and appropriate it to themselves.

Verse 199. Ruĉirā or Prabhāvatī (a variety of Atijagatī), containing thirteen syllables to the Pāda or quarter-verse, each Pāda being alike.

$$\cup - \cup - \mid \cup \cup \cup \cup \mid - \cup - \cup - \parallel$$

INDEX.

In the following Index the first number refers to the page, the second to the line. When, however, a number is followed by one of the letters ᵃ, ᵇ, ᶜ, ᵈ, the number and line of the verses are indicated.

n. after a number = note; after a word = neuter; ind. = indeclinable participle.

° denotes that the word or part of the word under reference has to be supplied.

A hyphen before a word denotes that the word occurs at the end of a compound.

Prākṛit words have been referred to under their Sanskṛit equivalents.

Words explained in the notes but not found in the text are printed in Roman type.

a- in *a-tas, a-tra, a-tha,* &c.
a-, before consonants, in *a-kath-ita,* &c.; *an-,* before vowels, in *an-agha,* &c.
aṇśa, 106[d]; °*vivartin,* 78[c].
aṇśu, 20[b] (*hima*°); 116[b] (*gharma*°).
aṇśuka, 34[b]; 169[b].
aṇsa, 30[a]; 175[c]; du. 63[b].
a-kathita, 17, 14; 229, 11.
a-kāṇḍe, 46[a], n.
a-kāma, adj. 23[d].
a-kāraṇa, 222, 14; 247, 4.
a-kāle, 260, 1, 2.
a-kṛita, 51, 9 (°*satkāra*); 35[b].
a-kuilava, adj. 208, 12.
a-klishṭa, 120[a] (°*kānti*).
-*aksha* (for *akshi*), 78[c]; 124[c].
a-kshama, adj. 112, 4; *ā,* f. 8[d].
a-kshayya, adj. 47[b].
a-kshara, n. 53, 6; 78[b]; 144[h]; °*artha,* 184, 2.
akshi, n. 62, 2; 65, 7; (at end of a comp. -*aksha.*)
a-khaṇḍa, adj. 44[c].
a-grihita, 230, 8 (°*artha*).
agni, 10[b]; 28[b], &c.; °*śaraṇa,* 148, 4; 189, 4.
agra, 229, 6; 190[a]; °*tas,* adv. 76, 6. 13; 212, 2; °*bhūmi,* 263, 12; °*yāyin,* 190[a]; °*hasta,* 252, 10.
aṅka, 74[c]; 181[c]; 66[c], &c.
aṅkita, 14[d]; 140, 9; 176, 7.
aṅkura, 228, 1; 135[a]; 230, 3.
aṅga, 21[b]; 277, 1; °*bhaṅga,* 62, 5.
aṅganā, 27[d] (*hariṇa*°).
aṅguli or °*ī,* 48, 1; 78[a]; 143[d].
aṅgulīya, 53, 5; °*ka,* 54, 5; 233, 4.
a-ćala, adj. 175[d].
a-ćintanīya, 243, 5.
a-ćira, 6, 6 (°*pravṛitta*); *āt,*
99[c]; *ena,* 262, 8; °*m,* adv. 103, 2; °*bhās,* 171[b].
a-ćetana, adj. 145[c].
a-jayya, adj. 162[a].
a-jasram, adv. 58[a].
a-jñātrā, ind. 107, 11.
aṭarī, 60, 2; 72, 3.
a-taṭa, 142[d] (°*prapāta*).
a-tanu, 110[c].
a-tas, 27, 2; 72, 6; 125[a], &c.; °*param,* 97[d]; 315, 2.
ati-kramya, ind. 250, 8; 263, 11.
ati-krāmat, 195[b].
atithi, 17, 2 (°*satkāra*); 36, 2.
ati-dūra, 58, 6.
ati-nishkaruṇa, adj. 185[c].
ati-parisphuṭa, adj. 115[a].
ati-pāta, m. 16, 7, 8.
ati-pinaddha, 23, 8.
ati-mātram, adv. 29, 4; 30[a].
ati-mukta, 112, 12 (°*latā*).
ati-raṇhas, adj. 5[b].
ati-rush, adj. 124[d].
ati-lola, adj. 10[c].
ati-lohita, 124[c] (°*akshī*).
ati-vah, caus. 238, 9.
ati-śithila, 257, 10.
ati-śrama, 108[c] (°*apanayana*).
ati-san-dhā, pass. 99, 1, 2.
ati-sandhāna, 126[c] (*para*°).
ati-sandhāya, ind. 211, 7.
ati-sneha, m. 176, 11.
atīta, part. 142[c].
atītya, ind. 12, 2; 148[c]; 274, 2.
aty-antam, adv. 27[c].
aty-aya, 65[b] (*tapa*°).
aty-artham, adv. 175[b].
aty-āhita, 35, 6.
a-tra, adv. 91, 4; 311, 4, &c.; °*bhavat,* 194, 11; °*bhavatī,* 52, 11, &c.; °*antare,* 64[d].
a-tha, 1, 1; 196, 2; 81, 7; 296, 5, n.; °*kim,* 46, 7, n.; 90, 11; 188, 9; °*rā,* 30, 5, n.

adas, pron. 9, 8; 8[d]; 48[a]; 175[d], &c.
A-diti, f. 279, n. 3; 282, 4.
a-drishṭa, 263, 11 (°*rūpa*).
adbhuta, n. 215, 8.
adya, 4, 2; 147, 11, &c.; °*prabhṛiti,* 165, 7; °*api,* 30[b].
a-dhanyatā, 61, 6.
adhara, m. 21[a]; 24[c]; 77[c]; 286, 14; °*uttara,* 210, 7; °*oshṭha,* 78[a].
a-dharma, 213, 7, 8 (°*bhīru*).
adhas, adv. 104, 2; with gen. 14[a]; °*mukha,* 47, 1.
adhika, 20[c] (°*manojña*); 30[b] (*pramāṇa*°); °*taram,* 282, 7.
adhi-kāra, 40, 8 (*dharma*°); 189, 7.
adhi-kṛi, pass. 8, 1.
adhi-kṛitya, ind. 6, 4, n.; 6, 6; 77, 3.
adhi-kship, 210, 4, 5.
adhi-kshipta, 201, 8.
adhi-gata, 42[a].
adhi-gamya, ind. 189, 8.
adhi-jya, 6[a]; 37[a]; 49[d]; 164[b].
adhi-rūḍha, 271, 2 (*ratha*°).
adhi-rohat, 274, 9.
adhi-rohin, 203, 3 (*dūra*°).
adhi-śayāna, part. 105, 1.
adhi, pass. 126[c].
adhunā, adv. 167[c].
adhy-ākrānta, 48[a].
adhy-ās, 236, 8. 11.
an-agha, adj. 44[c]; 167, 3 (°*prasava*).
An-aṅga, 58[b]; 60[b].
an-atikramaṇīya, 68, 7; 280, 2.
an-atikruddha, adj. 313, 8.
an-atipātya, 187, 1.
an-atilulita, 66[c], n.
an-anurūpa, 24, 10.
an-antaram, adv. 194[b]; 5, 8.
an-anyaparāyaṇa, adj. 72[a].

an-anyamānasa, adj. 81ᵃ.
an-apatya, 258, 13; °tā, 258,
  14; 286, 10.
an-abhijña, adj. 207, 11; 248, 7.
an-abhyantara, adj. 107, 8.
an-abhyarthanīya, 77, 6.
an-artha, m. 237, 5.
an-avagata, 254, 8 (°artha).
an-avarata, 38ᵃ.
an-avalepa, 248, 2.
an-avāpta, 76, 10.
An-asūyā, 22, 3. 7, &c.
an-āgas, 11ᵇ.
an-āghrāta, 44ᵃ.
an-ātmajña, 230, 5.
an-āmaya, 198, 2 (°praśnu).
an-āyāsa, adj. 69, 2.
an-ārambha, m. 107, 12.
an-ārya, 144, 3; 208, 8.
an-āridtha, 44ᵇ.
an-āsrādita, 44ᵇ (°rasa).
a-nimitta, 181ᵃ (°hāsa).
a-niyata, 60, 3 (°velam, adv.)
a-niyantraṇa, 48, 6 (°anu-
  yoga).
a-nirvarṇanīya, 196, 9.
anila, 176ᵃ.
a-niśam, adv. 57ᵃ; 70ᵃ.
an-īśa, 67, 7.
anu-kamp, pass. 247, 4.
anu-kampanīya, 111, 3.
anu-kampā, 133ᵇ (°mṛidu).
anu-kampita, 299, 4, 5.
anu-kampin, adj. 54, 7; 207, 1.
anu-kārin, 50ᵃ; 238, 6; 21ᵃ.
anu-kūla, 41ᶜ; 88, 18; 91ᵈ.
anu-kṛita, 208, 10.
an-ukta, 122, 2.
anu-krama, 218, 10.
anu-krośa, 100, 1; 139, 8 (sa°).
anu-gantavya, 169, 4.
anu-gam, 180, 5; 214, 16.
anu-gṛihīta, 88, 16; 224, 4, &c.
anu-grah, 121, 2.
anu-graha, 42, 7; 197, 16;
  308, 3; 198ᵈ.
anu-cintya, ind. 43ᵈ.
an-uccalat, 29ᵇ.
anu-ja, 93, 7 (rājan°).
anu-jñā, 57, 5, 6; 89ᵈ.
anu-jñāta, 102, 6; 163, 5;
  198, 8.
anu-tāpa, 122, 2.
anu-tishṭhat, 291, 6.
an-utkhāta, 197ᵃ.
an-utsekin, 98ᶜ.
anu-divasam, adv. 108, 6.
an-uddhata, 114ᶜ.
anu-dhāvana, 60, 4.
anu-naya, 139, 7.
anu-patat, 7ᵃ; 10, 4.
anu-padam, adv. 89, 7.
an-upapanna, 240, 11; 309, 10.

an-upabhukta, 156, 12.
an-upayukta, 271, 5.
anu-prati-shṭhā, 212, 5.
anu-praveśa, 247, 10 (bhāva°).
anu-badhyamāna, 285, 8, 9.
anu-bandha, 95ᵇ; 285, n. 5.
anu-bodhita, 8, 3.
anu-bhavat, 153ᵃ.
anu-bhavitarya, 156, 3.
anu-bhāva, 305, 2.
anu-bhāvin, 254, 8, 9.
anu-bhū, 109ᶜ; 253, 3; 262, 5.
anu-mata, 111, 2; 90ᵃ; neut.
  135, 6.
anu-man, caus. 128, 2.
anu-manyamāna, 121ᵃ.
anu-māna, 208, 8 (hṛidaya°).
anumānālaṃkāra, 19, n. 1.
anu-yātrika, 58, 5; 93, 9, 10.
anu-yāsyat, 29ᵃ.
anu-yoga, 48, 6.
anu-yojya, 306, 4 (vāsava°).
anu-rakta, 151ᵃ.
anu-rāga, 68ᵇ; 121, 5, &c.
anu-rūpa, 21, 6; 29, 9; 134,
  5, &c.
anu-lipta, 171ᵇ.
anu-lepana, 96, 2 (uśīra°).
anu-vāćya, ind. 53, 6; 258, 11.
anu-viddha, 20ᵃ.
anu-vṛit, 71, 7; 113, 2.
anu-śaya, 139ᵇ; 247, 4 (°tapta);
  189ᵈ.
anu-śās, 214, 6.
anu-śāsanīya, 173, 2.
anu-shṭhā, 3, 2, 3; 93, 1;
  187, 9.
anu-shṭhāna, 178, 6 (tapas°).
anu-shṭhita, 211, 13.
anu-sāra, 61, 4, 5; 285, 8.
anu-sārin, 9, 2; 6ᵇ (mṛiga°).
anu-sṛi, 34, 14; 168, 2.
anu-smṛita, 233, 5.
anu-smṛitya, ind. 67, 10; 240,
  15.
an-ṛiṇa, adj. 53, 5; 54, 6.
anṛita-maya, 207, 7.
an-ekaśas, adv. 296, 11.
anta, 2, 1; 144ᵇ; 260, 1; 17ᵃ
  (śuddha°).
antar in °karaṇa, 22ᵃ; 276,
  2; °pura, 123, 2; pl. 137ᶜ;
  93, 14; °ātman, 102ᵈ; 276,
  2; °ita, 23, 5; 129, 3;
  °gata, 166ᵃ; °hita, 140, 6;
  83ᵃ; °tāpa, 66ᵃ; °tushāra,
  120ᶜ.
antara, 182, 4; 10, 7; 284,
  5; 104ᵈ, &c.; e, 13, 5;
  eṇa, with acc. 81, 7, n.;
  104, 5 (viṭapa°).
antarā, adv. 91, 6; 256, 9, &c.
antariksha, 123ᶜ (°gamana).

antika, 166ᵃ (°stha); cf. jana°.
antya, adj. 292, 14.
andha, 188ᵈ; °kāra, 262, 4, 5.
anya, 6, 2; 164ᵇ; °tama, 153,
  2; °tara, 124, 11; °tas, 36ᵃ;
  °thā, 72ᵃ; 119ᵇ; 111, 3, &c.;
  anyo-'nya, 121, 5; 198ᶜ.
a-nyāya, 294, 2.
anv-aya, m. 292, 13.
anv-ās, pass. 105, 1.
anv-ita, 146ᵇ.
anv-ish, 102, 8; 124, 9; 216, 3.
anv-esha, 24ᵈ (tattva°).
anv-eshin, 57, 2 (asmad°); 284,
  5 (antara°).
ap, pl. 160ᵇ.
apa-kṛishṭa, 112ᵇ.
apa-ghnat, 88ᶜ.
apa-ćarita, 111ᶜ.
apa-ćita, 38ᶜ.
apatya, n. 42ᵃ; °jāta, 123ᶜ.
a-patha, 112ᵇ.
apa-deśa, m. 83, 8. 10; 115, 2.
apa-nayana, 108ᶜ (atiśrama°).
apa-nī, 75, 5; 159ᶜ.
a-para, 43ᶜ; 83, 10; 228, 1.
apa-rakta, 138ᵇ (°adhara).
a-parājitā, 295, 14.
apa-rāddha, 137, 11; 309, 2.
apa-rādh, caus. 126, 2.
apa-rādha, m. 139, 14.
a-parikshata, 77ᵃ.
a-parićaya, 207, 2.
a-parićita, 292, 7.
a-parićchinna, 260, 15.
a-parićcheda, 111ᵈ (°ākula).
a-paritosha, 271, 7.
a-parinirvāṇa, 126, 4.
apa-vādin, 71, 4.
apa-vārya, ind. 88, 17; 203, 1.
a-paśyat, 170, 9.
apa-sṛita, 92ᵇ; 248, 12.
apa-hāya, ind. 148ᵃ.
apa-hāra, 40, 6, n.
apā-kṛi, 162ᵈ.
apāṅga, 24ᵃ; 66ᵇ; 206, 13.
api, 2ᵇ; 91, 3; 35, 9; 89, 11,
  &c.; °ća, 16, 8; 19, 1, &c.;
  °nāma, 30, 1, n.; 30, 5, n.
a-pīta, 89ᵃ.
a-pūrva, 8, 1; 255, 5; 308, 2.
ape, 188ᵃ.
apeksh, 90, 6; 257, 9.
apekshā in edhāpeksha, 179ᵇ.
apekshita, 118ᵃ; 258, 7.
apeta, 196ᵇ (°tamas).
apoh, 53ᵇ.
a-pragalbha, 82, 2.
a-pratipadyamāna, 124ᵇ.
a-pratibuddha, 229, 13.
a-pratiratha, 100ᵇ; 306, 8.
a-pratiloma, 292, 7.
a-pratihata, 209, 12.

a-pratyaya, adj. 2[b].
a-pramatta, 221, 10.
a-pramāṇa, adj. 126[b].
a-priya, 137, 10; 119[d] (tad[o]).
apsaras, f. 44, 12; 46, 5, &c.;
 [o]tirtha, 131[c]; 226, 4.
abalā-jana, m. 83[c].
a-bāndhavakṛita, 97[b].
a-bālasattva, adj. 285, 9.
a-bodhapūrvam, adv. 104[c].
a-brahmaṇya, 263, 3, n.
a-bhaya, 50[b].
abhijana-vat, 99[a].
abhi-jātam, adv. 253, 7.
abhi-jñā, 201, 11.
abhi-jñāta, 34, 11.
abhi-jñāna, 140, 4, 5, &c.;
 [o]sakuntala, n. 1, 1; 4, 3, n.;
 7, 8, &c.
abhi-tas, 149[b] (with acc.); 307,
 10.
abhi-dhā, 34, 11, 12.
abhi-nand, 72, 7; 84, 5; 112, 6.
abhi-nandaniya, 195, 2.
abhi-nandita, 76[b]; 147, 8;
 259, 15.
abhi-nandya, ind. 214, 11.
abhi-nandyamāna, 152, 8.
abhi-nayat, 134, 2.
abhi-nava, 61[b]; 192, 4; 19[c].
abhi-niveśa, 108, 2.
abhi-nīya, ind. 96, 3.
a-bhinna, 38[b]; [o]yati, 14[c];
 [o]sthiti, 112[a].
abhi-prāya, 64, 1.
abhi-preta, 251, 7; 308, 2.
abhi-bhava, 41[d].
abhi-bhū, pass. 264, 2.
abhi-bhūyamāna, 34, 4, 5;
 35, 7.
abhi-mata, 57[a]; 224, 11.
abhi-marśa, 121[a] (kṛita[o]).
abhi-mukha, 2, 2; 31[b]; 45[a], &c.
abhi-rāma, 7[a]; 78[b].
abhi-rūpa, 250, 11; 4, 2.
abhi-laṅgh, 252, 12.
abhi-lāsha, m. 78, 5; 94, 3, &c.
abhi-lāshin, adj. 22[b].
abhi-vad, caus. 88, 2; 197, 7.
abhi-vṛit, 21, 7; 32, 4; 23[a].
abhi-vyakta, 202, 11.
abhi-shiku, 156, 6; 176[b].
abhi-hita, 190[b].
abhiśu, m. 'a rein,' 10, 10.
a-bhūtala-sparśa-tā, 174[c].
a-bhūmi, 271, 11; 285, 7.
abhy-akta, 113[a].
abhy-adhika, 135[b] (pañćan[o]).
abhy-antara, 172[b]; 205, 12;
 218, 6, &c.
abhy-arkavimbam, adv. 175[d].
abhy-arth, 146, 1, 2.
abhy-arthanā, 42, 7; 78, 6.

abhy-arthita, 291, 6 (yathā[o]).
abhy-as, 40[b].
abhy-āsa, 207, 2; 209, 10.
abhy-ukshya, ind. 130, 5.
abhy-ut-thā, 120, 6.
abhy-udaya, 304, 8.
abhy-unnata, 61[a].
abhy-upayata, 211, 6.
abhy-upapatti, 122, 10; 156, 2.
abhra, 'a cloud,' 65[b] ([o]syāma).
a-maṅgala, 194, 8; 260, 4.
amareśvara, 272, 6.
amātya, m. 236, 10; 258, 6,
 14, &c.
a-mānusha, 67, 4; 123[a].
a-mṛita, 282, 7 ([o]hrada).
ambā, 90, 9; 92, 5; 294, 6, &c.
ambu, 114[b]; [o]rāsi, 56[b].
ambhas, 15[a]; 30[c]; 122[b], &c.
a-yathārtha, adj. 55[b].
ayi, interj. 210, 4; 253, 2, &c.
aye, interj. 21, 4. 5; 84, 11, &c.
ara, 171[a] ([o]virara).
araṇya, n. 40, 9; [o]okas, 86[c].
aravinda, 60[a] ([o]surabhi).
aruṇa, 143[c]; 32[c]; 82[b]; 168[c].
arka, 82[b]; 91[b]; 99[c]; 42[b].
argha or aryhya, 36, 3; 138, 4.
arćana, 229, 7. 9.
arćaniya, 136, 2, 3.
arćita, 196, 14.
artha, 52[b]; 102[a]; 216, 2, &c.;
 arthe, 93[a]; [o]m, 96, 1; 105[d],
 &c.; [o]jāta, 258, 6; [o]ban-
 dha, 169[c]; [o]vat, 197, 16;
 [o]sanćaya, 258, 13, 14.
arthin, 159[a] (sonita[o]).
ardha, 9[b]; 7[c]; 7[b], &c.
arpita, 79[b]; 100[c]; 138[a]; 148[b];
 150[a]; [o]vat, 141[c].
arvāk, adv. 15[c] (with loc.)
r. arh, arhati, 71[b]; 93, 1, &c.
arha, adj. 137, 10 (pūjā[o]).
arhat, 117[a].
a-lakshita, 95[c].
a-lakshya, adj. 38[c]; 180[c].
a-laṅghaniya, 8[c].
alam, adv. 48, 6; 54, 2; 166,
 9; [o]karaṇa, 154, 12; [o]kāra,
 24, 11; [o]kṛi, 39, 5.
alinda, 192, 5 (agni-śaraṇa[o]).
a-lūna, 44[a].
alpa, 135, 10; 233, 4.
r. av, avati, 1[d].
ava-kāśa, 196[d]; labdha[o], 47, 3.
ava-gata, 107, 14; 310, 1, &c.
ava-gam, 44, 4; 46, 5; 66, 2.
ava-gāḍha, 279, 4; 282, 7,
 8; 61[a].
ava-gāha, 3[a] (salila[o]).
ava-guṇṭhana, 201, 10; [o]vat,
 115[a].
a-vaćana, adj. 35, 10.

ava-ćaya, 134, 2 (kusuma[o]).
ava-ćita, 59[a].
ava-aṉsaya, -yati, 4[b].
ava-taraṇa, 278, 4; 309, 15.
ava-tāra, 46, 2 (vasanta[o]).
ava-tārya, ind. 224, 4.
ava-tīrṇa, 277, 1; 174[d].
ava-tīrya, ind. 20, 3; 282, 11.
ava-tṛi, 19, 10; 20, 2; 112,
 11, &c.
ava-dāna, 165[b].
ava-dhāna, 182, 4.
ava-dhi, m. 245, 9.
ava-dhīraṇa, 116, 9; ā, f. 67[b].
ava-dhīrita, 145[d]; 177[b].
ava-dhṛi, caus. 174, 3.
ava-nata, 147, 7; 265, 2.
ava-mānin, 117, 4; 260, 6.
ava-ruddha, 36[c].
ava-ruh, 172[a].
avarodha-gṛiha, 105[b]; 144[c].
ava-lamb, 122, 11; 212, 11.
ava-lambana, 105[d] ([o]artham).
ava-lambita, 150, 8 (śākhā[o]).
ava-lambin, 192, 6 (aṉsa[o]).
ava-lambya, ind. 62, 7.
ava-līḍha, 7[c].
ava-lepa, 248, 2.
ava-lok, 53, 6.
ava-lokayat, 58, 2.
ava-lokya, ind. 2, 2; 9, 3, &c.
ava-śishṭa, 142, 5.
ava-śesha in sa[o], 68, 11.
ava-śeshita, 89, 14.
avaśyam, adv. 91, 1; 111, 3.
ava-sad, caus. 108[a].
ava-sara, m. 34, 10; 77, 5.
ava-sāna, 240, 2; 310, 3.
ava-sita, 2, 3; 158, 2 ([o]maṉ-
 dana).
ava-seka, 248, 13.
ava-sthā, 107, 10; 186, 3; 234,
 15, &c.; [o]antara, 122, 9.
ava-sthāna, 247, 10.
ava-sthita, 214, 12.
ava-hita, 105[a]; 119, 4; 197, 3.
ava-hina, 61, 4.
avāp, 87[b].
a-vighna, 40, 8 ([o]kriyā).
a-vijñāta, 139, 13.
a-vitatha, 108, 9.
avidhā, 264, 8, n.; 266, 7.
a-vinaya, 25[b]; 285, 7.
a-vinīta, 252, 16; 286, 5.
a-viralam, adv. 60[b].
a-vilambitam, adv. 85, 5;
 113, 4.
a-vilambin, adj. 120, 5.
a-vilambya, ind. 295, 9.
a-viśrānta, 255, 7.
a-viśrāma, adj. 187, 3.
a-vishaya, adj. 173, 5.
avё, 165, 4; 84[b]; 113[b].

a-vaksh, 205, 10.
a-vakshi-tā, 202, 5 (dharma°).
a-vyakta, 181ᵇ.
a-vyabhichārin, adj. 237, 5, 6.
a-vyavasyat, 120ᵇ.
a-vyāju, 18ᵃ (°manohara).
r. aś, aśnāti, 60, 4 (pass.)
aśana, 80ᵈ (piśita°); 265, 15.
a-śarana, 124, 11; 240, 15.
a-śikshita, 123ᵃ, 126ᵃ.
a-śiśira, adj. 66ᵃ.
a-śuchi, 113ᵃ.
a-śūnya, adj. 75, 6; 236, 16.
a-śeshatas, adv. 158ᵈ.
a-śoka, 284, 4 (°vriksha).
a-śochanīya, 147, 10.
aśru, 65, 7; 66ᵇ; 147ᵇ, &c.
a-śruta, 232, 1 (°pūrva).
aśva, 17, 10.
ashṭau, 1ᵈ.
r. as, asti, 3, 2; 5ᵃ, &c.
a-samśayam, adv. 22ᵃ; 129, 2.
a-samskāra, adj. 187ᵇ.
a-samstuta, 34ᵃ.
a-sakta, 46ᵈ.
a-sat, n. 111ᵇ; 201, 4.
a-salya, 145, 7 (°sandha).
a-sannivritti, f. 142ᶜ.
a-sannihita, 136, 12.
a-sambaddha, 51, 6, n.
a-sambhārita, 57, 11, n.
a-savarṇa, 30, 5 (°kshetra).
a-sādhudarśin, adj. 22, 11.
a-sānnidhya, n. 88, 12.
Asura, 161ᵃ; 173ᵇ; 274, 9.
a-sulabha, 243, 7 (°sthāna).
asūyā, 225, 3; cf. sāsūyam.
asta, 82ᵃ (°śikhara).
astra, n. 266, 11.
asmad, 30, 1; 34, 7; 40, 8,
    &c.; 57, 2 (°anveshin); 93,
    14; 214, 8.
a-svastha, 96, 4; 105, 11.
r. ah, 1ᶜ; 24, 5; 27, 4, &c.
-aha (for ahan), 67, 5. 7, 8.
ahan, 158ᵃ.
ahi, 188ᵈ (°śankā).
aho, interj. 36ᵈ; 95, 4; 103, 5.

ā- in ā-tāmra, &c., 134ᵃ; 181ᵃ.
    189ᶜ.
ā, prep. with abl. 2ᵃ; 27ᵃ; 169,
    4; 126ᵃ.
ā-kampita, 176, 9.
ā-karn, 163, 3; 182, 8.
ā-karnya, ind. 13, 4; 185, 6.
ā-kāra, 41, 4; 291, 4.
ā-kārita, 244, 11.
ākāśa, 226, 2, &c.; e, 96, 2, &c.
ā-kīrṇa, 112ᵈ (jana°).
ā-kuṭila, 189ᶜ.
ā-kula, 67, 5; 99ᵇ; °ī-kritya,
    ind. 65, 7; °ī-bhūta, 92, 2.

ā-kulita, 147, 8 (dhūma°).
ā-kriti, 20ᵈ; 38, 10; 135, 2.
ā-krish, pass. 207, 7, 8.
ā-krishṭa, 9, 8; 33ᵇ.
ā-krishya, ind. 58ᶜ.
ā-krand, 34, 7.
Ā-khaṇḍala, 303, 14; 192ᵃ.
ā-khyā, f. 294, 13; 197ᵈ.
ākhyāyin, 24ᵇ.
ā-gata, 89, 7.
āyantuka, 141, 4; °tā, 232, 1, n.
ā-gam, 2, 3, 4; 34, 3; 133, 4;
    249, 8.
ā-gama, 221, 3; 223, 4; 114ᵃ.
ā-gamana, 187, 2, 3; 222, 1.
ā-gāmin, adj. 90, 17.
ā-ghāta, 33ᵃ (tīvra°).
ā-chakshita, 240, 3; 297, 11.
ā-char, 25ᵇ.
ā-charita, 144, 4.
ā-charitavya, 304, 8.
ā-chāra, 62, 2; 158, 7; 105ᵃ.
ā-chhādin, 19ᵇ (pariṇāha°).
ā-jīva, m. 219, 7; 223, 11.
ā-jñapta, 7, 8; 155, 4.
ā-jñapti, 90, 7 (°hara).
ā-jñā, caus. 3, 2; 10, 12, &c.
ā-jñā, 88, 6, &c.; °kari, 308, 11.
ājya, 15ᵇ (°dhūma).
ā-taṅka, m. 106, 8; 108, 5.
ā-tapa, 96, 4; 75ᵇ; °tra, 108ᵈ.
ā-tāmra, 134ᵃ, n.
ātitheya, adj. 16, 8.
ātithya, n. 36, 5.
ātura, adj. 170, 9.
ātta, 110ᵃ (°daṇḍa); °gandha,
    263, 9, n.; °śastra, 269, 1, n.
-ātmaka in dāha°, 41ᵇ.
ātman, 2ᵇ; 17, 10; ātmanā-
    tritīya, 13, 11; °krita, 209,
    12; °gatam, 38, 4, n.; °gati,
    293, 1; °jā, 42, 10; °bhū,
    191ᶜ; 199ᵈ.
ātmīya, 77, 2.
ā-dadhāna, 80ᶜ.
ā-dara, m. 227, 4.
ā-dā, 265, 8.
ā-dāya, ind. 95, 2; 153, 13, &c.
-ādi, 44, 5; 207, 7 (evam°).
Ādityas (twelve), 305, n. 3.
ā-diś, 151, 7; caus. 161, 4.
ā-dishṭa, 142, 4; 227, 1.
ādya, adj. 1ᵃ; 89ᶜ.
ā-dhū, 4, 4.
ā-dhāra, 14ᵈ (toya°).
ā-dhi, m. 98ᵈ; °hetu, 64ᵇ.
ānana, 31ᶜ; 63ᵃ; 68ᵃ.
ā-nanda, 158, 6 (°parivāhin).
ā-nī, 238, 11; 249, 6; 172ᵈ.
ā-nīta, 309, 1.
r. āp, āpnoti, 12ᵇ; 16, 2.
āpagā, 172ᶜ.
ā-paṇa, 225, 10 (śauṇḍika°).

ā-panna, 72, 2; 50ᵇ; 122, 4;
    °sattva, 146, 3, 4; 199, 1.
āpta, 126ᵈ (°vāch).
ābaddha, 219, 2; 222, 4. 7, &c.
ā-bharaṇa, 20, 5; 79ᶜ, 85ᵈ, &c.
ā-bhoga, m. 17, 14, n.
ām, interj. 100, 2.
ā-mantr, 128, 14; 165, 2, &c.
ā-marda, 178ᵃ.
ā-mrishṭa, 166ᶜ.
āmra, 230, 5 (°kulikā).
āyata, 57ᵇ (°nayana).
ā-yatta, 97ᵈ (bhāgya°).
ā-yāta, 40, 9; 232, 12.
ā-yāsa, 120, 8; 135, 11.
ā-yāsayitri, 109, 2.
āyus, 91, 1; 307, 8; °mat, 9,
    4, n.; 10, 6, 10; 281, 2.
ā-ruṭ, 170, 9.
āraṇyaka, 57, 5; 47ᵇ, &c.
ā-rabh, 136, 5; 230, 6.
ā-rabhya, ind. 106, 6.
ā-rambha, 227, 2 (nir-utsava°).
ārāt, 131ᶜ.
ā-rādh, 7, 5, 6.
ā-rādhayitri, 125, 6.
ā-rūḍha, 176, 13; 111ᵈ; 261, 8.
ā-ropita, 122, 10; 263, 12.
ā-ropya, ind. 236, 12; 265, 16.
ā-rohaṇa, 270, 9.
ārta, 11ᵇ; 159ᶜ; 263, 5.
ārti, 122, 4 (°hara).
ārdra, 20, 6 (°prishṭha).
ārya, 3, 2; 5, 2; 22ᵇ, &c.; ā, f.
    2, 3; °ka, 295, 1; °putra,
    196, 11; °miśra, 7, 8, n.
ā-laksh, pass. 63ᶜ; 138ᵈ.
ā-lakshya, adj. 181ᵃ, n.
ā-lapat, 38, 10 sq.
ālavāla, 22, 6 (°pūraṇa).
ā-lāpa, m. 21, 4; 39ᵇ, 4.
ā-likhita, 7, 4; 248, 14.
ālikhitu-kāma, 250, 11, 12.
ā-liṅg, 60ᵇ; 298, 7.
ā-lok, pass. 279, 5.
ā-loka, 9ᵃ; 33ᵈ.
ā-raraṇa, 75ᵃ (stana°).
ā-vahat, 57ᵃ.
ā-vāpa, 265, 7 (hasta°).
ā-vārya, ind. 252, 10.
ā-vid, caus. 313, 15.
āvilaya, -yati, 122ᵃ.
āvis, 'evidently,' in °krita, 82,
    10; 82ᵇ; 85ᵃ; °bhū, 116ᵇ.
ā-vrij, caus. 30, 3.
ā-vritya, ind. 129, 6; 209, 10.
ā-vega, 125, 6; 139, 4; 295, 6.
ā-vedya, ind. 92, 6.
ā-śaṁs, 177ᵃ.
ā-śank, 28ᵇ; 242, 2.
ā-śankamāna, 202, 12.
ā-śankā, 107, 2; 15ᵈ.
āśā, 293, 6; °bandha, 96ᵇ.

ā-śās, 160, 1; 312, 2.
āśis, 153, 8; 159, 6; 192^b.
āśu, 71^n (°klānta).
āśćarya, 278, 4; 215, 4, &c.
ā-śrama, 13, 3; 16, 7; 48^n;
    194,11(varṇa°); °pada,16^a;
    °sad, 88, 8.
ā-śraya, 181^c (aṅka°).
āśrayin, 230, 11 (tad^).
ā-śri, 170, 2.
ā-śritya,ind. 7,5; 21,10; 149,3.
ā-ślishya, ind. 150, 1; 174, 12.
ā-śvas, 140, 8; 261, 3.
āśvāsin, 35^n (darśana°).
āṣ, interj. 137, 4; 252, 11.
r. ās, āste, 284, 4; 202, 8.
ā-saṁya, 33^b.
ā-sajyamāna, 79^c (°īkshaṇa).
āsana, 88, 1; 153, 1 (°stha).
ā-sanna, 238, 8.
āsīna, 76, 3 (sukha°).
ā-stīraṇa, 105, 1.
āspada, 191^c.
ā-sphālana, 38^n.
ā-haraṇa, 16, 6.
āhavanīya, 149, n.
ā-hāra, 60, 4.
ā-hiṇḍ, 60, 2.
ā-hiṇḍat, 72, 3.
ā-hita, 37^b; 84^n; 106^c.
ā-huti, f. 147, 9.
ā-hṛi, 155, 5.
āho, 27^d; 130^b; °svid, 111^c.
ā-hve, pass. 69, 15.

i- in i-tara, i-tas, &c.
r. i, eti, 101^n.
ikshu, 265, 2.
iṅgudī, 14^b, n.; 81, 3; 94^n.
i-tara, 16, 1; 130,12; 248, 15.
i-tas, 2, 3; 141^n, &c.; itas—
    itas, 91, 3; °gata, 134, 11;
    °mukha, 222, 17, &c.
iti, 10, 6; 60, 1; 134, 5, &c.
iti-hāsa, 107, 9 (°nibaddha).
ittham, 207, 4; 209, 12; °gata,
    146, 4; °bhūta, 114, 9.
idam, 8, 3; 9, 8; 10, 4; 12^a;
    20^c; 22,11.12; 76,2; 171^n.
i-dānīm, 7, 5; 9, 8, &c.
iddha, 180^c (°rāga).
indu, 55^nc; 85^n (°puṇḍu).
indra, 107^d; °ka, 287, 5
    (mṛiga°); Indra, 284, 5.
indhana, 163^n (ćalita°).
iyat, 61, 2; 134, 6; 137, 2.
ira,adv.7, 5; 6^b; 239, 17, &c.
r. ish, ićchati, 44, 8; 88, 6;
    176, 2; 119^c (pass.)
ishu, 39^c; 266, 12.
ishṭa,197,9; 83^c; °jana,64,1.
ishṭi,88,12(°righna); 134,10;
    267, 10 (°paśu-māram.)

iha, 16^n; 44^d, &c.; °stha,88,8.

īkshaṇa, 27^c; 72^c; 79^c.
īkshita, n. 45^n.
īdṛiś or °a, 39^d; 86^c; 90^d, &c.
īpsita, m. 67^d.
īrita, 26, 2 (vāta^).
Īśa, 'Śiva,' 1^d.
īśvara,272,6; 168^b; 191^b,&c.
ishat, adv. 4^n; 248, 14.
r. īh, īhate, 122^n.

ukta, 121,6(punar°); 203, 11.
ugra, 44, 11; 102,9 (°ātapa).
ućita, 38, 2; 201, 2; 137^c, &c.
uć-ćaya, 43^b; 139, 5.
uććais, adv. 141^b; °kula, 97^n.
uć-ćhid, 162^c.
uć-ćhvasita, n. 97, 2.
uć-ćhvāsa, 147^b (varṇikā°).
Ujjayinī, 316, n.
ujjhita, 42^n; 44, 4. 7.
ujjhitvā, ind. 32, 3; 67. 4.
uṭaja, 36, 3; 57, 6; 101^b, &c.
uta, 123^b (kim°); kim—uta,
    74nd; 105, 11, 12.
ut-kaṇṭha, °kaṇṭhate, 178, 9.
ut-kaṇṭhā, 86^n; 150, 3. 5;
    70, 3 (ājñāpanotkaṇṭha).
ut-kaṇṭhita, 185, 7.
ut-karsha, 39^c.
ut-kīrṇa, 217, 5.
ut-kula, adj. 128^b.
ut-kshipat, 172^d.
ut-kshipya, ind. 131^d.
ut-kshepaṇa, 30^n (ghaṭa°).
ut-kshepam, ind. 131^b (bāhu°).
ut-khātin, adj. 10, 6.
ut-tam, 40, 4.
ut-tara, 189,9; 210, 7 (adha-
    ra°); 211, 13.
uttarīya, 256, 14.
ut-tānu, 204, 6 (°hṛidaya).
ut-tīrṇa, 156, 6; 157, 3.
ut-thā, 57, 9; 47^n.
ut-thāna, 39^n (°yogya).
ut-thāya,ind.88, 1; 107,5,&c.
ut-thita, 142, 2; 85^c; 187, 2.
ut-pakshman, adj. 95^n.
ut-pad, caus. 79, 4; 88, 13.
utpala, 18^c (nīla°).
ut-prekshā, 95, n. 3.
ut-phula, 137, 13.
ut-sarpin, adj. 283, 8.
ut-sara, 89^c; 232,9; 234, 4.
ut-sah, 187, 3; 241, 11.
ut-sāha, 71, 4; 72, 2; 75, 2.
utsuka, 67^n; 124, 8; 234,16.
ut-srijya, ind. 75^n; 267. 1.
udaka,36,3; 97,3; 157^d, &c.
ud-agra, 7^d (°phula-tva).
uda-dhi, 49^a (°śyāma-siman).
ud-anta, 'news,' 226, 6.

ud-aya, 152, 7 (sūrya°); 82^c.
udara, 39^n; 19^d; 118, 10, &c.
udāra, adj. 205, 7; 279, 2.
ud-āhṛita, 47, 3, 4.
ud-i, 26^b; 194^n.
ud-gata, 32, 3.
ud-gama, 15^b (ājya-dhūma°).
ud-gulita, 92^a.
ud-gāra, 219, 4 (jāla°).
ud-diś, 265, 15.
ud-diśya, ind. 122, 9; kim°,
    192, 7.
ud-dishṭa, 153, 1; 214, 9.
ud-deśa,103,5; 237,3; 244, 8.
ud-dhuta, 8^c.
ud-dhṛita, 167^b; 302, 2.
ud-bhinna, 248, 12.
ud-bheda, 85^d (kisalaya°).
udbhrāntaka, 263, 1, n.
ud-yamya, ind. 13, 12; 16,
    1, &c.
ud-yāna, 17^b (°latā); 227, 5.
ud-runta, 248, 11.
ud-rikshya, ind. 166^b.
ud-rega, 261, 2 (riguṇa°).
ud-rejita, 78, 4.
un-nata, 95^c; 247, 11.
un-namita, 68^a; 78^d.
un-nidra, adj. 137^b.
un-majjat, 172^a.
un-matta, 228, 8; 254, 3, &c.
un-mādayitṛi or °ka, 46, 2, n.
un-mūlita, 174, 13.
upa-kaṇṭha, 58^c (śravaṇa°).
upa-kārin, 114^d (para°).
upa-kṛitu, 165^a.
upa-klṛip, caus. 138, 4.
upa-gata, 26, 9; 207, 3, &c.
upa-gama, 14^c.
upa-gamya, ind. 87,9; 188, 3.
upa-ghāta, 65, 5 (gātra°).
upa-ćar, 97, 1.
upa-ćāra, 71^b.
upa-ććhandita, 207, 2.
upa-jīvin, 223, 3 (jāla°).
upatyakā, 188, 4.
upa-dishṭa, 173, n. 3.
upa-deśa, m. 37^d; 174, 2.
upa-nata, 120^n; 130, 8; 201,
    5 (sukha°).
upa-nipātin, 237, 5.
upa-nī, 256, 10; 258, 10.
upa-nīta, 40, 2.
upa-nīya,ind. 20, 5 (with gen.)
upa-nyasta, 200, 2.
upa-nyāsa, 116, 6; 200, 4.
upa-pad, 46, 9.
upa-panna, 19, 7; 85, 12;
    127^b, &c.
upa-bhoga, 85^b; °kshama, 6,
    6; 29, 2, n.
upa-mā, 208, 9 (kūpopama).
upa-mālinītīram, adv. 16, 7.

upa-yam, 198, 7.
upa-yamya, ind. 308, 11 sq.
upa-rāga, ' eclipse,' 186^b.
upari, prep. 61, 3; 42^b; 171^c.
upa-ruddha, 95^a (°vritti).
upa-rudh, 57, 2; 74, 5; 178, 6.
upa-rodha, 19, 9; 93, 9; 258, 4.
upala, 14^b.
upa-lakshaṇa, 142, 4.
upa-lakshita, 48, 3.
upa-labdha, 302, 11.
upa-labh, 32, 1; 227, 6.
upa-labhya, ind. 291, 6.
upa-lambha, 40, 9; 129, 2; 302, 11.
upa-lālayat, 292, 8.
upa-vana, 15^c (°bhū); 83, 4.
upa-rāsa, 90, 18.
upa-viś, 38, 3; 76, 3; 121, 3.
upa-riśya, ind. 37, 3; 153, 13.
upa-vishṭa, 76, 8; 117, 7, &c.
upa-vij, 105, 4.
upa-vijya, ind. 105, 5.
upa-reśita, 271, 12.
upa-saṃharat, 267, 7.
upa-sarpaṇīya, 222, 9.
upa-sritya, ind. 35, 1; 120, 1.
upa-sṛip, 70, 3; 90, 15; 152, 9.
upa-sthātavya, 4, 4.
upa-sthita, 13, 6; 81^b; 207, 1.
upa-hata, 196^c.
upa-hāra, 239, 6.
upa-hita, 19^a; 141, 2.
upa-hṛi, 36, 3; 84, 2; 88, 4.
upā-gata, 261, 13.
upādhyāya, m.188,11;196,14.
upāya, m. 113, 4; 140, 10; 219, 4.
upāyana, 154, 10 (°hasta).
upā-labdha, 102, 1; 184, 6.
upā-labh, 24, 2; 246, 11.
upā-lambhana, 184, 5.
upā-vṛit, 20, 6.
upā-vṛitta, 142, 4.
upe, 144^d.
upeksh, 108, 6.
upekshita, 189^a.
upeta, 12^b (guṇa°).
upetya, ind. 28, 5; 37^a; 71, 1.
upodha, 111^a (°tapas); 174^a.
upta, 260, 2; 156^d (°vija).
ubha, du. 34, 6; 41, 4; 85, 9, &c.
ubhaya, 35^b; 271, 7; 167^a, &c.
uras, n. 63^a; 196, 10; 175^a.
urvī, f. 7^d; 73^b.
ul-likhita, 138^d.
usīra, 62^a; 96, 2.
ushas, f. 180^d (nava°).
ushṇa, adj. 56^d; m. n. 109^c.

ūḍha, 233, 5; 309, 3 (°pūrva).
ūru, 74^c (karabha°).
ūrdhva, 8^b (°karṇa).

riksha, 72, 4 (jīrṇa°).
ṛic, 160, 1 (°chandas).
ṛitu, 6, 4; 134^b; 303, 5; °utsava, 227, 1.
ṛite, with abl. 102, 8; 155^b.
ṛitv-ij, 96, 1, n.
ṛishi, 18^a; 94, 2; 192, 7; 283, n. 4, &c.; °kalpa, 85, 12.

e, 52, 8; 76, 8; 156, 6, &c.
eka, 30^d; 49^b; 131^d, &c.; °tas —°tas, 82^ab; °deśa, 121, 2; °antara, 191^d; °aha, 67, 7, 8; °eka, 118^b; 144^n.
ckākin, 228, 6.
etad, 5^b; 10, 7; 26, 2; 151^a, &c.; °nimitta, 150, 9.
etādṛiśa, 67, 4.
etāvat, 145, 9; 174, 2; 281, 2.
edha, 179^b (°apeksha).
edhita, 52^a.
ena, 7, 5; 13, 1; 23, 5.9; 81, 2.
eva, 10, 4; 17, 2; 65^a; 93^a, &c.
evam, 30, 1; 55, 2, &c.; °vidha, 109^b; °vṛitta, 260, 2; °guṇopeta, 12^b; °tarkin, 291, 5; °darśin, 180, 10; °ādi, 207, 7; °prāya, 188^c.

aindra, 269, 1 (°ratha).
Airāvata, 267, n. 1.
aiśvarya, 201, 6 (°matta).

okas, 86^c; 173, 2; 169^d(diśa°).
oshadhi or °ī, 82^a; 295, 14.
oshṭha, 78^a; 187^b (pāṭala°).

autsukya, 108^a; 58, 5 (manda°).
aurasa, adj. 286, 9.
aurva, m. 56^b.

ka, 3, 2; 34, 7; 38, 5; 53^n; 62, 2; kasmāt, 145^d; cf. kim.
kac-cid, 239. 17.
kañcuka, 208, 9 (dharma°).
kañcukin, 186, 1. 2; 193, 3, &c.
kaṭu or °ka, adj. 60, 3.
kaṇa, 60^a (°vāhin).
kaṇṭaka, 167^b.
kaṇṭakita, 68^b.
kaṇṭha, m. 86^b; 136^c, &c.
kaṇḍita, 60, 5 (°sandhi).
kaṇḍūyamāna, 149^d.
Kaṇva, 16, 6; 22, 11, &c.
ka-tama, 6, 4; 7, 5; 39, 5, n.
ka-tara, 275, 1.
kati, 231, 8; °cid, 46^b; °paya, 88, 13 (°rātra).
r. kath, kathayati, 5, 4; 17, 6; 283, 11; 291, 4, &c.
katham, 10, 4; 40, 6, &c.; °api, 78^d; 97^b; °iva, 18, 2.
kathayitavya, 233, 4.

kathā, 53^a; 81^d; 293, 12.
kathita, 105, 2; °vat. 239, 15.
kadamba, 251, 5; °ka, 40^b.
kalā, 128, 6; °cid, 93, 14, &c.
kanaka, 66^d; °rasa, 279, 4.
Kandarpa, 102, 1; 238, 2.
kanyakā, 21, 5; 94, 3; 76^a.
kanyā, 25^b; 102^n; °jana, 82, 2.
kapiśa, 80^d; 176^b.
kapola, 229, 14 (°hastaka).
kapola, 63^a; 68^b; 147^b.
kamala, 103^c; 152^d.
kamalinī, 91^a (°harita).
kara, m. 24^c; 145^b; 180^b; °tala, 85^c; °ruha, 44^a.
-kara in madhu°, 32, 4. &c.
karaṇīya, 5, 8; 145, 5, 6, &c.
karaṇḍaka, 256, 4; 295, 4.
karabha, 74^c (°ūrū).
Karabhaka, 90, 7. 15. 16.
karuṇa, 212, 7 (°paridevin).
karṇa, 8^b; 24^b; 30^c; 21, 3, &c.; °patha, 232, 11.
kartarya, 125^a.
karman, 37, 5; 95, 5; 168^a, &c.
kala, 90^c; 182, 5 (°viśuddha).
kalatra, n. 196, 9 (para°).
kalaśa, 30, 3.
kalikā, 228, 8; 230, 6; 136^n.
kalusha, 86^b; 141^c.
kalpa, 280, 5, &c.; ṛishi°, 85, 12; °ṛriksha, 176^a; °latā, 169^b.
kalpanā, 201, 4 (a-sat°).
kalpita, 220, 4.
kalpishyamāṇa, 156^c.
kalyāṇa, 134, 5 (nirvṛitta°).
karala, 92^a.
Kaśyapa, 22, n. 3; 279, n. 3.
-kaśa in kūlam°, 122^b.
kashāya, 60, 2.
kashṭa, 258, 14; °tapas, 282, 2.
kāku, 264, n. 2.
r. kāṅksh, kāṅkshati, 176^d.
kāñcana, 138^b; 176^b (°padma).
kāṭhinya, 63^a (°mukta-stana).
kātara, 47, 4; °tā, 64^d; °bhāva, 130, 8; °ī-bhūta, 35, 7.
kādambarī, 225, 10.
kānta, 77, 2; ā, f. 127^a; 153^b.
kānti, 120^a (a-klishṭa°).
kāma, 69^a; 145, 6, &c.; °m, adv. 24, 10; 31^c, n.; 35^a; 112^a; Kāma-deva, 100, 1; 99, n. 1.
kāmayamāna, 107, 9, 10.
kāmin, 36^d; °jana, 99, 2.
kāya, 7^b (pūrva°); 8^a.
-kāra in balāt°, sat°, saha°.
kāraṇa, 65, 7; 66, 7; 191^a.
kārita, 145, 7.
-kārin, 44, 12; 187, 2; 153^b.
kārmuka, 6^a (adhijya°).
kārya, 149^a; 310, 13; 16, 7, &c.
kāla, 1^b; 28, 6; 156^d, &c.;

°kûṭa, 257, 6; Kâla-nemi, 268, 7; °haraṇa, 112, 4; °antara-kshama, 150, 9.
Kâlidâsa, 4, 2; 315, n. 2.
Kâśyapa. 22, 11, 12; 42, 9.
kâshṭha, 62, 7; 238, 2. 3.
kiṇa, 13[b] (°aṅka).
kitava, 212, 4.
kim, see ka; kim—uta, 74nd; 111[nb]; °api, 188[b]; °âkhya, 293, 7; °iti, 71, 1; 182[b]; °uta, 123[b]; °evam, 215, 10; °tu, 47, 3, &c.; °nimittam, 26, 7; °purusha, 279, 7.
kiyat, 13[b]; 142, 5; 244, 14.
kiraṇa, 38[b] (ravi°); 168[d].
kila, adv. 18[a]; 36[d]; 133[a],&c.
kisalaya (=kiśalaya), 59[b].
kisalaya, n. 44[a]; 115[b]; 15[b].
kîdṛiśa, 81, 7; 223, 11.
kîrṇa, 7[c] (°vartman).
kuṭila, adj. 124[c]; 189[c].
kuṭumba, 100[c]; 219, 4.
kuṇapa, 265, 15 (°aśana).
kutas, 8, 4; 16[a]; 55, 3, n.
kutûhala, 89, 11; 196, 6.
kutra, 112, 11; 217, 4, &c.
kunda, 120[c].
r. kup, caus. 269, 8.
kupita, 230, 4.
kubja, 66, 4, n. (°lîlâ).
kumâra,85,7,&c.; °ka,85,2.
kumuda, n. 129[a].
kumud-vatî, 70[b]; 83[a].
kumbhîla or °ka, 217, 4.
kuravaka, n. 58, 1; 136[b].
kula, 40[b]; 98[d], &c.; °pati, 16,12; 97, 2,&c.; °pratish-ṭhâ, 156[b]; °vrata, 292, 14; °ankura, 183[a].
kuliśa, 190[d].
kalya, 15[a] (°ambhas).
kuvalaya, 252, 9.
kuśa, 57, 16; 95, 2; 94[b].
kuśala, 198, 2 (srâdhina°).
kuśalin, 197, 17.
kuśe-śaya, 91[c].
kusuma, 4[b]; 19[d]; °ruṇa, 55[d]; °sara-tva,55[a]; °âyudha,99,
kûpa, 208, 9. [I.
kûrća, 251, 5 (lamba°).
kûlaṅ-kasha, adj. 122[b].
r. kṛi, karoti, &c.; 14, 6, &c.; 152[d] (caus.); padam kṛi, 100[d]; manasâ kṛi, 43[b], n.; hṛidaye kṛi, 42, 2, n.; 68, 4.
kṛita, 36, 5; 76, 2, &c.; °e, with gen. 178, 9; °m, with inst. 30,6; 105,13; °kârya, 201, 2; °praṇaya, 184, 4; °saṃskâra, 312, 2; °san-dhâna,9[b]; 11[a];°smita,166[b]; °artha, 41, 9.

-kṛitaka, 94[d], &c. (putra°).
kṛitin, 24[d], n.; 183[d].
kṛitya,n.51[a];93,1;99[b];110[d].
kṛitvâ, ind. 218, 4.
kṛitsna, adj. 49[b].
kṛiśa, 36[a] (°udara); 114, 7.
r. kṛish, karshati, 178[b].
kṛishṭa, 136[d] (ardha°).
kṛishṇa,'black;' °mṛiga,149[d]; °sarpa,182[d];°sâra,6[a];13.5.
klṛip, kalpate, 110[b]; 294, 15.
klṛipta, 88[a] (°dhishṇya).
ketu, 34[b].
kevala, adj. 164[a]; °m,adv. 22, 8; 48[d]; 108, 6.
keśa, 248, 11.
keśara, 4[a]; 26, 2; 150,9, &c.
keśariṇî, f. 286, 12.
kaitava, 207, 11; cf. a°.
kokila, 162, 1; 136[c].
koṭara, 14[a].
koṭi-mat, 190[d].
kopa, m. 208, 12; 56[a].
komala, 21[a]; 77[a]; 145[a].
koraka, 134[b] (ćûta°); 136[b].
kolâhala, 61, 1.
kosha, 59[a] (bandhana°).
kautuka, 146, 7 (prasthâna°).
kautûhala, n. 39, 3; 44, 7,&c.
kaulîna, 232, 12.
Kauśika, 43, 2, n.
r. krand, krandati, 131[b].
krama, m. 194[c].
kriyâ,13[a]; 176[b], &c.; cf. sat°.
r. krîḍ, krîḍati, 289, 2.
krîḍanaka, 287, 5; 295, 2.
krûra, adj. 141[d]; 38[a].
krodha, m. 39[b].
kraurya, n. 299, 2.
r. klam, klâmyati, 235, 7.
klama, 74[a] (°vinodin).
klânta, 102, 7; 79[b]; 192, 2; °tara, 63[b].
klinna, 171[d] (°nemi).
r. kliś, kliśnâti, 108[b].
klishṭa, 63[c] (madana°); 142[b].
kleśa-leśa. 38[b],n.; see 248,n. 2.
kva, 102,6; 160,6,&c.; kva—kva, 10[cd]; 52[a]; °ćit, 14[b].
kshaṇa,m.8,3; 69,9; kshaṇât, 278, 2; °m, adv. 9[d].
kshatu, 46[a].
kshati, 40[c] (mustâ°).
kshatra, 22[a] (°parigraha).
kshapâ, 137[b].
kshama,6,6;29,2(upabhoga°); 18[b]; 22[a];28[b](sparśa°);128[d].
kshayin, adj. 47[a].
kshâma,63[a]; 185[b](niyama°).
r. kshi, caus. kshapayati,199[c].
kshiti, 184[b] (°rakshârtham).
r. kship, kshipati, 230, 3.
kshipta, 188[d].

kshiṇa, 138[d].
kshîra, 59[b] (°snigdha); 160[b]; °vṛiksha, 170, 2.
kshetra, 30, 5, n.; 279, 8.
kshetrin, 202, 12.
kshepa in sa-dṛishṭi°.
kshobha, 163[b].
kshauma,85[a]; °yugala,158,3.
khaṇḍa-śas, adv. 220, 4.
kharjûra, 78, 4 (piṇḍa°).
khalu, 4, 2; 8, 3; 10[a]; 123[d].
khâdikâ, 69, 5 (modaka°).
khâditavya, 247, 2.
r. khid, khidyate, 109[a].
khilî-bhûta, 154[a].
khura, 32[a] (turaga°).
kheda, 189, 7; 253, 3.
gagana, 170[a] (°pratishṭha).
Gaṅgâ, 246, 2 (°srotas).
yaja, m. 33[d]; 195[a].
r. gaṇ. gaṇayati, 99[d]; 144[b].
gaṇa, 268, 7 (dânava°).
gaṇanâ, 254, 6 (°bahula-tâ).
gaṇḍa, 150[b]; 61, 3.
gata, 17, 3; 93[b]; 38, n. 1; neut. 171[c]; bhartṛi°, 141, 3; madana°, 107, 8; sakhî°, 42, 5, n.; cf. âtma°, sra°; °vat, 180, 4.
gati, 14[c]; 105[d]; 62, 2, &c.
gatvâ,ind. 19,8; 29[b]; 46[b],&c.
gandha, 88[c]; 263, 9; °raha, 106[b].
-gandhi, 221, 5 (visra°).
r. gam, gaććhati, 21, 5; 34[a]; 57, 8, &c.; caus. 102, 10.
gamana, 51, 10; 57, 6; 58, 5.
gamanîya, 38, 6.
gambhîra, 38, 10; 224, 12.
garbha, 259, 2; 14[a]; 55[c],&c.
garvita, 257, 2; 266, 11.
r. gâ, 36[c] (mâ gâs).
gâtra, 65, 5; 38[c]; 71[b], &c.
gândharva. 76[a]; 134, 4.
-gâmin,134, 5; 146, 2; 258,13.
gârhapatya, 149, n.
Gâlava, 313, 14.
r. gâh, gâhate, 40[a].
gir, 36, 5.
giri,60, 3; 188, 4; °ćara, 38[d].
gîta, 7, 4; 48[c]; 185, 6, &c.; °râga, 5[a].
gîti,182, 5; 183, 7; °kshama, 169[c].
gîtikâ, 118, 7.
guṇa, 1[b]; 17[b]; 70, 6; 135, 2; 138[c](tejas°);°vat,135,10.
guru, 71[b] (°paritâpa); 99[b]; m. 49, 4; 98[a]; 173[b]; °tâ, 36[b]; °jana, 81, 5; 91, 3;

tapat, 116[b].
tapas, 35, 9; 54[a], &c.; pl. 279, 7; 176[d]; °kshama, 18[b]; °vin, 13, 6; 21, 5; 48, 6; 150, 5, n.; °dhana, 13[a]; °vana, 17, 14, 15; 20, 4.
tapasya, -yati, 173[b]; 176[d].
tapta, 60[b]; 247, 4 (anuśaya°).
tamas, 116[b]; 140[b]; 188[c], n.
taranga, 60[a] (Mālinī°).
tarala, 26[b] (prabhā°).
Taralikā, 256, 9. 14.
taras-vin, 258, 13.
taru, 14[a]; 114[a]; °mūla, 184[d].
taruna, 248, 13.
r. tark, °ayati, 22, 5: 248, 9. 11.
tarka, 107, 14; 196, 6, &c.
-tarkin in evam°, 291, 5.
r. tarj, caus. 48, 1.
tarhi, 253, 11; yadi—°, 2, 3.
tala, 26[b]; 121, 2 (śilā°); 30[a], n.
tāḍayitvā, ind. 217, 3.
tāḍita, 40[a].
tāḍyamāna, 184, 9.
tāta, 22, 4; 154, 17; 168, 4, &c.
tādriśa, 107, 10; 135, 2, &c.
tāpa, m. 91[b]; 62[c]; 65[a], &c.
tāpasa, 61, 5; 94, 3 (°kanyakā); ī, f. 153, 2; °vriddhā, 208, 2.
tāmra, 74[d] (padma°); 134[a].
tāla, 74[b] (°vrinta).
tārat, 2, 3; 6, 6; 17, 8. 10; 158[a], &c.; °—yāvat, 19, 9, 10; mā°, 203, 5.
tintidikā, 78, 4.
timira, n. 162[d].
tiras-karinī, 227, 5; 266, 11.
tila, 111, 4, n. (°udaka).
tīkshna, 254, 2 (°danda).
tīrna, 197[a] (°jaladhi).
tirtha, 17, 3, n.; 151, 1, &c.
tivra, adj. 109[c]; 33[a] (°āghāta).
tu, 34, 11; 78[d], &c.; cf. kintu.
tura-ga, 32[a]; 60, 4.
turanga, 106[a] (yukta°).
tulya, 117[c] (°guna).
tushāra, 120[c] (antar°).
tūna, 136[d] (°ardha-krishta).
tūshnīm, adv. 182, 8.
trina, 208, 9 (°chhanna).
tritīya, 13, 11, n. (ātmanā°).
trishita, 151[a].
tejas, 41[bd]; 179[a]; 84[a].
taikshnya, n. 100, 2.
taila, 94[b]; 81, 3 (ingudī°).
toya, 176[b]; 14[d] (°ādhāra).
toshita, 165[b] (avadāna°).
tyakta, 156[b].
r. tyaj, tyajati, 127[a].
-tyāgin, 130[b] (dūra°).
-tra in ātapa°, 108[d].
traya, n. 191[b] (bhuvana°).
trāna, 11[b].

tri, tisri, f. 248, 4; °diva, 167[b]; °srotas, 170[a]; Tri-śanku, 91, 6.
tritaya, n. 193[b].
tretāgni, 148, n. 1.
r. trai, trāyate, 240, 9.
tva, 5, 4; 12[a], &c.; tvat-tas, 22, 4; in comp. tvad-, e. g. 169[d] (°charita); 164[a] (°mati).
tvach, 175[a] (sarpa°).
r. tvar, tvarate, 146, 7; 152, 2; 176, 13; caus. 26, 2.
tvarā, 229, 1.

r. dans, dasati, 296, 7.
Daksha, 191[d].
dakshina, 98[c]; ena, 21, 4; 165, 4.
dakshina, 149, n.
danda, 110[a], n.; 108[d]; 62, 7.
datta, 70, 3; 124, 8 (°drishti).
dattvā, ind. 21. 3, &c. (karnam°).
dadat, 6[a].
dadhāna, 84[a].
danta, 33[a]; 181[a]; 286, 3.
damana, 197[c] (prasabha°).
dayamāna, 4[b].
darpana, 196[d] (°tala).
darbha, 7[c]; 15[c], n.; 88[b].
darśana. 17, 10; 21, 7; 35[a]; 86[b].
darśanīya, 196, 7; 248, 5, &c.
darśayat, 221, 2.
darśayitavya, 310, 10.
darśita, 61, 6; 206, 4.
-darśin, 22, 11; 180, 10 (evam°).
dala, 74[b]; 75[a] (nalinī°).
daśā, 82[d] (°antara).
dasyu, m. 121[d].
r. dah, dahati, 70[a]; 141[d], &c.
r. dā, dadāti, 21, 6; 137[c], &c.
Dākshāyani, 283, 10; 304, 12.
dākshinya, 137[c].
Dānava, 268, 7; 167[b].
dāpita, 223, 13.
dāra, 293, 9; 294, 2; m. pl. 97[c], n.
dāraka, 298, 5.
dāruna, 124[a]; 245, 7; 161[d].
dāsya, n. 128[d].
dāsyāh-putra, 61, 1, n.; 75, 2.
dāhātmaka, 41[b].
div, 274, 9; divā, 69[a]; 107[d]; divas-pati, 269, 13.
diva, 106[b]; °okas, 271, 12; 169[d].
divasa, m. 3[b]; 126, 4; 144[a].
dishta, n. 59, 4.
dishtyā, 186[a]; 112, 10; 193[a].
dīkshita, 50[b].
dipa, 262, 4.
dipaka, 87, n. 1.
dipti-mat, 85, 11.
dirgha, 185[d]; °m, adv. 259, 16; °taru, 96[a]; °apānga, 206, 13; °āyus, 91, 1; 307, 8.
duhkha, n. 109, 5; 64[a], &c.;

ena, 130, 12; 164, 3; °śīla, 146, 1; °uttara, 189, 9.
duhkhita, 242, 10 (viyoga°).
dur- or dus- in °saha, 83[d]; °avāpa, 50, 2; °āpa, 67[d]; °āsada, 10, 8; °ita, n. 88[c]; Dur-jaya, 268, 7; °mocha, 290, 4; °labha, 17[a]; 154, 2; °la-lita, 289, 4; °vāra, 137, 13; Dur-vāsas, 137, 12; °vinita, 34, 4; 25[a]; °kara, 170, 9.
Durgā-pūjā, 227, n. 1.
r. dush, caus. 298, 5; 182[c].
dushta. 34, 4 (°madhukara).
Dushyanta, 5[b]; 95, 4, &c.
duhitri, 17, 2; 198, 7; °jana, m. 139, 13, 14.
dūyamāna, 132[b].
dūra, 112, 4 (°gata); °e, 9[d]; °m, adv. 9, 8; °tas, 53[a]; °ī-krita, 17[b].
dūrbā, 151, 1.
dūshita, 111[a].
r. driś, paśyati, 6[b]; 17, 5; 16, 7; 55[b], &c.; paśya. 7[d]; 10, 12; caus. 35, 7; 247, 8, &c.
driśya, 97[c]; 147[b].
drishta, 76, 11; 238, 5; 257, 14.
drishti, 24[a]; 70, 3, &c.; °rāga, 81, 7; °vibhrama, 23[d], n.
drishtvā, ind. 35, 4; 127, 5.
deva, 44, 11; 45, 2; 70, 7. &c.; devī, 90, 17; 184, 4; pl. 90, 7; °guru, 293, 4; °tā, 85[c]; 136, 2; 241, 11 (pati°).
deśa, 10, 8; 19[a] (skandha°); 39, 6; °antara, 175, 1.
Daitya, 49[c].
daiva, n. 17, 3; 135, 11; 299, 6.
dosha, 127, 6; 105, 12; 262, 5.
dauvārika, 69, 12; 70, 1, &c.
Daushyanti, 100[b].
dauhitra, m. 214, 10 (muni°).
dyo, f. 48[c].
drashtavya, 76, 10.
druta-padam, adv. 257, 7.
druma, 32[d]; 46[d]; 91[b].
dva, 1[b]; 52, 8; 85. 2; 73[a].
dvandva, 48[c] (chārana°); 191[d].
dvaya, n. 91, 3; 55[b]; 82[c] (tejas°).
dvādaśa-dhā, 191[a] (°sthita).
dvāra, n. 20, 11; 16[b]; 61[b], &c.
dvi- in °ja, 123[d]; 160[a]; °dhā, 229, 12; °pa, 107[d] (°indra).
dvitīya, 87, 3; 88, 13 (sārathi°).
r. drish, dreshti, 137[a].
dvīpa, 197[b] (saptan°).
dresha, 201, 2 (krita-kārya°).
dvaidha-, 'twofold,' in °ī-bhāva, 47, 4; °ī-bhū, 51[a].

dhana, 81[b] (tapas°); 97[a]; Dhana-mitra, 258, 12.

dhanu, 135ᵃ (gṛihīta°).
dhanus, n. 20, 5; 37ᵇ, &c.
dhanya, adj. 181ᵈ.
dhanvan, 159ᶜ (ātta°).
dhanvin, 39ᶜ.
-dhara, 24, 2; 156ᵈ; 297, 7.
dharitrī, 49ᵃ.
dharma, 22, 12 (āśrama°); 106ᵈ, &c.; °kārya, 187, 1; °kriyā, 116ᵃ; °chāraṇa, 49, 4; °chārin, 41,2; °dāra, 293, 9; °patnī, 156ᵃ; °adhikāra, 40, 9; °abhisheka-kriyā, 176ᵇ; °araṇya, 40, 8, &c.; °arekshi-tā, 202, 5.
dharman in ridita°, 127, 5, n.
dhātṛi, 43ᵈ.
dhārā, 18ᶜ (pattra°).
-dhārin, 62, 4 (mālā°).
r. dhār, dhārati, 8ᵈ; 34ᵃ.
dhik, interj. 57, 2; 137, 10, &c.
dhishṇya, 88ᵃ (kḷipta°).
dhī-mat, 173, 5.
dhīra, 84, 11; 196, 12.
dhīrara, 218, 6; 225, 9, &c.
dhur, 168ᵈ.
r. dhū, dhunoti, 188ᵈ.
dhūma, 15ᵇ; 147, 8.
r. dhṛi, caus. 52, 8; 175, 1, &c.
dhṛita, 20, 2; 108ᵈ; 185ᵇ.
dhṛishṭa, 34, 2; 252, 14.
dhenu, 192, 4 (homa°).
dhauta, 15ᵃ (°mūla); 157ᵈ.
dhyātvā, ind. 240, 8.
dhyāna, 176ᶜ; 235, 8; 310, 1.
dhruvam, adv. 18ᶜ.
dhvaṃsita, 75, 2.

na, 5, 2; 2ᵃ; na na, 64ᵇ, n.
mukha, 118, 10; 79ᵇ; 167ᵈ.
nagara, 58, 5; 61, 6; 49ᵇ, &c.
r. nat, nāṭayati, 13, 1; 270, 9.
naṭī, 3, 1.
nata, 95ᶜ; 167ᶜ (°parvan).
nadī, 60, 3; 66, 5, 7, &c.
nanu, 6, 6; 90, 13; 93, 9, &c.
r. nand, caus. nandayati, 83ᵇ.
nandana, 307, 9 (kula°).
-nandin, 193, 2 (su-charita°).
r. nam, caus. namayati, 37ᵃ.
namas, 282, 2.
namra, adj. 114ᵃ.
nayana, 9ᶜ; 36ᵃ; 151, 7, &c.
nara, 72, 3; °pati, 112ᵃ.
nartana, 92ᵃ (parityakta°).
nalinī, 96, 3 (°pattra); 74ᵇ, &c.
nara, 4, 3; 44ᵇ, &c.; °mālikā or °mallikā, 22, 5; 42ᵇ; °i-kṛita, 192, 2.
nashṭa, 15ᵈ (°āśaṅka); 172ᶜ.
nāka, 274, 3 (pṛishṭha).
nāga, 38ᵈ.
nāgarika, 185, 2; 217, 2.

nāṭaka, n. 4, 3; 8, 1; 316, 5.
nāṭayitvā, 10, n. 5; 105, 9.
nāṭitaka, 218, 1, n.
nāṭya, 128, 12.
nātidūre, with gen. 58, 6.
nātiparisphuṭa, 115ᵃ.
nāndī, 2, 1, n.
nāma, adv. 8,1; 20, 4; 62,6,&c.
nāman, 239, 17, &c.; °tas, 294, 1; °dheya, 28, 2, 3; 43, 2, &c.; °mudrā, 53, 6, &c.
nāyaka, 47, 5, n.
Nārada, 154, 15; 268, 9.
nārikera, 150, 8.
nāsikā, 72, 3.
niḥ-śvasya, ind. 59,3; 102,7,&c.
niḥ-saṃśayam, adv. 221,5, &c.
ni-kāmam, adv. 60, 5; 148ᶜ, n.
ni-kshipta, 150, 9; 118, 10 (°varya).
ni-kshepa, 166, 5.
ni-gṛihya, ind. 51, 11; 180, 4.
ni-chita, 175ᶜ.
nija, 145, 5 (°karaṇīya).
nitamba, 36ᵇ.
ni-darśana, 71, 8.
ni-dāgha, 62ᶜ (°prasara).
ni-deśa, 271, 4 (anushṭhita°).
nidrā, 3ᵇ (sulabha-nidra).
ni-dhāya, ind. 74ᶜ.
nindat, 131ᵃ.
nindita, 260, 8.
ni-pāta, 10ᵈ.
ni-pāna, 40ᵃ.
nipuṇa, adj. 249, 2; °m, adv. 184, 6; °tā, 247, 13.
ni-bandha, 107, 9 (itihāsa°).
ni-bhṛita, 8ᵇ; °m, 113,4; 114,2.
ni-magna, 145ᵇ; 175ᵃ.
ni-mitta, 20, 11, n.; 45ᵇ, &c.; cf. kim°, etad°; °naimittika, 194ᶜ.
ni-mesha, 118, 2 (vismṛita°).
nimna, 54ᵇ; 247, 11.
ni-yata, 184ᶜ; cf. a°.
ni-yantrita, 23, 8, 9.
ni-yam, 157ᵇ; 82ᵈ; 110ᵃ (caus.)
ni-yama, 44,12; 296,16; 185ᵇ.
ni-yamita, 91ᵇ.
ni-yukta, 22, 6; 40, 8.
ni-yuj, 22, 12.
ni-yujya, ind. 17, 2.
ni-yoga, 3, 2; 22,8; 75,6; 236,16.
ni-yojita, 117, 7.
ni-yojya, m. 168ᵃ.
nir-abhilāsha, 109ᵃ (sukha°).
nir-avalamba, 259, 17.
nir-ākaraṇa, 240, 14.
nir-ābādha, 130, 4.
nir-āyata, 8ᵃ.
nir-āśa, 266, 8.
nir-utsava, 227, 2 (°ārambha).
ni-rudhya, ind. 52, 3.

ni-rundhat, 174ᶜ.
nir-upaplava, adj. 95, 5.
ni-rūp, 17, 12; 22, 9.
ni-rūpya, ind. 10,12,n.; 21,7,&c.
nir-gata, 142, 5; 136ᵃ.
nir-gam, 79ᵈ.
nir-ghṛiṇa, 69ᵇ.
nir-ṇaya, 28ᵃ (sandeha°).
nir-diś, 222, 12.
nir-diśat, 307, 11.
nir-diśya, ind. 194, 10.
nir-dishṭa, 63, 1, &c. (yathā°).
nir-bandha, 109, 5.
nir-makshika, 76, 2, n.; 237, 2.
nir-mā, 149ᶜ.
nir-vap, 84, 4.
nir-varṇya, ind. 105, 13, &c.
nir-vartanīya, 226, 4.
nir-vartita, 226, 4.
nir-vah, caus. 123, 11, 12.
nir-vāya, 104, 6 (netra°).
nir-vāpaṇa, 97, 1.
nir-vāpayitṛi, 65ᵃ; 117, 4, 5.
nir-vāhita, 256, 15.
nir-vighna, 197, 11 (°tapas).
nir-viṇṇa, 59, 5.
nir-viśesha, 286, 5.
nir-vṛit, caus. 140, 13; 146, R.
nir-vṛita, 134, 5; 150, 6; 103ᶜ.
nir-vṛiti, 183ᶜ.
nir-vṛitta, 134, 4; 258, 18.
nir-vṛitti (for nir-vṛiti), 282, 7.
ni-vapana, 'oblation,' 157ᵇ.
ni-vartin, 207, 7 (ātmakārya°).
ni-vas, 27ᵈ.
ni-vasana, 167, 8.
ni-vāsa, 184ᵇ.
ni-vid, caus. 40, 6; 51, 7, &c.
ni-viś, caus. 58, 6.
ni-vṛit, 54ᵇ; 139,12,&c.; caus. 74, 4; 138, 3; 52, 9, &c.
ni-vṛitti, 313, 16 (śāpa°).
ni-vṛitya, ind. 212, 10.
ni-vedayitṛi, 167, 3 (priya°).
ni-vedita, 136, 9.
ni-vedya, ind. 222, 1.
ni-veśayat, 245, 2.
ni-veśita, 140ᵈ.
ni-veśya, ind. 43ᵃ; 100ᵇ.
niś, cf. a-niśam; niśi niśi, 66ᵇ.
ni-śamya, ind. 104ᵃ.
ni-śita, 10ᵈ (°nipāta).
ni-shaṇṇa, 149ᵇ; 151ᵃ.
ni-shad, 153, 12; 239, 8.
ni-shich, 94ᵇ.
ni-shidh, 285, 7.
ni-sheddhavya, 74, 5.
ni-shevitavya, 27ᵇ.
nish-kampa, 8ᵇ.
nish-kram, 61, 3; 222, 2.
nish-krānta, 8, 7; 20, 9, &c.
ni-shṭhyūta, 85ᵇ.
ni-shyūta, 200, 6.

praty-arpita, 102^d (°nyāsa).
praty-avekshita, 236, 7. 11.
praty-avekshya, ind. 20, 6.
praty-aham, 48^b; 67, 5; 137^a.
praty-ākhāta, 234, 4.
praty-āyata, 263, 4 (°prāṇa).
praty-ā-ćaksh, 204, 7.
praty-ādiśat, 309, 1, 2.
praty-ādishṭa, 216, 2; 132^a; 138^a.
praty-ādeśa, 80, 2, n.; 141^a, &c.
praty-ādeśin, 310, 7.
praty-āyana, 303, 2 (°kāla).
praty-ā-liṅg, 165, 6.
praty-āsanna, 55, 10.
praty-utpanna, 206, 2 (°mati).
praty-ūsha, 61, 1.
r. prath, caus. prathayati, 68^b.
prathama, 85, 10; 106, 6; 165^a; °m, 7, 8; 81^d; 89^a, &c.
prathita, 209, 5.
pradakshiṇī-kṛi, 159, 8; 280, 2.
pra-dāna, 27^a; 49, 5.
pra-dīpa, 15, 2.
pra-deya, 174, 10.
pra-deśa, 67, 5; 188, 13; 281, 4.
pra-dhāna, 41^a (sama°).
pra-panna, 1^d.
pra-pāta, 142^d.
pra-bala, 188^c (°tamas).
pra-buddha, 113^a.
pra-bodha, 236, 10.
pra-bhava, 44, 4, n.
pra-bharat, m. 234, 4.
pra-bharishṇu, 74, 2, n.
pra-bhā, 26^b (°tarala).
pra-bhūta, 62, 2; 142, 6.
pra-bhāva, 43, 3; 95, 4; 154, 17; °vat, 39, 1.
pra-bhu, 71, 7; °tā, 127^b; 196^b; °tva, 206, 4.
pra-bhū, 54, 10; 127, 3; 138, 1; 162^c; 173^a.
pra-bhṛiti, adv. 110, 2. 7; 165, 7 (adya°); 233, 6.
pra-bhrashṭa, 139, 4; 205, 13.
pra-matta, 81^d.
pra-mada, adj. 'wanton;' ā, f. 4^b; 119^d; °vana, 231, 9; 236, 7; 237, 3.
pra-māṇa, 21, 6; 22^d; °adhika, 30^b; °ī-kṛita, 230, 11.
pra-māda, 158^b (°skhalita).
pra-mārjita, 256, 2.
pra-mukhe, with gen. 186^a.
pra-mṛijya, ind. 159, 5; 189^d.
pra-yat, 57, 9.
pra-yatna, 10, 4.
pra-yam, 223, 14.
pra-yā, 7^d; 106^b; 158^c.
pra-yukta, 269, 5; 299, 2.
pra-yoga, 2^a; 8, 1; °tā, 5, 2.
pra-rūḍha, 183^d.

pra-lap, 71, 7, n.
pra-lāpin, 51, 6.
pra-lobhya, 180^a.
pra-vartamāna, 174^b.
pra-vartitavya, 232, 4.
pra-vartin, 66^b.
pra-vāta, 103, 5, n.; 240, 10.
pra-vāsa, 142, 4; 83^c; 146, 3.
pra-vibhakta, 170^b (°raśmi).
pra-viś, 9, 2; 20, 11; 33^d, &c.; caus. 85, 7; 214, 11.
pra-viśya, ind. 3, 1; 16, 8, &c.
pra-vishṭa, 7^b; 95, 4; 282, 5.
pra-vṛit, 77, 9; 164, 3; 199^a.
pra-vṛitta, 6, 6; 131^b; 205, 4.
pra-vṛitti, 22^d; 97^b; 181^b.
pra-vṛishṭa, 259, 15, n.
pra-veśa, 194, 2; 239, 9; 144^c; °ka, 97, n. 3; 217, 1.
pra-veśin, 208, 9 (kañćuka°).
pra-veshṭavya, 20, 4.
pra-śam, caus. 110^b.
pra-śānta, 84, 11.
pra-śithila, 62^a.
praśna, 198, 2; 201, 4.
praśhṭavya, 48, 4; 107, 3, &c.
pra-sad, 218, 2; 277, 1; 308, 9; caus. 67, 7; 134^b.
pra-sanna, 195, 9; 122^b.
pra-sabham, adv. 5^a, n.; 197^c.
pra-sara, 29^a; 62^c.
pra-sara, 167, 3; 214, 8; 111^c.
pra-sarlṇī, 153, 5 (vīra°).
pra-sāda, 223, 13; 263, 12; 161^c; 194^d; 196^c.
prasādana-tas, 6, 2.
pra-sādh, caus. 154, 6.
pra-sādhana, 154, 8; 251, 7.
pra-sārita, 287, 8; 180^a.
pra-sikta, 157^c.
pra-sūtā, 168, 3; 293, 4.
pra-sūti, 89^c; 268, 7; 157^c.
pra-sūya, ind. 99^c.
pra-sṛi, 65, 2; 145, 6; 196, 6.
pra-stāra, 294, 14.
pra-stāvanā, 8, 8.
pra-sthā, 160, 6; caus. 93, 10.
pra-sthānu, 82, 10; 105^d, &c.
pra-sthita, 16, 6; 51, 10; 110^a.
pra-snigdha, 14^b.
pra-harishyat, 140^c.
pra-hasana, 99, n. 1.
pra-hasita, 207, 4.
pra-hasya, ind. 254, 2.
pra-hṛi, 11^b; 57^b.
prāṃśu, 49^b.
prāgra, 117^a (°sara).
prājya, 198^a (°vṛishṭi).
prāñć, 'eastern;' prāćī, f. 99^c; prāk, adv. 194, 12; 123^c; 194^b.
prāṇa, 38^d; 176^a; °vat, 1^c.
prāṇin, 1^c; 111^b.

prānta, 88^b; 137^b; 147^a.
prāp, caus. 115, 3.
prāpita, 244, 9.
prāpta, 310, 8.
prāpya, ind. 173, 7.
prāyas, adv. 163^b.
prāyeṇa, adv. 102, 9; 201, 6.
prārth, 88, 8; 211, 11 (pass.)
prārthanā, 47, 4; 50, 2; 55, 3; 35^b; 93, 14, &c.
prārthayitṛi, 64, 2; 67^c.
prārthita, 131, 2; 189, 8.
prāsāda, 257, 7; 263, 12.
prāh, 191^a.
priya, 27, 4; 167, 3, &c.; 232, 9 (utsava°); ā, f. 35^a; 102, 8, &c.; °tara, 22, 5; °darśana, 63^c; °maṇḍana, 89^b; °sakhī, 35, 6; 98^a.
Priyaṃ-vadā, 27, 2; 24, 1, &c.; °miśra, 174, 7.
r. prī, caus. prīṇayati, 198^b.
prīti, 305, 4; °mat, 193, 8.
preksh, 29, 5; 62, 3; 83, 5, &c.
prekshaṇa, 57, 11 (°nimitta).
prekshaṇīya, 10, 4.
prekshya, ind. 38, 5; 46, 2, &c.
prerayat, 36^a.
prerita, 23^b; 192, 8.
preshita, 44, 12; 231, 9; 268, 3.
pluta, 7^d (udagrapluta-tva).

phaṇa, 163^a.
phala, 14^b; 16^a; 88, 4; 143^b.
phalaka, 238, 10, &c. (ćitra°).

baḍava, 101, n.
baddha, 7, 4; 30^c; 113^b; °dṛishṭi, 7^a; °pallava-tā, 29, 1, n.; °bhāva, 112, 5.
badhya, 222, 11; 160^a.
r. bandh, badhnāti, 136^a.
bandha, 30^d; 40^d (jyā°); 96^b (āśā°); 221, 5 (matsya°); cf. maṇi°.
bandhana, 59^a; 219, 4 (matsya°); 223, 9; 229, 13; 248, 11; 150^a; 152^d; cf. maṇi°.
bandhu, 90^b; 97^d; 309, 1, &c.; °jana, 123, 12.
bandhura, 145^a.
bala, 52, 9; 126, 7; °vat, adj. 240, 5; 188^b; adv. 2^b; 96, 4; 132^b, &c.; balāt-kāra, 178^b.
Bala-bhid, 86, 4 (°sakha).
bali, 135, 14; 101^b (nivāra°); 222, 17 (gridhra°).
balīyas, adj. 107, 4; 108, 2; adv. 69^b; 286, 14.
bahu, 76^a; 79, 6; 139, 10, &c.; °taram, 7^d; °titha, 105^c; °tva, 73^a; °dhana-tva, 258,

15; °dhā, 80[c]; °patnika, 258, 15; °mata, 87[a]; 224, 10; 307, 8; °mantavya, 154, 2; °manyamāna, 148[b]; °māna, 153, 3; 257, 2; °mukha, 239, 12; °vallabha, 123, 11; °śas, 24[a]; 64[c].
bahula, 'much;' °lā, 258, 6; °ī-bhūta, 232, 11.
bādhana, n. 32, 6.
bādhā, 32, 4; 100, 1.
bādhyamāna, 290, 4, 5.
bāla, 21, 6 (°pādapa); 152[a] (°taru); 285, 9, &c.; ā, f. 54[a]; 64[a]; °kā, 292, 6.
bāhū, 165, 7 (sūkhū).
bāhu, 16[a]; 16, 1; 30[a]; 248, 13; °utkshepam, 131[b].
bibhrat, 138[b]; 175[c].
bimba, 152[c]; see vimba.
buddhi, 208, 12; 240, 4.
r. budh, caus. 129[a].
bubhukshā, 247, 2.
bodhita, 81[c].
brahma-čārin, 95, n. 1.
brahman, n. 42, 9; m. 84[b]; 238, 5 (°varčas).
Brahma-loka, 272, n. 2.
brāhmaṇa, 195, 2; 218, 4.
r. brū, bravīti, 77, 3; 96, 4, &c.

bhakti, 17, 5 (vidita°).
bhaga-vat, 42, 9; 99, 1, &c.
bhaginī, 161, 4; 165, 2 (latā°).
bhagna, 124[d].
bhanga, 7[a]; 71[a]; 62, 5; 167, 7.
r. bhaj, bhajati, 112[b]; 172[c].
bhaṭṭa, 69, 13, n.
bhaṭṭāraka, 225, 5.
r. bhaṇ, bhaṇati, 108, 5, &c.
bhaṇita, 294, 11.
bhadra, 72, 6; 295, 2 (°mayū-raka); ā, f. 52, 11, &c.; °mukha, 290, 3.
bhaya, 7[b]; 23[d]; 39[b]; 80[c]; 127, 5.
bhara, 100[c] (kuṭumba°).
bharaṇa, 197[d]; 219, 4.
Bharata, 197[d]; 315, 3 (°vā-kya).
bhartṛi, 69, 13; 70, 3; 87[a], &c.; trī, f. 247, 8; °mat, 119[b].
bhava, 191[c]; 199[d] (punar°).
bhavat, 15, 2; 18, 4, &c.; ī, f. 48, 3; bhavati, voc. 40, 7, n.
bhavana, 184[a].
bhavitavya, 16[b]; 67, 5; 69, 3, &c.; °tā, 240, 4, 5.
bhasman, 56[d] (°avaśesha).
bhāga, 84, 2; 47[b]; 85[c]; 112[a], &c.; °dheya, 84, 4; 236, 2; pl. 297, 10.
-bhāgin, 212, 11; 301, 7.
bhāgya, n. 97[d]; pl. 98[c]; 131[a].

-bhāj in piṇḍa°, 261, 8.
bhājana, 135, 13 (pushpa°); 193, 5; 206, 8, 9.
bhānu, 160[a].
bhāra, 106[c] (bhūmi°).
bhāryā, 258, 16.
bhāva, 34, 11 (rājan°); 35[a], n.; 112, 5 (buddha°); 196, 11; 104[d]; 114[d] (sva°); 222, 14, &c.; °miśra, 218, 2.
bhāvin, 243, 4, 5; 311, 6.
bhāshamāṇa, 31[b].
-bhās in ačira°, 171[b].
bhāsura, 221, 1 (ratna°).
-bhid, 14[b] (phala°); cf. Bala°.
bhinna, 15[b]; 33[c]; 180[d]; 186[a] (smṛiti°); cf. a°; °deśa-tra, 51[a]; °artham, 66, 2.
r. bhī, bibheti, 90, 2, &c.
bhīta, 33[d]; 212, 11; 286, 14, &c.
bhīti, 218, 1.
bhīru, 67[b]; 127, 5; 213, 8; °ka, 93, 3; 116, 9; °tva, 45, 2.
r. bhuj, bhunakti, 49[b], n.
bhuja, m. 13[b].
bhuvana, 172[d]; 190[b]; °traya, 191[b].
r. bhū, bhavati, 10, 8; 16[b]; 19, 9, &c.; bhavatu, 17, 5, &c.
bhū, f. 15[c]; 84[a]; 260, 2; cf. ātma°; °tala, 174[c].
bhūta, 1[c]; 5, 4 (°artha); 240, 3.
bhūti, 84[a].
bhūtvā, ind. 47, 1. 5; 62, 6, &c.
bhūmi, 10, 6; 85, 2; 95[c], &c.
bhūyas, adv. 17, 12; 57, 11; 314, 15; bhūyasā, 7[b].
bhūyishṭha, 4, 2; 60, 4; °m, adv. 31[d]; 98[c].
bhūri, 114[b] (°vilambin).
bhūshaṇa, 156, 12.
r. bhṛi, bibharti, 38[d]; 185[d].
bhṛita, bhṛitika, &c., in para°.
bhetarya, 34, 10; 264, 10.
bheda, 124[c]; 264, 9 (yati°); °ka, 221, 8 (granthi°).
bhoktṛi, 44[d].
bhogya, 48[a] (sarva°).
bhos, interj. 13, 3; 69, 11; 136, 7, n.; 161, 7, n., &c.
-bhraṃsin, 7[c] (mukha°); 243, 7.
bhrama, 142[a] (mati°).
bhramara, 4[a]; 32, 4; 120[c].
bhrashṭa, 14[a]; 79[c].
bhrū, 23[c]; 124[c]; °bhanga, 52, 5, n.; °latā, 68[a].

ma, pron. 10, 4, &c.; see mad.
Makara-ketu, 57[a].
Magha-rat or -ran, 269, 4; 271, 4; 190[d].
mangala, 151, 1, 2; 154, 5; 134[b] (ritu°); 298, 5; cf. a°.

mañjari, 103[b] (čūta°).
maṇi, 138[d]; 239, 6; °bandha, 295, 4; °bandhana, 66[c]; 217, 4, 5, n.; °ī-kṛita, 66[a].
maṇḍana, 20[d]; 154, 2; 89[b], &c.
maṇḍapa, 104, 1 (latā°); 206, 8; 238, 9; 239, 6.
maṇḍala, 175[c] (jaṭā°).
mata in bahu°, 87[a], &c.
mati, 206, 2; 142[a]; 164[a].
matta, 201, 6 (aiśvarya°).
matsara, 299, 5 (parityakta°).
matsya, 220, 4; 245, 11 (ro-hita°); °bandha, 221, 5; °bandhana, 219, 4.
matsyikā, 225, 2 (°bhartṛi).
mad- in comps., e.g. °račana, 88, 20; 171, 6; °vidha, 55[b]; 56[c]; °samīpa, 90, 2.
mada, 229, 4 (°vibhrama).
madana, 27[b]; 45[d]; 100, 1, &c.; °lekha, 115, 2; °vāṇa, 72[d].
madira, 57[b]; 72[c] (°īkshaṇa).
madīya, 107, 14; 198, 7; 144[a].
madhu, 44[b]; 207, 7, &c.; °kara, 32, 4; 24[d], &c.; Madhu-karikā, 228, 8; °māsa, 239, 2.
madhura, 21, 7; 20[d]; 38, 10.
madhya, 63[b]; e, 115[b]; °stha, 195, 3; °ahna, 60, 1.
r. man, manyate, 2[a]; 112[d], &c.
manas, 47, 4; 51[a]; 140[b], &c.; °santāpa, 269, 7; manasi-ja, 35[b]; 140[c]; °gata, 64[b]; °jña, 20[c]; °ratha, 30, 3; 47, 3, &c.; °rama, 143[a]; °vṛitti, 51, 12; °hara, 18[a].
manushya, 232, 9; 278, 4.
mantavya in bahu°, 154, 2.
r. mantr, °ayate, 40, 4; 42, 2; 68, 4, &c.; caus. 39, 5.
manda, 58, 5 (°autsukya); 71, 4 (°utsāha); °m, 36[b]; 235, 8 (dhyāna°); °mandam, 15[d]; °ī-kṛita, 10, 7.
mandāra, 166[d] (°mālā); 282, 4 (°vṛiksha).
manmatha, 52[a]; 56[c]; 112, 4; °lekha, m. 79[b].
manyamāna in bahu°, 148[b].
manyu, 310, 12.
mayūkha, 55[c]; 91[b] (arka°).
mayūra, 92[a]; 294, 3 (mṛid°); °ka, 288, 4; 294, 10; 295, 2.
marīči, 150[c] (čandra°): Marī-či, 173[a]; 191[d] (°sambhara).
marut, 63[d]; 275, 1; Marut-°vat, 165[a].
marshayitavya, 139, 14.
mala, 196[c] (°upahata).
Malaya, 174, 13 (°taṭa).
malina, 20[b]; °ī-bhū, 181[d].
mallikā in nara°, 42[b].

rakta, 252, 9 (°kuralaya).
r. raksh, rakshati, 13^h; 127, 2; 257, 3; 160^a.
raksha in ćakra-rakshi-bhūta, 90, 4.
rakshaṇa, 110^b.
rakshaṇīya, 141, 7.
rakshas, 88, 12; 93, 3 (°bhī-ruka).
rakshā, 55, 9; 48^b (°yogāt); 295, 4 (°karuṇḍaka); 298, 5 (°mangala).
rakshita, 34, 7 (rājan°).
rakshitṛi, 110,3;194,11; 116^a.
rakshin, 217, 2, 3, &c.
rakshya, 160^a.
ranga, 7, 5, n.
raćayat, 68^a.
raćita, 150^d.
rajani, 128, 14; 142, 6; 96^a.
rajas, 91^c; 136^a; 174^h, &c.; 301, n. 1; pl. 8^c.
raṇa, 162^b; 190^a (°śiras).
rata, 152^b (°utsava).
rati, 35^h; °sarvasra, 24^c.
ratna, 28^h; 84,5 (°rāśi); 43^c (stri°); 44^b; 224, 10, &c.
ratha, 9, 2; 10, 6, 7. 12, &c.; °angu, 277,1; 174^a (°nemi).
rathya, 8^d.
randhra, 237, 5.
r. ram, ramati, 241, 6; caus. 237, 3.
ramaṇīya,3^b;28,6;32,6,&c.; °tā, 239, 7; °tva, 234, 15.
ramya, 13^a; 137^a; °tva, 294, 10; °antara, 91^a.
rava, 162, 1 (kokila°).
rari, 38^b (°kiraṇa); 107^c (°pratapta).
raśmi, 10, 6 (°samyamana); 8^a; 170^h (pravibhakta°).
rasa, 44^h; 77^d; 279, 4 (kanaka°); °adhika, 184^a.
rasanā for raśanā, 73^h (samudra-raśana).
rahas,124^h; 125^a, n.; rahasi, adv. 233, 5.
rahasya, 24^h (°ākhyāyin).
rākshasa, 89, 13 (°vṛittānta).
rāga, 7, 4; 5^a (gīta?); 15^h; 81, 7 (dṛishṭi°); 183, 7,&c.
rājakīya, 217, 5.
rājan, 5^h; 9, 2, 3, &c.; °kula, 221,6; 227, 2; °kārya, 67, 4; °dhāni, 314, 3; °bhāva, 34, 11; rājarshi, 39, 5, n.; 76^a, &c.; °lakshmī, 156, 3.
rāji, 60, 1 (vana°); 180, 2.
rājya, n. 108^d.
-rātra, 88, 13 (katipaya°).
rātri, 60, 5; 69^a; rātrin-diram, 106^b.

rāśi, 10^b (pushpa°); 84, 5 (ratna°); 56^h (ambu°).
rāshṭri or rāshṭrin, 233, n. 1.
rāshṭriya, 231, 8.
riktha, 259, 2.
r. ruć, roćate, 74, 2; 116,2,&c.
ruć, 15^h (kisalaya°).
ruj, f. 57^a.
ruta, 136^c.
r. rud, roditi, 154, 5; 209,10.
rudat, 168, 5; 215, 1.
rudita, 68, 5.
ruditvā, ind. 166, 9.
Rudras, eight forms of Siva, 2, n.
rūksha, 196^a (smṛiti-rodha°).
rūpa, 38, 8; 46, 2; 26^a; 44^c; °vat, 80, 2; °uććaya, 43^h.
rūpaka, 80, n. 2.
rūpayitvā, ind. 103, 5; 119, 1.
rekhā, 14^d; 146^h; 147^a.
reṇu,32^a;91^c;176^b(padma°).
Raivataka, 69, 15; 75, 5, &c.
roćanā, 151, 1 (mṛiga°).
roddharya, 54, 11.
rodha, 196^a (smṛiti°).
-rodhin, 30^c; 140^a.
romantha, 40^b.
roshaṇa-tā, 98^h.
Rohiṇī, 186^b.
rohita, 220, 4, &c. (°matsya).

r. laksh, lakshayati, -te, 52, 11; 209, 6; 145^c; pass. 39, 1; 39^h; 174^d.
lakshaṇa, 202, 11; 214, 10; 287, 10.
lakshita, 275, 1.
lakshī-kṛi, 293, 12.
lakshman, n. 20^b.
lakshmī, 20^h; 156, 3 (rājan°).
lakshya, 39^c; 135^b; cf. a°, ā°.
lagna, 33^a; 256, 14 (ṛitupa°).
laghu,39^a; 129,11(°santāpa); adv. 81, 2; 165^a.
r. langh, caus. 286, 12.
langhana, 96, 4.
langhita, 236, 4.
r. lajj, lajjate, 57, 12; 201, 10.
lajjā, 41, 3; 46, 3; 147, 7.
latā, 17^b (vana°); 26, 9; 28, 5. 6; 63^d, &c.; °maṇḍapa, 104, 1; °valaya, 130, 10; 132, 2; °ralaya-vat, 102, 9.
labdha, 104, 6; 181, 1; 108^h; °arakūśa, 47, 3; 55, 3.
r. labh, labhate, 30, 1; 62, 6; 40^d; 67^c; 211, 7 (pass.)
lamba, 251, 5 (°kūrća).
lambita, 149^c (sūkhā°).
lalāma, 77, 2, 3; 112, 5.
lalita, 116, 7 (°pada-bandhana).
lākshā, 85^b (°rasa).

lāghava, 213, 10 (guru°).
lābha, 36, 2.
lāvaṇya,146^h;115^a(śarīra°); 294, 4 (śakunta°); °maya, 108, 7.
r. likh, likhati, 169^d.
likhita, 238, 10; 249, 5; 258, 14.
likhitavya, 250, 9.
līna, 149^a (saikata°); °tā, 172^b (purṇābhyantara°).
līlā, 66, 4 (kubja°); 290, 4.
lubdhaka, 61, 1 (śakuni°).
lulita, 79^a (śarīra°).
lekha, 115, 2 (madana°); 79^b (manmatha°); 145, 9.
lekhana, 118, 8 (°sādhana).
lekhā, 113, 2 (śaśānka°).
leśa, 38^h (kleśa°).
loka, 82^d; 109^a (°hetos); 278, 4 (manushya°); °tantra, 187,4; °anugraha,197,16; 198^d.
loćana, 23^b (lola°).
lobha, 48, 3, 4 (śravaṇa°).
lobhanīya, 21^h; 152^a.
lola, 23^b (°loćana); cf. ati°.
lolupa, 72, 3 (nara-nāsikā°).
lohita, 30^a; 199^c; cf. ati°.
laukika, 173, 3 (°jña).
vaṃśa, 15, 2 (Puru°); 12^a; 39, 5, &c.
vaktavya, 171, 7; 203, 11.
vaktu-kāma, adj. 47.6; 107,6.
vakra, 9^c; 139, 7 (prakṛiti°).
vakshas, 166^c.
r. vać, vakti, 40, 7; 94, 1; 69, 7; 64^h; pass. ućyate, 88, 20; 206, 2; 214, 8, &c.; caus. 119. 5.
vaćana, 42, 2; 54, 6; 313, 14, &c.; mad°,88,20,&c.; cf.a°.
vaćanīya, n. 310, 5.
vaćas, 68, 11; 72, 6; 237, 6.
vajra, 49^d; °sāra, 10^d; °sūri-kṛi, 55^d.
vanćita, 294, 8.
vaṭu, in. 93, 14.
vata, adv. 10^c.
vatsa, 287, 5; 307, 8, &c.; ā, f. 130, 5; 159, 2, 8, &c.
vatsala, 294, 8 (mātṛi°); 313, 1 (duhitṛi°).
vatsalaya, -yati, 286, 10.
r. vad, vadati, 39^d; 79, 2; 128^a; 130^a; 141^h.
vadana, 32, 4; 30^c; 46^c, &c.
vadhukā,128,14(ćakravāka°).
vadhū, 28, 2; 97^d; 167, 2 (mṛiga°); °jana, 174, 2; °vara, 117^c.
vana,3^a (°vāṭa);176^a;°graha-

vaṇa-kolāhala, 61, 1, 2; grā-
hiṇ, 74, 4; °ćara, 67, 5
(°vṛitti); °jyotsnī, 28, 3;
29, 1, &c.; °devatā, 85°;
°pushpa, 62, 4; °rāji, 60,
1; 180, 2; °latā, 17^b; °rāsa,
252, 2; 90^b (°bandhu);
°okas, 173, 2.
vanas-pati, 155, 5; 156, 6, 7.
r. vand, vandate, 158, 9.
vandana, 307, 2 (pāda°).
vandamāna, 205, 12; 246, 2.
vapus,17^a;18^a;24,10;43^d,&c.
r. vam, ramati, 41^d.
vayasya, 59, 4, n.; 65, 2; 68,
11,&c.; °ka,225,9(priya°);
°bhāra, 59, 4.
vara, 30, 1; 49, 5; 159, 6;
117^c, &c.; cf. svayam°;
°prārthanā, 47, 4.
varāha, 59, 5; 40^c (°tati).
-varćas (=varćas), 238, 5
(brahman°).
-varjam, 153, 8 (Gautumī°).
varjayitvā,ind.112,11; 296,2.
varṇa,195,9(mukha°); 169^b;
118,11; 181^b (avyakta°);
pl. 47^a; 112^b; °parićaya,
182, 6; °āśrama, 194, 11.
varṇikā, 147^b (°ućchvāsa).
vartikā, 249, 6; 256, 4.
-vartin,10,8; 13,5; cf. ćakra°.
vartman, 7^c (kīrṇa°).
valaya, 33^b; 62^a; 102,9; 66^d
(kanaka°); 138^b, &c.
valkala,14^d; 23,8; 19^b;24,10.
valmika, 175^a.
vallabha, adj. 27^c; ā, f. 123,
11 (bahu-vallabha).
r. vaś, vashṭi, &c., 184^b.
vaśa in para°, 49, 4.
vaśin, 48^c; 129^b.
Vaśishṭha, 91, n. 3.
vasati, 48^a; 103^c; cf. saha°.
vasana, 185^a.
vasanta, 46, 2, n. (°avatāra);
°māsa, 134^a; °utsava, 227,
n. 1; 230, 5.
vasāna, part. 185^a.
vasu-dhā,214,18; 197^b; °tala,
26^b.
vasun-dharā, 156^d.
vasu-mati, 25^a; Vasu-matī,
184, 4; 256, 9, 10.
vastu, 4, 3.
r. vah, vahati, 1^a; 170^a.
-vah in srotas°, 51^b.
-vaha in ganḍa°, huta°.
vahat, 181^c.
vahni, 56^a; 88^d; 179^b.
vā, 39, 6; 40, 1. 6, &c.; ka-
tham°, 26^a; kim°, 116, 2;
168^c, &c.; cf. atha°.

vākya, 68, 7 (suhṛid°); 315, 3.
rāć, 31^a; 207, 7; 137^c.
vāćanaka, 152, 8 (svasti°).
vāćā,65,2,&c.; 288,2(°mātra).
vāćya, adj. 97^d; neut. 117^d.
vājin, m. 12, 2; 13, 8; 20, 7.
vāṭikā, 21, 4 (vṛiksha°).
vāṇa, 13, 5; 10^a; 53^a; 55^d,
&c.; 238, 2 (Kandarpa°);
°asana, 62, 3.
vāta, 3^a; 26, 2; 74^a, &c.
Vātāyana, 236, 16.
-vādin, 121,6; 211, 6(satya°).
vāma,98^d;141,2;138^a;149^d;
253, 9; °itara, 194, 6.
vāyu, 170^d.
vāraṇa, 252, 16.
vāri, 171^c (°garbhodara).
vārita, 29^a (°prasara); 45^c;
253, 7.
vāshpa, 86^b; 95^b; 189^bd.
vāsa, 90^b (vana°); 252, 2; cf.
saha°.
vāsantika, 230, 10.
Vāsava, 306, 4 (°aunyojya).
-vāsin, 19, 9 (tapovana°); 122,
4 (vishaya°); 188, 4; āśra-
ma°, 20, 6; 17^a; 188, 12.
-vāha in sārtha°, 258, 12.
-rāhin in kaṇa°, 60^a.
vāhyāntaḥ-karaṇa, 276, 2.
vi-karshaṇa, 99, n. 1.
vi-kala,62,5; 157^c(prasūti°).
vi-kāra, 38, 5. 6, n.; 107, 11;
297, 9; 195^d.
vi-kṛi, caus. 145, 8.
vikṛiti-mat, 39^b.
vi-kṛish, pass. 161^b.
vi-kḷip, pass. 116, 4.
vi-krama, 170^c (Harī°).
Vikramāditya, 316, n.
vi-kraya, 221, 2.
vi-kriyā, 296, 9.
vi-klava, 67, 11; 78^b; 105^d;
240, 14; 269, 8.
vi-gata, 189^d (°anuśaya).
vi-gam, caus. 137^b.
vi-guṇa, 261, 2 (°udvega).
vi-ghaṭita, 130, 9.
vi-ghna, 13^a; 40, 8; 44, 12;
88,12; 111^a; °vat,131, 2.
vi-ćar, caus. 202, 6; 258, 15.
vi-ćārayat, 202, 3.
vi-ćārya, ind. 48, 6; 214, 3.
vi-ćintayat, 81^a.
vi-ćintya, ind. 92, 5; 97^a, &c.
vi-ćchitti, 169^a (°śasha).
vi-ćchinna, 9^b.
vi-jaya, 49^d; 90, 6; 269, 1.
vi-jalpa, 240, 3 (parihāsa°).
vi-jalpita, 52^b (parihāsa°).
vi-ji,87,10; 89, 9; 190,3.&c.
vi-jñā, caus. 57,12; 188, 11.

vi-jñāna, 2^a (prayoga°).
ri-jñāpita, 139, 12.
vitapa, 21^a; 32^b; 104,5,&c.
vi-ḍamb, 66, 4; 64, 2 (pass.)
viḍāla, 266, 8.
Viḍ-aujas or Viḍ-ojas, 198^a.
ri-tala, 198^b (°yajña).
vi-tāna, 76, 3 (°sanātha).
vi-tṝī, 194, 9; 304, 1.
ritta, n. 193^b.
r. vid, vetti, 81^b; 128^c; 158^d.
vidita, 54^a; 88, 8, &c.; °dhar-
man, 127, 5; °bhakti, 17, 5.
viditvā, ind. 41, 4.
vi-dūshaka, 59, 2, 3, n.
riddha, 94^b (kuśa-sūći°).
vidyā, 147, 10; 126^d.
vidvas, 2^a.
ri-dhā, 1^b.
vi-dhātṛi, pl. 308, 9.
vi-dhāna, 2, 3 (nepathya°).
vi-dhi, 43^b; 44^d; 134, 4 (vi-
vāha°); 188,12;138^a;193^b,
&c.; °vat, adv. 196, 14;
°huta, adj. 1^a.
vi-nata, 63^b (prakāma°).
vi-naya, 29^a; 45^c (°vārita);
127, 2.
vinā, prep. with acc. 148, 4;
with inst. 168, 3; 96^a; 151^b.
vi-nindita, 133^a.
vi-nipāta, m. 211, 9. 11.
vi-niyoga,156,13(ābharaṇa°).
vi-nirvartita, 190^c (°kurman).
vi-nireśa, 147^a (anguli°).
vi-nīta, 20, 4 (°vesha).
vi-nud, caus. 102, 7; 150, 5.
vi-noda, 37, 3 (pariśrama°);
39^d; °sthāna, 236,8; 249, 5.
vi-nodin, 74^a (klama°).
vindu, 89, 13; 248, 12; 189^b.
vi-panna, 258, 13.
ri-paryaya, 214, 11.
vipula-tā, 9^a.
ri-pra-kṛi, 286, 5, 6; 154, 8, 9.
ri-prakṛita, 98^b; 163^a.
ri-prakṛishṭa, 10, 7 (°antara).
vi-pralabdha, 212, 4.
vi-pra-labh, 213, 3.
ri-buddhu, 139^b.
ri-budha, 176^c (°strī).
ri-bhara, 99^b; 110^c; 227, 3.
ri-bhā, 180^b.
ri-bhāta, n. 120^c.
vibhu-tva, 43^d.
ri-bhū,caus.29,7;141,4;143^b.
ri-bhettṛi, 168^c.
ri-bhrama, 23^d (dṛishṭi°);
229, 4.
vi-marda, 295, 6.
vi-marshṭavya, 221, 6.
ri-mānita, 235, 6.
vi-mānya, 121^b.

ry-alika, 188[a] (pratyādeśa°).
ry-avasita, 146,2; 141[a]; 204,3.
ry-ara-so, 18[d]; 89[a].
ry-avahārin, 258, 12; (samu-dra°).
ry-avahita, 215, 2 (śāpa°).
vy-asana, 39[d]; 258,12 (nau°); °udaya, du. 82[c].
ry-ādhi, m. 236, 4.
ry-ādhunvat, 24[c], n.
ry-āpādyamāna, 13, 1.
ry-āpāra, 27[b]; 58, 7. &c.; 294, 2; cf. yathokta°, ya-thoddishṭa°.
ry-āpin, 175[c] (aṃsa°).
ry-āprita, 164[b]; 296, 16.
ry-āpya, ind. 1[b].
vyāyata-tva, 38[c], n.
vyāhārālankāra, 91, n. 3.
r. vraj, vrajati, 9[a].
vraṇa, 94[a] (°viropaṇa).
vrata, 27[a]; 128[c]; 184[c]; 185[d].
vratati, 33[b].
vratin, 111[a].
vrīḍā, 156, 4; 137[d].

r. śak, śaknoti, 58, 6; 108, 3; 120[d]; desid. śikshate, 23[c].
śakuni, 61, 1 (°lubdhaka).
śakunta, 175[c] (°nīḍa-niṣila); °lāvaṇya, 294, 4.
Śakuntalā, 1, 1; 4, 3; 26, 1. 5, &c.
śakta, 37[a]; 79[d].
śakti, 158[d]; 199[d]; cf. yathā°.
śakya, 60[a]; 140,8; 158[b]; 288, 2.
Śakra, 'Indra;' °avatāra, 205, 12; 218, 6.
r. śank, śankate, 136[d].
śankā, 188[d] (ahi°); 309, 10 (aparādha°); 44, 11 (jāta-śanka).
-śankin, 176, 11 (pāpa°); 205, 4 (parapariyraha°).
Śaṣi-tīrtha, 205, 12; 246, 2.
śata, 58[a]; 198[c] (yuga°); Śata-kratu, 162[a]; 273, 2.
śapta, 310, 7.
śaptvā, ind. 137, 13.
r. śabd, śabdayati, 257, 7.
śabala,14[c]; 44.7 (ujjhita°); 48[d], &c.; °anusāra, 285, 8.
śabdāya, -yate, 152, 3 (pass.)
r. śam, caus. 17, 3; 109[d].
śama, 101[a]; °pradhāna, 41[a].
śamī, 18[d] (°latā); 84[b].
śayana, 107, 5; kusuma°, 71[a]; 75[a]; °bhūmi, 216, 7.
śayita, 147, 2 (sukha°).
śayitavya, 60, 5.
śayyā, 79[a]; 137[b] (°prānta).
śara, 7[b]; 10[d]; 13, 1, &c.; °asana, 124[d]; 161[b]; 265, 7.

śaraṇa,159[d]; agni°,148.4.&c.
śarad, 150[c] (°ćandra).
śararya, n. 161[a].
śarira, 10[b]; 44, 4; 97, 1, &c.; °bhūta, 226, 7.
Śarmishṭhā, 87[a].
śalabha, 32[d] (°samūha).
śalya,141[d]; 302,2 (rishāda°).
śaśa, 'a hare;' °anka, 70[b]; 129[a]; 113, 2 (°lekhā).
śaśin, 83[a]; 186[b].
śaśvat, adv. 112[c].
śastra, 11[b]; 269, 1 (ātta°).
Śākalya in vriddha°, 283, 9.
śākhā,58, 1 (kuraraka°); 46[d]; 149[c]; °bāhā, 165, 7.
śākhin, m. 15[a].
śāṭhya, 126[a].
śānta, 16[a]; 91[d]; 100[d]; °m, interj. 204, 9.
śānti, 97, 3 (°udaka).
śāpa,140,5; 145,8; 215,2,&c.
Śāradvata, 193, 7, &c.
śārnga, 265,16; °hasta, 265, 6; Śārnga-rava, 161, 5; 193,6,&c.; 160,6(°miśra).
śārdūla, 59, 5; 159[b].
śālā, 182, 4 (sangīta°).
śālīna-tā, 82, 10.
Śālmali, 312, n.
śāva, 52[a] (mriya°); 295, 6.
śāsrata, 42, 9.
śāsat, 25[a].
śāsana, 222, 1. 16; 230,11,&c.
śāsitri, 25[a]; 252, 16.
śiksh, śikshate, 23[c]; see śak.
śikshita, 2[b]; cf. a°.
śikhaṇḍaka, 184, 8.
śikhara, 172[a].
śikhā, 8[b]; 14[d]; 152, 7; 4[a] (kesara-śikha).
śithila, 40[d]; 42[b]; 248, 11.
śithilaya, -yati, 23, 9. 11.
śiras, 130, 5; 188[d]; cf. raṇa°; °dhara, 265, 2.
śirisha, 4[b]; 30[c]; 150[b].
śilā, 79[a]; °tala, 76, 3; 176[c]; °paṭṭa, 105, 1; °paṭṭaka, 239, 6.
śiva, adj. 91[d]; 179, 4.
Śiva, 2, n.; 315, n. 1.
śiśira, 136[c]; 237, 2.
śiśu, 294, 1; 15[d] (hariṇa°); 178[b](simha°);182[d](sarpa°).
śishya, 95, 2, 3; 142, 2, 3, &c.
śikara, 171[d] (klinna-nemi).
śīghram, adv. 114, 2.
śīta, 107[d]; °raśmi-tva, 55[a].
śītala,37,2 (praćchāya°);74[a].
-śīrsha, 81, 3 (ćikkaṇa°).
śīla, 59, 4 (mrigayā°); 146, 1 (duhkha°); 185[c] (śuddha°).
śuka, 14[a]; °udara, 118, 10.

śuć, f. 99[d].
śući, adj. 113[a]; 125[c].
śuddha, 196[d]; °śila, 185[c]; °hridaya, 145, 7; °anta, 17[a]; 214, 11.
śubha, n. pl. 194, 8; 188[c].
śūnya, 79[d]; 266, 5; 205, 9 (angulīyaka°); hridaya, 137, 11; 310, 9.
śūla, 224, 4.
śūlya, 60, 4 (°māṃsa).
śringa, 40[a]; 149[d].
śringāra, 41, 3 (°lajjā).
śesha, 115, 2 (devatā°); 157[d]; 169[a] (viććhitti°); Śesha, 106[c].
śaithilya, 309, 1 (smriti°).
śaila, 51[b]; 172[a].
śaivala, 20[a].
śoka, 101[a]; 180, 5; °pātra, 240, 12 (°ātman).
śoćanīya, 123, 12 (bandhu-ja-na°); 204,3; 243,7; 244,6.
śoćya, 63[c].
śonita, 159[a] (°arthin).
śobhana, 218, 4.
śobhā, 19[c]; 83[b].
śobhin, 252, 9 (pallava°).
śoshaṇa, 63[d].
śauṇḍika, 225, 11 (°āpaṇa).
śyāma, 49[a]; 65[b] (abhra°).
śyāmāka, 94[c].
śyāla, 217, 2, &c.
śrad-dhā, 193[b].
śrad-dheya, 211, 11.
śrama, 7[c]; 102, 7 (°klānta); 108[c].
śravaṇa, 48, 3; 58[c]; °kātara-tā, 64[d].
śrāddha, 111, n. 1.
śrānta, 107[b] (°manas).
śrī, 67[c]; 24, 11 (alankāra°); 260, 1 (Pururavsa°).
r. śru, śriṇoti, 21, 4 (pass.); 105, 2, &c.; desid. śuśrū-shate, 98[a].
śruta, 47,4; 110,9; 233,2; 313, 1 (°vistāra); °vat, 242, 1.
śruti, 96, 3; cf. yathā°; °pra-sādana-tas, 6, 2; °mahat, 199[b]; °vishaya-guṇa, 1[b].
śrutvā, ind. 188, 5; 297, 9.
śreyas, n. 260, 6; 177[b]; 314, 13; pl. 280, 2.
śreshṭhin, 258, 18.
śrotavya,110,9; 206,6; 232,6.
śrotriya, 133[b], n.
śrotra, 188, 12.
ślāghanīya, 198[d].
ślāghya, 99[a].
śvan, 222, 17.
śvā-pada, 67, 6 (°anusaraṇa).
śvāsa, 30[b]; 138[b].

sam-udra, 279, 4; °rasana, 73[b]; °vyavahārin, 258, 12.
sam-un-nam, caus. 128, 12.
sam-upagata, 186[b].
sam-upa-sthā, 44[d].
sam-ūha, 32[d] (śalabha°).
sam-riddhi, 114[c].
sam-etya, ind. 58, 5, 6.
sam-patti, 312, 4.
sam-pad, 189, 8; caus. 113, 5.
sam-pad, f. pl. 260, 1; 194[d].
sam-pādita, 303, 13.
sam-pīḍita, 175[b] (atyartha°).
sam-prati, 6,7; 10,8; 132,1, &c.
sam-pravṛitta, 80[a].
sam-prasthita, 140, 9.
sam-prahāra, 274,9 (°utsuka).
sam-prāpta, 188, 5.
sam-preshya, ind. 102[b].
sam-bandha, 226, 7; 293, 3.
sam-bhava, 30, 5; 46, 5; 26[a].
sam-bhāvanā, f. 257, 9; 269, 4; °guṇa, 168[b].
sam-bhāvanīya, 305, 2.
sam-bhāvayitavya, 91, 1.
sam-bhāvita, 64, 1; 236, 11.
sam-bhārya, ind. 54, 2.
sam-bhū, caus. 26, 3, n.; 93, 5.
sam-bhṛita, 157[a]; 210, 4 (°do-sha).
sam-bhrama, 32, 3 (°udgata).
sam-bhrānta, 35, 4; 56, 8.
sam-mata, 224, 8.
sam-mārjana, 192, 4.
sam-mita, 223, 13 (mūlya°).
sam-mīl, 59[a].
sam-mukha, 31[c] (ānana°).
sam-moha, 242, 4; 188[b]; 309, 10.
samy-ak, adv. 8, 3; 24,5; 48,3.
sam-rāj, 87[b].
-sara in prāgra°, 117[a].
saras, 91[a]; 169, 5 (°tīra); sarasi-ja, n. 20[a], n.; Saras-vatī, 199[b].
sa-rosham, 41, 6; 51, 1; 72, 1.
sarpa, 175[a] (°tvać); 182[d] (°śiśu); 296, 7.
sarva, 1[c]; 19, 7; 38, 3. 7, &c.; °tas, 7, 5; 127[b] (°mukha); °tra, adv. 16[b]; °thā, 16, 2; Sarva-damana, 286,7; 294, 4; 197[c]; °bhogya, 48[a]; °sva, 24[c], n.; cf. rati-sarvasva, jīvita-sarvasva.
sa-lajja, 121, 3.
salila, 3[a]; 32, 3; 40[a], &c.
savana, 80[a] (°karman).
sa-vāṇāsana, 88, 20.
sa-vāshpam, 244, 13.
sa-vāhyāntaḥkaraṇa, 276, 2, n.
sa-vitarkam, 105, 11.
savitṛi, 176, 13; 129[a].

sa-vimarśam, 180, 10.
sa-visha, 141[d].
sa-vishādam, 200, 13; 205, 10.
sa-vismayam, 10, 3; 149, 1, &c.
sa-vyājam, 58, 2.
sa-vrīḍam, 158, 8.
sa-śara, 265, 8; °ćāpa-hasta, 9, 2.
sa-śishya, 17, 8.
sa-śrīka, adj. 192, 4.
sa-sakhījana, 102, 10.
sa-sambhramam, 13, 7; 32, 2, &c.
sa-strīka, 188, 4.
sa-sneham, 105, 5.
sa-spṛiham, 32, 5.
sa-smitam, 34, 6; 47, 5, &c.
r. sah, sahate, 14[c]; 112, 12; caus. sāhayati, 96[b].
saha, prep. with inst. 21, 12; 58, 3, &c.; °kāra, 28, 2; 29, 2, &c.; °ćara, 128, 14; 170,8 (priya°); °ćāriṇī,242, 1; °ja,133[a]; °dharma-ćara-ṇa,199, 1; °dharma-ćāriṇī, 180, 4; 310, 2; °yāyin,179, 5; °vasati, 37[c]; °vāsa, 168, 2; °aya, see sahāya.
sa-harsham, 12, 1; 89, 3, &c.
sahasā, adv. 9[a]; 108, 2; 120, 1.
sahasra-kiraṇa, 168[d].
sahāya, 69, 2.
sa-hāsam, 24, 1.
-sahita, 193, 3; 265, 7; 307, 2 (dāraka°); 314, 2.
sahishṇu, 38[b] (ravi-kiraṇa°).
sahya, 109, 6 (°vedana).
Sāketaka, 258, 18.
sākshāt, adv. 6[b]; 148[a]; 153[a].
sākshika,225,10(kādambarī°).
sāyara, 112, 10.
sādaram, 90, 8; 188, 6.
sādṛiśya, 294, 8. 14.
r. sādh, caus. 18[b]; 17,8; 284,9.
sādhana, 118, 8 (lekhana°).
sādhāraṇa, 122, 13; 150, 3 (utkaṇṭhā°).
sādhu, adj. 2[a]; 146[a]; 193[a]; m. 214,9; adv. 7, 4; 32,6; 11[a], &c.; °jana, 226, 5.
sādhvasa, 35, 10.
sānukrośa, 139, 8; 301, 5.
sānu-mat, m. 279, 5; Sānu-matī, f. 226,2,3; 239,10,&c.
sānuśaya, 130, 9.
sāndhya, adj. 279, 5.
sānnidhya, 226, 4.
sābādha, 62[b].
sābhilāsha, 28[a]; °m, 105, 13.
sāmānya, 97[c].
sāmpratam,adv.61,6; 76,2,&c.
sāyaka, 11[a]; 37[b].
sāyan-tana, adj. 80[a].

sāra,38[d](prāṇa°);cf.krishṇa°, vajra°.
sāraṅga, 5[b]; 9,8; °yūtha,33[c]; °akshī, 139[a].
sārathi, 88, 20; 267, 8 (ma-hendra°); °dvitīya, 88, 13.
sārtha, 99, 2 (kāmi-jana°); °vāha, 258, 12; 261, 2.
sārdham, adv. with inst. 100[c]; 304, 10.
sāvadhānam, 252, 11.
sāvaśesha, adj. 68, 11.
sāsūyam, 36[c]; 210, 6.
siṇha, 286, 3; °sāra, 295, 6; °śiśu, 178[b].
sikatā, 61[b] (pāṇḍu-sikata).
r. sić, sińćati, 111, 3; 141, 9.
siddha, 84, 9 (°artha).
siddhi, 131, 2 (artha°); 155, 2; °kshetra, 279, 8; °mat, 198, 2.
r. sidh, sidhyate, 39[c]; 168[a].
sindhu, f. 122[b].
sīman in udadhi-syāma°, 49[a].
su- in su-kara, su-tarām, &c.
su-kara, 114, 2.
su-kumāra, 4[a]; 116, 2; 118, 10; °tara, 40, 1.
su-kṛita, n. 93[b].
sukha, n.64[a]; 109[a]; cf. yathā°, °mārjana, 153, 10; °saṅgin, 113[b]; °āsīna, 76, 4; °upa-nata, 130, 8; 202, 5.
sukhāya, sukhāyate, 105, 6.
sukhita, 104[b].
sukhin, 189, 8.
su-ćarita, 143[a]; 193, 2; 301, 4 (°pratibandhaka).
suta, m. 87[b]; 192[a]; ā, f. 67, 10; 121[b]; 140[a].
su-tanu, 103, 2; 188[a]; 189[a].
su-tarām, adv. 200, 6.
su-duḥsaha, 83[d].
sundara, f. ī,123,5; 126,4,&c.; sura-sundarī, 169[a].
supta, 113[a]; 139[a]; 142, 2 (°utthita).
su-bhaga, 3[a]; 103, 5 (pra-vāta°); 62[d].
su-manas, 115, 3 (°gopita); 151, 5; 222, 11; °mūlya, 225, 5.
su-mukha, f. ī, 186[a].
sura, 49[c]; °yuvati, 42[a]; °sakha, 167[a]; °sundarī, 169[a]; °asu-ra, 173[b] (°guru).
su-rabhi, 3[a]; 60[a]; 71[a]; 229,13.
su-labha, 3[b]; 35[a]; 85[b] (upa-bhoga°); °kopa, 137, 12; °avakāśa, 196[d].
su-vihita, 5, 2 (°prayoga-tā).
Su-vratā, 288, 2; 296, 16.
su-śishya, 147, 10.

su-hrid, 68, 7; °jana, 161°.
r. sū or su, sūte, 191[b].
sūkshma, 9[a]; 19[a] (°granthi).
r. sūc, sūcayati, 14[b] (pass.)
sūcaka, 153, 3 (bahumāna°);
  Sūcaka, 218,10; 221,10,&c.
sūcayat, 20, 11.
sūcayitvā, ind. 162, 1; 194, 5.
sūci, 57, 16 (kuśa°); 94[b].
sūcita, 114, 6; 148, 2; 156, 2.
sūta, 9, 2. 3. 8; 17, 10, &c.
sūtra,150[d] (mriṇāla°);°dhāra,
  2, 2, n.; 3, n. 2, &c.
sūnrita, 36, 5.
sūrya, 102, 9; °kānta, 41°;
  °udaya, 152, 7.
srishṭi, 1[a]; 43° (strīratna°).
seka, 32, 3 (salila°).
secana, 22,9 (vriksha°); 52,8.
  11; °ghaṭa, 21, 6.
senā-pati, 69, 15; 70, 2. 5,&c.
r. sev, sevate, 137[a] (pass.)
serā, 156, 7 (vanaspati°).
sevita, 224, 14.
saikata, 149[a] (°līna-hansa).
sainika, 74, 4, 5.
socchvāsam, 310, 4.
sodara, 22, 9 (°sneha).
sodarya, 165, 4 (°sneha).
sodvegam, 295, 3.
sopāna, 265, 16 (°mārga).
Soma-tīrtha, 17, 3.
Soma-rāta, 188, 11.
saukumāra, 252, 2.
saubhāgya, 274, 3; °devatā,
  136, 2.
saumya, 161° (prasāda°).
sauhārda, n. 38, 8, n.
sauhrida,104[d]; 125[b]; 225,10.
skandha,224,4(hastin°);172[b];
  °deśa, 19[a].
r. skhal, skhalati, 247, 11.
skhalita, 139, 3; 136°; 137[d].
stana, 19[b] (°yuga); 30[b] (°ve-
  pathu); 62[a]; 150[d] (°antarc).
stambhita,86[b](°vāshpa-vritti).
stimita, 197[a] (°gati).
stutya, 273, 2.
stokam, adv. 7[d]; 19,8; 274, 2.
strī,123[a],&c.; °ratna,43°; 78,
  5; °saṃsthāna, 131°.
straiṇa, n. 206, 2.
-stha,195, 3 (madhya°); 166[a]
  (antika°); āsana°, 153, 1;
  182, 2, &c.
r. sthā, tishṭhati, 29, 2; 35,
  10, &c.; caus. sthāpayati,
  13, 10; 19, 9, 10, &c.
sthāṇu, 175[d].
sthāna, 131, 1; 236, 8 (vino-
  da°); 291, 4 (°pratyaya);
  sthāne, adv. 118, 2; 194, 2;
  286, 6.

sthāpaka, 2, n. 1.
sthāpayitvā, ind. 282, 9.
sthita, 1[b]; 21, 11; 68, 7; 99[a];
  229, 12; 136[b], &c.
sthiti, 112[a] (a-bhinna°).
sthitvā, ind. 34, 2. 13; 130,
  10, &c.
sthira,104[d] (bhāva°); °tā,95[b];
  °pratibandha, 71,6; °ī-kar-
  tarya, 166, 9.
snāta, 113[a].
snāna, 157, 3 (°uttīrṇa).
snigdha, 59[b]; 169, 4, 155[a],
  &c.; °m, adv. 36[a]; °jana,
  109, 5; °drishṭi, 114, 6.
r. snih, snihyati, 286, 9.
sneha, 22, 9 (sodara°); 121, 5
  (sakhī°); 86°; 89[b], &c.;
  °pravritti, 97[b]; 180, 10.
r. spand, spandate, 177[a].
sparśa, 103, 5; 130[b] (para-
  strī°); 174°, &c.; °kshama,
  28[b]; °anukūla, 41°.
r. spriś, spriśati, 24[a]; 48°.
sprishṭa, 63[d].
r. sprih, sprihayati, 289, 4.
r. sphur,sphurati,16[a]; 222,11.
sphuliṅga, 179[b] (°avasthā).
sma, 98[b] (mā°).
smara, 124[d], n.; Smara, 65[a];
  136[d].
smaraṇīya, 140, 9, 10.
smārita, 204, 3.
smita, 166[b] (krita°); smitaṃ
  kritvā, 64, 1; 88, 19, &c.;
  cf. sa°.
r. smri, smarati, 134,12; 104°;
  202, 11; 132[a], &c.
smrita, 117[a]; 224, 11; 162[b];
  301, 7.
smriti, 215, 2; 302, 11, &c.;
  °mat, 313, 16.
smritvā, ind. 165, 1.
syandana, 7[a]; 33[d].
syāla, see śyāla.
sransin, 30[d].
sraj, f. 188[d].
srashṭri, 1[a]; 191[d].
srasta, 66[d]; 30[a] (°ansa).
srotas, 51[b]; 246, 2; cf. tri°;
  °vah,51[b];°vahā,148°;149[a].
sva, adj. 19°; 75, 5; °kārya-
  paratā, 241, 6; °gatam, 34,
  11; 67, 9, &c.; °cchanda-
  cārin, 209,8; °cchanda-tas,
  51, 10; °jana, 141[a]; °tā,
  36[d]; °pramāṇa, 21,6(°anu-
  rūpa); °bhāva, 114[d]; 204,
  6 (°uttāna); °stha, see a°;
  °adhīna, 140, 10 (°upāya);
  198, 2 (°kuśala); °apatya,
  314, 2 (°dāra-sahita); °ī-
  karaṇa, 202, 10.

r. svan, svanati, 24[b].
svapna, 142[a]; 154[a].
svabhāvokti, 73, n. 1.
svayam,65,7; 140,5.10; 188,
  12, &c.; °vara, 28, n. 1;
  °vara-vadhū, 28, 2.
svara, 84, 11; 263, 5 (ārta°);
  °saṃyoga, 182, 5.
svarga, 272, n. 2; 282, 7;
  °mārga, 275, 1.
svargin, 198[b].
sv-asti, 152, 8 (°vācanaka).
sv-āgata, 120, 5; 153, 12;
  267, 8. 10.
svātantrya, 212, 11.
svādu, 303, 13 (°phala).
svāmin,70,6; 71,1; 74,11,&c.
Svāyambhuva, 173[a].
svāsthya, 181, 1.
svid, 111° (āho°); 115[a].
svinna, 147[a] (°anguli).
sveda, 248, 12 (°vindu).
svaira, 113[b] (°gati).

hansa, 149[a]; 160[b]; Hansa-
  padikā, 182, 6; 184, 6.
hata, 24[d], n.; 32[a]; 72[d].
r. han, hanti, 159[b]; 160[a].
hanta,interj.84,9; 142,6,&c.;
  °bhoh, 180, 10.
hantarya, 13, 3. 13.
-hara, 90, 7 (ājñapti°); 122,
  4 (ārti°); cf. manas°; Hara,
  56[a].
haraṇa, 112, 4 (kāla°).
hari, m. 12, 2, n.; 171[b]; Hari,
  161[a]; 268, 2; 166[d]; 167[a];
  °candana, 166°; °vikrama,
  170°.
hariṇa,149[b]; °ka, 10°; °śiśu,
  15[d]; °anganā, 27[d].
harit, m. 12, 2, n.
harita,91[a] (kamalinī°);°pāṇ-
  dura, 134[a].
harshaṇa, 99, n. 1.
halā, interj. 22,4. 8; 26, 5, &c.
havis, n. 1[a].
havya, 88° (°gandha).
r. has, hasati, 289, 2.
hasita, 45[b].
hasta, 9, 2; 13, 12; 115, 3,
  &c.; °ka, 229,14 (kapola°);
  °abhyāsa, 207, 2; 209, 10;
  °āvāpa, 265, 7.
hastin, 224, 4 (°skandha).
Hastinā-pura, 152, 2.
hā, interj. 137, 10 (°dhik);
  180, 2, &c.
r. hā, jahāti, 94°; 120[d].
-hāraka, 130, 10 (santāpa°).
hārin, 5[a]; 188, 4; 188, 7
  (sandeśa°).
hāsa, 181[a] (a-nimitta°).

ADDITIONS TO THE INDEX.

ADDITIONS AND CORRECTIONS.

Page 34, line 7, for राम रकिखदाइं read रामरकिखदाइं

  ,, 51, ,, 11, for ग्रहोतुम् read ग्रहीतुम्

  ,, 60, ,, 7, for कटूणि read कटूनि or rather कटुकानि

  ,, 66, ,, 8 of notes, for *sphutārtham* read *sphuṭārtham*

  ,, 108, ,, 14, for निवेदितुम् read निवेदयितुम्

  ,, 124, ,, 4, for °रसना read °रशना

  ,, 147, ,, 4 of notes, for *-pracchikā* read *-pricchikā*

  ,, 196, ,, 6, for पडिहिदो read पडिहदो

  ,, 196, ,, 15, for प्रतिहितो read प्रतिहतो

  ,, 198, ,, 10, for मूर्तिमितो read मूर्तिमती

  ,, 265, ,, 2, for पञ्चावयाद्° read पञ्चाधयाद्°

Clarendon Press, Oxford

A SELECTION OF
BOOKS
PUBLISHED FOR THE UNIVERSITY BY
HENRY FROWDE,
AT THE OXFORD UNIVERSITY PRESS WAREHOUSE,
AMEN CORNER, LONDON.

ALSO TO BE HAD AT THE
CLARENDON PRESS DEPOSITORY, OXFORD.
[Every book is bound in cloth, unless otherwise described.]

LEXICONS, GRAMMARS, &c.

ANGLO-SAXON.—*An Anglo-Saxon Dictionary*, based on the MS. Collections of the late Joseph Bosworth, D.D., Professor of Anglo-Saxon, Oxford. Edited and enlarged by Prof. T. N. Toller, M.A. (To be completed in four parts.) Parts I and II. A—HWISTLIAN (pp. vi, 576). 1882. 4to. 15*s*. each.

CHINESE.—*A Handbook of the Chinese Language.* By James Summers. 1863. 8vo. half bound, 1*l*. 8*s*.

ENGLISH.—*A New English Dictionary, on Historical Principles:* founded mainly on the materials collected by the Philological Society. Edited by James A. H. Murray, LL.D., President of the Philological Society; with the assistance of many Scholars and men of Science. Part I. A—ANT (pp. xvi, 352). Part II. ANT—BATTEN (pp. viii, 353-704). Imperial 4to. 12*s*. 6*d*. each.

—— *An Etymological Dictionary of the English Language.* By W. W. Skeat, M.A. *Second Edition.* 1884. 4to. 2*l*. 4*s*.

——Supplement to the First Edition of the above. 1884. 4to. 2*s*. 6*d*.

—— *A Concise Etymological Dictionary of the English Language.* By W. W. Skeat, M.A. *Second Edition.* 1885. Crown 8vo. 5*s*. 6*d*.

GREEK.—*A Greek-English Lexicon*, by Henry George Liddell, D.D., and Robert Scott, D.D. Seventh Edition, Revised and Augmented throughout. 1883. 4to. 1*l*. 16*s*.

—— *A Greek-English Lexicon*, abridged from Liddell and Scott's 4to. edition, chiefly for the use of Schools. Twenty-first Edition. 1884. Square 12mo. 7*s*. 6*d*.

—— *A copious Greek-English Vocabulary*, compiled from the best authorities. 1850. 24mo. 3*s*.

—— *A Practical Introduction to Greek Accentuation*, by H. W. Chandler, M.A. Second Edition. 1881. 8vo. 10*s*. 6*d*.

HEBREW.—*The Book of Hebrew Roots*, by Abu 'l-Walîd Marwân ibn Janâh, otherwise called Rabbî Yônâh. Now first edited, with an Appendix, by Ad. Neubauer. 1875. 4to. 2*l*. 7*s*. 6*d*.

—— *A Treatise on the use of the Tenses in Hebrew.* By S. R. Driver, D.D. Second Edition. 1881. Extra fcap. 8vo. 7*s*. 6*d*.

—— *Hebrew Accentuation of Psalms, Proverbs, and Job.* By William Wickes, D.D. 1881. Demy 8vo. stiff covers, 5*s*.

ICELANDIC.—*An Icelandic-English Dictionary*, based on the MS. collections of the late Richard Cleasby. Enlarged and completed by G. Vigfússon, M.A. With an Introduction, and Life of Richard Cleasby, by G. Webbe Dasent, D.C.L. 1874. 4to. 3*l*. 7*s*.

—— *A List of English Words the Etymology of which is illustrated by comparison with Icelandic.* Prepared in the form of an APPENDIX to the above. By W. W. Skeat, M.A. 1876. stitched, 2*s*.

—— *An Icelandic Primer*, with Grammar, Notes, and Glossary. By Henry Sweet, M.A. Extra fcap. 8vo. 3*s*. 6*d*. *Just Published.*

—— *An Icelandic Prose Reader*, with Notes, Grammar and Glossary, by Dr. Gudbrand Vigfússon and F. York Powell, M.A. 1879. Extra fcap. 8vo. 10*s*. 6*d*.

LATIN.—*A Latin Dictionary*, founded on Andrews' edition of Freund's Latin Dictionary, revised, enlarged, and in great part rewritten by Charlton T. Lewis, Ph.D., and Charles Short, LL.D. 1879. 4to. 1*l*. 5*s*.

MELANESIAN.—*The Melanesian Languages.* By R. H. Codrington, D.D., of the Melanesian Mission, 8vo. 18*s*.

SANSKRIT.—*A Practical Grammar of the Sanskrit Language*, arranged with reference to the Classical Languages of Europe, for the use of English Students, by Monier Williams, M.A. Fourth Edition, 1877. 8vo. 15*s*.

—— *A Sanskrit-English Dictionary*, Etymologically and Philologically arranged, with special reference to Greek, Latin, German, Anglo-Saxon, English, and other cognate Indo-European Languages. By Monier Williams, M.A. 1872. 4to. 4*l*. 14*s*. 6*d*.

—— *Nalopákhyánam.* Story of Nala, an Episode of the Mahá-Bhárata: the Sanskrit text, with a copious Vocabulary, and an improved version of Dean Milman's Translation, by Monier Williams, M.A. Second Edition, Revised and Improved. 1879. 8vo. 15*s*.

—— *Sakuntalā.* A Sanskrit Drama, in Seven Acts. Edited by Monier Williams, M.A. Second Edition, 1876. 8vo. 21*s*.

SYRIAC.—*Thesaurus Syriacus*: collegerunt Quatremère, Bernstein, Lorsbach, Arnoldi, Agrell, Field, Roediger: edidit R. Payne Smith, S.T.P. Fasc. I-VI. 1868-83. sm. fol. each, 1*l*. 1*s*.

Vol. I, containing Fasc. I-V, sm. fol. 5*l*. 5*s*.

Fasc. VII. sm. fol. 1*l*. 11*s*. 6*d*. *Just Published.*

—— *The Book of Kalîlah and Dimnah.* Translated from Arabic into Syriac. Edited by W. Wright, LL.D. 1884. 8vo. 21*s*.

GREEK CLASSICS, &c.

Aristophanes: A Complete Concordance to the Comedies and Fragments. By Henry Dunbar, M.D. 4to. 1*l.* 1*s.*

Aristotle: *The Politics,* translated into English, with Introduction, Marginal Analysis, Notes, and Indices, by B. Jowett, M.A. Medium 8vo. 2 vols. 21*s.*

Heracliti Ephesii Reliquiae. Recensuit I. Bywater, M.A. Appendicis loco additae sunt Diogenis Laertii Vita Heracliti, Particulae Hippocratei De Diaeta Libri Primi, Epistolae Heracliteae. 1877. 8vo. 6*s.*

Herculanensium Voluminum Partes II. 1824. 8vo. 10*s.*

Fragmenta Herculanensia. A Descriptive Catalogue of the Oxford copies of the Herculanean Rolls, together with the texts of several papyri, accompanied by facsimiles. Edited by Walter Scott, M.A., Fellow of Merton College, Oxford. Royal 8vo. *cloth,* 21*s.*

Homer: A Complete Concordance to the Odyssey and Hymns of Homer; to which is added a Concordance to the Parallel Passages in the Iliad, Odyssey, and Hymns. By Henry Dunbar, M.D. 1880. 4to. 1*l.* 1*s.*

—— *Scholia Graeca in Iliadem.* Edited by Professor W. Dindorf, after a new collation of the Venetian MSS. by D. B. Monro, M.A., Provost of Oriel College. 4 vols. 8vo. 2*l.* 10*s.* Vols. V and VI. *In the Press.*

—— *Scholia Graeca in Odysseam.* Edidit Guil. Dindorfius. Tomi II. 1855. 8vo. 15*s.* 6*d.*

Plato: *Apology,* with a revised Text and English Notes, and a Digest of Platonic Idioms, by James Riddell, M.A. 1878. 8vo. 8*s.* 6*d.*

—— *Philebus,* with a revised Text and English Notes, by Edward Poste, M.A. 1860. 8vo. 7*s.* 6*d.*

—— *Sophistes and Politicus,* with a revised Text and English Notes, by L. Campbell, M.A. 1867. 8vo. 18*s.*

—— *Theaetetus,* with a revised Text and English Notes, by L. Campbell, M.A. Second Edition. 8vo. 10*s.* 6*d.*

—— *The Dialogues,* translated into English, with Analyses and Introductions, by B. Jowett, M.A. A new Edition in 5 volumes, medium 8vo. 1875. 3*l.* 10*s.*

—— *The Republic,* translated into English, with an Analysis and Introduction, by B. Jowett, M.A. Medium 8vo. 12*s.* 6*d.*

Thucydides: Translated into English, with Introduction, Marginal Analysis, Notes, and Indices. By B. Jowett, M.A. 2 vols. 1881. Medium 8vo. 1*l.* 12*s.*

THE HOLY SCRIPTURES, &c.

STUDIA BIBLICA.—Essays in Biblical Archæology and Criticism, and kindred subjects. By Members of the University of Oxford. 8vo. 10s. 6d.

ENGLISH.—*The Holy Bible in the earliest English Versions*, made from the Latin Vulgate by John Wycliffe and his followers: edited by the Rev. J. Forshall and Sir F. Madden. 4 vols. 1850. Royal 4to. 3l. 3s.

[Also reprinted from the above, with Introduction and Glossary by **W. W. Skeat, M.A.**

—— *The Books of Job, Psalms, Proverbs, Ecclesiastes, and the Song of Solomon:* according to the Wycliffite Version made by Nicholas de Hereford, about A.D. 1381, and Revised by John Purvey, about A.D. 1388. Extra fcap. 8vo. 3s. 6d.

—— *The New Testament in English*, according to the Version by John Wycliffe, about A.D. 1380, and Revised by John Purvey, about A.D. 1388. Extra fcap. 8vo. 6s.]

—— *The Holy Bible:* an exact reprint, page for page, of the Authorised Version published in the year 1611. Demy 4to. half bound, 1l. 1s.

—— *The Psalter, or Psalms of David, and certain Canticles*, with a Translation and Exposition in English, by Richard Rolle of Hampole. Edited by H. R. Bramley, M.A., Fellow of S. M. Magdalen College, Oxford. With an Introduction and Glossary. Demy 8vo. 1l. 1s.

—— *Lectures on Ecclesiastes.* Delivered in Westminster Abbey by the Very Rev. George Granville Bradley, D.D., Dean of Westminster. Crown 8vo. 4s. 6d.

GOTHIC.—*The Gospel of St. Mark in Gothic*, according to the translation made by Wulfila in the Fourth Century. Edited with a Grammatical Introduction and Glossarial Index by W. W. Skeat, M.A. Extra fcap. 8vo. 4s.

GREEK.—*Vetus Testamentum* ex Versione Septuaginta Interpretum secundum exemplar Vaticauum Romae editum. Accedit potior varietas Codicis Alexandrini. Tomi III. Editio Altera. 18mo. 18s.

—— *Origenis Hexaplorum* quae supersunt; sive, Veterum Interpretum Graecorum in totum Vetus Testamentum Fragmenta. Edidit Fridericus Field, A.M. 2 vols. 1875. 4to. 5l. 5s.

—— *The Book of Wisdom:* the Greek Text, the Latin Vulgate, and the Authorised English Version; with an Introduction, Critical Apparatus, and a Commentary. By William J. Deane, M.A. Small 4to. 12s. 6d.

—— *Novum Testamentum Graece.* Antiquissimorum Codicum Textus in ordine parallelo dispositi. Accedit collatio Codicis Sinaitici. Edidit E. H. Hansell, S.T.B. Tomi III. 1864. 8vo. half morocco. Price reduced to 24s.

GREEK.—*Novum Testamentum Graece.* Accedunt parallela S. Scripturae loca, etc. Edidit Carolus Lloyd, S.T.P R. 18mo. 3*s*.
On writing paper, with wide margin, 10*s*.

—— *Novum Testamentum Graece* juxta Exemplar Millianum. 18mo. 2*s*. 6*d*. **On writing paper,** with wide margin, 9*s*.

—— *Evangelia Sacra Graece.* Fcap. 8vo. limp, 1*s*. 6*d*.

—— *The Greek Testament*, with the Readings adopted by the Revisers of the Authorised Version:—

    (1) Pica type, with Marginal References. Demy 8vo. 10*s*. 6*d*.
    (2) Long Primer type. Fcap. 8vo. 4*s*. 6*d*.
    (3) The same, on writing paper, with wide margin, 15*s*.

—— *The Parallel New Testament*, Greek and English; being the Authorised Version, 1611; the Revised Version, 1881; and the Greek Text followed in the Revised Version. 8vo. 12*s*. 6*d*.
The Revised Version is the joint property of the Universities of Oxford and Cambridge.

—— *Canon Muratorianus:* the earliest Catalogue of the Books of the New Testament. Edited with Notes and a Facsimile of the MS. in the Ambrosian Library at Milan, by S. P. Tregelles, LL.D. 1867. 4to. 10*s*. 6*d*.

—— *Outlines of Textual Criticism applied to the New Testament.* By C. E. Hammond, M.A. Fourth Edition. Extra fcap. 8vo. 3*s*. 6*d*.

HEBREW, etc.—*The Psalms in Hebrew without points.* 1879. Crown 8vo. 3*s*. 6*d*.

—— *A Commentary on the Book of Proverbs.* Attributed to Abraham Ibn Ezra. Edited from a MS. in the Bodleian Library by S. R. Driver, M.A. Crown 8vo. paper covers, 3*s*. 6*d*.

—— *The Book of Tobit.* A Chaldee Text, from a unique MS. in the Bodleian Library; with other Rabbinical Texts, English Translations, and the Itala. Edited by Ad. Neubauer, M.A. 1878. Crown 8vo. 6*s*.

—— *Horae Hebraicae et Talmudicae*, a J. Lightfoot. A new Edition, by R. Gandell, M.A. 4 vols. 1859. 8vo. 1*l*. 1*s*.

LATIN.—*Libri Psalmorum* Versio antiqua Latina, cum Paraphrasi Anglo-Saxonica. Edidit B. Thorpe, F.A.S. 1835. 8vo. 10*s*. 6*d*.

—— *Old-Latin Biblical Texts: No. I.* The Gospel according to St. Matthew from the St. Germain MS. (g₁). Edited with Introduction and Appendices by John Wordsworth, M.A. Small 4to., stiff covers, 6*s*.

—— *Old-Latin Biblical Texts: No. II.* Portions of the Gospels according to St. Mark and St. Matthew, from the Bobbio MS. (k), now numbered G. VII. 15 in the National Library at Turin, etc. Edited with two Facsimiles by John Wordsworth, D.D., Bishop of Salisbury, W. Sanday, M.A., and H. J. White, M.A. Small 4to., stiff cover, 21*s*. *Just Published.*

OLD-FRENCH.—*Libri Psalmorum* Versio antiqua Gallica e Cod. MS. in Bibl. Bodleiana adservato, una cum Versione Metrica aliisque Monumentis pervetustis. Nunc primum descripsit et edidit Franciscus Michel, Phil. Doc. 1860. 8vo. 10*s*. 6*d*.

FATHERS OF THE CHURCH, &c.

St. Athanasius: Historical Writings, according to the Bene-
dictine Text. With an Introduction by William Bright, D.D. 1881. Crown
8vo. 10*s*. 6*d*.

—— *Orations against the Arians.* With an Account of his
Life by William Bright, D.D. 1873. Crown 8vo. 9*s*.

St. Augustine: Select Anti-Pelagian Treatises, and the Acts
of the Second Council of Orange. With an Introduction by William Bright,
D.D. Crown 8vo. 9*s*.

Canons of the First Four General Councils of Nicaea, Con-
stantinople, Ephesus, and Chalcedon. 1877. Crown 8vo. 2*s*. 6*d*.

—— *Notes on the Canons of the First Four General Councils.*
By William Bright, D.D. 1882. Crown 8vo. 5*s*. 6*d*.

Cyrilli Archiepiscopi Alexandrini in XII Prophetas. Edidit
P. E. Pusey, A.M. Tomi II. 1868. 8vo. cloth, 2*l*. 2*s*.

—— *in D. Joannis Evangelium.* Accedunt Fragmenta varia
necnon Tractatus ad Tiberium Diaconum duo. Edidit post Aubertum
P. E. Pusey, A.M. Tomi III. 1872. 8vo. 2*l*. 5*s*.

—— *Commentarii in Lucae Evangelium* quae supersunt
Syriace. E MSS. apud Mus. Britan. edidit R. Payne Smith, A.M. 1858.
4to. 1*l*. 2*s*.

—— Translated by R. Payne Smith, M.A. 2 vols. 1859.
8vo. 14*s*.

Ephraemi Syri, Rabulae Episcopi Edesseni, Balaei, aliorum-
que Opera Selecta. E Codd. Syriacis MSS. in Museo Britannico et Bibliotheca
Bodleiana asservatis primus edidit J. J. Overbeck. 1865. 8vo. 1*l*. 1*s*.

Eusebius' Ecclesiastical History, according to the text of
Burton, with an Introduction by William Bright, D.D. 1881. Crown 8vo.
8*s*. 6*d*.

Irenaeus: The Third Book of St. Irenaeus, Bishop of Lyons,
against Heresies. With short Notes and a Glossary by H. Deane, B.D.
1874. Crown 8vo. 5*s*. 6*d*.

Patrum Apostolicorum, S. Clementis Romani, S. Ignatii,
S. Polycarpi, quae supersunt. Edidit Guil. Jacobson, S.T.P.R. Tomi II.
Fourth Edition, 1863. 8vo. 1*l*. 1*s*.

Socrates' Ecclesiastical History, according to the Text of
Hussey, with an Introduction by William Bright, D.D. 1878. Crown 8vo.
7*s*. 6*d*.

ECCLESIASTICAL HISTORY, BIOGRAPHY, &c.

Ancient Liturgy of the Church of England, according to the uses of Sarum, York, Hereford, and Bangor, and the Roman Liturgy arranged in parallel columns, with preface and notes. By William Maskell, M.A. Third Edition. 1882. 8vo. 15*s.*

Baedae Historia Ecclesiastica. Edited, with English Notes, by G. H. Moberly, M.A. 1881. Crown 8vo. 10*s. 6d.*

Bright (W.). Chapters of Early English Church History. 1878. 8vo. 12*s.*

Burnet's History of the Reformation of the Church of England. A new Edition. Carefully revised, and the Records collated with the originals, by N. Pocock, M.A. 7 vols. 1865. 8vo. *Price reduced to* 1*l.* 10*s.*

Councils and Ecclesiastical Documents relating to Great Britain and Ireland. Edited, after Spelman and Wilkins, by A. W. Haddan, B.D., and W. Stubbs, M.A. Vols. I. and III. 1869–71. Medium 8vo. each 1*l.* 1*s.*

> Vol. II. Part I. 1873. Medium 8vo. 10*s. 6d.*

> Vol. II. Part II. 1878. Church of Ireland; Memorials of St. Patrick. Stiff covers, 3*s. 6d.*

Hamilton (John, Archbishop of St. Andrews), The Catechism of. Edited, with Introduction and Glossary, by Thomas Graves Law. With a Preface by the Right Hon. W. E. Gladstone. 8vo. 12*s. 6d.*

Hammond (C. E.). Liturgies, Eastern and Western. Edited, with Introduction, Notes, and Liturgical Glossary. 1878. Crown 8vo. 10*s. 6d.*

> **An Appendix to the above.** 1879. Crown 8vo. paper covers, 1*s. 6d.*

John, Bishop of Ephesus. The Third Part of his Ecclesiastical History. [In Syriac.] Now first edited by William Cureton, M.A. 1853. 4to. 1*l.* 12*s.*

—— Translated by R. Payne Smith, M.A. 1860. 8vo. 10*s.*

Leofric Missal, The, as used in the Cathedral of Exeter during the Episcopate of its first Bishop, A.D. 1050–1072; together with some Account of the Red Book of Derby, the Missal of Robert of Jumièges, and a few other early MS. Service Books of the English Church. Edited, with Introduction and Notes, by F. E. Warren, B.D. 4to. half morocco, 35*s.*

Monumenta Ritualia Ecclesiae Anglicanae. The occasional Offices of the Church of England according to the old use of Salisbury, the Prymer in English, and other prayers and forms, with dissertations and notes. By William Maskell, M.A. Second Edition. 1882. 3 vols. 8vo. 2*l.* 10*s.*

Records of the Reformation. The Divorce, 1527–1533. Mostly now for the first time printed from MSS. in the British Museum and other libraries. Collected and arranged by N. Pocock, M.A. 1870. 2 vols. 8vo. 1*l.* 16*s.*

Shirley (W. W.). Some Account of the Church in the Apostolic Age. Second Edition, 1874. Fcap. 8vo. 3s. 6d.

Stubbs (W.). Registrum Sacrum Anglicanum. An attempt to exhibit the course of Episcopal Succession in England. 1858. Small 4to. 8s. 6d.

Warren (F. E.). Liturgy and Ritual of the Celtic Church. 1881. 8vo. 14s.

ENGLISH THEOLOGY.

Butler's Works, with an Index to the Analogy. 2 vols. 1874. 8vo. 11s. **Also separately,**

 Sermons, 5s. 6d.   *Analogy of Religion,* 5s. 6d.

Greswell's Harmonia Evangelica. Fifth Edition. 8vo. 1855. 9s. 6d.

Heurtley's Harmonia Symbolica: Creeds of the Western Church. 1858. 8vo. 6s. 6d.

Homilies appointed to be read in Churches. Edited by J. Griffiths, M.A. 1859. 8vo. 7s. 6d.

Hooker's Works, with his life by Walton, arranged by John Keble, M.A. Sixth Edition, 1874. 3 vols. 8vo. 1l. 11s. 6d.

—— the text as arranged by John Keble, M.A. 2 vols. 1875. 8vo. 11s.

Jewel's Works. Edited by R. W. Jelf, D.D. 8 vols. 1848. 8vo. 1l. 10s.

Pearson's Exposition of the Creed. Revised and corrected by E. Burton, D.D. Sixth Edition, 1877. 8vo. 10s. 6d.

Waterland's Review of the Doctrine of the Eucharist, with a Preface by the late Bishop of London. Crown 8vo. 6s. 6d.

—— *Works,* with Life, by Bp. Van Mildert. A new Edition, with copious Indexes. 6 vols. 1856. 8vo. 2l. 11s.

Wheatly's Illustration of the Book of Common Prayer. A new Edition, 1846. 8vo. 5s.

Wyclif. A Catalogue of the Original Works of John Wyclif, by W. W. Shirley, D.D. 1865. 8vo. 3s. 6d.

—— *Select English Works.* By T. Arnold, M.A. 3 vols. 1869-1871. 8vo. 1l. 1s.

—— *Trialogus.* With the Supplement now first edited. By Gotthard Lechler. 1869. 8vo. 7s.

HISTORICAL AND DOCUMENTARY WORKS.

British Barrows, a Record of the Examination of Sepulchral
Mounds in various parts of England. By William Greenwell, M.A., F.S.A.
Together with Description of Figures of Skulls, General Remarks on Pre-
historic Crania, and an Appendix by George Rolleston, M.D., F.R.S. 1877.
Medium 8vo. 25*s.*

Britton. A Treatise upon the Common Law of England,
composed by order of King Edward I. The French Text carefully revised,
with an English Translation, Introduction, and Notes, by F. M. Nichols, M.A.
2 vols. 1865. Royal 8vo. 1*l.* 16*s.*

Clarendon's History of the Rebellion and Civil Wars in
England. 7 vols. 1839. 18mo. 1*l.* 1*s.*

Clarendon's History of the Rebellion and Civil Wars in
England. Also his Life, written by himself, in which is included a Con-
tinuation of his History of the Grand Rebellion. With copious Indexes.
In one volume, royal 8vo. 1842. 1*l.* 2*s.*

Clinton's Epitome of the Fasti Hellenici. 1851. 8vo. 6*s.* 6*d.*

—— *Epitome of the Fasti Romani.* 1854. 8vo. 7*s.*

Corpvs Poeticvm Boreale. The Poetry of the Old Northern
Tongue, from the Earliest Times to the Thirteenth Century. Edited, clas-
sified, and translated, with Introduction, Excursus, and Notes, by Gudbrand
Vigfússon, M.A., and F. York Powell, M.A. 2 vols. 1883. 8vo. 42*s.*

*Freeman (E. A.). History of the Norman Conquest of Eng-
land;* its Causes and Results. In Six Volumes. 8vo. 5*l.* 9*s.* 6*d.*

Freeman (E. A.). The Reign of William Rufus and the
Accession of Henry the First. 2 vols. 8vo. 1*l.* 16*s.*

Gascoigne's Theological Dictionary ("Liber Veritatum"):
Selected Passages, illustrating the condition of Church and State, 1403-1458.
With an Introduction by James E. Thorold Rogers, M.P. Small 4to. 10*s.* 6*d.*

Magna Carta, a careful Reprint. Edited by W. Stubbs, M.A.
1879. 4to. stitched, 1*s.*

Passio et Miracula Beati Olani. Edited from a Twelfth-
Century MS. in the Library of Corpus Christi College, Oxford, with an In-
troduction and Notes, by Frederick Metcalfe, M.A. Small 4to. stiff covers, 6*s.*

Protests of the Lords, including those which have been ex-
punged, from 1624 to 1874; with Historical Introductions. Edited by James
E. Thorold Rogers, M.A. 1875. 3 vols. 8vo. 2*l.* 2*s.*

Rogers (J. E. T.). History of Agriculture and Prices in
England, A.D. 1259-1793.
> Vols. I and II (1259-1400). 1866. 8vo. 2*l.* 2*s.*
> Vols. III and IV (1401-1582). 1882. 8vo. 2*l.* 10*s.*

Saxon Chronicles (Two of the) parallel, with Supplementary
Extracts from the Others. Edited, with Introduction, Notes, and a Glossarial Index, by J. Earle, M.A. 1865. 8vo. 16*s.*

Sturlunga Saga, including the Islendinga Saga of Lawman
Sturla Thordsson and other works. Edited by Dr. Gudbrand Vigfússon.
In 2 vols. 1878. 8vo. 2*l.* 2*s.*

York Plays. The Plays performed by the Crafts or Mysteries
of York on the day of Corpus Christi in the 14th, 15th, and 16th centuries.
Now first printed from the unique manuscript in the Library of Lord Ashburnham. Edited with Introduction and Glossary by Lucy Toulmin Smith. 8vo.
21*s.*

Statutes made for the University of Oxford, and for the Colleges
and Halls therein, by the University of Oxford Commissioners. 1882. 8vo.
12*s.* 6*d.*

Statuta Universitatis Oxoniensis. 1885. 8vo. 5*s.*

The Examination Statutes for the Degrees of B.A., B. Mus.,
B.C.L., and B.M. Revised to Trinity Term, 1885. 8vo. sewed, 1*s.*

The Student's Handbook to the University and Colleges of
Oxford. Extra fcap. 8vo. 2*s.* 6*d.*

The Oxford University Calendar for the year 1886. Crown
8vo. 4*s.* 6*d.*
The present Edition includes all Class Lists and other University distinctions for
the five years ending with 1885.

Also, supplementary to the above, price 5s. (pp. 606),

The Honours Register of the University of Oxford. A complete
Record of University Honours, Officers, Distinctions, and Class Lists; of the
Heads of Colleges, &c., &c., from the Thirteenth Century to 1883.

MATHEMATICS, PHYSICAL SCIENCE, &c.

Acland (H. W., M.D., F.R.S.). Synopsis of the Pathological
Series in the Oxford Museum. 1867. 8vo. 2*s.* 6*d.*

De Bary (Dr. A.) Comparative Anatomy of the Vegetative
Organs of the Phanerogams and Ferns. Translated and Annotated by F. O.
Bower, M.A., F.L.S., and D. H. Scott, M.A., Ph.D., F.L.S. With two
hundred and forty-one woodcuts and an Index. Royal 8vo., half morocco,
1*l.* 2*s.* 6*d.*

Müller (J.). On certain Variations in the Vocal Organs of
the Passeres that have hitherto escaped notice. Translated by F. J. Bell, B.A.,
and edited, with an Appendix, by A. H. Garrod, M.A., F.R.S. With Plates.
1878. 4to. paper covers, 7*s.* 6*d.*

Price (Bartholomew, M.A., F.R.S.). Treatise on Infinitesimal Calculus.
  Vol. I. Differential Calculus. Second Edition. 8vo. 14*s.* 6*d.*
  Vol. II. Integral Calculus, Calculus of Variations, and Differential Equations.
    Second Edition, 1865. 8vo. 18*s.*
  Vol. III. Statics, including Attractions; Dynamics of a Material Particle.
    Second Edition, 1868. 8vo. 16*s.*
  Vol. IV. Dynamics of Material Systems; together with a chapter on Theo-
    retical Dynamics, by W. F. Donkin, M.A., F.R.S. 1862. 8vo. 16*s.*

Pritchard (C., D.D., F.R.S.). Uranometria Nova Oxoniensis.
  A Photometric determination of the magnitudes of all Stars visible to the
  naked eye, from the Pole to ten degrees south of the Equator. 1885. Royal
  8vo. 8*s.* 6*d.*

—— *Astronomical Observations* made at the University
  Observatory, Oxford, under the direction of C. Pritchard, D.D. No. 1.
  1878. Royal 8vo. paper covers, 3*s.* 6*d.*

Rigaud's Correspondence of Scientific Men of the 17th Century,
  with Table of Contents by A. de Morgan, and Index by the Rev. J. Rigaud,
  M.A. 2 vols. 1841–1862. 8vo. 18*s.* 6*d.*

*Rolleston (George, M.D., F.R.S.). Scientific Papers and Ad-
  dresses.* Arranged and Edited by William Turner, M.B., F.R.S. With a
  Biographical Sketch by Edward Tylor, F.R.S. With Portrait, Plates, and
  Woodcuts. 2 vols. 8vo. 1*l.* 4*s.*

*Westwood (J. O., M.A., F.R.S.). Thesaurus Entomologicus
  Hopeianus,* or a Description of the rarest Insects in the Collection given to
  the University by the Rev. William Hope. With 40 Plates. 1874. Small
  folio, half morocco, 7*l.* 10*s.*

𝕿𝖍𝖊 𝕾𝖆𝖈𝖗𝖊𝖉 𝕭𝖔𝖔𝖐𝖘 𝖔𝖋 𝖙𝖍𝖊 𝕰𝖆𝖘𝖙.

TRANSLATED BY VARIOUS ORIENTAL SCHOLARS, AND EDITED BY
F. MAX MÜLLER.

[Demy 8vo. cloth.]

Vol. I. The Upanishads. Translated by F. Max Müller.
  Part I. The *Kh*ândogya-upanishad, The Talavakâra-upanishad, The Aitareya-
  âra*n*yaka, The Kaushîtaki-brâhma*n*a-upanishad, and The Vâ*g*asaneyi-sa*m*hitâ-
  upanishad. 10*s.* 6*d.*

Vol. II. The Sacred Laws of the Âryas, as taught in the
  Schools of Âpastamba, Gautama, Vâsish*th*a, and Baudhâyana. Translated by
  Prof. Georg Bühler. Part I. Âpastamba and Gautama. 10*s.* 6*d.*

Vol. III. The Sacred Books of China. The Texts of Con-
fucianism. Translated by James Legge. Part I. The Shû King, The Reli-
gious portions of the Shih King, and The Hsiâo King. 12*s.* 6*d.*

Vol. IV. The Zend-Avesta. Translated by James Darme-
steter. Part I. The Vendîdâd. 10*s.* 6*d.*

Vol. V. The Pahlavi Texts. Translated by E. W. West.
Part I. The Bundahi*s*, Bahman Ya*s*t, and Shâyast lâ-shâyast. 12*s.* 6*d.*

Vols. VI and IX. The Qur'ân. Parts I and II. Translated
by E. H. Palmer. 21*s.*

Vol. VII. The Institutes of Vish*n*u. Translated by Julius
Jolly. 10*s.* 6*d.*

Vol. VIII. The Bhagavadgîtâ, with The Sanatsugâtîya, and
The Anugîtâ. Translated by Kâshinâth Trimbak Telang. 10*s.* 6*d.*

Vol. X. The Dhammapada, translated from Pâli by F. Max
Müller; and The Sutta-Nipâta, translated from Pâli by V. Fausböll; being
Canonical Books of the Buddhists. 10*s.* 6*d.*

Vol. XI. Buddhist Suttas. Translated from Pâli by T. W.
Rhys Davids. 1. The Mahâparinibbâna Suttanta; 2. The Dhamma-*k*akka-
ppavattana Sutta; 3. The Tevig*g*a Suttanta; 4. The Akankheyya Sutta;
5. The *K*etokhila Sutta; 6. The Mahâ-sudassana Suttanta; 7. The Sabbâsava
Sutta. 10*s.* 6*d.*

Vol. XII. The *S*atapatha-Brâhma*n*a, according to the Text
of the Mâdhyandina School. Translated by Julius Eggeling. Part I.
Books I and II. 12*s.* 6*d.*

Vol. XIII. Vinaya Texts. Translated from the Pâli by
T. W. Rhys Davids and Hermann Oldenberg. Part I. The Pâtimokkha.
The Mahâvagga, I-IV. 10*s.* 6*d.*

Vol. XIV. The Sacred Laws of the Âryas, as taught in the
Schools of Apastamba, Gautama, Vâsish*th*a and Baudhâyana. Translated
by Georg Bühler. Part II. Vâsish*th*a and Baudhâyana. 10*s.* 6*d.*

Vol. XV. The Upanishads. Translated by F. Max Müller.
Part II. The Ka*th*a-upanishad, The Mu*nd*aka-upanishad, The Taittirîyaka-
upanishad, The B*ri*hadâra*n*yaka-upanishad, The *S*veta*s*vatara-upanishad, The
Pra*sn*a-upanishad, and The Maitrâya*n*a-Brâhma*n*a-upanishad. 10*s.* 6*d.*

Vol. XVI. The Sacred Books of China. The Texts of Con-
fucianism. Translated by James Legge. Part II. The Yî King. 10*s.* 6*d.*

Vol. XVII. Vinaya Texts. Translated from the Pâli by
T. W. Rhys Davids and Hermann Oldenberg. Part II. The Mahâvagga,
V-X. The *K*ullavagga, I-III. 10*s.* 6*d*

Vol. XVIII. Pahlavi Texts. Translated by E. W. West.
Part II. The Dâ*d*istân-î Dînîk and The Epistles of Mânû*s*kîhar. 12*s*. 6*d*.

Vol. XIX. The Fo-sho-hing-tsan-king. A Life of Buddha
by A*s*vaghosha Bodhisattva, translated from Sanskrit into Chinese by Dhar-
maraksha, A.D. 420, and from Chinese into English by Samuel Beal. 10*s*. 6*d*.

Vol. XX. Vinaya Texts. Translated from the Pâli by T. W.
Rhys Davids and Hermann Oldenberg. Part III. The *K*ullavagga, IV–XII.
10*s*. 6*d*.

Vol. XXI. The Saddharma-pu*nd*arîka; or, the Lotus of the
True Law. Translated by H. Kern. 12*s*. 6*d*.

Vol. XXII. *G*aina-Sûtras. Translated from Prâkrit by Her-
mann Jacobi. Part I. The Â*k*ârâṅga-Sûtra. The Kalpa-Sûtra. 10*s*. 6*d*.

Vol. XXIII. The Zend-Avesta. Translated by James Dar-
mesteter. Part II. The Sîrôzahs, Ya*s*ts, and Nyâyi*s*. 10*s*. 6*d*.

Vol. XXIV. Pahlavi Texts. Translated by E. W. West.
Part III. Dînâ-î Maînôg-î Khirad, *S*ikand-gûmânîk, and Sad-Dar. 10*s*. 6*d*.

Second Series.

Vol. XXVI. The *S*atapatha-Brâhma*n*a. Translated by
Julius Eggeling. Part II. 12*s*. 6*d*. *Just Published.*

Vols. XXVII and XXVIII. The Sacred Books of China.
The Texts of Confucianism. Translated by James Legge. Parts III and IV.
The Lî *K*î, or Collection of Treatises on the Rules of Propriety, or Ceremonial
Usages. 25*s*. *Just Published.*

The following Volumes are in the Press:—

Vol. XXV. Manu. Translated by Georg Bühler. Vol. I.

Vols. XXIX and XXX. The G*r*ihya-Sûtras, Rules of Vedic
Domestic Ceremonies. Translated by Hermann Oldenberg. Parts I and II.

Vol. XXXI. The Zend-Avesta. Part III. The Yasna,
Vispa*r*ad, Âfrînagân, and Gâhs. Translated by the Rev. L. H. Mills.

Vol. XXXII. Vedic Hymns. Translated by F. Max Müller.
Part I.

Vol. XXXIII. Nârada, and some Minor Law-books.
Translated by Julius Jolly. [*Preparing.*]

Vol. XXXIV. The Vedânta-Sûtras, with *S*aṅkara's Com-
mentary. Translated by G. Thibaut. [*Preparing.*]

*** *The Second Series will consist of Twenty-Four Volumes.*

Clarendon Press Series

I. ENGLISH.

A First Reading Book. By Marie Eichens of Berlin; and
edited by Anne J. Clough. Extra fcap. 8vo. stiff covers, 4*d.*

Oxford Reading Book, Part I. For Little Children. Extra
fcap. 8vo. stiff covers, 6*d.*

Oxford Reading Book, Part II. For Junior Classes. Extra
fcap. 8vo. stiff covers, 6*d.*

An Elementary English Grammar and Exercise Book. By
O. W. Tancock, M.A. Second Edition. Extra fcap. 8vo. 1*s.* 6*d.*

An English Grammar and Reading Book, for Lower Forms
in Classical Schools. By O. W. Tancock, M.A. Fourth Edition. Extra
fcap. 8vo. 3*s.* 6*d.*

Typical Selections from the best English Writers, with Intro-
ductory Notices. Second Edition. In Two Volumes. Extra fcap. 8vo.
3*s.* 6*d.* each.

    Vol. I. Latimer to Berkeley.   Vol. II. Pope to Macaulay.

Shairp (J. C., LL.D.). Aspects of Poetry; being Lectures
delivered at Oxford. Crown 8vo. 10*s.* 6*d.*

A Book for the Beginner in Anglo-Saxon. By John Earle,
M.A. Third Edition. Extra fcap. 8vo. 2*s.* 6*d.*

An Anglo-Saxon Reader. In Prose and Verse. With Gram-
matical Introduction, Notes, and Glossary. By Henry Sweet, M.A. Fourth
Edition, Revised and Enlarged. Extra fcap. 8vo. 8*s.* 6*d.*

An Anglo-Saxon Primer, with Grammar, Notes, and Glossary.
By the same Author. Second Edition. Extra fcap. 8vo. 2*s.* 6*d.*

Old English Reading Primers; edited by Henry Sweet, M.A.

    I. Selected Homilies of Ælfric. Extra fcap. 8vo., stiff covers, 1*s.* 6*d.*

    II. Extracts from Alfred's Orosius. Extra fcap. 8vo., stiff covers, 1*s.* 6*d.*

First Middle English Primer, with Grammar and Glossary.
By the same Author. Extra fcap. 8vo. 2*s.*

The Philology of the English Tongue. By J. Earle, M.A.
Third Edition. Extra fcap. 8vo. 7*s.* 6*d.*

A Handbook of Phonetics, including a Popular Exposition of
the Principles of Spelling Reform. By H. Sweet, M.A. Extra fcap. 8vo. 4*s.* 6*d.*

Elementarbuch des Gesprochenen Englisch. Grammatik,
Texte und Glossar. Von Henry Sweet. Extra fcap. 8vo., stiff covers, 2*s.* 6*d.*

The Ormulum; with the Notes and Glossary of Dr. R. M. White. Edited by R. Holt, M.A. 1878. 2 vols. Extra fcap. 8vo. 21s.

English Plant Names from the Tenth to the Fifteenth Century. By J. Earle, M.A. Small fcap. 8vo. 5s.

Specimens of Early English. A New and Revised Edition. With Introduction, Notes, and Glossarial Index. By R. Morris, LL.D.. and W. W. Skeat, M.A.

> Part I. From Old English Homilies to King Horn (A.D. 1150 to A.D. 1300). Second Edition. Extra fcap. 8vo. 9s.
>
> Part II. From Robert of Gloucester to Gower (A.D. 1298 to A.D. 1393). Second Edition. Extra fcap. 8vo. 7s. 6d.

Specimens of English Literature, from the 'Ploughmans Crede' to the 'Shepheardes Calender' (A.D. 1394 to A.D. 1579). With Introduction, Notes, and Glossarial Index. By W. W. Skeat, M.A. Extra fcap. 8vo. 7s. 6d.

The Vision of William concerning Piers the Plowman, by William Langland. Edited, with Notes, by W. W. Skeat, M.A. Third Edition. Extra fcap. 8vo. 4s. 6d.

Chaucer. I. *The Prologue to the Canterbury Tales;* the Knightes Tale; The Nonne Prestes Tale. Edited by R. Morris, Editor of Specimens of Early English, &c., &c. Fifty-first Thousand. Extra fcap. 8vo. 2s. 6d.

—— II. *The Prioresses Tale; Sir Thopas;* The Monkes Tale; The Clerkes Tale; The Squieres Tale, &c. Edited by W. W. Skeat, M.A. Second Edition. Extra fcap. 8vo. 4s. 6d.

—— III. *The Tale of the Man of Lawe;* The Pardoneres Tale; The Second Nonnes Tale; The Chanouns Yemannes Tale. By the same Editor. Second Edition. Extra fcap. 8vo. 4s. 6d.

Gamelyn, The Tale of. Edited with Notes, Glossary, &c., by W. W. Skeat, M.A. Extra fcap. 8vo. Stiff covers, 1s. 6d.

Spenser's Faery Queene. Books I and II. Designed chiefly for the use of Schools. With Introduction, Notes, and Glossary. By G. W. Kitchin, D.D.

> Book I. Tenth Edition. Extra fcap. 8vo. 2s. 6d.
>
> Book II. Sixth Edition. Extra fcap. 8vo. 2s. 6d.

Hooker. Ecclesiastical Polity, Book I. Edited by R. W. Church, M.A. Second Edition. Extra fcap. 8vo. 2s.

Marlowe and Greene. Marlowe's Tragical History of Dr. Faustus, and *Greene's Honourable History of Friar Bacon and Friar Bungay.* Edited by A. W. Ward, M.A. 1878. Extra fcap. 8vo. 5s. 6d. In white Parchment, 6s.

Marlowe. Edward II. With Introduction, Notes, &c. By O. W. Tancock, M.A. Extra fcap. 8vo. 3s.

Shakespeare. Select Plays. Edited by W. G. Clark, M.A., and W. Aldis Wright, M.A. Extra fcap. 8vo. stiff covers.

The Merchant of Venice. 1*s.*	Macbeth. 1*s. 6d.*
Richard the Second. 1*s. 6d.*	Hamlet. 2*s.*

Edited by W. Aldis Wright, M.A.

The Tempest. 1*s. 6d.*	Midsummer Night's Dream. 1*s. 6d.*
As You Like It. 1*s. 6d.*	Coriolanus. 2*s. 6d.*
Julius Cæsar. 2*s.*	Henry the Fifth. 2*s.*
Richard the Third. 2*s. 6d.*	Twelfth Night. 1*s. 6d.*
King Lear. 1*s. 6d.*	King John. 1*s. 6d.*

Shakespeare as a Dramatic Artist; a popular Illustration of the Principles of Scientific Criticism. By R. G. Moulton, M.A. Crown 8vo. 5*s.*

Bacon. I. *Advancement of Learning.* Edited by W. Aldis Wright, M.A. Second Edition. Extra fcap. 8vo. 4*s. 6d.*

—— II. *The Essays.* With Introduction and Notes. By S. H. Reynolds, M.A., late Fellow of Brasenose College. *In Preparation.*

Milton. I. *Areopagitica.* With Introduction and Notes. By John W. Hales, M.A. Third Edition. Extra fcap. 8vo. 3*s.*

—— II. *Poems.* Edited by R. C. Browne, M.A. 2 vols. Fifth Edition. Extra fcap. 8vo. 6*s. 6d.* Sold separately, Vol. I. 4*s.*; Vol. II. 3*s.*

In paper covers :—

Lycidas, 3*d.*　　L'Allegro, 3*d.*　　Il Penseroso, 4*d.*　　Comus, 6*d.*
Samson Agonistes, 6*d.*

—— III. *Samson Agonistes.* Edited with Introduction and Notes by John Churton Collins. Extra fcap. 8vo. stiff covers, 1*s.*

Clarendon. *History of the Rebellion.* *Book VI.* Edited with Introduction and Notes by T. Arnold, M.A. Extra fcap. 8vo. 4*s. 6d.*

Bunyan. I. *The Pilgrim's Progress, Grace Abounding, Relation of the Imprisonment of Mr. John Bunyan.* Edited, with Biographical Introduction and Notes, by E. Venables, M.A. 1879. Extra fcap. 8vo. 5*s.* In ornamental Parchment, 6*s.*

—— II. *Holy War, &c.* Edited by E. Venables, M.A. In the Press.

Dryden. Select Poems. Stanzas on the Death of Oliver Cromwell ; Astræa Redux ; Annus Mirabilis ; Absalom and Achitophel ; Religio Laici ; The Hind and the Panther. Edited by W. D. Christie, M.A. Second Edition. Extra fcap. 8vo. 3*s. 6d.*

Locke's Conduct of the Understanding. Edited, with Introduction, Notes, &c., by T. Fowler, M.A. Second Edition. Extra fcap. 8vo. 2*s.*

Addison. Selections from Papers in the Spectator. With Notes. By T. Arnold, M.A. Extra fcap. 8vo. 4*s. 6d.* In ornamental Parchment, 6*s.*

Steele. *Selections from the Tatler, Spectator, and Guardian.* Edited by Austin Dobson. Extra fcap. 8vo. 4*s.* 6*d.* In white Parchment, 7*s.* 6*d.*

Pope. With Introduction and Notes. By Mark Pattison, B.D.

—— I. *Essay on Man.* Extra fcap. 8vo. 1*s.* 6*d.*

—— II. *Satires and Epistles.* Extra fcap. 8vo. 2*s.*

Parnell. *The Hermit.* Paper covers, 2*d.*

Johnson. I. *Rasselas; Lives of Dryden and Pope.* Edited by Alfred Milnes, M.A. (London). Extra fcap. 8vo. 4*s.* 6*d.,* or *Lives of Dryden and Pope* only, stiff covers, 2*s.* 6*d.*

—— II. *Vanity of Human Wishes.* With Notes, by E. J. Payne, M.A. Paper covers, 4*d.*

Gray. *Selected Poems.* Edited by Edmund Gosse. Extra fcap. 8vo. Stiff covers, 1*s.* 6*d.* In white Parchment, 3*s.*

—— *Elegy and Ode on Eton College.* Paper covers, 2*d.*

Goldsmith. *The Deserted Village.* Paper covers, 2*d.*

Cowper. Edited, with Life, Introductions, and Notes, by H. T. Griffith, B.A.

—— I. *The Didactic Poems of* 1782, with Selections from the Minor Pieces, A.D. 1779–1783. Extra fcap. 8vo. 3*s.*

—— II. *The Task, with Tirocinium,* and Selections from the Minor Poems, A.D. 1784–1799. Second Edition. Extra fcap. 8vo. 3*s.*

Burke. *Select Works.* Edited, with Introduction and Notes, by E. J. Payne, M.A.

—— I. *Thoughts on the Present Discontents; the two Speeches on America.* Second Edition. Extra fcap. 8vo. 4*s.* 6*d.*

—— II. *Reflections on the French Revolution.* Second Edition. Extra fcap. 8vo. 5*s.*

—— III. *Four Letters on the Proposals for Peace with the Regicide Directory of France.* Second Edition. Extra fcap. 8vo. 5*s.*

Keats. *Hyperion,* Book I. With Notes by W. T. Arnold, B.A. Paper covers, 4*d.*

Byron. *Childe Harold.* Edited, with Introduction and Notes, by H. F. Tozer, M.A. Extra fcap. 8vo. 3*s.* 6*d.* In white Parchment, 5*s.*

Scott. *Lay of the Last Minstrel.* Edited with Preface and Notes by W. Minto. M.A. With Map. Extra fcap. 8vo. Stiff covers, 2*s.* Ornamental Parchment, 3*s.* 6*d.*

—— *Lay of the Last Minstrel.* Introduction and Canto I., with Preface and Notes, by the same Editor. 6*d.*

[9]   c

II. LATIN.

Rudimenta Latina. Comprising Accidence, and Exercises of a very Elementary Character, for the use of Beginners. By John Barrow Allen, M.A. Extra fcap. 8vo. 2s.

An Elementary Latin Grammar. By the same Author. Forty-second Thousand. Extra fcap. 8vo. 2s. 6d.

A First Latin Exercise Book. By the same Author. Fourth Edition. Extra fcap. 8vo. 2s. 6d.

A Second Latin Exercise Book. By the same Author. Extra fcap. 8vo. 3s. 6d.

Reddenda Minora, or Easy Passages, Latin and Greek, for Unseen Translation. For the use of Lower Forms. Composed and selected by C. S. Jerram, M.A. Extra fcap. 8vo. 1s. 6d.

Anglice Reddenda, or Easy Extracts, Latin and Greek, for Unseen Translation. By C. S. Jerram, M.A. Third Edition, Revised and Enlarged. Extra fcap. 8vo. 2s. 6d.

Passages for Translation into Latin. For the use of Passmen and others. Selected by J. Y. Sargent, M.A. Fifth Edition. Extra fcap. 8vo. 2s. 6d.

Exercises in Latin Prose Composition; with Introduction, Notes, and Passages of Graduated Difficulty for Translation into Latin. By G. G. Ramsay, M.A., LL.D. Second Edition. Extra fcap. 8vo. 4s. 6d.

Hints and Helps for Latin Elegiacs. By H. Lee-Warner, M.A., late Fellow of St. John's College, Cambridge, Assistant Master at Rugby School. Extra fcap. 8vo. 3s. 6d.

First Latin Reader. By T. J. Nunns, M.A. Third Edition. Extra fcap. 8vo. 2s.

Caesar. The Commentaries (for Schools). With Notes and Maps. By Charles E. Moberly, M.A.

    Part I. *The Gallic War.* Second Edition. Extra fcap. 8vo. 4s. 6d.

    Part II. *The Civil War.* Extra fcap. 8vo. 3s. 6d.

    The Civil War. Book I. Second Edition. Extra fcap. 8vo. 2s.

Cicero. Selection of interesting and descriptive passages. With Notes. By Henry Walford, M.A. In three Parts. Extra fcap. 8vo. 4s. 6d.

    Each Part separately, limp, 1s. 6d.

    Part I.   Anecdotes from Grecian and Roman History. Third Edition.

    Part II.   Omens and Dreams: Beauties of Nature. Third Edition.

    Part III. Rome's Rule of her Provinces. Third Edition.

Cicero. Selected Letters (for Schools). With Notes. By the late C. E. Prichard, M.A., and E. R. Bernard, M.A. Second Edition. Extra fcap. 8vo. 3s.

Cicero. *Select Orations* (for Schools). In Verrem I. De Imperio Gn. Pompeii. Pro Archia. Philippica IX. With Introduction and Notes by J. R. King, M.A. Second Edition. Extra fcap. 8vo. 2s. 6d.

Cornelius Nepos. With Notes. By Oscar Browning, M.A. Second Edition. Extra fcap. 8vo. 2s. 6d.

Livy. *Selections* (for Schools). With Notes and Maps. By H. Lee-Warner, M.A. Extra fcap. 8vo. In Parts limp, each 1s. 6d.

> Part I. The Caudine Disaster.
> Part II. Hannibal's Campaign in Italy.
> Part III. The Macedonian War.

Livy. Books V–VII. With Introduction and Notes. By A. R. Cluer, B.A. Extra fcap. 8vo. 3s. 6d.

Livy. Books XXI, XXII, and XXIII. With Introduction and Notes. By M. T. Tatham, M.A. Extra fcap. 8vo. 4s. 6d.

Ovid. Selections for the use of Schools. With Introductions and Notes, and an Appendix on the Roman Calendar. By W. Ramsay, M.A. Edited by G. G. Ramsay, M.A. Third Edition. Extra fcap. 8vo. 5s. 6d.

Ovid. *Tristia.* Book I. The Text revised, with an Introduction and Notes. By S. G. Owen, B.A. Extra fcap. 8vo. 3s. 6d.

Plautus. *The Trinummus.* With Notes and Introductions. Intended for the Higher Forms of Public Schools. By C. E. Freeman, M.A., and A. Sloman, M.A. Extra fcap. 8vo. 3s.

Pliny. *Selected Letters* (for Schools). With Notes. By the late C. E. Prichard, M.A., and E. R. Bernard, M.A. Second Edition. Extra fcap. 8vo. 3s.

Sallust. With Introduction and Notes. By W. W. Capes, M.A. Extra fcap. 8vo. 4s. 6d.

Tacitus. *The Annals.* Books I–IV. Edited, with Introduction and Notes for the use of Schools and Junior Students, by H. Furneaux, M.A. Extra fcap. 8vo. 5s.

Terence. *Andria.* With Notes and Introductions. By C. E. Freeman, M.A., and A. Sloman, M.A. Extra fcap. 8vo. 3s.

Virgil. With Introduction and Notes. By T. L. Papillon, M.A. Two vols. Crown 8vo. 10s. 6d. The Text separately, 4s. 6d.

Catulli Veronensis Liber. Iterum recognovit, apparatum criticum prolegomena appendices addidit, Robinson Ellis, A.M. 1878. Demy 8vo. 16s.

—— *A Commentary on Catullus.* By Robinson Ellis, M.A. 1876. Demy 8vo. 16s.

Catulli Veronensis Carmina Selecta, secundum recognitionem
Robinson Ellis, A.M.   Extra fcap. 8vo. 3*s.* 6*d.*

Cicero de Oratore.   With Introduction and Notes.   By A. S.
Wilkins, M.A.
     Book I. 1879. 8vo. 6*s.*   Book II. 1881. 8vo. 5*s.*

—— *Philippic Orations.*   With Notes.   By J. R. King, M.A.
Second Edition. 1879. 8vo. 10*s.* 6*d.*

—— *Select Letters.*   With English Introductions, Notes, and
Appendices. By Albert Watson, M.A. Third Edition. 1881. Demy 8vo. 18*s.*

—— *Select Letters.*   Text.   By the same Editor.   Second
Edition. Extra fcap. 8vo. 4*s.*

—— *pro Cluentio.*   With Introduction and Notes.   By W.
Ramsay, M.A. Edited by G. G. Ramsay, M.A. Second Edition. Extra fcap.
8vo. 3*s.* 6*d.*

Horace.   With a Commentary.   Volume I.   The Odes, Carmen
Seculare, and Epodes. By Edward C. Wickham, M.A. Second Edition.
1877. Demy 8vo. 12*s.*

—— A reprint of the above, in a size suitable for the use
of Schools. Extra fcap. 8vo. 5*s.* 6*d.*

Livy, Book I.   With Introduction, Historical Examination,
and Notes. By J. R. Seeley, M.A. Second Edition. 1881. 8vo. 6*s.*

Ovid.   P. Ovidii Nasonis Ibis.   Ex Novis Codicibus edidit,
Scholia Vetera Commentarium cum Prolegomenis Appendice Indice addidit,
R. Ellis, A.M. 8vo. 10*s.* 6*d.*

Persius.   The Satires.   With a Translation and Commentary.
By John Conington, M.A. Edited by Henry Nettleship, M.A. Second
Edition. 1874. 8vo. 7*s.* 6*d.*

Tacitus.   The Annals.   Books I–VI.   Edited, with Intro-
duction and Notes, by H. Furneaux, M.A. 8vo. 18*s.*

Nettleship (H., M.A.).   Lectures and Essays on Subjects con-
nected with Latin Scholarship and Literature. Crown 8vo. 7*s.* 6*d.*

—— *The Roman Satura :* its original form in connection with
its literary development. 8vo. sewed, 1*s.*

—— *Ancient Lives of Vergil.*   With an Essay on the Poems
of Vergil, in connection with his Life and Times. 8vo. sewed, 2*s.*

Papillon (T. L., M.A.).   A Manual of Comparative Philology.
Third Edition, Revised and Corrected. 1882. Crown 8vo. 6*s.*

Pinder (North, M.A.).   Selections from the less known Latin
Poets. 1869. 8vo. 15*s.*

Sellar (W. Y., M.A.). *Roman Poets of the Augustan Age.*
VIRGIL. New Edition. 1883. Crown 8vo. 9s.

—— *Roman Poets of the Republic.* New Edition, Revised
and Enlarged. 1881. 8vo. 14s.

Wordsworth (J., M.A.). *Fragments and Specimens of Early*
Latin. With Introductions and Notes. 1874. 8vo. 18s.

III. GREEK.

A Greek Primer, for the use of beginners in that Language.
By the Right Rev. Charles Wordsworth, D.C.L. Seventh Edition. Extra fcap.
8vo. 1s. 6d.

Graecae Grammaticae Rudimenta in usum Scholarum. Auc-
tore Carolo Wordsworth, D.C.L. Nineteenth Edition, 1882. 12mo. 4s.

A Greek-English Lexicon, abridged from Liddell and Scott's
4to. edition, chiefly for the use of Schools. Twenty-first Edition. 1884.
Square 12mo. 7s. 6d.

Greek Verbs, Irregular and Defective; their forms, meaning,
and quantity; embracing all the Tenses used by Greek writers, with references
to the passages in which they are found. By W. Veitch. Fourth Edition.
Crown 8vo. 10s. 6d.

The Elements of Greek Accentuation (for Schools): abridged
from his larger work by H. W. Chandler, M.A. Extra fcap. 8vo. 2s. 6d.

A SERIES OF GRADUATED GREEK READERS:—

First Greek Reader. By W. G. Rushbrooke, M.L. Second
Edition. Extra fcap. 8vo. 2s. 6d.

Second Greek Reader. By A. M. Bell, M.A. Extra fcap.
8vo. 3s. 6d.

Fourth Greek Reader; being Specimens of Greek Dialects.
With Introductions and Notes. By W. W. Merry, M.A. Extra fcap. 8vo.
4s. 6d.

Fifth Greek Reader. Selections from Greek Epic and
Dramatic Poetry, with Introductions and Notes. By Evelyn Abbott, M.A.
Extra fcap. 8vo. 4s. 6d.

The Golden Treasury of Ancient Greek Poetry: being a Col-
lection of the finest passages in the Greek Classic Poets, with Introductory
Notices and Notes. By R. S. Wright, M.A. Extra fcap. 8vo. 8s. 6d.

A Golden Treasury of Greek Prose, being a Collection of the
finest passages in the principal Greek Prose Writers, with Introductory Notices
and Notes. By R. S. Wright, M.A., and J. E. L. Shadwell, M.A. Extra fcap.
8vo. 4s. 6d.

Aeschylus. Prometheus Bound (for Schools). With Introduction and Notes, by A. O. Prickard, M.A. Second Edition. Extra fcap. 8vo. 2s.

—— *Agamemnon.* With Introduction and Notes, by Arthur Sidgwick, M.A. Second Edition. Extra fcap. 8vo. 3s.

—— *Choephoroi.* With Introduction and Notes by the same Editor. Extra fcap. 8vo. 3s.

Aristophanes. In Single Plays. Edited, with English Notes, Introductions, &c., by W. W. Merry, M.A. Extra fcap. 8vo.

    I. The Clouds, Second Edition, 2s.

    II. The Acharnians, 2s.   III. The Frogs, 2s.

Cebes. Tabula. With Introduction and Notes. By C. S. Jerram, M.A. Extra fcap. 8vo. 2s. 6d.

Euripides. Alcestis (for Schools). By C. S. Jerram, M.A. Extra fcap. 8vo. 2s. 6d.

—— *Helena.* Edited, with Introduction, Notes, and Critical Appendix, for Upper and Middle Forms. By C. S. Jerram, M.A. Extra fcap. 8vo. 3s.

—— *Iphigenia in Tauris.* Edited, with Introduction, Notes, and Critical Appendix, for Upper and Middle Forms. By C. S. Jerram, M.A. Extra fcap. 8vo. cloth, 3s.

Herodotus, Selections from. Edited, with Introduction, Notes, and a Map, by W. W. Merry, M.A. Extra fcap. 8vo. 2s. 6d.

Homer. Odyssey, Books I–XII (for Schools). By W. W. Merry, M.A. Twenty-seventh Thousand. Extra fcap. 8vo. 4s. 6d.

    Book II, separately, 1s. 6d.

—— *Odyssey,* Books XIII–XXIV (for Schools). By the same Editor. Second Edition. Extra fcap. 8vo. 5s.

—— *Iliad,* Book I (for Schools). By D. B. Monro, M.A. Second Edition. Extra fcap. 8vo. 2s.

—— *Iliad,* Books I–XII (for Schools). With an Introduction, a brief Homeric Grammar, and Notes. By D. B. Monro, M.A. Extra fcap. 8vo. 6s.

—— *Iliad,* Books VI and XXI. With Introduction and Notes. By Herbert Hailstone, M.A. Extra fcap. 8vo. 1s. 6d. each.

Lucian. Vera Historia (for Schools). By C. S. Jerram, M.A. Second Edition. Extra fcap. 8vo. 1s. 6d.

Plato. Selections from the Dialogues [including the whole of the *Apology* and *Crito*]. With Introduction and Notes by John Purves, M.A., and a Preface by the Rev. B. Jowett, M.A. Extra fcap. 8vo. 6s. 6d.

Sophocles. For the use of Schools. Edited with Introductions and English Notes. By Lewis Campbell, M.A., and Evelyn Abbott, M.A. *New and Revised Edition.* 2 Vols. Extra fcap. 8vo. 10s. 6d.
Sold separately, Vol. I, Text, 4s. 6d.; Vol. II, Explanatory Notes, 6s.

Sophocles. In Single Plays, with English Notes, &c. By Lewis Campbell, M.A., and Evelyn Abbott, M.A. Extra fcap. 8vo. limp.

    Oedipus Tyrannus, Philoctetes. New and Revised Edition, 2s. each.
    Oedipus Coloneus,   Antigone, 1s. 9d. each.
    Ajax,   Electra,   Trachiniae, 2s. each.

—— *Oedipus Rex:* Dindorf's Text, with Notes by the present Bishop of St. David's. Extra fcap. 8vo. limp, 1s. 6d.

Theocritus (for Schools). With Notes. By H. Kynaston, D.D. (late Snow). Third Edition. Extra fcap. 8vo. 4s. 6d.

Xenophon. Easy Selections. (for Junior Classes). With a Vocabulary, Notes, and Map. By J. S. Phillpotts, B.C.L., and C. S. Jerram, M.A. Third Edition. Extra fcap. 8vo. 3s. 6d.

—— *Selections* (for Schools). With Notes and Maps. By J. S. Phillpotts, B.C.L. Fourth Edition. Extra fcap. 8vo. 3s. 6d.

—— *Anabasis,* Book I. Edited for the use of Junior Classes and Private Students. With Introduction, Notes, and Index. By J. Marshall, M.A., Rector of the Royal High School, Edinburgh. Extra fcap. 8vo. 2s. 6d.

—— *Anabasis,* Book II. With Notes and Map. By C. S. Jerram, M.A. Extra fcap. 8vo. 2s.

—— *Cyropaedia,* Books IV and V. With Introduction and Notes by C. Bigg, D.D. Extra fcap. 8vo. 2s. 6d.

Aristotle's Politics. By W. L. Newman, M.A. [*In the Press.*]

Aristotelian Studies. I. On the Structure of the Seventh Book of the Nicomachean Ethics. By J. C. Wilson, M.A. 8vo. stiff, 5s.

Aristotelis Ethica Nicomachea, ex recensione Immanuelis Bekkeri. Crown 8vo. 5s.

Demosthenes and Aeschines. The Orations of Demosthenes and Aeschines on the Crown. With Introductory Essays and Notes. By G. A. Simcox, M.A., and W. H. Simcox, M.A. 1872. 8vo. 12s.

Hicks (E. L., M.A.). A Manual of Greek Historical Inscriptions. Demy 8vo. 10s. 6d.

Homer. Odyssey, Books I–XII. Edited with English Notes, Appendices, etc. By W. W. Merry, M.A., and the late James Riddell, M.A. 1886. Second Edition. Demy 8vo. 16s.

Homer. A Grammar of the Homeric Dialect. By D. B. Monro, M.A. Demy 8vo. 10s. 6d.

Sophocles. The Plays and Fragments. With English Notes and Introductions, by Lewis Campbell, M.A. 2 vols.

    Vol. I. Oedipus Tyrannus. Oedipus Coloneus. Antigone. Second Edition. 1879. 8vo. 16s.

    Vol. II. Ajax. Electra. Trachiniae. Philoctetes. Fragments. 1881. 8vo. 16s.

IV. FRENCH AND ITALIAN.

Brachet's Etymological Dictionary of the French Language, with a Preface on the Principles of French Etymology. Translated into English by G. W. Kitchin, D.D. Third Edition. Crown 8vo. 7s. 6d.

—— *Historical Grammar of the French Language.* Translated into English by G. W. Kitchin, D.D. Fourth Edition. Extra fcap. 8vo. 3s. 6d.

Works by GEORGE SAINTSBURY, M.A.

Primer of French Literature. Extra fcap. 8vo. 2s.

Short History of French Literature. Crown 8vo. 10s. 6d.

Specimens of French Literature, from Villon to Hugo. Crown 8vo. 9s.

Corneille's Horace. Edited, with Introduction and Notes, by George Saintsbury, M.A. Extra fcap. 8vo. 2s. 6d.

Molière's Les Précieuses Ridicules. Edited, with Introduction and Notes, by Andrew Lang, M.A. Extra fcap. 8vo. 1s. 6d.

Beaumarchais' Le Barbier de Séville. Edited, with Introduction and Notes, by Austin Dobson. Extra fcap. 8vo. 2s. 6d.

Voltaire's Mérope. Edited, with Introduction and Notes, by George Saintsbury. Extra fcap. 8vo. cloth, 2s.

Musset's On ne badine pas avec l'Amour, and *Fantasio.* Edited, with Prolegomena, Notes, etc., by Walter Herries Pollock. Extra fcap. 8vo. 2s.

Sainte-Beuve. *Selections from the Causeries du Lundi.* Edited by George Saintsbury. Extra fcap. 8vo. 2s.

Quinet's Lettres à sa Mère. Selected and edited by George Saintsbury. Extra fcap. 8vo. 2s.

L'Éloquence de la Chaire et de la Tribune Françaises. Edited by Paul Blouët, B.A. (Univ. Gallic.). Vol. I. French Sacred Oratory Extra fcap. 8vo. 2s. 6d.

Edited by GUSTAVE MASSON, B.A.

Corneille's Cinna. With Notes, Glossary, etc. Extra fcap. 8vo. cloth, 2s. Stiff covers, 1s. 6d.

Louis XIV and his Contemporaries; as described in Extracts from the best Memoirs of the Seventeenth Century. With English Notes, Genealogical Tables, &c. Extra fcap. 8vo. 2s. 6d.

Maistre, Xavier de. Voyage autour de ma Chambre. Ourika, by *Madame de Duras;* La Dot de Suzette, by *Fiévée;* Les Jumeaux de l'Hôtel Corneille, by *Edmond About;* Mésaventures d'un Écolier, by *Rodolphe Töpffer.* Second Edition. Extra fcap. 8vo. 2s. 6d.

Molière's Les Fourberies de Scapin, and *Racine's Athalie.* With Voltaire's Life of Molière. Extra fcap. 8vo. 2s. 6d.

Molière's Les Fourberies de Scapin. With Voltaire's Life of Molière. Extra fcap. 8vo. stiff covers, 1s. 6d.

Molière's Les Femmes Savantes. With Notes, Glossary, etc. Extra fcap. 8vo. cloth, 2s. Stiff covers, 1s. 6d.

Racine's Andromaque, and *Corneille's Le Menteur.* With Louis Racine's Life of his Father. Extra fcap. 8vo. 2s. 6d.

Regnard's Le Joueur, and *Brueys and Palaprat's Le Grondeur.* Extra fcap. 8vo. 2s. 6d.

Sévigné, Madame de, and her chief Contemporaries, Selections from the Correspondence of. Intended more especially for Girls' Schools. Extra fcap. 8vo. 3s.

Dante. Selections from the Inferno. With Introduction and Notes. By H. B. Cotterill, B.A. Extra fcap. 8vo. 4s. 6d.

Tasso. La Gerusalemme Liberata. Cantos i, ii. With Introduction and Notes. By the same Editor. Extra fcap. 8vo. 2s. 6d.

V. GERMAN.

Scherer (W.). A History of German Literature. Translated from the Third German Edition by Mrs. F. Conybeare. Edited by F. Max Müller. 2 vols. 8vo. 21s.

GERMAN COURSE. By HERMANN LANGE.

The Germans at Home; a Practical Introduction to German Conversation, with an Appendix containing the Essentials of German Grammar. Second Edition. 8vo. 2s. 6d.

The German Manual; a German Grammar, Reading Book, and a Handbook of German Conversation. 8vo. 7s. 6d.

Grammar of the German Language. 8vo. 3*s.* 6*d.*

> This 'Grammar' is a reprint of the Grammar contained in 'The German Manual,' and, in this separate form, is intended for the use of Students who wish to make themselves acquainted with German Grammar chiefly for the purpose of being able to read German books.

German Composition ; A Theoretical and Practical Guide to the Art of Translating English Prose into German. 8vo. 4*s.* 6*d.*

Lessing's Laokoon. With Introduction, English Notes, etc. By A. Hamann, Phil. Doc., M.A. Extra fcap. 8vo. 4*s.* 6*d.*

Schiller's Wilhelm Tell. Translated into English Verse by E. Massie, M.A. Extra fcap. 8vo. 5*s.*

Also, Edited by C. A. BUCHHEIM, Phil. Doc.

Goethe's Egmont. With a Life of Goethe, &c. Third Edition. Extra fcap. 8vo. 3*s.*

—— *Iphigenie auf Tauris.* A Drama. With a Critical Introduction and Notes. Second Edition. Extra fcap. 8vo. 3*s.*

Heine's Prosa, being Selections from his Prose Works. With English Notes, etc. Extra fcap. 8vo. 4*s.* 6*d.*

Heine's Harzreise. With a Life of Heine, a Descriptive Sketch of the Harz, and an Index. Extra fcap. 8vo. *cloth,* 2*s.* 6*d.,* stiff cover, 1*s.* 6*d.*

Lessing's Minna von Barnhelm. A Comedy. With a Life of Lessing, Critical Analysis, Complete Commentary, &c. Fourth Edition. Extra fcap. 8vo. 3*s.* 6*d.*

—— *Nathan der Weise.* With Introduction, Notes, etc. Extra fcap. 8vo. 4*s.* 6*d.*

Schiller's Historische Skizzen ; Egmont's Leben und Tod, and *Belagerung von Antwerpen.* Third Edition, Revised and Enlarged. With a Map. Extra fcap. 8vo. 2*s.* 6*d.*

—— *Wilhelm Tell.* With a Life of Schiller; an historical and critical Introduction, Arguments, and a complete Commentary, and Map. Sixth Edition. Extra fcap. 8vo. 3*s.* 6*d.*

—— *Wilhelm Tell.* School Edition. With Map. Extra fcap. 8vo. 2*s.*

Modern German Reader. A Graduated Collection of Extracts in Prose and Poetry from Modern German writers :—

Part I. With English Notes, a Grammatical Appendix, and a complete Vocabulary. Fourth Edition. Extra fcap. 8vo. 2*s.* 6*d.*

Part II. With English Notes and an Index. Extra fcap. 8vo. 2*s.* 6*d.*

Part III in Preparation.

VI. MATHEMATICS, PHYSICAL SCIENCE, &c.

By LEWIS HENSLEY, M.A.

Figures made Easy: a first Arithmetic Book. Crown 8vo. 6*d.*

Answers to the Examples in Figures made Easy, together with two thousand additional Examples, with Answers. Crown 8vo. 1*s.*

The Scholar's Arithmetic: with Answers. Crown 8vo. 4*s.* 6*d.*

The Scholar's Algebra. Crown 8vo. 4*s.* 6*d.*

Baynes (R. E., M.A.). Lessons on Thermodynamics. 1878. Crown 8vo. 7*s.* 6*d.*

Chambers (G. F., F.R.A.S.). A Handbook of Descriptive Astronomy. Third Edition. 1877. Demy 8vo. 28*s.*

Clarke (Col. A. R., C.B., R.E.). Geodesy. 1880. 8vo. 12*s.* 6*d.*

Cremona (Luigi). Elements of Projective Geometry. Translated by C. Leudesdorf, M.A.. 8vo. 12*s.* 6*d.*

Donkin. Acoustics. Second Edition. Crown 8vo. 7*s.* 6*d.*

Euclid Revised. Containing the Essentials of the Elements of Plane Geometry as given by Euclid in his first Six Books. Edited by R. C. J. Nixon, M.A. Crown 8vo. 7*s.* 6*d.*

—— Books I–IV. By the same Editor. Crown 8vo. 3*s.* 6*d.*

Galton (Douglas, C.B., F.R.S.). The Construction of Healthy Dwellings. Demy 8vo. 10*s.* 6*d.*

Hamilton (Sir R. G. C.), and J. Ball. Book-keeping. New and enlarged Edition. Extra fcap. 8vo. limp cloth, 2*s.*

Harcourt (A. G. Vernon, M.A.), and H. G. Madan, M.A. Exercises in Practical Chemistry. Vol. I. Elementary Exercises. Third Edition. Crown 8vo. 9*s.*

Maclaren (Archibald). A System of Physical Education: Theoretical and Practical. Extra fcap. 8vo. 7*s.* 6*d.*

Madan (H. G., M.A.). Tables of Qualitative Analysis. Large 4to. paper, 4*s.* 6*d.*

Maxwell (J. Clerk, M.A., F.R.S.). A Treatise on Electricity and Magnetism. Second Edition. 2 vols. Demy 8vo. 1*l.* 11*s.* 6*d.*

—— *An Elementary Treatise on Electricity.* Edited by William Garnett, M.A. Demy 8vo. 7*s.* 6*d.*

Minchin (G. M., M.A.). A Treatise on Statics with Applications to Physics. Third Edition, Corrected and Enlarged.
Vol. I. *Equilibrium of Coplanar Forces.* 8vo. 9*s.*
Vol. II. *Statics.* 8vo. 16*s.* *Just Published.*

Minchin (*G. M., M.A.*).   *Uniplanar Kinematics of Solids and Fluids.*   Crown 8vo. 7s. 6d.

Phillips (*John, M.A., F.R.S.*).   *Geology of Oxford and the Valley of the Thames.*   1871. 8vo. 21s.

—— *Vesuvius.* 1869.   Crown 8vo. 10s. 6d.

Prestwich (*Joseph, M.A., F.R.S.*).   *Geology, Chemical, Physical, and Stratigraphical.*   Vol. I.   Chemical and Physical.   Royal 8vo.   25s.

Rolleston's Forms of Animal Life.   Illustrated by Descriptions and Drawings of Dissections.   New Edition in the Press.

Smyth.   A Cycle of Celestial Objects.   Observed, Reduced, and Discussed by Admiral W. H. Smyth, R. N.   Revised, condensed, and greatly enlarged by G. F. Chambers, F.R.A.S.   1881. 8vo. *Price reduced to* 12s.

Stewart (*Balfour, LL.D., F.R.S.*).   *A Treatise on Heat*, with numerous Woodcuts and Diagrams.   Fourth Edition.   Extra fcap. 8vo. 7s.6d.

Vernon-Harcourt (*L. F., M.A.*).   *A Treatise on Rivers and Canals,* relating to the Control and Improvement of Rivers, and the Design, Construction, and Development of Canals.   2 vols. (Vol. I, Text.   Vol. II, Plates.)   8vo. 21s.

—— *Harbours and Docks;* their Physical Features, History, Construction, Equipment, and Maintenance; with Statistics as to their Commercial Development.   2 vols. 8vo. 25s.

Watson (*H. W., M.A.*).   *A Treatise on the Kinetic Theory of Gases.*   1876. 8vo. 3s. 6d.

Watson (*H. W., D. Sc., F.R.S.*), *and S. H. Burbury, M.A.*

    I. *A Treatise on the Application of Generalised Coordinates to the Kinetics of a Material System.*   1879. 8vo. 6s.

    II. *The Mathematical Theory of Electricity and Magnetism.*   Vol. I. Electrostatics.   8vo. 10s. 6d.

Williamson (*A. W., Phil. Doc., F.R.S.*).   *Chemistry for Students.*   A new Edition, with Solutions.   1873. Extra fcap. 8vo. 8s. 6d.

VII. HISTORY.

Bluntschli (*J. K.*).   *The Theory of the State.*   By J. K. Bluntschli, late Professor of Political Sciences in the University of Heidelberg.   Authorised English Translation from the Sixth German Edition.   Demy 8vo. half bound, 12s. 6d.

Finlay (*George, LL.D.*).   *A History of Greece* from its Conquest by the Romans to the present time, B.C. 146 to A.D. 1864.   A new Edition, revised throughout, and in part re-written, with considerable additions, by the Author, and edited by H. F. Tozer, M.A. 7 vols. 8vo. 3l. 10s.

Fortescue (Sir John, Kt.). The Governance of England:
otherwise called The Difference between an Absolute and a Limited Monarchy. A Revised Text. Edited, with Introduction, Notes, and Appendices, by Charles Plummer, M.A. 8vo. half bound, 12s. 6d.

Freeman (E.A., D.C.L.). A Short History of the Norman
Conquest of England. Second Edition. Extra fcap. 8vo. 2s. 6d.

—— *A History of Greece.* In preparation.

George (H. B., M.A.). Genealogical Tables illustrative of Modern
History. Second Edition, Revised and Enlarged. Small 4to. 12s.

Hodgkin (T.). Italy and her Invaders. Illustrated with
Plates and Maps. Vols. I. and II., A.D. 376–476. 8vo. 1l. 12s.
  Vols. III. and IV. *The Ostrogothic Invasion,* and *The Imperial Restoration.*
8vo. 1l. 16s.

Kitchin (G. W., D.D.). A History of France. With numerous
Maps, Plans, and Tables. In Three Volumes. *Second Edition.* Crown 8vo.
each 10s. 6d.
    Vol. 1. Down to the Year 1453.
    Vol. 2. From 1453–1624.   Vol. 3. From 1624–1793.

Payne (E. J., M.A.). A History of the United States of
America. In the Press.

Ranke (L. von). A History of England, principally in the
Seventeenth Century. Translated by Resident Members of the University of
Oxford, under the superintendence of G. W. Kitchin, D.D., and C. W. Boase,
M.A. 1875. 6 vols. 8vo. 3l. 3s.

Rawlinson (George, M.A.). A Manual of Ancient History.
Second Edition. Demy 8vo. 14s.

Select Charters and other Illustrations of English Constitutional
History, from the Earliest Times to the Reign of Edward I. Arranged and
edited by W. Stubbs, D.D. Fifth Edition. 1883. Crown 8vo. 8s. 6d.

Stubbs (W., D.D.). The Constitutional History of England,
in its Origin and Development. Library Edition. 3 vols. demy 8vo. 2l. 8s.
    Also in 3 vols. crown 8vo. price 12s. each.

—— *Seventeen Lectures on the Study of Mediæval and*
Modern History and Kindred Subjects. 8vo. half bound, 10s. 6d. *Just*
Published.

Wellesley. A Selection from the Despatches, Treaties, and
other Papers of the Marquess Wellesley, K.G., during his Government
of India. Edited by S. J. Owen, M.A. 1877. 8vo. 1l. 4s.

Wellington. A Selection from the Despatches, Treaties, and
other Papers relating to India of Field-Marshal the Duke of Wellington, K.G.
Edited by S. J. Owen, M.A. 1880. 8vo. 24s.

VIII. LAW.

Alberici Gentilis, I.C.D., I.C., De Iure Belli Libri Tres.
Edidit T. E. Holland, I.C.D. 1877. Small 4to. half morocco, 21*s.*

*Anson (Sir William R., Bart., D.C.L.). Principles of the
English Law of Contract, and of Agency in its Relation to Contract.* Fourth
Edition. Demy 8vo. 10*s.* 6*d.*

—— *The Law and Custom of the Constitution.* Part I.
Parliament. Demy 8vo. 10*s.* 6*d.*

*Bentham (Jeremy). An Introduction to the Principles of
Morals and Legislation.* Crown 8vo. 6*s.* 6*d.*

*Digby (Kenelm E., M.A.). An Introduction to the History of
the Law of Real Property.* Third Edition. Demy 8vo. 10*s.* 6*d.*

Gaii Institutionum Juris Civilis Commentarii Quattuor; or,
Elements of Roman Law by Gaius. With a Translation and Commentary
by Edward Poste, M.A. Second Edition. 1875. 8vo. 18*s.*

Hall (W. E., M.A.). International Law. Second Ed. 8vo. 21*s.*

Holland (T. E., D.C.L.). The Elements of Jurisprudence.
Third Edition. Demy 8vo. 10*s.* 6*d.*

—— *The European Concert in the Eastern Question,* a Col-
lection of Treaties and other Public Acts. Edited, with Introductions and
Notes, by Thomas Erskine Holland, D.C.L. 8vo. 12*s.* 6*d.*

Imperatoris Iustiniani Institutionum Libri Quattuor; with
Introductions, Commentary, Excursus and Translation. By J. B. Moyle, B.C.L.,
M.A. 2 vols. Demy 8vo. 21*s.*

Justinian, The Institutes of, edited as a recension of the
Institutes of Gaius, by Thomas Erskine Holland, D.C.L. Second Edition.
1881. Extra fcap. 8vo. 5*s.*

Justinian, Select Titles from the Digest of. By T. E. Holland,
D.C.L., and C. L. Shadwell, B.C.L. 8vo. 14*s.*

Also sold in Parts, in paper covers, as follows :—
Part I. Introductory Titles. 2*s.* 6*d.*   Part II. Family Law. 1*s.*
Part III. Property Law. 2*s.* 6*d.*   Part IV. Law of Obligations (No. 1). 3*s.* 6*d.*
Part IV. Law of Obligations (No. 2). 4*s.* 6*d.*

Lex Aquilia. The Roman Law of Damage to Property:
being a Commentary on the Title of the Digest 'Ad Legem Aquiliam' (ix. 2).
With an Introduction to the Study of the Corpus Iuris Civilis. By Erwin
Grueber, Dr. Jur., M.A. Demy 8vo. 10*s.* 6*d.* *Just Published.*

Markby (W., D.C.L.). Elements of Law considered with refer-
ence to Principles of General Jurisprudence. Third Edition. Demy 8vo. 12*s.*6*d.*

Twiss (Sir Travers, D.C.L.). The Law of Nations considered
as Independent Political Communities.
Part I. On the Rights and Duties of Nations in time of Peace. A new Edition,
Revised and Enlarged. 1884. Demy 8vo. 15*s.*
Part II. On the Rights and Duties of Nations in Time of War. Second Edition
Revised. 1875. Demy 8vo. 21*s.*

IX. MENTAL AND MORAL PHILOSOPHY, &c.

Bacon's Novum Organum. Edited, with English Notes, by
G. W. Kitchin, D.D. 1855. 8vo. 9s. 6d.

—— Translated by G. W. Kitchin, D.D. 1855. 8vo. 9s. 6d.

Berkeley. The Works of George Berkeley, D.D., formerly
Bishop of Cloyne; including many of his writings hitherto unpublished.
With Prefaces, Annotations, and an Account of his Life and Philosophy,
by Alexander Campbell Fraser, M.A. 4 vols. 1871. 8vo. 2l. 18s.
The Life, Letters, &c. 1 vol. 16s.

—— *Selections from.* With an Introduction and Notes.
For the use of Students in the Universities. By Alexander Campbell Fraser,
LL.D. Second Edition. Crown 8vo. 7s. 6d.

Danson (J. T.). The Wealth of Households. Crown 8vo. 5s.

Fowler (T., M.A.). The Elements of Deductive Logic, designed
mainly for the use of Junior Students in the Universities. Eighth Edition,
with a Collection of Examples. Extra fcap. 8vo. 3s. 6d.

—— *The Elements of Inductive Logic,* designed mainly for
the use of Students in the Universities. Fourth Edition. Extra fcap. 8vo. 6s.

Edited by T. FOWLER, M.A.

Bacon. Novum Organum. With Introduction, Notes, &c.
1878. 8vo. 14s.

Locke's Conduct of the Understanding. Second Edition.
Extra fcap. 8vo. 2s.

———

Green (T. H., M.A.). Prolegomena to Ethics. Edited by
A. C. Bradley, M.A. Demy 8vo. 12s. 6d.

Hegel. The Logic of Hegel; translated from the Encyclo-
paedia of the Philosophical Sciences. With Prolegomena by William
Wallace, M.A. 1874. 8vo. 14s.

Lotze's Logic, in Three Books; of Thought, of Investigation,
and of Knowledge. English Translation; Edited by B. Bosanquet, M.A.,
Fellow of University College, Oxford. 8vo. *cloth,* 12s. 6d.

—— *Metaphysic,* in Three Books; Ontology, Cosmology,
and Psychology. English Translation; Edited by B. Bosanquet, M.A.
8vo. *cloth,* 12s. 6d.

Martineau (James, D.D.). Types of Ethical Theory. 2 vols.
8vo. 24s.

Rogers (J. E. Thorold, M.A.). A Manual of Political Economy,
for the use of Schools. Third Edition. Extra fcap. 8vo. 4s. 6d.

Smith's Wealth of Nations. A new Edition, with Notes, by
J. E. Thorold Rogers. M.A. 2 vols. 8vo. 1880. 21s.

*Wilson (J. M., B.D.), and T. Fowler, M.A. The Principles
of Morals* (Introductory Chapters). 8vo. 3s. 6d. *Just Published.*

X. ART, &c.

Hullah (John). The Cultivation of the Speaking Voice.
Second Edition. Extra fcap. 8vo. 2s. 6d.

Ouseley (Sir F. A. Gore, Bart.). A Treatise on Harmony.
Third Edition. 4to. 10s.

—— *A Treatise on Counterpoint, Canon, and Fugue*, based
upon that of Cherubini. Second Edition. 4to. 16s.

—— *A Treatise on Musical Form and General Composition.*
Second Edition. 4to. 10s.

Robinson (J. C., F.S.A.). A Critical Account of the Drawings
by *Michel Angelo and Raffaello in the University Galleries, Oxford.* 1870.
Crown 8vo. 4s.

Ruskin (John, M.A.). A Course of Lectures on Art, delivered
before the University of Oxford in Hilary Term, 1870. 8vo. 6s.

Troutbeck (J., M.A.) and R. F. Dale, M.A. A Music Primer
(for Schools). Second Edition. Crown 8vo. 1s. 6d.

Tyrwhitt (R. St. J., M.A.). A Handbook of Pictorial Art.
With coloured Illustrations, Photographs, and a chapter on Perspective by
A. Macdonald. Second Edition. 1875. 8vo. half morocco, 18s.

Vaux (W. S. W., M.A.). Catalogue of the Castellani Collec-
tion of Antiquities in the University Galleries, Oxford. Crown 8vo. 1s.

The Oxford Bible for Teachers, containing supplemen-
tary HELPS TO THE STUDY OF THE BIBLE, including Summaries
of the several Books, with copious Explanatory Notes and Tables
illustrative of Scripture History and the characteristics of Bible
Lands; with a complete Index of Subjects, a Concordance, a Diction-
ary of Proper Names, and a series of Maps. Prices in various sizes
and bindings from 3s. to 2l. 5s.

Helps to the Study of the Bible, taken from the
OXFORD BIBLE FOR TEACHERS, comprising Summaries of the
several Books, with copious Explanatory Notes and Tables illus-
trative of Scripture History and the Characteristics of Bible Lands;
with a complete Index of Subjects, a Concordance, a Dictionary
of Proper Names, and a series of Maps. Crown 8vo. *cloth*, 3s. 6d.;
16mo. *cloth*, 1s.

LONDON: HENRY FROWDE,
OXFORD UNIVERSITY PRESS WAREHOUSE, AMEN CORNER,

OXFORD: CLARENDON PRESS DEPOSITORY,
116 HIGH STREET.

The DELEGATES OF THE PRESS *invite suggestions and advice from all persons
interested in education; and will be thankful for hints, &c. addressed to the*
SECRETARY TO THE DELEGATES, *Clarendon Press, Oxford.*